Centaur's Champion

E. R. Kallus

ISBN: 0-6154-4669-8
ISBN-13: 9780615446691

Dedication

TO CHUCK

Chuck drove a car with a license plate that read "BURMA." In the back window, a sticker bore the legend, "Horse Cavalry." I wanted to learn about this man. Over two or three years, I spent many hours with him.

I found him to be a prolific storyteller with a ready grin, the soul of a historian and an attic full of memorabilia. His store of vivid reminiscences went on seemingly forever. For hours I would work with him on some of his exquisite woodworking projects, listening while he told me of his days in the 124th Cavalry, at Fort Brown and in Burma. For a time I checked his details for accuracy. One after another, they rang with truth.

Centaur's Champion couldn't have been written without him: not without the American soldier with the heart of an Irish patriot. Chuck Harney is Danny Flynn.

Acknowledgments

Anna Lou Harney graciously agreed to the use of her photograph of Captain Chuck Harney for use on the cover.

Rudolfo Losoya: U.S. Naval Academy classmate; adjunct instructor, South Texas College and lifetime Rio Grande Valley resident. Together, Rudy and I toured the Rio Grande Valley forts from Fort Brown to Fort Ringgold in Rio Grande City. We crossed the river on a rope-powered ferry and visited tiny, almost invisible settlements along the river. He introduced me to professors of history and related his experiences as the son of an itinerant farm worker.

Sergeant Major Emil Rohraker, a man I never actually met. We were introduced by Paul Dauschmidt of the U.S. Cavalry Association. Emil sent me photographs and we conversed frequently by telephone, until one day he didn't answer.

About The Author

In his new novel *Centaur's Champion*, historian and native Texan E.R. Kallus explores a rarely studied corner of American history, the last mounted cavalry unit in the U.S. Army. He acknowledges that writing about horse soldiering doesn't immediately appear congruent with his background as a Naval Aviator. But his birth and early years in Fayette County, centrally located in a part of Texas where Czech and German were first languages and are still spoken, explains his interest. It's the voices of real Texans the reader hears in reading the exploits of Irish Danny Flynn.

chapter

ONE

Berlin: Irish ministers meet with Adolph Hitler to discuss an alliance.

"Make way for Danny Flynn," roared Phil Coffey, ignoring the insistent cries of men demanding service. The Bantry Maid's most privileged patron had rushed in from the street on business that wouldn't wait for the whims of a rowdy Friday night mob.

Coffey—bartender, bouncer and keeper of the peace—rolled his sleeves above the elbow, a certain sign of his intention to uphold rock-ribbed discipline, and pounded the polished oak with the flat of his hand. "Step aside, now! Right here! Step aside!" His regulars obliged willingly enough, elbowing and shoving to push a path through the pack of bodies. They recognized Danny and understood exactly why Coffey was giving him preference. A small knot of vocal laborers from outside the neighborhood didn't know him from Adam. Not being local, they didn't have the slightest idea of the profound nature of meeting nights at the Maid. To them he was just a college kid off the street and they resented what they considered an imposition on thirsty workingmen enjoying a well-deserved schooner of beer.

A tall, rawboned man in his worn blue working garb, craggy faced, hands gnarled and heavily calloused from handling bricks and troweling mortar, balked at Coffey's order to move aside. "Just who the hell is Danny Flynn to have Liam Kelly pushed around?" he bellowed in protest. "Is his money better than mine?"

Clenching and unclenching his great fists, the bartender glowered at the challenger. One man's opinion didn't count much here in Phil Coffey's domain. "Get a move on now," growled Coffey with color rising in his face. Kelly glared back at the bartender, but the challenge was brief and the uneven struggle ended with Kelly turning away and lowering his eyes.

Phil Coffey planted his ample middle against the bar and reached out with his bare forearm, sweeping bottles and mugs from under the noses of several astonished patrons, to clear a space a yard wide. "Here," he decreed, polishing the cleared surface with a towel, "Danny stands here."

Seeing Kelly put in his place extinguished any further thought of rebellion. The disgruntled laborer's drinking companions shuffled aside, grudgingly making way for this man whose arrival was interrupting their evening's pleasure. A few turned to see who he was. They saw a man barely in his twenties—lithe, but powerfully built, cheeks flushed from running in the cold evening air. Flynn snatched off his knitted cap and hastily stuffed it into a pocket of his dark wool pea jacket. He shrugged himself out of the damp coat and flung it on one of a row of pegs mounted on the wall. A few stabbing movements with his fingers only partially helped in taming the unruly mane of coppery hair tumbling around his ears. The instant he saw a narrow opening, Danny plunged into the space cleared by Coffey, shouting greetings, shaking hands and trading lighthearted barbs with his mates.

Out of the corner of his eye, Danny caught another glimpse of the fractious bricklayer looking him over. It might be a good idea to settle matters with the affronted man before something started. He stretched an arm toward Kelly, offering his hand to make amends for taking another man's place at the bar.

From his vantage point, Coffey became aware of an astonishing comparison. At a distance Danny's muscular shoulders and arms created the impression of a bull of a man, but standing near the towering Kelly, his stature seemed less imposing—the bricklayer stood almost a head taller. Neither spoke for a moment while they sized each other up. The laborer, who considered every handshake a measure of his manhood, winced, surprised by the strength of Danny's grip. "Good to meet you, Flynn," Kelly grunted at being bested a second time. Danny nodded with a grin and turned his attention to Coffey.

Kelly felt a light tap on his shoulder. A short, smiling man in a dark sweater, one of the regulars, pointed to a recently framed photograph hanging on the wall behind the bar. The photo was of a gymnast performing on the rings. A quick nod gave Kelly to know that Flynn, the man with the steely grip, and the Fordham gymnast in the picture were one and the same.

"That's him, is it?" Kelly asked, gaping at the shot of Danny on the rings, arms outstretched horizontally in an iron cross pose. "Jaysus," he blurted, imagining the kind of strength required for such a feat. If Kelly had retained any lingering doubts which of them could demand the bartender's service, they were now extinguished.

As much as Danny relished the noisy, boisterous companionship of men he'd known all his life, he could spare only a few moments with them. Time was short. At any moment, Patrick Brady might be arriving at the Bantry Maid with the latest word of matters in the old country, but before official business could begin, Danny still had a duty, informal, but an obligation nevertheless, to perform before the Maid's patrons.

Coffey hovered impatiently nearby, poised and ready. As obligations went, this was one Danny rather enjoyed. He nodded almost imperceptibly to the waiting bartender, who ceremoniously produced a special bottle kept locked away for meeting nights and poured a fine trickle of the amber liquor into the short glass—only a sacramental amount. Holding the glass high, Danny toasted, "To the Cause," and tossed the whiskey down with a flourish. As custom required, Flynn slapped a bill on the bar in payment. The change, he pushed in the direction of an unmarked widemouthed gallon jar sitting prominently at the end of the bar. "Would you be addin' this too, Phil," he proposed. The Maid's regulars understood the signal. Several dug into their pockets for something more to contribute. By now the vessel was nearly filled with a mass of wrinkled green bills piled high above a thick sediment of coins—impressive enough—but not quite acceptable. So Flynn made a final appeal, "Have you all made your offering tonight?" The significance of these collections for the Cause was common knowledge at the Bantry Maid, and widely considered a matter of an inborn duty. Still, it never hurt to prick consciences a trifle. "Come on then, dig into your pockets...it's for the Cause." A few more coins rattled into the jar. Satisfied at last, Danny turned to ask for the jar. "When you're ready, Phil, I'll be takin' it up."

While Danny collected his pea jacket, Coffey wiped his hands carefully on his apron and cleaned the sides of the jar with a fresh, dry towel. He grasped it carefully in his powerful hands and raised it with the devout solemnity of an altar boy. This show of reverence was both symbolic and precautionary. Once, a jar slipped through his fingers when he carelessly grasped it with his hands wet. The heavy thud and the crash of glass shattering into fragments lodged firmly in his mind. Now, whenever he handled the collection jar, the dull glistening of a cascade of coins spreading among the kegs and cases under the bar sprang vividly into his mind. With each of these transfers, he dried his hands thoroughly and concentrated on nothing else but handing the heavy jar over the bar. This public ceremony was a thing they'd done with some regularity since Danny had accepted the fund-raising responsibility from Francis O'Leary almost a year ago. Once the jar changed hands, Coffey would replace it with another—almost empty, but not quite. The show of money lying in the bottom served as a reminder that donating to the Cause was a lively practice at The Bantry Maid.

Flynn gingerly cradled the weighty offering in the crook of his left arm, cushioned on his jacket. Deliberately, he sidled away from the bar—a smile here, a handshake there and an occasional nod. "Thank you all," he spoke to the tightly packed mass of revelers. "They'll be waitin' upstairs, y'know." He worked his way deliberately toward a dimly lit flight of bare wooden stairs in the far corner.

The Maid's Friday-night patrons were typical of the neighborhood gin mills in this part of New York. Tradesmen and laborers like Kelly in canvas or blue denim coats, heavy boots and cloth caps dropped by to slake their thirst after a hard day's work and to mix with their neighbors in a thick, smoky atmosphere spiced with the muskiness of sweat and wet wool. A smaller cohort of college men in sweaters and scarves knitted in the colors of their universities added a sprinkling of color.

Friday-night crowds, especially on meeting nights, never failed to bring out local ward politicians who stood out from their constituents in suits and felt hats. Two of them elbowed their way toward the bar to be seen at the ceremony, to sample the neighborhood gossip and be available to their constituents. Danny sensed that with the jar of their donations on his arm, he was far more visible to his neighbors than the politicians. Generations of men before him had collected the funds on Fridays, and how he behaved now that the honor was his remained a matter of great interest.

With only a few seconds to spare, he stopped for an obligatory chat with a few mature women seated on benches reserved for them a few steps away from the bar by custom. Here they sat, sipping shandy from small glasses, chatting and keeping an eye on their men—and their brazen daughters edging closer to the college men at the bar. All the women at The Maid knew Michael and his boy Danny. Age didn't matter much—they flirted shamelessly as he passed, each quite sure his parting wink had been for her alone.

Only a step or two farther , he paused to make his manners with a group of older men collected around a table. A silver-haired man in a worn black suit leaned on the curved handle of his well-used cane, watching a group of his cronies playing cards. Danny greeted him politely, "Good evening to you, Mr. Tiernan. My father sends his regards. The boys at the precinct station have been asking why you don't visit, he tells me." Pleased to be remembered, the white-haired Tiernan smiled broadly with his new teeth. Danny cracked a little joke with a wicked smile, "I see your bum leg isn't keeping you home, so I gather Da and the other beat cops can assume it's their company that keeps you away."

Tiernan threatened playfully with his cane. "Tell Michael Flynn he has a very cheeky son," he scolded.

Danny moved away, passing out of the lights into the shadow where an indistinct figure waited. Without that man's permission, no one would be allowed to set a foot on the stairs leading to the Upper Room.

Gaining entry could be a simple matter, but only for one of the Faithful. Becoming one of them was quite an accomplishment, however. It took regular attendance at meetings, very much as Holy Mother the Church required at mass and, of course, demonstrated loyalty and regular contributions to the Irish Republican Army. These basic steps assured recognition by the sharp-eyed sentinels guarding the entrance. To a man who was accepted, it meant the privilege of climbing these dimly lighted stairs and preference in service at the bar by Phil Coffey, but also precious introductions to those with local influence.

The rules for entry to the sacred upstairs precincts were to be committed to memory, never set down on paper. Neither was there a written list of the Faithful. They knew one another by sight and no stranger could enter without prior approval—and an escort. Most were young, and in the way of young men, passionately hotblooded and given to supporting stirring causes. Unlike men like Tiernan, who fought and shed their blood for Irish freedom, only a bare few had been born in Ireland. The older men approved supporting the Cause, but these days they left the affairs of heart and country to their sons.

The shadowy sentinel at the bottom of the stairs moved forward to welcome Danny with a handshake and a quiet greeting: permission to climb to the top of the steps where another guard waited.

The Upper Room boasted nothing much in the way of decoration except for an Irish flag and a few framed photos of Irish patriots displayed on the drab, poorly painted walls. Prominent in the display was a portrait of President Eamon de Valera, a man born in New York and immigrated to Ireland. The serviceable but unfinished furniture was as simple as the wall decorations. Beneath a single tiny circular window at the far end of the room, a narrow pine table set up with three chairs on the side nearest the wall would serve as a place of honor for tonight's speaker. In the intervening space between the table and the door, an irregular jumble of worn benches without backs could provide seating for about fifty—more if the men crowded together. The spare furnishings allowed a bit of extra space for standing room on special occasions.

In the Upper Room, the Faithful were guaranteed privacy, whether to hear men like Brady or to listen to reports on how well they were meeting their duty to the Cause. Visceral, frequently exhilarating, even inflammatory, their discourses behind the guarded door held a power to transform allegiances so that the Faithful felt Irish to the core no matter where they were born. Tonight, a hum of excited, expectant conversation hung over groups of young men standing wherever they could find room, speculating on what Brady might have to say.

"He's here!" A shout came from just outside the door. The inside sentinel sighted Flynn's distinctive curly red mane rising into the pool of light at the top of the gloomy stairs. The conversational drone in the Upper Room changed to shouts of approval mixing with applause growing as he entered holding the donations jar over his head.

"Evenin', lads," Danny shouted in a general greeting, nodding and smiling, working his way directly to the table where Martin Smith puttered with the finishing touches on his preliminary chores. No one could be certain when the guest of honor would arrive, because Brady seldom paid attention to a schedule, but Danny's presentation of the contributions with the Faithful looking on had to take place before any other business could begin. As always at these formal meetings, the roundish, balding Smith wore the same tweed coat and black necktie he wore to mass on Sundays. He loved ceremony almost as much as he did making elaborate speeches.

Danny waited for Smith to call for silence. Then he shifted the weight of the jar easily into his right hand, raised it and held it high amid shouts of approval. As the shouts ebbed away, he lowered the jar and its heavy burden of money slowly and gracefully to the table. Again, the Faithful cheered with justifiable pride in their generosity. The jar would sit prominently on the table during the evening's proceedings, contents clearly visible as a reminder of their duty to support the Cause. Smith produced a small, much-used, brown leather case filled with packets of neatly stacked bills, the consolidated contents of many evenings' collections. This was Patrick Brady's goal in coming to the Bantry Maid. All those coins and wrinkled greenbacks had been carefully counted and the amounts entered into a ledger. Smith's bag contained far more money than the jar contained, but the sight of paper currency piled on a glinting metal base of coins constituted a tangible reminder of what could be accomplished by tossing in small amounts of money, a little at a time. The case and the jar would be joined by a bottle of whiskey and an assortment of small glasses. Setting out the bottle was a certain sign that profound oaths would be taken and sealed before the evening was over. With the meeting duly opened and the contributions in place, preparations were complete.

As usual on these visits, Brady had been spirited from Cork on a small freighter bound for New York with legitimate cargo. A boat came alongside the freighter off Sandy Hook to transfer Smith from the larger vessel to the smaller before either of them docked. The boat slipped into the busy traffic and took Brady ashore at some secret location. Smith had been made aware of these general facts, but no one ever learned much about Brady's itinerary, which varied a lot, for the visitor's security.

Danny felt John Keenan's large hand on his shoulder drawing him aside for a confidential question. "How did it go in Montreal?" Keenan inquired in an expectant whisper. The two were first-grade classmates at the parish school and had remained fast friends ever since. In fact, of Danny's mates only Keenan knew of his recent hasty visit to Canada, applying for service as a pilot in the Royal Air Force.

Danny's face told the story before he ever spoke a word, but he knew he could confide in Keenan with the details. In a low, almost tearful whisper, he shared his disappointment. "Twas the devil, John boy," he said, shaking his head. He swallowed as if to get rid of the bitter taste. "They turned me down," he said, thinking back to the military doctor's physical examination. This was the final hurdle to be cleared before the signing-up formalities. From the enthusiastic welcome he was getting during the preliminary testing, Danny knew the Royal Air Force regarded him as a prime candidate. The doctor asked if he were fit. Danny did a one-armed pull-up on an exposed pipe running near the ceiling and gave the examiner a look at a picture of him winning a boxing championship in the Police Athletic League. Danny sensed what Keenan's questions would be. "No. T'wasn't any lack of fitness, or m' height, but another failing entirely," he admitted, hanging his head in dejection brought.

Keenan too, well aware of Danny's athletic prowess, realized it must have been something quite unexpected. "What was it, then?"

Danny stared at the bare boards underfoot and scratched at some imaginary itch at his ear, working out a graceful explanation, "There was a little problem with m' eyes, y'see." He clenched his fist, remembering the light combinations and the charts displaying swirls of color. "I was to tell them what I saw," he murmured, barely moving his lips. The bitter truth was that he hadn't seen the right things.

The medical staff encouraged Danny to try the colored swirls again, and yet again, not wanting to disqualify a prime candidate for color blindness. "When it became final that I couldn't tell the difference between blue and green," Danny confided to Keenan, "the doctor almost cried." With his hands spread in a show of helplessness, Flynn described the end of his quest to become an RAF pilot, "'Well,'" I asked him, "'what difference does it make, doctor? I can still see that fuckin' swastika. It's black and red, not green and blue.' But at the end of it all, he couldn't let me pass." Taking care to see if anybody else was listening, Danny heaved a heavy sigh. "They had a paper all ready for me to sign if I wanted to be a soldier in the ranks." Flynn slumped in utter disappointment. "I said no, John. I told the doctor straight out, 'A man who's performed on the rings and the high bar cannot be bound to sloggin' in the mud with a rifle,' and I reminded him I hadn't yet tried our own Army Air Corps." Keenan felt the melancholy in the disappointing scene as Danny described it. "He thanked me for coming such a long way, shook my hand, and I came home." They rejoined the milling crowd waiting restlessly for the speaker to arrive. Danny drew his nickel-plated watch from its pocket. "Brady's a little late," he observed to no one in particular.

Billy Driscoll overheard. "It's Brady, after all. He always keeps us waiting," he said nearby. He knew Brady as well as any of the Faithful and had gotten a word or two about the visitor's message. "I understand he's gotten some firsthand word about the bad blood between De Valera and Churchill over Ireland's neutrality and their coziness with Germany," he added.

At the top of the steps, Jimmy Collins the sentinel shouted, "Here they are! Patrick Brady and...and..." His voice trailed away. "A guest!" The heavy drone of excited conversation dropped suddenly and the Faithful turned to see Brady and someone unknown to them pass through the door. Bringing a guest to the Upper Room wasn't all that unusual an event. After all, none of the men in the room were born as one of the Faithful. But, Danny recalled, on their first visit, every one of them had been specifically invited and announced beforehand. Maybe Smith had approved this to keep Brady's itinerary secret.

Tim Reilly, the escort, came first, leading the way to the table. Danny, sharing a bench with Keenan, immediately recognized Patrick Brady's massive frame and florid features. But then a third person, following closely behind Brady and dwarfed by his bulk, emerged from the stairway, creating a stir of astonishment. "A woman!" someone said. Could this be a woman in the Upper Room? Indeed it was a woman's face—swallowed up by a man's cap and jacket, but at a second glance, obviously feminine.

Danny elbowed his friend, whispering excitedly, "Will you look at that, Johnny? He's not married, is he?"

"Oh, no. At least I don't think so." If he had a woman, it was his affair, but why didn't he leave her downstairs with the ladies? "He knows how we do things here."

"It's how things are with Brady," Danny said, shrugging.

Keenan bobbed his head in agreement, wondering aloud, "Y' don't suppose she'll be speakin' tonight too? Do ya?" Danny didn't answer. His attention was on Brady and his woman.

Martin Smith knew about Brady's woman from rumors crackling through New York's Irish neighborhoods, but hadn't let on. It would have required delicate diplomacy with many of the Faithful, and he didn't like confrontations. At Smith's invitation, she slumped into the chair between him and the speaker, deliberately holding her head down so that the visor of her cap partially hid her face. The critical inspection of Brady's woman that began the instant she entered continued with a low rumble of appraisals, hardly abating when Smith began his windy welcome. Out of anxiety over the stir her presence was causing, Martin hurriedly described the mystery woman as an agent embarking on an important project, and changed the subject. If he planned to give her a special introduction, it would come later.

While Smith droned on with his usual comments about the sanctity of the Cause, Flynn and Keenan indulged in some whispered speculation of their own. Who the woman was, they couldn't say. Brady, on the other hand, was nearly as well known here at the Bantry Maid as he was in Ireland—as a spellbinding speaker as well as an aggressive brawler. Keenan came to a practical conclusion: A man with Brady's reputation as a street fighter could bring his woman with him, or anybody else he wanted, with no trouble a'tall. Keenan nudged Danny. "Maybe he just felt he needed somethin' like her along with him..." he whispered with a knowing wink. "F'r travelin', I mean."

With the briefest glance at his friend, Keenan could see the thought of Brady's something to travel with appealed to Danny. An identical grin once prompted Sister Theresa to order her adolescent pupil directly to the priest's office to make his confession immediately—no questions allowed. "No boy can have such a look as that on his face without something on his conscience," the nun sniffed.

At last Smith took his seat, and it was Brady's turn. Rising slowly, the speaker took his time preparing his audience. Brady could have been in an empty room for all the attention he paid the Faithful while carefully removing his bulky seaman's jacket and draping it on the back of his chair. Then he looked up briefly, slid the plain wooden chair against the table and stood behind it. With his shoulders thrown back, arms crossed in front of him, the visitor cut an imposing figure indeed; clothed simply as he was, in a bulky, pale sweater of undyed wool, the kind Irish fishermen wear, and dark, coarse workman's trousers. Brady waited, motionless and expectant, for the Faithful to become silent. The technique was one he had learned from Father Murphy, the firebrand priest celebrated for his service to the Irish Cause during the Troubles. Conversations died away completely, but Brady wasn't satisfied. He swiped his fingers impatiently through his curly brown hair, waiting until their bodies became motionless too, and then until the creaking of the benches died away. The man knew how to get attention, Danny thought, giving him his due. At last, the visitor began his well-practiced remarks without wasting a syllable on pleasantries.

Brady spoke fervently of the progress being made by the Irish ministers in Berlin, and of the excitement raised by sightings of German submarines outside Kinsale harbor near Cork, and the unusual opportunities the war in Europe presented for furthering the Irish cause. "I've been to Berlin myself," he boasted. Those words stirred a scattered, uncertain mixture of approving nods and nervous laughs. It wasn't until he described Prime Minister Churchill's rage at Irish President de Valera's resolve to keep the Irish neutral that he received the enthusiastic applause he expected.

"Now then," said Brady, leaning forward with the tips of his fingers touching the table, "we of the IRA would prefer our president to square his public policy with his private one of support for the Cause. While the British are busy with their war in Europe, we have our best opportunity to reunite Ireland." Brady spoke confidently of gaining German help in wresting the northern counties from England's control. "Let me be clear. We want German support. With their money and weapons, we can accomplish miracles." He struck the plain table with his great fist until the glasses rattled. "It galls me to think of Irishmen forced yet again to bend a knee to the British, refueling British aircraft whose pilots make emergency landings in Ireland." Such talk drew foot stamping and applause from the Faithful. He carefully chose not to say that German aircraft were being given the same privilege.

Down below in the bar, the Bantry Maid's customers heard the applause rise and fall away slowly, even if they couldn't hear Brady's words. Here and there a head nodded knowingly and hands pointed proudly toward the Upper Room.

By habit, Flynn listened intently to Brady, but as the speaker returned to a more familiar message, he found his attention being drawn to the smallish figure sitting tensely on her chair behind the table. Throughout Brady's patriotic oration, she sat with her elbows on the table, occasionally allowing her chin to rest on her intertwined fingers. How many times must she have heard these same words this very day? From what Danny saw of her so far, the woman was unimpressive—small, round-shouldered and nervous. If she was Brady's woman or even if she played some important role in his work, she didn't appear to be a particularly striking creature. Granted, it could have been the formless man's gray tweed jacket hanging loosely over her shoulders, or even the visor of the wool cap obscuring much of her face. What he could see of her hair was shining and black—most of it pushed up under the cap. To Danny, her only remarkable feature was a pair of penetrating green eyes with which she steadily met the inquiring looks of the hot-blooded young men examining her so critically from the benches.

A rising hum of speculation from the members appeared to distract Brady. Any more and he would have called it insolence and stamped out of the room, but unfinished business required his attention, and this was a good time to address it. He raised his hands to quell the stir created by the woman's presence. "Friends, this is Maureen Gallamore. She is one of us," said the Irishman, gesturing offhandedly in her direction. Expectantly, the Faithful grew quiet again. Brady proceeded with Miss Gallamore's story. In order to slip away from English scrutiny, he told them, she had come first to Boston months earlier to melt into the neighborhoods there where the patriotic sentiment was so strong. Recently she moved to New York, working and living in Spanish Harlem while attending a nursing program at a local hospital. At the mention of her work, Maureen's posture stiffened and she folded her hands before her on the table—strong nurse's hands with neatly manicured, unpainted nails.

Danny snorted skeptically at Brady's claim that she lived in Harlem. Couldn't be, he thought. Apparently Brady didn't know much about the neighborhoods of New York. No Irish woman would be living in such a hellhole among those strange-talking people. Not a self-respecting one, anyway. Brady was well regarded and usually well informed, but surely this time he had his facts muddled.

At Brady's invitation, Miss Gallamore rose to be properly introduced, shrugging out of the jacket and tossing it on the table. Now, instead of lowering her shoulders to avoid notice, she stood haughtily erect, a patriot among pretenders. She snatched off the cloth cap and shook her head to allow her black hair to cascade to her shoulders. Boots scraped the floor and a low appreciative "Ahhh" rose from the benches. Keenan whispered something to Flynn. Obviously this agent, if that's what she really was, knew something about attracting attention herself.

Brady implored them fervently, "Look at this woman. She is a living symbol of the patriotism to which all who support the Cause should aspire." After the briefest pause, he confided, "She has embarked on a difficult and dangerous project; one crucial to our effort to further the cause of a united," he repeated, "united and free Ireland." Pleased by the applause and shouting erupting from the benches, he allowed the excitement to ebb only slightly before raising his voice above it, "Hear me, men." This, Brady saw as his opportunity to place an essential piece of business before them. His voice rolled through the crowded room, "Do I have your solemn pledge to aid her, without reservation, wherever and whenever she asks it?"

In a unanimous, full-throated voice, they answered instantly, reflexively, and in unison, as they might have added an amen at the end of a prayer, "You have it!" When it came to matters of patriotism to the Cause, the Faithful could be counted on for an enthusiastic response.

Hearing only applause and shouts of approval, Brady searched their faces for signs of dissent. Seeing none, he rumbled his approval. "Good." Abruptly he grasped the bottle by its neck in his huge right fist and presented it to them at arm's length. The room grew quiet while Brady and Smith prepared to seal the oath just sworn by the men on the benches. Brady poured a small splash of the whiskey into each of the glasses on the table. Smith passed them among the Faithful until every man stood expectantly with a charged glass in hand. Brady scanned the room to be sure no one remained seated. Not standing would mean publicly foreswearing the oath.

By the time Smith challenged them to drink, a familiar emotion held Danny in its grip. He drained the ceremonial glass without leaving a drop and passed it along to be taken away. At the table, Martin Smith beamed his satisfaction at this unanimous affirmation of the oath. "Well done," he intoned proudly to the Faithful.

Maureen nodded to the men, mouthing her thanks to them and to Brady before taking her seat.

Brady wiped perspiration from his face with a handkerchief as he turned again to the burning questions glaring daily in the headlines of American papers. The president of the Irish Free State proclaimed the Irish neutral in the European war being waged against the rampaging forces of the Third Reich. Brady reminded the crowd, "De Valera feels that Ireland, a small country standing alone, has no choice but to look to the high probability that the Germans will reduce England to impotence, if not capturing it altogether." Ireland then had three choices. The Irish could ally themselves with the Germans, who would in all likelihood be the leaders of a new world order, or with the British, who would almost assuredly become a new German colony. Even if England were to prevail, to continue the alliance with the English would be encouraging the former colonizers across the Irish Sea to reclaim their old domain. The third choice, then, was for the Irish to remain neutral. The speaker explained to the Faithful seated on the benches, "Neutrality was the only choice De Valera could make."

The Irish choice had outraged Churchill, but the cagey politician limited his public statement to one of strong protest. Instead of punishing Ireland militarily or economically, he took his case to the entire English-speaking world, asking his allies how the Irish could ignore their responsibility to defend the freedom of Europe.

According to Brady, De Valera made not the slightest effort to placate Churchill. He could have simply made a public statement reminding the crusty British Prime Minister that Irish volunteers from the south were flocking across the Irish Sea to take up the defense of Britain, but he didn't want to give him even that small grain of comfort. Quite the opposite, De Valera made no secret of receiving a German emissary who came seeking rights for Hitler's U-boats to refuel and refit in southern Irish harbors.

"Maintaining the public awareness of an independent Ireland is paramount, if we are to maintain our precious freedom," Brady told them, his voice swelling, expecting another burst of applause. Instead, he heard opposition.

Danny Flynn stood alone among the shocked Faithful, demanding to know about this business of U-boats carrying German diplomats docking in Irish ports with impunity while the widely ranging submarine fleet of the German Kriegsmarine systematically hunted and torpedoed British shipping—American ships too—then allowing the crews to die in their stricken vessels, or to drown in the open sea. Perhaps these practices could be expected in the case of Royal Navy vessels, and maybe even with the British merchant fleet because Great Britain and Germany were at war. "But the U.S. is not at war with Germany.

How can you ask us as patriotic supporters of the Cause to condone such a thing?" Danny demanded.

To the surprise of every man in the room, Maureen Gallamore, eyes flaring angrily, shot to her feet to refute this impudence. Brady stood aside and allowed her to speak. In the shocked quiet, she began to speak in a low husky voice welling up from deep within her. "What do any of you know about the Cause?" If any of them still held the slightest notion she was no more than Brady's traveling companion, it was now swept away. This was not a woman willing to take a seat quietly in the ladies' area downstairs. If by chance her American listeners were weak on facts, Gallamore refreshed their knowledge of the history of the Irish under British rule, a melancholy tale of brutal subjugation for the better part of a thousand years. "We owe them no allegiance," she hissed her hatred for England and the British in general. "Not even the perception of it. They've been spilling our blood for centuries, starving us, swindling us of our own sacred land and squeezing our heritage from our souls. Why on God's earth should we be offering to shed even one more drop of our blood for them—unless it means the return of the North to combine with us once again in one, single, united Ireland?" The Upper Room shook with the Faithful stamping their feet and roaring their approval.

She stood visibly taller, strengthened by their vocal support. "The English transported thousands of us into slavery in the Carribbean and even into these United States, when they were colonies." She shook her fist, crying out, "Remember the foul atrocities they committed against our people in those years." The Faithful responded enthusiastically to this, the same sort of speech they had heard in their fathers' dinner-table orations as long as they could remember. The woman in the black sweater and workman's boots stabbed her finger savagely at the air, making her points in a voice rising with a growing emotion. "Didn't the Germans stand with us through the Troubles during the years of the Great War, after all?" She tossed her head defiantly, glaring her antipathy to the British and their plight. "We owe Churchill nothing—no allegiance, no support, no comfort and no assistance. Let the British learn to speak German, exactly as our forefathers were forced to abandon their own sacred tongue." More applause, the kind that tells of swelling emotion, brought the Faithful to their feet screaming their agreement.

"Please, let her speak," shouted Brady in his practiced orator's voice, banging his fist on the table for silence. Stirring speech was good, but time was precious to a man charged with funding the Cause, and the Bantry Maid was only one of several meeting places on the night's itinerary.

Her listeners quieted reluctantly and resumed their seats, scraping the benches across the floor into their proper places. Only Danny Flynn remained standing, still and silent. Maureen Gallamore waited uncertainly. But he did not address her. In the strained quiet,

Flynn turned to confront the emotional men packed tightly on the benches. He rebuked them, speaking slowly, "What can you be thinking of then, friends?"

"Sit down, Danny. Let her speak," someone shouted.

Facing this challenger, Danny addressed him and the rest of the Faithful. "Think of what we've just heard," he said, referring to Miss Gallamore's scathing recitation of England's abuses of the Irish. In contrast to the shrillness rising into her voice, Flynn's tone was one of reason. "I'm well aware of the English attempt to stamp out the Irish language; and they are guilty of all those other crimes as well. Don't take my words as condoning any of that—not for an instant." He raised a hand for emphasis and the room fell silent. "But striking an alliance with Mr. Hitler is risking total enslavement of Europe and England—Ireland as well. Mark my words," he warned, "Germany will never stop short of the Irish Sea and the Irish will surely join in their neighbors' fate." He gave them a moment to think about it. "To support a misbegotten alliance with Germany against England will never right the wrongs of centuries. I say it is a perilous gamble that could result in the total enslavement of Europe."

Flynn turned to the agent who stood tensely, ready to rejoin the debate, "Miss Gallamore, it's utter rubbish to think that if the English are forced to speak German, the Irish will be spared the same fate." He proceeded to set himself farther from her view. "You may have a taste for it, but I'll be damned if I can bear the thought of the language of yet another oppressor being heard in the land of my forebears. And damned if I'll countenance condemning the British to speak German either."

"I'm with you, Danny," cried Frank Eagan impulsively.

Another took instant exception. "Screw the Brits."

Gallamore tried to speak over the growing uproar, but it was no use. Danny's words had released an eruption of emotion that had been building among the Faithful for months. At its heart lay the question: Just what does the Cause stand for? Martin Smith called sharply for quiet and pounded the tabletop with his fist, but his calls went unheeded. Danny, the one who could have stopped the pandemonium with a word or two, passively let it rage, while Smith and Brady appealed strenuously for quiet.

Brady fidgeted in his seat, rubbing his brow with his fingers, impatient for an end to this tiresome acrimony among the Americans. What did these coddled imposters know of the dangers facing Europe? He'd come only to collect the money displayed on the table, not to entertain these louts. The Bantry Maid was a prolific source of vital funds and he could ill afford to see these dependable donors split by dissent that could upset the expected flow of contributions. Damn Flynn and his contrary comments! Now, instead of making a timely exit with the bag of money, he was being forced to sit and squirm while these suddenly aroused Americans debated the sanctity of Ireland's plight.

Neither Brady nor Smith would publicly oppose Danny because they might lose his ability to convince these squabbling men and their friends to fill jar after jar with their contributions. Helplessly, they allowed Flynn the floor, holding the attention of the Faithful, still on their feet, waiting for his words.

"I've been thinking a lot," he said quietly. In fact, he and his father, a veteran of the trenches in the king's uniform in the Great War as well as a patriotic fighter during the Troubles, discussed this same topic night after night. How should Ireland's neutrality in these crucial times affect the passionate immigrant Irishmen who came to America in the hope of opportunity for themselves and their family? "Danny, lad, I love the old land more than I love m'self," the senior Flynn would say. "More than once I've shed blood for it, and I pray you never will. I long for the day the cause of Irish unity becomes a goal gained through peaceful negotiation rather than with shooting and bombing and the burning of homes. Danny, I'm sick to death of Irishmen killing Irishmen."

In the Upper Room, the Faithful hung onto Flynn's slow, careful words. "The struggle of the Irish people against the English is not over. I'm well aware of it, and I am firmly supportive of our efforts supporting them. But here is where I must disagree with our visitors."

Here and there, a few of the Faithful made thoughtful throat-clearing sounds.

"Failing to stop the Germans from crossing the Channel will result in the end of Western Civilization as we know it—all of it—including the sacred culture of Ireland." He allowed them a moment to consider the thought. "Let me make my view clear. I want my money and my energies to support a cause holding Irish independence as its goal."

He knew they were puzzling over the apparent contradiction in his statement. If Flynn wanted Irish Independence, why not faithfully support the policies of the Irish government? He gave them his answer. "Now we see the Irish government in the throes of making a monumental decision amid a collision of forces they are powerless to control. Mr. Brady has told us of their dire choices. For the moment, Ireland balances between the two combatants, cloaking itself with the mantle of neutrality." A deathly silence settled over the room. "While it teeters, our two guests ask us to support them in helping Ireland cast its lot with Germany," Danny said.

This time, a low murmur of discussion spread through the Upper Room. He tolerated the interruption momentarily. Then he drew their attention to the feminine figure still standing defiantly at the table. "Tonight we've heard the words of Miss Gallamore. She tells us plainly that the road to Irish freedom lies through an alliance with a nation systematically destroying European culture and murdering people who disagree with them, and Mr. Brady concurs." His hand waved toward Brady. "This simply cannot be. Though the Cause itself is sacred to me, I cannot support making common cause with the Germans." He lowered his head.

The young men crammed on the creaky benches, only moments ago besotted by the taste of the bloodlust for the Irish cause, sat silently for the most part. Some narrowed their eyes or pursed their lips in thought, trying to absorb and understand this surprising assessment from their outspoken colleague.

One, feeling a duty to rebuke Flynn for his apostasy, stood in opposition. Peter Kerrigan, a portly, freckled man with a wisp of a ginger-hued beard, rose to second the remarks of the belligerent colleen. Kerrigan, a history student at Columbia, reminded Flynn of the ancient grievances held by the Irish people against the English.

Flynn dismissed him with a withering look. What Kerrigan had to say was ground they'd gone over only minutes before. Danny deliberately allowed his words to roll in a round-voweled Celtic timber as thick as his father's, "I know me hist'ry, Paedar." Hand outstretched, he pointed at Kerrigan, chiding him, "Ye'd be advised to look at the future. Consider Herr Hitler's intentions." Flynn spoke quietly in a voice low and rough with emotion. "Only yesterday, I got off the train from Montreal. I was there to join the Royal Air Force." An emotional charge crackled among the men on the benches, setting them chattering among themselves in disbelief, gaping at Flynn, expecting a denial or at least some explanation, but Danny wasted no time before moving on. "Surprises you, doesn't it, Daniel Flynn asking to join the RAF? They're recruiting Americans in Canada to fly fighters over England...but they turned me down." For a moment, the sting of rejection rushed back to him, but he saw the faces of his fellows. A majority of them were younger than thirty and, except for two or three, all born in the local neighborhoods. A man's birthplace shaped him, in a way. "Let me remind you of another thing," he said. "We're Americans, no matter how much our parents and grandparents bled in Ireland. What if we're drawn into the war against the Germans? If we've supported the Irish who are now telling us they want Ireland to support the Germans, what will our countrymen say of us?" Leaving the question hanging, Danny took his seat, allowing the emotional clamor of loud, heated argument on both sides of the issue to continue around him.

At the table, Martin Smith and Patrick Brady sat huddled together in hot, animated discussion. To Brady, all this overheated fervor was pointless. He wanted it stopped immediately. Smith, intimidated by Brady's poking at his chest and mortified by the behavior of the Faithful, stood and climbed on a bench, shouting strenuously for quiet. "Stop. In God's name, give me your attention." Their voices lowered enough for him to be heard. "Obviously we have our own opinions, but we needn't forget our manners," Smith pleaded. "Our guests have come for the material support we promised them and I take pride in presenting it to Mr. Brady to help the cause in Ireland itself. We must also remember that Miss Gallamore, to whom we've sworn our support, lives with us here in New York and requires help in her project. While Mr. Brady makes his final comments, let's be generous to Miss Gallamore. I've given my permission for her to pass a hat for your contribution."

With his money on the table in front of him, Brady stood for a departing speech. He planned to use a shortened form of his usual statements of gratitude and make a quick getaway, but Smith's suggestion that Maureen make an impromptu collection effectively crossed his plan. He stood quietly impotent, fighting to control his anger at being forced to cede her time that was rightly his while more money that could have been his collected in her gray wool cap.

Maureen, in preparing to leave with Brady, had donned the gray coat again, but after her speech the garment had lost its diminishing effect. She moved among the men on the benches with an easy grace, smiling her thanks as they gathered around to add their money, offering a special word or two here and there. "God bless you, Mr. Kerrigan," she said to Peter, whose words Danny cut short.

Quickly lowering her gaze, she answered another man's question. "Oh, but I do live in Harlem—with a family." As she moved among them, Maureen's lustrous black hair spilled down her back and her eyes flashed from one face to another. Each man in his way felt the green-eyed beauty's charm.

Brady fumed at the sound of the arguments being rekindled, upset by the mixed jumble of patriotic fervor created earlier by Flynn. The visitor saw time trickling away and Gallamore's captivating presence commanding far more attention than anything he might say. Impetuously, he grabbed the money and stalked angrily toward the stairs, pushing his way through the Faithful with the humiliated Martin Smith trailing behind, desperate to placate his guest. "Just a moment, please, Mr. Brady," he was saying.

A confused uproar obliterated whatever Brady meant to say to Smith. He threw a glance at Miss Gallamore and shrugged. She could find her way, and with Smith still apologizing and pleading for understanding, Brady cursed Flynn accusingly. "Damn you. The Cause can do without your muddled views. You Americans are a sorry lot, thinking you understand the Irish Cause better than those of us who stayed to carry on the fight." He turned abruptly and clattered noisily down the steps with a firm grip on the leather case and its precious contents, leaving a suddenly quiet room behind him.

The Faithful stood in two general groups, waiting for the return of Martin Smith, whose solicitous tones could be heard at the foot of the stairs still attempting to placate the vocal visitor. "We are not a treasonous element, Mr. Brady," he could be heard saying.

The smaller group, an insignificant minority really, laughed and joked with masculine abandon, completely taken with the Irish agent still circulating with her cap. "Did you notice how quickly I swore the oath to be assistin' her?" someone was saying. "S'pose she'd want some assistance later this evenin'?" he guffawed.

In the larger group, where the political questions continued to rage, Peter Kerrigan took Miss Gallamore's points to heart, arguing hotly in favor of Irish neutrality and an active courtship of Hitler's Germany."

Danny stood alone, hands in his pockets, emotionally spent and physically weary, mulling over the reproofs mouthed at him by Smith throughout his spontaneous speech. From behind him, a hand touched his shoulder. He turned to see the green eyes of Maureen Gallamore fixed on him. Automatically, he fumbled in his pockets for something to add to the coins collected in the cap, but she waved away his gesture. "Another time, Mr. Flynn. Even if you are misguided in your politics, I'm quite positive your Irish heritage runs strong and true." Placing a fingertip near her right eye, she reminded him, "I saw you drink the whiskey and heard you swear the oath."

He felt a flush climbing from his collar to burn in his cheeks.

"*Slan go foill*," she said with a slight flash of a smile and clomped hurriedly away in her oversized boots to catch up to Brady and their escort, leaving Danny groping helplessly for a response.

chapter

TWO

New Orleans: U.S. War Department sources report sightings of the German freighter *Aruaca* off Vera Cruz, Mexico. The vessel is thought to be involved in supporting U-boats.

In the days of westward-rolling wagon trains, the U.S. Cavalry made a home on the plains of Kansas and never left. Generation upon generation of cavalrymen regarded Fort Riley as the wellspring of the lore and learning of waging war on horseback. There in the sprawl of barracks, school buildings and stables ruggedly constructed from the strong native limestone, cavalrymen earned the privilege of wearing spurs and the distinctive crossed-sabers insignia—rights that set them apart from their less-favored comrades in the other branches of the army. Once the long line of stables hummed with activity. Today, they lay almost completely still. If the planners in Washington had their way, this lone class of officer candidates would be the last group trained for duty in mounted regiments.

Nine young men in khaki uniforms, faces and necks deeply tanned from weeks of exposure to the Kansas sun, stood bantering anxiously among themselves in a loose group on the neatly raked sand outside the stable door. This morning's exercise would be their initial live firing session on the mounted pistol range—their first opportunity to prove themselves at this critical skill. If they qualified at shooting targets with a pistol from the back of a galloping horse, they progressed toward becoming lieutenants in the U.S. Cavalry. Failure meant dismissal from officer training. Their instructor had his students report early for a bit of extra preparation before the horses were led out.

It wasn't that shooting was new to them. The entire group had already qualified with the reliable old .45 caliber pistol, but that was dismounted, standing comfortably on the firm, level surface of the firing line, shooting at stationary targets. Today Danny Flynn and the rest of the officer candidates would take their first crack at riding through a twisting course of fourteen man-shaped targets, shooting at each one in turn.

Lean and wiry Sergeant Leonard Willman, closely cropped hair showing nearly white beneath his flat-brimmed hat, moved from student to student, dispensing advice he intended that all of them hear. Each, in his own way, tried to relieve the tenseness as best he could: stretching, bending and shrugging his shoulders to encourage the stiff webbing straps of his field gear to settle a bit more comfortably on his body while the instructor moved methodically from one student to another, tugging at straps and belts, making small adjustments as he dispensed advice.

Willman loved shooting and he believed firmly that a man could shoot his best only if he was confident and comfortable. "This ol' webbin' feels different now that ye're gonna shoot from hossback, doesn't it?" he joked to one in a confidential tone. "That'll loosen with a little wear and sweat, and then if it's too loose, ye'll feel it slippin' around on ya, and it'll rub," he said, giving a pistol belt a hard yank. "That's not tight enough," he said, delivering his judgment. On another he checked the leather thong that went through the lower end of the pistol holster and around the rider's leg to keep the weapon from flapping as the horse galloped. "May want to loosen it," he suggested.

As he moved among them, the eager students followed Willman intently with their eyes, absorbing his suggestions and subconsciously imitating his mannerisms. They'd already learned that the slightest bit of the sergeant's wisdom lost through inattention could cost them later, so they listened hard.

Decades of soldiering had tempered the crusty veteran's voice with a richly mixed complexity of regional accents, giving it a quality that exuded experience and knowledge. "Now," he demanded, "listen to me about this field gear yer wearin'." The green webbing combination of belt and suspenders distributed the weight of weapons and ammunition over shoulders and waist. To hear him explain it, the stiff straps possessed magical properties that could enable a man to work steadily through a day of riding and shooting with a comparative degree of comfort. Obviously then, failure or even harm could befall them if they failed to follow his instructions. He went over the main points again, stressing snugness, of course, and enough freedom of motion to draw the heavy, awkward pistol and shoot with steady, reliable marksmanship.

But then Willman suggested something contrary to anything they'd heard in their weeks at Fort Riley: He suggested the instructions laid out in the training manual might not be the only way of qualifying on the mounted pistol range! One modification he had in mind involved the lanyard that connected the rider to his pistol to prevent the weapon from being lost if he dropped it during a moment of clumsiness. All nine wore their lanyards—because they were issued to them.

Occasionally, to remind them that soon they'd be lieutenants, Willman allowed the slightest hint of deference to creep into his well-practiced delivery. "Ya wouldn't want to be shootin' for score and get tangled up in yer lanyard and fall on yer ass. Right, Gennelmen?" They all laughed at Willman's practical humor, but if the sergeant intended it as a joke, he never let on. "I'll give ya a little advice—leave the lanyard behind while yer out here on the range tryin' to qualify." A distant flock of crows could be heard in the quiet that followed his unexpected suggestion.

From years of training new officers, the sergeant knew this new revelation would create a little confusion, and he called them closer to be sure they all understood his message. "Look, it's OK ta think." A detail as trivial as a uniform regulation could be ignored if performance was at stake. After a second or two, Willman resumed his well-rehearsed briefing on thinking and practicality. "This exercise is f'r accuracy, and f'r time, too, see. If ya trot through this range and hit every target, ya won't qualify, any more than if ya tear through it at a scorchin' gallop and miss every damn one of them. But ya gotta have the piece in yer hand, firin' at them targets, see." Willman saw them nodding. "So it ain't goin' ta make a gnat's ass wortha difference if ya drop the piece somewhere between the targets—ya still don't have it when ya need. In the dirt or bouncin' on the end of a string, it won't matter a damn why." He grinned broadly, displaying most of his coffee-stained teeth, and made his point. "Ya still won't be shootin." In seconds, nine lanyards became excess baggage. Smiling with satisfaction, Willman added one more suggestion. "Leave 'em hangin' on that nail over there and pick 'em up later."

Willman moved several yards to the side—so they wouldn't miss anything by having to squint into the sun. "Now, one more time, let's go over the most important maneuver ya have to be able ta perform—reloadin'." He wanted them to think the problem through once more, before he sent them onto the range. "Didn't want ta think about that one, did ya?" In his well-rehearsed way, he raised an eyebrow to signal the importance of his next point. "Fourteen targets and only seven rounds in the magazine." Students preparing to shoot for the first time on the mounted pistol range always smiled nervously here.

"Now remember, this little chore of reloadin' takes at least two hands," Willman reminded them. The crow's feet at his eyes crinkled as the truth began to settle and he enjoyed a pregnant little laugh. "Heh, heh." The sun warming the morning air sent little droplets of sweat rolling down their backs as Willman explained the process. "One hand fer the reins and one fer the pistol," he said, pausing to demonstrate, holding a standard issue .45-caliber pistol in his right hand and imaginary reins in his left, and to be sure they were absorbing his lesson: "The pistol has to go from your shootin' hand to the one with the reins." Talking all the while, he transferred the imaginary pistol, frowning with mock distress at the awkward handful of pistol and reins that resulted. "Then ya remove the empty magazine, put it into yer shirt pocket, take out th' new one and..." Willman hesitated, his face a perfect picture of bafflement. "I'll need another hand, won't I?" he suggested.

"No, Sergeant." One of them gave him the response he required. "Take the reins in your teeth until you have control of a loaded pistol in your shooting hand."

Willman beamed his satisfaction. "'At's right, gennelmen. Ye've been listenin'." Over the heads of his students, the sergeant saw their horses being led out. "Jes one more thing. We bin teachin' ya ta keep the second magazine safe in one a these pockets on yer belt." He fingered the ammunition compartments on his own faded, well-worn belt. "See? Mine'll open real easy." His snap, all bright and brassy from long use, functioned smoothly. Theirs were stiff and the brass hardware still had its dull black finish. "Ya may have trouble opening the flaps while yer on the course. My advice is t' put a loaded clip into yer shirt pocket." He tapped his chest over the left pocket. "Here," he said. "Yeah, I know the magazine is heavy and it'll bang 'round 'gainst your chest while ya ride, but 'cha won't notice it after a while. An' the empty one? Ya can put it into yer shirt, where the new one was, or throw it away if it means missin' the next target. That's what ye'd do if you were bein' shot at." His homily delivered, the sergeant waved a hand to signal the range master that his students were ready. Time to mount up.

One of Willman's students was having trouble calming his skittish mount. While they waited for him to get the horse under control, Danny and Eddie Pierce talked about the hand dealt them by fate. The two had been together in San Antonio trying vainly to convince the army doctors at Randolph Field that they were truly made of the stern material the army required in its pilots. Pierce reached over to give Flynn's belt a playful tug. "Just like the ones in an airplane cockpit. Huh, Danny?"

Danny glowered under the brim of his hat, "Ah. Don't you be tormentin' me, Eddie. Life as an aviator has eluded both of us." Danny looked away, in the direction of the mounted pistol range. "The cavalry is where Flynn is seekin' his glory now."

Only three months ago the prospect of becoming a pilot still consumed him. Waiting in the doctor's office, the sound of aircraft engines droning over the field captured Danny's attention. He could see them through the window—a flight of four silver-and-yellow bi-wing trainers, student pilots returning from a training flight: four lucky devils, living his dream.

The doctor had bad news, as disappointing as it had been in Montreal. "I'm sorry, Mr. Flynn. I simply can't clear you to fly. We gave you all the tests we know to give, but you didn't pass any of them." Danny felt his spirits falling as he heard the doctor's final verdict, "I can't give you a waiver for color blindness."

The doctor, brown hair flecked thickly with silver, gold oak leaves on the collar of the khaki shirt stretched snugly over his middle, recognized the deep dejection in the slumped shoulders of the youth in the chair. He scribbled something on a scrap of paper and pushed it across the desk. "While you're here in San Antonio, why don't you visit Sergeant Stokes at the recruiting office to see what he has to offer?" He peered over the tops of his glasses silently at the downcast Flynn, watching the disheartened youth staring numbly at the toes of his shoes. "We're going to be in a war soon and the nation will want you—only not as a pilot," the major said to the young man whose dreams he had just dashed. To Danny, it was a door slamming in his face. Surely there was another way, Danny thought, to get around a physical defect so trivial as not being able to tell the difference between blue and green. He pleaded shamelessly, "Doctor, please," but it was no use. Dejectedly, he folded the paper and pushed it into his pocket.

Sergeant Stokes had met many young men like Danny Flynn, faces wracked by bitter disappointment over a lost opportunity, presenting the crushed paper given them by a doctor as a prescription for rejection. The hurt in their eyes told of their lost dreams of entering the European war as pilots. In his heart, Stokes admired their pluck and zealous motivation to enter the fight against the spreading German menace. The nation was lucky to have men like these. He swallowed hard as the redhead approached tentatively; wondering whether achieving monthly quotas made him an enabler of patriots or merely a salesman filling orders. No matter how often he asked the question, the answer was always the same: some of each.

Danny's eyes swept the recruiter's office wall. There was Old Glory in its position of honor in a show of brightly hued posters and regimental banners, a carefully contrived world of color and pageantry designed to put the army on display. Here and there—on his large, government-issue oak desk, for instance—Stokes had set out a few items emphasizing the hard, cold side of a soldier's service: a polished hand grenade, a dark bayonet with a brightly honed, menacing edge, and a nickel-plated .45-caliber pistol. For this new prospect referred to him by the flight surgeon, he brought out a pair of highly polished cavalry boots and set them on the floor near the desk. Altogether Stokes felt satisfied with his raw, powerful message of future excitement.

The crisply starched and polished recruiter greeted Danny warmly, inviting him to take his time looking. There was plenty of time for talk. Stokes sat quietly at his desk, erect, hands together on the spotless white blotter, taking careful note of what his visitor was finding interesting.

Flynn's eye found the boots as Stokes expected and paused for a long moment scrutinizing a drawing of a mounted cavalry trooper, carbine nestled in the crook of his arm. In his depiction of "Old Bill," artist Frederick Remington had captured a man at once assured and truculent, the heart and spirit of the U.S. Cavalry. Stokes walked around the desk. "Have a seat, Mr. Flynn," he said, suggesting a carefully positioned chair. "I think I may have something for you."

Sergeant Willman led his nine charges to the range at a slow trot, pointing out a group of photographers in khaki uniforms setting up a tripod. "See 'em up thah? They're gonna be around again today," he said of the cameramen. "Don't let 'em bother ya." The photographers had come out early, attracted by the promise of easily photographed action, stationing tripod-mounted movie cameras around the mounted pistol range.

Throughout the training, rumors had been running rife that this group of nine might be the last class of officer candidates to be trained for duty in the horse cavalry. The word was, last or not, this small group was the centerpiece in a rite marking the beginning of the end of a historic era in the U.S. Army: the dying days of an ancient mode of warfare and, maybe equally important, a way of life. Of course, there were plenty of voices raising contrary opinions. By now, though, these young men had become accustomed to the inquisitive lenses of the bulky, professional cameras the Signal Corps crews set up daily all over Fort Riley.

Willman brought his students to a halt at the range master's station, leaving barely enough time for a final piece of advice. "Now, lissen," he said, turning in his saddle, speaking over his shoulder, "if you're out there gallopin', getting ready to reload and everything goes to crap..."

"Sergeant Willman," a voice called, "a word with you, please." Until he spoke from somewhere behind them, none of them had noticed the mounted figure of Major Sam Chamberlain approaching, gliding smoothly as a gentle breeze on his finely gaited bay.

They'd seen Chamberlain nearly every day when he came to observe the class at their training, always at a distance. On these occasions he appeared heroically tall (although he stood a full three inches short of six feet), a bit of gray in his moustache, uniform expensively cut and meticulously pressed, boots gleaming. Officially Chamberlain bore the title of Acting Commandant of the Cavalry School, a position that struck awe in the minds of cavalrymen because it meant that Sam Chamberlain was also captain of the U.S. Equestrian Team and an Olympic champion.

Throughout the training the sergeants informed their candidates in the most respectful of tones that a man who rode like Major Chamberlain couldn't be merely human. "He's got to be part horse," they would say. In tones suggesting to their trainees that they must never think of using the term themselves, they admitted that around Fort Riley, the Major was "Centaur."

On hearing Chamberlain's call, Willman instinctively straightened his posture and sat in his saddle as if he were passing in review. Centaur's attention had that effect on a rider. The sergeant left his class and rode smartly to place his horse alongside the major's, so they could watch the nine mounted students waiting in a line.

Out of the side of his mouth, Pierce said to Flynn, "They're talking about us. See the sergeant nodding."

Chamberlain vanished as suddenly as he'd come, and Willman was again in his customary position with his students, with the air of Moses returned from the mountain. What priceless words had Centaur shared? They might never know, but it really didn't matter. Far more important to them was what they needed to know if everything went to crap on the range.

The sergeant pressed his lips together into a tight line, searching for exactly the right words to convey his message. His face brightened a bit. What had passed between the sergeant and the major should come first because it wasn't as important as what they needed to know about shooting. "Ah bin tellin' the major that some of ye've been doin' perty well." He cleared his throat. "He's gonna watch all of ya shoot yer first round." Again he made that light coughing noise and let his eyes rest momentarily on Danny before sweeping the entire class. "Now's the time to impress him."

Without the slightest hesitation, Willman returned to his favorite subject, shooting from horseback. "As I was sayin', when things go to crap, the best thing to do is the simplest—trust yer mount. These horses know the course better'n you do," said the master trainer.

It was time to do some shooting. While Willman and the range master discussed final details, most of the shooters used these last few moments to recheck the extra magazines in shirt pockets and adjust the fit of their belts.

Pierce whispered to Flynn, "See him up there?" He meant Chamberlain, positioned on the slope of a nearby hill. "I got a silver dollar right here that says you won't do it." He patted his pocket to emphasize their bet.

Flynn grinned mischievously. He'd been preparing for an opportunity like this for weeks—ever since he discovered that riding horses came very easily and naturally to him.

Deliberately, he removed his hat and attached it to one of the rings on the saddle by its strap. Both feet came out of the stirrups. The left, he kicked over the pommel behind the horse's neck, so that momentarily he was sitting on the saddle facing to the right. He rolled onto his stomach, grasping the pommel with his right hand and the cantle with his left. Danny's luck held—the old troop horse beneath him had been a silent partner to many an unannounced shenanigan over the years and he endured this one too, standing steadily as a rock.

Danny pushed himself up from the saddle and into a handstand he'd practiced a few times during free riding periods, showing off for Eddie and the others. Otherwise, it was no more than standard fare for a gymnast. The weight of the ammunition and the pistol gave him an awkward, out-of-balance feeling, but not enough to interfere. For a moment, no one spoke. Eight officer candidates, about a half-dozen sergeants—range masters, instructors and scorers, even Major Chamberlain at a distance—every one of them eyed Danny poised and motionless in his improbable handstand. The Signal Corps photographers kept the film cameras grinding, catching him holding his position for several seconds, then reversing the process easily and taking his seat, as if this were a little something he did every day to loosen up. As a final gesture, he recovered his hat from the ring and saluted the major.

Sergeant Willman, with as much dignity as he could gather, rode up to Danny and grabbed his horse's bridle, glaring at him. "Jes' what the hell're ya doin', young fella?" he growled.

"Impressing the hell out of Major Chamberlain, Sergeant," said Danny with a grin much like the one that drove Sister Theresa to order him to the confessional.

Willman, veteran of the war in Europe and decades of training new cavalrymen, fought to maintain his composure but failed. He spat into the sand and grimaced. The sergeant gritted his teeth before finally admitting helplessness, "Somethin' mus' be wrong with it, you doing a thing like that." He spat again. "Damn, young fella." He shook his head and grumbled mostly for effect, "I seen some people do crazy things in the saddle to show off, but they bin ridin' f'years. I'll damn well admit I ain't seen enybody try that, p'tic'ly after jus' a month'r so heah at Fort Riley. Now let's stop this foolishness." Clearing his throat loudly, he kicked his horse into motion, and in an afterthought, pointed his finger at Flynn in a final warning, "You better be damn good with that forty-five," he yelled over his shoulder.

Like most firing ranges, the mounted pistol range was laid out in an arrangement of protective earthworks meant to contain errant shots. To keep order and to make sure the shooting was done safely, several strategically placed observation towers provided vantage points allowing the range master and his assistants to keep an eye on the operation of the range. A red flag fluttered on a pole as a warning that live shooting was being conducted.

The range master used his long pointer to step them through the fourteen stations on a map of the serpentine course—slightly more than a quarter mile in length. "This will be your first of several runs," he said in a harsh, slightly nasal voice. Frowning, he made the same observation he always offered to first-time shooters, "Mounted shooting is hard to get the hang of. Most trainees take a few days to qualify." Then his words were all about the business of riding and shooting safely, concluding with a recitation of the rules. They'd heard them a dozen times, he knew, so he allowed himself to finish on a light note. "Points will be deducted for hits on your horse or saddle...or any other qualifiers."

The mounted qualifiers laughed nervously, waiting for the shooting to begin. The speaker horn blared a long, loud string of new orders, words that meant imminent shooting. One or two sneaked a glance at Willman, but he purposely avoided eye contact and rode away a little distance, leaving it to his students to perform.

The horn squealed, "Number one shooter, Harkins, on the range. Number two, Pierce, be ready." The order of firing had been determined at the barn by drawing slips of paper from a hat. Flynn counted himself lucky. He would go next to last.

Eight viewers watched intently, mentally picturing the targets and the course, trying to stay relaxed despite the noisy hammering of the range master's commands. Wesley Harkins, a blond, rawboned farm boy from a small town near Salina, Kansas, appeared nervous and slightly intimidated by the presence of the photographers and their cameras. Under Willman's careful training, he had already handled the loaded pistol on the range, firing at targets set to jump up unpredictably. His was a sensation everybody felt. It didn't matter how experienced the shooter might be. Somehow it was different when the scores would be recorded. Not one of the remaining eight failed to see Harkins flinch the instant he cycled the first round into the chamber.

He was still in view when he saw his first target, forward right. He flinched again, jerking at the trigger, but nothing happened. "Harkins, it's the safety," somebody shouted. Most of the waiting candidates assured themselves that they wouldn't be making that error. The Italian kid from Boston made the sign of the cross.

Harkins's second target came up much sooner than he expected: right rear. He passed on that one too. Now the newness was behind him. His posture relaxed, his arm steadied and he felt ready for the third, dead ahead. All eight of them felt relief for the first man when they saw the recoil raise the gun in his hand and they heard his shot. If he didn't get the shot on the target, at least it was close.

The range master had seen these things many times. Harkins was making mistakes expected of any shooter qualifying for the first time. His head, for instance: It was jerking around from left to right in nervous movements, anticipating the fourth target. He fired impulsively the instant the target appeared. Another miss! Wide. The sergeants in the tower saw him shake his weapon, berating himself, and they understood. Watching quietly in his saddle, Sergeant Willman mused aloud to no one in particular, "That ain't gonna do him any good."

Wesley Harkins worked hard, negotiating the course mostly through determination, never quite finding his confidence. He recovered his composure far too late to try a shot at the fifth, but the idea of how to shoot from horseback became clearer to him. He began to feel the timing and allowed his horse to run more freely. In the next few seconds, he improved visibly, scoring his first hit on the sixth target. From his tower, the range master looked down to Willman to be sure he had taken note of Harkins's improvement.

The screeching loudspeaker prompted the next shooter to be ready, but Harkins was far too intent on his target for the racket to affect him. He anticipated the next target to be front left, and his luck held. The target seemed suspended, asking to be shot. He fired twice—to make sure. With the first, he scored a well-placed hit. The second round splintered the target frame.

Harkins left the course red-faced with embarrassment, chiding himself for not being ready to fire often enough to empty even one magazine. But it was a good first run, they all knew, because every one of them watched Willman for his reaction and they saw his smile as he checked something on a clipboard.

Watching the earlier shooters produced a slight calming effect on those still waiting, although not enough to make them comfortable. At the moment, it was Clyde Sommers from Arkansas entering the course. Shooting dismounted, Clyde shot the black bull's-eyes out of the circular, stationary targets. He was an experienced rider before reporting to Fort Riley and, as expected, rode smoothly and scored well on the early targets; but turning to fire at the sixth target, the pistol slipped from his hand. Cursing his clumsiness, the favorite to qualify deliberately pulled off the course. Willman took note of his student's reactions. Dropping the weapon could wreck a qualifier's confidence. He'd have a word with Sommers.

Watching and waiting, Danny reverted to his gymnast's training, imagining the rhythm of his mount's gait, counting through seven targets, the reload, and seven more. With two more qualifiers to go before him, Flynn placed himself mentally into a little sphere of his own, relying on his mount to keep his place in the line qualifiers approaching the range while he visualized the targets popping up. He patted the horse's neck and spoke quietly to the animal, hoping a lot of solid pistol marksmen had trained him well. Old Jubal here would probably put his rider in perfect position to hit every target if his rider would be sensible enough to let him.

The horns squealed, "Number eight shooter, Flynn."

At the warning, Danny felt a familiar emotional surge that came to him when it was time to perform. He leaned to give his mount a final pat on the neck and drew a long breath.

On the signal, he tapped Old Jubal lightly with the reins, but the veteran was already running. Flynn felt solid on Jubal, but fired early on the first target, hitting it, but outside the scoring area. Forcing himself to breathe, he fired three times at targets popping up, barely aware of their numbers. It could have been luck, or maybe that his peripheral vision was working, but he saw the next two targets clearly and got hits with his shots. At the seventh shot, the slide of his pistol stayed open, a certain sign of an emptied magazine, but the mental shift from shooting to reloading threw him out of rhythm. To keep from having to slow down, he tore the button off his shirt pocket, grabbed the next magazine and inserted it. After that it came easily. The tricky reload maneuver that froze several of the previous shooters had played out like a slow-motion film and left Danny confident enough to urge Jubal to a little more speed. Reacting to the target positions, he turned and twisted, firing once at each target, getting hits.

Through the field glasses, it looked like fourteen targets hit for a first-time qualifier! Excitement edged into the range master's voice. "Damn! That's the redheaded wiseass that did the trick on his horse," he shouted to the assistants with him in the tower. The sergeant picked up the sound-powered microphone that connected him with the scorers at targets, shouting, "Mark these."

Danny, out of breath and grinning broadly, rode over to join the crowd waiting for the targets to be spread on long tables for inspection.

"How'd you do that, Flynn?" asked Pierce in frank admiration. The two were standing back with the other seven, watching and listening while the instructors compared their views as to progress of the class. Jerry Harkins moved close to Danny to congratulate him, adding a bit of rueful humor. "I hope they didn't bring my targets up here."

The troopers who marked the targets brought them to the range master's station and spread them on the table, pointing out the marked holes excitedly to one another, moving aside as the sergeants arrived to inspect the targets. Willman watched intently during the scoring, anticipating a qualifier. The range master looked Flynn's targets over twice, looking to one of the scorers for verification. "Looks like a damn machine was doing this shooting," he said softly in frank admiration.

Sergeant Willman beckoned to the Signal Corps cameramen, leaning against a canvas canopied truck a short distance from the range, smoking, chatting, killing time until the shooting began again. He wanted a picture with his prize pupil. In the few minutes while the range crew reset for the next round of qualifying, a photographer worked with his still camera, popping dozens of flashbulbs. In the lull between rounds of shooting, he wrote delivery instructions for the photographer on a sheet from his notebook, looking up occasionally to keep an eye on Major Chamberlain.

On his arrival, the gawkers stepped back, giving the major room to get a look at the scoring table without dismounting. "Who shot that round, Sergeant?" he inquired, inspecting the faces of the nine students. None of them spoke. They weren't accustomed to talking to majors. In their experience, only the sergeants did that.

"It was Flynn, Major." Willman pointed to Danny standing with the others. "That's him, the redhead," he added, "th' one who did that trick on Old Jubal."

Would Centaur have anything to say to the trainees? To their great disappointment, he spoke only a few quiet words to the sergeant. Willman nodded his understanding of something the major said and saluted as Chamberlain cantered away.

Returning to his waiting students, Willman said curtly to Flynn, "Wait for me over there, near that gate," and turned his attention to his other students. Only when his remaining shooters were busily reloading their empty magazines under the hawk-like eye of the range master did he find time for his lone qualifier. "Flynn," he said, speaking hurriedly. "Heah's what Major Chamberlain said. He wants to see ya this evenin': kinda late, so lissen. Yer excused fer the afternoon. Get yer evenin' meal early, then report to the stable sergeant's office at eighteen hundred hours. Sergeant Long'll have a horse ready fer ya." He gave Danny the once-over, taking in his dusty uniform and field gear, sweated up in the heat. "Ya won't need the webbing—or the weapon," he said, "and I'd change the uniform, too, if I was you."

Danny opened his mouth to ask a question, but Willman had already shifted his attention to his remaining eight candidates.

⚜

Seated in a wooden swivel chair in his cluttered office, First Sergeant Amos Long pushed his steel-rimmed eyeglasses higher up his nose and allowed himself a discrete smile at the tentative approach of a very inquisitive trainee, the one whose riding ability Major Chamberlain wanted to assess more closely. The stables sergeant was thoroughly unlike Centaur. Where Chamberlain was lithe, trim in his uniform and taciturn, Sergeant Long was rotund and comfortable in his faded denim fatigue trousers held up by red suspenders, and garrulous. He walked with a limp that sidelined him from operational assignments, but the army was happy to have him exactly where he was. Talk among cavalrymen held that the veteran sergeant had no peer as a judge of horseflesh—or of men, for that matter. In ordinary conversation, Long was known simply as Amos to thousands of cavalrymen of all ranks, but such is the way of military protocol with famous soldiers that few would presume to address him except as Sergeant Long. Plenty of generals proudly claimed the colorful sergeant as a confidant on a broad range of subjects. The sergeant tilted his head back to get a look at the young man in khaki closing the screen door behind him.

Danny closed the office door carefully behind him, and allowed his eyes to adjust to the dim light in the office before speaking. "Sergeant Long? My name is Flynn. I'm here to report to Major Chamberlain." He hesitated before adding, "Sergeant Willman told me you'd want to see me before the major arrives. Can you tell me why the major wants to see me?"

Long rummaged elaborately through his pockets for a mislaid corncob pipe and searched the office for it. Finally, he found it lying atop a steel bookcase. His comfort restored, the sergeant inspected the bowl carefully before answering Danny's questions. When he finally spoke, it was in a surprisingly high, nasal drawl. "Well yes, I do kinda know what the major wants you for." Pursing his lips, the sergeant blew through the pipestem to clear it. "You and him are going for a ride," he said. "Le's go outside."

Long ushered Danny through the back door of his office to a small paddock, where a single horse stood quietly near the fence in the lengthening shadow of a line of tall elms. The sergeant explained as they walked, "Major Chamberlain'll be here d'rectly, but for now the only thing he told me was to saddle up this here black mare and show you the tack." Long caressed the horse affectionately on her nose. "Her name is Lena," he said.

Two months here at Fort Riley, give or take a few days, had been a constant challenge for Danny to work out the mysteries of how the army worked. Physical demands presented no real problem. He'd taken to riding and shooting like a duck to water. His uncertainties came in the form of questions about when to salute or how to remember the differences between brigades and battalions, squadrons and companies, and exactly who was really in charge of these groups of men. Right now his mind was on Centaur, but Sergeant Long persisted in telling him about the horse.

"Lena, is it?" Danny looked the mare over in the fading light of a once-brilliant sunset, taking in her strong, graceful conformation. He felt himself rattling his questions in a stream, but he couldn't help it. "She looks a bit small to me, but strong. In fact, she looks very much like the horses the major rides. Is there something unusual about the tack he wants me to see?"

"Easy with the questions. Not all at once," said Long. The sergeant scratched his nose and took stock of this Flynn fellow—strong and eager—and promising, too. Through his bifocals he appraised the young man who would soon be a lieutenant, grunting his approval of the youngster's good sense in showing up looking smart and polished. Beyond shadow of doubt, Major Chamberlain treated riding with the reverence of a religious rite, and when he arrived for the evening's ride, he would be attired as smartly as if he were competing in an international competition. *Attired*: Not a word Amos Long uttered aloud very often, but it came to him when he thought of Sam Chamberlain.

Satisfied with the raw material, he expelled a long breath that conveyed a sense of the great burden entrusted to him. Motioning Danny to follow, Long led the way to the tack room, limping on a knee that had been mangled years before, handling new horses at a remount station. "Now look here, boy." He stopped at a bench to point out a few features of a recently repaired saddle. "See, you've been ridin' on a McClellan saddle like this—the kind that ordinary sojers use. It's a good workin' saddle that can make a raw rider look like a military man." He watched Flynn to be sure he was paying attention. "It kinda makes 'em sit up straight. We want you to have an idea of what your men'll be sittin' on when you take 'em out in the field. That old McClellan saddle's been around since about the Civil War. It's made for hanging things on it: stuff y'might need, like food for you and grain for the horse—and your men will have their rifle in a boot over here on the side—it rides just under their left leg. And if they don't throw 'em away, they c'n carry their tin hats behind 'em too." Troopers hated wearing the heavy, flattish steel helmets.

Flynn, watching every movement and hanging onto every word, found himself imagining the colorful sergeant as some sort of wizard. His hands, gnarled from years of broken and sprained fingers, yet still surprisingly sensitive, caressed the beautiful new leather of a light, graceful saddle resting on a stand about two steps away, just asking to be admired. Long had plenty to say about it. "This here saddle, though, is one of the major's. He has 'em put aside for teachin' the army equestrian team some of the fine points of ridin'." Danny's eyes widened admiringly at the saddler's exquisite workmanship and luxuriated in the smoothness and tang of brand new leather. Satisfied with the reaction, the sergeant nodded permission for Danny to heft the featherlight saddle. "The major wants ya to use it this evening," he said deferentially. "Le's try it on Lena."

The sergeant moved spryly around the horse for a man with a damaged leg, making minute adjustments to straps and saddle position, paying particular attention to how Danny examined the horse and her tack. He nodded approvingly at the way the younger man approached Lena and opened her mouth to inspect the bit. "Looky here," he said, his voice sounding his approval. Long patted the mare on her rump and ran his appreciative hands over her well-groomed flanks. "This little lady ain't one of your troop horses. For one thing, she stands a full hand shorter than them troopers. The major likes horses that's smaller 'n more agile. And look here too." He watched his student absorbing the idea of using his hands travelling smoothly along the large muscles of her hindquarters and shoulders to appraise the horse's condition. "Feel the power she's got. She c'n jump almos' like a deer." As if it were a thing to be kept secret, Long shared a little about her pedigree. "She ain't exactly a thoroughbred," he confessed. "Got some Morgan in her."

The sergeant clearly enjoyed being entrusted with one of Centaur's hand-selected pupils. "Take another minute 'fore the major gets here. Pick up Lena's feet and look at th' shoes." They were light, specially crafted and fitted to the mare's feet, not even half the weight of the heavy standard, durable things he saw on troop horses. Danny looked up to ask about the shoes and saw the sergeant standing at attention. They both saluted the major, mounted as usual, trotting toward them out of the gathering gloom. Danny wondered whether the major ever dismounted. And where were his horses kept, if not here under the watchful care of Sergeant Long?

Chamberlain came directly to the point. "Mount up, Mister Flynn. Ride with me, so I can get an idea of what you can do on a horse."

They rode away from the stable with Danny out in front, first at a walk and then at a slow trot. When the last of the limestone buildings passed behind them, Chamberlain rode beside his new pupil and slowed to a stop. This was by far closer than Danny had ever been to the legendary rider. The major appeared much older than he looked to be from a distance, with surprisingly deep crow's feet etched around a pair of gimlet eyes that looked as if they could bore right through him. A dark, pencil line of a moustache lent Chamberlain the look of some of the prominent movie stars. Danny suspected this man could penetrate his very core to learn how well his senses served him and how he thought. Such a realization made him very uncomfortable. What would Centaur see? Would the major deem him inferior? What was it the man wanted? Of course Danny had been making every effort to ride as gracefully and naturally as he possibly could, but if riding was all that Centaur wanted, he probably would have said something by now. So Danny watched Major Chamberlain, to learn better how this great rider sat his horse—and Danny experienced a revelation. Even with their horses standing still, he realized that compared to Chamberlain, he was nothing more than a competent rider: that despite his highly developed balance and strength, he was little better than a burden Lena would be forced to carry.

Chamberlain, however, was something different. Centaur and his horse were athletic partners, interacting physically and communicating with each other even when standing quietly. Is that what the major looked for—hoping Danny had that kind of latent sensitivity hidden somewhere within him? Centaur spoke in a voice both kind and penetrating. "You haven't been around horses much, have you?" he inquired, but it was more a statement of evident fact. "But I think I see some feeling for them. Right? Where did you get that?"

Danny blurted the first thing that came to him. "Maybe from helping Mr. Brennan with his milk rounds." Foolish words, he knew as soon as he uttered them. His face reddened with embarrassment. If he had some rare sense of ease with horses, it was something he was born with.

He would soon discover Major Chamberlain to be a man of considerable innate powers, enabling him to discern the special gifts he expected to find in an international class rider. That Danny couldn't identify the source of his skill with horses, told Chamberlain that his gift was natural and not a result of special tutoring. Centaur had seen enough. "All right," he said. "We'll ride for a while to loosen up on the way to the exercise areas. Follow closely behind me and do what I do. If you become unsure or frightened, trust Lena."

Without a word of warning, Centaur tore out into the rolling hills of central Kansas with no more than faint moonlight to see by, staying off the army roads crisscrossing the hills, leading Danny on a ride far more challenging than any he'd ever experienced before. From the beginning, the major rode at speeds that made Danny fear for his safety, but the celebrated horseman felt confident of how much speed his pupil could tolerate. For miles they raced across the landscape, slowing only when it was dangerous for the animals, laboring up steep hills and plunging down the reverse slopes, leaping off rocky outcroppings and scrambling across dry washes, sending cascades of stones rattling behind them. At times Danny suspected this hair-raising scramble might be a calculated punishment for his brash handstand demonstration, but punishment isn't generally meted with such trust and care. Before long, he felt the fear leaving him. Lena was teaching him what it truly meant to let his mount run, to relax and trust her confidence and skill.

Eventually Centaur and his breathless new student clattered onto an unpaved road cut by army bulldozers through a field of boulders broken from the chalky bluffs, and they trotted in silence for a time, until the Major spoke again. "Ride ahead of me as I direct." He followed a few lengths behind Danny, watching him cantering, galloping and trotting—without a word except to call for a change of gait. Once more they paused for a critique. Then they rode again, sometimes together and at other times with Danny following. The drilling and inspecting didn't stop until they saw the lights of the stables, and the major rode stirrup to stirrup with his pupil.

Sitting as erect as he knew how in the new saddle Sergeant Long had taken such pains to fit on Lena, Danny waited for Major Chamberlain's judgment. Only the horses' breathing and their hooves hammering on the patterned brick pavement broke the silence—until the major spoke again. "Mister Flynn, gymnastic feats on the back of a horse aren't what we teach here at Fort Riley, but your antics out there this morning showed me that you have great athletic ability—if not particularly good sense. A gymnast as talented as you are should have the potential to become a great horseman." Allowing Danny a few moments to think, Chamberlain finished his assessment. "Tonight I've satisfied myself that you're capable of riding at very high levels—with work, of course."

"Thank you, sir," said Danny, very much uncertain of what was to come.

Sergeant Long met them, taking Lena's reins. Chamberlain gave the sergeant a wink and a conspiratorial whisper Danny couldn't hear. "He'll do, Sergeant Long. I think he'll do."

"Thought as much, Major Sam," said old Amos, leading Lena away.

Chamberlain, tersely as always, had only a few words for his new protégé. "I'm not excusing you from your duties tomorrow morning, but I'll expect you at the stable sergeant's office daily, thirty minutes after your last training period." Danny took that to mean a final forgiveness of his handstand antics."

Thus began the rigorous sessions under the unforgiving eye of the fabled Centaur. For the entire week, Chamberlain continued the confidence-building exercises in the maneuvering ranges around Fort Riley. Nightly Centaur led Danny across the landscape, with few reductions in speed or any other consideration for his lack of experience. Nor did Chamberlain ever once turn to see how his student was faring. He learned all he wanted to know by listening. "Good," Chamberlain would say tersely while he and Danny walked their horses into the stables area. "Better get some rest before tomorrow's training."

Soon the emphasis shifted to skills requiring patience and fine control in taking jumps and guiding Lena through the range of gaits, with Chamberlain making minute criticisms delivered in monosyllables. Then, suddenly it seemed, at the conclusion of an afternoon's training during which Danny succeeded in demonstrating complete control of his mount with the most miniscule possible movements of his hands and body, Centaur relaxed, speaking more and more familiarly as the work progressed.

One night, as Danny's training at Fort Riley was coming to an end, the major said, "Young man, you're one of the finest natural riders I've ever met, and I'd like to help you become a finished horseman," a statement as pregnant with possibility as he could have made it. To someone in his first months of riding, it could mean practically anything, but Danny had come to appreciate his own accomplishments. He knew for sure he was a far better horseman already than he ever expected to be.

Chamberlain had been thinking far ahead of his student, yet he spoke as if his expectations were something well known. "It's a pity the next Olympic Games have already been cancelled because of the war in Europe." Shaking his head regretfully, he said, "We're going to be fighting in this war, you and me. How long it will take is the only question. If it's over by forty-four, we could have another Army Equestrian Team in the Olympics, and if I'm still the captain, I want to include you in my planning. We did well in 1936, and a rider of your potential could someday be an outstanding representative of the United States in international competition."

A trooper on stables duty appeared in a lighted doorway and Chamberlain dropped the subject abruptly. He didn't believe in wasting time on speculation. "Come with me," he said, sharing a few more thoughts as they walked. "I've been on the telephone a lot this week. The War Department is making a final review of the continuing need for horse cavalry units at a meeting in Washington. They want to convert some of the larger units, divisions like the First Cavalry, and train them as infantry or armor." For a long moment,

Chamberlain pursed his lips as if confronting an important decision. "I'm leaving tomorrow morning on the train for Washington to help in preparing arguments for keeping horses in army service. I could be there a week, or a month. In fact, I may not get back here to Fort Riley at all before I'm sent off to my first war assignment."

Chamberlain led Danny to the stable sergeant's office, which was as neat as his personal appearance was not. Long had made the required arrangements and had been awaiting their arrival. Now he deferred to Major Chamberlain, who led a little procession into the tack room where they kept the special saddles, and then into a smaller room where five exquisitely beautiful saddles sat on individual stands. A sixth stand stood empty. Chamberlain and Long stood back for Danny to inspect this collection of brand new, full sets of russet brown leather tack: saddlers' masterpieces. With all the gravity of a grand master of a chivalric order investing a new knight, the major ceremoniously strode past the saddle display, showing Danny a trunk, an ordinary army tack box, painted olive green, except that this one was stenciled 2nd Lt. D. C. Flynn in white letters. He heard the Major saying, "We issue this kind of tack to riders whose promise justifies the expense."

For an instant, he forgot the saddles, thinking only about becoming a lieutenant in two days. Until this moment, Danny had been acutely aware he and his group of nine were condescendingly referred to as ninety-day wonders, and thus hadn't allowed himself to think of the day actually happening. He felt a surge of excitement at seeing his name painted on the wood, and he struggled to keep it to himself.

Chanberlain opened the lid with almost reverent care to reveal a saddle and its matching tack—the sixth saddle. "The finest available anywhere," he was saying. "Colonel Podhajsky at the Spanish Riding School in Vienna doesn't have a better one." He reached into a canvas packet tacked inside the lid, withdrawing an envelope and an army-issue lock. He handed Danny the envelope. "This is your authorization to have the gear." Then finally Centaur handed him the lock. "To help you keep it safe," he said.

Danny opened his mouth to voice his appreciation to his mentor, but he managed only to mutter, "Thank you, sir." What would his father think? A Flynn at a loss for words!

Chamberlain took his watch from its pocket and glanced at the time. "I have an appointment," he said, excusing himself. At the door, he turned with an additional thought. "I may have disappointed you with my talking about the uncertain fate of the horse cavalry. And it's quite possible that none of us may enter the war on horseback, but this kind of speculation has been going on for years and we're still here. I'm confident the men in the War Department have nothing yet that can replace us. So don't worry. I'll do what I can to make sure that you're ordered to a horse cavalry regiment after you've completed training." Then Centaur was gone, leaving his apprentice to work out what he had just heard.

Danny felt a hand on his shoulder and heard Sergeant Long speaking to him. "Come help me with Lena. You worked her pretty hard." And under the pretense of needing some help in wiping Lena down with straw, walking her to cool down before giving her water and feeding her a carefully measured ration of oats, he began to teach his pupil how an expert takes care of his horses.

Long carefully inspected each of Lena's feet for injuries, quite aware of the sort of terrain she had been ridden over. "Look here," he said, pointing to subtle signs of wear. "These were new yesterday. Keep an eye on them shoes."

"I will, Sergeant," Danny said, staring into the darkness where Centaur had just disappeared. At the moment he was far more interested in the man who had singled him out for special treatment than he was in horseshoes. Who was he? What did those vague warnings about fewer cavalry units mean? "Tell me about Major Chamberlain, Sergeant Long."

The wizard in denim stood slowly, favoring his gimpy knee, and felt for his pipe. He patted Lena on the rump, allowing her to move across the paddock to a spot where she felt comfortable. She didn't need to be taken to her stall for a few minutes yet. Considering where he would begin in answering the question, Long struck a match on the leg of his trousers and held it to the tobacco until the fire glowed, puffing noisily at the pipe until a cloud of smoke engulfed his face.

"Everybody in the army knows Major Sam," he began. Amos Long knew about infantry and artillery units, but only in a vague kind of way. They didn't count to him because he was a cavalryman, a horse soldier. To him, every morning's reveille added another link to a long chain of historical tradition of military horses going back thousands of years. Hell, armies always had cavalry. But lately he'd been hearing more and more disturbing news from the major about the beginning of the end for this glorious tradition. He didn't want to believe it, but he'd been told directly that the young man facing him was among the last to be trained here at Fort Riley. "Sam..." He corrected himself. "Major Sam's the best rider in the world," said Amos Long of Sam Chamberlain, because he was sure it was true.

Only months ago, Chamberlain was riding the crest of a wave of optimism. He was acknowledged as the army's preeminent horseman. Promotions were picking up and at times like these, every eye in the army would be on the man who held the job now occupied by Sam Chamberlain. For decades the foregone conclusion held that an officer with tickets like Chamberlain was certain to be promoted and given command of a cavalry regiment. Now, though, with war almost certain, well, his future was anything but that.

The Germans were swallowing up Europe, sending waves of tanks in a series of strikes they called blitzkrieg, and those tanks couldn't be stopped by men on horseback. The army was buying tanks and promoting tankers as fast as they could be retrained. But the same war that was speeding up promotions was also sounding the death knell of horse cavalry. The thinkers in Washington felt certain that horses couldn't stand up to modern vehicles, particularly fast-moving tanks. Long's sources were bringing him word of the political battles being waged in the War Department to retain the mounted units. He knew beyond a shadow of doubt that the highly placed general who had been Chief of Cavalry rashly threw away a career-making opportunity to become the first Chief of Armor. His old friend George Marshall, the Army Chief of Staff, was saying, "We must phase out the horse cavalry and..." The cavalry general blurted, "Over my dead body," before Marshall could make him the generous offer he intended. General Herr never got another chance.

Long winked. "I hear lots of stories here at the stables. General Marshall fired him right there in his office," said the sergeant, shaking his head with evident distaste for the whole thing. Now with the future looking murky at best, Sam Chamberlain was bound for Washington to take the case for horses to Congress.

Long stared out into the dark, thinking over all these things Danny wanted to know about. "Major Sam's the best in the world at what he does, but he's goin' to Washington lookin' for work." He puffed slowly on his pipe and exhaled with a long, mournful sigh. "Fer all of us, I expect."

chapter

THREE

Washington: U.S. State Department spokesman today decries continuing tanker
sinkings by German U-boats.

New York to Brownsville had taken an eternity. At least it seemed that way to Second Lieutenant Danny Flynn, who'd been living in a railroad car—sitting, eating, dozing—lulled by the rhythmic clacking of wheels carrying him steadily south and west. At each stop, he'd unfold his timetable and elaborately strike through the name of the station with a pencil. If the weather allowed, he walked to stretch his legs and reacquaint himself with the feel of solid earth under his feet. If a newspaper was available, he bought a copy, hoarding it for slow, careful reading during the long monotonous stretches of low rolling hills covered with scrub growth or flat land marked off by barbed wire strung on countless fence posts. After thoroughly digesting the paper, he saved a few pages to fan himself in the sweltering heat rising steadily, mile by mile.

In the last hour, Danny's pencil slashed through McAllen and Harlingen: two of the last stops in the valley, as Texans called it, before the train reached Brownsville. He had the car to himself now, with plenty of time to get into his uniform. He spread everything out, smoothing away the folds as best he could and busied himself in polishing the stovepipe legs of his russet brown cavalry boots.

Satisfied with his handiwork, Danny stood in the aisle pulling on the khaki uniform last ironed by his mother just before he left home, moving from side to side in the car, bending down for a look at the flat earth shimmering in the heat—gritty, rosy-brown earth laid up over millennia by the meanderings of the Rio Grande seeking its way from the Rockies to the Gulf of Mexico. Crossing to the right side of the car, he looked west to where the Rio Grande had to be, but thick stands of trees hid the river from view. He could only guess at the crops being raised in the irrigated fields or what strains of cattle grazed among the scraggly, thorny trees scattered on the arid ranchland.

The train slowed noticeably, passing irregular little settlements of low, unpainted wooden dwellings roofed with overlapping sheets of rusting metal. Almost there, he smiled to himself, happy that his journey was finally ending. He held onto the back of a seat to steady himself against the train jolting from one set of rails to another as the switches guided it through a large railroad yard littered with industrial clutter. Every tree, every structure—even the faded paint on the metal signs—showed signs of scorching by the relentless sun. A rusty water cistern towered over mounds of coal and split firewood partially hidden behind corrugated metal fences meant to deter pilferage. Nearly illegible, the faded letters on the cistern told him he'd finally reached Brownsville, the southern terminus of the Missouri Pacific Railroad. To travel any farther south by rail, a passenger would have to cross the river to transfer to a Mexican railroad.

At the now-familiar sounds of squealing brakes and hissing clouds of steam vented by the locomotive, he pulled on his newly shined boots and straightened his khaki tie. Anxiously, he waited for the signal to open the door. Generally satisfied with his appearance, Danny fidgeted with his handkerchief to brush a few specks of dust off his hat before pressing it on his head—with a little forward tilt. He folded his handkerchief, put it away, and stepped off the train.

For a month, he had been Danny Flynn, son of the crowded, dingy Irish neighborhoods of New York, but now, on the Brownsville platform, he once again became Second Lieutenant D.C. Flynn, the army horseman whose name was stenciled on the new tack box the army sent ahead from Fort Riley. Making his way down the paved walkway between the tracks, however, he felt niggling doubts setting in. Everything he knew about soldiering, every single scrap of knowledge about the army, he'd learned at Fort Riley under the watchful eye of men like Willman and Long, and Major Chamberlain, of course. After a month at home, those days of training suddenly felt faint and inaccessible in his memory.

The Brownsville passenger depot wasn't anything like he imagined it would be. Between here and St. Louis, the railroad depots in the little towns were mostly small, wooden structures with wide awnings providing a little shade—usually no more than three or four rooms, counting the stationmaster's office, and an outdoor privy painted in the same color as the station. Here, at the southmost tip of the United States of America, he found him-self in a stuccoed art-deco beauty elaborately enhanced by doorways and ornately deco-rated windows, reproductions of architectural features like those in the Spanish missions of California. A wide green awning extended along the broad platform for the length of the first two or three cars, and the rest of the train stretched along the track to the baggage car, where sweating workers were already transferring luggage and freight onto steel-wheeled carts. Danny walked out to the street and set his cardboard suitcase on the curb. The worn telegram in his pocket assured him he would be met with transportation to Fort Brown, so he waited anxiously, scanning the roadway for some kind of army vehicle. A black taxi with red lettering waited for a fare, and a few private sedans stood idling near the main door, but nothing in sight resembled an army truck. A few passengers moved away confidently from the front cars in the direction of the two-story brick hotel visible about three blocks away. Others stood waiting impatiently: three soldiers and a few salesmen in straw hats and rumpled suits with sample cases to collect.

With no army vehicles in evidence, Danny considered hailing the taxi driver, but he didn't know how far it was to Fort Brown. It might be a long way and he had only two dol-lars in his wallet and a few coins in his pocket. He began to wonder if the army had forgot-ten about him because he'd stayed at home too long. Maybe taking a full month before reporting to his first assignment wasn't the best way to get off on the right foot.

Actually the army encouraged new lieutenants to take home leave after completing training. Having Danny, fit from hard work and browned by the sun, walking the streets of his New York neighborhood in his flat-brimmed campaign hat, riding breeches and spurred boots was a recruiter's dream. His mother proudly did her share by ironing his uniform each Saturday, insisting he wear it to Sunday mass.

After another fruitless search for an army vehicle of any kind, Danny pulled out his handkerchief again to wipe the sweat from his face. He removed his hat and applied the handkerchief to the inside leather band. Catching a reflection of himself in a window, he used it as a mirror to press the wispy red strands of a month-old pencil-line moustache into place with the tip of his finger.

"Lieutenant Flynn!" a voice called from a black army sedan rolling to a stop at the curb. Danny turned self-consciously to see a painfully thin, sandy-haired man emerging from the passenger door, extending his hand in welcome. "I'm Doug Cameron," he greeted the anxious arrival. "Welcome to Fort Brown and the 124th Cavalry." The man who called to him stood slightly taller than Danny, an inch perhaps, though his high forehead may have lent that illusion, and he might have been that much narrower at the shoulders.

"Thank you, sir," Danny said, saluting at the sight of the silver bar on Cameron's col-lar.

Doug ignored the salute with a wave of his hand. "Forget it, Flynn. I'm only a first lieutenant," he explained in his deep resonant voice "Hardly senior at all." This time Danny shook the proffered hand, thinking Cameron looked older than a lieutenant should be. It could have been because of the man's surprisingly prominent, chiseled facial features outlining his bladelike nose. Cameron made a few brief, polite inquiries about the journey from New York.

At some signal from Lieutenant Cameron, the driver jumped from behind the wheel of the sedan to whisk the new lieutenant's flimsy suitcase into the trunk. At a glance, Flynn took him for one of the Mexican men handling baggage around the station. On closer look, however, he saw that the driver wore a khaki uniform of shirt and riding breeches, identical to his passengers' except that his brown laced boots came only to mid-calf, quite different from the tall, smooth riding boots worn by the two lieutenants—and he wore no mark of rank whatsoever—not on his collar or on his sleeves like the sergeants. In his training at Fort Riley, the sergeants had his complete attention. Of course there were very few army uniforms in New York. That made this wiry young man the first private Danny had ever seen: so short he could barely be seen over the top of the sedan. Before sliding behind the wheel again, the soldier gave Danny a long stare, as if to size him up very carefully.

Cameron held the rear door open for Danny. "Hop in," he invited with a sweeping flourish, before taking the front passenger's seat, continuing to talk. "I'll give you a look at your new home as a lieutenant sees it," promised Cameron with a wry grin. "It's going to be a quick tour because Colonel Chamberlain wants you in his office in about two hours." Danny, accustomed to long periods of silence on the train, failed to understand much of Doug's message.

At Doug's signal, the driver pulled slowly away from the depot and into the Brownsville business district, which began immediately across the street from the railroad station. In the first few blocks Cameron pointed out a few useful landmarks—the hotel, a small collection of municipal buildings and a saddler's shop where Fort Brown officers went occasionally went to have special modifications made to their tack, or to buy sporting saddles for polo. Beyond that, Brownsville didn't have a lot to offer off duty soldiers. If it was entertainment they wanted, they had only to cross the bridge to the Mexican city of Matamoros, in plain sight directly across the river.

Brownsville couldn't actually claim a founding date. Rather, it sprang up as one of those opportunistic commercial settlements, which during America's westward expansion, grew outside army posts to sell things to soldiers, and it took its name from the fort, which itself had been built opportunistically opposite Matamoros to establish the American claim of a border on the Rio Grande. Mexico held the contrary opinion that the border was actually many miles to the east, on the Nueces River. But the Mexican War settled the border issue in the mid-eighteen hundreds. These days Brownsville owed its continued existence and commercial growth mainly to commerce with Mexico. "Look over to the right," said Cameron, drawing Danny's attention to the international bridge spanning the Rio Grande.

The driver pulled out of the traffic a few dozen yards from a bridge cluttered with signs in English and Spanish. "Mexico, sir," said the driver helpfully, speaking with a slight accent. The flags displayed at the Mexican checkpoint across the river appeared so near, Danny could make out the distinctive emblem of an eagle with a snake in its beak depicted in the white center panel. Absorbed by the novelty of an international boundary just a few yards away, he watched intently the steady stream of traffic working its way into the United States through the nearer checkpoint, marked by American flags.

Cameron took his role as tour guide seriously. "That's your gateway to foreign enchantments," he said, breaking into the new man's preoccupation. Danny had hardly gotten a look at the border crossing before the diminutive driver swung the sedan into the light stream of international traffic crossing the bridge, almost immediately slowing for an army sentry post at a wide iron gate mounted on massive stone posts. All this occurred too quickly for the realization to sink in with Danny that the railroad station, downtown Brownsville and the bridge to Matamoros, Mexico were all within a quarter mile of the Fort Brown gate.

Once inside Fort Brown, it was only a few hundred yards more before they turned into the circular drive at the entrance to a sprawling building constructed of limestone blocks. As the driver slowed to a stop, Cameron informed the new man, "You're home. This is the Bachelor Officers' Quarters. It's where you'll live with the rest of us. Let's get out of the car. We'll drop off your luggage before we get you oriented on the major landmarks of the post."

But there was one more bit of important business that couldn't be delayed. Having met Danny, Cameron felt that learning about the private at the wheel could turn out to be a delicate matter. No time like the present, he concluded. While he had them together on the concrete sidewalk, Doug made it direct and brief. "Lieutenant Flynn, meet Private Francisco Garza. He's been assigned to be your dog robber. The two of you will soon get to know each other very well."

What was that Cameron said? Dog robber? None of this made the slightest sense to Flynn. It struck him as a vile thing to call a man. In New York, where young men are extremely touchy about what other people may call them, using a name like that might have provoked a fight, but Private Garza apparently took no offense. In fact, he was smiling.

Cameron watched the new lieutenant's face for his reaction. Good thing he'd waited till now to make the introduction. As he expected, Flynn truly hadn't understood. Maybe he'd been asleep at Fort Riley the day they mentioned orderlies. Doug explained to Danny that Private Garza was assigned to be his orderly. "That's all, an orderly," said Cameron, trying to reassure the agitated Flynn that in no way was Private Garza being abused.

Doug's explanation awakened something in Danny's memory. Somewhere in a drowsy classroom, he'd learned that a cavalry officer was assigned an orderly to take care of his horse and equipment and generally do things for him. The principle of the custom was that an officer didn't have the time to do all the things required of a platoon commander, like training, riding, and supervising his soldiers, plus taking care of his horse and equipment, so cavalry officers were permitted to hire troopers as orderlies. All right, thought Danny; so he would have an orderly, if they did things like that here. "But I'll not be calling him a dog robber," he insisted.

Cameron offered a slightly longer explanation. "The story is that the term stems from the loyalty that frequently develops between officers and their orderlies. They say a good orderly'd steal food from a dog so that his lieutenant wouldn't go hungry." Cameron didn't wait to learn whether this story eased the new man's objections. This trivial matter musn't permit Lieutenant Flynn to waste precious time on a pointless Irish lament—he had a very important appointment in a little more than an hour. "For now, Flynn, let's be practical about this and accept it," Cameron advised impatiently. Private Garza in particular would be no ordinary dog robber, Doug assured Danny, because his family lived in a small town here in the valley. "Raymondville, isn't it?" he asked, to give Garza an opportunity to speak. What Cameron meant was that Danny's new orderly could help him learn about life in South Texas, and from all appearances, he would need a lot of help.

"That's right, sir. Raymondville," said the private. Glancing at his new boss, he suppressed the urge to break into a broad grin at the man's discomfort. "We don't need to talk about dog robbers anymore," said Cameron, impatient to get on with his indoctrination. The new lieutenant and his orderly could work out their agreement on their own.

Danny's thoughts still churned over this dog robber business. What was an orderly or a dog robber but a servant? He didn't begin to know how to treat a servant and fully expected to be embarrassed by the practice. Shifting uneasily, he whispered a question to Cameron. "I'm to pay Private Garza, am I?"

Cameron nodded. "Yes."

"How much, Doug?"

Cameron saw no difficulty in talking about honest compensation in Garza's hearing. "Twenty-one dollars a month—in cash," he said, "And that's equal to what the army pays him." He'd leave it to Flynn to realize later that doubling a man's income wasn't such a bad deal. Cameron gave Garza orders to take Lieutenant Flynn's suitcase up to his room.

Danny rushed to stop his surprised orderly from handling his luggage, protesting loudly, "I'll do that."

Cameron intervened. "It's his job, Flynn. Let him do it, for god's sake." He stepped between Flynn and the private holding his flimsy cardboard suitcase. "Look," said Doug with a shrug, "Put your difficulty behind you. Look at this as a division of labor. That's the way the army sees it. You'll be very, very busy, and Private Garza's assistance will be of great benefit to both of you. Remember, he's new to the army too. Your part in this partnership is to use his help wisely and teach him to become a cavalry trooper." He motioned to Garza to take the luggage into the building and slipped behind the wheel, inviting Danny to take the passenger's seat. "I want to explain a few things while you get a look at the post." Impatiently, Cameron urged his passenger to pay attention to the general layout of the post and to pay specific attention to the signs on its principal limestone buildings. "You know how the army likes to label everything," said Doug, "but now we've got to get moving."

He pulled away from the BOQ and drove slowly along streets lined with orange trees and tall palms. "Now, Flynn, here's what I have in mind," he explained, a quick spin to locate the landmarks a brand new lieutenant would need to recognize and find without having to ask a lot of questions. As best he could without a map to show it, Cameron described the older buildings, the original fort, as being located in an almost circular loop created by the Rio Grande—all but surrounded by Mexico. "I think we'll drive down to the parade ground, and start there," suggested Cameron, "Every important building on the post is located nearby." The broad, beautifully groomed stretch of lawn, unmistakably the parade ground, could have been the one at Fort Riley, except for the palm trees that didn't grow in Kansas. Doug leaned on the steering wheel to see past his passenger, "See there, the Chapel and the Post Theater plus those large barracks buildings on the far side."

Driving a little farther, Doug pulled the sedan to the curb across the parade ground from a two-storied building of honey-colored bricks, surrounded by porches trimmed in white-painted wood. "See how the builders set the headquarters building on a slightly elevated plot to accentuate its importance," Doug said quietly, shifting gears and edging the sedan ahead. Nearing the handsome structure, Doug raised a finger from the steering wheel to make a point. "The colonel's office is up there on the top floor, and for some reason he wants you there in about an hour." Cameron checked his watch to be certain, adding another thought; he glanced at Danny to be sure he was getting this information. "See, the colonel wouldn't ordinarily have you in this soon after your arrival, but tomorrow he has to travel to Austin to meet with the governor." Improbable as it might seem, the commanding officer was positive he knew this Lieutenant Flynn. His instructions had been very explicit: "Make sure he reports to my office at fifteen hundred hours. I want to welcome him personally."

If Cameron was certain about the details, Danny was perplexed. "Colonel? I know a Major Chamberlain."

Cameron shrugged. That was more than he knew. The colonel was new here too.

Flynn queried Cameron more about Colonel Chamberlain. "Superb horseman? Gray at the temples? Moustache?"

Doug nodded. "Yes, the colonel looked like that."

"Do they call him Centaur?" Danny suggested.

"Has to be the same man. I can see you know him—and that you think a lot of him," said Doug, stroking his lip as if drawing a moustache. He suggested with a wry grin, "May want to get rid of that mousy pink growth under your nose. Otherwise he may think you're trying to imitate him."

Whether Flynn remembered him or not didn't matter. Cameron was acting on the colonel's express orders to take pains introducing Lieutenant Flynn to the post as quickly and thoroughly as possible. "He said something about looking forward to riding with you," said Cameron with a puzzled expression. "Maybe he wants to see how you ride." Even if Flynn didn't realize his huge advantage in having the CO for a personal mentor, Cameron knew what it meant, and he was clever enough to realize the good it would do for his own reputation if this new man were to say something complimentary about his introduction to the post. Right now he was going to make sure Flynn could say something about the post.

"The stables are over there." Cameron pointed through the open window at a collection of low buildings half hidden among mesquite and live oaks, and that reminded him: "Garza can get your tack ready and saddle a horse whenever you need it. But he can't read minds. You have to tell him."

Danny studied the stables; they were much smaller than the massive structures at Fort Riley, but still impressively large. Oddly, here it was the middle of the afternoon and hardly a soul was to be seen working with horses, or anywhere else for that matter. "Doug. Could you be tellin' me where all the soldiers are—and the horses?"

Cameron indulged himself in a superior smile. "Look, this is a little complicated for somebody with experience going back, what, four...five months?" Out of the corner of his eye, he could see Flynn struggling to get all this information together to help him form a picture. Understandable. But if this new guy was already having difficulty, this next point might prove to be beyond him. Cameron began slowly, "Our regiment, the 124th Cavalry, is a Texas National Guard outfit that's being mobilized: federalized, the army likes to say. They're not here yet—but that's why the colonel and the governor are meeting."

Cameron felt sorry for Flynn. There was so little time to bring him up to snuff. Cameron worried about taking too much time. Just now, he was slowing to point out the hospital, the biggest building on the post. Army people were proud of two medical icons, Reed and Gorgas, the army doctors who stamped out malaria and yellow fever at the Panama Canal. They served here at Fort Brown too. "But look," Doug suggested, "let's continue this at the officers' club when you're done with your call on the colonel. I'll introduce you to the lieutenants' caucus, a bunch of guys like you and me, waiting for honest work to begin. They've all been here for a while and they can help answer some of your questions, I hope. Knock on my door when you get back. I'm right down the hall."

Danny took the steps two at a time, dashing to his room, relieved to find Private Garza waiting for him. Somehow Garza knew! By talking with another dog robber, Garza learned of his lieutenant's appointment with the commanding officer—and that he'd be needed. For a man appalled at first by the thought of having an orderly, Flynn suddenly saw the arrangement in a new, positive light. "I need to get rid of this mustache," he said to Garza, who'd been occupying himself by putting the room in order. He pointed to his suitcase. "How about unpacking the bag and getting my other uniform ready. Can you iron it a little?"

"Yes, sir," said Garza calmly, quite comfortable with doing these personal chores for his new lieutenant, and he left the room with the lieutenant's uniform rolled up under his left arm, clutching an iron in the other hand.

Satisfied with the results of a few frantic minutes of work with his razor, Danny fumbled with his tie and found still more requirements for his orderly. "I sent a tack box ahead from Fort Riley. Looks as if I'll be going riding soon. Think you can locate it?" He remembered another thing. "I've sent a trunk too."

"I have them both at the storeroom in the stables, sir," said the quick, dark-eyed Garza, pantomiming a motion of turning a key in a lock. "If you'll give me the keys, we're in business."

At the stroke of 1500 hours, Second Lieutenant Daniel Flynn, clean-shaven and respectably turned out by his new dog robber, arrived for his call on the commanding officer of the 124th Cavalry Regiment. The man rising from his seat behind the massive desk was indeed Major Chamberlain from Fort Riley: the elegant, legendary horseman who, two months ago, assured him they'd very likely never meet again. Now, to add to the novelty of his situation, here was Centaur dismounted and a colonel. He'd never spoken to a colonel before. Only once, in his days at Fort Riley, had he even heard such a senior officer speak. Danny saluted and stood at attention,.

Yes, he recognized Chamberlain as the man who bid him goodbye at Fort Riley, but today his manner was far more relaxed and personal. "Have a seat, Lieutenant Flynn," he offered, indicating a plain oak chair set across the desk from him. "Welcome to Fort Brown and a special welcome to the 124th Cavalry Regiment."

Taking his seat in a large leather-upholstered swivel chair, the colonel reached for a rosewood cigarette box. Carefully, he withdrew one and busied himself in a practiced ritual of lighting it and deeply inhaling the fragrant smoke. Centaur contemplated the effect a nearly deserted post might have on a brand new officer. "You've found Fort Brown a rather quiet place after Fort Riley, I would think," he said, quite certain that Doug had already acquainted him with the layout of the post and its temporarily empty buildings and streets. "It's a perfect time for a new officer to arrive," he explained. "The 12th left a little over a month ago, and my new command, the 124th, won't be here for another two weeks; when the major part of it arrives by train." The swirl of numbers must be confusing to his newest officer, Chamberlain knew, and he began a condensed lecture he hoped would somehow help Lieutenant Flynn make a little sense out of the apparent confusion. "Things are changing rapidly, but let's go over some things you need to know before training begins in earnest."

The Texas regiment was still scattered in its separate troops, each located in one small city or another across the state. When they received their mobilization orders, the troops would travel by railroad to a collection point in San Antonio, and then the entire regiment would board a single train for Fort Brown. Horses, vehicles and weapons could be loaded in a few hours, but the citizen soldiers needed time to lay their civilian lives aside.

Mobilizing the regiment had begun almost two weeks ago and today or tomorrow the individual troops would be leaving their homes. Chamberlain brought up a few more complicating matters. "Its former commanding officer and a number of senior officers have been promoted and transferred, because the War Department needs their experience in organizing the training of new, inexperienced men now that the army's expanding." As if to reassure the new lieutenant of his own legitimacy, Chamberlain said, "I've taken command here even though most of the men of the regiment are still at home."

After the few months at Fort Riley, immersed in the regular army way of doing things, Danny found the concept of the citizen soldier puzzling. Not surprising, since few regulars knew much about the national guard. Chamberlain took one more precious bit of time to explain. "The guard is nominally an organization of state militias," he said. "Each state may raise militia units as the state government sees fit." Centaur asked Danny if he knew about guardsmen and reservists.

"No, sir," said Danny, shaking his head. The topic hadn't come up at Fort Riley.

Centaur recognized his new lieutenant faced more immediate challenges than learning the fine distinctions between the army and the national guard, and he settled for a short explanation. "Right now these men are civilians—farmers, lawyers, salesmen—reservists who train a few days a month. Normally they take their orders from the governor. But in time of war or other national emergency, state militias may be called to active duty by the War Department, and then they're under the command of the president of the United States as commander in chief—no different than you or me."

The picture of a confusing flow of men into and out of the regiment didn't square well with the organizational block diagrams they taught Danny at Fort Riley. "Don't be concerned," said Chamberlain. "The men of the 124th have been at this for a long time. They know the army and they're very experienced soldiers."

Centaur's assessment of the 124th was something of an understatement. The Texans had been coming to the Rio Grande for their annual training for years. Besides, many visited the valley every fall to hunt Whitewing doves at the invitation of friends, if they didn't own the land themselves. "They know Fort Brown and the country for hundreds of miles to the north almost as well as the locals. A few of them are already here. Lieutenant Colonel Newman is at work as the executive officer, my second in command. So have a few others like your dog robber, a Private Garza, I think. He's one of them. Colonel Newman and I are in touch with the smaller units daily by telephone."

Happily thankful for Doug's timely education about dog robbers, Danny said, "I've met Private Garza, sir."

Chamberlain smiled approvingly: something the trainees at Fort Riley never saw him do. As he talked, the old Centaur emerged, speaking nostalgically of equestrian competitions to come. He proposed a schedule for continuing their sessions. They could do that in the afternoons until the main body of the 124th arrived. Then, thoughts of the deadly serious process of preparing for war clouded his features, and Chamberlain talked to his new lieutenant as commanding officers always have: Learn your business. Work hard and the rest will take care of itself. After a few brief minutes of this standard advice, Centaur placed his hands on his desk, expectantly eying the lieutenant seated across his desk. "Now, do you have any questions for me?" he asked.

The offer took Danny by surprise. At Fort Riley nobody cared what he wanted to know—only about what he knew. He stalled a moment and blurted the first thing that came to his mind, something he'd been asked about in New York. "Colonel, I'm not sure exactly why we're here at Fort Brown. The Rio Grande Valley doesn't seem to have much to do with the war in Europe."

Chamberlain smiled approvingly. Few lieutenants ever asked a question at all, much less about current politics. Usually, all they wanted was to get out from under the CO's magnifying glass. "Good question," he said. The answer required some care in framing his thoughts in simple terms. "War is consuming Europe." On that, he agreed with Danny. "And we Americans will soon be on the other side of the Atlantic. The War Department is preparing this country as fast as it can be done until the Congress releases more money. A lot of politicians think we should stay out of the war at all costs," he said. "But Americans are already in the war! They're being killed at sea—frequently—by German U-boats sinking our ships." Like many military officers, Chamberlain found it frustrating to see these atrocities happening without a thing being done to prevent them. The best he could say was, "And, in the army, we're preparing ourselves to fight a new kind of war."

Danny's face told Centaur that he was losing his new lieutenant in a cloud of abstract thought. "I know, this doesn't answer your question, does it?" he asked, grinding out his cigarette in a shiny brass ashtray fashioned from the base of an artillery round. "See, Lieutenant Flynn, while we're rearming, we can't afford to ignore our borders. The government is worried about the Rio Grande border. I can tell you that for a fact. We don't know where Mexico stands, but we're certain that the Germans are trying to send spies through Mexico into Texas."

Danny's eyes widened. "Spies? Is that why we're here, sir?"

"Well, spies might be oversimplifying it, but all right, call it spies, or maybe saboteurs." Colonel Chamberlain had in mind the vulnerability of the refineries and oil fields of Texas and Louisiana, but he didn't have time to explain all that. He concentrated on the 124th. "Cavalry is ideally suited to patrolling the border, and the Texans are outstandingly qualified for that, so all the pieces fall into place."

Chamberlain intended to end his explanation there, without touching on any further possibilities, but another thought occurred to him, something he wanted this young man to know, trusting it would be helpful to him. "The horse cavalry generals consider assigning the 124th to Fort Brown as the end of an era because the future is in mechanization. They offered me this command as something of a bonus, making it clear that everything we do between now and the day we're dismounted will be a historical event." Chamberlain considered himself the perfect man for the job. In the certainty that he, better than anyone else, could make this brief, but golden opportunity historically memorable, he offered a little more personal insight. "If fate deals me even an ordinary hand of cards, the 124th will live in memory as the finest, most accomplished horse cavalry regiment ever assembled in the U.S. Army."

God! Talk of having a destiny in the history of the military horse invigorated him, but Chamberlain knew Danny couldn't possibly feel the same keen interest as a career cavalryman might. He was so green, so unaware of thousands of years of warhorse lore and the glorious history of the U.S. Cavalry. If only he could keep Flynn with him! But Chamberlain faced the difficult realization that it was time to return to the present and to permit his protégé to capitalize on the opportunity and learn his trade the way all new officers have to do it, by trying and failing, and trying again.

Centaur walked Danny to the door: Not something commanding officers do as a rule, but Flynn's innate potential stirred another urge to smother him with mentoring. With an effort, Chamberlain sent Danny off with a lighthearted order. "Check with Doug Cameron for the particulars on the tea dance next Saturday." The colonel smiled as if something about tea dances amused him. "We'll expect you."

Suddenly the interview was over. Danny felt disappointed. After bringing him to an emotional crest by a warrior's introduction to the horse cavalry, the army's greatest horseman was ushering him out of his office speaking of tea dances. He had only the foggiest idea of what Centaur was talking about, but he knew he could fall back on Doug for advice. "Thank you, sir," he said, saluting. The sound of his heels echoing in the empty corridors drove home a message that getting along in the army would be no simple proposition.

Cameron led the way, picking up where he left off earlier in the afternoon. "We'll walk to the officers' club. It's not very far." Danny fell in step, striding briskly along the sidewalks lined with ornamental orange trees, past the tidy white bungalows built for the married officers' families and partway around the smooth, green parade ground at its best in the afternoon light. Only a few residences were occupied now—a few families from the 124th had been arriving during the last few days, but most of the houses still looked out on the world with the blank stare of empty windows.

Had there been more time, Doug could have pointed out more of the architectural fine points of Fort Brown and its buildings designed and laid out by engineers who appreciated the charm and grace of the Moorish arch enhanced by lines of tall, majestic palms. But it was Friday and happy hour at the officers' club would begin soon. "You should see a few things before the other lieutenants get there," he said. "Once things get started, there won't be time." At Doug's hot pace, they arrived comfortably early, striding up the curved, shrub-lined drive leading to the Club entrance. Only a few cars occupied the lot, but it was still early. When the regiment arrived in full force with their families, the streets would be busy and the officers' club would be crowded on Fridays.

Doug eagerly took the steps at a run, still keeping up his tour guide's commentary. "Calling on the commanding officer is thirsty work, and all that time on the train only makes the matter worse, but I think we can find a remedy here." He would see, Danny thought. So what that Fort Brown was a border fort. Nothing about it evoked the faintest imagination of the gritty, rough-hewn frontier forts Danny had read about in novels or seen in the movies. He'd say that gave Fort Brown an advantage as a pleasant place to learn his job. As they walked, Doug explained that the unmarried women who lived and worked on the post had standing invitations to Friday happy hour. Not wanting to miss a thing, he followed Doug eagerly in answering the compelling lure of music, strong drink and the prospect of the company of women.

Lieutenants are the same as any other young men with a little education and professional training, except that new army officers have all been given a light coating of army civilization—the better to fit them acceptably into the social structure that lives in parallel with the military society. But the civilizing layer is frequently thin and brittle, and the lieutenants sometimes find that it chafes, or when they find it constricting, they burst out of it like an insect shedding an outgrown shell. Danny, unaware and distracted, dutifully kept pace with Doug's swinging gait, under the arches and through a broad entry area lined with carefully tended tropical plants, barely noticing the architectural grace or the view through the open doors of an impressively spacious ballroom.

Cameron snapped his fingers, suddenly remembering that this ballroom was where the tea dances were held and he'd altogether forgotten about Mrs. Chamberlain's request to explain the upcoming tea dance to Lieutenant Flynn and issue an invitation. Mrs. Chamberlain was explicit in her instruction to him, and to do his duty to her and Danny Flynn as well required an explanation, but the Friday meeting of the lieutenants' caucus was about to convene. With so little time, he'd settle for something short and sweet. "These tea dances are a major event around here. Don't treat any part of regimental social life as trivial." If his body language conveyed anything, Doug meant what he said. "The one next Saturday is going to be a small affair, since so few junior officers are here and there's no regimental band to play. No more than a combo, I'd guess. Mrs. Chamberlain—Helen is her name—is a stickler for that stuff. I've heard her say she's waited a long time to be the colonel's lady, and she isn't going to waste a minute of it."

For the moment, however, Doug forgot about the tea dance and ignored further mention of any of the Club's other features, leading Danny directly to what he considerd Fort Brown's greatest attraction: a wooden platform extended daringly over the twisting, steeply banked Rio Grande River on a system of heavy wooden pilings. "Look," said Doug simply, pointing toward the opposite bank, where a tightly packed clutter of rusty-roofed buildings stood crammed together—low, unpainted warehouses for the most part. A few taller structures might have been home to Mexican shipping companies. Lord knows what really went on over there in those buildings.

Doug found a table that suited him and pulled a few chairs around it. Without waiting for Danny to take his seat, he placed an order with a young Mexican man in an immaculate white jacket. Flynn, meanwhile, became lost in studying the greenish waters of the Rio Grande rolling and eddying directly below the stout planks of the platform. Since arriving in Brownsville several hours earlier, Danny had been clutching desperately at the shreds of worldly seasoning doled out by the sergeants at Fort Riley, hoping to avoid sounding like a gaping tenderfoot. Now, suddenly the view from the platform helped him work out some of his guide's rapid fire litany of information.

Doug's suggestion that originally Fort Brown had been built in a loop of the Rio Grande became much clearer. "That's Mexico?" he mused, working on orienting himself by the sun and the direction the roiling water was moving. He brightened suddenly, realizing that from the serpentine looping of the river around Fort Brown, he could look north or even east and look into open windows in Mexico. Danny succumbed to the realization. "Right there, Doug. Look!"

But Cameron was forgetting his own fascination on his first look at Mexico with nothing separating him from a foreign country except a few yards of water and air. Otherwise he would have reminded the new man why the fort was built there in the first place. But a first lieutenant with almost a year of service in the valley had more practical and interesting things to show this shavetail than a taste of forgotten history. "Of course it's Mexico," he snorted. This boy had been leading a sheltered life, wherever he was from.

"Here's something you'll really like. Watch carefully so you can see something worth joining the army to see." Cameron pulled a chair around for Danny so he could view the entire breadth of the river. "Look at this." He asked Danny to concentrate on a point above the edge of the platform where two slender steel cables stretched across the river toward the buildings on the other side. Flynn might not have noticed them without prompting. Those two strands, stretching tautly from the building behind them, made up the visible part of a single endless loop that spanned the Rio Grande, threaded over wheels on either side. Cameron waited for Danny to follow the cables before talking him through the beautiful utility of it. "The American wheel is above the ceiling a few yards behind us—above the bar." For a time Danny studied the international span with a polite interest, but what good did it do?

Cameron assured Danny that this cable was far more than a mere curiosity. It served a most practical purpose. He insisted that the new guy turn toward the bar to witness an essential part of the operation. "Over here, Flynn. Watch the waiter."

The white-coated man fussed with a small platform partitioned into many compartments of varying sizes and hooked it onto the cable. Next, he carefully attached a scrap of paper with a wooden clothespin. "That's my order," said Doug, pointing. "Keep watching."

Long ago, according to Cameron, some officer assigned to Fort Brown, an engineer of no mean skill designed the contraption to shuttle smoothly between the U.S. and Mexico while keeping the cable and its cargo out of the water. An unlikely legend held that the ingenious devil was none other than Robert E. Lee, an officer known to have been at Fort Brown for at least a short time during the Mexican War. Whoever he was, the imaginative engineer rigged a driving mechanism of toothed wheels and bicycle chain so that a waiter could operate the entire apparatus with very little effort by cranking a pair of handles hanging behind the bar at a convenient height. In order to satisfy the fort's guard force, the only driving handles were on the Fort Brown side. As an added security feature, the apparatus could be locked when the officers' club wasn't open for business.

Flynn watched with great interest as the dangling platform dipped low over the river and ascended steeply into Mexico to pass through a window in one of the unpainted walls on the far bank. Minutes later, an arm waved through the window and the Fort Brown waiter cranked the partitioned platform and its load of drinks back from Mexico. "Ingenious, isn't it?" Cameron suggested proudly.

A bottle of tequila arrived with a tray of small glasses. Cameron arranged them in a line and poured. Watching the clear liquid filling the glasses, Danny broadly smiled his heartfelt approval. "Ah, Doug," he said, "my father would love to be here. He could sit out here watching the river and enjoy the booze coming across the border without worrying about what the sergeant at the station house thought about it."

Doug's attention wasn't on the new Irish kid and his reflections. He watched two lieutenants approaching. "Look at these guys, Flynn. It's the happiness twins here for the meeting. They stayed behind when their old regiment left." Danny turned to see a couple of young officers walking over from the bar; both second lieutenants like Flynn. One with curly black hair, whose shirt strained across a comfortable middle, set a plate of tacos on the table and helped himself to the tequila, but the other one, a rangy, serious-looking fellow with short brown hair, hung back. His left shirtsleeve hung unbuttoned over a heavy wrap on his right wrist and forearm. Doug introduced them hastily. "Mike Pinelli here hasn't kept up his riding—see, now he waddles." Pinelli, chewing noisily on a mouthful of a crispy taco, mumbled something. Doug pushed a glass to a muscular, sunburned man who, like Cameron, wore silver bars on his collar. Harry Jenks, a wrestler at West Point a few years earlier, nodded a reserved greeting. "Harry's just the opposite of Mike. He's been entering rodeos on weekends, occasionally winning a little prize money riding broncos, but he got himself banged up a week ago."

"Pleased to meet you, Flynn," said the bronc rider without offering to shake hands.

Cameron left the three to chat while he searched for the fifth member, George Kincaid, another second lieutenant. He spied him a few tables away, chatting with three women. "Come on, George. We got a new man to initiate." But the broad-shouldered lieutenant with all the freckles and red hair waved at Cameron to go away.

Danny wondered aloud why the entire caucus didn't postpone the meeting and join the women. Doug mumbled something about their being married to men in the 12th Cavalry. The word going around held they were remaining at Fort Brown until their husbands reached their new assignments and arranged housing there.

Five junior officers, who were second lieutenants except for Cameron and Jenks, sat around a bottle of tequila. Their common interest, Cameron informed Danny, was that all five were slated to lead platoons in the 124th when the regiment arrived. Until then, their time was their own: to ride and sharpen their horsemanship, or if they were unwise, to waste. In such circumstances, lieutenants could fade from view and be overlooked by the senior officers until they did something to draw attention. On Fridays they gathered here to drink tequila, swap gossip and pick up women. Danny's eyes posed a silent question: other officer wives? Doug drew his breath in noisily through clenched teeth and shook his head.

Forget George. Four of five around the table constituted a quorum as far as Doug was concerned. He topped off the glasses. The old hands drank a welcoming toast while Danny smiled uncomfortably. All together, the lieutenants left behind at Fort Brown by the departing 12th could boast a combined army experience of not quite eight years, but this new arrival, fresh from Fort Riley, instantly elevated them to a higher caste. Another toast followed, proposed by Jenks, a Californian, to the Republic of Mexico, for sharing the gift of tequila with the gringos. Pinelli disagreed with the history, but drank anyway. His idea was that tequila was a Trojan horse given to gringos in revenge for the Mexican War. The lieutenants drank toast after toast, smothering Danny with advice and snippets of the latest post gossip. Cameron withdrew from the chatter. He'd let them compete among themselves telling the new man one outrageous story after another about life on a cavalry post. His attention followed George Kincaid and the three women. Damn! He could get us all in trouble, he thought. All three of the women with George were married to men he knew well. The dark-haired beauty nearest George was Julie Breaux. It happened on posts: screwing around with somebody else's women—often with bad consequences. But George had been around enough to know better. Centaur had warned them against it just a few weeks ago. Dumb! Flaunting it right here in the club was simply asking for trouble.

While Doug mused, Mike Pinelli presided over the meeting, keeping them all laughing with stories about being a new guy in a cavalry unit. He reached across the table to take the tequila bottle by the neck. The initiation couldn't be called complete until the new kid took his turn. "Look here, Flynn," he said, "my glass is dry...and the bottle is almost empty. I'd say you were guilty of dereliction of duty." Amid some expectant tittering at Danny's expense, Pinelli pushed the bottle across the table. "It's time you got a little training in international commerce," he said, waving for the waiter. "See, I'll get you started." When the new bottle arrived, Danny awkwardly followed Doug's example in opening the bottle and pouring. Doug beamed happily at his apprentice, but there was one more thing. Cameron reminded him, "Pay the waiter, Flynn. It's a quaint little custom we have here."

Now that Danny was suitably initiated, they wanted to know the details of his afternoon call on Colonel Chamberlain. "The current propaganda—straight from Centaur's mouth," Pinelli put it. Danny sensed that the request was as much about hazing the new guy as it was about expressing real interest. So out of a sense of loyalty he chose his words carefully, omitting the personal stuff and keeping mostly to the work-hard-and-keep-your-nose-clean parts. If Colonel Chamberlain wanted them to know of his interest in the junior lieutenant, he would have told them himself.

George Kincaid surprised them, breaking in with his loud abrasive voice, "So, Iron Bottom Chamberlain gave you his line about keeping the border secure, did he?" For a moment, at least, George appeared to be dropping his liaison with the ladies. Kincaid didn't introduce himself, nor did he wait for an invitation. He swept up a glass and helped himself to the tequila, posturing loudly, "What else would he tell you but the standard crap? Somebody, in Washington, probably, thinks that German spies are coming across the river in droves and we're supposed to catch them wading across." Eventually George M. Kincaid III introduced himself, as he always did, as a product of North Georgia College, the only coeducational military school in the country. He tossed down the tequila, looking Flynn over from head to his shiny boots. The sturdy, red-faced Georgian momentarily interrupted his indoctrination of the new boy, waving to the women to join them. He set his glass on the table to have both hands free for dramatic gestures. With his left, he indicated the river flowing by, and he swept grandly to the north with his right to suggest the awesome challenge of patrolling its length. "Hell, most of the way to Eagle Pass, and maybe farther, the land along the river is owned by ranchers and some of the larger farmers, and they don't much want us on their bottomland," he said, searching Flynn's face for a response. "Now, if I were a spy, I'd sure as hell wade across at some lonely stretch of some rancher's property and stay the hell away from the roads where the army likes to stay 'cause it's federal property." Kincaid tossed back another tequila hastily—Julie Breaux and the other two were approaching. George finished laying out his opinion with, "We ain't gonna catch any spies that way." He turned away to mouth something to Julie.

Kincaid dropped any thoughts he might have had about joining Doug and the others. Picking up the half-full tequila bottle, he left them to join the three women who had taken seats nearer the lieutenants. Quiet and thoughtful Harry Jenks elbowed George as he edged through a narrow space between chairs. "Keep it in your pants, George," he warned through barely open lips. "You could get yourself shot." He didn't expect a response from Kinkaid, but he mumbled another warning anyway. "Don't think the word won't get around."

"And why don't you mind your own business, cowboy?" Kincaid hissed.

Jenks let the comment pass, but he saw the color rising in Danny's face and warned him quietly, "Stay where you are, Flynn. See, we're not very busy around here right now, so George got started on the tequila early this afternoon. He can be a nasty SOB, with or without it."

Cameron attempted to channel the conversation away from the women with an explanation of Kincaid's comment. "We didn't go across private property too much in the

12th if it wasn't arranged with the rancher ahead of time—but we did it some. I took my platoon down to the river to do a little looking around, and so did George, I guess."

The Georgian was already taking a seat near Julie Breaux, but that didn't keep him from taunting the new man, "Don't worry about legal questions, you dumb Yankee Mick. You'll probably be too lost to know whose property you're on anyway."

Cameron knew he should have warned Danny about Kincaid, but there hadn't been time. In a bare few months, George's troop commander had reprimanded him twice for brawling. The other two lieutenants knew how Kincaid could be and tried to keep the matter from flaring into something. Jenks glared at Kincaid and Pinelli touched Danny's shoulder to dissuade him from standing up. "Don't let him get to you," he warned. "Start misbehaving at happy hour and you'll get the book thrown at you. Whether you were enticed into it or not won't mean a damn to the colonel."

Pinelli saw that if something weren't done immediately to lighten the mood, Flynn could easily become involved in a scrape on his first night in the real army. Ignoring Kincaid, he said, "It just occurred to me. Our new member needs a car." He turned to Danny. "Life can be pretty tedious here without transportation." Cameron's suggestion brought a babble of assent. "You're trapped here without a car."

Pinelli, who spent more time working on his cars than in getting in extra riding, expanded on the idea. "Yeah, you can walk to Matamoros, and Brownsville, of course, but it's a long way to any other town here in the valley." He was thinking of Rio Grande City and the border towns to the north. "Even with a car, it'll take you most of a day to get to San Antonio."

A car? Danny wasn't at all sure about owning an automobile. "I can't afford one," he said, mentally tallying up his expenses, especially his new obligation to pay his dog robber twenty-one dollars a month. He hadn't been paid since Fort Riley, so he couldn't even pay Private Garza until he made a visit to the paymaster's office on Monday.

The truth was he'd never driven a car. Hardly anyone owned a car in the city—certainly not Irish immigrants. Until now, the necessity of owning one had never crossed his mind.

"You can afford one in Matamoros," said Harry Jenks, trying to be helpful. "But you're gonna need cash." Jenks did a little figuring. "Hmm. You'll get paid this coming week, and we can spot you a little money." Jenks looked for agreement from the others. "Yes, that would work." Next Saturday's auction would be the time, they all agreed, nodding their heads. There was so much to think about.

"It's happy hour," Kincaid complained loudly from where he sat with his arm around the back of Julie's chair. "Talkin' about cars is wastin' time when ladies are sitting here. It's not polite to ignore them." He stood and Julie took his hand to follow him inside where the music was playing.

If the caucus didn't recognize a pair of unaccompanied women as an opportunity as their colleague Kincaid did, others agreed with George and they acted. A captain Danny hadn't noticed earlier took a chair between the remaining two women. He seemed to know one of them quite well. He moved his chair closer to hers and said something that made her laugh.

When Kincaid and the raven-haired Mrs. Breaux didn't return to their seats, it occurred to Danny with sudden clarity that even though he was developing a smoldering dislike for the opinionated Georgian, he'd give the rogue credit for pretty well demonstrating the merits of having a car on Friday nights. At that, he turned to ask the opinion of Mike Pinelli, who professed to be an authority on the Matamoros used car market.

"I've bought two of them over there," bragged Pinelli, proceeding to lay out a dry, rather complicated method of selecting cars and how to convert the price from pesos to dollars. Danny's attention wandered to the lone woman remaining at the table. She could have been thirty years old, and she wore a wedding ring, but if that wasn't an invitation in her smile, what was it? Should he go to her? While Danny listened with waning interest, Cameron recognized the opportunity and accepted, shrugging helplessly as if to say that it was all right as long as the woman did the initiating. Over his shoulder, he said to the others, "Tell him about Captain Franklin's Whitewing hunt tomorrow."

chapter

FOUR

Washington: Congress passes the Burke-Wadsworth Selective Service Act, symbolizing a growing need for the nation to arm.

A pair of Whitewing doves swirled overhead, dashing to the Rio Grande for water before the light failed. Danny tracked the lead bird with the muzzle of his borrowed shotgun and missed. Instinctively, he worked the smooth action and fired again, sending the dove falling to the thick brush below. With his two shots echoing along the riverbanks, he visually marked the spot where his bird had fallen in a patch of grass dried to the same subdued grays and browns as the dove's softly shaded feathers.

Danny collected two empty red-and-shiny-brass shells from the ground where they had fallen and stuffed them into his pockets with the others. The spectacular red ball of the dying sun still hung a finger or so above the low treetops, but its light was already fading. Carefully he worked his way through masses of rough bushes that sawed at his clothing and around broad clumps of flat-leaved prickly pear cactus. After a brief search, he found the bird and dropped it into a makeshift game bag fashioned from a flour sack and a length of twine. With this final bird plucked out of the grass, he probably had a dozen doves, a good day for a beginner. Many of his earlier shots had been misses and how many were lost he couldn't say. Twice he saw downed birds lying tangled in the thick, tangled growth, but couldn't work his way through the impenetrable barriers of thorns and cactus spines to retrieve them.

From somewhere out of sight on the higher ground behind him, Danny heard a car horn sounding—five separate, deliberate honks: Captain Franklin's signal that hunting was over for the day. For most of the afternoon, the sound of shooting echoed through the bottomland, hardly ever stopping, but now a serene quiet lay in the valley. He hefted the bag, slung it over his shoulder and glanced around him in the vividly colored light of the fading sunset playing on the quiet sweep of the river bottom for anything he might have forgotten. Satisfied, he picked his way deliberately along cattle trails toward the sound of the horn, cradling Walter Franklin's borrowed Winchester Model 12 in the crook of his arm, enjoying the soft feel of the early evening on his hands and face.

Getting back to the camp required only a short walk—less than ten minutes, but perhaps a little more for the others, who were stationed farther out because Captain Franklin wanted the new man handy, in case he encountered some unforeseen problem. Pinelli, Jenks and Cameron would be along soon. George Kincaid hadn't been seen since Friday at the officers' club.

The captain and the orderlies returned to the camp earlier to get things organized. The moment the lieutenants arrived with their birds, they'd have an accounting of sorts to determine how they stood in the numbers brought down. That's the way it was with Franklin, a slender, thoughtful man with a hint of crow's feet growing at the corner of his eyes; he wanted nothing left to chance. For a hunt in the flesh-tearing growths of the river bottom, many hunters might have simply worn some old, barely serviceable clothing. The orderlies wore parts of their denim fatigue uniforms—so did Danny, out of consideration for his meager wardrobe of civilian attire—but not Franklin. He wore heavy trousers of a brown ducking material sheathed with thorn-defying leather patches, and he carried his ready ammunition in loops on the front of his shooting jacket.

For the Franklins of South Texas, shooting Whitewings in the valley was a longstanding family tradition. His father, a prominent lawyer in Fredericksburg, situated in the limestone heights of the Texas Hill Country, looked forward to getting away from the office on fall weekends for bird hunting in the valley and his sons learned to enjoy it as much as he did. Walter first came to this piece of land with his father when he was ten, as guests of the elder Franklin's law school classmate. These annual pilgrimages continued through his college days. This year, as a new captain who would soon command a troop of the 124th Cavalry, a Whitewing hunt gave him a splendid opportunity to look over the crop of lieutenants before deciding which of them he might request to command the three platoons in his troop.

Danny looked up from cleaning his borrowed shotgun to see Franklin approaching, nodding approvingly at the lieutenant's luck with the birds. The captain probed an inside pocket of his hunting jacket for a slim flask. He unscrewed the top of the leather-covered vessel. "Shooting's done for the day," he said, offering it to be sampled. "Guess it wouldn't hurt to have a little sip of whiskey to celebrate some pretty good shooting." He left the flask with Danny and strolled away to supervise things at the fire and lend a hand plucking the birds. It made quite a sight, that heap of birds: It might even amount to more than a hundred when the others came in with their bags.

When they arrived in the camp minutes later, Franklin welcomed the other three lieutenants in the same way. "Drop your birds, gentlemen. Have a sip from the flask. Then join us here with the chores." A Whitewing hunt organized in the Franklin family style didn't stop with shooting the birds. The high point of the day was still ahead: prodigious feasting washed down with cold beer. With everybody pitching in with the plucking, roasting the small pigeon-like birds could begin in half an hour. The captain's orderly pulled a faded green shelter half from a tub of beer that had been on ice all afternoon. Franklin and his dog robber demonstrated how the feast was to be prepared—beginning with the plucking. Ten men at work soon produced an impressive drift of feathers—yet stripped of its feathers a single dove wouldn't amount to much more than a bite. The breasts of the birds were to be wrapped with slices of bacon and placed on a skewer, four or five at a time, with generous bits of onion between them for moisture and added flavor. Then, with the skewers placed over the glowing coals, they roasted nicely, with the hunters taking turns at the basting.

Stories about the afternoon's shooting along the river began almost immediately After a while, Danny wandered away from the storytelling with a brown bottle of a good Mexican beer in hand to look at the cars parked in the clearing and to do some thinking about his finances. Could he really afford a car, he wondered? He stood alone, reflecting on how far all this seemed from New York; thinking on all he was learning from Cameron and Franklin—about cars and women, polo and dove shooting...and about tomorrow morning when he would face his first working day as a second lieutenant.

Seven officers of the 124th Cavalry stood at attention in a single straight rank facing Major Wilmer Perkins, the adjutant. Four lieutenants and three captains were in for a special ass chewing. Another face should have been included in the line of officers standing at rigid attention, but Lieutenant George Kincaid hadn't been seen since Friday. Danny stood wide-eyed and motionless at the incendiary developments of his first officers' call.

With so few officers of the 124th on hand at Fort Brown, little faults could become magnified and larger transgressions like having an officer absent from a normal, scheduled meeting under illicit circumstances set Centaur off like a skyrocket. Somehow the commanding officer knew the details about George and Julie Breaux leaving happy hour together. This kind of thing happening right under his nose embarrassed him. All weekend he stewed and by Monday morning he'd had the connected events into a single offense that stained them all equally. The colonel, seething with displeasure, worked at maintaining his composure, but it was useless. "Wait here for Major Perkins," he snarled in a voice gone gravelly with disappointment in his officers, and stamped out of the room.

Yes, Sam Chamberlain understood how this whole thing could look to some like making a mountain out of a molehill. Sure, Kincaid and Mrs. Breaux were adults, but this was treachery to a fellow officer. He viewed it as something of a family matter. And, yes, dammit, some of the culpability lay with him. In the weeks between the departure of the Twelfth and the scheduled arrival of his new command, he didn't require the junior officers to be present at a daily officers' call. In rational moments he was aware that his own failure in permitting this laxness could have been the root of this problem. Nevertheless he vented his displeasure to Perkins, who stood respectfully silent while the commanding officer raged at full volume about his officers not having enough personal responsibility to make the most of a light schedule. "Even Lieutenant Flynn, who's been here only three days, knows we have precious little time to prepare for the regiment's arrival by train," he growled, hoping it was true. The irritant that wouldn't go away was Lieutenant George Kincaid's publicly flaunting his questionable morals and thorough lack of common sense. Centaur couldn't abide it, particularly the public part. He interrupted his tirade long enough to light a cigarette and slam the lighter on the desk. "Find Kincaid and drag him out of wherever he's shacked up with that woman. Then send him to me," he directed the major. "I'll deal with him myself." Chamberlain strode back and forth angrily, shouting ideas as they came to mind. "They have too much time on their hands," he snapped at his adjutant. "You get moving and whip that rabble into shape. Make damn sure they're busy."

Sometimes a cigarette had the power to calm him—but not today. Irritably, he ground it out and left the stub in the ashtray with several identical butts.

⌁

The major carried more weight than most cavalry officers, but Colonel Chamberlain had asked specially that Perkins be assigned to his command because of his reputation for making things work. Like many regular army officers, Perkins had been promoted only recently. For ten long years in a moribund army strangled by the tight-fisted budgets of the Depression, he languished as a captain, but at last he wore the brand new gold oakleaf insignia on his collar. This chore the colonel assigned could be a defining moment as an emerging leader in the eyes of the commanding officer. The new major knew how to deliver a scathing tongue-lashing and was quite willing to do it, but the best tirades spring spontaneously from the soul, and Lieutenant Kincaid, the subject of this blotch on the regimental reputation, wasn't even present. He knew he looked the part with a constantly florid face framed in curly, dark, almost-black hair cut short and a moustache beginning to show a few lines of gray, but Perkins searched deep within himself for the inspiration to make this chewing-out truly authentic.

"Which one of you is responsible for Lieutenant Kincaid?" he demanded, glaring separately at each one in turn to make them realize accountability for a fellow officer rested equally on each of them. They'd failed as leaders and in their duty to a fellow officer. Pacing back and forth, scarcely more than a foot away from the toes of their boots, Perkins reminded them of Simon Breaux, stationed somewhere in Virginia by now, struggling to whip thousands of draftees into fighting trim. "Have you the morals of gutter-running alley cats, not to keep one of your brother officers from a breach of principle and honor?" He shouted so it could be heard in Centaur's office.

"All right," he warned them, "the country club existence is over." This was something he truly felt. Perkins singled out each of them for special assignments. The work would be a remedial correction for their lapses in responsibility and what he referred to as blatant disregard for duty. Walter Franklin, the senior of the group, reported to the post engineer to supervise the renovation work on the barracks, and as the junior officer in the regiment and likely to remain so when the train arrived, Danny took charge of the stables. The others were to be assigned duties suited as much as possible to their seniority and experience. Until further notice, they would report personally each day to Perkins, to inform him of their progress.

Doug Cameron could help only a little in advising Danny about running the stables. His best guess was, "All they have is a few dozen horses and some mules, with a few soldiers to do the work—some of the dog robbers, I think." Luckily, he'd escaped that nasty little detail. "Probably the job doesn't involve much more than signing inventories for bags of oats and bales of hay."

Centaur knew about lieutenants and the character flaws of young men. He knew how their attention wandered and how infrequently good sense and the principles of good order and discipline entered their minds. Especially, he understood their fragile, easily bruised egos. The regiment wouldn't work well with its young officers cringing like a pack of whipped puppies any more than it would with its platoons led by coddled prodigals. True leaders know very well that nothing restores confidence like a clear sign of approval from the commanding officer. So far this week, he'd spoken with Captain Franklin and Lieutenant Jenks. Major Perkins had expressed satisfaction with what he called a visible improvement in conditions at the stables. It wasn't that he didn't trust Perkins's observations implicitly. Centaur liked to see these things for himself.

Without calling to have his horse saddled or allowing himself to be driven in a sedan, he walked the quarter mile to the stables, chiding himself for not exercising and riding as frequently as he should. He stopped in the shade of a widely spreading, gnarled live oak tree with long beards of Spanish moss dangling in long thick beards from its widely spreading branches. Here he could make a leisurely observation, unobserved and unescorted. The smell of a charcoal fire and the sound of a hammer told him the farrier was plying his art nearby, and here and there he heard the quiet voices of men at work among the stable buildings. Two troopers worked to calm a skittish horse having troubles with its new shoes. He took a moment to watch them and make a general survey of the activity. As far as he could tell, no one in the stables crew had noticed the silent arrival of the single man on foot. Good. He hoped it was because the troopers were much too busy to notice him.

Some movement at the small building where the stables sergeant had his office caught his eye. A smallish trooper, almost lost in his stiff new blue denim fatigues, emerged from the door carrying a bucket of paint, blinking in the bright sunlight. He set the bucket down on the step, balanced a brush on its rim and walked toward the live oak where Chamberlain stood obscured by the Spanish moss. Unaware of the colonel's presence, he wiped the sweat from his face with a much-used red bandanna. On hot days like this, they set a galvanized container of water on a low wooden platform under the tree to keep it out of the sun. The trooper took an enameled metal cup from a nail driven into a low-hanging limb and filled it. He gulped thirstily, allowing a little trickle to run down his chin and neck. Only then did he notice the commanding officer standing at the trunk of the tree. Uncertain what to do first, the soldier hung the cup back on the nail, recalling the lieutenant's strict instructions to "Come get me immediately if any senior officers come to ride." But he couldn't very well run for the lieutenant with the colonel standing right in front of him.

Sweaty and spattered with paint, Private Francisco Garza swiped his fingers through his black hair, stepped smartly up to the CO and saluted. "Good afternoon, sir. Can I help you, sir?" Impulsively, he said, "I'm the acting stables sergeant."

Chamberlain returned the salute, struggling to suppress a broad grin at the soldier's bold greeting. "You're Private Garza, aren't you," he said, eyeing the paint-spattered soldier. "Who appointed you stables sergeant?"

Nobody had, of course, but the situation was a bit unusual. "We're paintin' today, sir," Garza said by way of explaining things in general. Across the fences where the newly shod horse was being led away, several bare-shouldered figures in partial working uniforms worked industriously with ladders and large brushes, spreading white paint with varying levels of skill. Garza pointed them out with a finger heavily caked with the light green government-issue paint selected for the office walls. "Lieutenant Flynn got us nose down and ass up at work." He poked around in a large pocket, fumbling for the floppy denim hat he stuffed there earlier.

With a little wave of his hand, Centaur let Garza know he didn't require something as trivial as a hat or anything as formal as a salute from men who were nose down and ass up. He intended to leave Garza in peace to quench his thirst. "I'd like to ride, if anybody is available to saddle my horse. Otherwise, I'll do it." The colonel squinted, taking in all the work. "Is the lieutenant in the office—or is he riding?" he asked. Chamberlain thought he ought to explain that he expressly directed Lieutenant Flynn to keep up his riding.

But the acting stables sergeant knew exactly what his boss was doing. "He's awful busy, Colonel. I tell you, that man has ever'body workin'." He made a follow-me motion. "Come see, sir," he urged with a hint of pride. Garza knew a short way to where Lieutenant Flynn was working, but he didn't take it. Garza had an innate sense of how other people viewed things. It made sense that when the entire regiment occupied the post, every single one of the long, low-roofed stable buildings would be full of horses. Then the place would be full of activity, but nothing could be more forlorn than an empty stable, so he escorted Colonel Chamberlain through the only building with any occupied stalls at all. That's probably where the boss man intended to go anyway, but he wasn't certain. When the commanding officer stopped for a look at his own horses, Garza waited discreetly a few steps away until the colonel was ready to move on. What he wanted the colonel to see wasn't far anyway, less than a hundred yards. "We can see from here, sir," said Private Garza, stopping at the broad stable entrance doors blocked open for air.

Standing near Garza, Chamberlain saw the stocky gray-haired farrier laboring with his younger assistant, both stripped to the waist in the sweltering heat like most of the men at the stables, except that these two wore heavy leather aprons. The skilled craftsman bent over, intently absorbed in supervising the assistant at work on the right forefoot of a mare, nearly black, with a little Morgan in her.

"That's one of your horses getting some new shoes, sir," the private said, watching the colonel's face to be sure he recognized his lieutenant as the apprentice trimming the horse's hoof. In a whisper, Garza spoke with unalloyed appreciation of the redheaded lieutenant who burned to know everything about horses. "See the assistant, sir? He sure is gettin' good with them tools." Chamberlain made a sound of acknowledgment, and for a long, attentive moment, they stood together watching the work on his horse.

At a familiar noise from close behind him, Centaur stepped back into the gloom of the stable. A compact bay gelding, being led to the door by the colonel's orderly, saddled and ready for his afternoon ride, made a half-snorting sound of recognition.

Sam Chamberlain took a few moments checking the fit of the saddle and ran his hands over the horse's neck, talking affectionately to the animal the whole time, the same familiar ritual he taught Danny at Fort Riley. He wanted his mount to hear the familiar sound of his voice and recognize the smell of him before he put a foot in the stirrup. "Your paintbrush is drying, Acting Stables Sergeant," he said, excusing the private.

Shifting his weight in the saddle, the colonel spoke to Garza, "Remind Lieutenant Flynn about the tea dance tomorrow afternoon. Tell him, no excuses."

chapter

FIVE

Washington: The U.S. Border Patrol requests FBI assistance in coping with spies attempting to cross the Mexican border.

Danny counted his precious wad of cash one final time before leaving his room. At the Fort Brown gate, he turned left, heading straight for the bridge. Mexico, the alluring land of cheap booze and affordable cars, beckoned in the morning sun. According to Pinelli, the Saturday used-car auction in Matamoros wasn't easy to find—because it wasn't always held in the same place. "A taxi driver will know," he advised, but he added a warning that carried the clear ring of experience. "Don't use a Brownsville cab: too expensive—so are the ones that wait at the bridge to pick up tourists. Walk a little way before you decide to take a taxi."

The border guards recognized a Fort Brown soldier when they saw one. They nodded a friendly greeting, and that was it for formalities—he was in Matamoros. A few more steps and the distinctly foreign flavor of the scene struck him: chaotic traffic, signs in Spanish, taxi drivers honking to attract tourists and hawkers selling souvenirs and food.

Flynn thrust his hands into his pockets to guard his money from pickpockets and walked straight ahead on the uneven concrete sidewalk, resisting the temptation to gawk at the endless rows of ceramic animals and Aztec symbols in the brightly lettered windows of souvenir shops. Walk! The direction didn't matter much. Just get away from the scoundrels preying on tourists, he told himself repeatedly until it dawned on him that he might be wasting time heading the wrong way. Somebody might already be buying the car meant for him! He waved to signal a passing taxi. After a short ride through twisting, poorly paved streets, Danny paid his fare in a place the driver called a plaza, an expression that implied something far grander than a patch of weedy land enclosed only on two sides. Where there were no buildings, the plaza was separated from a deserted stretch of cactus and mesquite by a single strand of rusty barbed wire strung on a few irregular fenceposts. In a few places, mounds of rubble piled up in rough lines helped enclose the roughly rectangular plot.

"I wait here, *senor?*" asked the driver.

Danny waved the taxi away with a snippet of Spanish he learned from Garza, "*No, no. Gracias.*" His express goal was to drive away from the sale in his own car, but a quick look around the plaza squelched his optimism. Seventeen cars, scattered in no particular order over the dusty, untidy lot, comprised the entire offering, and he counted at least fifty potential buyers roaming among them, kicking tires and raising hoods to look over the engines. Danny recalled Pinelli's final bit of advice, "If I had your experience with cars, pal, I'd stay with the newer ones."

The Matamoros used car sale was clearly a seller's market: long on promise and short on documentation. No surprise. Danny knew he didn't really have a choice. Back on the Texas side, a second lieutenant without family money had little chance of buying a new, reliable automobile—especially now, with Detroit concentrating on building military vehicles and aircraft. He wandered through the random assortment, doing his best to identify them by make and year, looking mostly for American cars built in the previous five years. Unfortunately, not many in the plaza met that description. Most of them were a mixed bag of older American models and wheezing European derelicts of uncertain ancestry. Judging from all the gringos, most of the competing bidders would be from north of the border; hopeful young men hovered near the newest cars. Of those, quite a few hung together in small groups; soldiers from Fort Brown probably, pooling their money to buy some transportation. Following the collective wisdom gathered from Pinelli, Cameron and Private Garza, Danny planned to hang back at first, keeping an eye on the bidders as much as the cars. "The competition'll sort itself out," Doug had suggested.

A smartly dressed couple stood out from the mixed crowd of mostly masculine buyers. He took them to be local landowners, people who could afford to hire maids. Here, the house help would be Mexican, whereas in New York, they would have been Irish. Instantly, he detested them. Danny envied the man for his obvious wealth and his striking woman, who was standing aloof from the grimy details of selecting a car while concentrating intently on the three or four newest ones. She wore a broad-brimmed straw hat and a flowered Mexican shawl over her shoulders to shield her fair skin from the sun. A pair of very dark sunglasses completed an air of protected detachment from the business in the plaza, probably from the rest of the world and the ugly realities of life. Why they were here on this littered patch of bare ground rather than looking at new cars in a legitimate dealer's shop? Danny couldn't answer the question.

Pretending to be absorbed in the details of a Buick roadster, Danny watched the woman standing near her husband, idly running her fingers over the paint on the fenders of an older Dodge while he squatted for a close inspection of the tires. The man was quite thorough, and his methodical inspections reminded him of Pinelli's advice about inspecting the tires carefully, because war production was consuming most of the rubber on the world market, making tires extremely hard to come by—almost as difficult as the cars themselves. The man stood from his scrutiny, smoothing his well-cut tan suit, coldly glaring at Danny for ogling his striking woman. She showed no awareness of any of this, but Danny felt his face burning at being caught in the act. He moved away, making a clumsy show of interest in the older cars, confirming his suspicion they were mostly tired old wrecks with flaking paint and balding tires. Crude, inexpert repairs of crunched metal fenders and bumpers warned him to stay away from several that had survived collisions of varying intensity.

Instead of making his selection on color or sportiness, he forced himself to think of reliability and an affordable price. A dark blue 1938 De Soto sedan with a decent finish, acceptable tires and Texas license plates drew Danny's interest, but at least four other potential buyers hovered around it, waiting for the bidding to begin. The way things were shaking out, it would be very spirited, particularly for the newer vehicles. He walked away from the cars and the crowd for a moment to sort out the possibilities calmly and analytically; but with a final glance over his shoulder, his eye caught the letters "DF" standing out from the numerals on the De Soto's license plate. Oh, man. DF! The car was calling to Danny Flynn.

The auctioneer began with the least desirable cars; the ones with the most obvious defects, and the bidding proceeded far more quickly than Danny expected. He wrote down the winning bids, calculating and recalculating. With each sale, he agonized over his plan. If he waited too long, the remaining automobiles would be out of reach. He needed transportation. That much was sure, and almost any of the few still on sale would do. But the De Soto with the DF license plate was the one he wanted.

A rising breeze from the Gulf of Mexico blew dust across the plaza. It pressed the light fabric of the wealthy woman's white skirt against her body and forced her to steady her wide-brimmed straw hat with a hand to keep it from blowing away. Danny glanced around the plaza to locate the husband. He didn't want to be caught again staring open-mouthed at her seductive figure. The wealthy couple, so out of their element in this place of flying dust and litter, could have any car on the lot, and it disturbed his thinking.

During the rapid-fire bidding, he watched three soldiers drive away in the best of the older automobiles. After that, the bidding intensified. Now, only four of the newer models remained. Danny took a final critical look at the De Soto and a Ford coupe parked near it.

"Pardon," said a voice from behind him, interrupting Danny's deliberation and sending a warning tingle up the back of his neck. It was the man in the suit—without the woman. At close range, his air of privileged wealth and taste for expensive business suits showed even more starkly. Danny balled his hands into fists, expecting an unpleasant confrontation with a haughty Mexican aristocrat. Instead, the man spoke pleasantly in English, but in an accent Danny couldn't place. It wasn't a Texan's English like the kind Captain Franklin spoke, certainly nothing like the Spanish inflections in the cabdriver's speech, nor anything of the sound of Garza's English. "The lady is especially fond of the blue car," he was saying, watching Danny's face for a reaction. Probably the man didn't think he was being understood, because he spoke more deliberately. "I intend for her to have the De Soto, and I will outbid you," he said, stressing De Soto and outbid. "You can save us both some money if you just refrain from bidding."

Relieved somehow that an expected unpleasant confrontation over ogling the man's attractive wife hadn't materialized and still tense about the threatening scowls he'd gotten earlier, Danny shook the man's hand in agreement. The woman had moved closer during their brief conversation, appearing only a few steps away as the men made their agreement, approving with a slight patrician nod.

Flynn settled for the black Ford coupe—serviceable, if not particularly racy. Its major attribute was good tires and an engine that looked good to him. No matter, the deal was concluded. Satisfied, he cast a final glance at the blue De Soto and its new owners poring over a Texas road map spread on the hood, using their hands to keep it from flying in the breeze. The letters "DF" on the license plate stood out sharply in a final rebuke.

Danny couldn't count the times he came within a whisker of meeting his death or the destruction of his new automobile in the baffling maze of narrow Matamoros streets. Not once before seating himself in his new purchase did it occur to him that returning from Mexico in his new car might be more complicated than a simple stroll across the bridge. The seller who took his money spoke rather good English. Hiding his amusement at Danny's obvious unfamiliarity with his purchase, he generously taught the gringo from Fort Brown how to start the engine and coached him in shifting the gears. But the buyer's hesitant manner suggested a problem in the making. If there were to be an accident, an investigation would certainly follow, and as the seller, he would likely be involved. Probably out of self-protection, the seller led the way to the bridge in one of the battered hulks that hadn't drawn enough bids, all the while keeping a solicitous eye on the American teniente lurching apprehensively behind him in the traffic.

Once Danny was safely in the line of cars leading to the bridge, his Good Samaritan sped away, leaving him on his own to negotiate the international crossing. A weary, perspiring border guard in a blue uniform watched the black Ford jerk roughly to a stop before him, wincing when he saw the driver's embarrassed smile. This guy looked like a soldier— no older than his own son, the guard guessed—and the kid couldn't drive a lick. From the window of his booth, the guard looked over the car, scratching the gray stubble on his chin. He assumed the car to be a new purchase from the Saturday auction. That would mean the kid probably didn't have any papers either. "Well, damn," said the man in a pragmatic frame of mind. If he were to order this driver out of the line of traffic for a check of papers and to fill out the proper Customs paperwork, there would almost certainly be an accident—and then a traffic snarl at the very least. Afterward, there would be all the bureaucratic formalities and a list of international consequences a block long, particularly if the other driver were to be a Mexican. Worse yet, the guard knew, the police would want him to stay after his shift to answer questions.

Under the painful circumstances confronting him, the veteran of years of watching the border peered over his glasses and made a Solomon-like decision: Best for everybody to ignore a few laws and avoid the problem in the first place. He simply waved the youngster through with a knowing wink. "Right. Nothing to declare," said the defender of the border, gambling that Danny would make it clear of the bridge before he crashed. "Move on, please," he urged, waving him on. "Gotta keep the traffic movin'."

Danny gripped the steering wheel tightly, hands trembling. He hadn't shifted gears a single time since the man from the auction lot left him, and he wasn't going to try it now. Timidly he aimed his Ford slowly along Fourteenth Street, up the slight incline to the Fort Brown gate, ignoring the honking horns of the traffic around him. Fighting to appear calm and unconcerned, he brought the Ford to a fairly smooth stop. His luck held. The guard recognized the redheaded lieutenant and waved him through. By the time Danny placed a telephone call to the barracks with a message for Private Garza, it was almost noon. Someone there would try to find him. "But it's Saturday, you know, sir," said the voice from the barracks.

A knock on the door announced the arrival of his dog robber. Danny berated himself for slipping so easily into thinking of his orderly by the dreadful term, but he promised himself never to use it in public. "Come in, Private Garza," he called. "Have a seat, I need to tell you about a little problem I have."

Garza sat on a straight chair, listening to his boss recounting the morning's adventures, struggling to suppress his amusement. "This ain't anything hard to fix, sir," said the private reassuringly afterward. "We can take care of the driving part right now," he suggested confidently. He moved to the window for a better view of the parking lot. "Where's your car, sir?" he asked.

Danny took the passenger's seat, attentively watching Garza manipulate the clutch and shift gears as they drove through a grove of low trees to a clear area in one of the less-populated parts of the post.

They parked on a high bank of the river—but something wasn't right. Danny could tell it wasn't really the river, and it confused him. "What's this water here, Private Garza?" he asked, very much conscious of having to rely on his orderly for almost everything. Only a couple of days ago, during his whirlwind introductory tour, Cameron explained to Lieutenant Flynn in some detail how the meandering Rio Grande almost encircled the old parts of Fort Brown, but this thing that looked like the river seemed to be out of place, on the wrong side of the parade ground.

Here we go again, thought Garza, but in this case the lieutenant's mystification was understandable. Lieutenant Cameron probably forgot about showing it to him. "It's a re-saca, sir," he said, never quite getting around to explaining to Lieutenant Flynn that the Rio Grande delta has many such formations between Brownsville and Boca Chica, where the river meets the Gulf of Mexico. Using his hands to describe the curves a meandering river makes as it forces its way to the sea, Garza explained, "Sometime, when there's a flood, the river kinda straightens itself out and breaks off one of the loops. Then, when the water goes back to its normal level, the loop stays cut off—isolated. It still looks like part of the river, but by then it's a lake." Garza turned away to look at a clump of cattails in the shallow water, mostly to hide another shy smile. His new boss was going to need a lot of teaching to have a chance of making it in Texas. "I worked for a man in Austin—a gringo like you," said the orderly, continuing the tutorial. "He told me about resacas back East. According to him, the Mississippi has some near St. Louis. But there they call 'em oxbows." Garza opened the door and slid out of the seat. "Let's get a look at this car of yours, sir," he said.

For a few minutes, the lieutenant followed the private through an inspection of the new purchase, learning about the mysteries hidden under the hood: radiator cap, oil dipstick, battery, fan belt—that sort of thing. "Having a car is more than just driving, sir. You need to know about oil, gas and air," said Garza, rummaging in the trunk, making a cursory inventory of the hardware. "Hmm."

"What do you mean, 'Hmm'?"

Garza shrugged uncomfortably at what he'd found. "Well, sir, you got a jack. That's good, but your spare's got a lot of air showin' through." The private pretended to be interested in something in a clump of huisache trees before he dared reveal another deficiency. "No tire pump either," he said.

"Tire pump? Why would I need a tire pump?"

Garza rolled his expressive eyes, diplomatically deferring the question, steering the project back to the urgent issue they were trying to solve. "I think we should work on the driving now, sir."

Now that he'd seen Garza driving, Danny took the driver's seat with a confidence that had eluded him on the streets of Matamoros and Brownsville. With a few simple corrections from his orderly-instructor, he ironed out most of the jerkiness in shifting gears. They practiced the basics over and over until he felt a certain assurance about handling the car. So he asked, "You said, 'The driving part.' What else?"

"*Ay, yi,*" whispered the orderly, staring at the distance. This naïve New York lieutenant amazed him with his ignorance about these essential things that every savvy valley kid learned just by being awake and alert. Francisco Garza was only a little younger than his lieutenant, but the differences between them were proving to be as wide as the Rio Grande. To give the man his due, the lieutenant probably knew his way around the raucous, teeming canyons of Manhattan, but not one damn thing about how to handle himself in the Rio Grande Valley. And the lieutenant was a college man too, while Panchito Garza missed much of his schooling during the family's annual migrations north along the Rio Grande, or the Rio Bravo del Norte, as the Mexicans called it. Year after year, it was the same, following the cotton harvest as far north as Colorado. Schooling came only when he wasn't in the fields snatching the fluffy lint from the spiky five-pointed bolls one by one, stuffing it in a sack until it became heavy with cotton and dumping it again and again, until he and many other pickers filled a wagon that was hauled away to a gin to be baled. The work of picking went on that way until sunset.

From the Gulf of Mexico to the Rocky Mountains, Francisco found life stacked against him. Often the schools wouldn't admit the children of migrant workers. But the family's fortune improved in time, allowing them to give up the annual migration and settle permanently in Raymondville, where Panchito finally got to school regularly. He was twelve the year he first completed a school term. Poking around the lieutenant's new car and helping him with it, Garza couldn't guess how life might have been in the immigrant neighborhoods of New York. Some day, he'd ask. Not now, though. The lieutenant needed a lot of help.

"You gotta get a driver's license so you can drive the car around, sir," said the orderly. "And papers." He scratched his cheek thoughtfully and suggested to the lieutenant that they could get the job done, "one day this coming week, up in Raymondville, Where people know Panchito."

Danny wanted to know more about this man. If they were going to work together, he was going to have to learn about Garza and the valley. Learning what name he called himself would be a good start. "You're Panchito, right?"

"Yes, sir. My father named me for Francisco Villa." He looked expectantly at the lieutenant. "You know about Pancho Villa, don't you, sir?"

"No," said Danny. The sisters hadn't taught him about men described as outlaws.

No matter. They'd take care of the history too—but later. "My family's been here in the valley for a long time—on both sides of the river," said Garza. He contrasted himself with the Texas guardsmen who would be arriving at Fort Brown in a few days. "Most of the men in the 124th are from Austin and San Antonio—maybe Houston and all the little towns around there." He waved a hand in a vaguely north direction. "One of the troops is from somewhere in the Panhandle."

Danny scowled, not fully appreciating what he was hearing about Texas and Garza's people, but he was discovering his orderly to be a surprisingly talented fellow with an uncanny natural ability in communicating. Garza answered the lieutenant's next question before it was asked. "How did I come to be in the 124th? I joined in Austin. I was up there playing guitar and trumpet in a Mexican band. Last year, on November the eleventh I saw a troop of the 124th riding in the Armistice Day parade and I joined the next week, to ride the horses."

"What kind of band?"

"Oh, we played *mariachi* stuff. Weddings sometime. Anything," said the private, shrugging, confessing his real goal was a job playing the guitar for Bob Wills. He laughed at his own audacity, a Mexican kid thinking of playing with the legendary Wills. "But then, a few weeks ago, the 124th got called up. When I heard we were going to be at Fort Brown, I asked to come home to wait for them." He spread his hands as if to say, isn't that the way life is?

"And who would Bob Wills be?" inquired Danny, lagging a thought behind.

"The king, sir! The man who wrote 'San Antonio Rose,'" said the guitar player, incredulous that a New Yorker could be so abysmally ignorant. "You wanna dance in Texas, sir, Bob Wills is the king! At least he is for gringos."

"I see," said Flynn, without the slightest comprehension.

This man would never fit in with the Texans, thought the dog robber. With all his education, how could he be so unaware? "Better check the time, sir. You're not forgetting the tea dance, are you?"

"Dance! Tea dance!" Lieutenant Flynn had allowed the business of buying a car to push the regiment's social requirements completely from his mind.

The army community at Fort Brown carefully nurtured its own society—partly as a necessity and partly from a sense of duty. The custom stemmed from a tradition arising in the tiny isolated frontier forts of the Indian Wars when, if an army garrison didn't make its own entertainment, there wasn't any at all. So long as a handful of couples resided at the post, particularly if there were unmarried men and women, there would be balls and tea dances—no matter what. That was practically the situation at this evening's affair. Fort Brown sat nearly deserted for almost a month while the army dithered in moving the 124th Cavalry to Fort Brown, and until they arrived, the population of eligible bachelors would remain sparse. So would the supply of unmarried teachers. Army tradition, however, would never allow social standards to slip for such a flimsy excuse. The colonel's lady and her committee solicited their husbands' help in an all-out effort to encourage attendance at the Saturday afternoon tea dance. Their reputation as guardians of the social life of Fort Brown was at stake.

As a rule, young men in their early twenties aren't disposed to go gladly to an event called a tea dance. The very name gives this kind of entertainment an aura of formality and effete stuffiness that conflicts with their natural urges. Fort Brown could be considered an isolated post, but it couldn't be thought of as a pool of monotony, especially not with Matamoros a short walk away. To many, the Mexican city's bars and brothels offered a long list of activities far more enticing on a Saturday afternoon than pretending to be cheerful over sipping colored punch and making small talk.

An invitation to a tea dance carried its own set of especially uncomfortable requirements for lieutenants struggling to find their place in the army. It's the kind of social affair that requires the regiment's lieutenants to give up free time to don a dress uniform and mingle socially with people who hold nearly absolute power over them. Understandably, it can be extremely awkward for them to converse easily with the colonel at a tea dance when their usual part in a conversation with the commanding officer is limited to, "Yes, sir." And when they suspect that even the colonel would rather be riding his jumper than catering to his wife's social urges, the whole thing can turn out to be an excruciating obligation. So what if a few unmarried women have been invited to meet the bachelors? It's not a particularly enticing prospect—not if the word gets out that those likely to come are spinster schoolteachers and librarians from Brownsville.

The Danny Flynn who parked his newly purchased car and ran up the steps through the ornate club entrance was not the same man as the brand new, uncertain lieutenant who arrived on the train less than a week ago. The sunburned redhead in a dress uniform regarding him from the hallway mirrors was the far more confident product of many men's remolding efforts. But the transformation wasn't quite thorough enough to leave him comfortable in this new situation.

He hesitated timidly at the wide entrance to the ballroom, peering furtively around an ornamental plant in a large terra cotta pot, vaguely remembering the room from a quick glimpse during Cameron's lightning tour. Then, they were in a rush to be the first of the lieutenants at the bar, but today the ballroom was open for an unfamiliar, intimidating business. But he had no choice and he knew it. Finding company in this obscure duty would help. Once more, he scanned the earlier arrivals for the other lieutenants, but from the door, he saw only a group of senior officers in dress uniforms and their ladies in party dresses arranging themselves in an obscure order he could only partly understand.

A little farther into the room, Danny found some of the friendly faces he was hoping to see. Doug Cameron and a few other younger officers stood along the wall, hoping to avoid notice. Walter Franklin and several other captains, some of those who lined up for Perkins's ass chewing, plus a few from the post engineer's office and the hospital, stood in a more visible group farther out on the ballroom floor. These experienced men knew their job was to mix with the guests from Brownsville, dance with the ladies, and make conversation with their seniors, but they too appeared disinclined to break away from the comfort of their own chatter.

Danny kept his distance from both senior groups, slipping away toward the other lieutenants. They'd chosen a location conveniently near the lavishly decorated refreshment table and partially hidden from the senior officers' view. It allowed them to talk and drink while looking over the smallish clutch of equally nervous women who had come in response to Helen Chamberlain's handwritten invitations.

Two glass bowls graced the large table. One, filled with a vivid red punch, was being sampled far more frequently than the other, which contained something of a pleasant pink color. Danny ladled some punch from the red bowl into a cup, unaware that it was a cavalry staple, mixed according to a not-so secret recipe favoring wicked strength over subtlety. His first sip sent a comforting sensation moving up from the collar to warm his ears. Quite satisfied with its effects, he topped off his glass and joined Doug Cameron and a few of the men he had met at happy hour. His plan was simple: when Cameron moved, he would follow, but until then he meant to bide his time.

Mike Pinelli thumped him on the shoulder with the back of his fist, full of eager curiosity. "What about the car, Flynn? Did you get a car? For the moment, Danny forgot all about the wicked punch or his obligations to Mrs. Chamberlain and the army's ancient traditions. His face brightened. "It's outside, all shined up," he said. "Let me show it to you before it gets dirty with all the dust being kicked up in this wind."

Cameron would have gladly bolted with the other two to see the car, but he knew better. He stood his ground, concentrating on the bottom of his empty punch cup. Flynn and Pinelli chose to ignore his implied warning and steered for the door. It was Captain Walter

Franklin, doing his duty, who stopped them in their tracks. "Gentlemen you'll not leave to go look at cars," he said quietly but sternly. "You may not ignore Mrs. Chamberlain." Franklin didn't want to risk another tirade from Major Perkins.

Meekly, Danny turned to follow Franklin's nod to where Colonel Chamberlain stood with his wife, chatting amiably with Major Perkins, Lieutenant Colonel Newman and their ladies. His memory perfidiously chose this moment to suppress every trace of the knowledge dispensed in a Fort Riley classroom about receiving lines and calling cards and other frothy niceties. Instead, his mind flooded with vivid memories of Irish weddings, exhilarating affairs where everybody was family and neighbors who drank whiskey and frolicked according to ethnic tradition born into the Irish, generation after generation. But the captain recognized their apprension and called them aside. Flynn and Pinelli listened closely to Franklin's icily delivered directions. "You'll go stand in the line—it's a receiving line—introduce yourselves and make a little small talk. Got it?"

They nodded and answered dociley, "Yes, sir."

But Franklin wasn't finished. "And afterward, you're going to dance with the ladies, and stay 'til it's over. Helen Chamberlain has put out the word on that score." Satisfied that lieutenants Flynn and Pinelli were safely in the fold, Franklin called over Danny's shoulder, beckoning to another lieutenant. Quietly, he spoke to Cameron, "Don't you run away, Doug. Where's George Kincaid?"

Cameron recognized Franklin was taking his new rank seriously. "Christ, Captain, I'm not sure." Lowering his voice, he said, "George knows, and I think he'll be here, but he and Julie Breaux've been playing house in his room all week."

The new captain was hearing things he would have preferred to ignore. For one thing Kincaid had been restricted to quarters during his free time. That meant without visitors. Even worse, Simon Breaux had called Franklin long distance, asking that he drop by to oversee the movers who would arrive on Monday to move his wife to Louisiana to live with her family until the war was over. Franklin's face clouded over with displeasure and he muttered for the benefit of his lieutenants, "Friend Kincaid better pray the tongues don't wag, or he'll will be in deep trouble." He remembered to draw deeply on his self-control and smile so the Chamberlains wouldn't see signs of brewing trouble. "All, right, Doug, we'll forget Kincaid for now. Help me herd this bunch of mavericks into line to talk to the boss and his missus." He put Pinelli, Jenks and Cameron at the head of the lineup because they'd done this before. Danny would follow the other three lieutenants and learn from them.

Centaur followed Walter Franklin's progress with the lieutenants and suppressed a smile. He remembered with crystal clarity how he felt in an identical situation one rainy afternoon at Fort Sheridan on the western shore of Lake Michigan when he was a lieutenant. This wasn't for the colonel's ego, nor did he approve the tea dance solely for Helen's sake—although she probably derived more enjoyment from an affair like this than any-one else. After all these years in the army, he knew an entire community benefited. It could truthfully be said, he was at his animated and cheery best when he was with his men and that he actually enjoyed these social formalities.

Then came Danny, the lone new arrival. As he approached, Colonel Chamberlain beamed and presented him to his wife as if he were unwrapping a present. "Helen, meet Second Lieutenant Danny Flynn, our newest officer. He's the superb, instinctive horseman I've been telling you about."

Mrs. Chamberlain looked up at Danny with undisguised delight, taking him in, from the glossy toes of his brown shoes to his closely cropped blaze of red hair. "Delighted to have you in the 124th, Lieutenant Flynn," she cooed. "I've heard my husband speak of your riding skills."

Pinelli, Jenks and Cameron, only a few steps away, couldn't help overhearing the fuss being made over the most junior officer on the post—and they craned their necks to eaves-drop when Helen Chamberlain leaned slightly toward Danny, whispering a question, "Is it true? Can you really do a handstand on horseback?"

Danny reddened. "Yes, ma'am. I was a gymnast in college," he explained.

"And that you're quite a student of the farrier's art?" she probed, arching an eyebrow. Not another soul at Fort Brown knew such information—only Centaur, and Danny glanced up at him for his intervention, or a reassuring sign, but Colonel Chamberlain obviously ap-proved of the grilling his wife was giving him. But her questions were only part of a plan. With a wicked smile, the colonel's lady impulsively cast protocol aside. Taking Danny by the hand, she excused herself from her position in the receiving line. "I won't be a moment," she whispered to her husband. Leading him across the dance floor, Helen Chamberlain confided impishly, "I want you to meet Molly Blankenship, a delightful young woman who teaches in the post school." The colonel's lady seemed to know exactly where to find Miss Blankenship—near one of the ornamental trees artfully placed throughout the ballroom. "Ah, there she is, the pretty girl with the lovely auburn hair," she said, squeezing Danny's hand to show how much she was enjoying this bit of unalloyed meddling.

Molly wore a simple black dress with narrow straps over the shoulders. In her left hand, she demurely carried her small shiny black purse and a pair of white gloves. A slight stiffness in her posture suggested she wasn't quite comfortable in dressing up and acting with propri-ety. She nodded to Mrs. Chamberlain, greeting her politely in a manner suggesting both con-fidence and the shyness of one unaware how pretty she is. With such a fair complexion and the slightest hint of freckles, Danny wondered if she mightn't be just a little Irish. Yes, and he thought he saw a becoming hint of red in her dark brown hair. She had to be.

Molly Blankenship, he repeated the name to himself while Helen Chamberlain completed the introductions. "Molly, I want you to meet Lieutenant Flynn. He's just the man to teach you to ride." Molly was nearly as tall as he was, he judged—maybe it was the heels—and slender. Quite athletic, Danny guessed. Very likely she wasn't one of the women who came here to the Club on Fridays for happy hour. If she were, he'd have certainly noticed her. Danny should have been listening to Mrs. Chamberlain. He knew it, but he found himself concentrating on the girl in the black dress instead.

"Pleased to meet you, Lieutenant Flynn," said Molly, her eyes flashing between the matchmaker and the man she'd just introduced. Neither noticed Helen Chamberlain slipping away to rejoin her husband in the reception line.

Several seconds passed before either spoke, and it was Molly who broke the awkward pause. She held her head to one side and stepped back slightly, standing on one foot with the other supported on the tip of one high heel. "So you're the Lieutenant Flynn Mrs. C. mentioned when she invited me. What should I call you?" she asked.

"Danny will do."

She held her purse self-consciously, as if she'd rather be carrying a tennis racquet. "I'm Molly...the schoolmarm," she said, running a forefinger under the narrow strap over her right shoulder, shrugging slightly to make some unnecessary adjustment. "Mrs. Chamberlain seems to think a lot of you," she said in a soft voice flavored with the accents of South Texas, much like Walter Franklin's. "You must know the Chamberlains quite well."

Danny saw an opportunity to impress this young woman. But he didn't want to lie, and it wouldn't do to admit Helen Chamberlain had never laid eyes on him until a few minutes before. "Mrs. Chamberlain is very kind," he fudged. "How about some punch?"

"Yes, please, Danny," she said with a silvery little laugh, pointing with her little finger to the newly refilled bowl on the left, "I like the red kind."

Helen Chamberlain was not one to embark upon a project and simply leave it to run its course untended. From time to time, she cast surreptitious glances to check on the progress of her handiwork. She saw Danny bringing Molly a cup of the lethal red punch, wearing the same grin the nun recognized as a certain sign of mischief in the planning. Why, that devil, she thought with justifiable satisfaction. Quite pleased with herself, she and the colonel circulated about the floor, chatting happily with the guests at the Officer's Club, reveling discreetly in her indisputable social accomplishment as the colonel's lady.

Throughout the afternoon, Danny felt the envious looks of the other lieutenants who weren't lucky enough to have Mrs. Chamberlain as a patroness, or the captains too, for that matter. A rich sunset glowed in the west, gilding a layer of low clouds scudding before the wind—a sunset worthy of an oil painting set Flynn struggling under a heavy burden. Providence had miraculously dropped hm in the middle of a young man's dream. That's what the guys in the lieutenants' caucus were probably thinking. Now what would the lucky SOB do about it? He felt the irresistible pressure of a young man's powerful instincts—not following through on them would mean ridicule by the other lieutenants—and the humiliation of failure. His peers would list the signs in his favor: a lieutenant in his dress uniform, with a car on a Saturday night, alone with a beautiful woman and a glorious sunset. Absolutely, the signs were with him.

Opposite those signs and masculine urges ranged a procession of powerful scruples crafted by society. Danny felt the presence of judgmental feminine faces looking expectantly over his shoulder: Helen Chamberlain's, his mother's, Sister Theresa's—but not Molly's. Well, there it was. The truth burst in his mind with brilliant clarity. His choice lay behind him. Buying a car in Matamoros had given him a new power to change his life, just as he had expected it would. He dare not fail!

As they walked toward the car, Danny felt perspiration forming on his lip and sensed his confidence wavering. Everything would go well until they reached the car, but failure lurked in taking the first step. What if Doug Cameron were to be walking by when he tried to start the engine, and failed. Christ! How would he live that down? Or even if he got it started; what then? Very soon he would have to admit he knew nothing about Brownsville—even that he hadn't driven a single inch on a public highway when he wasn't terrified of crashing. He'd never be able to admit those things to Molly. Well, too late. He'd just smile and hope for the best. She sensed something.

Without ever letting go his hand, she looked at him openly. "What now, Danny?" she asked without the slightest negative note to cloud the moment. "I'll bet these army people haven't even allowed you off the post, have they?" she suggested helpfully.

He was so relieved. "Molly, I don't know a thing about Brownsville," he said, opening the passenger door for her, holding it steady in the wind that had noticeably freshened since before the tea dance began. "You're my first passenger," he admitted.

Her little laugh restored his confidence. It told him she was delighted to be with him. "I know where things are around Brownsville," she suggested lightly. They rolled the windows down to let the warm breeze blow through. "First," she said, "We'll go out to South Padre Island for a wade in the surf. You'll like that. Then, there's a place in Port Isabel where they make wonderful tacos. We could go there." Port Isabel, at least, had a familiar name. Somebody mentioned it as the port through which the army received its heavy supplies brought in by ship.

If Molly suspected any of his fears, she didn't show it. She giggled at Danny driving slowly, with his hands clamped onto the steering wheel, never allowing his eyes to leave the road. "Don't worry. I won't get you lost," she assured him. Did she have any inkling of the weighty burden he carried? For Molly he'd try to relax, and it worked to a degree. Extremely light traffic on the road to the beach helped his confidence grow.

The warm, humid wind blowing through the open windows wasn't particularly refreshing. "Maybe you should take off your tie—on a hot night like this," she invited, pushing her flying hair away from her face with her fingers. Danny tried driving with one hand while working awkwardly at untying his tie with the other. He glanced at Molly sliding across the seat to help him remove it, allowing her skirt to move up in the process. "Cooler this way," she winked. She placed his tie on the seat and rested her head on his shoulder for the ride along the causeway leading to Padre Island and the Gulf of Mexico. He drove tentatively for a few miles, vaguely aware of a sign indicating a road veering to the right toward Port Isabel. There should have been more lights, he thought, but it wasn't a big town, after all. For a time the only lights to be seen came from a few single bulbs shining in the windows of scattered beach houses.

For a while Danny drove along a narrow causeway for a short way, guessing when the car was again rolling on solid earth that they were now on Padre Island, where Cameron said people went to the beach. Before long, however, the highway from Brownsville ended at a crossroads, leaving only an option to turn right or left onto a rough, narrow road paved with crushed oyster shells. In his headlights he could make out the tall flanks of a broad line of sand dunes rising above the tall, bearded grasses tossing furiously in the wind. Anxiously he asked, "Where are we?"

Molly pointed to the left. Not much of a road at all compared with the streets of New York, but he followed it, bumping tentatively over lines of sand drifting across the surface. "Corpus Christi is this way about two hundred miles," she said. He stared ahead into the dark, swallowing, but not willing to admit his anxiety over what he could do if something happened to the car. A little later she said, "We seem to have the island to ourselves. You can park anywhere." He pulled the car onto the sandy roadside where the grass wasn't so tall, relieved that his first real drive was over. He walked around the car to open the door for Molly.

Never in his life had Danny been in a place so dark and lonely—not even the Kansas hills around Fort Riley. The scudding clouds hid everything—no moon, no stars—nothing was very apparent but the threatening wind and the roar of the surf. He rolled his uniform trousers up to his knees and waited while she carefully rolled down her stockings. Barefooted, they made their way through the sand, holding their shoes in their hands, stopping at the top of the dunes, feeling the strength of the wind pressing against their bodies, holding them back. Every now and then, the moon broke through the clouds, illuminating the chaotic beauty of the surf dashing far up the beach.

If it'd been daylight with plenty of people around, the waves might not seem so intimidating, but with just the two of them alone in the dunes and the noises of the wind and the crashing surf, the scene looked menacing. Danny felt Molly's hip press against his, and he slipped his arm around her waist. "Is it like this all the time?" he asked.

She reassured him, speaking calmly, "It looks a bit dangerous down there. But there's always a wind at the beach. We'll just be careful and most likely the water won't even come up to our knees." The two made their way down the soft sand slope toward the water, excitement growing as they neared the surf, which by now looked mountainous to Danny. Once on the firm beach, they stood at the point where the waves stopped and began to recede, feeling the cool of the wet sand on their feet. The spray flying from the tops of the breakers told them that if they went any farther, it would be far more than wading through shallow water. Well, he'd come with Molly, and if she wasn't concerned about the foam and spray, neither was he. "We'll probably get wet, but it's OK with me," he shouted above the wind.

She turned thoughtful all of a sudden. "Oh, this dress isn't mine. I borrowed it from Mrs. Chamberlain—to impress you. I can't risk giving it a soaking in salt water." He heard her melodic laugh.

"There's nobody here to see you but me, Molly," said Danny, unbuttoning his shirt, walking back to a place beyond the crashing waves.

"I will, if you will. Help me with the back?" she asked. She tensed slightly as he undid the buttons, and admitted in a sheepish tone, "Ah...Mrs. C. said I should wear a girdle—to show off my figure. I borrowed it too."

Danny watched her slip out of the loaned garments, scarcely breathing. One by one, she handed him her things as she removed them, to keep them out of the sand. He asked himself, "Oh, man. Can this be happening to me?" The moon broke through clouds as he helped her with her bra hooks, and he heard her inhale as the last one came undone. Funny how you can hear one tiny sound through a rush of noise, he thought—if you're listening for it.

By the time she wore only the borrowed girdle, Molly's inhibitions had disappeared. She wriggled out of it without a hint of self-consciousness and tossed it on top of the pile on his arm, striking a pose with a hand on a hip and the other arm above her head. Danny put his arms around Molly and spoke with his lips to her ear—to be heard over the wind. "I believe I'll tell Mrs. Chamberlain," he teased. "I'll say I saw your figure without the girdle—and I think it's beautiful."

Neither said anything while Danny set their clothing on a clump of sea grass: her delicate things piled atop his clumsily folded shirt and trousers. He thought about the safety of his wallet in the pocket of his trousers, but only for an instant. Who else would be out here on the beach? There sure as hell weren't any cars on the beach road. He ran to catch up to the naked beauty waiting at the place on the beach where the largest waves ran out of momentum, pointing her toe to test a rolling bit of foam driven up by the wind.

"It's frightening," she yelled over the wind, her voice trembling a little. "I don't think I've ever seen the surf so rough. Is it dangerous, do you think?"

To Danny, who knew beyond doubt that the other lieutenants would see hesitation as cowardice, this was no time to turn timid. He'd been to Coney Island a few times, on quiet summer days when the Atlantic waves lapped gently on the beach. This kind of ocean surf was something a kid from the neighborhoods didn't know about. "It looks that way because it's dark," he guessed. He shifted his gaze back and forth—at Molly, then at the mountainous, pounding surf. When the clouds obscured the moon, it was very dark...but Molly waded in up to her knees, apparently having overcome her fear of the booming surf. Not to be outdone, Danny followed.

They could have been the last two people on the earth for the loneliness of the dunes and the endless line of the crashing waves. Danny and Molly walked along the sloping sand hand in hand, wading timidly at first in the sheets of water driven dashing past their legs and far up toward the dunes and back down the beach, receding into the sea. Little by little, they ventured deeper, till the rolling waves and the flying spray drenched them, and they tasted the salt on their lips. The water's warmth lured them into the breakers, diving awkwardly and tumbling happily in the churning foam when the waves broke over them. Step by step, Danny led Molly into deeper and deeper water, pleased she shared his sense of excitement in the power of the surging water. Laughing, he caught Molly's hand to help her up from a long tumble in the rolling foam. The wind swept away their laughter.

Something moved in the dunes—Molly saw it and her scream shrilled through the wind's roar. At that instant, a brilliant, heart-stopping beam of light swept over them, reflecting blindingly off the white surf! From the way it played back and forth, it could only be from a powerful flashlight searching the seashore and sweeping the surf for the occupants of the car parked by the shell-paved road. The light found them again and held them steadily in its beam. Danny felt his heart pounding in his chest like a hammer. Mad thoughts came to him. Bandits! Mexican bandits! They found my car! We've got to hide! Or run for help. The probing light beam held them steadily. It wouldn't go away.

"Stay down in the water, Molly," he said, trying to sound calm. It came out more like a shout, but she didn't hear him. Trembling and on the verge of panic, he yelled for her to move away from him so the probing light couldn't hold them both in its beam. He dived into deeper water, hoping to lose it, holding his breath until he was afraid he would drown by gasping involuntarily, but when he came up for air, the light was on him. Whoever held the flashlight already had the car, but now he wanted them! That was clear. "Take the money and leave us alone," Danny yelled, but he couldn't hear a response. Was it because the bandits were planning something or maybe that the wind carried his words away? No way could he know.

For a few seconds, they bobbed fearfully in the water just beyond the breaking waves, hiding behind the tumbling white water as much as they could. Each time, the light fixed on them immediately after the wave passed. After a bit, Danny and Molly fell silent, gasping excitedly for breath, thinking their own fearful thoughts about what was happening to them. But they didn't see anything any more menacing. Only the light flashing on them occasionally as if to keep them in sight, and Danny's panic subsided after a bit. His thoughts became more rational. If somebody wanted the car, they could've taken it and driven away without looking for its driver. "There's probably only one of them," he yelled to her over the noise, with no particular basis for his assumption.

But Molly didn't hear him and was panicking. "Danny, I can't get back to you," she yelled. Realization washed over them both that, in trying to avoid the light, they were being carried farther down the beach and out into waves easily capable of drowning them, and the situation was getting worse. For all they knew, the dunes could be infested with bandits or who knew what. Their only alternatives were dismal at best: stay out here in the waves a little longer with the risk of being swept away, or wade in to stand naked and helpless in the shallower water where a man waited with his flashlight.

Danny wasn't very good at cursing, but some of the most foul and colorful oaths he'd heard at Fort Riley burst from him in a torrent. He kept at it until he realized it wasn't helping anything. He wasn't much of a swimmer either, and the worsening seas made it even more difficult. He reached the floundering Molly in a few seconds of desperate, awkward strokes. Gasping from their exertions, and on the point of panic, they found the sandy bottom and struggled toward shallower water.

She clung to him tightly. "Danny, what'll we do?" He heard the fear in her voice.

Trying to sound reassuring, with his mouth near her ear so she could hear over the noise of the storm, "Molly, I see only one light. If there were more, they'd be on us. I think so, anyway. Let's go down the beach a bit farther. Maybe he'll leave us alone if he sees we're staying away from him."

But her trembling told him that moving along the beach and farther away from the car in the water wasn't something she wanted to do. The futility in it became pretty clear to him too. One bad guy playing cat and mouse with them just didn't make sense. Danny didn't have a clue. "If it's a bandit, there isn't too much he could want from us now. He's already got the car, our clothes and money: everything we left in the dunes. Our footprints would probably have led him to our stuff."

She listened quietly, clinging to him tightly, but her frightened gasping betrayed her anxiety. Danny tried his best to sound confident. "But if he is...um...if he wants to do something to us, I'll try to take care of him while you run for the car." The flashlight snapped on again. The man in the dunes began to draw the beam from them, through the surf and directly to him, repeating the motion every few seconds. Helpless to do anything else, they moved obediently toward the light.

Momentarily, the moon broke through the low clouds, giving them a glimpse of the man with the flashlight, waving a round white hat. Now he held the light on himself, a reassuring sign he probably didn't intend to kill them.

Danny led Molly, clutching her by the wrist, wondering aloud at an improbable sight, "I can't imagine what he wants, but I think he looks like a sailor!"

Trembling, hearts thumping with fear, the two frightened nude figures climbed warily up the soft, sloping sand, Molly huddling behind Danny, toward a man in dungarees standing in the lower dunes. Flynn made his voice as deep as he could. "Who are you?" Then, with as much dignity as he could muster, he demanded, "What do you want?"

"Coast Guard," the sailor shouted into the wind, sounding peeved about something. "Come up here and identify yourse'f," he said in a nasal drawl. Once they stepped onto the soft sand between the beach and the dunes, he dropped the blinding beam from their faces, and now they could see him better in the glow. Molly clung to Danny, hiding herself behind him, still shivering from fear and embarrassment.

"I'm Lieutenant Daniel Flynn, Army."

The sailor wasn't impressed in the slightest. "Yeah, I saw the bar on your shirt. Who's the lady with you?"

Molly peered around Danny's shoulder, "I'm Molly Blankenship," she piped.

With a sour expression equaling the peevishness in his voice, the sailor looked over the two cowering figures and said disgustedly, "Y' may be an officer, sir, but it's sure plain to me that yer just plain stupid."

At the moment, Danny, standing in the sand, dripping, feeling the flying sand stinging his naked skin, being upbraided for something dangerous, no doubt, and probably illegal, did indeed feel stupid.

The sailor rolled his tongue around in his cheeks and lips as if to be rid of a vile, bitter taste before letting fly with a righteous lecture. "The beach's been closed since before sunset. Y'drove right by the sign about a mile up the road. Never even read it, did ya?" he accused in a voice raspy with disgust. We've had hurricane warnings out since noon. Damn near everybody who lives on the island left for high ground hours ago. Lucky thing y'weren't hard to find. I saw yer car and followed yer tracks through the dunes to yer clothes." Those were the facts as viewed by a tired man at the end of a long day of patrolling an area threatened by an approaching storm, but he couldn't resist delivering his judgment. "Who but a army lieutenant would think of going skinny-dipping in a hurricane...sir?"

The man in dungarees turned to lead the way through the dunes toward the car, slogging through the soft sand. He shouted over his shoulder, "Now, follow me back to yer clothes." He didn't address them directly anymore, but grumbled loudly to himself about the general lack of common sense among the sort of people holding officers' commissions in the army.

The sailor moved on, leaving them to dress in the dark. They saw his light moving toward the road. While Danny and Molly hurriedly pulled on pieces of clothing without taking the time to shake out the sand thoroughly, they heard the sound of the Coast Guard vehicle being started, but the sailor didn't drive away. He waited behind Danny's Ford with his headlights glaring through the rear windows, intending to follow until they were safely on the causeway before high winds and steadily rising water made passage impossible.

Being dressed again helped restore his personal dignity, at least partially, but Danny felt his hands continuing to shake nervously when he tried to insert his key into the ignition. He hoped Molly didn't notice, but of course she did. She reached for his hand and squeezed it. He would have fought a Mexican bandit for her! Danny drove at a slow, careful speed across the causeway and most of the way into Brownsville, half-expecting the headlights of the Coast Guard car to reappear in the rearview mirror at any moment. Only when he saw the bright lights at the Fort Brown Gate shining in the distance did he give much thought to what he must look like, covered with sand, wearing only his ruined dress uniform trousers. He drove a little farther to a small parking area in front of a hardware store, long closed for the night. But it was a place with a single light bulb still shining enough so that he could shake the sand out of his shirt and get straightened up a bit before approaching the sentry at the gate.

Molly opened the window, calling to Danny, "I don't have a car on the post. Can you take me home? I'll give you directions."

chapter

SIX

The hurricane clawed its way northward over the Gulf through the night, driving ashore somewhere near the mouth of the Rio Grande in the early hours. On Sunday the storm hurled its terrible fury at Brownsville and Matamoros, tearing down power lines, toppling telephone poles and sending roofs flying. Gradually it pushed inland, battering the smaller towns in the valley before veering eastward. Before exhausting its strength, the hurricane lashed hundreds of thousands of square miles with high winds and deluged the earth with the full burden of water it carried up from the Gulf.

In Monday's pre-dawn calm, residents of Mexico and South Texas emerged cautiously to assess the damage. The most optimistic of them counted their blessings and the devout lit votive candles and prayed for an early return to a normal life. Fort Brown's post engineers set the garrison to work filling sandbags for bolstering the post's flood defenses. For several tense hours they kept a watchful eye on the water level inching up the scale, but the rise of the water slowed and peaked below a critical level—and now appeared to be ebbing. Restoring electrical power and telephones and telegraph lines took only a few hours. Afterward, the engineers concerned themselves mainly with repairing leaky roofs, replacing broken windows and cleaning up broken limbs and uprooted trees. The post's strongly-constructed, well-maintained buildings escaped major storm damage.

Except for wind damage to structures and citrus trees, the Rio Grande Valley itself fared well. Before the storm, the river had been flowing at barely a trickle, thus its basin had ample capacity to contain the storm waters. The rains refilled reservoirs, and the abundant moisture absorbed by the fields would refresh the citrus orchards and assure a grass crop that meant money in ranchers' pockets. Levels ran high in the streambeds but only in a few places did the water overflow to flood the countryside widely.

Conditions were far different a little farther to the north and east. In nature's capricious way, torrential rain swelled the streams of the Hill Country and the coastal plain, sending the rivers over their banks to inundate the low-lying flatlands in a shallow, turgid flood. Texans all over the state heard reports of widespread flooding in the lightly populated southern counties where the waters continued to rise. In the headquarters, Colonel Chamberlain and his staff followed the progress of the transport train from San Antonio to Fort Brown with growing apprehension

Lieutenant Flynn drove through the gate in a particularly good mood. Rapidly clearing skies promised the first truly fine day since the storm struck on Saturday night. A new sunrise sent its first rays filtering through the orange trees, assuring him of plenty of time to have a good breakfast before reporting for a new week's duty. He parked his car and strolled up the sidewalk at the Bachelor Officers' Quarters with parts of his dress uniform balled up under his arm.

Well before Danny reached the door, an agitated Private Garza ran down the steps to meet him, beckoning excitedly. "Hurry, Lieutenant, you gotta hurry," he yelled. Mouth agape and uncomprehending, Danny lurched ahead, staring at his overwrought orderly. Garza snatched the balled-up uniform parts and ran up a flight of stairs, keeping up the urgent flow of news that the colonel required all his officers at the headquarters building without delay. Confused by all the fuss, Flynn moved mechanically, blinking his eyes in the stream of furious scolding.

"Where you been, sir?" Private Garza ran up the steps to hold the door open, yapping like a terrier to rouse his boss into a sense of urgency. "You tryin' to make me look bad, Lieutenant? The colonel's had his people lookin' for you half the night! You gonna be the last one to show up." The dog robber shook out the sand-encrusted uniform parts, looking over his shoulder at Danny, but the orderly's best efforts were only partially successful.

"Lieutenant!" he screamed. "You're still in your uniform from Saturday, and you look like...well, you look like a dog pile," he said, shaking his head. Flynn closed the door behind him, but Garza wasn't done with him. He held a pressed khaki uniform shirt ready, rushing his boss with his shaving, scolding him for a long list of transgressions. "If you'd at least checked in with somebody, Lieutenant, you'd know that Centaur and Colonel Newman have been in the big office since Sunday morning." Finally, with his handiwork complete, the private sent his lieutenant speeding down the stairs, sounding more like a disappointed parent than a dog robber. He yelled through cupped hands to be heard over the sound of the engine, "Everything's packed and ready to go, sir."

Sweating from anxiety over the confusion and the rush of making himself presentable, Danny drove to the headquarters through the quiet streets as fast as he dared, still trying to guess the cause of all the fuss when everything on the post seemed so peaceful and calm. He looked at his watch to assure himself this was really happening. Jeez, it wasn't even seven o'clock yet. Then he saw all the cars parked outside the headquarters building and all the lights on inside. This wasn't some mistake. Something big's stirring. "Damn." He ran up the steps to Centaur's office with a panicky string of baseless excuses running through his mind. "What the hell am I supposed to apologize for?" he asked himself. Sweat beaded on his face and trickled down his back. At the top of the stairs, he stopped to collect himself. No way he'd barge into the room sweating and panting. He mopped his forehead with a handkerchief and stared at a shiny brass doorhandle he lacked the courage to twist and pull. Urgent words filtered through the crack under the door. He heard a voice he didn't recognize, and took another few seconds to collect himself so they wouldn't hear his anxious breathing. The voice inside was saying that the Signal Corps people had been collecting sporadic emergency messages sent yesterday and last night. Now it had become inescapably clear: The train carrying the 124th was stranded somewhere south of San Antonio.

<hr />

The first news of an impending calamity came in during the night, disturbing Chamberlain as he prepared for bed. Except for the men on the train, no one else knew exactly where the train lay trapped, much less any verifiable information on the condition of the men on the train. After a brief, restless sleep, he was on the phone from his quarters, conferring earnestly with staff officers in Washington and embarrassed railroad officials all over the country. A picture formed and with each new telephone call, the truth became more apparent: A train loaded with a regiment of cavalry had been completely stranded by floodwaters. A railroad dispatcher called to add a few details: The train and its passengers were probably in no physical danger, and except for flooding, the tracks had incurred little, if any, damage. But another call from San Antonio led Chamberlain to suspect the dispatcher's information wasn't solid. They were inferring a lot, feeling optimistic the train wasn't in danger because the tracks were laid on an elevated railroad bed. What was certain, though, was that the train carrying the 124th was unable to move toward Brownsville because of a weakened bridge and prevented from backing down in the direction of San Antonio by flooding behind the train. The railroad management staff assured the colonel they were still trying to learn exactly where the 124th was and how the men and animals were faring.

Maybe they were doing their best, but more was unknown about the situation at the train than was known. More time passed and all the railroad could say was that they hadn't heard anything from the train because the telegraph line along the tracks was broken at several points in the flooded area. From other sources, they learned that the shallow, muddy floodwaters spreading slowly through the mostly flat terrain would be several days subsiding. Of course, nobody knew exactly how quickly the waters would recede, but even when the water level was well down, the railroad officials said, they'd have to deal with the question of what damage the prolonged soaking might have inflicted on the roadbeds. Only then would they begin to assess exactly what measures could be taken to free the train. If it meant rebuilding large sections of roadbed, it could take a long time.

Centaur learned from a major in San Antonio that the train left for Brownsville with next to nothing in the way of food supplies for hundreds of men and their horses. Understandably, the thinking had been that, since the run from San Antonio to Brownsville took only a few hours, there had been no apparent need to provision the train for more than a couple of days. Having listened to all the reports, Centaur summarized his conclusions in a single word on the writing pad he kept on his nightstand, "Disaster!"

Shortly before midnight, the governor of Texas telephoned—concerned and irate. At first his words were polite and statesmanlike, but his message turned hard and accusatory, "Colonel Chamberlain, we Texans want to know what's being done to assure the safety of the men of the 124th. The voters want me to assure them that their husbands and sons are in good hands. I'm sure you're hard at work on this unfortunate problem, but you keep me informed. Hear?"

Nor was the governor the only one calling. The division commander and generals up the chain of command wanted regular reports on the 124th. Centaur wasn't accepting calls from the newspapers, but ignoring the reporters couldn't help matters much—the papers would print whatever they could scrape up, and it probably wouldn't be good. Sleep was out of the question, and his fuming and fretting were disturbing Helen, so a little before two, he left for his office, where some of his small staff had been at work, manning the phones, poring over maps and sifting through the stacks of telegrams.

The information collected so far painted a confusing picture at best, yet it could have been worse. Before the storm struck, Lieutenant Colonel Jerry Newman, Chamberlain's second in command, a lawyer in his civilian career, had been conferring with an advance party of sergeants to organize the arrival of the regiment, but now the effects of the storm and the resulting entrapment of the train by floodwaters knocked all their preparation into a cocked hat. Still, their work wasn't entirely wasted. Before the train rolled from San Antonio, they set up an office to communicate with the officers on the train and the railroad company offices along the line. This organization proved to be an advantage in collecting valid information. By the time Chamberlain arrived in his office, Newman and Major Perkins had been busy for several hours collecting information and notifying the officers of the regiment to report to work as soon as possible. They now saw a situation far less confusing than it had been when the governor called.

The unflappable Newman enjoyed a good reputation—always prepared: never at a loss in selecting the right words. He pointed with a pencil to a spot on the map unrolled on the large table in Chamberlain's office, speaking quietly as if all this were merely one of many potential difficulties he had been planning for right from the start. "This is where the train is isolated, sir: somewhere between this flooded river"—he drew a pattern of lines to show where the floodwaters had inundated the countryside—"and this bridge." He tapped the spot with his pencil, scanning faces around the table for signs of understanding. "We got word through the railroad before the telegraph line went dead that the engineer felt the train swaying dangerously on the embankment leading to the bridge, causing him to suspect the tracks just ahead of the train might have been weakened. Crossing the bridge was out of the question, so he felt it prudent to stop the train and back it down as far as he could; stopping at a place safe and stable enough to wait for the waters to subside." Newman waited for questions.

Wait? Wait, hell, Chamberlain's mind was buzzing, jumping ahead. He leaned over the table, staring at the predicament clearly laid out on the maps, agonizing over how this must look in Washington. Here's old Chamberlain, they'd be saying. He twisted arms to get his cavalry regiment and, first crack out of the box, the poor devil lost his entire command before laying eyes on it. Irritable from lack of sleep, the colonel turned again to his executive officer accusingly. "You've been talking to them since their orders went out. How in God's name did they get themselves into this fix, Jerry?" Chamberlain was inclined to like Newman. In fact he was prepared to accept him and the officers on the train as efficient, professional military men, but getting a train stranded on some forlorn patch of scrub growth sounded pretty damn stupid—on the face of it, at least. Chamberlain swept his hand across the map where Newman marked the flooded area. "The whole army's going to know about this by noon. Can't you imagine how they're going to be talking about this as soon as they go home and get a few drinks in them, Jerry?" questioned Chamberlain. As he talked, his voice grew shrill and louder. "Chamberlain's gotten his men into a damned flood in a desert! That's what they'll be saying."

Newman, well experienced in dealing with anxious clients and impatient judges, agreed, "Yes, sir. It does look bad," but he calmly spelled out a few more key factors in how the predicament had developed. "Fully three-quarters of the horses, and of course, men and equipment, were already aboard the cars when the hurricane came ashore," he said, setting the stage. "About then, the eye of the storm was still over the Gulf of Mexico, but they were already feeling some strengthening winds as far away as Galveston. I talked to our officers on the train by telephone while they were collecting the last of the outlying units and loading them onto a single train at San Antonio." It was while the final cars were being coupled up that Newman last conversed with them. "They reported a steady rain, but we talked over the possibilities, Colonel," he assured Chamberlain. "At most, they were a half-day by train from Fort Brown. They preferred to keep the regiment aboard and press on to their destination to avoid the disruption of another unloading and reloading." Chamberlain frowned. He didn't need to hear anymore to imagine how this freakish disaster played itself out.

Newman left the office for a cup of fresh coffee, and to give the colonel time to come to grips with the facts he had already presented. Returning to Centaur's office, he sipped his coffee and offered more detail about the discussions in San Antonio. Their decision to go for Fort Brown was sealed when the general, he didn't know the name, urged them to stay with their plan because the sprawling army posts in San Antonio were already overcrowded. Four large posts and still they lacked the extra facilities to devote to the unplanned arrival of a unit as large as the 124th. "When our troop commanders on the train assured me that their grain and fodder was sufficient for the last leg to Fort Brown—but no more, I agreed that our options were all used up." Newman watched Chamberlain's face fall when he reminded him about the animals, "You recall, sir, we no longer have horses at San Antonio."

Chamberlain acknowledged grimly that, put in this light, the decisions seemed more understandable. He listened reasonably to Newman's assurance that the railroad officials were staunchly confident the train wouldn't be slowed down by anything this storm could throw at them. He reached for the cigarette lying on the ashtray. "OK, Jerry," he said, carefully tapping away the long gray ash, "I'm convinced it was unavoidable." He drew deeply on the cigarette before finishing his thought. "But what I see is a trainload of well-intentioned men marching, step by blameless step, down the road to disaster," he said, exhaling. He ground out the cigarette in glum silence. "Go on," he grunted to Newman.

The executive officer moved to the large wall map and reached for a pointer to better describe the situation. He tapped a point south of San Antonio. "See, this is about where they are. Right between the Frio and the Nueces Rivers."

Chamberlain followed the pointer. Inescapable! An army regiment bogged down in the middle of a mostly flat area of farmers' fields carved out of stretches of mesquite trees and cactus. "Tell me again. What do we know about their condition?" he snapped. The colonel was working on something.

Newman knew what this man called Centaur was thinking of the officers on the train, but he didn't want him to think his new command was waiting helplessly for a rescue after the flood ebbed. "They're resilient, talented men, Colonel," he said, "They don't have an engineer unit with them, but some of the men from the train have been at work repairing telegraph and telephone lines. They reestablished telegraph contact with San Antonio less than an hour ago, and we're getting information routed through there." He beckoned to a sergeant waiting with a clipboard of copied telegraph traffic.

Silently Chamberlain invited Newman to take a seat before briefing him on the latest reports. The spare, fit lieutenant colonel drew out a chair from the large table and self-consciously eased into it. He sipped at his coffee, riffling through the papers, selecting a few reports that brought reassuring details. "Take a look at these, sir," he said, pushing the copies to Chamberlain. "Since they got stranded, our people have made pretty good progress." Newman spoke proudly of his fellow Texans, painting a picture of self-reliance and good organization, "They found a good place to camp and got the horses unloaded. There's still a little hay and some grain on the train. They're doing all they can to stretch it, but the horses are going through it fast. Some dry hay's available from the local farmers, but many of the roads are flooded. Working with the farmers, they're working out a route they can use to bring their wagons through."

Centaur grimaced at the images of a lifeline of tractors sloshing through waist-deep water. But Newman maintained his optimism. "Doubtless, the situation will improve. A workable camp is being erected and organized, and they're concentrating on the supply of drinking water for men and horses." Newman spoke with smug satisfaction of the ingenuity the stranded Texans were showing. "It's coming together, Colonel."

Chamberlain appreciated Newman's view of the matter. He, more than most, knew how professional pride could induce the men on the train to endure hardship, just to show their new commanding officer they didn't need help to get out of the situation. But he couldn't find enough assurance in Newman's stack of telegrams to suit him. "A regiment of men and their horses need a lot of clean water," he said, probing for more information.

"Yes, sir," he agreed, "and right now, we're working on finding good wells and coordinating the farmers' tractors. We've got the county law enforcement helping on that."

<hr>

Chamberlain pursed his lips and drummed his fingers on the desk. He wanted a point clarified. "What about the river water, Jerry? I think I know the answer, but tell me. Can they drink it?"

"Not really, sir. They've done some testing, and the regiment's been warned not to let the horses drink straight out of the floodwater." Newman shifted uncomfortably and told the truth they both knew. "Of course, if comes to it, they'll make sure it's as clean as possible."

Next, Chamberlain wanted to know what kind of help the army could expect from the people in the nearby cities. "See, here, Tilden and Three Rivers. They're not far. What about them?"

"Those aren't big towns, sir," said Newman. He knew the country quite well. "Tilden's the county seat, but the entire population of McMullen County doesn't add up to a thousand people, total. There's not much help readily at hand—in the way of trucks and road building equipment, I mean." Newman knew what Chamberlain was getting at. With the right equipment, they could even drill a well. "They need food—for both men and horses, but water is critical. As soon as they work out the problem of getting the water they need, they'll be all right," the exec said reassuringly.

Chamberlain couldn't be satisfied with mere reassurances. "We haven't even talked about how long it'll be before the railroad repairs the roadbeds." Shrugging powerlessly, he pushed his chair back and walked around the table to get another look at the situation. Critically, he squinted at the highly detailed map, examining the spacing of contour lines to get a better idea of the terrain. "Right here. This must be where they're setting up their camp," he thought aloud. "This bridge," he tapped the spot with the eraser of a yellow pencil. "Can we get any railroad rolling stock across it?"

Newman thought he understood what Centaur had in mind, but he wasn't sure. He answered the question directly. "Yes, sir. It's unsafe for the locomotives, but the railroad says it'll take some light loads." That much was true, but the CO had to see the dilemma in this. "We could get out there with one of those track inspection vehicles that look like an automobile to see for ourselves. Then maybe we could get some light loads to them," said Newman. Centaur's face brightened, but he hadn't yet heard the full story. "Colonel, the truth is that the bridge might fail unexpectedly. Listen, sir. Here's what I see. We can probably get to them, bringing a little help, but with a likelihood of failure. Or we can let them work it out by getting help from San Antonio or some other place on the other side of the flood with a likelihood of success. Why don't we give it a few hours, Colonel?" he said, trying to find something positive in the situation. "The farmers and some railroad repair crews will be there by noon, in all probability. In the grand scheme of things, those men will be fine where they are."

Centaur walked back to the table and stood behind a chair. Oh, he saw the scheme, all right, but he saw the situation spelled out in big, sharp black headlines: Emergency! No

Food! No Water! Army unwilling to accept risk! "Goddamn it, Jerry. Don't you see the politics in this? We've got to act."

Newman shook his head. No, he didn't agree that it was worth the risk of making matters worse by making an unnecessary effort and failing. The farmers would come through. There wasn't any reason to rush out there before they knew a lot more.

Centaur wasn't buying that line of reasoning. "Like hell we don't need to rush," he shouted, pacing the polished floor. "Sounds to me as though they don't have enough water for even one water call! Think of how it must look in Austin, or Washington, to every damned politician and every general in the army." No, they wouldn't waste a single second looking into the good reasoning by a lieutenant colonel at Fort Brown explaining the decision to send the train on from San Antonio. From their detached vantage points, they'd draw the kneejerk conclusion that, without any basis whatsoever, an overzealous commanding officer sent his entire command right into the howling maw of a hurricane."

Centaur stopped pacing. The more he thought about it, the more certain he became of the bleak view they'd take in Washington. "And now with the train sitting helpless on a railroad track, forcing his regiment to go slogging in the mud, hungry and thirsty, Chamberlain is sitting on his ass at Fort Brown, waiting for help from a few farmers and the railroad." Feeling isolated and frustrated, the colonel pounded his fist on the table. "That's what they'll be saying," he yelled. "That's why we have to rush." The commanding officer of the 124th wanted the people of Texas, the press and the army to see him as a concerned, decisive commander, taking strong action to bring a stranded cavalry regiment to safety. "We've got to rescue 'em...whether they want rescuing or not! Let's get moving on this."

Actually, Newman and Perkins had assumed all along that Chamberlain would want to jump into action, and they anticipated him. According to the wall clock in the headquarters building, the time was 0500 hours when Major Perkins began systematically alerting the 124th at Fort Brown, every one of them, to report as soon as possible: First, of course, the troop commanders and their lieutenants—orderlies too. "Make sure they understand it's an emergency." After the first round of calls, one sergeant contacted the Fort Brown post engineers, who were still keeping a close watch on the Rio Grande's high waters. Others notified some medical officers and a chaplain, calling them at home to be ready when Colonel Chamberlain went to the aid of the men stranded on the train.

One by one, the 124th received their notification that the train was in trouble and they would be needed for urgent action. Walter Franklin, Jenks and Pinelli, even George Kincaid, had been reached by telephone, or their dog robbers knew where to find them. Kincaid saw the large chalked sign at the sentry post. No one asked him how he happened to be absent from his room. In the anxiety over the predicament of the men on the train, his dalliance with Julie Breaux was quickly forgotten. The only officer who failed to respond to the recall within an hour was Lieutenant Daniel Flynn. A tense atmosphere of high emergency prevailed in the meeting room, stifling any talk other than essential conversation.

After listening at the door for a minute or more, Danny decided to sneak in on his tiptoes to keep his hard leather boot heels from ringing on the polished flooring tiles. He might as well have arrived with a siren screaming.

Major Perkins stopped in the middle of his instructions at the slight sound of the doorknob turning slowly. The clock showed 0655 hours, still early for a normal schedule, but sinfully late under the current circumstances. "Join us please, Lieutenant Flynn," he bellowed in a parade-ground bass. Danny slunk into a vacant chair under the reproachful stares of a battery of accusing eyes while the major waited behind a lectern with a map pointer in his hands. Flynn was spared an elaborate tongue-lashing by a shout from a sergeant at a side door. "The colonel's on his way, gentlemen."

Chamberlain, in uniform and ready to make something happen, returned from his office to issue orders. His eyes found his tardy junior lieutenant. "Good morning, Lieutenant Flynn. You're here at last," he snapped irritably, more from having his command stranded than from Flynn's tardiness. But nothing could have hurt Danny more cruelly than disappointing the man he wanted so much to please.

The colonel put the matter of his errant lieutenant aside and faced the men in the room, composed and energized, ready to act. "The hand-wringing's over," he said, keeping them standing. "Here's what we're going to do. Since our people can't join us here, we'll join them there. We're going to load a train with food, fodder and water especially—in any container we can find—and take it to them." Centaur set the priorities: Water was first, but food for the men and the horses stood as an urgent second. "The railroad has located a tank car, but it's somewhere in Arkansas. It is coming, however, and we might find a use for it later, if we don't find a good water source near the train. We don't need the medical team from the hospital. They've got their own medical people on the train.

"I know the railroad is working on the tracks. We can't help with that job. Our first action is to get there fast, bringing whatever we can to meet their requirements and then to become part of the 124th." His manner made it clear he wouldn't entertain questions. "I'm leaving now, with Colonel Newman, via the rail inspection car." Once he arrived at the stranded train, his first action would be to take personal command, establishing regimental headquarters on the train. So there it was: short and to the point. Chamberlain stood and left the room. Newman paused only long enough to assign one of the captains to call the newspapers.

The details of organizing the rescue train were left in the capable hands of Major Perkins. His directions were just as terse as Centaur's: "Our train leaves in two hours—sooner if the railroad can get an engine on our siding. Whatever we can't get on this train with us will come later. Every officer assigned to the 124th will be aboard. No exceptions. You're dismissed." Perkins hung the map pointer on its hook and left hurriedly to join Chamberlain and Newman.

The apprehension and confused emotion that swirled in Danny's head on his arrival in Brownsville was nothing compared to what he felt now. The day had hardly begun and he was already in trouble. That first day he was being met and escorted around the post. This time he was expected to lead a platoon. And there was Molly to think about. When he left her a few hours earlier, he hadn't the slightest notion of anything like this happening, and in a matter of less than two hours he would be leaving for god knows where or how long. If things went as Captain Franklin seemed to think they might, by nightfall he'd be facing a platoon of skeptical troopers.

Danny acted on an impulse to telephone Private Garza. But he knew nothing about the dog robbers' highly efficient network. To anticipate their employers' needs, these indispensable men contrived ways to spread information to one another with the speed of light. Every order, every scrap of gossip overheard in officer housing, classified information, anything—the orderlies made it their business to learn about it and spread the news. Garza reminded him, "All set, Lieutenant. If you'd'a listened, I told you the gear was already packed. You can trust me, sir. You gotta learn to trust me," scolded the private. "Your stuff'll be on the train before you get there."

His second call was to Molly, a call made without the slightest idea of what army men say to their women when they're sent away on short notice like this? Danny didn't quite recall the exact words he used, but Molly cried a little at first. She composed herself as she had seen her mother do so many times, and spoke bravely about not wanting to be late to work.

The rescue train pulled away two hours after Perkins closed the meeting, exactly as scheduled. Yet not sixty miles from Brownsville, it encountered the first delay. They were forced to wait for railroad crews to reach the switch opening the track to the weakened bridge and the isolated train. Two further stops delayed them, so night had fallen by the time hissing steam and squealing brakes roused the weary men who'd fallen asleep sprawled on the floor of the car or propped against grain sacks hastily thrown aboard at Fort Brown. Railroad flares and flaming wood scraps cast a spotty glow over the confused industrial clutter stretching along the track. Danny and Doug Cameron stood in the open doorway of a freight car, staring at the stark spectacle below them: men laboring amid piles of heavy tools and repair materials by the glaring light of gasoline lanterns.

This little godforsaken island isolated by shallow floodwaters had been selected as an industrial yard and a kind of logistics depot because it was a bit less than five miles to the weakened bridge, and it provided cramped but adequate working room immediately adjacent to the railroad tracks. According to an agreement hastily worked out by Perkins and a railroad supervisor, the army shared this convenient plot of ground with the railroad's maintenance crews. The idea of the army cooperating with the railroad proved to be extravagantly over-optimistic. What useful ground remained above the flood waters was almost entirely covered with piles of gravel, sand, crushed rock, shoring timbers, steel beams and a jumble of portable equipment brought in by the railroad. To the newly arrived men, the army seemed to have gotten the worst of the bargain, crammed into an impossibly small scrap of uneven, rocky soil sparsely overgrown with clumps of tall, reedy Johnson grass and a healthy stand of low, menacing patches of dull-green prickly-pear cactus.

Cameron and Flynn jumped down to the crushed stone of the railroad bed before the train came to a complete stop. If their first impression from the freight car door was one of clutter and disorganization, once down on the rocks, any sign of organization at all appeared miraculous. How on earth could there be room to stuff the supplies still on the train? Soldiers toiled furiously unloading crates and sacks to be sent over to the regiment, piling the material wherever they could, sometimes between the jumbled heaps of building materials assembled to repair the bridge. For the time being, where didn't matter. The army had to get their cargo away from the tracks immediately, so the railroad crews could get back to work.

A single gasoline lantern hanging on a makeshift pole fashioned from a piece of new lumber drew them to Major Perkins. His command post consisted of boards laid across the ends of two steel fuel drums. A sergeant and two privates kept track of things with a dozen or so clipboards and two field telephones connected to Centaur's headquarters on the train. The lumber and barrels had been borrowed from railroad stocks, and troopers from the train strung the wire across the bridge. On Centaur's express orders, the Texans returned to the train after hooking up the telephone wires. How would it look if even one man from the stranded train were to straggle into Fort Brown on one of the shuttling supply trains before the stranded train crossed the bridge?

Perkins hadn't slept for nearly two days and, from the looks of things, wasn't likely to get any rest for many hours. Without wasting time on pleasantry, he grunted a greeting to the two lieutenants. "Here, give me a hand," he said. "Take these flashlights and check the cars. If you find anybody still inside, rouse them and get 'em off the train so they don't get sent back to Fort Brown by mistake. Direct them here to me so we can find a place to put them for the night." He explained the operation of his tiny domain. The place was a constantly moving puzzle: nothing standard the way the army liked it to be. The major and two sergeant assistants, wearing loaded .45s had been struggling with it since the moment they arrived. A dozen men from the camp on the other side of the river erected the tents and built the temporary loading dock with materials furnished by the railroad, but they had gone back to Camp Centaur for the night. Now that the first train from Fort Brown was here, the major had something to work with. As soon as the cars were unloaded, supplies and replacements like Lieutenants Flynn and Cameron would be shuttled across the weakened bridge on flatbed rolling stock pulled by whatever light engines the railroad could provide. "Look over there on the tracks," said the unflappable Perkins, giving every impression of a man struggling against impossible conditions to make a sketchy plan work. Sergeant Bowers had the soldiers unloading the remaining cargo hastily tossed into the three boxcars before departing from Fort Brown.

Until now, almost everything Danny knew about Major Perkins was from Doug and Mike Pinelli, who described him as a jovial, sociable man, and they called him "Ma" after the radio soap opera character "Ma Perkins." Of course Danny knew from experience the man could be a willing disciplinarian. He'd already seen some of the major's skill this morning at headquarters. Out here in the damp heat and unnatural light, though, they began to see Perkins differently—as an energetic, no-nonsense leader—a man who could straighten out confusion and get men to work for him.

Once Perkins laid out the project and assigned responsibilities, he took time to explain the general working rules of his postage-stamp domain, stressing the tight priorities on access to the weakened bridge. "The repair crew has first priority on the tracks. Don't get in their way," he told the younger officers. Then, in the brief periods when the track was clear, the army could bring in a train shuttling more supplies from Fort Brown and unload it, but no shuttle from Fort Brown could remain there for any appreciable time. Without delay, it had to be backed away nearly fifteen miles to the nearest siding. The trick was to be ready to take advantage of the smallest bits of time to keep army traffic moving.

Chamberlain and Newman wanted updates at unattainable rates. Perkins understood the urgency and did his best. Rubbing his eyes, he peered at a clipboard in the pool of light cast by the lantern to check his schedule. The weary major tried to be patient with the captains and lieutenants. "Now listen up. I do have a transportation scheme, but we have to be flexible, ready to move as soon as the railroad crews back off the bridge." The lieutenants expected to be excess baggage around the camp until late afternoon, but the bridge work schedule allowed more army traffic than anticipated. Perkins surprised them: "Colonel Chamberlain wants to get the lieutenants over as soon as possible. At first light, those of you who will be platoon commanders will get high priority in getting across the bridge. So be ready."

"First time a second lieutenant got priority in anything," a voice drawled. It sounded like Captain Franklin.

Perkins explained how things were being run on the other side of the bridge. River Camp, they called it. "Colonel Chamberlain and his deputy have set up shop in one of the cars. That's regimental headquarters, and I'm in charge over here." The harried major demonstrated flexible sense of humor. "Here's a little something to remember," he warned with a quick grin. No sooner had Colonel Chamberlain crossed the river to take command than his headquarters popularly acquired the name Camp Centaur. He smiled broadly at the thought. "The name spread everywhere in minutes, but the colonel hates it. Remember, with him it's the River Camp."

Then Perkins was all business again. "Let's go find your tents now," he said, waving his flashlight to show the way. "Any questions?"

Danny asked, "Why are you wearing your pistol, Major?"

"Snakes," snapped Perkins. "The floodwater flushed rattlesnakes out of their holes all along here—huge, fat diamondbacks—big as your arm, some of them. We caught two near the tracks just before you arrived. We must have shot half a dozen of the damn things at least. Better be wary down here closer to the river." He shook his head, expressing regret about the location of the tents. "It's the only place we could put 'em. But be careful." Perkins had one more warning for them. "Think about where you're going to shoot when you decide to kill a snake. Lot of people around here." The major bustled away, leaving a sober silence hanging over the knot of lieutenants.

Searching among the weeds for a coiled rattlesnake is a fully absorbing endeavor. Only after digging out their weapons and loading them did they dare to point their flashlights into the low, sway-backed tents to assure themselves they were completely unoccupied. Flynn and Cameron agreed to fit themselves into one tent, leaving George Kincaid and the others to pair off. The lieutenants deferred to Captain Franklin, who got an entire tent to himself. Over the noise of steam engines shuttling shoring materials to the bridge, they lay uneasily among the tall weeds and the knifelike shards of broken limestone rocks, sorting out their thoughts after a day of disrupting events.

For a long time, Danny tossed on the rocky ground thinking about so many things—about rattlesnakes, about the men of the 124th settling into sleep nearby and about Molly, who suddenly seemed so far away. Eventually he fell asleep despite the shrieking and banging of the railroad gang's steam-powered tools at work fabricating braces and cutting beams to size—and awakened a few hours later when the raucous night noises fell silent. He guessed it was because work on the bridge was being halted to let the army use the tracks. Stiff and sore but unable to go back to sleep, Danny groped around to locate his pistol and dragged himself out of the tent. With a growing excitement, he pulled on parts of his uniform hastily and crept off in the glow of the work lights to find the orderlies. He located Garza and shook him awake. "Might as well get an early start on getting over the bridge," he whispered. The two scrounged coffee and hard bread from some out-of-date field rations available in the makeshift field kitchen. By the time the lieutenant and his orderly arrived at the hastily knocked-together loading ramp for transportation across the river, they could discern a faint gray light edging weakly into the eastern sky.

Danny left Garza piling their bags and tack on the rough new-lumber platform while he approached one of Perkins's sergeants about the transportation schedule. As brightly as he could manage under the circumstances, the lieutenant approached the fatigued non-com almost apologetically. "Good morning, to you, Sergeant," he said, making a show of checking his pocket watch. "It's early, I know, but I heard the noise stop. My orderly and I had our breakfast a few minutes ago. We're raring to go. Got any transportation over to Camp Centaur?"

The sergeant, a man he didn't know, rubbed his stubbly chin and peered up the track toward the bridge. The man squinted through his bifocals at the handwritten schedule on his clipboard, absorbed in filling every available space on anything capable of crossing the bridge. "Look heah, Lieutenant," he spoke in a voice roughened by cigarettes and, from the smell of it, an occasional taste of cheap whiskey. He shrugged his shoulders, assessing the situation. "These railroad fellas just told me our engine is still back on the sidin', so I may not be able to get you officers over theah before, say, noon." The sergeant rubbed his chin again, scrutinizing the lieutenant and his diminutive dog robber over the top of his glasses, sizing them up for something. Apparently satisfied, he suggested, "But I got this heah handcar that's got to go back right now." The rickety vehicle sat on the rails a few feet away, a little flatbed of a thing with wheels much like the ones on rail cars, but smaller. The ingenious machine was designed for two men to propel by pumping a set of handles up and down in seesaw fashion, operating gears that drove the car along the tracks. True, it was small and required manpower to move it, but it offered plenty of room for the two of them and their gear. "It'll save me sending my men with it if you and your orderly can take it over there. But it ain't first class travel, as y'can plainly see," said the sergeant, chuckling at the very thought of a lieutenant and his dog robber pumping their way along the tracks. "Y'd be workin' up a prett' good sweat."

Danny saw opportunity in the handy little car. Getting to the River Camp before the rest of the officers who came with Major Perkins might help remove the stigma of being the last to arrive at headquarters the day before. "We'll take it," he said without hesitation. The two early arrivals stacked saddles and the rest of their tack on the handcar, added a couple of sacks of clothing, securing the resulting heap with a piece of rope the sergeant gave them. Then they stripped to their underwear for the labor of pumping the handcar across the bridge, and then the several more miles to Colonel Chamberlain's River Camp— so as not to sweat up a uniform.

The light car moved smoothly and steadily along the tracks and the work didn't keep them from talking. Just to make conversation, Danny asked his orderly, "Looking forward to meeting your old friends, Pancho?" A quick flash of amusement in Garza's quick brown eyes told his boss that he still didn't comprehend this little detail of how these guard units worked. Garza stopped working the handles, allowing the car to coast a little way before he answered the question. "You forget, *Teniente,* I really don't know these people very well."

No, Lieutenant Flynn hadn't forgotten. He didn't understand in the first place. "How can you be in the regiment and not know them?" he asked for perhaps the third time.

"There was only the one troop of the 124th in Austin, sir." The orderly reminded his lieutenant that in about six months in the regiment—his time with the troop actually amounted to a mere twelve days—he had gotten to know only a few men. "Besides, people don't notice privates much, sir," Garza said shyly.

"Yes, but..." Danny wasn't sure what question to ask. Groping for a comfortable way to continue the conversation, it occurred to him there might be some advantages in being paired with an orderly who wouldn't be noticed around the camp. For a few minutes they pumped without speaking, until they started across the weakened bridge, letting their handcar coast while they watched the railroad crew working on shoring up the rickety bridge.

Cupping his hands at his mouth, Danny called, "How much farther to the train?"

"Two, three mile, mebbe," said the foreman in a brand of English heavily accented by his native Mexican dialect. "Hey, Army," he called after the two men in their underwear, "what happened to you' clo'es?"

Private Garza echoed the foreman. "Lost 'em in a crap game with some Mexicans workin' for the railroad." They laughed with the foreman and picked up the pumping again. The sun had barely climbed above the horizon by the time they'd traveled the remaining distance to the River Camp where the 124th had organized themselves along the track on a slightly elevated tract of what had been plowed farmland before the hurricane.

The train sat helplessly still and quiet on the raised roadbed where the engineer stopped it when he ran out of options: Its firebox had long ago gone cold—to conserve fuel for the final leg to Brownsville. An impressive string of cars stretched behind the locomotive—most of them nearly empty, with their doors yawning open. The roadbed supporting the tracks and keeping the train above the damp, still-marshy ground served fairly well as an awkward but workable thoroughfare for transporting equipment from the train to the firm ground where they set up the camp. The regiment's vehicles, trucks mostly, which might have made life in the camp far more bearable, remained useless on the cars. Someone had decided to defuel them in San Antonio after loading. Even if the farmers could have been persuaded to sell gasoline, the trucks might have been ineffective anyway because the narrow, wooden-spoked wheels would mire easily in the water-soaked ground. Otherwise the stranded men had taken advantage of their equipment and every bit of land the location offered them to organize a workable camp.

chapter

SEVEN

San Antonio: A special train of the Missouri Pacific Railroad carrying the 124th Cavalry Regiment, a unit of the Texas National Guard, lies trapped by floodwater.

Danny braked the handcar to a stop a few yards from the locomotive, where a waiting work party of troopers prepared to board it for transportation back across the bridge. The Texans had prepared a crude, but workable staging area by strewing the still wet earth between the track and the door to one of the first railroad cars with straw. Even an hour before a normal workday might begin, a large crowd had gathered at a crude bulletin board where the latest information was regularly posted.

He and Garza, still in their underwear, moved away from the roadbed and searched for a dry patch of ground to stack their gear and get into presentable uniforms. At that moment they saw the familiar figure of Colonel Chamberlain pointing from the steps of a railroad car coupled just behind the engine. "Who is that man? What's he doing here?" they heard him shouting.

Flynn, still in his underwear, stopped his search, thinking the colonel might be referring to him. But it wasn't Flynn drawing the CO's ire. The faces around the headquarters car were all turned in another direction.

Lieutenant Colonel Newman, who'd been circulating among the crowd, climbed a couple of steps up from the heavily trampled straw to get a better look. The object of Centaur's displeasure, a stocky civilian in an immaculate seersucker suit and straw hat, ignored the fuss. He knew army people and their habit of shouting all the time, and he didn't let it concern him. The man shifted a boxy black camera slung over his shoulder on a strap and continued his conversation with an equally short corporal. Neither the man in the suit nor the corporal in a fatigue uniform paid the colonel any further heed.

"Get the guy out of here," screamed Centaur, waving his arms.

Newman climbed up to the top of the platform to speak privately to the colonel. "It's OK, sir," said Newman soothingly. "I know him. He's a reporter from San Antonio."

Chamberlain exploded at the thought of the mischief the press could get into out there: "A reporter roaming in the middle of my command as if he owned it?" He turned on Newman, yelling, "What the hell do you mean, 'It's OK,' Jerry? Where in god's name did he come from? I didn't authorize any reporters to be here."

Newman wiped his face and neck with his bandanna. "Colonel, the man in the seersucker suit is Max Gindler. He writes for the *San Antonio Express.* I talked to him a few minutes ago. He's been here at the train since before you and I arrived. Came out as soon as he heard of the stranding, he says." Newman thought about Gindler and his statewide reputation for digging out the news, wherever it was. But in this case the ingenious reporter had outdone himself. "Colonel, Max found somebody with an airplane to land on a dry country road not far from here. Then he walked to a farmhouse and made arrangements to room with the family." Newman knew from talking with Gindler a bit earlier that the farm belonged to the man in blue overalls standing alone near a stack of the newly arrived material from Fort Brown, drinking a cup of army coffee and amusing himself by watching the soldiers. "The farmer who drives him over here on his tractor has offered to give us a hand," he said to the colonel.

Newman prided himself on being able to read body language and facial expressions. He watched Chamberlain's eyes narrowing, and when the expected outburst didn't materialize, he added a bit more he thought Centaur should know. "That's not just any corporal the reporter is talking to, sir. His name is John Sulak. He's been our press representative for years."

For decades Centaur's world had been centered on a small, sometimes shrinking army led according to rockbound tradition and unchanging regulation by men he knew personally. Here, Newman was introducing him to the concept of an army in which corporals did press relations work for a regiment. It would take some getting used to, but he conceded he had much to learn about these guardsmen. Chamberlain told himself he'd better get used to listening to the circumspect Newman. The man possessed the right combination of skills to guide the regular army colonel through this transition.

The executive officer pointed at the corporal and the cigar-smoking reporter. By now the two men on the ground were aware of being discussed by the pair of men standing on the steps at the train. Gindler waved with his straw hat, which produced a frown from Chamberlain. Newman ignored the reporter's gesture and expanded on his explanation. "Colonel, in civilian life Corporal Sulak is the owner of the *Fayette County Record*. He and Gindler went to college together." Here was even more novelty—corporals who owned newspapers. "By being in the business, Sulak is on a first-name basis with most of the newspaper people in the state," said Newman.

Chamberlain relented and relaxed visibly. "All right, Jerry," he agreed reluctantly to the situation and returned to his cluttered desk. Thoughtfully he sipped at his coffee, shuffling aimlessly through a personnel record, still preoccupied by images of Gindler and Sulak. After a time Chamberlain turned back to Newman to share his thoughts, "Jerry, let this be the last day for Mr. Gindler. The corporal can send reports to him in San Antonio by telephone." If Newman answered, nobody else heard it.

Flynn and Garza found their gear being unloaded and dumped on the track by a pair of the soldiers who met them. Without so much as a by your leave, the new operators jumped aboard and sped away, pumping strongly at the handles, leaving the strange lieutenant and his orderly standing abandoned on the railroad track. In the mud and growing heat, and the absolute lack of laundry facilities, no one seemed to pay the slightest attention to two men in baggy undershorts hauling their gear across the straw-littered mud. Danny borrowed a bucket to collect river water to use in washing and shaving before climbing into the uniform and boots so carefully preserved from the stains of labor. He felt his chin where he'd nicked himself in a couple of places with the razor before deciding that he'd done everything possible to make himself presentable. Garza stood back, hands on hips, eyeing his lieutenant critically. He nodded his approval. "Not bad, *Teniente*, for out here in the mud."

Francisco Garza had been brought up by his father to be honest, hardworking, free of most vices, but somehow, from the roughly organized chaos of a provisional camp, a siren sang to him of opportunity and endowed him with a special understanding of his role as a dog robber. After just a few minutes among these stranded men, the term took on a new meaning that meant more than orderly or just plain old trooper. He couldn't exactly put his finger on it, but he sensed power in being an unnoticed private who answered directly to his lieutenant—and he knew he was going to be good at using it. "While you're checking in with the colonel, I'll see what I can find over there in the camp, sir," he said, nodding to where long lines of the old-style white canvas tents had been erected. "We need some transportation. Maybe some real breakfast," he mused with a confident smile growing at the corner of his mouth. If the lieutenant didn't detect a new swagger in Pancho Garza after this metamorphosis, he would soon.

⚜

Immediately upon his arrival in the inspection car, Chamberlain made a cursory inspection of conditions in the fields along the track, but as Newman predicted at their Fort Brown meeting, the men of the 124th had gone to work with a will to organize a functioning camp. His tour assured him that, with ingenuity and hard labor, the problems of providing food and potable water would be solved. Centaur felt something as he rode through the camp that first day, speaking briefly to his citizen soldiers. They said the right things, politely and correctly, but a feeling of reserved uncertainty hung palpably in the air. It was the men themselves: the way they stood and the way they looked at him. In their voices he heard embarrassment at being stranded by a hurricane. Mainly, though, the message was that they were Texans, and they didn't know him. The real difficulty would be much harder to surmount. He saw it as a matter of pride. Call it morale, maybe dignity—the indefinable stuff that makes good soldiers. With it, they do their jobs well, even heroically, for only miserly pay. Without it, they can turn into a grumbling rabble.

As his first real business, Centaur meant to acquaint himself with these Texans, to learn how they reacted to adversity and to install the "fill-ins" from Fort Brown in the billets still vacant. If he succeeded in rearranging his new command to his satisfaction, his next goal would be preparing the regiment for an arrival at Fort Brown with as much noise and fanfare as possible.

Since their arrival, he and Newman had more or less secluded themselves in the headquarters car going over personnel records, especially those of the officers and senior sergeants, going outside on brief occasions to be seen by the Texans. Late into the night, they worked by the light of a lantern, checking records, writing lists, comparing notes and interviewing some of the men Newman recommended as troop commanders. Chamberlain wanted the assignment lists complete and typed before the replacements from Fort Brown arrived. Except for short periods of sleep, he'd been working without rest since getting the word about the train being stranded.

Centaur appreciated the Texans' circumstances and recognized that closeting himself in a railroad car with the regiment's records spread before him would excite a lot of anxiety and sharpen the guardsmen's suspicions of their regular army colonel. But Jerry Newman was the right man to send out into the camp at frequent intervals as a spokesman. He, if anybody, could assure the inquisitive, vocal Texans that their new colonel understood their concerns. He'd also spread the word that from now on, things were going to be done Centaur's way.

Danny saw that, even now, before the field kitchens had breakfast ready, a curious crowd milled around outside the headquarters cars, scanning the bulletin board fixed to the temporary entryway platform for any new information, awaiting their interviews, killing time smoking, drinking coffee and loudly speculating on what this "reg'lar" was going to do with the regiment.

Lines of communication weren't quite as primitive as the size of the insistent crowd made it seem. Field telephones connected the headquarters car with the troop offices in the tents, so they could have waited there; but with everything in upheaval and a new man making wholesale changes in affairs that, until yesterday, were handled largely by tradition, waiting for a call on the field telephone couldn't begin to satisfy the burning need for firsthand information. They had real lives, and they wanted the headman to realize what kind of stress was being laid on them. This business of being called up for active duty by the President without knowing when they'd be home again could upset anybody.

Danny carefully worked his way into the curious crowd, getting plenty of stares from the Texans, but he didn't care so much about them, because it was the other replacement lieutenants from Fort Brown he felt concerned about, and he was way ahead of them—by hours. Having the foresight to take the handcar might have made up for nearly missing the recall. Newman easily spied his clean uniform among those of the men who had been coping with the mud and primitive conditions for a couple of days. He beckoned vigorously. "Come on around to the steps, Lieutenant Flynn. The colonel has been looking for his people. He'll be glad to see the first arrival from Fort Brown."

Immediately, Danny noticed how haggard Chamberlain looked after several nearly sleepless nights. Maybe it was the morning light slanting through the window. He appeared to have aged considerably—but many of the lines dropped away from his face when he looked up to see Newman guiding one of his lieutenants into the cluttered car. "Good to see you, Lieutenant Flynn," said Chamberlain, smiling cheerfully. "You're the only thing operating on schedule this morning," the colonel was saying. He motioned to Danny to have a seat with him for some urgent business.

While a trooper with corporal's chevrons poured coffee, Newman produced a folder containing sheets of yellow paper from a folder: carbon copies of new assignment lists.

Centaur hesitated. This lieutenant had just surprised him with a show of initiative. He was so green, but the kid was trying hard: finding a way to get a jump on the others to get to his objective ahead of time and all shined up like a new dime. It might be worth the trouble, even if surrounded by chaos, to give this young officer an inside look at how a professional saw things. "This camp may look like a hopeless mess, but these Texans have done a damn good job," said Chamberlain reassuringly. "They're working hard, and we— the ones from Fort Brown—have to catch up with them." Laying the flat of his hand on the document as if to impart a special authority, the colonel pushed it across the table with a terse announcement; "I've assigned you to E Troop. Effective right now, you have the First Platoon." At his makeshift desk, Newman checked his watch and selected another yellow sheet of paper. Chamberlain plainly saw the need to move along with a busy schedule, but he had a little more advice for Lieutenant Flynn. "I want you to go over there." He pointed toward the tents. "Find them, your platoon, and get to know them while we're here, without the distraction of families or girlfriends. Get them working for you. First impressions count a lot." Danny thought he saw something, perhaps a slight tightening at the corners of the colonel's mouth for an instant. It could've meant anything, or nothing at all, but their sessions at Fort Riley taught him never to shrug off anything Chamberlain said—or did. He saluted and made for the door, where the impatient men outside could be heard calling for Newman's attention. "Who's next, Jerry?" called Chamberlain. At the top of the stairs, Danny got a suspicious glare from a major clattering up the steps for his interview with the new colonel.

No sign of Private Garza. Still exploring, Danny guessed. He could use the time to study the E Troop roster. Taking care to avoid sinking his boots into the sloppy mire, he found a seat on a wooden crate and spread the paper on his knee. A few handwritten notes in the margin suggested some last-minute changes. Right off the bat, he felt relieved to see Captain Franklin listed as troop commander. Franklin had been away in the regular army for a time, but he was a born Texan too. That counted for a lot. It would help in getting along with these men who'd been together so long. Danny read down the roster of First Platoon names. One quick run over the list, and he knew there'd be trouble in pronouncing most of them. He saw Garza's name, of course—the only Mexican name on the roster. But the rest were hard to place. Wieczorek, Bednarski, Zientek—Polish maybe? How about some of the others: Bohuslav, Cernosek, Kovar, Rohan? Matthijetz? He found the German names much easier to identify: Niemeyer, Oeltjendiers, Reimers, von Minden, Warnken. There were others, though, he saw, including at least one he could pronounce, a man named Henry Moore.

"Lieutenant Flynn," he heard Garza calling his name through all the conversation going on around him. Amid the ragged stream of men and animals approaching from the direction of the camp, Danny saw his orderly mounted on one big troop horse and leading another, waving and grinning like a possum.

Flynn folded the paper and placed it carefully between the pages of his notebook before slipping it into his pocket. Garza had gotten hold of the two horses by offering to exercise them. "Tall, strong horses, *Teniente*, and a little old," said the dog robber, appraising the borrowed mounts. "But I checked the shoes. Brand new."

Danny hesitated before swinging up into the saddle. There was a little detail he thought he should straighten out before he reached First Platoon. "Private Garza. Why did you say 'Lieutenant' when you called me, but Teniente when I was close enough for us to talk quietly? You do know you shouldn't be using Spanish words."

Garza didn't answer immediately. "Sure, sir, I know. But teniente means lieutenant in Spanish, and to me it sounds more elegant." He flashed a mischievous, disarming smile. "I think it suits you, sir," he said.

Together, they walked their horses slowly, picking their way through the traffic. The Texans had done well erecting a camp on this ground loaned to them by a man who considered it his duty to help the Texas National Guard. The bivouac itself wasn't large—barely the size of the parade ground at Fort Brown, he guessed—set up on an irregular plot of dry land almost surrounded by water and brushy land dotted with low trees. This jumble of tents and people looked very little like anything he'd been taught at Fort Riley, where the manuals assumed plenty of room on dry level ground, which resulted in camps depicted in precisely measured intervals along straight lines.

Here, the stranded Texans were forced to make do, pitching their tents in disorderly clumps, jammed together to use the available dry land but avoiding stumps and mudholes. Men could fit in anywhere, but a kind of order could be discerned among the swaybacked shapes of faded tents by locating flags and platoon guidons. Field kitchens required a bit more room, but two had been set up, one at either end of the farmer's field. Both were open for business, sending up a pall of white wood smoke hanging over the entire field in a low-lying layer. Troopers patiently waiting in line for breakfast watched cooks and their assistants laboring professionally at pink carcasses strung up on tripods for butchering—beef carcasses, from the size of them—probably brought in from neighboring farms. Garza studied the camp with a keen interest.

With cavalry, the horses mattered more than anything else, so the lion's share of the land, the flatter part of the field, was given over to the essential effort of caring for them. Danny surveyed the scene spread before him. If the headquarters was the communication hub at River Camp, the picket lines at the far western corner of the field, where horses were being fed and watered, constituted the regiment's industrial center. That part of the camp could be reached without too much difficulty by farmers' tractors pulling wagons over an unpaved, still-flooded road. The water wasn't more than waist deep at the most and fence posts showed the drivers where the road was. Three wagons with small loads of hay and one with a few sacks of grain stood in a row near the picket lines, waiting to be offloaded.

Feeding, watering and exercising the horses, plus farriers' and saddlers' work, required the constant labor of many men; yet despite all the activity, the peculiar thing about the camp was the quiet. The only sounds were the voices of men at work using hand tools.

The train itself stretched still and silent. No vehicles could be heard either, except for the puttering of one or two farmers' tractors.

Neither Flynn nor Garza had ever seen anything like this jumble of sweaty men in khaki and blue denim. If they went on business near the train where the new colonel was holding court, they wore the cleanest khaki uniform they could find, but looking smart was almost impossible when the ground was saturated and muddy river water was all they had for washing. Some of the sergeants continued to wear their khakis around the troop tents, but most of the troopers, especially the ones working with the horses, wore their shapeless blue fatigues held up by suspenders. Too hot for anything else.

The two newcomers stuck out like sore thumbs in their clean khakis. But it wasn't only the uniforms. Most of these stranded soldiers had been together in the regiment for so long that they knew each other as well as they did their own families. To them this new lieutenant and his dog robber were strangers, interlopers whose every move must be watched, and word of their movement spread before them. Both felt the constant probing of curious, occasionally hostile eyes. Garza somehow looked familiar to many of the Texans, but only one, a man from Austin, actually recognized him. Danny, though, felt the intense scrutiny of many eyes analyzing his every move. Who was this man riding one of their horses, and where was he from? If he really was from up North, as the rumors said, they wanted to hear how he talked. Most hadn't ever seen a real Yankee before.

Strangely enough, he found, when forced to pass at a short distance, almost all the troopers gave the impression of innate friendliness, unfailingly saying something like, "Hahdy, sir." Another trooper, a young black-haired man from Seguin, recognized Garza with a broad smile. They exchanged a few words in Spanish.

Danny needed to know where to find things around the helter-skelter camp. If a lieutenant is going to command a platoon, he doesn't want to be seen drifting around like a tourist. He hailed a white-haired sergeant making his way toward the train afoot. "Good morning, Sergeant."

For a time the man said nothing. He took his time inspecting the lieutenant and his orderly mounted on the regiment's horses with the kind of look people have always reserved for invading armies. The sergeant, whose legs bowed so severely he appeared lost and miserable without a horse, saluted awkwardly. "Hahdy, Lootenant," he said.

Danny met the man's stare, taking in the leathery skin and deep crow's feet around the eyes. He returned the hesitant salute as formally as only a brand new second lieutenant can, thinking this was the oldest man he'd ever seen in uniform. "Can you help me, Sergeant? I'm new in the 124th. Where's E Troop bivouacked?"

The sergeant cleared his throat noisily and turned toward the mass of tents erected around the field, pointing out the landmarks leading to the E Troop tents with his finger.

"Look yonduh," he said. "Y' kin fahnd 'em right over thah, where you see them two fahrs burnin'." He searched Danny's face, straining his memory for vestiges of army protocol plainly atrophied over decades in the neighborly workings of the all-Texan regiment and gave it up as an impossibility. Finally the sergeant reverted to his native habits, extending his hand to introduce himself. "I'm Leon Springer, fuhm 'round Longview, 'n ah don't think ah know you, suh." Springer inquired impulsively, "Not f'hm Texas, ah yuh?" It sounded less like a question than an admission of disappointment.

"Danny Flynn, from New York City," said the new lieutenant, leaning down from the saddle to shake Springer's hand.

"Lootenant, ah've nevuh met anybody f'hm New Yohk befoh." He thought over what he had just said, and how it must have made the Yankee lieutenant feel. "N' neither has anybody in E Troop, ah can assure yuh." Springer's sunburned face wrinkled into a smile. While the sergeant held healthy reservations about having yankees in the 124th, he was vastly amused that the E Troop men from the small rural communities on the edge of the coastal plain would have to deal with one. "Them old boys're Polaks 'n Bohemians 'n hah-dhedded Dutchmen, f'm down 'round Brenham 'n La Grange. 'Mong themselves, they talk thayah own languages—f'm th' ol' country, y'know. 'Specially when they don't wantcha' ta understand 'em." Springer was having difficulty in keeping from laughing at what was in store for this obviously green lieutenant in the clean uniform. He almost succeeded except for the furious working of his long, untidy eyebrows. "Hearin' 'em talk's gonna sound funny foh a while, but don't give it another thought." He waved a dismissive hand in the direction of E Troop. "They don't mean nothin' by it." Sergeant Springer touched the brim of his hat and rolled in his bowlegged gait in the direction of the train, still enjoying the look on the Yankee lieutenant's face.

Danny thought carefully about meeting these "Polaks, Bohemians and Dutchmen" who Springer found so amusing. Now or later? He decided on later, disguising his reluctance with a plan to kill some time. To Garza he said, "I'm going to ride around the camp and have a look." He nodded in the general direction of a field kitchen where a line of troopers waited for breakfast. "Why don't you walk around over there and see what you can learn. Talk to them if you like, but I want you to listen to what they're saying among themselves. I'll come find you."

He rode slowly in the general direction of the picket lines, stopping occasionally to avoid disturbing the troopers at work. When he could without appearing to stare, Danny sneaked looks from under the brim of his hat, surveying the frenetic activity. In the days since the engineer stopped the train in this forlorn spot hemmed in by slowly receding floodwaters, the feet of hundreds of men and even more horses pounded the borrowed farmer's field into a flat, muddy paste, and the smells of the animals and cook fires hung oppressively in the hot, humid air. From where he sat quietly astride his horse at the center of it all, the outlook appeared far more intimidating than from the rutted patch where he and Sergeant Springer stood talking a few minutes earlier. Back and forth Danny scanned the activity moving between the irregular jumble of tents and horses arranged in picket lines, looking to hit upon a way to introduce himself to the 124th Cavalry Regiment.

The putt-putting noise of a farmer's tractor struggling to pull its load into a line of grain and hay wagons sounded a little louder now above the voices of men working the horses. Several farmers in faded overalls and straw field hats were having a grand time visiting with the soldiers, making themselves at home near the field kitchens. It didn't matter whether they came to deliver water or fodder or if they only wanted to satisfy their curiosity. Their fields were still too wet to work anyway because of the flood, so they were staying to talk with the cavalrymen and be entertained by watching them ride.

The Texans had a lot of horses, and they liked them big. Danny remembered Amos Long's observations: "The major likes smaller, more agile hosses. If they're over fifteen hands, two inches, they're too danged tall." Danny's general impression was that the 124th had too many horses, perhaps half again as many as they were allowed, and since such a high percentage of them were past their prime, he assumed the Texans simply kept their favorites, a benevolent practice that wasted food and robbed a cavalry regiment of its maneuverability. But every horse, Danny realized, was well exercised and in tiptop condition. They knew how to take care of their mounts, and they were good, experienced horsemen—even if most of them had a tendency to slouch in the saddle and allow their legs to dangle down to low stirrups.

On a sudden impulse, he decided to show them how a soldier should ride, if his horse could remember how to cooperate with a skilled rider. The Yankee lieutenant on the borrowed mount, fell in with the mounted traffic, putting his mount through a drill of varied gaits at faster and faster speeds. Suspicions confirmed, the troop horse responded awkwardly.

At a small pile of grain sacks recently unloaded from a farmer's wagon, he took a low jump to see what this troop horse had in him. The horse labored awkwardly over the jump, but at least he didn't shy away from it. Danny felt his mount gaining confidence and a willingness to show his strength. The horse's response helped his own confidence enough to try two more slightly higher jumps. He expected some response from the soldiers, but for the attention they paid him, he might as well not have existed. Self-consciously he gave up the effort and walked the troop horse toward the field kitchen to find Garza.

Throughout the lieutenant's riding exhibition, the dog robber had been watching: paying more attention to the troopers around him than to the riding itself. When he saw his lieutenant approaching, he mounted and tied a small sack to a ring on his saddle. Together, they walked their mounts, talking, comparing observations.

"Learn anything?" Flynn wanted to know.

"Yes, sir. A few recognized me. Some were surprised that I hadn't come with them on the train. They asked me where I'd been and what I was doing—that kind of thing. I didn't say much—just that I missed my breakfast, so we all had something to eat and coffee." He patted the sack. "Got some biscuits for you, sir." He shrugged. "It's all they had."

Flynn nodded. "Thanks."

Garza reported one conversation while Danny hungrily chewed a stout biscuit and sipped coffee from a canteen cup. "The troopers seemed to be a little embarrassed that we didn't just wait for them at Fort Brown. Somebody asked me, 'Why does Colonel Chamberlain think we need to be rescued?' I didn't know. What could I say? I didn't see any of their officers at the field kitchen."

Flynn helped himself to another biscuit. "Anything else?" he asked with his mouth full of warm bread.

Garza's young face blushed deeply. "Well, sir. They watched you every step of your ride. 'That smart-ass lieutenant rides like a damn pansy,' I heard one say. And when you took the little jumps?" He hesitated.

"Yes."

"I heard a few of 'em calling you an asshole."

A deep thundering sound rising from somewhere near the picket lines interrupted Garza's report. They both heard it at about the same time and turned to locate the source. Danny recognized it as the low rumble of many men's voices, increasing gradually into a full-throated roar rolling through the camp. Over the sound of surging voices, they heard the drumming hoof beats of horses galloping fast toward them. "*Teniente*, look out!" Garza shouted a warning barely in time for Flynn to avoid a pair of horses galloping shoulder to shoulder, barreling straight at him.

A daredevil in blue trousers, riding with a bare foot on the back of each horse, thundered by, screaming, "Try this, you redheaded son of a bitch!" If Danny's savvy old troop horse hadn't shied away instinctively, they might have ended up in a tangled mess of humanity and horses. A roar of approval spread through the camp: saddlers, men at breakfast, sergeants with clipboards and idler privates, all cheering their man for showing up the fancy riding intruder. What would the new lieutenant do now?

Flynn's first impulse was to trail the shirtless rider and thrash him on general principles, but he felt dissuaded by the paralyzing force of the combined stares of the entire regiment. Swallowing hard, he thought the better of it, and the lieutenant and his dog robber rode slowly toward the E Troop tents in silence. Danny chewed on the last biscuit, considering what might happen when he found First Platoon. To break the mood and perhaps to restore his confidence, he hailed a trooper leading a newly curried horse. Now that he knew how the Texans regarded his attempt to impress them with his riding, Danny thought he'd try an appeal to their innate sense of hospitality. "Good morning, Trooper. I'm Lieutenant Flynn. Can you help me find E Troop?"

The sunburned, stubble-cheeked soldier squinted in the sun to inspect the two mounted figures, shifting a huge wad of tobacco in his cheek—doing everything but saluting. Deliberately, he ran his hands over the horse's carefully groomed rump, taking in the spectacle: officer, orderly and horses. When he was quite satisfied that this was the man he thought it was, he aimed a squirt of tobacco juice at the ground between the forefeet of Danny's mount and jerked his thumb to the nearest tents, where a red and white troop guidon marked with the letter *C*, fluttered on its pole. "This here is C Troop, as y'kin plainly see." With a toss of his head, he drawled, "Back there is D." He worked elaborately on the tobacco wad in his cheek for several seconds before looking straight at the lieutenant. "Now, even a damn Yankee kin probably figger out where E Troop is." Without further attempt at conversation, the trooper led the horse away, shaking his head in amazement at the abysmal ignorance of Yankees in general, but particularly lieutenants.

Impotently watching the trooper swaggering toward the picket line, Danny remembered what Centaur had pointed out only an hour or so earlier: "First impressions are important." Well, he'd tried to impress them by showing the regiment how well he rode, and his total accomplishment was that they knew a redheaded lieutenant was assigned to E Troop, and some of the troopers didn't think much of him.

All of a sudden the decision came to him. He'd start over at E Troop. "I think I'm going over there to meet them this instant," he announced, watching for his dog robber's reaction.

Garza leaned back in his saddle, eyes wide, and took a deep breath. Exhaling slowly, he leaned forward confidentially, speaking frankly, "Right now, sir? It might be a little hostile around the tents, don't you think?"

All right, so Garza didn't think much of his first impression either. But if he didn't act now, he'd lose his advantage over the other lieutenants. Danny ignored Garza's warning, thinking aloud for the dog robber's benefit, working out what he would do at E Troop. Somewhere in this sea of tents was a small patch of men who'd just become his new neighborhood, and nobody was going to push him out of it. The way he saw it, the Texans were giving the green lieutenant a testing a new guy should expect. He hoped old, white-haired Leon Springer really did have the right idea about the Texans in saying, "They don't mean nothin' by it." Suddenly, recalling Springer's comment explained Centaur's faint, fleeting smile. Both knew something like this was bound to happen. Danny saw the situation clearing up. He looked at his dog robber with a look that meant business, but maybe not all business. "What would you do, Private Garza?" Danny asked.

Garza could read decision in the teniente's face. No harm in saying what he thought about it, "No choice, sir. I know how miserable it was to be treated like dirt for no more reason than being a peon's son, and if you feel anything like I did then, you ought to go show 'em who's boss."

Danny dismounted, handing the reins to Garza, laying out his plan. "I guess it'll be better if I approach the E Troop people alone." The dog robber waited while the teniente tilted his hat a little farther down over his forehead and rearranged his shirt. The man understood machismo pretty well, for a gringo. Damned if the teniente didn't remind him of the gamecocks his father liked to put his money on.

Flynn sent his dog robber away with a swat on his horse's rump, hoping his actions would impress these people watching him as being casual and confident. "See if you can get our tack and the other gear up here from the railroad."

Garza didn't truly agree with the idea leaving his lieutenant to the men of E Troop until he saw the grin forming under the flat hatbrim. Even so, he voiced some reluctance. "I'll do it, if you want, sir, but why not leave the tack at the train a while, till this afternoon? If things get settled down."

Letting any part of the matter ride simply didn't fit with the lieutenant's freshly made decision. "Listen here, Private Garza," said a determined Flynn, wrinkling his nose. "I'm as much a member of the 124th as these people are, but they're forgetting their manners. I'm sleeping here tonight, after I introduce meself to them." From now on, he was playing a new game. The men of E Troop knew the new First Platoon commander was nearby, alone, for all practical purposes. Without a soul from the 124th to introduce him and vouch for his reputation, they saw him as meddling in a private matter. All right, thought Flynn, that kind of thinking might be understandable with a new arrival, but enough was enough.

E Troop's tents weren't far away, just past a heap of D Troop equipment. He picked his way through the littered troop area watching warily, hoping to learn something, maybe to see some of the officers or the sergeants, or perhaps to get an idea of how the men of E Troop did their chores. From the looks of it, many of the troopers were away from the Troop area with the horses or some other work. There was plenty of it to do, obviously. Of those he did see among the tents, most were conveniently finding something interesting to watch: in the direction of the picket lines, maybe or down toward the train; anywhere but where the lieutenant happened to be. Conversations stopped at the new officer's approach, creating a circle of silence that followed him wherever he went. This treatment was so deliberate, it set him seething: To be more outrageously snubbed would be impossible. Danny knew the full weight of army discipline was on his side, but it wasn't worth much to a brand new lieutenant out here among the tents. Stepping carefully over the helter-skelter arrangement of tent pegs and ropes, Danny made his way as directly as he could toward the E Troop guidon, where he found a smallish, dark-haired master sergeant sitting on a folding seat at a folding table in front of a tent, making out work assignments while three corporals waited to pick up the afternoon's orders. The sergeant puffed on a cigar, finishing a joke about a farmer's mule. The largest of the three troopers, a man with graying temples and a prominent belly, forced a laugh and groused irritably, "C'mon, Pappy. We're ready to go to work and we need the assignments." If any of the four noticed the lieutenant standing a few steps from the table, they didn't show it. Flynn, irritated more and more by this active shunning, walked slowly and deliberately to the table, fighting back the temptation to kick it over. One by one, they gave way silently as he approached, grudgingly allowing him a few inches to pass.

The sergeant, his sleeves impressively adorned with the chevrons and rockers of his grade, looked up with the exaggerated dignity of a Byzantine potentate interrupted in the act of issuing a royal decree. "Kin I help you, Lieutenant?" Without waiting for a response from the lieutenant, the sergeant observed, "We seen you out theah, ridin' around, n" takin' a look at owah hosses." The statement hung over the group like a pall of acrid smoke.

Struggling to remain cool, Danny said, "Look, Sergeant. I'm here to report to E Troop: First Platoon.

"Well, good. That's good. But there ain't a thing I can do about it," said the sergeant with a pained expression. "See, all our records're in the train, and Lieutenant Dietrich, First Lieutenant Dietrich, is the acting troop commander. Now, Lieutenant, ah...?" The question hung expectantly.

"My name is Flynn, Daniel Flynn," said the lieutenant.

"Yes, sir, Lieutenant Flynn. Lieutenant Dietrich ain't here right now."

So what about Dietrich? "As of this morning, I have First Platoon," Flynn announced with the insistency growing inside him. "Why don't you get up and escort me over to the platoon for an introduction?"

"Well, suh, that'd be nice, Mister Flynn," said the sergeant, not the least bit impressed by this brand new lieutenant. "But Sargint Wieczorek is in charge there, and he's doin' a good job. I know you'll learn a lot from him as time goes on." The sergeant studied his cigar and held his mouth as if he'd tasted something bad. "See, Lieutenant, we're used to officers with a little bit'a experience. We're kinda partic'lar that way in E Troop." He took a moment to sign the orders lying on the camp table. Then slowly and deliberately he passed them out to the corporals. Handing the last paper to a slouching gray-haired corporal, he introduced him. "By the way...sir, this here is Corporal Frank Cernosek. He'll take you over to report to Sargint Wieczorek." The sullen trooper said nothing at all, but moved away from the table with painful deliberation without a glance backward to see if the lieutenant was following him.

Chafing under the studied abuse, Danny trailed Cernosek, stepping carefully, raising his feet high to avoid tripping in the maze of ropes and stakes. He knew there had to be a better path. What he saw was a mixed picture of idleness and industry. He heard the derisive banter and taunting laughter—no damn different than they did on Manhattan street corners, it occurred to him. Never allowing Cernosek to draw away from him, he listened to the troopers speaking in a sprinkling of English and whatever else they spoke. He steeled himself for what he was sure to come, but he was determined to put an end to the game. And he meant to do it today.

Two hatless privates with sunburned faces sat in the meager shade of a scrub cedar, killing time at a game of dominoes. They hardly moved except to push the black tiles around on the upended crate they were using for a table, but when their corporal led the red-haired lieutenant straight for their sergeant's tent, they halted their game to get a better look at him.

A few feet away, three more soldiers showed hardly any interest at all. One, Danny saw, energetically rubbed oil on a leather strap freshly mended by the saddlers. Another rolled a cigarette, shaking tobacco out of a small pouch. They had just hung their laundry out to dry over the limbs of a low bush. He could hear them talking in English. "I hate warshin' clothes in that rivuh watah," said one, wringing water from a khaki shirt into a galvanized bucket. "It's got s' much mud in it." Their conversation stopped abruptly as Cernosek deliberately led the new officer between their table and the tents.

The circle of silence followed Danny every step of the way: real and oppressively heavy. As soon as they thought he wouldn't be able to hear their chatter, they went back to their conversations, but it didn't matter much—they weren't speaking English anyway. Right down to the newest privates, and some of them weren't all that young, they felt violated by the arrival of this "American." All this forced Danny to reconsider Sergeant Springer's comments. Right now the man was wrong, dead wrong, about these men not meaning anything by it. It might be simply that he surprised them by being early, but this was the army and their behavior couldn't be allowed to persist. The corporal stopped in front of an unmarked tent pitched with an extra foot or two of surrounding space around it. Without a single word, he pointed at the closed flaps.

"First Platoon?" Danny called, to be certain he was heard.

A sleepy response came from inside the tent. "Yup. Who're you?" In a moment the flaps were tossed aside roughly by a strongly built man in khaki riding breeches and a regulation undershirt over his belly, emerging from the tent, yawning, eyes blinking, running his fingers through the thinning brown hair over his white forehead. If the troopers in the 124th were the size of this platoon sergeant, they might need all those big horses. According to the typed list in his pocket, this had to be Sergeant Wieczorek.

The anxious corporal spoke first, "Sarge, I got the orders from Pappy." But the sergeant, looking straight at the new lieutenant, shuffled past Cernosek in brown boots with the untied lacings trailing behind him on the damp earth.

Here was another situation Fort Riley hadn't prepared him for. The rude idlers in this confused collection of tents bore no resemblance to the troopers in the school troop, or the few at Fort Brown, for that matter. These men were behaving like street bullies. That's it; he thought to himself. In fact, this burly lout of a sergeant reminded him of a loudmouthed Italian kid who swaggered into the Irish neighborhood one afternoon, looking to expand his territory beyond Scanlon's grocery. The Italian's posturing and threats didn't work when it came to a showdown in the alley, and it wouldn't work for this man either.

Danny took his time searching the sergeant's face. "Second Lieutenant Daniel Flynn, First Platoon, E Troop, 124th Cavalry," he said slowly, so there could be no question.

The sergeant was no more civil than the rest of them. "I'm Elwin Wieczorek, platoon sergeant. I'm in charge here." He stood to his full height and crossed his arms defiantly.

Centaur's smile came to mind again, setting Danny wondering how much of this kind of behavior the colonel had anticipated. He guessed the sergeant's flagrant challenge was as much for the benefit of his impressionable troopers as it was for Lieutenant Flynn. Out of sight behind the clustered tents, Danny heard the shameless chipping among the denim-clad troopers increasing. Weech had intimidated their last two lieutenants, and they wanted to see how he handled this one. Two, speaking out plainly out of confidence they couldn't be understood by the new officer, speculated on how this confrontation would go. One proposed a bet, but none of the others would back the lieutenant.

This wasn't quite what Springer's warning led him to expect, but Danny had a good idea of what was happening. "What are those troopers saying?" he demanded.

"Sonny," growled the hulking Wieczorek, thrusting his jaw at the impertinent lieutenant, "they're talking Polish. We all talk our own languages when we don't want outsiders to know what we're saying." Wieczorek's smirk advertised his annoyance at having a nosy new lieutenant to straighten out. "And they're saying, 'See what a tit-sucking baby the army sent us. God help us when we have to fight real men.'"

Flynn felt the rising taste of fight filling his mouth. Shaded by the hat brim, his blue eyes blazed at Wieczorek. "So much for the cheekiness, Sergeant," he said in the lowest voice he could manage. "We're going to start over right now. From now on, we won't have this insolence."

Out in the tents, the eavesdropping troopers heard—and nodded knowingly. Two other lieutenants had balked too, but in the end Weech had always won. The first accepted being a figurehead. The last wouldn't—but repeated hints of a disabling accident in the near future intimidated him. After two months the lieutenant had gone to the captain and quietly asked for a reassignment. Just as quietly, it was granted. Conversations stopped dead—this was going to be interesting.

The corners of Wieczorek's eyes tightened, and he stood a little straighter, letting his arms fall loosely to his side. He'd fix this uppity little pissant.

Danny wasn't going to let this become a personal thing between the sergeant and the new lieutenant. If First Platoon had even the faintest trace of military discipline lingering in their memories, they would respond reasonably when faced with a decision between order and intimidation. "Call them to attention, Sergeant," he ordered. None of the troopers remembered a lieutenant giving Weech an order.

Now it was Wieczorek who had a problem—one that couldn't be handled with a physical threat. Before witnesses, he'd been given a reasonable order by a man he fully expected to knuckle under. For the slightest instant, the sergeant's eyes wavered, flickering between the lieutenant and a brawny, scowling, sandy-haired soldier he relied on for support.

Danny saw a tiny opportunity in the sergeant's momentary indecision. He pressed his advantage, speaking a bit louder for the troopers' benefit. "We'll drop this sloppiness as of this second, Sergeant." He restated his order as if explaining it to a school kid. "Get them standing in nice straight lines, right here, where there's a bit of room," he said through clenched teeth. "Then you fall in with them and I'll be thankin' you to keep your yap shut." He wanted the men hiding in the tents to hear what he was saying to the sergeant. If they heard him at the troop commander's tent, then so much the better.

Two troopers, returning from picket line duty, sweaty and stripped to the waist, stumbled into the volatile confrontation, dropping their tools in surprise. Hurriedly, they pulled on the blue fatigue jackets they carried slung over their shoulders, shuffling away in confusion to lose themselves in the scattered fringe of wide-eyed soldiers. The platoon hadn't ever seen Wieczorek give ground to a lieutenant, except for form's sake around senior officers. This little Yankee may have surprised the sergeant so far, but if it came to anything serious, Weech could break him in his hands.

Danny never allowed his hard stare to leave Wieczorek's face. He had no fear of the troopers—they'd take their cue from their sergeant, who'd already showed that his reservoir of self-confidence wasn't bottomless. From hard experience, Flynn knew of disputes where the issue turned on a momentary weakness of resolve. He took advantage of Wieczorek's surprise. "If you don't want the troopers to see you lying in the dirt, twitching, then you'll be gettin' them in ranks at attention," the lieutenant said.

Wieczorek swallowed involuntarily. Flynn saw it, and so did every trooper in the expectant circle in front of the sergeant's tent. Another win for the lieutenant. Weech turned toward the men in blue with glacier-like deliberation. It pained him to do it, but he gave the necessary orders. And the troopers obeyed, shuffling awkwardly into ranks, eyes downcast so Wieczorek wouldn't see the surprise in their faces. The platoon sergeant saluted slowly, reluctantly. "First Platoon all present or accounted for, sir," he said in a voice shaking with boiling resentment.

So much for the first step: They knew how to stand like soldiers, if they were forced to do it, but now they had to learn that the lieutenant's approval was a more powerful force than the sergeant's wrath. He knew he could work with them, and the sergeant too, damned bully. Keeping them standing at attention, he introduced himself. "I'm Lieutenant Daniel Flynn, son of an immigrant from Ireland. My hometown is New York City, and I, like you, am in the 124th Cavalry." Danny motioned the sergeant to stand closer—so there would be no excuses for not hearing. "Now," he said, stabbing at Wieczorek with a finger, "you miserable excuse for a soldier. I want you to introduce each one of these men to me, pronouncing each name clearly."

Danny didn't take much time with the introductions. All he wanted was for them to get a close look at the man who now commanded First Platoon. When it was done, Wieczorek saluted without prompting.

"Take charge of the platoon, Sergeant. I want to see every one of these men, one by one, alphabetically—and privately." Without looking at Wieczorek, Danny walked away and sat in the nearest folding chair. Moving deliberately, he took out his notebook, sharpened a pencil with his pocketknife and waited for Wieczorek to send the men to him. Flynn chatted briefly with each soldier, asking easy, gentle questions about family and schooling, just to get him talking. As the trooper answered with his name and hometown, the lieutenant made entries in his notebook, adding more personal information after each brief interview.

Adamcik, Pvt. Arnold: Schulenburg—plumber
Bednarski, PFC. Lorenz: Brenham—butcher
Bohuslav, PFC. Jaroslav: La Grange—carpenter
Cernosek, Cpl. Frank: Roznov—farmer
Matthijetz, PFC. Leroy: Dime Box—farmer
Moore, PFC. Albert: Navasota—bank teller
Reimers, Pvt. Gerhard: Industry—farmhand
Sevcik, PFC. Anton: Fayetteville—school custodian
Von Minden, Pvt. Otto: Round Top—farmhand

Zientek, Pvt. Stanislaw: Brenham—drugstore clerk

The rest were away on work details elsewhere in the camp. All right. The word would reach them soon. These were strong, honest young men brought up with a strict work ethic, but they were reticent to converse freely, very much unsure if this new lieutenant would last. If Danny had it worked out correctly, the troopers were shocked at seeing their sergeant so thoroughly humbled, confused that things weren't working out like they always had before. It wasn't over yet, and Danny knew for certain that the sergeant would take each of them aside to learn what the lieutenant wanted to know about them.

After a little over an hour of interviews, Private Zientek stood, waiting for the lieutenant to dismiss him. "Find Sergeant Wieczorek," said Danny. "Tell him I'm ready to talk to him." Zientek saluted and hustled away, searching among the tents. "Weech," he yelled.

Waiting for the sergeant, Flynn went over the results of his interview. Except for Cernosek, the gray-haired corporal and Wieczorek, all were privates in their twenties or possibly even a bit younger. All appeared wiry, lean and fit from hard work and hard riding. Bednarski, the blond one Wieczorek depended on for support, could have been the sergeant's younger brother in size and appearance. The lieutenant had strong reservations about the sergeant and the corporal. How well could these oversized men with their youth behind them take hard riding day after day? He would see. Without exception, all his troopers learned their soldiering right here in the regiment. From what they told the new lieutenant in their interviews, they thought of themselves as Poles or Czechs, or some other nationality, first. Some of them, such as Private Moore, were sometimes referred to by the rest as Americans, whatever that meant. Then they were Texans second, and lastly members of the 124th. To most of these men, brought up in the insular rural communities of South Central Texas, the regular army was a vague, distant government organization calling them away from home because of a war somewhere. None of them knew much of Fort Riley—except Wieczorek, maybe. This was a tightly knit club of Texans with their own traditions overlaid heavily on army discipline, nearly smothering it. To his surprise, Flynn learned a little of the odd twists in the intermixture of civilian lives and the structure of the National Guard. Private Moore guardedly informed Lieutenant Flynn of cases where the officers were civilian employees of the soldiers they commanded. "Captain Davis is a loan officer in my daddy's bank," Moore said offhandedly, referring to the F Troop commander. Situations like these confused a new lieutenant without any background for judging them. Maybe they worked in the cultural context of the National Guard, but Flynn didn't much think those practices would work out in the active-duty army.

These short talks with his soldiers left Danny with a glimmer of assurance, but working with Wieczorek would be another thing, he suspected. Before calling Sergeant Wieczorek in, he stood to stretch and survey the area around the tents. Only two troopers were visible: one busily applying something from a can to the leather of his worn McClellan saddle, the other methodically threading a new string through the eyelets of his lace-up boot. This scene of quiet industry was all too neat, too convenient to be anything but a facade. Danny would have bet a week's pay that a good many others were close by, probably lying in the tents, listening.

Weech lumbered around a corner of the tent to avoid being seen until he was almost upon his new platoon commander. Somewhere he had collected a complete uniform and laced up his boots. He had even taken pains to clean the encrusted mud from them and apply some leather dressing. "You wanna talk, Lootenan'? I'm here."

"Have a seat, Sergeant. This may take a while," said Flynn.

The arrogant and immensely powerful, but unsophisticated Wieczorek stood stiff-legged and red-faced, a few steps from the table the lieutenant appropriated to use as his office. "I'll stand," he blurted, "and this ain't gonna take long." He crossed his arms over his chest in the same aggressive posture as before. The lieutenant shouldn't draw any conclusions that he was welcome in the platoon or that he was in control of anything, and Wieczorek growled, "The 124th is a Texas outfit, an' nobody in it is gonna work for anybody who ain't a Texan. You and the new colonel fella got to get things straight, Lootenan'," said Wieczorek in his rasping nasal tone.

Flynn decided that rather than trying to lead him with questions, he would learn more by simply allowing the sergeant to talk.

Taking the lieutenant's silence as a kind of capitulation, Wieczorek felt a bit bolder. "I sure as hell ain't goin' to take orders from a snot-nosed, pissant lootenan' who ain't dry behind the ears." Crossing his arms again, he waited to see how this pronouncement went down.

Danny stood without a word and walked around the crate standing between them to confront the recalcitrant sergeant, who stared straight ahead at the lieutenant's red hair.

Wieczorek hissed a warning. "Watch your step, sonny. You embarrass me in front of the troops again, and your're mine—right here—tonight, maybe."

Danny wasn't going to be lured into a threat-swapping match. He moved forward warily, closing the gap between him and Wieczorek until the two stood a mere few inches apart—and he grinned at Wieczorek. Before the platoon sergeant realized what was happening, he felt the weight of the lieutenant standing on the toes of his boots, grinding at them with his soles of his own boots before stepping away. The man looked down at his toes, forehead furrowed, so astounded he could only sputter. Danny reached toward the sergeant with both hands, grabbed him by the shirtfront...and lifted. Feeling Wieczorek stiffen in surprise at being raised to his tiptoes by a smaller man, Flynn released him.

The new lieutenant intended news of this latest encounter to get out fast. Loudly enough for his hidden platoon to hear, he threatened his headstrong platoon sergeant. "You're a lazy sack of dung, Wieczorek. If I don't get instant obedience from you, you'll be Private Wieczorek on permanent dung-shoveling detail. Now get to work on making those boots presentable." Coolly, Danny stalked away in search of Captain Walter Franklin.

⚔

At the train, Centaur stepped out of his headquarters car to stretch and to say a few words to the waiting crowd. He heard one voice clearly shouting for attention. "Colonel Chamberlain." It was the portly, dapper reporter waving his panama hat for attention. "I'm Max Gindler of the *San Antonio Express*." After the colonel's tacit approval two days earlier, Gindler had made himself a fixture in the camp. Daily, a little before nine, a versatile little yellow aircraft chartered by the reporter landed on a narrow strip of paved road no more than two miles from the train. The farmer who was putting him up at his house would drive Gindler to the plane on his tractor so he and the pilot could exchange deliveries. The pilot's job was to pick up a packet of the reporter's dispatches and film for delivery in San Antonio before the paper's deadline, but the cargo he delivered was almost as important: a hefty stack of copies of the final edition of the *Express*. The first copy, of course, went immediately to the headquarters car for Colonel Chamberlain; the rest were for circulation around the regiment—several copies per troop. The papers passed quickly from hand to hand, with the soldiers avidly devouring Gindler's articles and photos that daily informed their families and the entire state of Texas how well their men were coping with the flood.

Another fairly large package contained necessities such as clean suits and shirts. One more, a smaller, more confidential delivery marked "Photo Supplies," held more film and paper for Gindler's typewriter, plus a few half pints of bourbon and a supply of cigars.

Some reporters might have chosen to share the grimy life of the marooned 124th, but Gindler saw his role a bit differently. To be the only man in camp in a clean, starched shirt and an immaculate, freshly pressed suit was a sure way to be noticed. Cigars and whiskey worked wonders in collecting the candid personal views that add spice to news items. Gindler, the man in the seersucker suit, became a fixture at Camp Centaur, a lifeline to the people at home. Wherever he went, troopers gladly posed and pressed notes into his hands to be sent to their families with the pilot.

Chamberlain bore a curious resentment toward Gindler and the way he had inveigled himself into the camp. Damn it, the man had infiltrated a cavalry regiment. Instead of being allowed to stroll around the River Camp on the gradually drying land, looking like a bandbox dandy among the unwashed troopers, the man should've been locked up. Up to now, he'd been resolutely maintaining a bald deception of ignoring the reporter, but to a soldier starved for something to read out here on this soggy farm plot, a daily delivery of a fresh newspaper was a pretty good morale builder. Besides, Gindler's favorable articles in the *Express* were thoroughly erasing any hint of the proposition that an absentee commanding officer rashly ordered the train into a life-threatening situation. And dammit, Chamberlain had to admit that the man was good with his camera.

"Go away, Gindler, before I have the MPs run you out of here," said Chamberlain, leaving his office for a practice parade on the cramped field near the tents.

The cagey reporter puffed on his cigar, unconvinced by Chamberlain's show of brusqueness. "Colonel, you may be surprised at what I know about your command. For instance, I know you don't have any MPs in the 124th, and I know your people are far too busy to be making a prisoner of a reporter who's been making them look good in the papers." Waiting for a response, he interested himself in the long ash on his cigar. Chamberlain turned away and took a step or two toward the saddled horse held by his orderly, but Gindler recognized tentative behavior when he saw it.

"Colonel," he said suggestively, "I wasn't born yesterday. I know that if a cavalry regiment gets itself stranded, somebody stands a strong chance of being embarrassed, or worse." The reporter knew he'd touched a sensitive spot and didn't have to elaborate. "I have a proposition, sir," said Gindler.

Chamberlain took the reins from his orderly and motioned irritably with his head toward the mass of mounted men awaiting him in the camp. "Be quick, Gindler. I have an entire regiment waiting for me."

The reporter came well prepared for this opportunity. "I know this regiment and its men...and I think I'm getting to know you. I've learned what you intend to accomplish before you leave for Fort Brown." Gindler paused, watching Chamberlain's face. "You want to get this collection of civilian soldiers looking like professionals for a grand arrival on the parade ground."

Leather squeaked under the colonel's weight as he placed his foot into the stirrup and eased himself into the saddle. Gindler, a veteran observer of powerful men, saw something. Perhaps it was a subtle tightening of posture, or the easy balance in the seat. Maybe it was something in the eyes. Whatever it was, the change was profound. In that moment the reporter sensed the charisma that compelled people to refer to the man as Centaur. He raised his camera and snapped a picture.

"So?" he heard the mounted colonel asking.

Gindler saw opportunity beckoning to both of them. He laid out his proposal. "I'll stay here and ride the train with you to Fort Brown to cover your..." He gestured with his hands, searching for the right word. "Your triumphal return to Fort Brown with your new command." Confident of his salesmanship, the reporter was on it like a Bible-thumping country preacher going for the altar call. He put it to Chamberlain, whose suspicion appeared to be waning noticeably. "It's a great idea you have, to exploit this unfortunate accident of nature to make the 124th look good in the eyes of their fellow Texans. I think it'll push the embarrassment of getting caught by a hurricane right out of their minds. This story will be picked up by every significant paper in Texas...maybe the national press too."

Centaur shifted lightly in the saddle, staring at some imaginary spot in the trees across the encampment and flicked at something with his riding crop. Abruptly, he leaned over to shake hands with the reporter. "All right, Mr. Gindler. Join me in my office in the railroad car around eighteen hundred hours, and we'll get started on this."

chapter

EIGHT

Washington: Two U.S. merchant ships, a tanker and a freighter, sunk by U-boats off Iceland.

Gindler and Chamberlain stood together at an open window, two satisfied conspirators looking out over the manicured parade ground, where less than an hour before, the 124th had passed in review. "It's a great day for you, Sam," said the reporter, offering one of his long, aromatic cigars.

His story and photos hit the Texas papers and hours later, the evening editions of the eastern papers. In a single day, an obscure National Guard unit came to symbolize victory over adversity, setting off celebrations in Texas country towns, the governor's mansion in Austin, even at the War Department. Chamberlain eagerly accepted, congratulating himself on his impulsive agreement to collaborate with the brash, aggressive reporter.

"Let me light that," said Max. If asked, he would've claimed his journalistic *tour de force* to be nothing more than a good day's work. Usually he carefully avoided becoming emotionally involved in a story, and yet here he was, celebrating another man's success with unalloyed delight. He struck a large kitchen match, allowing the flame to flare and burn the sulfur away before holding it ready to light Chamberlain's cigar. The delighted colonel puffed contentedly, watching the flame dwindle to a glowing ring at the end.

"You did all this, Max," said Centaur, grinning, thumping the reporter heartily on the back. "Take a look at these." He ushered him across the room to view an array of large glossy photographs on the table. Some were Gindler's, taken at the River Camp. The rest were the work of army photographers—including a few truly excellent shots of the 124th riding proudly, full of piss and vinegar just an hour earlier: Captivating scenes, and undeniably successful, but they were yesterday's news. The real cause for today's celebration was the deluge of telegrams piling up on a tray set opposite the photographs.

Chamberlain selected several to show the reporter, "They're coming in from all over the army. Look," he said, reaching for one set aside in a folder, "this one's from the former commander of the 124th. It's my favorite." He passed it to Gindler.

Max smiled too—picturing his friend, Governor Ned Pennington, at his desk in his Capitol office, penning the short note. He read it aloud. "The Eyes of Texas are upon you, and the entire state is proud to have you leading her sons." He closed the treasured folder carefully and returned it to Chamberlain. They stood at the table for a moment, chatting, leafing through telegrams, matching them with photos—reliving their triumph. The temptation was strong to linger with the images: the band playing on the platform, welcoming the 124th to their new home as the train pulled in; Centaur mounted, leading his men from the railroad siding; and many late examples of Gindler's artistry. But neither had time to dwell on pleasantries.

Centaur left it to the man of words to capture the moment. "You're a gifted leader, Colonel, and I agree with the governor. You found a way to make Texas proud of her militiamen. I was lucky to be there to report it," said the reporter, shaking Chamberlain's hand, taking his leave reluctantly. An army sedan waited to whisk him to the Brownsville station. Now it was time for the regiment to celebrate.

Hundreds of troopers packed into the mess hall cheered and applauded, almost drowning out the regimental band blasting out a stirring march. Centaur stepped nimbly onto a flag-draped platform set up under a large banner that read *Golpeo Rapidamente*. He waited at the lectern for the sound to die away.

"I'm proud of you," he began. "In the days after the hurricane, you rose above the humbling ordeal in the River Camp. While some would have blamed the railroad company and waited passively for help, you overcame a nasty turn of luck like the veteran soldiers you are, and you made the most of it." He nodded proudly. "Together, you and I, we've gotten to know each other, and I like what I see." Applause and foot stamping boomed through the bare rafters, telling him that the Texans were accepting him too.

"Two days ago, you made a splendid show for the army and civilian populations here at Fort Brown and Brownsville, and thanks to the modern miracles of aviation and photography, most of the country is aware of your pluck and determination." He waved a sheaf of papers—the same congratulatory telegrams he and Gindler shared earlier. "These come from all over the army."

The troopers knew from their families and neighbors how well Gindler's work was received. Texans all over the state clipped articles and photographs from the newspapers and passed them to their neighbors. They were mightily pleased and proud of their men.

Chamberlain set the stack of telegrams aside. "That's in the past," he said. "Now, in facing the future, we must confront a harsh truth. We of the 124th aren't ready, at least not yet, to defeat the massive well-equipped forces of our enemies rampaging in Europe and Asia." He recognized them as capable, veteran soldiers, he told them, but every troop in the regiment was short of men—for a variety of reasons. The State of Texas had no pressing need of a large cavalry regiment. Nor could the treasury support it either. Also, many of the troopers were already being reassigned all over the army, where their experience was needed to train new recruits. Another round of applause rolled through the long building. "First," he told them, "we've got to fill the gaps in our ranks." Bringing each platoon and troop up to full strength was the first order, and then to rearm the regiment with newer, more capable weapons. After that would follow many days of hard training before they could live up to the motto on the banner hanging from the rafters. Translated from Spanish, it said, "I strike quickly."

He scanned the sea of faces, keenly aware of how important this message was to their impression of him. "You're thinking to yourselves, the war's already going on in Europe, and here we are, safe in the Rio Grande Valley, not very far from home. Maybe you're asking yourselves why. Nobody's afraid of Mexico." Chamberlain saw a few heads nodding. "Of course not, but we aren't here because we fear the Mexicans, but because we have plenty of enemies. The War Department is concerned about foreign agents coming into the United States. While we train and rearm for war abroad, we'll help protect the long, undefended border." The men in khaki understood. He hardly needed to remind the Texans about the depredations against American shipping. Some of these men came from coastal towns, such as the island city of Galveston. Almost certainly they had seen the fires of burning ships casting a glow into the night skies. And that was his point: "German U-boats have been killing Americans at sea for months in an undeclared war. I'll bet my next month's paycheck that you and I will be in the middle of a fight before we know it, sent overseas by an outraged nation to avenge those killings."

He signaled for a large map to be moved to the center of the stage and took up a long wooden pointer. "We're here because Germany knows war against the United States is inevitable—and they're preparing for it!" He placed the pointer on the map at the Mexican city of Vera Cruz, not far south of Matamoros and Brownsville. The old port served the

Germans as an essential harbor in their heavy commercial traffic with Mexico, an enduring interest that began before the turn of the century and didn't completely die out during the First World War. "See here? This is where the Germans are fueling and rearming their submarines—from ships at sea, of course. Then, loaded with fuel and torpedoes, the U-boats can lie in wait outside Galveston or New Orleans to sink our ships putting to sea with oil for Britain, or entering port to unload cargoes of ore or rubber." He smacked the pointer against the map with a loud pop. "Bastards!" he fumed.

Hardly a week went by without the press reporting a ship sinking somewhere along the eastern coast. The trumpets of war were calling, ever closer. The 124th would have a definite role to play—soon. It could be at any time. This was why Centaur had assembled the troopers in the mess hall today. These details bordered on a classification of "Secret." The S-2 had cleared it with the intelligence office at brigade headquarters. That explained the armed troopers at the doors, checking identification.

From Vera Cruz, Chamberlain moved the pointer north across the Rio Grande River, following the curve of the Gulf of Mexico to the port cities and oil fields where FBI agents had been arresting Germans: not those from the immigrant communities in Texas, but agents from Hitler's Germany, caught with radios capable of transmitting to U-boat commanders that a tanker was leaving port laden with oil. Many of the troopers on the benches before him, especially the young ones from the rural towns farther inland, may never have traveled outside their home counties. It wouldn't be surprising that they might be unaware of how very simple it could be for Germany to send spies across the Rio Grande River. With his pointer, he drew their attention to the valley north of Fort Brown, saying, "Beginning today, much of our time will be used to stop people from coming into Texas. As soon as I think we're ready—as we update physicals and issue new weapons—we'll be out there patrolling for them." Wishing fervently that things were really as clear as the words he had spoken to his men, Centaur stepped down from the platform, leaving it to Major Perkins, now the operations officer, to map out a rigorous training schedule that met the War Department's expectations.

⊰⊱

The euphoria that energized the Texans after Centaur's mess hall address lasted less than a month. Danny sat on a bench outside Captain Franklin's office, staring at a carbon copy of the First Platoon roster. The E Troop commander had called him in to review some troubling reports about his troopers. It didn't involve the entire platoon: The captain's interest focused on one man, maybe even two or three miscreants who were regularly calling in sick. Day after day First Platoon's sergeant and a couple of his privates were reporting in sick. What was it now, three or four days? Wieczorek's loutish behavior was being pointed out as the main cause of E Troop's declining performance. In fact, a few of Major Perkins's operations staff had gotten telephone calls from the brigade headquarters at Fort Ring-gold. Usually, the inquiries began, "What's happening with your troopers?"

Up to now, the brigade was accepting, "We're looking into it. The medical people aren't entirely convinced there isn't a health problem" as an adequate response. But if they were honest about it, the problem wasn't afflicting only Lieutenant Flynn's platoon, or even E Troop alone. The whole damn regiment was affected by a kind of malaise. It seemed that they weren't taking well to being in the army on a full-time basis. Centaur had been heard calling it malingering. Comparing experiences with their platoons, Flynn, Cameron and Pinelli were referring to it as the guard flu. But Franklin keyed in on Weech's influence with the other sergeants as being at the center of it.

The word was that Weech and his most trusted privates were at the head of nightly forays into Matamoros, getting howling drunk at a favorite little cantina every night, and reporting sick the next morning. A growing contingent of Weech's fellow sergeants were seen to be joining in, but First Platoon's sergeant was almost always seen as the leader. None of this was new to Captain Franklin, who was disposed to think well of Lieutenant Flynn, green as he might be, but Centaur had been calling his troop commanders in, putting on the heat. Of course, most of them were guardsmen who viewed his inquiries as a witch hunt.

Then, speaking to all his officers, from Lieutenant Colonel Newman to Second Lieutenant Flynn, Chamberlain reminded them of the regiment's proud arrival at Fort Brown. If asked then to comment on their readiness to go to war, he would have made a glowing report. The hell of it was: their first day at Fort Brown might've been their high point. Since then morale had plummeted. "It was little things at first—their attitude, for instance; they still think they're good," he shouted at his officers. "A little arrogance is a good thing in soldiers, if they can back it up, but gentlemen, the troopers of the 124th aren't showing me much." In his mind, they'd become a collection of whiners unwilling to make the adjustment from citizen soldier to plain old work-every-day soldiers. "Granted, they know more about the valley than anybody else at Fort Brown—in the whole army, maybe—but it isn't worth a damn if they're malingering in the barracks."

The State of Texas hadn't insisted on physicals and inoculations. So the Texans had been spending far too much time lined up at the hospital in their underwear for thorough physical examinations and a battery of shots required by the army. Twenty percent of the 124th reported sick with fevers after those shots. "Days of training lost, gentlemen," Centaur leveled with the officers. "We're falling behind in a race we can't afford to lose. We've got to be physically fit, properly equipped and trained to fight when the call comes—and it could come this afternoon. These men have to live up to their press clippings. No more whimpering out of them. If anything, life is going to get harder.

Indeed life did get harder, and First Platoon's reputation declined even further. Big, strapping Bednarski, one of Weech's favorites, fell flat on his face on the clinic floor, breaking a tooth on the tile—even before he reached the innoculation station. It could have been merely fright at the sight of a needle, but more likely that a colossal hangover played a major part in Bednarski's swoon. Wieczorek, far back in the line, hadn't seen the incident. Nevertheless he lurched up and upbraided a young medic giving the shots. First Platoon, E Troop and its sergeant were becoming altogether too well known.

Danny turned the door knob apprehensively and entered. The man behind the desk was not the courtly Walter Franklin who entertained his lieutenants on his family land. This captain sat stiffly erect, lips pressed into a straight line, peering through reading spectacles at a copy of the troop muster records. "I had such high hopes for you," said Franklin, disappointed and hurt. When the commanding officer informed him of assigning Danny to First Platoon, Franklin readily concurred. Lieutenant Flynn would be the man to straighten out the problem platoon. Now he questioned his own ability to judge men.

"What's your sense in this, Lieutenant? Is Wieczorek too much for you? Maybe he's not fit to be in the army. Do we charge him with some offense and get rid of him? Damn," Franklin pounded the desk. "There's plenty we could slap him with," he suggested, "but we don't have another sergeant, you know. So you'd have to use Corporal Cernosek as an acting platoon sergeant." The odd thing was that Lieutenant Colonel Newman saw potential in those odd ducks of First Platoon. At the moment Franklin was truly perplexed, but Centaur wanted results, not excuses. He looked at Flynn over his reading glasses with an eyebrow arched, waiting for answers.

Danny met the captain's stern glare with far more confidence than he felt. "Don't make any changes, sir," he pleaded. "I know it's my men who're at the center of this, but I can make First Platoon work." Shaking his head firmly, he added, "Wieczorek can be a good platoon sergeant. I can do it, sir."

Captain Franklin rolled a new idea over in his mind, eyes closed, lips still tightly pursed. He breathed deeply before telling Danny how things stood. "All right, Lieutenant. Let's see how you and your sergeant can work together. I'm volunteering you to take the regiment's first patrol. That'll be in a couple of days, after you're issued new equipment." He issued a final warning, "You can bet your ass that Centaur will have his eye on First Platoon. So will I."

❧

"Sargint's sick again, Lieutenant," reported the gray-haired Corporal Cernosek. Every eyeball in the platoon focused on the Yankee lieutenant to see what he'd do about it.

Checking his watch, the lieutenant turned to Private Bednarski, who was still wearing a bandage where his broken tooth had cut his lip. "You go with the corporal and bring

Sergeant Wieczorek here. Drag him if you have to." To Cernosek, he merely nodded. "Five minutes," he yelled, holding up a hand with the fingers spread, letting the platoon know this was a showdown. Urging the two sent for the sergeant to move faster, Danny yelled again, "The whole regiment knows he's malingering. No more sick in quarters, or I'll make sure he does time in the stockade." Five minutes later an ashen-faced Wieczorek tottered unsteadily in place before his troopers and began issuing orders.

For the next few days, the platoon worked well together, with hopeful signs that Wieczorek would regain the respect a good platoon sergeant needed to run the platoon. But Flynn wasn't satisfied. The sergeant was pissing away precious time inspecting field gear and drawing new equipment because they hadn't done it on their own—boots, clothing, that sort of thing.

Then it came to turning in their beloved Springfields—beautiful things, those rifles, cared for and coddled for years—for the new Garrand M-1s now being issued. It hurt to see these weapons, so well trusted and thoroughly proved by years of experience, thrown onto the bed of a dump truck to be hauled away like a pile of trash. Lieutenant Flynn fully expected his troopers wouldn't take that kind of indignity without complaint. But Weech surprised everybody by acting like a real sergeant, taking control while they stood in line to sign for their new M-1s. "Yeah, it hurts to get rid of them '03's, but good soldiers don't bellyache when it comes to weapons." Merely by being there, listening, he imposed calm and began to establish his control, letting them blow off steam as long as the general tone of it was constructive.

"That M-1 is a lot heavier'n the '03, Sarge," complained one.

"Well, sure, but th' M-1's semi-automatic, so you can put lead on the target faster with it."

Another trooper complained, "Not that much faster. You take that M-1 and gimme my '03. They both take the same damn ammunition. We'll shoot f'r fifteen seconds and I bet I'll put more holes in th' target than you will."

Evidently, way down deep, Elwin Wieczorek could be a man of some complexity—limited perhaps, but not quite the obtuse, churlish lout of the past few days. The sergeant didn't have a subtle bone in his body. He worked best among his own people, and he thought clearly when he felt sure of himself. Wieczorek, it seemed, normally worked with only one idea at a time, and once the idea had been chewed over to his satisfaction, he shouted it out at the top of his voice. Not a recipe for a diplomat, but not altogether a bad trait in a platoon sergeant.

Lieutenant Flynn didn't feel charitable about the way his troopers were taking to being assigned the regiment's first patrol. Every time they had a few minutes—at water call or standing in a line to draw new equipment—the troopers huddled together to bitch and complain like a bunch of old women, contemptuously referring to it as a job of raising dust for the Border Patrol. For far too long, the 124th hemmed and hawed in getting ready...and yet, serious questions lingered in many minds as to how capable they really were.

Finally Centaur insisted. "I won't make one more excuse to the Border Patrol. Brigade headquarters keeps telling me to light a fire under the 124th. No more goddamn excuses. Get a platoon out there," he yelled at Newman and Perkins. At headquarters they called this a patrol. Danny knew better and so did every trooper in the platoon.

According to the briefing, it was nothing much more than navigational training, and only incidentally to help the Border Patrol slow down the Germans waiting for an opportunity to cross the Rio Grande unnoticed.

First Platoon wasted a lot of time in getting geared up, ignoring the fact that they were being scrutinized by skeptical observers from Fort Brown all the way up the Rio Grande to division headquarters at Fort Bliss near El Paso. Time to get these malingerers covering ground.

Danny snapped to Weech, "All right, Sergeant. Get 'em moving," and for a short time the platoon looked like soldiers, clattering through the gate and down the paved streets of Brownsville, smiling and waving at the girls in the stores, but then it was out to the north and west over the Military Highway paralleling the river. In a few places, crankcase oil had been sprayed on the patchy surface it to keep the dust down, but mostly the road was a rutted strip of gravel or crushed stone and cinnamon-brown grit.

The big black troop horse stamped and tossed his head at his rider's roughness with the reins. The lieutenant felt partly to blame for the surly mood infecting the whole platoon, because he and his platoon sergeant still hadn't worked out their differences. When there's feuding among the leaders, the troopers can hardly be expected to perform worth a damn; and once out of public view, the whining and carping began in earnest. At first it was the idea of wearing steel helmets in the South Texas sun. When they wanted him to know what was eating them, they screamed in English, "These damn pots'll bake a man's brains out, Lieutenant." Before long, a couple of them started chipping to Weech in Polish. The sergeant smiled at the change because, it increased his confidence they'd side with him and not the lieutenant.

As usual, Private Garza had been keeping an eye on his lieutenant, riding at the head of the platoon since the platoon first mounted up. At the first water stop, he waited for an opportunity to talk when he was sure they wouldn't be overheard. "You ever done this before, sir?" he asked.

"Why do you ask?"

"Well, sir. You acting kinda like you did the morning we brought that handcar over the river."

Flynn looked around, not wanting his answer to be overheard. "You're right. It's my first time off the post with a platoon."

"You're a smart man, *Teniente*. It'll work."

The teniente had his doubts. Even without Weech, chances were that the troopers would be critical of him for a long time. A lot of these men were older than Danny, and they'd been coming to the border forts in the valley each summer ever since they joined up. If they weren't familiar with every geographical detail, at least they knew the nature of the rolling land and the people living in the valley. Flynn fingered the bandanna around his neck. He'd never worn one before, but in the steaming humidity at the River Camp, he noticed the Texans using them to wipe the sweat away and keep it from trickling down the neck. The young dog robber perceived his boss sitting noticeably taller in the saddle and rode away to his place in the platoon.

The patrol laid out for First Platoon had been conceived as a simple exercise: pretty much going straight out toward the river from a point designated on the road and back, to return and re-enter Fort Brown just before sunset. "If you get way behind schedule, you can consider crossing this bit of ranchland—here." The operations briefer stabbed his short pointer at the map at a point where the road made a bend. He was a captain from one of those small towns near Austin. Danny knew him only vaguely. "Don't worry about the ranchers," the briefer began an explaination. "Our people cut through the ranches every year—on summer training. Once in a while, however, the ranchers' hands get a little touchy." He warned Danny that some of the vaqueros carried weapons. "Never know what you're going to find in the brush, so do your best to stay on the military highway, or close to it, except if you have to cut through the ranchland," said the captain, noticeably concerned about Centaur's interest in making these first patrols work smoothly. He reminded Danny to be careful and follow orders explicitly. "Don't try anything fancy. Take 'em out and bring 'em back. That's all we want you to do." It seemed so simple.

It was about half past noon before First Platoon completed the outward leg of the patrol—a little behind schedule, but they could catch up. Danny felt his confidence growing. So far his navigation skills had been up to the task. The troopers were resting by the side of the road under the shade of some low Huisache trees after feeding their horses from the small sack of grain each trooper carried on his saddle. Their own diet wasn't much to write home about—nothing more than the standard field rations of hard bread and some kind of meat: beef, according to the legend on the cans. Flynn stood alone taking a pull from his canteen, poring over a map laid open across the saddle, fretting about finding watering places for the horses.

"Car comin'," somebody yelled. The cry came from the rear of the platoon strung out along the narrow shoulder for about a hundred yards.

"Car comin'."

This wasn't the first car to pass them, and they reacted to the inevitability of the coming dust cloud the car would dump on them as it passed by. Hurriedly the troopers pulled bandannas over their noses and urged their mounts farther off the road. Some cursed colorfully and shook their fists at the oncoming car. "Slow down, you son of a bitch." The dust thrown up by the dark, dusty sedan took what seemed to be forever to settle. Under the bandanna, Danny swore to himself. Damn driver was probably going fifty miles an hour.

"Did ya see the babe driving that car?" someone shouted. It sounded like Private Moore.

"S'pose that was her husband with 'er?" another wondered. "Lucky devil."

"Yeah. He's in there with that good-lookin' black-haired gal, and we're eatin' their dust."

"What kinda car was that?" It was Rohan, one of the Czechs, asking.

"Dunno. Too dusty," said little Zientek. "Maybe a Dodge or somethin'. Blue, though. That's all I could see."

Flynn fought to keep from coughing. He didn't give a damn about the driver, man, woman or child. She had to know the car trailed a long plume of road dust curling thickly behind it, choking the soldiers and horses. Obviously the woman at the wheel didn't care. He emptied his canteen, washing the dust from his nose and throat—conditions stressing the need to get to a well. In desperation he searched the map, looking for a cistern or a waterhole near enough to the road to meet the captain's orders.

"Lootenan'." Weech, leading his mount, came stamping up the road toward him, scuffing the dust off himself, complaining, "What th' hell we doin' out here, lettin' people dump all this dust and dirt on us? F'god's sake, we gotta git off this eff'in' road." Hearing the younger troopers voicing their own unhappiness to the lieutenant, Wieczorek sensed a swing in the loyalty in his favor and he took advantage of it. "We look like a buncha idiots lettin' civilians like them in th' car dump all that crap on us." He pointed down the road to the still-visible plume of dust trailing the car. "We already lookin' like a buncha dumb assholes with all this gear we carryin'." The sergeant shook his bandanna and wiped his face with it. He saw this as a good time to test the lieutenant again. "These ranchers don't give a damn if we pick our way through their land. Whatsa matter, Lootenan, you think you gonna git lost?" Weech taunted loudly enough to be heard.

The sergeant's sarcastic complaining opened the floodgates—only the troopers weren't as direct about it. "Right, Weech. What we doin' out here on the road fightin' the cars when everybody else in the whole army is trainin' their asses off to fight Germans?"

They wouldn't talk that way directly to the lieutenant, but Flynn heard it and hoped they'd stay on the road. He sought comfort in what the sergeants said at Fort Riley: "It's when they ain't bitching that you got to worry."

He rolled his eyes upward, allowing a prayer to escape his lips: Lord, just this first time, let me get them back to the post this afternoon. If he could only keep them in a coherent group clattering along the road—it didn't have to be a smart military unit today; things would get better.

"Jesus Christ, Lootenant," he heard from somewhere down the line of horses. They were at it again. "We know this country." This time it was Bednarski, the butcher, doing the complaining, following Wiecorek's lead. Since his fainting incident began to recede, he'd been showing signs of becoming a real malcontent. "Been here three or four times in the last few years, n' we ain't done nuthin' as dumb as this. If we gotta stir up a cloud of dust, let's do it taking a shortcut across some of this ranchland. Ain't gonna be no spies out here on the public road anyhow," he snorted.

Danny made a show of dusting himself off before calling out to Sergeant Wieczorek, "All right, get 'em mounted up." While the platoon sergeant gave orders, the lieutenant held a private council with himself. Saints preserve us! They'd told him to keep them on the road—unless there was a good reason! Water was his good reason—that and they needed to make up a little time. According to the map, there should be a good windmill and a cistern an hour or so from here, he judged. Water and time, that's what he'd tell them at the debriefing if anybody asked.

The sergeant got them mounted and moving, but Flynn still felt a little apprehensive. The Mitchum property was so vast that nobody covered it with any regularity. That was all right, but he remembered the captain's warning about the ranch hands wearing loaded pistols. Not so good. According to the briefer, no army unit had been across the ranch in six months or so—depending on what part of the sprawling property was in question, maybe not for a long time before. What was it he'd heard from Captain Franklin? "If you do go in there, even with a good reason, it's smart to be a little wary. They've shot at us before."

Danny looked up and down the road. Sure as hell, there was another car approaching—this time from the other direction—only not as fast as the blue one that went by them a few minutes earlier. His decision was solidified when he saw how much dust it was scattering. Trotting down a public road in the heat, standing aside and enduring the dust raised by these automobiles didn't seem like an honorable way to make a living.

"Weech," he called, waving the sergeant to him. "Here's what I want," said the now-resolute platoon commander, collecting three men around him to show them his map. He intended to send them into the Mitchum land in a line abreast, spread out with fifty yards between riders. Two scouts would ride out ahead. Flynn would ride the left flank, with his messenger taking the next position and Garza the next position after the messenger. Wieczorek, he put out on the opposite flank so he wouldn't have to listen to the man's constant complaints. He instructed the scouts to look for the watering hole or for cattle tracks leading toward it. One would be out ahead of the lieutenant on the left, and the other was to scout the area at least a quarter of a mile in front of the sergeant at the far end of the line. "Use your compass and lead us south southwest. Here, look at the map." Danny saw an uncomprehending look from one of the scouts. Holding the man by the shoulders, he pointed him in the direction he wanted him to lead. "See how the sun strikes your face? Keep the sun like that and keep moving along."

At the lieutenant's relayed order, they moved forward in a line that extended about a quarter of a mile. At least they weren't eating dust, and for the moment, the troopers weren't grousing. For the first half hour or so, Flynn felt the elation a tinkerer feels when his backyard invention works the first time, but they ran into a patch of taller mesquite trees growing more thickly than before; suddenly, even at the fifty-yard spacing, Weech was completely out of sight, obscured by the brush. In fact, most of the time Danny could see fewer than half his troopers. Uncertainty set in and destroyed his early confidence in the orientation of his line. He began to worry that he might lose contact if the far end of the line had to slow their advance for some reason despite the guide's best efforts. He sent his messenger down the line with instructions to blow his whistle when he got to the platoon sergeant's end, and then to come back. A short time later, Flynn heard the whistle, quite a bit ahead of where he thought it would be. He used his compass to check the orientation of the line. Out of kilter, from the looks of it. In a few minutes the sweating messenger verified the lieutenant's suspicions. "Sergeant Weech's moving the line perty hard, sir."

Up to now, Flynn had been pretty well satisfied with his scouting line—but again he felt the sergeant's challenge. As he rode, he referred to his compass frequently and double checked his navigation by referring to the sun—the same way he instructed his scouts. To hide his uneasiness from his line of mounted troopers, he stopped behind clumps of small trees to consult his map. The last landmark he recognized was the pronounced bend in the road at the point where he and his men had left it. He had some general confidence in the direction they were heading, but the diabolical brush was always tall enough so that he couldn't pick out a landmark to aim for. And the spines on the prickly pear cactus! Out here when a man didn't exactly know where he was, the stuff looked even more menacing than it would to the same man on a well-known trail. Skirting around a broad patch of those vicious spines would divert anybody off a straight line of advance. Danny told himself a more-experienced platoon commander would've found this little excursion a simple matter, but then a more-experienced lieutenant wouldn't have let Weech get away with his treachery either. Danny knew he had to check regularly to tell how fast the right half of the line was moving. Once more the messenger went down the line with his whistle. This time the sounds showed a fairly satisfactory orientation. An hour passed in this uncertain kind of travel while Lieutenant Flynn worked at keeping his concentration clear and on not getting lost.

⚒

A few head of widely ranging, stringy cattle popped out of the brush and vanished as quickly as the line of mounted soldiers swept through. To the eye of a boy from New York City, they were thin and longlegged, with a formidable spread of horns. He paid careful attention to the split-hoofed prints left by the cattle. Maybe cattle tracks would lead them to water, even if his map wasn't all that helpful. Here and there he saw a few hoofprints left by horses—smaller than army horses, judging by the size of the marks, but shod—thin little shoes. Somebody had been riding this land not long ago. Then, rather suddenly, the hoofprints disappeared. No, he decided, he couldn't rely on the tracks to lead him to water. He whispered a half-remembered prayer for help in spotting a windmill.

From the road, this mixed growth of wiry scrub trees and prickly pear cactus hadn't looked so tall. Just a few feet higher and he could see over most of it. He rode ahead a bit and stopped on a slight rise. He motioned his messenger to stop, and Garza to ride on, keeping this end of the line moving.

For a few moments, he sat motionless in the saddle, then dismounted and let the reins fall on the ground. He made some soothing sounds to his steady, veteran mount and ran a hand over the horse's neck. Then he placed his left hand on the pommel and his right on the cantle, stepped into the stirrup with his left foot and raised himself; but instead of swinging his right leg over, he swung it high to step directly behind the cantle. In a smooth movement, he placed his left foot on the saddle seat and stood straight up. Unperturbed by the odd shifting of the load on his back, the old troop horse stood as steady as a rock, allowing Danny to keep his balance comfortably. A few feet of additional elevation gave him a view of a little more than half of his platoon, but the spacing was ragged, as he feared it might be. He couldn't see the platoon sergeant, but from the way the line was tending, he assumed the man had slowed his pace and was almost where he should be. Out to the southwest, exactly where he thought they might find it, he made out the upper tips of windmill vanes ahead in the distance. Now there was a sight to elate an uncertain navigator! Once again confident and far more sure of himself, Danny sent the messenger down the line to move the stragglers along and encourage Weech to bring his end of the line into position, the smart ass. Now, if that scout didn't get lost, the platoon would be under control.

In ten minutes or so, his scout came back to the line from his position with news he had found the windmill. He relied on the scout on the far end of the line to bring the news to Sergeant Wieczorek. In a less than half an hour, the final three troopers were entering the large clearing.

⌖

"Water call, Sergeant," ordered Flynn as the platoon closed on the windmill. Before he moved away, Danny reminded him of a common precaution. "Don't let the horses drink too much water."

Resentment flashed in Wieczorek's eyes. Under his breath he slurred his responses to the orders into a drone, "Yessuh, Lootenan'. Yes, Lootenan'. We'll watch the water. We'll check for sore backs." He changed his tone sharply so that it cracked like a whip. "We know how to take care of hosses, suh." Danny let it ride. This was something to take care of back at the post.

First Platoon had come across a well-established camp, one the enormous ranch must have built as an outlying cattle-tending facility. A windmill with *Aeromotor* stenciled in red towered over a large galvanized cistern and a pen with a loading chute where the cattle could be collected and moved into trucks or trailers. The Mitchum hands had set out a few salt blocks on low posts, and although there wasn't a dwelling, the troopers found several recently-used fire rings.

Danny stood alone watching the Texans care for their horses. He'd have to recognize they were very good at it and didn't need all the orders he was giving. All those were for the benefit of the whole platoon—he wanted them to get used to seeing the sergeant taking orders. Under the windmill, his messenger held court at the center of a group of troopers filling their canteens. Danny pretended to be engrossed in his maps and notebook, but he sneaked a few glances. The private gestured animatedly with his hands and legs, showing them how Lieutenant Flynn vaulted to a standing position on the saddle. He noticed their eyes turned his way, and he could read Wieczorek's lips forming, "I'll be damned."

He felt pretty satisfied with his day's work so far—satisfied enough to take a seat on a salt block that the cattle hadn't licked out much yet. He was studying his map to memorize the landmarks along the route home, when in a sudden clatter of hoofbeats, four emaciated figure with faces burned dark by the sun; small, quick and wiry as their agile ponies—swept into the clearing like a flock of starving birds, raising clouds of dust and shouting excitedly. Two carried pistols. Flynn, already jumpy from a day of contending with his own shaky confidence, jumped up from the salt block brandishing his .45. Who were these untamed men in broad sombreros? He saw coiled *riatas*, high-heeled boots with narrow toes and large-roweled spurs.

A string of excited shouts popped up from his troopers. "No, no, no. Lieutenant. Don't shoot! They're ranch hands."

The vaqueros, tense in the company of gringos and agitated by something out in the brush, sat lightly but never quite still on their skittish ponies, as much like specters as men. They rattled away in a Mexican dialect that didn't sound like anything he'd ever heard. But he could understand a few words of a call for help. "*Senores. Ayudo, por favor.*" They pointed into the brush. "*Socorro,*" was another word he thought he understood.

He holstered his service pistol, cursing himself for being as jumpy as an old woman. "Garza! Where the hell is Garza?" The orderly came running up from the picket line.

"Talk to these men, will you?" Danny shouted to the dog robber. He wasn't quite sure what they wanted, but he was pretty sure they were in distress. They spoke earnestly to Garza, pointing and gesturing with their hands to show that they had somebody, another vaquero most likely, out there in those wiry thickets with a problem. Occasionally they looked anxiously toward Flynn.

Garza turned from the vaqueros to translate, "Their *compadre* is out here somewhere in a little clearing. He's sick, they say, and his stomach is hurting bad. He's rolled up in terrible misery. They want us to take him to a doctor."

Flynn realized he was being faced with a decision he hadn't anticipated. "Appendicitis, do they think?" He looked to his dog robber for an opinion.

Garza shrugged. "Who can say, sir? I don' know about appendicitis."

"Tell them we'll be happy to take him." The lieutenant waved for his platoon sergeant. "Let's get the sick man in here and rig a litter for him." The sergeant forgot about his sputtering dispute with the lieutenant. His sullen mood dropped away the instant he took charge of bringing the sick vaquero in to the camp. Danny called for two more troopers to make for Fort Brown. He pointed them in a direction that would take them to the Military Highway, with instructions to get the word back as fast as they could. One should try to hitch a ride if possible. The other would then go for a telephone. "We need some medics sent out to meet us with an ambulance," he said, wishing like the devil they had a radio that could reach to Fort Brown. "We'll be back on the road, moving as best we can with the vaquero."

Darkness had already fallen when Flynn and the remainder of his platoon cantered into the stables. Danny handed the reins to Garza, hearing, "Lieutenant Flynn. Come here, please." It was Walter Franklin, checking on First Platoon.

"Yes, sir."

"What happened out there? Have some trouble? I've been hearing rumors."

"No, sir. We found some Mitchum vaqueros out in that nasty tangle of brush. One had a case of acute appendicitis. At least that's what I think it is. I once saw my friend Liam Duffy actin' like that vaquero and that's what he had."

Franklin knew about the Mexican and where they had found him. Having the platoon out there at the Mitchum cattle handling pen raised a question about it. "Why were you on the Mitchum land? You were supposed to be on the road, weren't you?"

"Yes, sir, that's quite true, but we had to divert to get some water for the horses."

"Water?" asked Franklin, suspicious there had been a deliberate deviation from orders. "There's water along the road. Don't think I haven't gone over the maps." Being at the vaqueros' camp probably meant that his lieutenant had exceeded his orders.

"Maybe so, sir, but I didn't see any on the outbound leg—I would have marked my map. The heat and traffic on the road were killing the horses."

"We'll come back to the water later," said the captain. "Did you see anything out there?"

"Heat, buzzards, a coyote. I guess they had a calf that died...and the Mitchum vaquero with the appendicitis case. That's all, sir. What were we supposed to see?"

"Don't be flippant with me, Lieutenant Flynn. We have a real problem here. Somebody eluding the Border Patrol is what I'm talking about. Right in broad daylight." The Border Patrol had a shootout with a couple of suspected German agents coming across the river at a place a few miles south of where First Platoon had left the road, but on the Mitchum Ranch, nevertheless. Franklin had briefed himself well on the terrain up there. "It was pretty far south to be attempting a crossing, because the water's deep and the bottom's full of quicksand. But they tried it and got across. Border Patrol captured one of them, but the other illegal got into a blue car that was waiting for them. The intelligence people thought the car might have been driving up the road you were patrolling."

Flynn's shoulders slumped. "Oh, damn."

"I see," said the captain, understanding what First Platoon had probably seen. "The S-2 people want you to come tell them about what you saw before you do anything else."

Flynn felt an apprehensive, prickly feeling creeping up his spine. "That all, sir?" he asked.

The Texan drew a deep breath and exhaled. "No. It isn't."

Franklin had more news for Danny. "First Platoon isn't going to the rifle range tomorrow."

While the rumors about spies buzzed hotly in the mess hall and the stables, Centaur was moving fast to reshape the 124th to meet his own expectations.

"For some reason he wants you and your platoon standing by to help in the stables," said Franklin. "Have your platoon there at 0600 hours. Uniform is fatigues."

Oh, man! Danny was thinking, if they only knew what he was facing with Wieczorek and his band of thugs. "You're kidding, aren't you, sir? We've been working hard."

"So's everybody else," snapped the troop commander without a hint of sympathy. "This is fact, Lieutenant. Centaur specified First Platoon, E Troop." If First Platoon thought they were suffering, Franklin thought they ought to do some thinking about the afternoon's showing. He reminded Danny, "Maybe it's because you took off skylarking cross country and found everything but that car and the agents eluding the Border Patrol." The seriousness of the matter was sinking in, but Lieutenant Flynn wasn't willing to admit his faulty judgment. Franklin challenged him. "Now, if you have the cojones to take on the colonel because his orders don't suit you, Lieutenant, you have my permission to take it up with him." The captain shrugged. "But he and Colonel Newman went up to Fort Ringgold to meet with the brigade commander. It'll be nearly midnight before they get back."

Franklin wasn't telling his lieutenant all he knew about First Platoon's assignment. With the veterinarian, the colonel meant to inspect every horse in the regiment personally and ship out the ones that didn't measure up. The troop commander had been let in on First Platoon's assignment, but all he was permitted to tell Danny was, "It's very simple. Have your people there on time, ready to work."

The assignment wasn't a military secret—only a matter of wanting to get a sensitive job done before the whole regiment got wind of it. Centaur knew the men of the 124th had tender spots in their hearts for their horses and, if asked, thousands of reasons for keeping them. But now wasn't the time for sentimentality. The colonel knew what they were looking for. Furthermore, he insisted that each horse be inspected separately.

The next morning Chamberlain waved to Wieczorek to start bringing in the horses. At first the troopers used halters to lead them one by one, but that proved too time-consuming. This wasn't some fancy horse show, after all. Danny and his troopers sweated with gates and ramps, using their hats, brooms, anything that came to hand, urging the horses along through chutes and into holding pens. Chamberlain had the final say on each horse—nobody around Fort Brown would dispute the man's skill in judging horses. He used one of those heavy wooden canes they use at cattle auctions. Sometimes he prodded a horse or he pointed at the animal and signaled his decision, up or down, with the cane tip. Up meant that the horse met his standards for size, age, and conformation—even color. In that case, the horse went back to the stables. Down meant a trip to the remount station at Fort Reno, near Oklahoma City. The rejected animals got an X daubed on their rumps with white paint to prevent some misguided sentimentalist from spiriting them out of the holding pen and slipping them back among the horses that were to be kept. A positive and irreversible process, it seemed to the colonel and his operations officer. Altogether the 124th was getting rid of nearly two hundred head of horses at Fort Reno, for an unspecified number of replacement mounts. Temporarily, the trade might leave them a little thin, but not for long.

Centaur felt well satisfied with his work. He stopped in the stable sergeant's office to use the telephone. "Put the word out, we'll give the regiment a little slack tomorrow," he said to someone in the Headquarters Troop.

While First Platoon handled horses in the heat and dust of the stables, the rest of E Troop marched to the rifle range, sweating, shooting, marking targets and becoming accustomed to their new M-1s. The merciful part of a day on the rifle range was that the work usually stopped well before nightfall, when the light got too dim for any real marksmanship. Captain Franklin relaxed with two of his three lieutenants at a table overlooking the river, chatting and watching the international shuttling of the trolley bringing drink orders from Mexico. They waited for news from the stables. All they knew was that the colonel had placed a guard on the horses. One rumor, and speculation was running rampant, held that the horses weren't really going to Oklahoma, but were to be shot and the carcasses plowed under. The word from Centaur's office was that the regiment was getting a one-day pass: to Matamoros, or Brownsville, if they didn't have the patience to go as far as Mexico to get their beer. The announcement about the passes spawned a different version of the rumor. The horses would be disposed of while the troopers were getting drunk on Mexican beer.

As Danny joined Captain Franklin and his officers on the veranda, he overheard the troop commander suggesting an early-morning Whitewing hunt on one of the army's exercise areas a few miles north. "Can't go far on a one-day pass anyway," Franklin was saying, but he didn't look too serious about going out for the birds.

Kincaid protested loudly. "C'mon, Walter. We get a day off and you want to go back out into the bushes?" George was the only one of the lieutenants who didn't go out of his way to defer to Franklin as a captain. As far as he was concerned, Walter had been a lieutenant when they met and was still one of them. He shrugged and shook his head; shooting birds wasn't official business.

Franklin, stopped in the act of aiming a retort at Kincaid by the arrival of a waiter with a tray of tequila, saw Danny approaching. Now they'd learn about the horses. "Come join us, Flynn," called the captain while the drinks were being passed around. "We're voting on a bird hunt in the morning."

"OK, sir. I'm voting no on the bird hunt," Danny snapped.

The junior lieutenant didn't usually talk that way to a captain. Pinelli sensed something. "Hey, Flynn, you got something against bird hunting and a few drinks? The pass starts tomorrow. You can't always be sniffin' around that schoolteacher lady."

Danny came right back at him. "That's what you think, pal. I'm going to Brownsville after I finish this drink. The only reason I'm here is to tell my troop commander."

"So there is some news," Franklin said, testing the air. He thought he knew what Centaur wanted, but he could have easily changed his mind after looking the horses over. "He gave you days off for culling the horses, did he?"

Danny nodded. "Only tonight, sir—'til 0730 hours tomorrow. Then we load and leave as soon as they hook up the locomotive."

Franklin asked, "How many horses did Centaur finally select?" The word was getting around anyway.

"A hundred and eighty-two—about all we have room for," said Danny. He gave Franklin all he knew about the revised plan, which wasn't all that much.

Any conversation between the lieutenant who witnessed the culling of the Texans' horses and his troop commander was sure to attract the keenest interest in the growing crowd of officers collecting on the veranda. Several came over to listen, and the buzz of questions spread.

"Train?"

"Horses?"

"What's all this sneaking around with our horses? Are they really gonna shoot 'em?"

Lieutenant Colonel Newman had given Franklin the barest details to use in keeping baseless rumors from spreading. The captain decided that if things were to remain calm, he'd better share what he knew. "Centaur has given orders for Lieutenant Flynn here to take some horses to the remount station in Oklahoma." Lieutenants and troop commanders pressed closer to hear.

"What goddamn horses are they talkin' about?" demanded an officer in a voice shrill with annoyance. The man had recently left his schoolteacher's desk in Cuero. He preferred a tall, strong horse with a comfortable gait—not the quicker, more agile mounts Centaur liked. The former teacher sniffed. "And who's taking them?"

"That redheaded guy over there," shouted another captain, the B Troop commander.

Danny felt he was being surrounded in a fight he couldn't win. "Hey, get off my back," he yelled, turning to confront them. "I'm not taking your damn horses—or any other damn horses, for that matter. My platoon had a work detail at the stables today, handling horses while the colonel and the vet inspected them. The ones they picked out are going to the remount station for replacements." A crowd of curious, agitated men packed tightly around the E Troop commander and his lieutenant.

The B Troop captain stubbornly clung to the rumor that the rejects were to be shot. "You're not destroying my horses, by god," he insisted.

Franklin pushed his chair back and approached the shorter, round-shouldered former schoolteacher, trying to placate him with a friendly hand on his back. "Calm down, Allan," he said, and laid out the facts as clearly as he could. "Some horses were selected for replacement. It happens all the time in the regular army. The boss man is swapping horses he doesn't like for ones he does. Don't look at this as a personal reprimand or condemnation to life as a grunt infantryman." Under the soothing effects of Franklin's logic, the shouts slowly subsided.

Franklin waved for the waiter. "Better send over for some more drinks here. My treat." As the order sped away to Mexico, the E Troop commander raised his hand for silence, so he could be heard. "Centaur called Ma Perkins and me into his office yesterday to tell us he wanted my First Platoon for a special job of handling the horses while he and the veterinarian looked the animals over." None of this was brand new information, of course. Centaur's preferences in horses had been a point widely discussed throughout the regiment from the first look he took at them. He made it clear out there at the River Camp while the train was still stranded. The man didn't like those horses the Texans had brought with them. "Some were big and heavy—too damn big for him," Franklin reminded the crowd of men drinking his tequila. "And the little pintos slipped onto the post one night about a week after the hurricane were the others."

Airing the secret of the spotted horses released a burst of spontaneous laughter throughout the room. Half a dozen painted ponies had been smuggled into the stables from a moving van. Well, so they'd been caught with those agile little mounts. They laughed even harder when Franklin described what had happened. "The pintos were spirited out of the stables when word of this inspection leaked out. But someone must have thought Colonel Chamberlain had already gone home when the trucks rolled back in."

Walter Franklin nodded, rendering his judgment. "That wasn't smart, gents. The old man was mad as a wet hen when he saw those pintos being slipped back. But they're as good as gone now." He waved a hand as if he were erasing them. "So Lieutenant Flynn, with his platoon and some others from my troop, forty troopers total, are loading up a train and taking—How many did you say, Lieutenant? A hundred and eighty two horses to the remount station as soon as possible."

A few Texans muttered more foul threats against anyone taking their horses, but it was mostly alcohol talking and Franklin put it off as that. "Lieutenant Flynn has specific orders from the commanding officer, so don't harass him. If you have a problem with any of this, you should go to the colonel." Danny slipped away to Molly's while Franklin calmed the agitated Texans.

The arrival of two bottles of tequila took the heat off Franklin and the talk switched to women and bird hunting. Even at a nickel a throw, standing drinks to appease all these men could put a dent into a captain's budget, but Franklin felt it easily worth the cost.

As far as Danny Flynn was concerned, this assignment was a mixed blessing. Ma Perkins actually congratulated him. "This is a giant plus for you, Lieutenant Flynn, to be singled out for this assignment." Grudgingly, Danny agreed that it was. What brand new lieutenant wouldn't be proud to be told, "I'm sending you because you've got a reliable sense for horses and I know you understand what kind of horse I have in mind." The colonel had some advice too, as he usually did. "Watch those people at the remount station. They know me and I've spoken to them on the telephone, but they may try to give you horses we don't want." He repeated himself on some points. "You, better than anybody here at Fort Brown, know what I want and I'll support your decisions."

Danny wondered how it could be that all this knowledge and judgment that Centaur mentioned didn't reside in one of the troop commanders, maybe in captain Walter Franklin. And he surely didn't relish being cooped up on that train with a sergeant who'd been overheard suggesting the lieutenant might "have an accident someday." But Danny had saluted crisply and left the colonel's office holding his breath until he was well away from the door.

The length of the railroad journey from the extreme south of Texas to the remount station in the middle of Oklahoma was probably one of historic magnitude, but with the horse cavalry dwindling, Fort Reno turned out to be the closest place to go. Danny got a flood of advice—far more than he wanted. Many of the officers and senior sergeants offered stories about dealing with the horseflesh brokers at remount stations, but no one at Fort Brown had actually undertaken anything quite like this trip.

Regulations called for one man for each five horses being transported. For that, Danny had thirty-six troopers—First Platoon, including Garza and Wieczorek, plus more than a dozen extras assigned by Lieutenant Colonel Newman. Then there were specialists for jobs plain old troopers weren't trained to do. A sergeant assigned to supervise the care of the horses came along with an assistant to handle trunks of hardware and veterinary supplies. And since a substantial purchase of additional supplies along the way was highly likely, another sergeant, this one an armed quartermaster, rolled his safe aboard with cash and boxes of forms. The fortieth man was a cook to preside over a mess car, actually a modified boxcar with a field kitchen installed, where he was to prepare a hundred and twenty-three meals a day for the lieutenant and his forty-trooper detachment. The men would feed and care for the horses, plus they would be expected to help load cordwood when the train stopped to refuel. According to railroad calculations, most trains should make it to Fort Reno in two days, but the wood-fired locomotive was slow and required frequent water and wood stops. Its lack of speed was sure to result in diversions for higher-speed, higher-priority trains. Just to be conservative, the army put aboard food and fodder provisions for four days.

At the pleading of his dog robber, Danny walked the platform turned out as if for inspection. Earlier Garza had made an irrefutable counter to the lieutenant's insistence on wearing his blue fatigue uniform: "If you don't care about your reputation, sir, think of mine." Garza compared Danny's responsibility for the regiment's horses to his uncle taking his crops to town. "My Uncle Rudolfo don' go to the market looking like a peon. He gets dressed up, 'cause he's proud of what he does." Fussing a little, he laid out a fresh khaki uniform and polished boots. "See what I have here, *Teniente*: One good uniform to leave Fort Brown and another for getting off the train at Fort Reno. I'll do 'em again at the remount station."

Danny fretted about making the upcoming departure on time, checking and rechecking the list on the first of many dog-eared papers stacked on his clipboard. For the benefit of the lieutenant, a waggish clerk had titled the first entry, "One train." Danny penciled a large check next to it.

What the locomotive and the stoves in the cars needed for fuel and other railroad business didn't concern him much. Well, it did in a way, because the locomotive was old, rickety and slow; and if the weather turned very cold, they might easily not have enough wood for the kitchen and the troopers. He shrugged his worry away as being nothing he could control.

The train included a car to serve as an office and quarters for him and his orderly, one for the extra sergeants, and two cars for quartering the troopers and cooking facilities. One hundred and eighty-two horses, side by side, would ride in six cars. One extra car, a closed car of uncertain origin, carried hay, sacked oats, assorted tools and an impressive variety of tack for handling and exercising the horses. They called it a utility or a cargo car and hooked it on at the end of the train. Probably they did that because it may have been a caboose once or maybe simply because it was an ordinary boxcar modified with the necessary signal lights. What to call any particular car was another detail the railroad people could worry about.

Some of the cars were army property and others belonged to the railroad. Who owned them wasn't a real concern of his either, but when all the cars were first collected, it became apparent that the soldiers in this detachment wouldn't be able to move from the accommodations cars to look after the horses or to reach the utility car in the rear. Colonel Chamberlain asked the post engineers to work out some way to modify the cars to make it easier to care for the animals. Some cutting through wood and steel, a bit of welding and a lot of ingenuity worked minor miracles, considering the amount of work that had to be done. A system of ladders up the sides of the cars, catwalks to cross them, and a few handrails fashioned of galvanized water pipe stretched over the six cars with the horses. Now, if necessary, Danny or one of the troopers could make his way from his car in the front, through the commissary car, the berthing cars, and all the way to the end of the train to the utility car to inspect the horses on the long stretches between stations. Moving back and forth over the catwalks wouldn't be comfortable, or even particularly safe, but it could be done if necessary. That was the critical thing.

For the third time this morning, he recounted the horses—expecting a last minute effort to rescue a favorite mount. Probably not the pintos, though; they were too visible. Then he walked back along the track to make another quick inventory of the supplies. Three days of exposure in those cars—the railroad company's best guess as to the duration of the journey—might be hard on the animals. Danny appealed to Colonel Chamberlain, who agreed and ordered some modifications to be made. For the greater part of a day, the stables sergeant and one of the versatile army engineers worked on a design for an arrangement of makeshift stalls, but they were forced to settle on loading the horses side by side, facing the sides of the cars, in a nose-tail alternation. Nets, fabricated by the saddlers of rope and straps, would to keep the horses separated in the cars. With the stabling problem more or less solved, exposure remained a concern, because snow could fly and be piled up in the open cars by the howling winds this late in the year on the plains of North Texas and Oklahoma. Actually, the horses might be able to withstand the cold, but their appearance would suffer. Experience showed that their coats would grow long, and the horses had a tendency to chew each other's tails off. Centaur wouldn't have any of that. The brain trust convened by Major Perkins to consider the problem didn't find a good solution. Shortly before scheduled departure time, a veterinarian's assistant reported to Danny that somebody had made a last-minute decision to store a supply of shelter halves and other tenting material in the utility car to cover the horses if the weather became nasty. He wrote a note on his long checklist. After that matters deteriorated.

Three hours late and still the train sat stationary at the siding. From a railroad agent, Danny learned the reason given for the delay was that a shipment of cordwood had arrived late. Some faceless railroad dispatcher decided it would be better to wait for one more shipment of wood. That way, the reasoning went, the horses wouldn't have to stand unprotected in the cars on some forlorn siding, waiting for heating fuel. The Brownsville stationmaster climbed into the locomotive to consult with the engineer. The army load, including people and horses, was already aboard, and the two of them discussed how much fuel it would cost to keep steam up in the engine while they waited. Apparently there had been progress. The fireman had steam built up in the boiler and at last the wailing of the locomotive's steam whistle cut the air. The one-minute warning Danny had requested.

"Weech," he called out. "Form 'em up. I want to see eighty eyeballs staring back at me before I let this train go." Leisurely, Wieczorek called for Trooper Bednarski, and together the two ambled toward the end of the train, passing the lieutenant's order. That pair gave him some anxious feelings. The sergeant had yet to break a regulation or deliberately dis-obey an order, but an opportunity to embarrass Lieutenant Flynn by creating a delay might be more than he could resist. "Sergeant Wieczorek," Danny yelled. "Now!" He wasn't about to let Wieczorek ignore him that way, not here on this siding. Shortly, thirty-nine appre-hensive, denim-clad troopers stood in ranks with the platoon sergeant out in front. The lieutenant consulted his clipboard a final time. "Get 'em aboard, Sergeant," he ordered qui-etly.

Once more the whistle sounded insistently. Time to go. The whole train shuddered noisily in the first few inches of movement. Taking a final look down the tracks from the steps, he was surprised to see Centaur striding up to him from his car, with Newman and Ma Perkins close behind. "Safe trip, Lieutenant Flynn," said the colonel. "I expect you back for the competition," reinforcing news he'd given Danny only the day before. The three senior officers, plus several Texans he didn't know well, shook his hand and wished him well as the train crept ahead. Anxiously, Danny saluted and boarded the train at the first car forward of the horses.

Danny made his way through the cars to his office, counting troopers, spending a moment here and there for a word with one or two, stopping for a cup of coffee in the cook's field kitchen. The brick buildings of downtown Brownsville slipped quietly past the win-dow, giving way to a dwindling row of dwellings built largely of corrugated metal, trailing away to open fields and stands of mesquite. He settled into a chair at the handy wooden surface built by the carpenters to serve as both table and desk, concentrating his thoughts on how the next few days would go and when he might return to Fort Brown and Molly in Brownsville.

Oklahoma City and back, locked up in a rickety train with a malcontent sergeant, and Centaur tells me he wants me to be ready for the competition when I get back. He shouted, knowing he wouldn't be heard over the noise of the train, "Saint Patrick and Saint Brigid! How can I possibly do it?" He removed a sheet of paper from his clipboard to review the skills involved. Running, mounted pistol, navigation, rifle marksmanship, horsemanship, swimming perhaps—an imposing list—and for more than a week, he'd have no leisure time to devote to getting ready.

From his instructors at Fort Riley, Danny had learned that cavalry commanding offi-cers typically used these competitions to determine their younger officers' progress in the crucial military skills of horsemanship, fitness and marksmanship. The entire post might be there to watch, and since Brownsville had grown up at the army's very doorstep, the local community could be expected to pour through the gates to sit in the parade ground seats to watch at least the start and finish. As a guard unit, the 124th hadn't scheduled a competition like this in years, but the tradition appealed to Colonel Chamberlain. If nothing else, he thought, it might inject some real competitive spirit into his lieutenants.

Danny had been looking forward to the competition as a way to impress Centaur, but when ordered to take the horses to Fort Reno, and nothing said to the contrary, he assumed he'd be excused. So did the other lieutenants, but when they heard that he would compete, there wasn't a rush to help him. All of them, including Cameron and the others, saw it as a matter of fate: If Flynn couldn't practice, well, too damn bad. But Captain Franklin helped a little, offering some workable suggestions. At every stop, as long as he had as much as fifteen minutes, Danny had a horse saddled, and he rode until time for the horse to be loaded. If a makeshift jump could be fashioned in some manner, he practiced jumping. On the shorter stops, he worked on his own fitness. Sometimes, if a stretch of smooth ground was available, he ran along the track. Otherwise, he climbed the slatted sides of the horse cars for exercise. Marksmanship practice with a brand-new weapon presented a thorny problem. Harry Jenks, excused because of his injury, had no reason to withhold help. He suggested shooting at targets along the railroad right of way—jackrabbits would make good targets, or coyotes or fence posts—particularly from a train trundling along at the slow speed of a wood burner. There'd be plenty of longlegged rabbits on the lonely stretches across Texas and Oklahoma. Interesting idea maybe, and fun, unless somebody started shooting at the train, but the competition called for shooting at stationary targets. The solution he hit upon: safe, if not exciting, included daily sessions of dry firing both weapons—his .45 automatic pistol and the newly issued M-1. It wasn't his brainchild, or even Walter Franklin's. They had done a lot of that at Fort Riley, and it was rather effective.

Every day he practiced at shooting, holding his sights on spots on the wall, concentrating on squeezing the trigger with steadily increasing pressure until he felt the click. Sometimes he practiced loading and unloading with inert ammunition, until he could do it blindfolded. At other times he took the firearms apart blindfolded and reassembled them with the blindfold still in place. He couldn't know exactly how the competition would be conducted: The format wouldn't be announced until the competitors were assembled at the start, but daily he tried to picture how it would go. Watching the other lieutenants ride, he hadn't seen many who could beat him. But shooting? That was a question, because everybody would be firing the new rifle. He suspected the Texans hadn't been working on their mounted marksmanship very much. All together, he assessed his chances as good—as long as he got back in time.

chapter

NINE

Berlin: Three million German infantry soldiers supported by thousands of aircraft and tanks cross the Russian border on the opening day of Operation Barbarossa.

Weather and higher priority traffic had already cost them more than two days: fifty-three hours, to be exact. All the waiting on isolated sidings had consumed more fuel and water than expected and naturally added stops for water and fuel. Four days from Fort Brown, and the railroad dispatchers were now estimating an arrival at Fort Reno just before noon of the sixth day. In daily reports Lieutenant Flynn telegraphed all these pertinent details to Fort Brown. That is, he mentioned all the stops. Plus, he was candid about the delays encountered in waiting for higher priority traffic. But for him to include his difficulties with the troopers would mean admitting failure as a leader. Morale and training were his responsibility, and that malcontent Wieczorek was constantly inventing ways to create trouble.

Today was a good example. He felt the train slowing for a scheduled water stop in Fortney, Oklahoma—another one of those dreary little towns built entirely on one side of the track, on land carved out of the railroad right of way expressly for building a town. The train's crew and the troopers could have continued on to Fort Reno on field rations, but fodder was already below minimum acceptable levels. A railroad dispatcher telegraphed the recommendation they try to buy hay or grain for the horses in Fortney to tide them over. Water too, if the locomotive didn't take it all. After a brief consultation, the local stationmaster agreed.

Days of being packed into these swaying, lurching railroad cars exposed to rain and wind had taken their toll on the horses. The generally well-intentioned troopers tried everything, even draping thin but nearly waterproof shelter halves over their hindquarters, tied around the neck with a length of binder twine to protect them from the elements. Little by little, conditions worsened—kicking and biting—some of the horses had lost most of their tails to the teeth of the nervous horses next to them. Small wonder the animals had a shoddy, plucked look. Despite Danny's constant insistence on caring for the animals, the troopers allowed even the essential chores like exercising and currying to slip. Laxity in common duties like that didn't go into his daily reports. If the lieutenant had been specifically required to include a comment on the privates and corporals, it would be that they were hard and willing workers, but at the moment their loyalties were confused. When the lieutenant was in sight, they could be model soldiers, but when he wasn't watching, they turned to their sullen platoon sergeant, who wanted nothing more than to take his platoon back. From what Garza had been overhearing, Weech viewed these days on the train, with the little detachment isolated from scrupulously enforced army organization, as his opportunity to bend matters more to his way of thinking. Day by day he increased the pressure, physically threatening troopers who didn't see things Erwin Wieczorek's way.

Something had gone wrong in the relaxed ways of the hometown militia to make the previous lieutenants content to knuckle under. Who knew what pressures distorted the simple, clear organization of First Platoon? Garza mentioned a rumor that the previous lieutenant had been employed by the sergeant's uncle, but the dog robber wasn't from the right part of Texas to be privy to such local matters. Reality was that Wieczorek had cultivated a good-sized circle of troopers who faithfully took their cues from him. Somehow Weech's twisted reasoning set him thinking his supporting clique would see him as a failure if he didn't dominate the new lieutenant too.

The train hadn't quite stopped when the quartermaster sergeant jumped from the train with a leather satchel full of forms and greenbacks—followed by a gaggle of troopers scrambling for the utility car to collect tools equipment. Each one had an assigned task to perform. Lieutenant Flynn's specific priorities were for water, food and sanitation, which amounted to mucking out the cars, putting down new straw and as much exercise as time would allow. Danny swung down to the gravel along the track and ran back along the train to inspect the condition of the horses. Already some were being led out of the cars. Most of them showed the wasting effects of a general lack of food and inattention by the troopers. Garza hurried up from the utility car leading Stinker, a coffee-colored gelding that Wieczorek had been riding occasionally at Fort Brown. The dog robber had the horse, which hadn't been exercised in the past several days, all tacked up and ready for the lieutenant to ride.

Danny followed his usual routine of carefully inspecting his mount. Checking the saddle adjustment, he let his eyes wander up the track to the locomotive taking on water from the cistern through a long galvanized spout. But where the hell were the troopers? Even if he allowed for a half dozen loading firewood on the opposite side of the train, he saw far too few working with the horses.

He called to Corporal Cernosek, "Where is everybody?" The portly farmer looked down at his feet and twisted a pair of leather gloves in his hands.

"They're with Sarge," he mumbled. The man shifted uneasily, anticipating a response from the lieutenant. Something was up. One thing about Cernosek: he was honest. The corporal might be a quiet, plodding sort, but he wouldn't act this way, slouching, avoiding eye contact, except for the sergeant's influence.

"With the sergeant, are they?" asked Danny, more in acknowledgement than as an inquiry. Cernosek nodded across to the elevated sidewalk along Fortney's main street. A collection of weather-beaten wood structures flanking the solid-looking red brick bank building, every commercial building in town fronted the street running parallel to the tracks. The frowning corporal didn't offer any more information, but his eyes wandered involuntarily to where three tractors were parked with wagons hitched behind them. From the looks of it, Fortney's business life was centered in those buildings. The sign painted right on the rough-sawed board facade of the larger of the two read "Bentley's Feeds." Next door, according to a slicker professional signboard supplied by the Coca-Cola Bottling Company, Jimmy's saloon stayed open to serve its customers twenty-four hours a day. Green neon letters in the dusty, fly-spattered window conveyed the one-word message, "Beer." In the middle of the street, a farmer driving a team drawing an empty wagon stopped to take a long look at the soldiers and their horses.

All right then, something in Danny's Irish soul spoke to him. Sometime a man has a thirst that needs quenching. This little inspiration told him that if he allowed the troopers a cold beer, it might help set matters straight.

"Take a message to the sergeant for me, Corporal," he said. "Here's what I want Weech and the troopers in there with him to know. We've been on this train for a long time. They can have their beer. I'll let them have whatever they can drink in ten minutes." Flynn drew his watch from its pocket and showed the corporal the time. "See this? It's almost on the hour, and I'm going to finish riding. I'll be troubling you to walk over there to Jimmy's and tell Sergeant Wieczorek I want all forty men accounted for on this side of the of the road by the time the train whistle stops blowin'." He watched

Cernosek's pinched face for a sign of understanding. "That's ten minutes from now," he said, wagging a finger. "Tell the sergeant I said, 'No excuses.'"

Cernosek nodded and wet his lips with his tongue. He wasn't a man to refuse an order, but he didn't want to go.

Quite aware that they'd be watching from inside Jimmy's, the lieutenant made a show of restoring military discipline. "Stand at attention and salute, Cernosek, or you and I will have a little trouble right here in the street." The corporal raised his right hand in an awkward stab toward his forehead and hurried across the rough street.

The lieutenant trotted away on Weech's overfed horse. Straight out from Fortney for five minutes, he rode slowly. Turning back, he asked Stinker for an easy gallop. At the town limit, he allowed his mount to slow to a walk before halting at the locomotive cab.

Cernosek had dutifully carried the lieutenant's message to Jimmy's before returning to the train to supervise a handful of men unloading baled hay and grain from a line of wagons, but they hadn't gotten even half the job done. He saw trouble brewing—the lieutenant was talking to a man in striped overalls—the engineer, he guessed. Weech and his cronies were still at Jimmy's, and the work detail was still short of men. Then a five-second blast of the train's steam whistle screamed across the Oklahoma prairie.

Danny dismounted and took a turn with the reins around the utility car door handle. He said a few words to Garza, working inside with a push broom. The dog robber frowned and pointed across the tracks. "They're still over there, sir."

At a wave from Danny, the steam whistle tore the air again for several seconds, leaving a stillness settling over Fortney. The few troopers still toiling steadily unloading the wagons stopped their work and watched Jimmy's front door.

Cernosek stood aside, watching the lieutenant. What would happen now?

"You tell Sergeant Wieczorek what I said?" Flynn asked.

"Yessah."

"And you heard the whistle?"

"Yessah."

"Good. I might need a witness," snapped the lieutenant, screwing his face into a scowl.

Nearly a minute passed before three of the youngest troopers burst from Jimmy's, running across the street to the train. Others emerged a few steps behind, scurrying like the first three in a trickle of individuals. Most shouldered a case of beer each. Flynn stood near the feed wagons, counting his errant soldiers one by one, imagining what Wieczorek must be telling them inside. Whatever the sergeant's message was, it lost its influence out in the daylight and fresh air—particularly when they felt the lieutenant's auger-like glare. One by one, they set the beer on the graveled loading area and huddled with the others to watch. Every few seconds, one would look up, expecting Wieczorek to emerge and take charge of things. In the open door of the utility car, Garza crossed himself instinctively, rummaging around for something to use as a weapon in case something broke out in the next few minutes. His .45 was in the car up front.

At last Wieczorek lurched through the doorway at Jimmy's—flushed, weaving across the street with a cardboard beer case on either shoulder, swearing loudly, "Goddamn it! Nobody rides Stinker but me." Shuffling across the dusty street toward the stack of beer cases, he stopped, probably to get an idea of how things stacked up. The men he counted on, the few hanging nearby, were outnumbered slightly by the troopers at the wagons. But if Weech paid the slightest attention to them, or that they'd stopped work to be ready to defend themselves with their intimidating steel hay hooks, nobody saw it.

The sergeant nodded toward Stinker, shouting a challenge no one mistook. "I'm gonna kick the ass of whoever was ridin' my hoss."

Danny reckoned the insolent oaf wouldn't dare risk violence in broad daylight, so he didn't respond to the blustering. With his feet spread slightly, hands on his hips, he confronted the sergeant. "You've kept me waiting, Sergeant, and I won't have it," he said, watching Wieczorek teetering unsteadily, blinking his eyes in the bright sunlight, but listening—the man wasn't gone that far. "Put the beer down on the gravel."

Without being asked, Bednarski moved quickly to help the sergeant with one case. Weech set his case on top the irregular stack.

"Now, dammit, form 'em up and get a muster," the lieutenant stormed at the weaving, red-faced sergeant. "When you have forty, put them to work."

Weech clenched his fists angrily, but he obeyed the order. Every soldier on the train knew that the sergeant's lightning binge had nothing to do with a man's natural thirst. He'd been guzzling Jimmy's beer to build up his courage and brought the extra cases along to keep himself and his followers stirred up.

A blind man could see the trouble building, but Danny knew the real danger wasn't here in Fortney. It was far too public out here and the little town probably had at least a constable to keep the peace, but all that would change once the train rolled out of town. He had only this opportunity to set things right. "Now gather 'round so you can hear me," he said to the troopers, excusing the cook and the two sergeants assigned to care for the animals. The trouble was a First Platoon matter. The remaining troopers, including Garza, stood in a semi-circle of men in baggy blue denim fatigues, listening to the lieutenant laying down the law. "Two days from now I expect us to arrive at Fort Reno, and I intend for these horses to look as if they were cared for by professional soldiers. We're not leaving here before we exercise each horse thoroughly and have them all looking as good as we can. Be especially careful to inspect the hooves and look them all over thoroughly for sores."

The platoon sergeant spat a line of tobacco juice, and a few troopers tried to look bored by the lieutenant's orders. Their faces betrayed their responses to Wieczorek's play for their loyalty, but Danny pretended Weech didn't even exist. "I've looked the cars over and the whole train is a disgrace," he told them. One by one, he singled out individual soldiers for eye contact. From the number of men who looked away, he could tell that the platoon sergeant had been more successful at winning them over than he thought. "We're already late, but it doesn't matter anymore. We'll take whatever time we need to get things right." The men kept an uneasy silence, glancing apprehensively at Danny, then Wieczorek. Deliberately, Flynn inquidred of his sergeant, "Have I made myself clear to you, Sergeant Wieczorek?"

Painfully, the sergeant dragged out the words from the depths of his soul, "Yes suh'." This Yankee was asking for it.

The last of the brilliant, rosy glow of a visibly waning winter sunset ebbed behind the rolling hills before Danny was satisfied. Forty troopers had boarded, assuming Wieczorek was in the car up front. Good, thought Flynn, waving his signal forward to let the crew in the locomotive know he was ready to move the train. He waited until the train had finally begun inching away, leaving the abandoned beer cases along the track. Then he jumped into the utility car. At all previous stops, he boarded the train up front, at the car used for an office and quarters, but leaving Fortney, he chose the utility car because he had seen Garza pulling the door closed. There had to be some reason for it, because for the orderly, it meant having to remain in the remote utility car until daylight at least. Those catwalks terrified him, even when the train wasn't moving, and never would he attempt to negotiate them at night. Besides, the explicit orders were that no one was allowed on those catwalks at night without the lieutenant's specific approval. The dog robber knew something. He was certain of it.

The wood burner struggled up the long, gentle grade out of Fortney, flinging bright sparks from its stack into the darkening sky. Even now, the train was rolling so slowly he could've run to catch up with the accommodations cars up front. Danny meant to hear out Garza and get them both over the catwalks before the train got up enough speed to set the cars swaying. He pulled the door closed. Tonight, with the smell of danger sticking in his nostrils, no small matter could be allowed to stand unresolved.

Despite the purchase of additional hay and grain, the utility car still gave the impression of cavernous space. Garza sat on a stool in the glow of a safety light, oiling and polishing his saddle with nervous energy. Danny tried an indirect approach. "How many times can you go over that saddle, Pancho?" In the few months they had been working together, he couldn't recall seeing Garza shaken by anything—except for his fear of the catwalk—but this was more than that.

Garza looked up, wiping his hands with a rag. "I feel more comfortable back here, sir. Weech…" He stopped.

"Go on," said Flynn, trying to reassure his orderly, and himself too.

Garza's eyes probed the dark shadows behind the sacks and bales of hay, fearing being overheard by one of Weech's men. "I meant Sergeant Wieczorek. He's had a crazy, mean look all afternoon. I don't know where he's got it hidden, but I know he's been drinking whiskey since he came out of Jimmy's. I smelled it on him."

Danny grunted, hoping to reassure the dog robber. "I'll have it out with him at the remount station, where we can do it in private. You stay here until you're ready, and call me on that telephone the engineers installed—I'll come get you." Trying to make light of the prospect of negotiating those catwalks at night, he reminded Garza that the rest of the troopers were having their evening meal. "I'll make sure the cook saves you some bacon." But Flynn wasn't all that confident either. There'd be trouble before they got to Fort Reno. Tonight, probably.

Food wasn't Private Garza's concern. "*Teniente*," he said hesitatingly, "you got to listen to me. It's dangerous. That man's gone *loco*…and he's got some of the others stirred up too— th' Polish guys mostly. They've all been at that whiskey."

Up till now, Danny had been feeling pretty satisfied about the work at Fortney and pleased at averting a brawl. He'd actually found himself thinking Weech was under control…until this warning from Garza. The thought of that treasonous snake of a sergeant roaming the train drunk on whiskey sent a spike of fear through him. "Stupid," he berated himself, realizing that by jumping into the utility car, he may have given Wieczorek the idea he was afraid and hiding. No telling how that might encourage him in his drunken state.

Danny took stock of the situation, swallowing to fight back the fear. He was unarmed—his pistol was locked in his office with all the other weapons. Of course it was possible that Weech and his crowd might have broken the locks by now. Danny felt the sweat rolling along his spine. He forced himself to think seriously about the danger and the fear subsided a little. The first step was clear—he had to work his way up there and establish control of those cars. "Pancho," he said, "we've got to go up there—I'll need you."

"Should I bring this, sir?" asked Garza, holding up the lieutenant's .45. It looked huge at the moment. "I went to the office and got it after you talked to us out there." How the dog robber unlocked the weapons was a question Danny didn't want to delve into at the moment, but having his dog robber armed shifted the odds.

"Loaded?" asked the lieutenant.

"Si, *Teniente*." Garza had been thinking about what'd happen to him if he hadn't been able to warn Lieutenant Flynn. He lowered his head, admitting, "I thought I might have to defend myself, sir."

Danny opened a large cabinet where they kept tools. A few things that might serve as clubs appealed to him, but something like a club would be an encumbrance on the catwalks. He took out a couple of flashlights from the toolbox and inspected the dog robber's pistol. They talked for a few minutes, the private nodding his understanding. The last thing Danny said before leaving the car was, "Here, you keep the piece with you. Leave this door open. Then watch for my light as I make my way." He would flash the light at each car: once for the first and two for the second and so on. "But if you don't see my light flashing at you from each car, it means I need help. Wait a little while. Then come forward with your weapon."

Garza listened to the lieutenant's plan calmly, biting his lip; otherwise he showed no sign of fear. He tested the flashlight and assured himself that his pistol was ready, and patted his shirt pocket, checking for the extra magazine. "How about you, *Teniente*? You don't have a weapon at all." He took a hay hook from the wall, where its fearsome point had been stuck into the wood, offering it as something that might help, "How about one of these, sir?"

Flynn shook his head. "No. It's better this way."

Carefully—it was almost dark—Danny began to crawl his way forward. In the daylight, the rickety scheme for checking on the horses seemed like a pretty good idea, but in these conditions, he couldn't see a damn thing. If a drunken Weech wanted to be rid of an uppity lieutenant, it wouldn't take much. After a few feet of crawling along the catwalks over the swaying cars, Danny stopped to collect himself, wishing there'd been time for the engineers to install lights. God, it was cold in the swirling night air!

He inspected the first three cars carefully with his flashlight. One after another, he found the horses standing nose to tail, calm and undisturbed, swaying with the movement of the train. The shelter halves over the animals' backs and rumps seemed to be working. After each car he aimed his light at the orderly standing in the door of the utility car and sent short flashes to account for his progress. By the time he reached the fourth car, he felt better—taking note of clean straw on the floors except for what the horses had deposited in the last hour or so.

Four cars now, and everything looked to be in order. He was feeling calmer. Maybe this thing with Weech had been a false alarm. Moving faster and with more confidence, he entered the next-to-last car thinking of getting up front in time to have his supper.

Nothing too remarkable here, except that the front three horses had kicked or pulled off the shelter halves draped and tied over their rumps. One stamped skittishly at a corner of flapping fabric, and its jumpiness affected the others. Whatever the problem was, it had to be fixed to keep the horses from injuring one another. He slipped down onto the floor at the rear end of the car. He found enough space between the horse and the side of the car so that he could inch his way forward, putting a reassuring hand on the nose or the rump of each successive horse, making low sounds to calm them. After all this time, he knew most of the animals by name, but this one was easy. It was Stinker, Wieczorek's favorite—the one he'd ridden earlier. He took hold of Stinker's halter in his right hand. With his left he stroked the gelding's right cheek, talking softly into his ear.

Something heavy thudded into his face: above the cheek, near the temple. Not pain at first—only brilliant flashes of light filling his vision. He fought to stay up by hanging onto Stinker's halter, but he felt himself sagging, and his fingers let go. The flashes merged into a single large bright spot. He was barely conscious of horses rearing and screaming with fear. In his last moment of awareness, he felt himself being slammed into the wall and a twisting pain burning in his left shoulder. Hooves crashed into the floor and walls. Before flopping face down into the straw, Flynn glimpsed boots: huge, brown, laced boots, through a forest of madly stamping legs. A hand plucked the loose flashlight out of the straw and then everything was dark.

Garza climbed warily down to the floor of the car. The horses stood in their places, still jumpy and spooked, but their skittishness had pretty much subsided. He shined his light over the inert form lying half covered by straw, watching for signs of danger. Danny groaned when the dog robber moved his arms and felt for breaks. They didn't find anything broken, but the injured lieutenant had to be dragged away from danger from the hooves.

When he was as safe as possible, propped against the side of the car, Garza gave him a canteen. "Come on, Lieutenant, stand up if you can," he shouted over the wind and the rattling noises of the open car. "You got to get outa here. If you stay on the floor where these horses can stomp on you, you jus' gonna get hurt more." He pulled on Danny's left arm to stand him up.

"Ahhhh, not that arm," he heard the lieutenant groan. The dog robber dropped the arm, making Danny grimace with pain again. Garza watched him breathe deeply a few times to clear his head. When he could focus his vision better, he said, "I'm all right with these horses. It's that bastard Wieczorek who's trying to kill me!"

Garza pointed the flashlight at Danny's face and shouted, "*Teniente*, your face looks awful. Your uniform is ripped and you got horse manure all over you." In a momentary role reversal, it was the dog robber thinking for both of them. He talked while he rummaged in the first aid kit. He broke an ammonia ampule and held it under Danny's nose. "Here, sniff this. Then I'll go up to your car and get Sergeant Andrews. He knows about fixin' horses.

Maybe he can help you too?" Holding up a syringe of morphine, he asked, "How about some of this?" He waved the naked needle in the beam of the flashlight. "Maybe we should get you off the train at the next town."

The ammonia made Danny's head felt better. "No," he shouted over the noise, gritting his teeth with pain when he shook his head. "Stay here with me until I get my legs under me." He breathed deeply again and reached for the canteen. "Put that needle away. I'm feeling better now. Let me think a little." He tried his arm by holding himself up by boards in the side of the car, concluding it'd be serviceable if he needed it. Garza stabbed at the lieutenant's face with a bandage wet with water from the canteen, trying to wash the blood and horse manure from his face. "You'll feel better without that stuff on you."

"I'm not going to be satisfied until I set things right with Sergeant Wieczorek," gasped Flynn, blinking his eyes to clear his vision.

Garza had been thinking over Wieczorek's attack, and he feared how far he might go. And if it came to a fight...oh, Lord. "*Teniente*," he said, "he's huge! That man's been running his mouth for the past two days." The orderly indicated the direction of the troop car with a quick move of his head. "And remember, he's been drinkin'. He's mean and ugly drunk. Don't go up there, *Teniente*," he pleaded again. "Don't."

It wasn't that Garza's warning didn't register with Danny, but sergeant's attack opened a matter that had to be settled tonight. Retreating to the utility car would look as if he were hiding--and that would only encourage the man. He sucked in the clear, cold swirling air. It was better now that he could think better. To go up to the troop car, he'd have to be under control. Another good drink from the canteen helped; so did seeing the weapon strapped to Garza's waist. "Is that loaded?" he shouted over the wind and clacking wheels.

Garza nodded, saying, "Still loaded, sir."

"All right, then. Wait here for a few more minutes after I leave, and then..." He thought for a moment about the other sergeants and where the weapons were stored. He assumed that any potential assistance would be forward of where Wieczorek and probably Bednarski—maybe others—were getting worked up on whiskey. Sergeant Andrews would have dissuaded Weiczorek from breaking into the sergeant's quarters, so it was unlikely that Weech had gotten to their weapons. Danny felt he had to risk it, or Weech might work himself up to come looking for him to finish what he started. He said to his orderly, "Come forward with it and stand outside the troop car. I may need help."

Garza's eyes narrowed. He didn't like the thought of having to use a weapon on people he knew. "What do you want me to do with the piece, sir?" he asked.

Someday, but not right now, Danny thought, he'd find a way to thank Garza for his loyalty. For the moment the dog robber had to suck up his courage. Danny tested the shoulder, thinking things through again. If he could knock Wiecorek down—and with that big son of a bitch, he couldn't be sure—he might have to face some of his cronies. Damn, his mouth was dry. He hoped Garza didn't notice his shivering. "If it looks like I'm in danger... If things go very badly, just step into the car and show it in your hand." He swallowed before he spoke again. "Do not use it." He stressed the order, "Do not use it—except if you can't get out of the car any other way." There was going to be violence, no doubt of that, but Danny wanted it to be between him and the sergeant, without allowing the whole platoon to become part of the fight. He reassured Garza, "Even if they're pretty well liquored up, looking down the barrel of a forty-five should have a calming effect."

Danny stood leaning against the side of the car, thinking. He didn't want Garza going against the whole platoon for him. "I want you to keep a good eye on what goes on. Remember who does what. And listen to me, now. This is First Platoon business, and those sergeants up front shouldn't get into this. But! If anybody goes for you with any kind of weapon, run like hell—go forward, to Sergeant Andrews. If not that, then try to get into the locomotive. They won't go after you there. Get the crew to send a telegram to the next station. Tell them you want the police or the sheriff or whatever they have.

"Now give me your weapon while you go through the cars and see where everybody is. Don't admit you saw me. Come back as soon as possible—but don't rush, or they'll suspect something—and let me know how it looks."

The horses were calmed down now, and Danny waited for a long time, wrapped in a shelter half, thinking about the man who would probably like to see him dead. Finally he saw Garza on the catwalk, jumping down to give him his message. "A lot of people are still eating in the mess car, but they're not First Platoon, so their car was empty. I went through the platoon car, where Weech is, and it looks full," he warned, "and they're all listening to him."

Time to go. This might work. Might not, but what choice did he have? Weech, that son of a bitch, left him for dead, no doubt of it. Over his shoulder he shouted to Garza, "I'm going up there now. Follow me, but stay outside."

He didn't remember negotiating the catwalk, but that was behind him, now. Hand on the door handle of the platoon car, Danny squinted through the small grimy window for a look. Inside, a red-faced Weech, in his buttoned red undershirt and denim trousers, held court in the small open space around the wood stove, gesturing broadly to some of the troopers, who were laughing at something the sergeant said. A few, mostly the younger ones, looked away in embarrassment, pretending to be intent on cleaning tools or setting up a domino game on a field ration crate. Those, at least, he might be able to count on.

Lieutenant Flynn, bleeding, filthy, chest heaving, seeking revenge, swung the door wide open, letting in the cold and the noise of the train. He took a single step inside and slammed the door shut as hard as he could. A live grenade wouldn't've created more of a shock. "Sheeit, Weech. It's him!" screamed a voice from a dark corner off to the right. All over the car, troopers jumped hurriedly to their feet, spilling cards and dominoes to the floor in a scramble to clear a space. A few flashed frightened looks back and forth from the angry lieutenant to the stolid sergeant who had yet to turn to face this apparition returned from the dead. Bednarski and a couple of others threw glances at their lieutenant and looked away. Danny saw the behavior as a plain admission they were with Wieczorek.

Danny's shoulder injury wasn't apparent, but a swollen red bruise glared vividly on his right cheekbone, and his breath came to him in hard, excited gasps, so that he felt light-headed. But the troopers didn't know that. What they saw was a man smoldering with revenge, a furious specter in torn, filthy clothing smeared with horse manure.

"Turn around, Weech," Flynn yelled to cover the shakiness in his voice.

The sergeant turned slowly, bringing the trouble brewing all day to a head. "Kin ah he'p you, Lootenan'?" he sneered in his nasal drawl. "We noticed Pancho didn't come through heah with yuah food. I guess we thought you had a little something f'm that little town we jus' left."At the huge man's taunts, Danny's eyes darted from face to see where trouble might be lurking. Again he heard Wieczorek's taunts. "What happened to your face, Lootenan'? Some of them poor old horses get tired of you pattin' 'em on the ass?" He guffawed and half turned to his audience. A few of the young privates made nervous little sounds at Weech's crude, drunken joke, but even while forcing laughs, they hedged their bets, edging quietly toward the dim corners, fearing being drawn into the fight.

"Git 'im, Weech," somebody said. Another shouted a warning. Bednarski, Danny thought. "He got sumthin' on his right hand, Sarge." The sergeant sneaked a look at the khaki web belt wrapped tightly around Danny's right hand. Surprise registered on his flushed face. The lieutenant didn't come to negotiate. He had serious business on his mind.

Clack clack...clack clack, the wheels beat the time. Jesus, Mary and Joseph, the man was massive! The lieutenant flexed his hands and shifted his weight. He talked to Wieczorek as evenly as he could, reciting words he memorized while Garza went through the cars to get an idea of how things stood. "I'm here to teach you who runs the platoon, Weech. It's time to stop being a lout. You're a soldier. This is your chance to act like one." He waited for the platoon sergeant to make the first move.

Wieczorek wiped sweat from his face on the sleeve of his undershirt. Shouts exploded as the sergeant crouched and sprang forward, lunging for the lieutenant with arms outstretched, hoping to grapple him to the floor, where the power in his arms would be an advantage. In his drunken state, his move was slow and awkward—easily dodged. The brawler turned and charged again, grabbing awkwardly, but Danny moved deftly and the sergeant missed again. The third time, Weech came more cautiously, pawing and grabbing, but forgetting to protect himself against his opponent's protected fist. Flynn ducked under the grasping arms and stepped in behind the man's muscular left to plant his right, tightly-belted hand into the sergeant's ribs, blasting the breath out of him. A surprised Weech jumped back to recover, involuntarily feeling his ribs with his left hand.

Bednarski shouted encouragement, slurring, "Lucky shot, Sarge."

Again Wieczorek came at Danny, a little more cautiously this time, respecting that right hand. Instead of lunging, he crouched, moving deliberately with his arms out in front, groping for an arm, still intending to use his strength and weight to drag his smaller opponent to the floor. The powerful sergeant, surprised and unsure, shuffled sideways in the cramped space, trying to force a mistake. But the mistake was his, in clumsily trying to grapple with a boxer.

Again Danny risked a step inside those long arms and powerful hands. A popping left to the face straightened Weech up, snapping his head back long enough for Flynn to fire a punch with the belted right, landing it on the unprotected face with a loud crack. That shot probably shattered something, causing blood to spurt, but it would take more than one good right to bring that hulk of a man down. The blows forced Weech to back away momentarily, shuffling behind the stove, gasping for air through his open mouth. The arrogant sneer had vanished. Instead, his eyes flickered madly back and forth between the angry lieutenant and the shocked faces of his cronies.

Danny waited in the center of the small space, balancing on the balls of his feet, stalking the man who had clubbed him with a piece of lumber and abandoned him under the horses' hooves. Much more confident now, he goaded, "I already know you're stupid, Weech. For once, do something smart—sit on your ass and save your troopers from having to carry you off the train on a stretcher."

The taunt stung. Wieczorek's flushed and bleeding face told of embarrassment and humiliation. In taking the staggering blows without the slightest answer, his hold on the platoon, gained through years of brutish intimidation, was slipping away, unless he could batter this upstart. The unsteady sergeant shuffled warily toward the stove, eyeing the lieutenant in the hopes of finding an advantage, scanning for something to tilt the odds. Ha! The bucket of fire-tending tools—something Flynn had overlooked. A man could do formidable damage with the point and hook on a heavy iron poker.

Weech lunged for it and grabbed the tool in a huge fist, brandishing it out in front of him, jabbing at Flynn with the barbed point, trying to force him into a corner where he could batter him senseless or at least grab him. He'd been hurt before by better men and still brought them down. But the agile lieutenant slipped away into the middle of the car, still taunting, "You're whipped, Weech. Drop the poker and sit down."

Heedless of a broken face and battered ribs, Wieczorek clumsy launched another charge, swinging viciously with the sooty, pointed weapon, grazing Danny's shoulder, drawing blood and smashing splinters off the wood of one of the triple bunks fashioned of roughsawed lumber. Danny felt the blood trickling down his arm.

Weech wheezed for breath, positioning himself for another charge with the poker. Twice he looked at the fearful right hand wrapped in the belt. The sergeant never saw the left to the stomach that blasted the breath from him and left him gasping and wheezing for air that would not come. It would have been over then with most men, but the stubborn, immensely powerful Weech refused to go down. Danny let him totter with his hands on his knees, held in that position mostly by a sheer determination, straining loudly for his breath.

"Throw the poker down, Weech," said Danny. The calmness in his voice surprised him.

The sergeant, battered, bleeding and struggling to breathe, rolled his eyes, searching for help. But none came. Most of the troopers looked away to avoid the pleading eyes of the sergeant and backed farther away, making room for the rampaging lieutenant.

For a second time, Danny ordered, "Drop it, Weech, and go down to one knee."

Still the stubborn Wieczorek refused to go down or to drop the poker. A hoarse shout encouraged him. "Stand up, Sarge. Fight him." It was Bednarski's voice again, but Danny didn't dare take his eye off Wieczorek. If he left Weech standing, he might have to do this again, or worse, he might have to take on Bednarski too. He needed to silence them all. Pushing indecision out of his mind, he grabbed Wieczorek's hair with his left hand and jerked his head up, ready to smash him again with the right, but he saw surrender in the man's face and watched his mouth struggling to form the words, "No more."

Jerking the man's head up again, Flynn kicked Wiecorek's feet out from under him and let him lie, gasping in a crumpled heap. Nothing could be heard but the car creaking, the wind and the clacking of the wheels on the rails. No one moved to help him.

Danny moved deliberately to confront Bednarski to handle one more critical detail. He meant to see exactly how strongly this man held his allegiance to the insubordinate sergeant. He thought he saw a flicker of resistance. Suddenly he grabbed the strapping, liquored-up corporal by the front of his denim jacket and raised him till his heels came off the floor. Bednarski had been one of those watching when the new lieutenant did the same thing to Wieczorek at Camp Centaur. Now Weech lay motionless on the floor, and this new show of strength put fear into the corporal's wide-open, staring eyes. Shouting to be heard by every trooper in the car, Flynn threatened Wieczorek's thoroughly cowed henchman. "Make your choice right now, you stupid son of a bitch," he growled through gritted teeth. "If it's him, I'll put a knee in your crotch and drop you right here with your manhood gone. Or if it's me, you can..." Bednarski's bulky shape slumped.

Astonished by the turn of events, one of the younger troopers near the stove shrilled, "Look there, Leon peed his pants." Every man in the car saw the wet stain darkening his denim trousers, but none laughed.

"I see you've made your choice," Danny said, letting the jacket slide through his fingers like the skin of a snake.

Danny stood in the center of the swaying car near the stove and its small supply of wood, turning slowly, looking directly at each one, as he'd seen Centaur do. A few glanced at their sergeant before looking back at the man in the center of the railroad car. "Anybody else want to dispute whose platoon this is?" he challenged. "Come out here now."

Danny pointed at the slow-moving, solemn Cernosek, who had at least shown he could take orders. "Corporal, you're in charge here until we pull into Fort Reno." He nudged the inert form on the floor with the toe of his boot. "This lump of manure had better be fit for duty and standing tall when we do. None of that too-sick-to-work business; I don't give a damn how he feels."

With Garza close behind, Danny worked his way forward to his car and stripped out of his torn, filthy khaki shirt, feeling the painful stiffness setting in. Carefully he washed in a bucket of warm water brought from the kitchen by his dog robber and looked himself over. His left eye was nearly shut by a violent purple bruise and swelling rapidly, threatening to close his eye.

Garza asked, "Should I ask Sergeant Andrews to look you over, *Teniente?*" The dog robber, looking closely at the wounds on the lieutenant's face and over his body, made a wry face. "Man, you beat up, sir." He poked a spot on Flynn's left leg. "Looks like a horse kicked you here."

Flynn shook his head. But thinking how it was going to look when they got into Fort Reno late tomorrow afternoon with bruises and scrapes all over the platoon commander and his sergeant, he changed his mind. It might look better with a little doctoring. "But not by Andrews. The less he knows about what went on, the better. I want you to do it," he said to the dog robber.

With Garza working under a small dangling light bulb, they tested the lieutenant's wrenched shoulder gingerly and examined the cuts and scratches over much of his body. He hurt like hell everywhere, but he felt better now that the inevitable showdown with Wieczorek was done. Garza collected the bloody uniform and inspected the cuts and the ugly wound from the fire poker. He cleaned the wounds with alcohol from the medicine chest and applied something from a can Sergeant Andrews gave him to use on the larger bruises. "Works real good on horses," the sergeant said. After applying an inexpert bandage, Garza left for a few minutes and returned with a metal container of thick stew and a half loaf of bread bought at one of their recent stops.

Garza sensed the Teniente had no more talk in him for now, so he watched quietly from an office chair while the lieutenant sat at the tiny table in a clean suit of long underwear, wolfing down the stew with a large enameled spoon. He stayed until Flynn rolled his battered body into the narrow bunk. Before leaving, he whispered to see if the bruised lieutenant had fallen asleep, "*Teniente?*" The lieutenant opened his eyes, listening. "Corporal Cernosek was waiting when I went to get your food," he said.

"What are you telling me?"

"Don't worry about the troopers. They don't want to be locked up at Fort Reno. They all know Weech got what was coming to him—so they'll all say there was an accident when the horses got spooked."

chapter

TEN

"Lieutenant Flynn, we're hearing crazy talk from the people at Fort Reno," said Major Perkins, climbing the steps to the railroad car. "Tell me what really happened." He and Captain Franklin had driven a few miles from Fort Brown in an army sedan to board the train at a remote railroad junction while it waited to be switched to the Fort Brown siding. This way they could talk privately with Lieutenant Flynn before he disembarked to be questioned by one of any number of people who might be interested. Not about horses, though—they were pretty sure the new horses would be quite satisfactory. They worried that what they were hearing from Fort Reno wasn't adding up with the terse official reports he'd been sending from the train.

Franklin knew all along about the difficulties in First Platoon, and from stories going around, matters had come to a head. "It's all rumor so far," Franklin began. "We're here to try to get things straight with you, before the questions begin to fly."

Perkins didn't intend to say anything. Mainly he'd come to impress upon Lieutenant Flynn how seriously the stories from Fort Reno were being taken in the headquarters offices at Fort Brown. But Danny's bruised face, still swollen and vividly blotched with purple, still shocked the major. Involuntarily, he allowed his breath to escape in a long hissing sound.

Franklin began slowly, "The colonel isn't going to meet your train when it comes in. He's concerned about the regiment being pulled apart by reports of a nasty incident on the train."

Danny stared incredulously at the two men sitting across his makeshift desk. How could this be? Not a trooper in the platoon would have talked. Not even Wieczorek. He'd stake his life on it. Somebody up there at Fort Reno must've made some assumptions—a doctor at the clinic, probably, although the sergeants' mess was a likely source of the rumors.

Franklin referred again to the rumblings from Fort Reno, calling them, "Things we didn't see in your reports." Rumbling was hardly the word for the unofficial comments arriving at Fort Brown. Some calls speculated about mutiny and beatings, while the cryptic reports from First Platoon presented a different picture. "All you reported was, 'Lt. Flynn and Sgt. Wiecorek treated at clinic for minor injuries.'" Of course, the troopers at Fort Brown formed their own ideas from bits of confusing chatter they heard from news they were able to gather by telephone from Fort Reno. The danger lay in allowing false assumptions to circulate. "I've got my own ideas about what happened," said Franklin.

Acting unofficially for the colonel, Major Perkins took off his hat and dropped it on the table. He felt far too many people at Fort Brown were making calls to the remount station. "Listen, boy. The new adjutant is hell-bent on giving you a court-martial for beating up your platoon sergeant." The idea that Wieczorek, almost a foot taller and at least fifty pounds heavier than the lieutenant, could possibly have gotten a dose of bare-knuckle discipline was too hard to swallow; so Captain Tobolski was preparing charges based on the scraps of rumor he'd been able to pick up. He reasoned Flynn had allowed factions to build and some kind of riot took place. He wanted to say more, but if there were to be a court-martial, the convening authority would be the regiment's commanding officer, so it would be best for him to remain aloof.

Danny felt himself panicking over what he saw as a growing possibility of being drawn and quartered on the strength of a few rumors! What would anybody have done if he had found himself unconscious, face down in filth, with horses about to trample him? Would a reasonable man accept these baseless assumptions? These two, Perkins and Franklin, were on his side: it was obvious. "Can I talk to the colonel, so he hears my side of things?" he asked.

"Tomorrow morning," said Perkins gravely. "The colonel wants to talk to you early in his office. Take some time to get your story together."

Franklin tried to sound reassuring. "As soon as we get off the train, I'm going to the colonel to see if I can keep your meeting with him on a man-to man basis. You're the one who hasn't been able to present his facts." All three officers understood that Captain Tobolski and the legal people couldn't be allowed in Centaur's office during the meeting.

"What should I tell him?" Danny asked.

"If you're there with him alone, tell him the God's truth." That was Perkins's advice and Franklin agreed.

The train shuddered solidly. It meant the yard engine was being connected. Franklin and Perkins stood hurriedly. Both shook his hand and tried to sound optimistic about his meeting with Centaur.

Before turning to follow Perkins, Franklin called to his lieutenant from the step, "I'll try to get you out of the competition tomorrow."

"No," Danny shouted, but it was too late. The two visitors were hurrying to a waiting sedan.

Major Perkins's "tomorrow morning" turned out to be more like the crack of dawn, 0630 hours. Private Garza worked industriously, giving Lieutenant Flynn a trim, but not fast enough. "Cut. Cut. Cut," Flynn urged, moving his fingers like scissors. "I'm going to be doing a rug dance in a few minutes." The last thing he wanted to do was to be late at the headquarters building.

Flynn turned his head from side to side, inspecting the haircut with a small mirror. "That'll do. Thanks," he said, brushing his neck with a towel while Garza swept bits of red hair into a small heap. He scrambled into his uniform and gave some last-minute directions to the dog robber while he brushed the dust from the brim of his hat. "If Centaur doesn't have me in handcuffs or in the guardhouse an hour from now, I intend to ride in the competition. Saddle Bolter and bring him to the headquarters building."

"The colonel's ready, Lieutenant Flynn," a sergeant called from the door, beckoning him to enter the office. In the hallway, Franklin and Perkins paced nervously, expecting to be called in for comment. Franklin shrugged and gave Danny a smile, hoping his intercession with the colonel had helped.

"Lieutenant Daniel Flynn, reporting as ordered, sir," said Danny at attention and saluting. So far, Captain Tobolski hadn't appeared. Danny breathed deeply and concentrated on Colonel Chamberlain's face for a clue as to what he was thinking. Would he accept the charges made by Captain Tobolski, who knew Wieczorek personally? Or would he accept the word of the man who was there on the train?

Chamberlain looked up from the papers on his desk. He'd been in the army too long to let a lieutenant read his thoughts. Danny wanted to close his eyes to keep from facing up to that gimlet stare. When the colonel finally spoke, it sounded threatening. "Up till now," he said—by that expression he apparently meant he'd just read an account of the brawl on the train—"you've done good work."

Danny knew better than to reply.

Chamberlain's eyes didn't waver. "You seem to have an instinct for getting noticed, Lieutenant Flynn."

Danny waited, standing rigidly at attention. He wouldn't speak unless he was asked.

"The horses you selected are exactly what I was expecting. And they're in excellent condition."

Surprised to hear praise, Danny took heart. "Thank you, sir," he said.

"When horses survive a long confinement in open railroad cars fit and well kept, it says a lot about the man charged with their care." Centaur's words came slowly, carefully chosen to balance the accusations already presented with facts from sources he trusted before deciding the fate of the young man standing apprehensively before him. He felt quite certain that Lieutenant Flynn sensed none of the political pressures twisting and turning in his mind: Did he brush aside the charges and congratulate the lieutenant for personally disciplining a lout who had it coming, or did he allow the adjutant's charge to stand because a court-martial might clear the air once and for all?

Seeing the situation from his own inexperienced perspective, Danny thought Centaur's tone—this talk of how well the horses had been treated—was a strange way to start a court-martial or even an ass chewing. While the commanding officer talked, Danny's mind struggled to make some sense out of these conflicting signs. He sneaked a look at the long, brutally serious-looking legal document on the desk. No clue there, but what kind of weight did Centaur give Captain Tobolski's opinion? Saints preserve us! Why didn't the man get on with it?

And what would he say if he were given the opportunity to describe the events on the train? As it did frequently in difficult times, Danny's mind flashed to what his father would think about all this? Michael was proud to see his son in the uniform of an officer in the U.S. Army. If Colonel Chamberlain decided to court-martial him, all that parental pride could be a thing of the past. If he were discharged from the army, how could he go home and face his father? He'd wrestled with these questions a half dozen times already this morning. Now then, he reassured himself, if the commanding officer asked him what happened, he'd tell him the truth.

Apparently not everything was positive in Centaur's view. He came at Danny from an unexpected direction. "Lieutenant Flynn, I take a dim view of my men arriving at another cavalry post battered and abused, looking for all the world as if a lieutenant and his platoon sergeant have been brawling." Danny's sharp inhalation didn't slip by unnoticed, but the colonel moved on to other matters without interrogating the lieutenant on the events of the trip to Fort Reno.

After a pause, Chamberlain said, "It may surprise you how much I know about this... this regrettable event," reaching for the thick document on the desk and opening it to a page Captain Tobolski had marked for him. He read silently for a few seconds before looking up at the fearful lieutenant. "In a matter of an hour after your arrival, Lieutenant Flynn, virtually every sergeant at Fort Reno knew that a fellow sergeant had been beaten senseless by an officer under my command. Damn, Lieutenant, word like that gets around like lightning. It spread to the Provost Marshal, who did some investigating, mostly reviewing the clinic's records and listening to some talk. Just barracks talk, of course. In the clinic, your platoon sergeant said he slipped and fell heavily to the floor when the train lurched." Chamberlain left the desk to look outside over the parade ground where the steeplechase course was being set up. Turning back to Danny, he said, "You, it seems, told the doctors that there was some trouble with a horse in one of the cars after a watering stop—classic cover stories, both of them. The doctor didn't swallow either one. He drew the conclusion that the rumors were correct and telephoned. This paper is an order to commence an Article 32 inquiry. You know what this means, I presume?"

Danny swallowed. "Yes, sir." Was this the time to spill his guts in one final attempt to stave off a court-martial? No, he decided, at least not yet.

"You may stand at ease now, Lieutenant Flynn. What do you have to say?"

Danny felt pretty certain the permission to stand at ease meant he was in the clear. "My statement to the doctor was correct, sir. A horse slammed me into the side of the railroad car."

"And the sergeant? Wieczorek, I think his name is?"

"Wieczorek. Yes, sir."

"What do you think the sergeant would tell me if he were standing here?"

Danny had prepared himself for a question like that. He didn't gulp or swallow. All he said was, "He'd say he slipped and fell. That's what he said at Fort Reno, sir."

"Hmm. What if I were to ask the corporal or the quartermaster sergeant?"

"The same, sir." He wasn't all that sure about either of the two sergeants.

To Danny's immense relief, Centaur relaxed visibly and smiled. He'd heard enough, most likely. "That's exactly what they did tell me after the train came in," he said, adding, "and I'm prepared to believe them." His tone softened even more. "How's your platoon performing now?" he asked.

"Never better, sir," said Danny with his broadest grin, hoping it really was true.

"I would think so too," said the colonel, beginning to sound more like a proud uncle than a commanding officer. He tore the intimidating document in two lengthwise and pushed it aside. "Sit down, Lieutenant Flynn, the matter is concluded."

Taking care not to exhale audibly or to grin foolishly, Danny took his seat, pretending he wasn't giddy from a huge flood of relief.

The colonel glanced over Danny's head to his wall clock. Time was short, but there were a few more details to handle. He drew another document toward him. Danny recognized it as the report he'd handwritten on the train, typed by one of E Troop's clerks."

"I've already told you what I think about the horses you brought me, but I want to compliment you on the clear, concise report you've written. Colonel Newman and I were both impressed by your recommendations for improvement in caring for horses on long railroad journeys. You'd think all the tricks had been learned by now, but this report shows some innovative thinking. Good job."

"Thank you, sir," Danny said, relieved and grateful for a narrow escape. God knows what might have happened—a single trooper whining was all it would've taken. His fervent wish was to get away from this meeting before something bad could happen. Why wouldn't Centaur let him go?

"One last thing," said the commanding officer. There was that jolt of panic again. How long would this torture go on? "That orderly of yours...Garza?"

Damn! Had his dog robber gotten them into trouble? "Yes, sir," he said evenly.

"He seems to be doing a good job for you?"

It was true, of course, but Danny would have agreed to almost anything to be allowed to go free. "Yes, sir, he certainly is," he said.

"Good. I want you to present this to him. It's his advancement to Private First Class."

Another flood of relief washed over Danny, who grabbed at the arms of the chair tightly with his fingers, unable for the moment to pick up the certificate without his hands shaking.

Another glance at the clock stirred Chamberlain into action. "I'm due to open the competition in a half hour. And you should be there too. But I'll excuse you if you think you haven't had time to prepare." He gave Danny a few seconds to decide. "Your withdrawal would certainly improve the odds for many of your competitors, but you could still make the start—if your horse were saddled," he suggested.

As the colonel stood, Danny leaped to his feet, barely aware of the words tumbling out of his mouth, "Private First Class Garza has him ready. All I have to do is to get into my gear, sir."

Colonel Chamberlain turned away before the lieutenant could see him smiling.

Danny had been far too worried about his own affairs to pay attention to the new rumors about his fate. They'd been flying thickly since his return from Fort Reno. The stories varied widely, depending on the bearer, but the common thread in nearly all the versions was that Danny Flynn had been summoned to headquarters for some unspecified reason; but whatever the motivation, the versions based on a sighting of him leaving Centaur's office held that Lieutenant Flynn had been banned from the competition.

Publicly, some lieutenants voiced noble sentiments. George Kincaid was one. "I hope Flynn's allowed to compete. I wouldn't want anybody to think I won 'cause he wasn't here." Privately, not one of them felt their chances of winning wouldn't have been improved if Flynn withdrew.

Meanwhile, Danny and his newly promoted orderly prepared for the first event. In the lofty language of official positions, the purpose of a regimental competition like this one was to improve morale by promoting development of the professional skills required of a junior cavalry officer through competition in a variety of martial arts. As usual, the official position had little to do with the true motivation. Competition in scored events can measure the lieutenants against one another, with the commanding officer taking official note. Usually, that meant a written report.

Among the lieutenants, it was mostly about public recognition and being able to brag about it. At its core, the all-day competition presented an opportunity for glory—public acknowledgement of being first among peers. Horse cavalrymen understand swaggering as part of their being, and deep down, men who swagger know it's a right to be earned and defended.

Having Flynn on the sidelines seemed a powerful motivator, because common thinking around Fort Brown held him to be the best rider in the regiment, with the presumption that he was the best athlete too. All Kincaid's grand talk of not wanting his probable victory sullied because Flynn was out of the competition was a case of shameless posturing. A win was a win, no matter who was in the race. And if Flynn were to be on the sidelines, for whatever reason, every lieutenant in the 124th knew his chances of standing out were greatly imporved.

By the time Danny rode onto the parade ground, the colonel had already begun his remarks stressing the importance he placed on each officer doing his best. With the same care and discretion he would have exhibited in arriving late at Sunday mass, Danny dismounted a short distance from the swarm of competitors milling on the grass before the temporary speaker's platform, hoping to mingle unnoticed with some of the lieutenants hanging back at the fringes. In the meantime Garza rode slowly around the crowd to where the other orderlies were busily currying horses and adjusting the fit of the tack, checking any minute detail that could affect the steeplechase event. One of the other lieutenants saw Danny attired for riding and nodded in his direction, setting heads turning and a low buzz of recognition rising among the contestants. Suppressing a smile, Colonel Chamberlain commented with a nod. "Join us, Lieutenant Flynn," he said, as if the scene in his office had never happened.

Competitions like these varied in format from post to post and from regiment to regiment, depending mostly on the surrounding terrain, and each had its own unique features. Here at Fort Brown, the 124th would begin with a steeplechase event on the parade ground, where the families could watch. The event, with spectacular jumps at a sedate, genteel pace, placed a premium on form and control and cooperation between horse and rider. The opening event would occupy the entire morning, with captains as well as lieutenants competing. After a little something to eat, the lieutenants-only competition would begin. Racing and shooting required a lot of room, but for the sake of spectators, the first of those events would start in front of the parade ground stands, and the final event would finish in the same spot.

Danny drew a square of pasteboard from Major Perkins's hat—number three—which meant he would ride third in the steeplechase and wear the number three in the afternoon competition. Garza led Bolter from the shade of the orange trees, allowing Danny a bit of precious time to prepare himself mentally for the event. The time he could have used to warm up and get the feel of the course had been taken up by his meeting with the commanding officer. In the few minutes remaining before his number came up, he intently watched the first two riders, learning from their performance over the obstacles, visualizing the course mentally, leaning and tensing through each turn and jump. All the while he stroked Bolter's neck, speaking softly to calm his mount and control his own racing pulse. He mounted a bit earlier than usual, to let Bolter get the feel of his rider's weight.

"Rider number three, ready?" Danny pushed his visored cap firmly on his head and fixed the strap under his chin. On the judge's signal, he held Bolter in check, concentrating on controlling his pace. They went well over the first two jumps, but he sensed Bolter shortening his stride. In urging the powerful, long-legged horse to lengthen it out, his lack of familiarity with the course, call it lack of practice, led to overcompensation and resulted in an impossible approach angle at the next jump. Coolly, Danny avoided the disaster of a certain miss by slowing and circling to set up at a more comfortable angle. The time it took to do the circle cost him in the standings—Doug Cameron, a veteran of these competitions, took the lead. Having Danny at even a small disadvantage may have raised the hopes of the competitors, but Flynn himself wasn't dismayed. A second place left him well positioned for the afternoon events.

After the elegance of the morning's steeplechase and a rather elaborate, but high-spirited lunch catered by the officers' club, the judges, including a Mexican Army major, gathered the competitors at the end of the parade ground to go over the complicated rules for a final time. The afternoon event would be a varied, grueling competition requiring riding ability, of course, but also a good familiarity with overland navigation, skill with firearms and above all, physical fitness. The course required crossing the Rio Grande twice, to the Mexican side and back, across a stretch of river chosen for comparatively safe conditions of depth and width.

Essentially, the afternoon contest was a continuous race around a closed course, so the lowest total time would win, but a complicated system of time penalties for rule infractions and time deductions for high marks in the shooting events would affect the eventual outcome. Doug Cameron, whose first place in the Steeplechase would reduce his total time by five minutes, asked a question. "What's the penalty for lost equipment, Major?"

"One minute per item. Throw away your helmet and add a minute to your total time." Major Perkins riffled through the papers on his clipboard to find the table he would use in adjusting scores. He reminded the riders, "If you leave the course for any reason, you're disqualified immediately. Cutting corners is considered leaving the course."

The first four hundred yards of the parade ground would be a foot race for all competitors from one line to another, just beyond which the orderlies held their horses ready. With the competitors standing nervously at a mark chalked on the grass, the judges checked that each of them wore a steel helmet and carried the required quantity of pistol and rifle ammunition. Rifles would not be carried on the first leg of the race, but a .45 caliber pistol and a full canteen completed the equipment required by each competitor at the start. Danny undid a button on his shirt pocket: just one less detail to concern him before he entered the mounted pistol range.

Perkins reported, "Colonel, I've checked with the observers around the course. Telephone lines and radios are loud and clear."

Centaur raised a starter's pistol and fired. The sharp report sent twenty-eight lieutenants breaking away from the line, in a flat-out run across a quarter mile stretch of grass to the line of horses. With a good time in the steeplechase, Danny chose not to sprint. Running in the heat, wearing boots and loaded down with gear, could be a waste of energy. He was well back in the pack of racers when he took Bolter's reins from PFC Garza. Mounting, he craned his neck for a glimpse of his competitors. Three of the least fit, laboring heavily, had yet to cross the line, and two men who rashly chose to sprint were now bent over, puking their lunch and beer onto the ground. That meant five with no realistic chance of figuring in the standings.

A trooper on the field telephone reported, "Number sixteen, Lieutenant Whiteman, is first mounted and away." At the judges' stand, Centaur watched a headquarters clerk move a white poker chip with the number sixteen painted in black numbers to a new position on a map of the course.

Bolter's eyes rolled in the excitement, but his rider had one more preparation to make before he mounted. He carefully fished a loaded magazine out of a pocket on his belt and buttoned it carefully in his shirt pocket to have it ready. Then they were off at a scorching gallop. Flynn let his mount burn off a little energy before slowing to conserve Bolter's strength for the tight turns and short sprints between targets of the mounted pistol course, and particularly for the long run to the river.

At the judges' stand located at the parade ground, a trooper passed information from the mounted pistol range. Number three entered the range in fourth place. The Texans of the 124th boasted a number of good shooters, but most of them would concede the best score with the pistol to Lieutenant Flynn of E Troop—partly because of his incomparable balance in the saddle. Entering the course, Danny felt comfortable and steady on Bolter, who turned out to be the best mount he could've hoped for: surefooted and powerful—a good platform for shooting the targets with deadly accuracy. The run through the figure-eight range went well. The score would depend on the tally of the targets, but Flynn sensed he'd improved his standing. He concentrated on his mental picture of the next leg.

The map showed the run from the mounted pistol ranges to the river crossing to be a nearly straight leg of almost three miles, an opportunity to let Bolter show his strength and speed on the level ground. If Bolter could get Flynn across the river first, he would have the huge advantage of having the first choice of the new mounts. Danny let Bolter run: Once he and his rider got across the river, the horse would be done for today.

In a spirit of international cooperation, the Mexican Army had cordoned off two or three acres of land on the riverbank for use in this competition and assigned several of their officers to help with judging the complicated process of crossing the Rio Grande twice. Since midmorning, a mass of horses, military vehicles and a swarm of busy men in uniforms jammed the area. Most of the judges, a mix of Mexican and U.S. Army officers, gathered under a large green tent with the sides rolled up, to stay out of the sun. From there they could view the open area where the competitors would change mounts. Horse handlers would work two picket lines: one for the wet, exhausted horses that had just negotiated the river, the other for fresh troop horses brought over from Fort Brown by vehicle, with plenty of space in between to reduce confusion. These waiting horses were already saddled with an unloaded M-1 in the rifle boot. It would be first come, first served—set up in that manner to create an advantage for the leading riders, who could mount any horse they chose. A veterinarian and two helpers stood by under a small tent near the picket lines.

Word of the competition had spread in Matamoros. Having gringo soldiers splashing through the water, negotiating both banks up and down and changing horses in between, promised to be quite a spectacle. The event attracted a crowd of civilians, mostly well-to-do people, from the looks of their clothing, who made the short drive to watch. Civilian cars packed the small parking area reserved for them, and the roped-off spectators' area filled early with curiosity seekers.

Rules for the complex event called for each rider to bring his horse down the American bank, ford or swim the river with his mount and then to climb up the Mexican side. There, before the spectators and judges, he would leave his spent mount with a waiting soldier. As quickly as possible, he would choose a fresh horse from the picket line, and cross the Rio Grande to the Texas side.

Danny felt optimistic about the double fording maneuver, despite the steepness of the banks, but luck would count a lot in the soft sand. Approaching the river, he allowed Bolter to pick his way down through the precipitous slope and plunge into the Rio Grande at his own pace. The river, which appeared quite narrow from up above, suddenly became perilous and wide. The current moved them downstream, to the left, but Bolter swam strongly, easily reaching footing in shallower water. Once across, Danny dismounted and allowed the horse to lead the climb up the bank. Danny heard the shouts letting him know he was first to arrive at the exchange point on the Mexican side.

A trooper took Bolter's reins and led him away. Danny followed a carefully thought-out routine. He ran past the judges and the spectators, more or less ignoring the applause, the flashes from reporters' cameras, even the shouts of encouragement, and snatched a cup of water offered by one of the troopers. Gulping a few swallows, Flynn let his eyes sweep the faces a few feet away. He returned the smile of a striking beauty whose face was shaded from the sun by a broad-brimmed white straw hat.

"Pick any horse, Lieutenant," called a trooper.

"This one," Danny shouted, touching the rump of a chestnut mare. Splashes of white in the blaze on her forehead and on her feet convinced him she could run with good speed. He took a moment to check the fit of the saddle and look the horse over. "What's her name?" he asked.

"Sabrina, sir," came the answer.

Before mounting, he gulped more water from his canteen, and gave a thought to getting rid of it, but losing the canteen would give him a time penalty. His pistol magazines already lay discarded in an empty ammunition can. Pouring away some of his water rid him of a few ounces of weight, and he surveyed the best route down the bank as he screwed the top firmly on the canteen.

The Mexican major judging the river crossings spoke quietly to the American communications team cranking the radio set. "Number three is first away from the river crossing. Second competitor approaching American bank." At the parade ground another communicator translated dots and dashes into words and handed the note to Major Perkins. Danny's chip advanced on the course map.

Leading Sabrina by her reins, he plunged boldly into the water, hoping to wade much of the distance. Two thirds of the way across, he stepped into a hole and the water engulfed him. He tried swimming: an awkward effort with his boots and rifle ammunition weighing him down. The buoyant half-empty canteen tugged upward at his waist. Probably it was instinct that prompted Danny to hold onto the reins. When he came up for air, he could see himself being swept downstream by the green water, but Sabrina swam strongly till her feet felt bottom, towing her distressed rider through the water by the reins until he felt a foot touch. That was enough. Then he was across, gasping for breath from the exertion in the water. But the keyed-up mare wouldn't be held back. Sabrina chose her own path up the American bank—and it cost them. The sand gave way under her forefeet, and she went down whinnying in fright, rolling onto her left side. Boots still full of water, Danny clambered with great difficulty up the bank to the laboring mare. "I'm coming, Sabrina, hold on," he called out.

The roll in the treacherous sand hadn't turned out to be disastrous. Sabrina scrambled to her feet in a few seconds. Near disasters like this had to be expected. Horse and rider cleared the bank shaken, lead reduced to less than a minute, but ready to run.

On the Mexican side, a judge nodded to the radio operator. The tapping key sent the terse message that rider number three was first to complete the recrossing. It omitted the difficulties in the river or the sand-covered spectacle of Sabrina watching her rider dump water from his boots.

After the river, the riders faced another three-mile run to the rifle range on a sketchily marked trail cut through patches of thick brush. The senior officers laying out the course intended this to be much more of a navigation challenge than the first leg, but they elected not to post judges at all the places where a rider could shorten the course by cutting a corner. "It would be the same as marking the course," argued one of the majors.

Centaur agreed with the man's argument, leaving navigation to a matter of honor. "My officers wouldn't be so unscrupulous," he insisted. The expectation might have been justified under ordinary conditions, but much was at stake. A man struggling in the later parts of the course might be tempted to take advantage of the absence of judges.

Out in front of the pack, Danny saw a real problem in his situation. As the leader he would be forced to ride cautiously, picking his way along the faintly marked track. Not only would being first cost him time, but Sabrina's tracks would give a huge advantage to those following him.

Less than a quarter mile from the crossing, Danny discovered that selecting the chestnut mare had been a cardinal error. Sabrina may have looked like a fast runner, and without a doubt she did save his bacon at the river. The sad truth was that Sabrina had a hidden flaw, an awkward gait that robbed her of speed. Still, he guessed, they were holding their own for now. The cutoff was something he couldn't afford to worry about.

The rifle competition at the end of the cross-country leg put him in a sweat because of his inexperience with the new piece. If the old reliable Springfield were riding under his leg, it would be a different matter. The lieutenants would be shooting from the relatively short range of two hundred yards, but because of the time factor, accuracy and maintaining a high rate of fire held premium importance. Each shooter was allowed only ten minutes on the range. That bit of time included loading, reloading and changing positions. A single white target with a black bullseye would remain visible the entire time, but the shooter was required to fire the semi-automatic weapon thirty times: ten times standing, ten more sitting, and the last ten from a prone position. Any mechanical difficulty with weapon or ammunition would be counted as hazards of the competition, and the shooter would be hammered with hefty time penalties for not getting the shots off.

The observer on the field telephone at the rifle range made his first report to the parade ground. "Number three is entering the range." The talker, probably bored by the long wait for the first sign of action at his post, added that he did hear another rider approaching. The competition committee had some concern about mounts straying into the nearby cactus thickets or even onto the range when the shooting started, if the lieutenants didn't tether them carefully enough. For safety's sake, the planners assigned a single trooper to handle the horses while the lieutenants did their shooting.

This exercise required the shooter to keep track of his shots carefully. It would cost him if he fired too many times from any position or if he fired too few. For safety's sake, unspent cartridges were to be left in a bucket at each shooter's station.

Danny jumped off Sabrina, hauling the M-1 out of the boot while a trooper held her head. Judges and their assistants heard his scream breaking the silence. "Damn. The boot's full of sand." In the range master's house, they watched, nearly helpless with laughter, at the sight of the leading competitor running to a canvas watercooler hanging at the end of the firing line to wash sand out of his rifle.

All this flailing cost him at least a minute. He inserted a clip, breathed several times to slow his breath, aimed and squeezed.

"Number three is firing standing."

"Number three has completed his standing rounds. Now firing seated."

All the time lost cleaning his piece put him in danger of running into the time limitations, and Flynn felt his concentration wandering. Damn, he felt rough and jerky on the trigger. The prone position would be steadier, and he'd have the benefit of twenty rounds of practice.

"Number three has completed his seated firing. He's now switching to prone."

Spreading out flat on a shelter half, Danny made a tripod of his belly and elbows, and shifted his concentration to steadying himself in the new firing situation. It looked good and felt smooth; saving seconds for Sabrina to use her speed to make up ground. Here's where Flynn clinches the win with ten quick shots, he thought. Squeeze the trigger, he urged himself, increasing the pressure. Three shots away smoothly. On the fourth, all he heard was a mechanical click, a soggy silence and nothing more—no recoil pushing against his shoulder. "Misfire! Damn! Misfire!" he yelled. He heard the steady popping of other shooters firing away. Frantically, he tried to clear the round. The M-1 was thoroughly jammed—probably the sand. The penalties mounted.

"Number three is having difficulty with his weapon and calling for assistance with a misfire."

His allotted time had only twenty-five seconds to run. Bad luck had dumped a penalty for seven missed shots on his head. Damn! He couldn't leave the range with a weapon jammed with a live round. "Take it," he said, handing the rifle over to the armorers. Out of time, in fact, over time, he ran for his horse and started for the finish line, gasping from strain and exertion. Danny was still in the lead for covering the course, but not by much: another shooter was mounting for the run to the finish. To Danny's surprise, his nearest competitor was George Kincaid. "Where the hell did he come from?" It would have taken a miracle; or taking a short cut.

"Number three departing the rifle range without his weapon." This news sent a wave of excitement through the judges' tent. The leaders would be in sight of the finish in the next few minutes. Some trained binoculars down the smoothly graded road leading from the post to the training ranges. Others gathered clipboards and checked stopwatches. Ma Perkins reluctantly rummaged for the table of penalties to calculate what the mishap on the rifle range was going to cost the man in the lead. Spectators had been waiting for nearly an hour to watch the finish, and the race was far from over.

If Sabrina was capable of any speed at all, now was the time to ask for it. Danny shouted at her and spurred the reliable animal that pulled him out of trouble in the river. He wanted speed and she responded with all she had, running with strength and courage but without the fluid motion that might have gained time.

Lieutenant Flynn crossed the finish line first to a roar of applause from the spectators, but until the judges compiled the final times and applied the complicated computations, the actual standings would be in question. Lieutenant Kincaid followed seconds behind, and several others with better luck in selecting horses finished in a desultory procession.

Danny rode to the far end of the long green stretch of the parade ground, where it was quiet and he could be alone with his thoughts while allowing Sabrina to cool down. Letting the mare walk back toward the finish line, he leaned over to pat her neck. "Good girl. You gave me all you had." He left her at the picket line, where several troopers waited to collect the spent mounts from their riders. Others took custody of rifles and any remaining unfired ammunition.

Only half the lieutenants had finished by the time Lieutenant Flynn handed the reins to a waiting trooper, but ten closely spaced finishers already across the line meant no remaining possibility for a rider still on the course to be declared the winner, or even figuring prominently in the standings. But to the men of regiment, each lieutenant represented the pride of his platoon; thus the order of finishing remained crucial, right down to the last to cross the chalk line. On matters like these, where bets rode and reputations were made or lost, the final standings would be a hot topic of discussion for days, with everyone from the commanding officer to the lowest private having opinions. Accuracy in tallying and computation of penalties was paramount. While the judges worked feverishly, checking and verifying each contestant's scores, the sweating, exhilarated finishers cooled off under the spray of sprinklers set out to water the parade ground.

Leaving the judges to work out the thorny details of deductions and penalties, Colonel Chamberlain led the way to the officers' club patio to await the final standings. Some of the spectators followed immediately, but Danny couldn't bring himself to join them: at least not yet. He hated talking about losing nearly as much as the loss itself. Standing apart from the generally boisterous participants, Danny closed his eyes, concentrating on pushing the memory of the disastrous rifle jam out of his mind. He overheard some voices speculating on the standings. "What do you think about Flynn's problems with the rifle?" said one. Danny didn't recognize the voice.

Thoughts varied. "Well, isn't that just too damn bad? Centaur's boy ran into a little bad luck," said the C Troop commander to another captain, who saw things another way. "I heard he skipped qualifying on the M-1 for that trip to Fort Reno. He shouldn't even have been in the race if he didn't know anything about the rifle."

Flynn boiled. The gall of the idiot! He'd show him. He was only a couple of steps behind the two troop commanders when a shout saved him from grabbing one by the shoulder.

"Hey, Flynn, wait up," he heard a voice saying, "You need to hear this. You've been screwed. I'm afraid that pompous ass George Kincaid is gonna get clean away with cutting that corner. It'll be a shame if he does." Danny saw John Sowell, an electric company engineer from Rosenberg running to catch up. Sowell had been in a pack of lieutenants riding behind Flynn, with Kincaid a few hundred yards ahead—well out of the lead. At a turn in the trail, Kincaid had checked over his shoulder; both right and left, before veering off the course, but Sowell spotted him through a gap in the scrub growth, leaving a dust trail showing plainly where he had veered off the course, cutting the corner. "I think you and I could go up to Perkins and report a foul," said Sowell.

Danny forgot about the outspoken captain. Sowell's information could help to set things straight, if he could get to the judges before they completed their elaborate calculations. "Come with me, John," he said, but it was too late. Perkins and his team of judges were rechecking the final tabulations. Danny's misfortune at the rifle range had done him in anyway. He knew his chances of winning the competition were gone. Instead, he kept his mouth shut and walked away to look for Mike Pinelli and Doug Cameron on the officers' club veranda.

Sam Chamberlain savored the thrill of mingling with his officers—whiskey glasses in their hands and the pungent smells of sweat and horses in their nostrils—celebrating a cavalryman's arts to nurture a spirit for the day it came to real fighting. Alone on the platform, he felt the heady sensation of being Centaur, an actor on a stage holding their attention by the power of his presence. He spoke to them. "All my life I've waited for the command of a regiment of mounted cavalry. Today I say we've collected all the elements essential to accomplishments that will burn our names into the annals of the U.S. Cavalry."

No longer were they citizen soldiers temporarily called away from home. At this moment they were Centaur's men, each watching his face and looking into his eyes, sensing the bond between them. "I have a strong sense of history in this," he said. "These are fateful days: perhaps the end of a golden era—the horse cavalry and its wonderful way of life. And these are also the first days of an undeclared war." He perceived a straightening of postures and a tightening around the eyes. Many chose this time to sip at their drinks, affirming Centaur's vision. Encouraged by the visible effect of his words, he narrowed his focus. "I don't know at this moment where we'll confront our enemies, but I assure you this regiment will not idle away the coming conflict in the warmth of the Rio Grande Valley." His voice softened ever so slightly. "But we will remember this idyllic period at Fort Brown as a preparation for greatness." He raised his glass, allowing them time to follow his gesture. "To the 124th Cavalry," he toasted.

"The 124th," they answered with the percussive clap of a rifle volley. A mass of men in khaki pressed around the colonel, falling in behind as he led them across the patio to the tables where the judges set up the blackboard under the spreading, moss bedecked branches of a live oak. As they scanned the columns of numbers tallying up the scoring, Centaur referred to the first of several cards prepared by Major Perkins, saying, "I'm gratified to see that, in the matter of completing this difficult course, the lead changed hands many times." Applause, mostly from spectators, answered the announcement immediately, but the lieutenants crowded closer to examine the results and apparently found some discrepancies.

Chamberlain raised his hand for quiet. Carefully, he explained the complexities of determining the standings. "First, remember the final result is determined by adding or subtracting from each officer's elapsed time from start to finish. The scores in the separate events are converted to times to be subtracted from total time."

Major Perkins, the chief judge, interrupted with some whispered information and stepped back. The colonel explained, "The judges inform me there were a number of penalties to apply." He drew Perkins aside and asked some questions about the final scores. Satisfied, he summarized the results in the individual events. "As the timed portion of the competition began, Lieutenant Cameron had the advantage because he won the steeplechase. Lieutenant Flynn led all shooters in the mounted pistol. He was the first to make the river crossings, first to reach the rifle range, and he rode across the finish line first." The CO paused momentarily, frowning at a group discussing private bets placed the morning of the competition. "In the rifle competition, Lieutenant Robert Helmcamp posted the highest score." Centaur pointed to the delighted Helmcamp, an accomplished marksman, and shifted to his next card to announce the official results. "You know this is a taxing test of military skills and fitness. We saw some uneven results at the beginning." Laughter scattered through the crowd with a few derisive jibes at the expense of the two who fell out of the competition after the quarter mile dash from the starting line.

"But adding in the penalties dictated by the rules, the standings changed. Lieutenant Flynn took two hefty penalties on the rifle range: They dropped him to third place." He beckoned Danny to him and shook his hand. "Fine work," he said in a quiet tone.

George Kincaid raised his arms above his head, crowing, "So much for the great Flynn."

Sensing the tensions developing, Centaur hurried through his announcements. Warmly, he congratulated Bob Helmcamp, one of the Texans' favorites, as a surprise runner-up, to enthusiastic applause. Setting his note cards aside, Colonel Chamberlain moved proudly through the program. "I want to congratulate the winner, the one who exemplifies our motto, 'I strike quickly.'" He spoke it as it appeared on the regimental colors, "'*Golpeo Rapidamente.*' Our winner is Lieutenant George Kincaid."

The winner received only an aenemic round of polite applause. If the lack of enthusiasm displayed by the men he out-performed troubled the outspoken Kincaid, he didn't show it. He swaggered forward to accept the colonel's congratulation, chin outthrust, hands waving, smiling broadly through the obligatory pose for photographers.

Still troubled, John Sowell whispered to Doug Cameron, "Jeez, that son of a bitch isn't the winner! Flynn doesn't want to contest it, but Kincaid cheated out there where there weren't any judges. I saw it 'cause I expected he'd do something shady if he got a chance. Hold my beer. I'm going up there to report it."

Cameron held Sowell by the arm. "Stop, Johnny. It's too late. The show's over." The soggy silence meeting the announcement of Kincaid as the winner had thrown a suffocating blanket of disappointment on Centaur's historical moment, smothering the surge of excitement evident only a few minutes earlier, and a few of the Texans found reasons to leave early.

Danny hung his head, studying the battered and muddy toe of his right boot. He looked over to where the rightful winner stood, waving weakly at him. "I feel terrible for Bob Helmcamp, though. He's the one getting screwed," he said sadly to Cameron and Pinelli.

Robbed of a cause for celebration, a clutch of junior officers remained behind, surrounding the reliable Major Perkins, who embodied credibility in analyzing the political workings of the army, while somehow being in tune with his junior officers' thoughts. Scraps of spontaneous speculation began to fly. "It makes sense to leave us here, doesn't it, sir? We're not going to fight panzers with horses."

Another suggested something different. "Maybe we'll get tanks. The tactics are similar, if you think about it."

Still another, an optimist, they would call him, said, "They'll always need some horses for scouting, probably for communication too."

To all these, the circumspect Perkins had no answers. "I flatly don't know yet," they heard him say time after time.

Now, all Danny wanted was to avoid the emotional speculation and any further discussions of Kincaid's questionable behavior. Drained by the combined experiences of his trip to Fort Reno and the last two gut-wrenching days, he drifted out to the edge of the veranda to watch the trolley shuttling along the slender cable on its way across the Rio Grande from Mexico. Molly would be expecting a call, but first he wanted a stout drink of whisky to wash away the bitter taste of the competition. "I'll be at the telephone booth in the hallway," he said to the white-coated waiter.

chapter

ELEVEN

Washington: In a Navy Day speech, President Roosevelt reported he has a map of Hitler's plan for South and Central America.

"Teniente," said the waiter holding a tray with a white envelope. No drinks. Nothing from the bar: only the envelope. *"El Teniente Rojo,"* it read, written in bold, purposeful strokes, but unmistakably a woman's hand. Ah. The red lieutenant! Who else could the red lieutenant be? What the hell was this all about? Suspecting a practical joke, Pinelli or maybe Cameron, he thought, Flynn pretended to be busy with the telephone for a moment, to deprive them of the satisfaction of seeing him tearing into the envelope.

"Who's it from?" he asked cautiously.

Sixto shrugged. He was new at the club. He didn't know who sent it, but he took pains to explain how it happened to get to the bar. "Matamoros," he said, pointing to the far side of the river, "It came with the drinks."

Flynn went through his own pantomime, wanting to be sure the question was understood. "From Mexico? On the wire?"

"Si, Teniente, si," the dark-haired waiter answered, smiling and nodding.

Danny walked away from the booth and took a seat in a tall-backed, upholstered chair screened from most parts of the club by an ornamental tree in one of the club's terra-cotta pots. This wasn't the work of a prankster lieutenant—the cream-colored stationery was too expensive. Cautiously, he opened the envelope and withdrew a folded sheet of paper. "Please meet me at the Matamoros bullring on Sunday—shady side. Be early, if you can," it urged. A graceful swirl substituted for a signature.

Sixto found Danny seated at a small table, with a telephone before him, still studying the mysterious letter. The waiter held his fingers as if he were holding the letter near his nose, enjoying the faint hint of a scent clinging to it. Smiling broadly, he asked, "The letter, Teniente? It's good?"

A noncommittal shrug turned out to be the best answer that came readily to mind. The message confused him. He didn't know who sent it or why, and his Spanish was too feeble for him to explain to the helpful waiter. Trying his best to appear unaffected, he paid for his drink, returned the card to its envelope and tucked it into the pocket of his shirt. Alone with his thoughts and the amber Irish elixir, he sat in the chair with his mind running furiously. The competition and its disappointing outcome jumbled his thoughts with a flood of new ones brought by the unexpected note. The level in his glass receded steadily without releasing a single answer. All right, he told himself—delicate, scented stationery, feminine script. The note was certainly from a woman. For certain, it wasn't from Molly; why would she go to the trouble of having it sent from Mexico? If the note were genuine, then who in the world could have sent it? How would he find her? Should he even try to find her? After emptying the glass, he left the club and walked the short distance to his quarters for a shower before driving to Molly's, but this letter stuck fast in his mind. Whoever wrote the note knew him, or at least what he looked like, and that he would probably be in the club after the competition.

That's it! It could have been one of those spectators at the crossing. A woman sent an anonymous note to a redheaded lieutenant who had been leading in the competition. Or was it somebody over there wanting to knock a soldier on the head and rob him?

By late Sunday morning, none of the other lieutenants had claimed responsibility for a joke, or the scented invitation on his desk which fired the timeless urges that inspire young men to impulsive actions that leave old men shaking their heads—but smiling understandingly.

After making an excuse to Molly, Danny left the post and walked across the bridge to Matamoros, hailing the first taxi he saw, rushing to meet a woman he did not know, at a bullfight in a foreign country. For the briefest of moments, he questioned himself, a thing that didn't happen often, and he felt an uneasiness stirring. Should he have discussed this with one of the other lieutenants: one with some experience in Matamoros—or anybody— even Cameron, or Pinelli?

Bumping along unfamiliar streets in the battered taxi, he wished he had sought some advice. Earlier, it occurred to him to go armed, but the .45 was so bulky. Besides, he was pretty sure he'd get into trouble for taking it to Matamoros. A knife? No, he wasn't good with a knife. At the prospect of being alone in the streets without some kind of protection, Danny felt uneasy and vulnerable, suspicious of a plot, plain and simple, by somebody who saw him from across the river.

Then too, there were the lies. Cameron waved good-bye to him on the way out, assuming, Danny guessed, he would be with Molly as usual. But it wasn't really lying and, for god's sake, Doug Cameron didn't need to know everything he did. It was another thing with Molly. She'd done her best to take his awkward explanation with good grace. While her lips said, "Of course, Danny. I understand things come up without much notice," her entire being told him his awkward excuse hurt her deeply. If Danny didn't want her to know exactly what he was going to do, she knew it must be a powerful enticement that lured him away from a luxurious Sunday afternoon of lovemaking. He felt like a rat, and the feeling wouldn't go away. What if something happened to a rat covering his tracks with lies? Would his friends care?

The taxi driver agreed to take him—not quite to the *Plaza de Toros*, but to a place nearby. This way Danny could mingle with the pedestrian traffic for a short distance while watching people streaming toward the plaza. If he could scan the assigned meeting place unnoticed, he might see her first and recognize her. For the dozenth time, he went over the possibilities: He was meeting someone, a woman probably, and she was fluent in English. His red hair would shout his identity to her, a thought that made him even more uncomfortable. He couldn't rid himself of the idea of somebody lurking for him. That kind of thing happened!

Danny became aware of the little tickle along his spine warning him of impending danger, but he convinced himself that if he encountered something he couldn't handle with his fists, he could outrun it. He patted his pockets for something to use in dissuading an assailant—just in case. All he had were his keys and a few coins: not much, but enough perhaps. He transferred them to his right-hand pocket, where they'd be handy to throw in an assailant's face if it came to such a thing. But a few minutes in the fine air of a bright clear day swept away his anxiety, replacing it with a strong feeling of expectancy.

He followed a small group of men in suits walking with women attired in bright, festive colors. They led him through a short narrow street, which after an abrupt turn ushered into a wide plaza way with a view of the bullring itself. It surprised him to find it looking so small and not stone or brick, but a wooden structure in need of a fresh coat of white paint.

Danny guessed the woman he was to meet must be quite near. He saw a kind of kiosk plastered all around with the large brightly colored posters advertising today's *Corrida de*

Toros. He used it as a blind, pretending to be engrossed in reading the names of the matadors while he scanned faces of people gathering early to talk and visit. Impatiently, he abandoned his vantage point near the kiosk and strolled slowly toward the bullring itself. The closer he approached, the noisier the crowd noise became and the greater grew his excitement. Groups of bullfight aficionados argued energetically in Spanish. Danny recognized a few of the words cropping up as names printed on the posters, which led him to conclude they were arguing the grace and courage of the matadors. Here and there, small crowds of American tourists visited the food vendors' stalls, chattering loudly, happily, enjoying the adventurous feeling of being in a foreign country. He rolled his thoughts over slowly and deliberately, attempting to solve this mystery, coming again to the same bare conclusion; it had to be a woman. Yet almost all the women he saw were accompanied by men.

A soft, low voice from very near at hand startled him. "Lieutenant Flynn, you've come." Somehow, she'd come close enough to touch him without being noticed. "I was afraid you hadn't gotten my invitation," she was saying pleasantly with a faint, but distinct Spanish inflection in her speech. Taken by surprise and unable to find words, Danny turned awkwardly to get a look at this mysterious woman. She took his arm boldly, leading him a few steps out of the crowd streaming toward the entrance. Anyone watching would have taken them to be friends: very good friends.

The American lieutenant, who only a few minutes before feared an attack, found himself being inspected by a fair-skinned beauty, elegant in the formal apparel affected by Mexican ladies on traditional occasions like this corrida. A *mantilla* draped over a tall, ornate comb in her black hair added an illusion of height while partially obscuring her features. A few sunburned tourists and several Mexican men in suits slowed as they passed to admire the grand lady and her copper-haired companion. A short, roundish man, one of a mixed group of strollers, recognized her. He bowed slightly in passing and greeted her, "*Buenos Tardes,* Dona Marina." She returned the man's greeting with a regal nod.

Tilting her head back and to one side, this Dona Marina briefly viewed the American soldier critically and admiringly through smiling, strikingly green eyes, coquettishly obscuring her features behind an elaborately carved ivory fan. "Ah, but you're a fine figure of an Irish man, Daniel Flynn," she said with an appreciation approaching boldness. With these words, the Spanish notes in her voice gave way to a broad Irish accent. She snapped her fan closed, revealing a bright, impish smile. As yet, Danny hadn't said a word of recognition. Dona Marina stepped a bit closer, looking him full in the face. "Daniel Flynn. Can you not remember me from the Bantry Maid? From the Upper Room!" she urged, lowering her eyes with a hint of wounded pride.

The Bantry Maid! This woman was at home here in Mexico. She was one of them, absorbed in the culture. And yet...she was neither Mexican nor Texan, and not so Irish either. Dear God, could this be the green-eyed hellion with whom he clashed in New York? Ah, so much had happened since then. He tried to imagine this softly spoken, feminine creature as the spitfire in laborer's denim and stout boots. Yes, she was. This was the very woman who had entered the Upper Room with her lustrous black hair hidden under a flat cloth cap!

He stammered, "You're, ah, Miss Gallamore."

She allowed herself a slight smile. "Maureen will do quite well...Danny." In a whisper barely loud enough to hear, she confessed, "I didn't dare use my name in my invitation, for fear you might not come."

Now he felt foolish for not recognizing her, and a recollection of the oath in the Upper Room stabbed into his memory. This couldn't be a coincidence, he told himself. At the moment, did it matter?

"But I'm here," he said. "Put it down to my spirit of adventure." Not very graceful, but the best he could do. "And I think I'm glad I came. But, if you'll forgive me for being direct, you have some explaining to do, Maureen."

"Oh?" She said it softly, suggesting she might have been hurt by his directness.

Faith! The woman was beautiful. It was hard to look at her and think clearly. "Maureen. I'll admit I was surprised to get a message delivered across the Rio Grande with my whiskey. Is the trolley to the Fort Brown bar your personal mail service?" No more had he said it, but he regretted the question.

Apprehensively, Dona Marina (for she strongly felt her Spanish persona at the moment) toyed with her large, elegant fan, opening and closing it as the whim struck her. Her uncertainty wasn't something she could explain easily. She took his arm boldly, guiding him toward the entrance. For a time they walked slowly through the gathering crowd, without speaking. A little later, she began to speak hesitantly of herself, more to explain her familiarity with the people of Matamoros than to answer his questions. "I came to Mexico with an introduction and quite naturally, I've developed some acquaintances."

Acquaintances! In Danny's mind her terse explanation didn't begin to cover the questions it raised. "You certainly have," he agreed in a voice hard with edginess. What kind of contacts must she have if her notes could be delivered across an international boundary to the Fort Brown Officers' Club? And how did she, or had it been her acquaintances, know he was there? He seriously doubted those contacts were the same people greeting her politely and respectfully here in the crowd.

She mentioned her presence in Mexico as they made their way to the bullring, but the words came with difficulty, and the accents and cadences of her adopted Spanish emerged again in her speech. "Actually, much reaches me about what happens on both sides of the river, she said," and immediately she saw the suspicions return to Danny's face. For a time she walked in silence, before addressing his questions from a fresh perspective. "I found the road along the river blocked by the police, so I parked my car out of curiosity and watched. By chance, I was there as you crossed and re-crossed the river at the change-over place outside Matamoros. Some competition, I believe—you were required to change horses between crossings of the *Bravo*?" She laughed brightly, a delightfully easy laugh that pleased him. With this scrap of a reason for her to know about his life on the other side of the border, he relaxed. She took his arm again with a coy glance, saying, "I think you look very handsome and manly in your uniform and riding boots—especially dripping wet."

Disarmed still further by her flattery, Danny's wariness and suspicion of Maureen's unexplained presence in Mexico dissipated, replaced by a sense of imminent adventure in this beguiling woman's company. "I've never been to a bullfight before," he confessed shyly, tearing his eyes from her to take in the brightly colored banners festooned over the rugged exterior beams of the bullring. His admission wasn't surprising. How would an Irish boy from New York have any way to experience anything like this?

"Ah," she said, with the soft Spanish inflections returning, "So you do not know the traditions of the Corrida de Toros?"

"Not a bit."

"No?" she pouted, searching his face. But Danny knew she wasn't disappointed. The excitement glowed in those expressive green eyes. Truly, as they approached the wooden temple of Spanish culture transported to Mexico, he followed willingly. This woman speaking of the corrida and calling the border river by its Mexican name was not the one who asked to be called Maureen. Momentarily, she allowed her hip to press against him, lightly, but firmly enough to tell him it was intentional. "Come with me," she said, leading the way through the entry, up the short ramp into the full light. It was Dona Marina, certainly, who hesitated involuntarily at the first sight of the sunbathed circle of sand where the afternoon's savage artistry would be enacted. He felt her distance herself from him—a matter of inches—consciously absorbing the electric hum of excitement created by her arrival. She turned slowly, regally, feeling the eyes of spectators following her. This woman must be very well known to receive instant recognition by the patrons scattered among the prestigious seats near the wall.

With her hand on his arm, Maureen allowed Danny to lead her in a stately progress, step by step to the wall encircling the golden sand. He barely noticed himself being guided by her subtle pressures on his arm. Frequently, she paused for brief exchanges with acquaintances while her redheaded gringo companion stood mute at her side, awkward in an unfamiliar role. Maureen played her part gracefully and instinctively, speaking animatedly in these ritual conversations, switching easily between the Mexican dialect and Castilian Spanish, and then to English, depending on the listener. Once she and Danny took the seats reserved for her in the lowest tier, she devoted her concentration to instructing him in this ancient ritual, leaning closely to him so that he could hear. His concentration on her tutorial faded occasionally, dissolving in faint traces of jasmine. Danny had long since succumbed to Maureen's spell by the time the trumpets blared the ancient, unvarying messages announcing the opening rituals of the corrida.

A large gate in the wall on the opposite side swung open to admit a dignified horseman wearing a long black coat. "The *alguacil*," she said of the figure leading a parade of the men who would be the active performers of the traditional artistry. Behind the horseman, the three matadors, majestic beings, each resplendent in a splendidly ornamented cape, moved into the sunlight with the lithe, self-assured stride only a matador can affect. Each man's manner exuded an unmistakable grace and courage—his physique accentuated by his "suit of lights," a richly decorated short jacket and tightly fitting *talleguia*. "Never pants. Not even pantaloons," she told him in a quick aside—and for a time she ignored everything but the matadors, leaving Danny to derive, as best he could, the roles of the assistants who followed.

The indispensable *banderilleros* entered next, attired similarly to the matadors, but in subdued colors and with far less adornment. Again Dona Marina explained, "They carry those *banderillas*" to be used at the *matador's* direction. She made a pantomiming motion to show how the *banderillero*, racing out at the matador's bidding, approached the bull, placing the short, decorated sticks, each with a barbed blade affixed, into the animal's powerful neck muscles. Danny, whose only references were the vivid images of the posters displayed outside the Plaza, found it difficult to grasp all she was describing. He hadn't ever actually seen a fighting bull, only those domesticated animals on the ranches along the Rio Grande, but the excitement this bewitching woman felt in the unfolding of this drama suggested an immensely powerful animal possessed of a kind of primeval magnetism. She was saying, "But first, these men will put the bull through a few passes, so the matador can assess the bull's courage and learn how he charges." As she spoke, her posture instinctively adopted the graceful tension of a matador's manner, and her voice took on an even stronger, more alluring Spanish timbre. Danny eyed the parade with interest, but his attention fixed mostly on her in the hope she would turn her green eyes back to him. But for the moment, at least, she remained transfixed by the pageantry. "Look." She pointed to the mounted horsemen carrying long wooden lances. "If the matador finds it necessary, these riders use the long lance to help prepare the bull for his artistry with the cape and sword," she said, breathing in growing excitement as the moment of truth approached. The narcotic effect of her jasmine scent overwhelmed his interest in the *picadores* and the elaborate course of the opening pageantry.

Then the procession was over. Dona Marina sat erect and attentive, lost in another world with a single man on the floor of the arena. The senior matador, who would take the first bull, stood motionless in profound silence, alone at the undisturbed center of a smooth circle of sand.

In a formalized gesture, at once graceful and workmanlike, he removed his voluminous, splendidly embroidered parade cape, folded it with a flourish, and approached the wall to select a special place where he would leave it until his afternoon's work was done. The matador came so near! Danny could see every detail of his sunburned features and hear the courtly cadences of his speech. With evident pleasure, he hung the cape over the wall directly before Dona Marina and removed his black *montero* from his head as a gesture of respect, to the thunderous approval of the crowd. Applause and shouting reverberated through the steeply tiered circle of seats. As if she were thoroughly accustomed to this kind of favor, Maureen nodded to her admiring *torero* and wished him luck. He bowed formally and turned his attention to the entrance of the first *toro bravo*.

"Watch there," Maureen said, pointing daintily. An explosive roar filled the arena before Danny could follow her direction. The gate slammed down behind the heels of the bull bursting into the bright sunlight—strong and agile, but quite small, he thought. To his surprise it wasn't black, but brown with a bit of white mottling. She slipped her arm around his and held it tightly. "That bull weighs over a thousand pounds, and he's looking for something—anything—to charge," she said, speaking in a faraway, aroused voice.

Briefly the bull ran free, ruling the sand, brandishing his intimidating horns with a rising awareness of impending danger. Tearing tracks across the face of the packed sand, the bull sought a visible enemy, something to destroy. In the eyes of hundreds in their seats, the brown animal grew larger and more imposing.

The matador stepped from his place behind the wall, signaling his assistants to begin their work. The banderilleros completed their testing passes with their capes and looked to the matador for his signal of satisfaction. At this defining moment the crowd hushed in anticipation of the emotional, artistically stimulating byplay testing the skill and nerve of the matador against the inbred bravery of the bull.

From that moment the matador controlled the eyes and emotion of thousands and claimed the rapt attention of Dona Marina, in whose veins coursed the blood of an Irish soldier and a Spanish great-grandmother. In total absorption she was drawn into the drama on the sand, mesmerized by the solicitous skill the matador lavished on each pass, allowing the bull to demonstrate his bravery. In these moments, her breathing grew short and heavy, her nostrils dilated. The ritual climax in the sacrificing of the bull was at hand, and until it was consummated, nothing would interrupt her sensual excitement.

Through the afternoon's cycle of presentation and sacrifice, of blaring trumpets and ritual, neither Danny nor Maureen gave a fleeting thought to the events that brought them together here in Mexico. When they spoke at all, it was of the stimulating drama unfolding before them, her voice trembling more huskily with each new bull presented. Danny felt genuine appreciation for the bravery and athletic skill of the men in the ring. Something in the earthy essence of the corrida awakened primitive pagan stirrings in his Celtic soul, but his grasp of the tradition could not extend far enough to balance his pity for an animal fighting against impossible odds. None of that mattered, really. Instead, his awareness fixed intensely on his aroused companion—on her eyes darting between the drama being played on the sand and the American Lieutenant at her side. Danny, giddily drunk in a warm, invisible cloud of her musky scents and fragrances, felt himself losing track of the whirl of bulls, fanfares and the deadly artistry of the matadors. He saw it all, but his consciousness was of Maureen's expressive green eyes, the hair curling at the nape of her neck and the touch of her hands. His thoughts concentrated increasingly on spiriting her away from the crowd in the Plaza to go somewhere else to satisfy his own stirrings. The place wasn't so important, as long as it was near and soon.

Perhaps the corrida had run its full course. Perhaps it hadn't—Danny didn't know for sure. The only thing certain about their departure from the bullring was her taking him by the hand, leading him hurriedly down ramps and steps and away from the crowd. She gave directions to the taxi driver in Spanish. From the position of the afternoon sun, Danny could tell the taxi was headed generally westward. Other details were lost, except perhaps a street name—Revolucion, maybe, seen in a fleeting instant of awareness, hardly more than a spark reminding him of the importance of knowing where he was being taken. But any thought of practical matters dissipated in the darkening evening. He followed his instincts, pulled her tightly against him, kissing and fondling her hotly and urgently, gratified by her eager responses. Desperately impatient to be alone with her, he paid scant further heed to the route. It could have been only seconds or as long as a half hour by the time the taxi stopped. Maureen paid the driver in pesos. To Danny it looked like a lot of money, and he heard genuine gratitude in the man's, "Muchas gracias, Dona Marina."

Then they were in her building. She led the way through an atrium at the entrance of a place surprisingly lavish for a volunteer in the Cause, far from her native country. He put the thought aside and followed her up the steps. Once inside, Maureen brushed her lips against his momentarily, stepping away from him for an instant to close the door, leaving them in near darkness. She deftly slid a large iron bolt home with a heavy thump.

He heard her breathing and felt her taking his hand, pulling him through the door into her bedroom, where a late-afternoon sun still slanted through the shutters. "A moment, please," she asked shakily in a breathy voice, and snatched the tall comb from her hair. Many long pins followed and her black curls tumbled around her neck and shoulders. Wordlessly they undressed with trembling hands, each pulling insistently at the other's resisting buttons and snaps, tossing their clothing on a chair. They stood for a moment in anticipation, caressing each other. Danny lifted her in his arms and carried her lightly to the bed.

He'd fallen asleep. The late, red light of the setting sun told him it might have been for as much as an hour. For the first time since Maureen had found him at the corrida, he was acutely aware of his surroundings. He felt for her with one hand, but the place where she lay earlier was now empty. Danny sat upright to find her seated on a chair beyond the foot of the bed, combing her long black hair with a pleased smile, watching him in the mirror. His eyes followed the gentle, graceful curve of her back upward to the neck, where she parted her hair and allowed it to cascade over her breasts. The fading light touched the few errant strands of her newly combed hair with a hint of reddish gold. Steadily but unhurriedly, she stroked with the comb, enjoying the feel of his eyes on her, allowing the spell to linger.

"Come here and lie with me," he said, touching the place beside him with his hand.

"I can't," she said, plaiting her hair in loose braids. "I'm needed north of here tonight." In the failing light he saw she'd already laid out a dark, simple dress like those the country women wore. The questions rushed back again. Who was this Maureen Gallamore? Not Dona Marina at the moment, certainly, but why was she here? Seeing the questions on his face, she whispered a brief explanation. "My people are waiting for me."

He rose from the bed without speaking and stood behind her, touching her with his fingertips. She moved slightly to caress him with her back, and he held her closely. They watched themselves in the mirror, each with their own thoughts. If she had to leave, so must he, because by daybreak he would be leading his platoon into the flat rangelands north of Fort Brown, but leaving Maureen Gallamore at this moment was a thing he hated more than anything. She took his left hand and held it between both of hers. Her eyes sought his with a questioning shadow flitting away, and she moved his hand to her breast, tempting him. "And when will you be coming back to me, Danny?" she breathed.

"Soon," he said, his voice trembling with emotions spinning madly between lust for her body and urgency to learn of her purposes for being in Mexico.

"Tomorrow, then," she urged. "I'll be back about nightfall."

His mouth went dry with the lustful thrill of the very suggestion. Tomorrow, he thought of her soft nakedness, savoring the prospect of being with her again. In a torment of disappointment, he closed his eyes. "I can't be here tomorrow, love. Tomorrow my platoon will be in the river bottoms for two days patrolling." Oh, he wanted to be with this tempting Irish creature holding him closely and pressing her hips against him. "Wednesday, then?" he offered, swallowing away the dryness in his mouth.

"Yes, Wednesday," she whispered, kissing away anything else he might have wanted to say.

chapter

TWELVE

Washington: Proposing lend-lease to England, FDR tells the Congress of four
freedoms: of Speech and of Worship, and freedoms from want and fear.

The first surprise hit First Platoon well before sunrise. Instead of a one-day operation, something of a training exercise as the preliminary order directed, they'd be out for
most of a week. The change in plans surprised Captain Franklin, the E Troop commander
too. His earlier briefing to Danny was, "Your platoon has been out of the loop for a couple
of weeks—with the special trip to Fort Reno and all these other things. Major Perkins feels
your platoon needs extra work to bring them up on a level with the rest of the regiment—at
least a couple of short out and back patrols—like your first one."

"Things change," said the captain from S-2, opening his briefing book. "If you're
expecting an apology for the change in plans, you won't get it here." He was one of those
who still thought of the railroad journey to the remount station as a pleasure excursion.
"We can't afford to coddle you anymore. Even E Troop platoons have to pull their share of
the load."

A sudden flood of illegal river crossings was taxing the Border Patrol to its limits. The
illegals weren't Mexicans, but Germans, so the army had been called in for hot and heavy
work along the river. Danny learned at the same time Walter Franklin did that E Troop—

all three platoons—would be moved upriver along the Rio Grande to help put a stop to these crossings. This operation would be a significant departure from last time, when they mostly kept to the roads under the assumption that the mere presence of mounted army patrols would dissuade the attempted insertion of spies. This time they'd be working right down in the thick underbrush in the bottomland, right to the river itself.

Already, the troopers were loading their horses into long, motorized vans. The veteran Texans knew about transporting horses in these cavernous vehicles they called portees—but Danny hadn't ever seen them in use. Each platoon would be dropped at a different location, to set up separate camps. Trucks would come from Fort Brown several times during the week to resupply them. Every few minutes Danny felt his mind slipping away to frantic thoughts about the Irish beauty waiting for him in Matamoros. Five days! Maureen would be expecting him. How would he get word to her?

A sergeant from Headquarters Troop stressed a vital point: "The first supply trucks won't be coming to resupply you at your campsites until late Tuesday. Before you leave, be damn sure the rations and fodder you need for the first two days are actually in the portees."

Walter Franklin and his lieutenants worked together quietly, coordinating their maps with the larger display on the office wall, preparing for the major's briefing. A five-day patrol by an entire troop represented a new wrinkle in operations for the 124th. Major Perkins would do the briefing himself to be sure they got it right. Pinelli and Cameron worked calmly and efficiently, sharing their recollections of that part of the valley from earlier experience, but the junior lieutenant fidgeted and fumbled, making foolish errors in data transposition, sometimes staring mindlessly into the distance for long periods.

The major came in early with a folder of papers under his arm, walking slowly among the map tables to assess E Troop's planning before he began his briefing. "Get yourself together, Lieutenant Flynn," he challenged. "This patrol should be nothing for the man who took the train to Fort Reno," he needled.

If only they knew, thought Danny, correcting some erroneous notation on a map.

Whether the three lieutenants were prepared or not, Major Perkins began the briefing by switching on the little reading light attached to the lectern.

"They want us to maintain coverage from here."—Perkins touched his pointer to the map at a point near the town of Mission—"to here," this time north, about halfway to Rio Grande City: about sixty miles altogether. According to Major Perkins, the Border Patrol was being remarkably closemouthed about what kind of activity they were expecting. "I don't think they trust us to do anything but make noise and raise dust," he said. Franklin and the lieutenants chuckled nervously at the major's little joke.

But they were running late. "Get these coordinates now, people," insisted Perkins. "First Platoon, we're going to drop you at this little crossroads here." He tapped with the pointer at a point where the road approached the river. "You have the exact positions, I believe," he said, looking to Franklin to verify his assumption. "Carry on, then, Captain," said Perkins.

The way Franklin arranged E Troop's coverage of their assigned area, First Platoon would be the northernmost of the three platoons. If Major Perkins didn't appreciate what Flynn had accomplished in taking the trip to Fort Reno, Walter Franklin did. First Platoon deserved a little slack. He gave Danny some help in getting his maps prepared. "It should look something like the place where you found the vaquero with the case of appendicitis. You'll recognize the same sort of windmill, the usual pens, and so forth. That's where you'll camp." The idea, Franklin said to all three of his lieutenants, was to patrol the riverbank, making themselves visible to interested observers on the other side. He left unsaid who the observers might be. To be getting serious about border crossings so far south was in itself something of a surprise. The lower river attracted fewer illegal crossings because the water usually ran deeper, and the quicksand was a hell of a lot more prevalent nearer the Gulf than farther upstream. So either the Border Patrol must have learned something special, or they were having the 124th fill holes.

Major Perkins didn't usually involve himself in a troop commander's business, but this request from the Border Patrol wasn't very specific, or perhaps not thought through well enough. He decided to spend a little time supervising E Troop's preparations, taking far more personal pains than he usually would. He pointed to places on the map where colored pins marking known fordable stretches of river became more closely spaced as the pointer moved north and the water depth decreased. They were to inspect every inch of riverbank for every crossing they could find—and report the coordinates. "Spend your time moving near the banks—on both sides of the river—where you find the places obviously being used as crossings." Speaking directly to the lieutenants, the major gave careful directions. "Not more than fifty yards from the river when you're across on the Mexican side." He saw Flynn's eyes wandering away from the map. "Understand, Lieutenant Flynn?" he barked to shock the dreamy lieutenant out of his reverie. In a confidential tone, he let them know that this direction to "leave hoofprints in Mexico" was from him personally. "This is to let them know we're in the valley, waiting for them."

Perkins left E Troop with some words of caution: "I want you to put some people down here on the river at night to watch. Don't pick a fight. Be particularly careful, because if anybody is crossing, it'll probably be Mexicans, and we're not specifically interested in them. Gringos are another matter. The Border Patrol wants a radio call if we see gringos coming across."

After taking the horses up north, Danny had reason to think he knew a lot about his troopers and how they responded to challenges. But every trooper in First Platoon felt a bit edgy today. Perhaps it was being dropped in the tangled bottomland of the Rio Grande with a real chance of being shot that generated the sense of excitement. Sergeant Wieczorek and Lieutenant Flynn had a lot to get worked out between them. The sergeant's nose still showed swelling from a recent job of surgical repair work performed at the hospital. Most of the time they worked together acceptably, but stiffly, feeling each other out, working on ways to make the platoon work smoothly without open friction. The troopers didn't talk much about it, but they realized this operation was the first independent work since the incident on the train and an explosion could easily erupt. Would the platoon sergeant carry out his duties as Elwin Wieczorek maintained things should work, or would he accept the lieutenant as the man in command? Perhaps the most important question might was: Could the sergeant put his public humiliation behind him?

The sun shone high in the east before the portees rolled to a halt to unload First Platoon with its horses and gear, plus several days' worth of rations and fodder. If a confrontation were to occur, it would be here in the quiet of this desolate place. Not right away, perhaps, but well after the dust plumes raised by the departing portees disappeared.

Lieutenant Flynn waited until the horses were led away to the picket line and the supplies inventoried to wave the drivers on their way. Now, free of outside distractions, he turned to face his platoon gathered in a silent group, waiting. "Form 'em up and report, Sergeant," the lieutenant ordered.

"Yes, sir," said the platoon sergeant, saluting. No trouble here. Taking a few seconds to muster his men, Weiczorek reported, "All present and accounted for, sir."

"Take charge, Sergeant," Danny said crisply. He opened his map case on an improvised table and made a show of working on locating their camp accurately. Actually, he was eavesdropping, listening for signs of trouble.

Garza stepped away from the rest of the platoon. "*Teniente?*"

"Yes?" Danny looked up impatiently at the dog robber. Garza of all people didn't need any special direction in getting his work done. He nodded. "Go ahead."

Garza knew he could communicate with the lieutenant better, sometimes, without speaking. The diminutive dog robber rolled his eyes around, taking in the vaqueros' campsite. It offered the usual primitive facilities: a windmill, cistern and a fire ring. Handling pens too. In the same manner, he drew Danny's attention to the bags of grain and the modest pile of crated field rations. "Pretty thin pickin's eh, sir?"

Well, yes, the pickings were indeed pretty meager, if that was all they had to last them until they were re-supplied. Plainly, the dog robber had something in mind. "What's on your mind, PFC Garza?" Danny resorted to the formality to make his orderly aware the *teniente* knew when he was being led on.

Garza turned away to take in a broad perspective of the bleak little campsite. Here was his sculptor's clay, and he would shape it into something worthwhile. "How 'bout if I stay here while you and the sergeant get the work started in the river bottom? I'll get this place organized, sir."

"Well, I believe y'have a little of the leprechaun in you," laughed Danny appreciatively. What Garza had in mind, he couldn't imagine, but to have a trooper volunteering to set up a camp was a novelty worth a gamble. "All right, find the platoon sergeant for me, and then you're in charge of organizing the camp."

Flynn rode with Wieczorek, searching for the nearest ford, speaking civily, working out a plan for locating all the fords in the twisting section of river assigned to them. Afterward, the sergeant rode downstream with Bednarski and Zientek toward Second Platoon's area while the lieutenant moved upstream with Bohuslav and Moore toward a point opposite the Mexican city of Reynosa to have a look at things.

The work of navigation was a damn sight harder than last time, when they worked along the roads as much as possible. Today, down in the lower bottoms near the riverbank, where some of the thickest, meanest undergrowth in Texas grew in thickets that would intimidate an armadillo, they found the work exhausting. At the pre-dawn briefing, Major Perkins used a familiar saying about this part of Texas. "Everything in those thickets either scratches, scrapes, stabs or stinks." Conceivably, a man might be able to get through the dense, thorny tangles where a hundred kinds of mean underbrush could slice like a knife or inflict nasty punctures, without knowing the animal trails—but he might kill himself doing it. The cruel joke was that Perkins had far understated the cruelty of the conditions.

Danny guessed that nobody, not even a man desperate to avoid detection, could go far without using some sort of established trail: even one worn over years and years by wild animals and freely ranging cattle. Through his glasses, it looked no better on the Mexican side, but he wanted to be sure. The barbed humor that spread through the regiment—about First Platoon clearing the road to allow a car full of spies to speed past—still stung. "We're going to try to work our way through this stuff, staying within two hundred yards of the river," he told his two young troopers. "If there's a way through, I want to know about it."

For their part, Bohuslav and Moore thought they could learn to like the lieutenant and they approved of the way he put the platoon sergeant in his place; but way down deep, they weren't sure what to expect when this city kid from up north was faced with having to cope with the matted brush. Until they learned through experience how he acted out here in the field, they meant to give him a wide berth. No telling what kind of behavior would set him off like that night on the train.

When he ordered them into those hellish thickets, they went, not so much without question as because the lieutenant was right behind them. The prickly pear menaced with plate-sized leaves armed with long yellow spines. Leather chaps, the kind the vaqueros wore like a second skin, might have helped, but he didn't think they would truly help unless the horses were protected too. The animals shied away from the stuff, so Danny had the troopers dismount for a try at picking their way through, leading their mounts. But he saw no particular improvement in that scheme either. He found that walking gave away the advantage of height of eye that might have helped to see potential openings through the cactus. After an excruciating half hour in the heat, sweating and cursing biting insects and painful stab-wounds and cuts from spines and grass with razor-like edges, they hadn't been able to make much more than a hundred yards. The upstream end of the area he planned to reconnoiter still lay far to the north. Wiping the sweat off his face, Danny decided that if he and his two native Texans couldn't get through the thickets, he could assume most of the riverbank to be impassable. "Let's move away from the river a little more," he said to Moore and Bohuslav, turning away from the impenetrable growth.

"I'm f'r that," sir," said one of the troopers. They knew they'd be able to find a little shade farther up the bank, under the ebony trees. Lieutenant Flynn hadn't appreciated their value before. One thing about the ebonies, or *ebanos,* as the locals called them, they were the tallest trees around and useful for climbing to get a look at the flattish bottomland. They grew in groves, creating a canopy dense enough to create a small clearing more or less free of the nastiest stuff. In fact, a man could make a respectable progress, going from one ebano's shade to another, but the big trees didn't grow everywhere.

Where there were no ebanos, they worked even farther away from the river, moving toward thinner, less-threatening stuff, until they could move more or less parallel to the river at an acceptable rate, but by this time they were a few hundred yards from the stream. What would Major Perkins do if he were in this fix? Danny asked himself. Move away as they'd already done. Nobody, not soldiers, spies or even the native Mexicans could get through that murderous matted stuff near the river. Nobody.

Flynn and his troopers did find trails that showed some promise. Exploring the narrow little paths on foot, they found four places that looked as if they might be useful as fords. Their maps showed only two. All four were well hidden in the brush. Presumably an agent could stay undercover long enough on the Mexican side to reach the river safely and then, once on the American side, get away from it rapidly without being seen. Three were located near clearings used by vaqueros and herdsmen to collect their animals, and two had primitive roads or dirt tracks leading almost to the water. All four showed signs of regular use. Danny marked his maps so the ones in Captain Michael's office at Fort Brown could be updated.

The lieutenant and his two troopers stopped to rest at a settlement so small, the army maps didn't even give it a name. Its only buildings were a tiny adobe church, actually more of a shrine since it had been built as an open building without a door, and a modest building of adobe and wooden poles built in the welcome shade of three ebony trees. He guessed it to be the general store for the people around here. The proprietor, who spoke some English, told Danny the people who lived there called the place Los Ebanos and that the soldiers were welcome to rest their horses. The store had gotten a little ice earlier, the proprietor said. Danny bought cold Coca-Colas, which they drank sitting on the ground in the shade, making a meal from the rations sacks tied to their saddles. No need to go any farther. "Reynosa is only a little way upstream, across the river," Danny said, spreading the map on a table and using his fingers as a pair of dividers. "Time to move south toward Second Platoon."

Sergeant Wieczorek waited for the lieutenant and his troopers under a line of leafy trees leaning toward the river, shading the sloping sand almost down to the water's edge. He walked slowly, hands in his pockets, kicking his toe at the sand disturbed by animal tracks. His troopers stripped naked, waded waist deep in the water, laughing and splashing their horses to cool them off.

The two privates with Danny heard the laughter a short distance ahead. Their faces plainly told the lieutenant they wanted to join in the frolic. Danny dismounted, handed Moore the reins of his mount and waved them ahead to join the others. "Give him a little coolin' too," he said, slapping the horse's rump. The lieutenant walked the short distance to where the sergeant waited.

Wieczorek was searching the bank for something. Danny called out, "Find anything of interest?" The sergeant shrugged in a way that suggested he noticed something the lieutenant was missing. Not wanting to risk giving Weech an advantage in his game, Danny made a safe observation, "Looks like the river's been low for a while."

Wieczorek shuffled out of the shade and toward the ford. "Must be two weeks' worth of cavalry tracks around this place," he said. Danny threw him a look that asked what he was getting at. "Well, Lootenan', Firs' Platoon may be out here in troop strength for the first time, but it ain't like the army ain't been here at all. Mebbe it was some'a them people fr'm Fort Ringgold."

No denying the truth of what the man said. The place bore plenty of the prints of shod hooves. Weech offered another observation. "We been lookin' at the mud in these fords all afternoon, and I ain't seen nothin' but horse tracks: heavy horses with shoes—troop horses, I'm purty sure."

The troopers in the river stopped splashing to listen to the conversation. "Sarge is right," one of them piped up.

Wieczorek spat into the scrub growth. "Could be our guys, but I don't know. They been splashin' 'round here so often, evabody on both sides of the river jus' knows to hunker down and wait for th' army to go away." One look at the sergeant expressed the futility he felt in doing this job for the Border Patrol. "That's why the onliest tracks a man can see 'round here are troop horses and goats. We done chased evahbody else away." He took his hat off and scratched his high white forehead and asked a very reasonable question. "How come the Border Patrol knows about the Germans and we don't see nothin' of 'em?" The sergeant didn't expect an answer. Wieczorek turned to watch the men laughing in the water. "Hey. Watch your horse there, Stan," he said to Zientek, swimming carelessly out into the stream, leaving his horse unsupervised. Weech motioned the trooper to collect his mount. "No more water f' him."

For a time Danny looked the place over and trying to discern any intelligence value at all in the deep hoofprints hardening in the drying mud. Wieczorek spoke as if he could read some kind of message in all those tracks, but Danny was skeptical. He heard the goats bleating on the other side and considered riding crossing the river to take a look. The idea enticed him, but Moore had already unsaddled his horse and led him into the river. Wieczorek's place was in the camp supervising setting it up, but Danny didn't want another confrontation, not with four days to go out here in these forbidding river bottoms.

"I'm going up to the camp, Sergeant," Danny said, trying to sound crisp and self-assured. He decided to keep the newly discovered fords to himself, for a while at least. Later he and the sergeant might be able to work out a way to exploit them.

Danny walked alone toward the vanes of the windmill rotating slowly in a whisper of a breeze. The closer he came to the camp, the more certain he became of the unmistakable savory aromas of meat roasting. If the sergeant and the lieutenant were returning with nothing of interest to show for a day's sweltering work riding in the heat, the troopers detailed to set up the camp had been quite successful—especially the lieutenant's dog robber. Primitive as they were, the rancher's facilities cut down the troopers' chores enormously. The livestock-handling pen simplified the job of setting up picket lines, and the wooden planks gave them a handy place for airing blankets. The windmill provided plenty of water. With so much of the work of caring for the horses taken care of, some of the troopers had time to play cards, smoke their hand-rolled cigarettes and drink coffee.

Still a hundred yards away in the brush, Danny got his first view of Garza's miracle from the trail. The diminutive orderly, in baggy peon's trousers and stripped to the waist, supervised two volunteers barbecuing a small goat over coals smoldering in the fire ring. A little sheepishly, the dog robber explained how he came to be dressed as he was. "I borrowed 'em, sir." He jerked his thumb toward his sweaty khaki uniform spread to dry on a low huisache limb. "Uniform's too hot f'r cooking," he said, and turned back to the fire ring with an elaborate show of inspecting the roasting goat, nodding his approval.

Danny took in the snug, neat camp, fumbling for the right questions to ask. He saw bags of oats and fodder sorted and stacked against the pens and a tarpaulin spread over a stack of supplies—rations filched from the barracks kitchens, he guessed. Moore took the lieutenant's horse to the picket line, nominally Garza's job. Flynn felt a growing realization that his platoon had done very well setting up the camp without any supervision from either the sergeant or the lieutenant. "What on earth is all this?" he asked, pointing to the dark green tarp.

"Beer, sir," said Reimers, as if having a load of beer in camp were the most normal thing in the world. Taking the lieutenant's silence as approval, Reimers explained, "It's awfully hot out here and we put some into the portees with the horses and bags of fodder." He watched the platoon commander expectantly.

Danny pulled up the tarp away and counted four cases. Hell, there could be ten times that hidden in the brush. He stalled for time, "Let me think about it," he said, walking slowly around the fire ring, taking a closer look at the general layout of the camp. He saw tents pitched in good order, the platoon guidon hanging limply in the still air—all good signs. Now that he knew about the beer, he searched for other little non-regulation comforts, not intending to make too much of a deal of it. A few sacks of grain for the horses and probably a few extra cases of rations were about all he found. Every good platoon needed a couple of midnight requisitioning specialists. A guitar case caught his eye. Garza's, he knew. He saw these things as ingenuity: nothing to be a hard-ass about. He beckoned to Garza to ask about his hand in provisioning the camp. "And the rest, Pancho? Talk to me."

The industrious orderly showed nothing but pride in his accomplishments. Gesturing vaguely toward the river and generally northward with the unmistakable air of genial hospitality, he explained how things were in this part of the world. "I know this land, sir and a lot of the people—both sides of the river. I write Raymondville as my hometown, but my people live all around here. If they aren't my relatives, I know them from fiestas, or weddings and funerals." He smiled shyly, pointing in the direction of the river. "See, *Teniente*, that way, across the ford a quarter of a mile away from the river itself? Esteban Vasquez has a little house there. When the people want to cross the river to visit or go to a little *fiesta*, they whistle or call to him. If the ford is clear, he whistles back. He brought me the goat and the clothes, and he made me promise we'd police the vaqueros' camp before we leave."

For the time being, the beer was forgotten. Danny leaned with his back against the boards of the cattle pen, arms spread along the top board, not speaking; just listening to his dog robber. Garza picked up a stick to rearrange the coals in the fire ring. Satisfied with the fire, he waved the stick, as a schoolteacher might use a pointer for emphasis at a blackboard—the burning end glowed and smoked in the early evening light. He shared what he knew about the countryside with the lieutenant. "Now, we're going to be up and down the river for the next four days, sir. That's all right—we need practice if we want to be good at it, but nobody's crossed this particular ford in the past two days and nobody's hiding on the other side, waiting to cross." He was sure of all that because, "Esteban told me so."

Danny thought about what he'd just heard from Garza. "What does Esteban say about gringos who speak German?" he asked.

Garza looked gravely into the coals sending up sparks as he poked them absently with his stick again. "Well, sir," he said, sharing more of what he'd learned from Esteban, "They came occasionally, according to a shepherd who kept a flock of goats and watched the ford. Somebody brought them by car and dropped them off on the river road on the other side. Sometimes the furtive gringos wore working clothes like the Mexican workers. Other times they came in workman's dungarees, or in street clothing. Their methods required little finesse or stealth. The country was far too vast to be watched. Most of the time, they hid for a while till it was quiet and the ford looked clear. Then they cross the water and move as fast as they can to the road on this side. Esteban thinks these gringos are picked up over here by another car." Garza poked the sizzling goat browning over the coals with a long-bladed knife lent him by Esteban.

"How much more do you know about this?"

The mercurial Garza had a pleasant way of beginning a sentence with a laugh. He looked over his shoulder at the boyish Gerhard Reimers, a private and perhaps the youngest man in the 124th. He waved him over. "My traveling buddy and I have something to tell you. We think so, anyway." Garza urged the young trooper to "Tell the lieutenant about our trip."

Danny recalled that Garza mentioned that the two did travel together on their first weekend pass, weeks ago. Instead of going to the bars and brothels of Matamoros, the two privates rode north on the river road to visit Vicente Morales, Garza's uncle. They took a bus through the string of towns stretching west along the river from Brownsville, then north toward Rio Grande City, only not quite so far.

The timid, fair-skinned Reimers, almost cherubic with his cheeks burned red in the sun, looked expectantly at Danny, who nodded encouragingly to him. "We was out there on the bus, sir—with nothin' else on the road, and not a house in sight, neither." The young private thought it was funny that the two rode in the last row of seats, with the Mexicans.

He recalled, "Pancho walked up front to ask the bus driver to stop an' let us off, but the driver called him a crazy Mexican and kept driving along."

In his mind, Danny envisioned a straight, dusty road across the broad plain sloping slightly toward the Rio Grande lying a few miles to the west.

Ordinarily painfully shy, Reimers seemed to be enjoying his role as storyteller. "Panch kinda got mad at the way the driver was treating him, so he yelled at the man. Everybody heard it."

Garza had been listening without a word, nodding occasionally to verify the facts. He walked over from the fire ring to embellish the story a little. "That's right, sir. The driver backed up about a quarter of a mile to let us off at a mailbox."

It occurred to Danny it was probably unusual, there in the remote stretches of the valley, for a white bus driver to do something like that for a Mexican kid. Maybe it was the uniform. Reimers's story was unusual too and far more than a simple account of a weekend outing, he recognized. Instead of silence when the lieutenant came around, these troopers were volunteering to talk. Sure, he had Garza to thank for it, but to Flynn it meant the platoon was accepting their Irish Yankee lieutenant.

Several troopers inched closer to hear. Reimers hesitated a second to shape his words before he picked up the story. "There was a little ranch road, just two tracks through the weeds, an' nothin' else anywheres. So we started walking." He recalled for the ragged circle of fascinated troopers that in about ten minutes, they saw a little truck coming from where they thought the river was. Reimers couldn't believe it at the time, he said, but the driver had come looking for Panchito and his army buddy from Fort Brown.

Garza explained, "When they go to the big towns, they use the bus, so they know when it comes. That's why they were coming—to get us." After a brief ride in the back of the truck, they arrived at a ranch house, where they were offered some tortillas and beans to keep the hunger away. Garza's friends loaned them some working clothes and hats, allowing them to leave their army uniforms there at the house.

Later in the afternoon, their hosts took the two young men another three, four miles in their truck down to a trail leading to the river. Reimers picked up the story. "There wasn't anybody there, Lieutenant—not like at the bridge in Brownsville with gates and guards. I was a little nervous about it, but Panch just stripped down buck naked and waded across with his shoes and clothes over his head." The blond soldier laughed at the thought. "I followed him. All I remember is how cool the water felt, and how wide and shallow the river is up there." Reimers held a hand just above his waist to show the water's depth. "It ain't nearly as deep as it is at Fort Brown, sir."

Danny closed his eyes to imagine the scene and how far from reality the thought of an international boundary must seem in a place like that. He asked Garza, "These people with the truck: Are they your relatives?"

"No sir. They're just friends of my uncle's." His usually impish face turned quite serious, and he spoke earnestly, trying his best to get the lieutenant to understand. "See, up there, everybody on both sides of the river knows everybody else. Pretty much, anyway.

Most of the time, it's...ah...ah, what's the word in English? Ah yes, inconvenient, to drive all the way down to some town with a bridge and then back up. They jus' wade the river and go visiting, so that's what we did."

Danny asked, "Does your uncle have land right on the river?"

"No, no, *Teniente*. My uncle ain't exactly a peon, but he don't own a lot of land on the river. We walked up the road a perty good piece before we got to a place where we could hitch a ride."

"Is there a town there?"

"Oh, no, sir. It's no more than a little store with a filling station—for gas." He shook his head to see if Danny understood. He did. "They sell a little food, some beer too—even a Coca-Cola. And people stop to see if anybody needs a lift."

"Not a place with a name, then?" asked Danny.

"Well, no, sir. Closest thing to a town with a church and a coupla stores is, I don't know, ten, twelve miles north."

"Well, what then? Did you wait for a ride?"

"Yes, sir. We waited long enough to get a ride with a farmer going south. But my uncle woulda come up to get us at nightfall if we hadn't gotten there by then."

Danny nodded to encourage the story, listening attentively.

"Gerhard here wanted a beer." He pointed to the fuzzy-cheeked Reimers. "Actually, we both did. We could pay in American money. The place doesn't have a porch, or any shade in front, so we sat on a bench in the back. They keep the doors open, back and front, to let a little breeze come through." His tone became confidential. "About then, a car drove up. They were gringos...but not American. You know what I mean? Big tall men. One's hair was kinda reddish brown, and the other one's looked more like Gerhard's." The orderly waved his hand nonchalantly. "Blond."

Garza tested the roasting goat with the knife, pursing his lips as if trying to recall something. "Funny thing. Here were these people, in Mexico, in an American car with Texas plates, and they were pale." With a wry smile, Garza explained, "In South Texas, even gringos are brown from being out in the sun." He waved the knife in his hand and made a face. "Kinda. Well, these men were sunburned on their faces. Bright red, I mean, like they weren't used to being in the sun. Mostly, though, they were pale. While the owner pumped their gas, they came inside and spread a map. We looked like a couple of orange pickers with our hats pulled down, so we didn't bother them any. They were talking, but I couldn't understand a word they said."

"What?"

"What I'm telling you, *Teniente*, is I couldn't understand them." He passed the story to Reimers again, "But Gerhard could."

The smallish private shifted uncomfortably, but seeing an encouraging gesture from Danny, he began tentatively, "They were speaking German, sir. *Hochdeutch*. We don't talk High German much here in Texas, but I could understand them perty easy. They'uz in a hurry to meet somebody in Navidad, I heard 'em say."

Garza interrupted, "That's the place up the road. The one I was talkin' about."

"One of them said somethin' about wantin' to be at work by tomorrow. They meant the next day."

"Did you hear any more?"

"Not much, sir. They seemed perty relaxed. The one with reddish hair said he'd give a lot to have life as easy as the peons in the back who didn't have anything to do all afternoon but drink beer and take siestas." Reimers grinned broadly at the thought of overhearing those Germans.

In the failing light, Danny watched a flock of Whitewings flying away from their watering stop at the river and heard the voices of the troopers going out to set up their observation posts at the fords. He recognized Bednarski's deep voice grumbling about riding horses in the valley when Hitler was overrunning Europe with tanks. "How many tanks you think we got in the army, Sarge? Six, maybe?"

The little group gathered to hear the story about the Germans didn't drift away when Garza moved away to put his last touches on the roasting goat. To a man, they were vitally interested in learning what the lieutenant was going to do about the beer. They all remembered what happened over the beer in that forlorn little Oklahoma town—but this time it was the dog robber's doing. It was up to the lieutenant to make his decision pretty soon.

Danny could feel their eyes following him, asking him for a decision, so he made one. On not much more than a whim, he said, "If there's beer, let's have some of it. I'm havin'a terrible thirst."

Cool beer in this heat could only mean there had been ice in the portee all day. Contraband beer packed with ice and insulated with bags of fodder: all that, and the lieutenant never noticed. Fully aware he'd been read like a book, Flynn made another decision: He'd walk away and let them enjoy it. "I'll just go over there to write my reports," he said, tapping the notebook in his shirt pocket, and carried away his slab of barbecued goat on a tortilla in one hand and the brown beer bottle in the other. At a discrete distance, he sat with his back propped against a tree stump, enjoying the beer and barbecue, writing his report in the fading sunlight. When the brilliant stars filled the heavens, he listened to Garza tuning his guitar by the fire and let his thoughts wander.

chapter

THIRTEEN

Washington: President Franklin D. Roosevelt issues orders transferring 25 percent of the Pacific Fleet to the Atlantic.

After the day's work was concluded and before night training began, things had gotten quiet at the stables. Horses rested comfortably in their stalls and most of the troopers detailed for stables duty had gone to the mess hall. Colonel Chamberlain found that spending a few minutes with the horses at times like this helped him clear his mind and put the office business behind him. Sometimes he called to have a mount saddled, but not this evening, because he planned to walk for a little workout and maybe to sort out some of the thorny problems troubling him. The quiet sounds and familiar smells of the stables could do that, but there were always things to be learned here too. Years before a wise sergeant told him, "You can tell a lot about a cavalry outfit by visiting the stables: The good ones know how to take care of their horses."

Bypassing the office, the colonel walked to the nearest stable building and let himself in. He would never think of himself as a slave to habit, but on most visits, it was his own horses he went to see first. Under the glow of a few electric bulbs spaced regularly down the length of the barnlike structure, he made out the names lettered neatly on a small sign at each door. At Peggy's stall, he slipped in to offer her an apple. While she enjoyed the little delicacy, he rubbed her flanks and told her how well she could jump. Centaur took a little more time to run his hand over her face and neck. Then just as quietly as he had entered, he slipped out of the stall and methodically checked the latch.

"Evenin', C'unnel," he heard a familiar voice greeting him.

"And a good evening to you, Sergeant Long," he said. "Isn't it a little late for a man of your seniority and influence to be here in the stables?"

"Not if the c'unnel's here too. No sir." They shared a comfortable laugh at the sergeant's little joke. Long drew his pipe from the pocket of his denim trousers and inspected the bowl. He took out his pocketknife, a rather dainty instrument, and opened a short, slim blade worn to a mere steel sliver by frequent applications of a whetstone. With Centaur observing silently, Long delicately carved away an insignificant bit of something from the blackened inner surface of the bowl. Satisfied, he put away the knife, blew noisily through the stem before clamping it in his teeth. Chamberlain loved Long's rituals: From them he could tell when everything was all right, or when it wasn't. Watching him fumbling with his tobacco pouch, he searched his memory for the last time he'd seen Master Sergeant Long in anything but a fatigue uniform.

The man-legend of the horse cavalry had come to Fort Brown to help Sam Chamberlain fulfill his sacred trust. Centaur put it to his old friend this way, "The 124th is destined to make cavalry history, Amos. I'd like you to come down to Brownsville, for a few months maybe, to make sure we do it right." A few phone calls to the right people at the War Department and Long was on his way.

"Are you all settled here, Sergeant?" Chamberlain knew very well Long would recognize the question included the stables as well as his living and working conditions.

"Yessir. Sure am. Ever'body's treatin' me real good," said Long, producing a large kitchen match. He set it alight with a quick swipe across a leg of his denim britches and drew on his pipe to get the tobacco going. Through the billowing clouds of fragrant smoke, he inquired, "Got time to go over and see how good th' hosses we brought in from Fort Reno are lookin'?"

"Lead on," said Chamberlain, following the proud, white-haired man making his way easily despite a permanent limp. Deferentially he inquired, "I can smell the bread baking at the mess hall. Isn't it time for you to be going for supper?"

Long turned to Chamberlain, looking over the tops of his glasses. "Hell, C'unnel Sam. You know me better'n that. I got me a little place over there above the office and I'll fix up somethin' later." They walked slowly together, speaking very little. Between these two men, communication didn't always depend on words. After a respectful silence, however, the sergeant puffed loudly on his pipe, a certain sign he was thinking on his mind. Odd how Long did that—like a bagpiper puffing air into his instrument before sounding off. "It sure is a pretty sight to see the regiment on the parade ground with each troop ridin' their matched horses," said Long, through the smoke. "The grays're my favorites," he said, falling silent. From years of friendship, Chamberlain knew Long liked to set the stage before offering his opinion on a delicate matter. Frankly, though, it wasn't clear where the sergeant was going just now.

Chamberlain's plans had been going smoothly in the last month or so. Hard riding and regular work on the weapons ranges were producing troopers who could ride and shoot with the best of them. Already, the 124th could be assured of a ready-made place in history as the last of the horse cavalry—unless something changed dramatically. Many, many cavalry officers already envied him, but Centaur sensed his appointment with destiny approaching. If it were to happen, the next few months would tell.

Long exhaled a cloud of smoke. "Big changes comin' up. Right, C'unnel?" he asked.

Chamberlain wouldn't even think of deceiving the sergeant. This man whose life centered on running the stables of a cavalry post knew precisely where to place his sensitive finger to measure the pulse of things. It worked simply. Whereas the center of official communications was the colonel's office, every trooper, every officer came to the stables nearly every day to work or to ride for a while, and almost always, they shared what they knew and thought with Sergeant Long.

Plenty was in the wind. Events pointed to it every day. Very probably the patrols into the Rio Grande Valley would be stepped up more and more to help staunch the flow of German agents attempting to cross the river into Texas. Early this morning the official traffic from Fort Ringgold informed the 124th and the rest of the brigade at posts up and down the valley that a cavalry patrol operating to the south from Fort Ringgold stumbled upon an attempted river crossing and captured a man without a passport. According to the report, the prisoner told the Border Patrol in accented English that he was a Mexican of German ancestry, traveling to visit his relatives in Fredericksburg, Texas. Possible: quite possible—but not very likely. The man was being held for questioning.

As it occasionally happened at times like this, Chamberlain wasn't sure Long was speaking at all, or whether somehow thoughts flowed from one man's mind to the other's. "So it looks like we're going to start some real training for the war. Right, sir?"

Rather than respond immediately, Chamberlain stopped to enter a stall to look over one of the grays. He ran his fingers through the mane and tail, checking on the grooming of an ordinary troop horse. Abruptly he turned, asking Long, "You said, 'For the war,' didn't you? What makes you think our training isn't real already?"

The sergeant and the colonel both knew what was happening to cavalry divisions, one by one. First Cavalry was already infantry, and most of the rest would end up as armored divisions, grinding around in noisy, smelly tanks. Rather than facing his friend directly,

Long took a long look in the general direction of the railroad spur, pointing with the stem of his pipe. "I was over there, coupla days ago, ridin' near the loading docks, when the railroad people backed them boxcars in. They were mighty heavy—them cars. I rode over and asked the train crew what was in 'em. The men couldn't tell me, they said, but they knew the cars were at maximum load and they knew where the loads came from. Th' cars had ammunition in 'em," said Long, glancing over his shoulder at Chamberlain. "I know what a train heavy-loaded with ammunition looks like when it rolls, C'unnel Sam," he said, relighting his pipe with another kitchen match.

The sergeant leaned on the top board of the wooden fence with the sole of his boot on the bottom one. Amos Long's pose sent the signal that this was the time for the chat. The two friends stood that way; a foot propped on the fence, hats perched forward on their heads. "What's really on your mind, Sergeant?" asked Chamberlain.

Long didn't hesitate. "Look here, C'unnel. Mebbe you're goin' in the wrong direction, stickin' with parades 'n polo. You got a few troopers 'round here that read newspapers. They know they's a training allotment of ammunition in them cars that's bigger'n anything they ever seen. They's lotsa talk about another trainload a' new weapons. Sojers know ammunition trains mean hard work comin'." He rolled his shoulders, one at a time. "Make's 'em itchy, see, when they know sumpn's comin' and they ain't sure what, 'n don't know when."

"Go on, Amos," urged the colonel. He waited patiently while Long worked on the pipe bowl again and slapped it into the palm of his hand to collect the residue before throwing the bits aside.

"C'unnel, they know th' army's fixin' t' send 'em someplace." Long pointed the pipe stem and talked to his friend like sergeants talk among themselves. "Who you hidin' it from? Them or y'self?" He saw the colonel's eyes narrow, but Long knew he could speak his piece here. "Look here. You may be hanging on too long to the hoss cavalry." For a time Chamberlain stared into the distance, rubbing his chin with his fingers. Long puffed on his pipe, waiting, giving the man time to get his thoughts together. By some unspoken agreement, they left the fence and walked together between the stalls, toward the office. At the door, the colonel placed a respectful hand on the sergeant's shoulder.

"Amos. It isn't a simple thing." It wasn't merely a matter of Chamberlain's obsession with prolonging the existence of the horse cavalry. He could take orders as well as the next man, but plainly the War Department was dithering, as large, unwieldy organizations do. A rumor would come from a confidant in the War Department, "Better get ready to start infantry training." Then a telephone call, probably generated by a plea from the FBI or the Border Patrol, would stop the unloading of the boxcars. "Do not cease cavalry operation," a frantic voice would say.

Institutional expectations at the War Department held that Germany would invade the U.S. through Mexico. For several decades and two wars now, it loomed as a factor: Keep the Rio Grande clear of Germans. If nothing else, that sort of thinking explained the erratic orders coming to Fort Brown. In the course of a rambling, speculative conversation, the possibility of a new mission altogether came up. Chamberlain shared a sensitive proposition with Long, "What if we trained the 124th for long-range reconnaissance?" The question set Long puffing furiously on his pipe. He hadn't heard that idea yet.

The colonel assured Sergeant Long that his message about the mood of the regiment had been clear and on target. "But you're right, Amos. I've got to do something to clear the air."

Danny handed the driver a mixed wad of dollars and pesos and waved him away. "No, don't wait," he said. Resorting to taking a taxi to find Maureen's house was adding up to nearly a week's pay. The driver he hired at the bridge wasn't very helpful, but what could he do if this gringo teniente didn't even know the address for his destination and couldn't speak more than a handful of Spanish? The best idea about her whereabouts was a hazy memory in a mind befogged by lust, of a hurried cab ride that began at the Plaza de Toros.

Danny brightened with a new street name. "Revolucion?" he suggested.

The driver shrugged elaborately. The barely remembered street name didn't help him. So the search had to begin anew at the Plaza de Toros. From there it was up to Danny and his addled memory to direct the taxi through the traffic-choked streets of Matamoros, praying for inspiration, calling for turns in the simplest way, *direcha* or *esquierda,* right or left. Danny berated himself for colossal stupidity: in not memorizing a route to Maureen's apartment, and for not learning more Spanish.

Maureen had been watching from the window for more than an hour, unsure of how he would arrive. At last she saw the taxi creeping up the street with a red-haired gringo craning his neck, looking for a building he had seen only once. She stood in the open door, watching him running up the steps. "Ah, Daniel, dear," she called from the top step. I waited for you." When he reached the landing, she took him by the arm and pulled him into her apartment. "When I hadn't seen you for more than a week, I was afraid it meant you wouldn't come again." The sound of her voice rounding vowels and the faint hint of her favorite Jasmine scent awakened the vivid memory of their urgent dash from the corrida. Danny tried for a moment to tell her of his frantic search, but they were together in a frenzied instant requiring no explanation, kissing breathlessly, fondling, groping with shaking hands for buttons and stubborn snaps. He heard the sounds of the door being closed and locked, shutting out the world and dispelling the questions disturbing him. If anything, she was the aggressor more than he, pressing urgently against him, feeling him responding. "I want you, Daniel. Now!" she said.

It seemed a long time later that they lay quietly with Maureen's head on Danny's chest, listening to his heart beating. She raised her head a little to ask a question. "Do you have the Irish?"

The question took Danny by surprise. He was born an American, as were the nuns who taught him. Never before, not once, did he feel the inclination to learn the Irish tongue. Of course, the old ones spoke it in their homes and when they met in the markets. And yes, he understood a little of what was being said at family dinners at his grandparent's house. Maureen's question, though, awakened an inexplicable sense of failure—as if he were betraying his ancestors. He answered slowly, hearing an apologetic tone in his voice. "No, Maureen my girl, I do not. I only know the tiniest bit I learned in the neighborhood in New York."

"What a pity," she said, laying her head on his chest again. "You should know it." For a moment she listened to his heart beating faster. She urged him, "Let me hear you call me *Mo Cuishle*. Tell me you want me."

"Mo Cuishle, yes," he tried the words and smiled, knowing that in the dark, she couldn't see how he struggled to form the words. "I do want you, Maureen girl."

"Yes, love," she purred happily, satisfied and pleased.

Danny felt very much the same way and wanting desperately to prolong the moment, he tried to swallow away the thirst parching his mouth and throat. Succumbing to practicality, he asked in a gentle whisper, "Could we have some water to drink?" A man can do without physical love and sometimes even food, but neither life nor love can endure without water. Danny's dry throat forced Maureen to leave her cherished role as lover to answer a request that cannot be denied. She rose, leaving the room to bring the water. When she returned, something had changed. He'd been thinking during those few seconds. She knew it. He sat up, gulped thirstily, and lay down again beside her. Suddenly Danny rolled onto an elbow. "Remember the meeting?" he asked. "In the place we called the Upper Room? You were with Patrick Brady and delivered that fiery speech."

She held him close, touched his lips with a fingertip and kissed them lightly. "But are you sure you want to talk about it just now, love?"

At first he shook his head no, but he changed his mind, whispering, "Maybe we should."

She held him even more closely. "Yes, I do remember it—very well," she said warily, in a voice barely above a whisper. "Everyone swore an oath to help me. An unconditional oath, it was, sworn fully and without hesitation. Patrick proposed the oath and all of you swore to it." From its intimate whisper, her voice had strengthened, rising bit by bit as the memory became more vivid.

He hoped she hadn't seen the slight tic of an eye he felt when reminded of that night. Gently he reminded her, "For some kind of special work, didn't he say?"

"Yes," she agreed quietly, but very deliberately. "He said that I was to work in a special project, but the oath as he gave it was to 'Help her whenever and wherever she asks it.'" She kissed him again, in case there was a question, and cradled her head in the hollow of his shoulder. Maureen allowed her voice to fall again to a whisper, reminding him further of their meeting, then strengthening again. "You were not very pleasant to me then, do you recall?"

"I do recall it," he said, not liking the hardness he heard in his own speech. He tried to avoid the memory, but there it was, vivid and raw. He shifted and raised himself slightly on an elbow. "Well then, Mo Cuishle. Are y' still doin' this special project?"

"I am," she said firmly.

Danny could think of nothing to say. A heavy, uncomfortable silence hung between them until Maureen spoke. "It's not what you think, Danny, and I haven't asked for any help a'tall, have I now?"

"And how would you know what I think your project might be?"

"You assumed. That's what. You assumed I was working to help the Germans strike England." A slight tightening of his body was enough to tell her she was quite correct, and he heard a wounded regret in her voice. "I think you've forgotten that Patrick told you, one and all, I was receiving special nursing training in New York—and improving my Spanish."

"I don't think I remember anything of the sort," he said uncomfortably.

"But it's true, I was being trained in midwifery by the staff at St. Barnabas Hospital." Once more she left the bed, gracefully nude in the soft light filtering through the shutters. Without dressing, she went directly to the table she used as a desk, switched on a light, and drew a sheet of paper from a shallow drawer, a letter written in a calligrapher's hand on expensive paper with an elegant, raised letterhead depicting a cardinal's hat. "Here, then, I'll show you." She sat with him on the edge of the bed so he could see it more easily. "From the Archbishop of New York to Bishop Salinas," she read, expecting him to recognize the name. She translated the letter smoothly from Spanish, reciting it more than actually reading.

"This is to introduce Miss Maureen Gallamore, a nurse trained in midwifery and feminine ailments at St. Barnabas Hospital in New York. She is a volunteer working in the service of the Irish Free State with all the good wishes of my office. She is prepared to establish a women's clinic in some deserving small village in Mexico. Please give her every consideration and assistance in her worthy endeavors.

> Fraternally yours in Christ
> Terrence, Cardinal Hanrahan,
> Archbishop of New York

Well, if that's the way the bishop said it was, Danny was convinced. "Put the paper away, Maureen. Come here," he said.

※

"Why is it always First Platoon? Exactly what in the hell is the matter down there?" screamed Walter Franklin, driven into an uncharacteristic rage by the confusion down along the road. It was the same wherever animals were being loaded; not only at First Platoon. From where he stood, the captain could hear his troopers cursing strenuously in at least three languages, blaming each other for clumsiness in heaving the heavy new weapons around. It was hard, unfamiliar work, and they were far behind schedule.

Had the troopers been asked, they would've complained about heavier and more complex loads than the ones they'd been accustomed to handling. Wasn't it plain to anybody who cared in the slightest that a larger, more lethal machine gun is harder to heave up onto the back of a horse? It takes a different, heavier saddle too. Same thing with the cumbersome hand-cranked radio and the rest of the equipment piled along the road—all bigger, heavier things. The Texans could aim a good, round, satisfying curse at an unfamiliar piece of equipment or a specific order demeaning their status as horse cavalry, and it made them feel better, but not even artful oaths were a satisfactory remedy for the vague atmosphere of uncertainty and change.

But they weren't the only ones complaining. Major Perkins had already walked down the line two or three times, boiling at what he saw as malingering and deliberate laziness. Captain Franklin chafed at the major's blunt, derisive comments, and E Troop's work this morning embarrassed him. He too knew damned well what the real problem was—his men were disgusted by the uncertainty coming from the headquarters building. Dammit. Were they cavalry, or what? Yesterday they rode out to the ranges in trucks, to fire machine guns—but that was yesterday. Today's training required them to load machine guns, mortars and radios onto horses—not to use all of the stuff, necessarily—but to learn it so well they could do it at night. Then they marched to the machine gun range with their rifles and full infantry gear.

Already pushed beyond his limits, Franklin scanned the area for his lieutenants. Finding none, he screamed in the general direction of several troopers he recognized as their dog robbers, "Where the hell are my platoon commanders?" But Franklin knew the answer.

They were out of sight, hiding from the senior officers' open derision of the lieutenants' failures in getting their troopers to follow orders and avoiding the vocal objections of the troopers themselves: disgusted, sweating, laboring at what they considered to be impossible tasks. No wonder the lieutenants looked for opportunities to scuttle off and hide. The broad truth was nobody could be sure which war or what contingency the 124th was training for! Not at Fort Brown, or even in Washington.

A colonel at Fort Sam Houston in San Antonio listened with a detached interest to Major Perkins, who called pleading for relief from the conflicting orders, or at least for explanations that made sense. Perkins had already exhausted the patience of the Brigade staff at Fort Ringgold with his questions, and now he was working up the chain of command to try to get this straightened out by somebody at division headquarters. "Colonel, our troopers think we've gone crazy, and I don't blame them." Perkins conveniently laid the blame on the generals doing the heavy thinking.

The faceless colonel in San Antonio appreciated the aggravation in the voice of this major from Fort Brown, but he couldn't offer any help. The War Department itself hadn't quite decided how to resolve the many complicated questions on how the army should reorganize itself to wage an inevitable war in Europe. What should be done with mounted regiments: infantry or cavalry? And if the answer wasn't infantry, then what kind of cavalry?

The Germans were tearing through Europe with their panzers. Everybody knew that, but would tanks work in the U.S. Army? Although the thinking generally favored converting cavalry units to armor, mounted cavalry still had its devotees. Meanwhile, troopers of the 124th, isolated in the Rio Grande Valley, filled the air with vile cursing.

In his office, Perkins heard the colonel at the other end of the telephone line shuffling through a stack of papers for something he could use in giving the slightest bit of guidance. After a few seconds the colonel gave up, frustrated. The best he could do in placating Perkins was his own personal view. "Tell Sam Chamberlain my advice is to improvise, Major. This confusion is a direct result of War Department politics. Sam knows it. If some of those friends he has in the War Department can win their arguments, things will work out in his favor. In the meantime, plan your training to give the troopers a taste of everything and get 'em used to marching."

But the men of the 124th were cavalrymen who, to a man, knew in their souls they weren't born to march. Anybody could tell at a glance, most of them were comparatively smallish, wiry men, naturally selected to be horsemen. If they hadn't been born to ride horses, they might have been content to be infantry, but walking into a fight, especially if burdened with a mountain of gear, presented a prospect that strained their souls. Centaur knew it and so did every trooper, right down to the new private from Michigan who arrived last week as a replacement for Corporal Frank Cernosek. It didn't matter who they were or where they stood in the chain of command: To their cores, they rebelled at the thought of trudging miles to a machine gun range this morning when the stables were full of perfectly good horses and mules.

Franklin felt it viscerally, even as he found fault with his troop. He shared those same feelings, but he knew more than they did about the uncertainty from on high. He said of the situation, "We're getting ready for war," knowing full well it wasn't really an answer. What optimism he felt in these trying days, he derived from his trust in Colonel Sam Chamberlain.

This surge of intense training had begun two weeks before, give or take a few days. It was hard to remember, because one day Centaur suddenly turned ruthless about the training and restricted his troopers to the post. The day the order came out was the day every trooper, married or not, moved into the barracks, and every officer jammed into the over-crowded Bachelor Officers' Quarters—Centaur included. Wherever a vacant plot could be found, tents went up to handle the overflow, and the dissatisfaction and moaning could be heard in Matamoros. All the regiment could expect in the way of time off was a pass to leave the post from noon to midnight on Saturday, with Sunday a free day on the post. From then on, the troopers hurled blue curses at every change and greeted every new day with a sullen suspicion that everybody outranking them had gone stark, raving crazy.

To begin with, there was the flood of new equipment, mostly weapons and radios, hauled by truck from the ships at Port Isabel. The backbreaking labor of unloading and storing it in underground bunkers, crate by crate, fell to men who had signed up to ride horses. Then there was more ammunition to unload from the trains and mass training sessions on the parade ground. Hundreds of men spread across the grass working on shelter halves laid out in a precise grid. Day after day, they learned each interlocking part of every one of the weapons, taking them apart and reassembling them over and over again in the heat of the Texas sun.

Every trooper in the regiment got identical treatment—band and Headquarters Troop included. All right, there was some sense to it. Take rifles, for instance: the M-1s were still new to them. And sure, most would agree at least grudgingly that training with the mortars and machine guns made sense too. In fact most of the troopers were almost completely new to machine guns—they had always been the sole purview of the Machine Gun Troop. But in seeing reason in the odious regimen, they might be missing a subtle message. The obvious good sense of becoming better with the tools of their trade obscured a warning—that some mysterious plan augured a reorganization in mind for the regiment, one that didn't allow for separate units to specialize in the heavier weapons while others galloped freely and relatively unencumbered.

At first they fired machine guns already set up for them so they could concentrate on safety and building confidence. Seeing the chattering weapon at work, spitting flame and spraying bright brass ammunition cases flying through the air, they watched earth embankments behind the targets torn into flying dust. It left most of them wide-eyed at the weapon's destructive capabilities. Its heavy staccato chatter excited Private Jerry Bohuslav. The normally quiet, introspective farmer from Fayette County instantly became a rabid machine gun enthusiast. Pretending his hands were still on the controls, firing downrange, he yelled, "Let me at that gun and I'll show you how to chew up a target." Had Centaur asked for volunteers for the Machine Gun Troop, fully a third of First Platoon would have stood to answer his call. That was in the morning.

An afternoon of closely supervised loading, firing and collecting spent brass casings by the bucketful took the initial thrill out of the training, and by the time the sun turned red over the Rio Grande, the temporary excitement had been replaced by weariness and a grudging touch of confidence. Nevertheless, to a few young troopers riding back to the post in the bed of a truck, much of the talk dwelt appreciatively on the guns sucking in belts of ammunition and spitting out an invisible stream of lead.

And then one black day, calamity descended on them. Some nameless somebody, an idiot quartermaster probably, unloaded bayonets from one of those railroad cars. God! Bayonets! The mere thought of it flung shame on the U.S. Cavalry's sacred crossed-sabers emblem and almost certainly consigned them to a life as mud-loving grunts. Issuing the bayonets must have been the result of a colossal mistake. Had to be! What good was a bayonet to a cavalryman? For fighting at close range, the traditional weapon had always been the saber, until a repeating pistol came along. For a time the cavalry carried both, because in the army, traditions die hard. The thinking in getting rid of the sabers was that if you found yourself close enough to reach an enemy with a saber, you should have already shot him with a pistol.

But what if the bayonets weren't a mistake? What if the .45s were taken from them? The terrible possibility began to dawn, but the stables were still full of horses. Until the horses were gone, there would always be the hope of remaining cavalry.

⚜

Responding to some intuitive sense young officers develop to prevent themselves from committing professional suicide, the lieutenants reappeared near the loading activity to find the pall of resentment hanging over the sullen, sweaty troopers hadn't dissipated the least bit. Danny found one of his men kicking one of the new packsaddles with contempt. Bednarski lamented to no one in particular, "Damn. My feet ain't made for marchin'!"

Then there was Weech. He'd backslid into his old ways, joining the griping like an undisciplined private. In fact, at the moment he stood waving the short, ugly knife meant to be clipped under the M-1's muzzle, raging. "Damn, Lootenan'. Did they have to drop this on us all of a sudden? Ain't it 'nough th't we been ridin' hosses f' a hunnerd years, 'n all of a sudden we gotta walk?" The bayonets were the dirtiest insult in a long line of indignities, dragging them into the lowest caste of fighting men in the army. "Lootenan'," yelled the big sergeant. "We' screwed."

Danny lashed out, "C'mon, Weech. Set an example. You're a sergeant crying like an old woman." He couldn't allow Wieczorek to slip into his old malcontent ways. "Sergeant, you're the one who's been saying, 'There's a war going on in Europe.' You have a platoon to get ready."

Despite all the profane references to the miniscule brainpower of the person who arranged this damn drill, as it was almost universally called, its real goal was to put the earlier training with individual weapons into practice. Each squad was to learn the cumbersome business of loading one of the new, heavier machine guns on an equally new and awkward packsaddle and get the whole arrangement onto the broad back of a horse. They would do all this until it was second nature. Then they'd march to the ranges to set up the weapons before a rushed meal of field rations gobbled standing up. Afterward, it would be an afternoon of firing on the range.

Sweaty, heavy labor didn't particularly faze the men of First Platoon—most of them made their civilian livings at hard work. It was this torture of a step-by-step descent into the abased station of a dogface infantryman. Of all people to join loudly in the discontent, his perpetually optimistic orderly surprised him the most. "I know, *Teniente*," said Garza, "this ain't s'posed to be a new thing. Cavalry troopers are s'posed to ride to the fight. Once we're there, we dismount to do our fighting on foot. Only now we don't ride the horses. We hear that all the time." He raised his steel helmet and wiped the perspiration from his forehead with his sleeve. "But walking and leading horses is just crazy."

Stan Zientek, the diminutive carpenter from Brenham, agreed. "Pancho's right. This ain't cavalry. It ain't exactly a pack train, neither. We got trucks parked all over the post." The little man shook with outrage. "Let's use trucks, f'god's sake!" He exploded with an astonishing string of loosely connected profanity, with which he was obviously unfamiliar, and looked over his shoulder to see if anybody was listening, but it didn't really matter.

Every platoon in E Troop felt the same sense of betrayal and complained just as bitterly. In a way, they were right; the clamp-down on the regiment had come with an almost savage vindictiveness, and Danny didn't feel any particular conviction in training like this either. They would've gladly done far more for Centaur, had he asked. But nobody had asked Centaur either, and now it appeared that the regiment would dissolve into a rabble, platoon by platoon if each lieutenant didn't do something.

"Is this weakness I'm hearing from First Platoon?" goaded Lieutenant Flynn. "Not long ago it was bitching because we were living a country club existence. Now, we're working too hard." He called for the sergeant. "Weech! Let's get these horses loaded and move out."

Wieczorek proved that down deep in his core, he knew how to be a good sergeant. He went into action immediately, bellowing orders at his men to get the machine gun loaded on the horse, but he didn't get the job done without one more complaint. "The colonel let the army take Corporal Cernosek outa here Monday, Lieutenant. Christ: Frank was an expert at this stuff. He woulda had that gun up on that old horse just like that," said the sergeant, snapping his fingers. "We don't understand why they had to go and get rid of him, or a lot of others like him."

So this was the latest excuse; First Platoon was down in the mouth because their circle was being broken up. "Come on, Sergeant, come on. I can agree the corporal had his strengths, but did you look at the man? This is young man's work and he was old, and fat, and slow. He'll be better off in the stables, or maybe in San Antonio, where he can help more than he did here."

Flynn turned away to supervise the loading. Behind him he heard Weech grumbling under his breath to the men struggling with the machine gun. "Send me to San Antonio with Frank Cernosek then."

That was enough of the sergeant's bellyaching. The lieutenant wheeled to confront the peevish sergeant, emphasizing his points like a choirmaster beating time with his hand. "The man was a fifty-two-year-old corporal. A slow-movin' fat corporal at fifty-two! Get it through your heads, people. We can't fight with soldiers like him."

"We ain't the same without 'im either," griped the sergeant in the infuriatingly nasal tone he refused to drop. He glared at the lieutenant and their eyes met. Expectant silence fell on the platoon. Every trooper felt the tension and froze expectantly. The contest of will teetered for a moment on an invisible balance. Wieczorek detected something in the lieutenant's face, maybe a slight shadow of confidence at the corner of his mouth, and it was enough for him. His eyes fell back to the packsaddle and the work resumed.

chapter

FOURTEEN

Washington: Navy destroyer *USS Greer* fires torpedoes at U-652. President Roosevelt declares it a response to piracy.

Sergeant J.R. Roper knew damn well something was up when he felt himself being shaken from a sound sleep. Centaur was standing over him, asking, "What are you doing asleep on the floor in the middle of the night, Roper?" Despite the time, an hour past midnight, the sergeant's office was open for business. Overhead lights glared and the ceiling fan whirred softly. A typewriter sat on its stand with an unfinished letter still in the carriage. "Go to the barracks and get some rest," the colonel ordered.

Roper felt awful and his uniform didn't fit so well. Ten pounds had melted from his slight frame in the month since Centaur's pronouncement that nobody in the 124th was exempt from the training whirlwind, not even the headquarters troop or the band.

Sometimes well-meaning men make mistakes through acts of well-intentioned zeal. Important details had fallen through the cracks in putting Centaur's order into effect. Some perfectly reasonable exceptions that should have been made were overlooked. In getting them out of their offices for weapons training and conditioning marches, nobody had thought about what would happen if Roper and his staff of typists and clerks weren't at their desks at least part of the time.

If the cooks had been reassigned like that, unfed troopers would have turned mutinous. And what if the hospital were left unstaffed? Unthinkable! Sure, assigning musicians and clerks to field training sent a powerful message that preparations for war had the highest possible priority. After all, office clerks were every soldier's example of something being as useless as tits on a boar hog. But somebody had to do the official paperwork and handle the colonel's daily schedule. With the whole regiment in a stew about where they would be ordered, and every single clerk working to exhaustion, the office work piled up in mountainous heaps. What would it have done to morale if even one trooper's advancement papers were lost?

Roper took it on himself to set up a work rotation for the clerks that included intense field training plus the clerical work that kept the regiment running. Night after night the sergeant ignored his bed in the barracks. Instead he returned to the headquarters building to catch up on the essential paperwork. What bits of rest he got came by sleeping on the floor. This was the first time he realized that the commanding officer wasn't taking things easy either.

Centaur decided on the spot to bend his own ironclad rules. "I need you in the office, Sergeant," he informed Roper after the sergeant returned from a couple of hours of sleep. "Effective right now, you're excused from the fieldwork." That's when Roper was cut in on Centaur's plan.

J.R. had joined the 124th ten years earlier, right after high school—to ride the horses. When he signed the enlistment papers at eighteen, it thrilled him to be accepted as a member of a select fraternity, and life in the Texas Guard grew on him. Through the urging of some of his fellow guardsmen, J.R. earned his degree at the Teachers' College at San Marcos and stepped into a job teaching English in the little city of Caldwell, where the high school principal held a captain's commission in the 124th Cavalry.

One summer, during the regiment's annual training at Fort Ringgold, Roper came into the office to apply for an officer's commission, only to learn that the Headquarters Troop sergeant, who knew how applications were handled, had been sent to the hospital at Fort Sam Houston with a broken leg. "You understand, Roper," he was told by a diffident corporal temporarily standing in for the sergeant. "Come back later

With his application on hold for a time at least, J.R. volunteered to fill the vacancy—and he made the regimental administrative process run like a top—but he hated the work. "I didn't join the guard to be a clerk," he complained loudly and frequently. Jerry Newman, a major at the time, talked him into staying on the job by appealing to some skewed sense of order. "Dammit, J.R.," he said, "we can't afford to let you go long enough to get you a commission." So here he was, an exhausted clerk with an assignment that amounted to being chained to the desk.

Centaur's snap decision, one he made to correct a mistake, appeared a stroke of genius. Roper turned out to be the ideal man to have around, a secretary, a driver, a special assistant and a confidant, all in one. Chamberlain and Newman knew he could be trusted with secret material and that he was scrupulously discreet with personal confidences. The last qualification might well have been the most valuable of all his attributes. It wasn't news to Sergeant Roper that about a month ago, Chamberlain had given Newman the responsibility of running the day-to-day training, but it did surprise him to learn that Centaur's daily schedule had little connection to long conditioning marches in the heat and endless days on the firing ranges. As the weeks wore on, Sergeant Roper learned more about the two men who ran the regiment and determined the destiny of the 124th.

Although they had come to their assignments in the 124th Cavalry via widely different routes, Chamberlain and Newman were both highly accomplished in ways that had no obvious connection to leading a regiment of cavalry. A particularly useful talent they had in common, however, was the art of persuasion, but even there, they differed.

Newman, of course, was primarily a civilian, not a professional soldier. As a lawyer with a University of Texas Law School pedigree, the executive officer possessed an innate skill in avoiding legal roadblocks altogether or finessing his way through the narrow openings other men weren't perceptive enough to notice. Fifteen years of Texas law practice and a term in the House of Representatives in Austin had left an indelible stamp on him too, giving him plenty of practice at a uniquely Texan form of persuasion known as jawboning. As the folksy expression went, the man could talk a possum out of a tree.

Chamberlain, on the other hand, saw things in a far more direct light. For one thing, professional soldiers are expected to refrain from participation in partisan politics—even when assigned to Washington. But necessity is a powerful stimulus to becoming skilled in arts not usually learned from army training manuals. Over decades in a moribund peacetime army where promotion stagnated and a rigid chain of command stifled the flow of new ideas, Chamberlain learned how to keep his seniors pacified while relying on a network of West Point classmates and professional mentors to carry his messages to exactly the right place. It took patience, tact, and considerable cojones, but the man was a past master at getting his ideas implemented.

Roper saw from the first day that the division of labor in the regimental front office wasn't exactly the way it was laid out in the manuals. Instead the two officers split the duties along a more goal-oriented set of functional lines. From placing the telephone calls, Roper learned that Newman's job was to run the regiment and to orchestrate a convincing barrage of communication up the chain of command, keeping the brigade and division commanders satisfied that the boys at Fort Brown followed orders to the letter. Meanwhile Centaur burned up the telephone wires to key offices all over the army, playing every friendship, every acquaintance, any opening, to find a sympathetic ear. The name and reputation of Sam Chamberlain could be big medicine in many headquarters offices, but in Washington he was a mere colonel—a high-stepping, front-running colonel to be sure, but even a world-class equestrian like Centaur needed help from generals. Desperately, he wanted the ear of a general with enough influence to carry a convincing message to the army chief of staff himself—that the army needed the horse cavalry.

Even though the regiment wasn't specifically ordered to conduct active patrolling in the valley, Captain Joe Michael had his intelligence specialists keeping close tabs on a rapidly-changing affair brewing a little way upstream from Fort Brown. With the 124th hard at work on infantry training, he could have been forgiven for leaving the concerns over the security of the Texas border to others. It wasn't his job anymore. Arguably, he should have switched his concentration to matters concerning the European ground war. But in maintaining his vigilance in Texas, he found something.

A Border Patrol agent called with an informal plea for help. "We got a funny situation here, Captain," the agent said, tossing out the bait. Fairly recently, almost to the day the 124th unsaddled their horses and began this infantry training, the FBI began picking up information about German agents becoming active around the Gulf Coast ports. "You didn't announce that you were giving up patrolling that I recall, did you Captain?" inquired the agent.

"No, we try to be sensitive to security matters like that," said Michael.

"Well, it looks to me as if somebody knew something," said the agent thinking aloud. Understood was that he meant somebody in Mexico, but neither of the two men knew who was running the spies across the border. The Border Patrol, stretched thin as always, had been doing their best. The Germans weren't crossing at the bridges anymore. That had been stopped by increasing scrutiny at the official gateways—but now the spies were filtering across at the fording places the Mexicans had been using for ages. "They're getting help from somebody—a local, we think, who knows where these fords are," said the agent. "We know that, 'cause one man the FBI picked up in Bay City, around the oil refineries, did a little talking." Occasionally they found one of these spies who would rather sit the war out in an American prison than fight it out in Europe or risk his life in espionage. This one had been talking freely.

Michael doodled on a pad of paper, letting the Border Patrol man talk. According to the agent, the German had an American passport but spoke only fair English. Something about the passport looked a little fishy to the FBI. They sent it off to Washington to be analyzed in the hope of learning how it had gotten into German hands. The Border Patrol was still waiting to hear from the State Department. These things take time.

When questioned on how he had made it so far on his own, the spy admitted that he'd gotten help from a woman in Mexico. He didn't have a proper identity, but he said they called her by a nickname of some kind. "So far, it doesn't mean anything to us," said the agent, preparing to set the hook. The Border Patrol agent wasn't bashful about admitting how badly things were going in the valley. "What if I was to send a request up my chain for Colonel Chamberlain to send some patrols into the valley?" he proposed. Then he set the hook. "You still got enough hosses to do that, Captain?"

Almost anybody else in the 124th would have jumped up, agreeing instantly to take up the enticing opportunity, but Michael understood how hard it would be to ignore explicit orders for all-out training and then to turn around and send out mounted patrols. He delayed for quite a while before answering the agent. "I'll take it to the colonel," he said finally.

The next day Sergeant Roper's daily routine included the chore of driving his boss to the S-2 offices for daily intelligence briefings on the growing problem with this new rush of spies crossing the river. Chamberlain, concentrating on convincing people in Washington that dismounting the 124th wasn't a good idea, found it helpful to see the detailed, wall-sized maps they kept in the S-2 office. He seemed especially fascinated by the possibilities presented by the Border Patrol's predicament. "You take shorthand, Sergeant?" he asked Roper.

"Yes, sir." In the slower-paced days before the orders to begin infantry training, Roper had been whiling away slow afternoons practicing the skill with one of his clerks. Yes, he could do it.

"Good. Bring your notepad with you tomorrow. One of the Border Patrol boys is coming to Captain Michael's office, and I'll want a record of what they have to say." He brushed aside Roper's concerns about recording the agent's exact words, feeling that if the headquarters in San Antonio wasn't ready to admit these Germans were slipping in, they probably hadn't classified it as secret yet. Some of this detail would be crucial in future telephone calls. "If it concerns you, Sergeant Roper, we'll put your notebooks in my safe," said Newman.

After that Roper detected a new tone in the phone calls to Washington. For one thing the discussions were becoming longer and more detailed. Also, the conversations, at least the side he could hear, were noticeably less plaintive. Once he heard Chamberlain making a hard sell. "No, General, I can't explain why the Germans are trying to sneak so many more spies across on foot these days. Very likely it's because they know we aren't sending mounted patrols out for them anymore." Another time Chamberlain reminded his listener, "If there's anything that'll put a scare into the War Department, it's a threat of being invaded by the Germans through Mexico," and, "Yes, sir. I'd bet a lot on it. I'm sure they still have drawers full of plans designed to stop that kind of incursion. I might suggest you have somebody in the War Plans section dust off the latest one—and I bet it'll include mounted cavalry."

Lieutenant Colonel Newman nearly spilled his coffee over his desk blotter at the sound of the door flying open. An animated Roper beckoned furiously from the doorway. "Come look, sir. You won't believe this." He led the way into the small cubicle between the two executive offices where the administrative clerks kept filing cabinets and beckoned again, even more insistently. "Come, come."

Newman dropped a report he'd been reading and pushed his chair back from the desk. "What the hell's going on, Roper?" he asked.

"Come on. Look through the peephole." The sergeant indicated a tiny circular window, a peephole that the clerks used, very discreetly, to peer into the CO's office before they entered, to be certain they could enter without interfering.

Newman put his eye to the hole, a quick glance, not wanting to be caught eavesdropping, and backed away, incredulous. He took Roper by the elbow, leading him into his own office and locking the door, so they could speak in privacy. "Sergeant, I saw Colonel Chamberlain puffing away on a cigar." Shaking his head, he admitted, "I think I saw him planting a hand on the desk, and jumping up kicking his heels—am I crazy?"

Roper grinned, agreeing, "Not a bit, sir. That's what I saw too."

"Who's he been on the phone with?"

"First General Truscott and then General Marshall, sir."

Newman squinted at Roper over the top of his glasses to be positive the sergeant was absolutely certain. "Not George Marshall, surely," he interrogated Roper, to be certain that it was *the* George Marshall who commanded the entire army.

Roper held his right hand up as if taking an oath. "I took the call from the War Department myself. A colonel had me put Colonel Chamberlain on the telephone to wait for General Marshall to pick up."

The two were still talking an instant later when an energized, elated Chamberlain erupted from his office and barged through Newman's door, trailing a cloud of cigar smoke, breathless and excited as a beauty pageant contestant, spewing a string of orders: "Shut it down, Jerry—all this marching and bayonet drills. Help's on the way." Centaur was in the saddle again. "The horse cavalry is still alive," he crowed. As more and more ideas popped into his head, he shouted them in a rapid-fire string. "I think we'll have a ceremonial parade," he said.

Newman watched quietly, not prepared to give in to sampling the sweet feeling of triumph until the Centaur's euphoria abated. It had happened before, rumors like this, and always there had been disappointments. He motioned to Roper to make notes of the machine-gun flow of orders from Colonel Chamberlain, just in case.

"No. No," Chamberlain was changing his mind. "Strike that about the parade." Pacing back and forth a bit calmed him to some extent: enough, anyway, for him to sit on one of Newman's chairs and stretch his boots onto the coffee table. He sat that way, smoking his cigar, recalling precious snatches of the conversation with General Marshall until he was ready to dictate his orders more calmly. "As of now, we resume operations as a horse cavalry regiment. Put out the orders to cease all other training immediately." Roper scribbled furiously while Newman watched over his shoulder, reading the sergeant's shorthand.

Colonel Chamberlain knew the transformation he had in mind couldn't be brought about in an instant, but he felt keenly the emotional highs and lows his regiment had been put through over the preceding weeks. It occurred to him momentarily that he had been too zealous before in bringing the entire regiment into quarters on the post. He wanted to let his troopers have some time at home with their families, or in Matamoros, if that's what they wanted, as soon as possible. "No waiting on that—tonight. Have the S-2 brief them on this German situation. Then send 'em out into town to have a good time."

In moments Centaur was up again, thinking aloud, pacing, puffing clouds of smoke. Taking a turn around Newman's office, he stopped suddenly, poking the smoking end of his cigar at Roper and Newman. This was hot, but it musn't get out until tomorrow. "Don't even tell the S-2." Yes, hell, he knew that the questions would come at them like a fire hose when it did get out. For the moment, only the three of them knew about it, and he wanted it to be kept secret. "Officers' call in the morning," Centaur said, blowing a smoke ring. "That's when we'll put out the new plan." He closed his eyes tightly, thinking. The troopers needed to know something before they went out to celebrate. He pointed to Newman. "In the meantime, let's have the S-2 people give 'em a little briefing before they leave the post."

For once Newman was caught by surprise. "Do we have a plan, Colonel? Maybe…I've been so caught up in other things that I'm not aware of one."

"Of course not, Jerry," Centaur placated Newman, "but we will in the morning. Just give 'em a pass for tonight." He puffed furiously at his cigar, his mind running a mile a minute. "Sure they'll think I'm crazy—but they already think that. Get all the heavy thinkers together as soon as you can, so that we'll have something to say in the morning."

He stopped in the door with another thought. "Roper, call Sergeant Long. Tell him I'd like to go riding. And, if he has the time, I'd like his company."

The order to cease training reached E Troop on the mortar range a few miles from the central post. "Truck transportation is on the way," said the caller relaying the message, setting the troopers whooping in celebration.

Captain Michael and his people set up a tent near the front gate, where every fifteen minutes the captain or one of his staff delivered a short warning. The substance of it was, "It's dangerous in those German bars. Stay away from them." Of course the troopers posed many questions and speculated broadly about what it meant to be drawn back into the fort from the training ranges, but the S-2 was as much in the dark as were the troopers themselves about what had come from Washington. "All of a sudden, Colonel Chamberlain approved passes, and he wants me to tell you that those people are giving Americans trouble across the river in Matamoros." He referred indirectly to the growing German activity in Mexico. "That's what we get from the Mexican police." He said this privately to Walter Franklin and his three lieutenants with the knowing look of a man sharing a secret. "I think it's pretty serious, and we can't send armed people over there to get you out of trouble."

After a quick change into civilian clothes, two E Troop lieutenants strode briskly across the bridge, eyeing every face in the thin stream of gringos crossing to the American side with great suspicion.

"Where we going, Danny?" asked Cameron, trailing his redheaded guide down streets completely new to him. Flynn ignored the question, walking ahead of Cameron, whose curiosity was turning to genuine worry. "You're heading straight to the part of Matamoros where they've been seeing those Germans, aren't you?"

Danny kept up a fast pace. "It never occurred to me, Doug m' boy," he said, panting from the exertion. "But now that you mention it, I do think it's a good idea..." He threw a look at the lanky Cameron, challenging him, "What do you say?"

If either of them had any idea of being the only ones of the 124th with the idea of exploring the most dangerous parts of Matamoros, they were mistaken. Plenty of troopers had thoughts of catching up to those Germans and exacting personal revenge for the U-boats depredations at sea. The intelligence officer's brief created a crackle of interest that spread with the speed of lightning and sent the troopers across the bridge in a khaki flood, choking the tourist areas and the better-known bars and strip joints. If the invading American troopers resisted the temptation to look for trouble, the most likely danger would be to each other, in letting go the pent-up energy in men who hadn't had a night off the post in more than a month. But if the men of the 124th pressed on to the known German areas, the problem could be far worse. The Mexican police kept watch at a discrete distance from the best known sensitive areas, hopeful that the lust for vengeance would diminish after learning how far away the known hotspots actually were from the safety of the border crossings. According to reports telephoned to Fort Brown by roving MPs, that's the way it appeared to be working.

Doug nudged Danny, pointing out two troopers in uniform moving along far ahead of them. In the next two or three minutes, a half dozen young troopers appeared from one of the alleys, shouting general threats of what they'd do when they found the Germans. None of these men in khaki looked familiar. It didn't matter, really, because after a few blocks, nearly all of them decided they'd looked hard enough for spies and turned back. Soon only the two they had seen earlier were still ahead of them.

Street after street, the two lieutenants kept pace, until the pair ahead hesitated at a narrow passage leading off to the right. The troopers elected a wider, better-lighted street to the left, leaving the route to the German bars to Flynn and Cameron alone. The two lieutenants felt that, with men in uniform around to attract attention, their civilian clothes assured them of anonymity. That might have been the case, except that in hurrying to distance themselves from the bridge, they automatically fell into step. Soldiers do that.

Danny's eyes scanned in quick movements like a predator's. He whispered, "See that guy over there, the one in the white shirt? I'll bet he's one of them. He looks German."

"You're crazy, Flynn. I think he's a civilian from Fort Brown. How do you know what a German looks like, anyway?"

"You can always recognize a German. A hundred percent." Flynn slowed the pace to keep his quarry in sight. They followed him for several minutes, keeping their distance whenever he paused to look at something that caught his interest, resuming when he walked. Danny wouldn't be talked out of tailing the man in the white shirt until he turned into one of the last streets leading to the safer tourist areas.

Before Flynn could refocus on people and signs, Cameron surprised him with a question right out of the blue. "Where've you been going when you're off duty?"

"Huh?"

Cameron hounded him. "Lieutenant Flynn, don't be coy with me. For the past few weeks, you've been a ghost around the fort. You're at work...or you're gone." Danny tried to plead innocence, but Doug kept the pressure on. "Your car's gone the second it's OK to leave the post."

"Why, I've been seeing Molly a bit more than usual."

"That's a bunch of bull," Cameron shot back. "You're doing no such thing." Doug wasn't the only one who had seen Molly moping around the base with the regiment ladies, looking like a sad, abandoned wallflower. He needled Danny a little more. "George Kincaid's noticed, and he's been doing a little sniffing." He knew his probe had struck deeply, but Flynn succeeded in ignoring the question, as if he were concentrating on inspecting street signs. Doug let the matter go for the moment.

By now they'd left the tourist areas were far behind them and found themselves in an area where streets barely wide enough for a handcart twisted and turned in an intricate maze. Out of a sense of self-preservation, Doug began memorizing landmarks to help him find his way back if things went to hell, but he wouldn't stop interrogating Danny. "You've been coming over here to Mexico, haven't you? Don't deny it, Flynn." If Danny heard the new question at all, he disregarded it.

Doug shouted angrily, grabbing Danny by the shoulder. "I want an answer," he demanded.

Danny pushed Doug away. He didn't like the tone. "Hey. Stop accusing me of things that aren't any of your damn business. What makes you think I come over here to Mexico?"

"An educated guess. The reason I ask is that any dumb ass can see you're not with that Blankenship girl. And because you've been leading the way, right from the bridge." Cameron stopped at a dimly lighted intersection verging on a seedy district of low, adobe commercial buildings, most of which could have used a coat of paint. "All I've been doing is following you," he said.

Danny mumbled something about some people being much too worried about other people's business. "Keep an eye out for those street signs, Doug. I think we're close." Flynn meant, of course, the signs mentioned by Captain Michael in his warning.

The two friends were feeling the exhilarating buzz of being isolated in a dangerous neighborhood. Doug had already convinced himself that these narrow streets marked a district where European expatriates congregated by nationality, handy to the riotous border-town nightlife, but far enough from the bridge to keep nosy American tourists from venturing in by accident. From their exteriors the buildings were the usual crude brick-and-wood border-town structures, but these were strikingly different from anything they'd seen in the last twenty minutes. Maybe it was the paint. More and more of the dilapidated adobe-front buildings had been tidied up recently with the application of a bit of fresh, brightly colored paint.

And then it became obvious; *Wilkommen* stood out vertically on a recently painted doorframe. Along the street, similar innocuous signs on windows and doors suggested strongly that the shops, bars and restaurants in this small area, catered to a thriving German colony.

Danny, intent on pursuing a building-to-building search for a bar where German belligerence was flaunted, never looked back to see if Doug was following, but every few steps Doug would suggest something like, "Maybe tonight's not the best time for this, Flynn," but the Danny couldn't be dissuaded. Darkness had begun to settle on Matamoros and the evening pulse was picking up. Here and there a few chalked signs read *Cerveza, Bier, Beer*, offering Pearl and Lone Star from breweries in San Antonio, suggesting that the local Mexican businessmen were carefully hedging their bets. Here, much the same as they did in the more familiar areas near the bridge, the jukeboxes blared a familiar mixture of Mexican music and Texas swing.

"Look here." Cameron pointed to a large whitewashed building on a corner. By itself the building presented no threat. Its windows advertised women's clothing, but someone had recently painted *Unter den Linden* on the adobe in an ornate Gothic script. "Aha. Good work, Doug. You found it," said Danny. "This is one of those streets the S-2 people were telling us about."

"Yeah, you crazy man. That's also the name of the main drag in Berlin. Wish I had my forty-five," complained Cameron, but his warning didn't slow Danny a bit. If anything, Flynn grew more eager, checking the signs with growing interest.

"*U-Boot Alee,*" Flynn read with fascination. "This must be new. Captain Michael didn't say anything about this one."

"You'd think the bastards would be a little more cautious, wouldn't you?" Cameron clenched his fists involuntarily. Being German wasn't a crime—there were plenty of innocent Germans in this part of Mexico. But here he was with Flynn in a deliberate, barehanded hunt for Germans—any Germans—in the Mexican bars. In Cameron's mind, this was stupid stuff, not the kind of adventure he wanted tonight. He hung back warily, letting Flynn lead the way. His own instincts were screaming retreat, but the aggressive Irishman simply had a nose for this kind of thing. If he let Flynn go on sniffing out the Germans with the determination of a bloodhound, the two of them could be up to their necks in trouble in a heartbeat. He closed the distance between himself and Danny so they couldn't be separated easily. Damn Flynn anyway. "Let's get out of this place," he said.

Danny held up a finger. For silence? For one more moment? Or was it one more bar? Doug waited motionless until Flynn changed the hand signal to one meaning follow me, and suddenly there it was: *Die Lorelei.* This had to be what they were looking for. The jukebox blared German beer hall music and, painted on the window, a buxom, rosy-cheeked blonde in a blue and white alpine dirndl smiled her *Wilkommen* in large, elaborate Gothic letters.

Flynn barged through the open door of Die Lorelei and angled toward the jukebox, sweeping his eyes around a room lighted dimly by a few small, shaded bulbs over the bar and blue neon signs on the windows. At the moment only a few patrons stood in the gloom near a row of tall wooden stools. A single bartender in a white jacket made small talk in Spanish while he arranged a row of heavy glass beer mugs: a chalked price called them steins. At one table near the far wall, two men, most likely Mexican businessmen he guessed, sat quietly talking over small glasses of tequila. Nearer the jukebox, three gringos lounged on chairs around a circular table, laughing and chatting with Mexican women in tight, brief skirts.

Doug pointed to an incongruous note on the jukebox, handwritten in English, informing German and Mexican customers that the jukebox took only American nickels. "Crazy," said Doug, mostly to himself. "Everything about this escapade of yours is crazy—even the jukeboxes."

As their eyes became accustomed to the dim light, the lieutenants moved toward a table that would give them a good view of the room. Two Fort Brown soldiers, a private and a PFC, had slipped in from the street and gone directly to the bar, leaning against it stiffly, surveying the room—hunting Germans probably—very likely unaware that their khaki uniforms could attract unpleasant attention. Perhaps these two were the same ones he and Doug saw a few minutes earlier. Either they were crazy, or they had the biggest cojones at Fort Brown. They'd been served their beers, and from the little rings of foam inside their nearly empty beer steins, they'd drunk most of the contents in a few large gulps. Flynn and Cameron didn't recognize them, and for all the attention the soldiers paid them, the slim, almost painfully thin Cameron and Flynn with his flaming red hair hadn't sparked any recognition in them either.

Cameron ordered in his limited Spanish, *"Dos Cervezas, por favor."* At first the two lieutenants sipped tentatively from their glass steins, speaking quietly in some vague intention of remaining inconspicuous. With about a quarter of his beer consumed and nothing bad happening so far, Cameron felt comfortable enough to resume pumping Danny about his interests on this side of the river. "So, tell me, Lieutenant Flynn. This chiquita you have over here: Where does she live? Matamoros? Or in some dusty little town upriver?"

Danny, tense and quite intent on searching the corners of the room, didn't answer immediately. He took a long thoughtful pull at the stein before he said anything. When he did, it sounded like a challenge. "Now pray tell, what might you be driving at, friend?"

Doug's eyes swept the other tables warily, suspecting they would be drawing attention by now, but no one in the place appeared to be paying the slightest heed. Nevertheless, he lowered his voice even more. "When you come back to Fort Brown, your car is covered with dust, white dust from limestone country, not the kind from around here. You don't talk about it, so I ask Garza where you go. All I get from him are shrugs."

Danny signaled the startlingly pretty young Mexican woman drying her tray at the bar. She nodded and luxuriated in a slow, sultry smile and made her way slowly to their table. Without a word, she stood with a hand on her hip, taking in the redheaded gringo with her eyes. She ran her fingers up from the nape of his neck through his hair, and gave it a playful tug. Danny closed his eyes. Fuzzily he heard Doug's voice, "The waitress wants your order, Flynn." Before he could answer, she stiffened at a look from the bartender and left the two without taking an order.

Danny asked Doug, "You were saying something, weren't you? What was it?" He hadn't noticed the bartender's frown disapproving the girl's lingering with the two gringos. Bad business.

Doug, however, had seen the entire exchange, which left him even edgier. He thought if he could make Danny uncomfortable enough with questions about Molly, he'd leave this place. "Damn you, Flynn. It was dust I was talking about, white dust from someplace else—not this pinkish stuff from around here. So where does she live?"

The question caught Danny by surprise. Maybe offended would be more accurate. The nerve of Doug Cameron, interrupting like that while he talked to a pretty girl! "You're not my mother, Doug," he snapped, immediately regretting how petulant he must have sounded.

For a while the two sat silent at the table; Doug knew he'd been pushing Danny too hard. Very likely he'd get farther by biding his time. He raised his nearly empty stein, draining it. Almost immediately two fresh beers appeared, without a word from the waitress to either of the two lieutenants. In the corner of his eye, he noticed the bartender tallying up the delivery on a small sheet of paper.

Flynn took a long swallow, delaying in answering these questions. But what was he to do? It wouldn't hurt if Doug learned a few things. "She lives here, my inquisitive friend. And she isn't a chiquita! She's an Irish lady...from Ireland." He tapped the table with the flat of his hand to affirm his statement and pronounce the matter closed.

Cameron wasn't to be satisfied just because Flynn thought he should be.. "Oh, I see—an Irish lady, from Ireland," he mimicked, rolling his eyes.

What business was it of Cameron's where he went? Would this stubborn fellow never give him peace? They hadn't come here to talk, after all. "Well now, Lieutenant Cameron," he said, feeling pressed. "If it'll satisfy you, I met her in New York. She's a nurse, a midwife, who runs a clinic up north. Sometime I pick up supplies from the hospital and take them to her in..."

Cameron's gaze fixed on two men, not Americans, entering Die Lorelei from the dark, narrow street. They stood inside the doorway, squinting at the customers while their eyes adjusted to the dark, much the same way he and Danny had done. But these new arrivals were taking a keen interest in the two troopers. No matter which corner of the room they searched, their eyes returned to the two in uniform. The men standing at the doorway appeared ordinary enough. One with curly brown hair, very likely in his late twenties, was of average height but muscular. He swirled the remains of a dark beer in the bottom of a stein he brought with him from another bar. His companion, about the same age, stood noticeably taller and wore his dark, almost-black hair combed straight back. The smaller of the two gestured toward the soldiers with his stein and said something to the other, who nodded.

Doug didn't like their aggressive behavior. "Let's get out of here, Danny," he said. But Flynn, watching the scene like a hawk, wouldn't budge. He shook his head without speaking. The pretty Mexican waitress passed their table, sweeping by without stopping, but her wide-eyed expression conveyed a frightened warning. Danny tensed visibly. This is what he'd come for.

At the door, the short one said something to his companion and both of them made one more precautionary scan of the tables. By some invisible sign of agreement, the two advanced toward the uniformed troopers.

The stalkers may have overlooked Danny as a casual, relaxed gringo who'd strayed from the usual tourist haunts, but Doug knew who the real predator was. Sure as hell, Danny was going to drag him into a scrape. Now, did they have to sit here and wait for it to happen? No, he thought, and said as much. "Danny, I don't know if those two are German or not, but they're about to kick those troopers around."

The pretty waitress, carrying tequilas to the soldiers seated at the table near the wall, stopped to deliver an ominous message. "Fort Brown?" she asked, nodding at Doug and Danny. The lieutenants shifted uncomfortably. "You. *Bueno*. OK." She touched Doug's collar. "*Mas*"...she drew out the Spanish word, nodding in the soldiers' direction, "*Perigo,* danger. In civilian clothes, Doug and Danny would likely be safe, but not the soldiers in uniform.

The soldiers knew about trouble in these German bars from the obligatory briefing, and like the two lieutenants, they had come straight to the source of it. But coming in uniform, particularly to this place, was stupidity, plain and simple. Weren't these two aware they were being singled out for a humiliating thrashing?

The laughter and conversation from the group near the jukebox died away when the smaller, more aggressive one stepped over to the PFC and bumped him with his hip and shoulder. The soldier had seen it coming and bumped back immediately. The civilian, still carrying his stein, pushed the trooper with his free hand. "Get out," he snarled in English, tossing his head slightly in the direction of the door. "You are not wanted here."

The larger one pushed his hair back with his free hand. He followed the first man's lead, bumping into the other soldier hard enough to spill a little beer. The two in civilian clothes began mouthing insults about the manhood of the foolish U.S. cavalry. "Where are your horses, the ones you are parading up and down the Bravo? Now you come to Mexico, to our bar. What kind of preparation is this for war? Come to Europe and face some real men. We will send you home to your mother in a box."

It was English they were speaking, at least the larger one was, but certainly not the kind valley people spoke. English, German, it didn't matter to Danny. He knew the belligerent pair weren't a pair of innocent tourists straying from their usual haunts.

The soldiers showed no intentions of backing down. The PFC pushed back hard. "You're asking for it, you goddam kraut." The aggressor, beer stein clamped in his fist, stood with his legs spread directly in front of the soldiers, brandishing it like a weapon. The larger gripped the handle of his stein and joined the confrontation, twisting his mouth into a condescending sneer.

Conversations stopped and for an instant the only sound was loud singing from the jukebox, "*Du, du liegst mir im Herzen...*" The gringos at the table with the Mexican women scrambled from their chairs. They didn't look like Americans. Were they leaving, or were they taking sides? Whatever the men's sentiments, the women scuttled away through a door in the dark obscurity at the back of the room.

From the looks of it, the PFC wanted a piece of these arrogant people. He threw his khaki tie aside and began rolling up his sleeves.

Running footsteps clattered outside in the narrow street. The three men deserted by the Mexican women had slipped out the front door.

The private's resolve melted at the sounds of the place emptying. He didn't say so, but it was obvious in the way his eyes searched the room.

That was enough for Danny. Without bothering to look over his shoulder to see if Doug was with him, he stepped into the middle of it, facing the two men threatening the soldiers. "You heard him. Leave these two alone," he said, sounding more annoyed than like a man picking a fight.

None of this, the posturing by the Germans or the emptying of the room, had caused Danny to show the slightest concern. He spoke confidently to the soldiers. "I'll take care of this. Be getting yourselves across the bridge before more of these people come—or the police get here." At this close range, the two soldiers recognized the lieutenants, even in the dim light—the redheaded one particularly. The private took heart and the two troopers stood quite ready to make it a four-man stand.

Cameron urged them to leave, even though he would have welcomed the company. "Go," he ordered, "You're too visible in uniform." Reluctantly, the two troopers collected their ties and left by the front door, glancing back to see if the redheaded lieutenant might have changed his mind. Their footsteps moved hesitantly down the alley. Cameron thought they might have stopped.

Danny made a slight mistake by looking back at Doug. Either that or he intended to lure one of the two men into making a move. But he heard a warning scream—the waitress was on his side. The instigator, the feisty little one bellowed, "*Gottverdampten Asel,*" but it was the big man coming at Flynn first, swinging his heavy stein.

Doug watched the German's attack from two steps away. The man was mean and vicious, but the stein in his hand slowed the blow, almost as if it were in slow motion.

Stupid, Danny thought, drunken brawlers almost always open with a roundhouse move. In a smooth instant, he stepped inside the sweeping attack and blasted the attacker with a combination: a right to the stomach, a blow that bent him forward; then one more, a shot to the head that turned the lights out, sending him sprawling over one of the chairs recently abandoned by the Mexican women. Now bullying was out of the question for the remaining aggressor. His survival was at stake, forcing him to fall back on gutter-fighting experience. The man crouched momentarily, reaching down to his ankle. Something flashed in his right hand when he stood. A woman's voice somewhere near the door, maybe, screamed a warning about the knife. It could have been the pretty waitress.

The knife reversed the odds. Now Danny's quickness and boxing training might not be enough. He might have a chance, though, in forcing the knife wielder to keep moving and making him think. Something about the way he handled the knife suggested the man didn't really want to use it, except for intimidation. Danny circled his antagonist, changing directions, coming in on him cautiously, then retreating—always watching his reactions. That in-and-out movement made the man uncomfortable enough to try an awkward lunge—in a vague hope of pressing the advantage his knife gave him. He missed with a wide slashing move, without losing his balance or taking his eyes off Danny. He shuffled to get back in position with his back to the bar, brandishing the knife in his outstretched hand. Every eye in the place fixed on the fearful sight of the naked knifeblade. In the silence, the few people still in the room gave way and backed into dark corners, watching in fascination, keenly aware of feet scuffling and the gasping breaths of the two combatants.

Doug smashed a heavy chair over the knife wielder's head, sending spindles and slats flying, knocking him to the floor, stunned. The crouching knife wielder never saw the blow coming. The man's knife rattled across the dirty wooden floor, inches out of his reach. He scrambled with astonishing agility, crawling to retrieve it. The lout found his feet and rushed at Danny, thrusting with the knife. Another chair slammed down on his head and shoulders, sending him to the floor again.

Cameron stepped on the man's wrist, pinning it to the floor, smiling reproachfully. "Stay down. Forget the knife or I'll break your arm," he threatened.

Danny kicked the knife away and collected it. It was over. The entire fracas hadn't lasted much more than a minute. The shocked quiet hung in the room another few moments before the few customers remaining in Die Lorelei bolted for the door, knocking over furniture in their haste to avoid the official inquiry that was certain to come. Cameron and Flynn stood together in the center of the room, allowing the battered pair to pick themselves off the floor and escape into the night. "Good work with the chairs, Doug," said Danny. "That little one had me sweating with that knife."

"Senores, please leave," pleaded the bartender, relieved that his place had survived the disturbance without a bleeding body left on the floor. "Please, the police will be here soon."

The edgy Cameron was completely willing to comply with the man's plea. "Are you satisfied, Flynn?" He wanted to be gone well before the two came back with help, looking for a redheaded American and his skinny compadre. Who knew how the police would handle the matter? Cameron headed for the door, pleading, "We know they're here now, don't we? Lead the way, Flynn. I want to get my butt back across that river."

With Danny in the lead, they hurried through dark twisting streets heading toward the bridge, stopping now and then to listen, prepared to run if they heard sounds of being followed. When the expected pursuit didn't materialize, they slowed their pace to catch their breath. Once again amazed by a Flynn performance, Cameron had questions. "How'd you do that, Danny? That monster with the stein went down like a sack of potatoes."

Flynn, sucking at a scraped knuckle, mumbled, "Police Athletic League." Recognizing that more explanation was necessary, he said, "My father took me there to get boxing lessons because the Italian kids were beating me up in the streets. So I boxed before I took up gymnastics." His body bent into a boxer's pose and his hands blurred through a combination. "I was a lightweight then," he boasted with a grin.

New orders posted all over Fort Brown spread the word. "Officers Call 0600 hours. Troopers remain in the barracks for further orders." Soldiers fear uncertainty—some big deal officer changing his mind. Back and forth changes upset them and destroy their trust in the system.

For a time Sergeant Wieczorek waited with his men in the barracks, but the longer Centaur kept the officers, the more persistent became the troopers' pleas for wisdom from the man of experience, but he had nothing to offer. Abruptly he snatched his hat off a bunk by its stiff flat brim and pointed it at the new corporal. "You got it here, Wilson. I'll be at the office with the other sergeants," he said, knowing the troopers would feel more comfortable in their waiting and fretting without the platoon sergeant listening to every word.

First Platoon killed time, profanely questioning the sanity of the people in charge. The latest rumor sweeping the barracks was that they would board a train by the end of the week for Indio, California, for training in tanks. "I heard a sergeant talking about it when I went to the latrine," said a trooper walking by First Platoon's bunks.

When they ran out of rumors, a few pulled out playing cards or dominoes. Some turned to writing letters or repairing their uniforms. As the headquarters meeting went longer and longer, they drifted into small groups, drawn by the comfort of talking together in languages from their hometowns. Somewhere toward the far end of the barracks, a trooper played a plaintive song of old Europe on his accordion.

The Germans collected in a corner to speculate among themselves about what was going on at officers' call. The news on the radio was all about the war in Europe. Herbert Warnken, an old man of nearly thirty, thought about it a lot these days. His Uncle Max used to tell him stories about being in France during the last war. On the dull days, they would kill time swapping insults and curses in German across the no man's land between trenches. One of the men in the opposing trenches knew the Warnken family and the ones who moved to Texas.

"It made me think different 'bout things," Uncle Max admitted, but that was in the last war.

Schulze sat on a bunk, head in his hands. "It's gonna be differen' fer them Czech 'n Polish boys than f'r us." The whole world knew it was the German army that had run over Poland and Czechoslovakia. The troopers knew it shouldn't have made a difference in the United States, particularly in the army, but they felt it strongly.

Warnken brought the matter to a head with a question. "Hey, Gerhard. Didn't you say you got an uncle in Germany? In the army, right?" It was the first time he had dared to bring up the subject, but it had been eating at him since the regiment came to Fort Brown. Among themselves, the German boys knew the rest of the platoon had been thinking about it too, wondering what to expect of the Germans. Who would they side with when it came down to hard decisions?

"Yeah. He's a *Feldwebel,* I think," said Gerhard, explaining the word. "That's kinda like a master sergeant or somethin'. Mama had a picture of him taken a year or so ago. He's her youngest brother."

"Would you know him if you saw him?"

The rest knew what Herbert Warnken meant, but Reimers seemed unaware. "Oh, *ja, ja.* He came to visit us one summer. Helped with the cotton crop." Reimers laughed happily, remembering how he and Manfred would sneak away from cotton picking to steal a watermelon and break it open, scooping out the sweet, juicy red heart with their fingers.

Harbers, who didn't know of any relatives in Germany—though he knew there had to be some—posed the question this way: "If you saw him. Over in the war, I mean. Would you shoot him?" Up to now, asking the question had been taboo, but it had to be brought into the open sooner or later.

Reimers didn't have an answer. Suddenly he thought of the young relative, only a few years older, working side by side with the rest of his sister's family in the heat of the Texas summer. Could he shoot the man who went with him to meet the farm girls at the Saturday night dances? The thought left him weak and nauseous. Lips trembling, he stammered for words that wouldn't come. Reimers clasped his arms around himself to stop the shaking. "No. No," he moaned. He couldn't bear to think of it.

The can of oil he had been using to clean his rifle fell to the floor with a clatter, and everyone's eyes followed it.

Could he pump a round into Manfred with that rifle? He wiped his face on the shoulder of his undershirt and turned away to avoid eye contact. The blond boy sat sobbing, afraid of becoming a traitor to both his family and his country. He held his face in his hands to hide the shame. In a way he couldn't blame the rest for questioning his loyalty to them when it came down to kill or be killed. How could the others trust him? Could he trust himself?

Sergeant Wieczorek, returning from the Troop office, stood silent and unnoticed between the lines of double-decked bunks, listening to the innocent admission. It was plain from the silence and the somber faces that every trooper in the platoon agonized over the same problem, or something just like it: Matthijetz, Bednarski, Jaroslav Bohuslav and Henry Moore too.

Weech felt an urge to turn and leave, hoping they'd forgive him for not facing up to his duty as platoon sergeant, but it would be sneaking out. If he moved at all, they'd see him. He knew it. Instead he sucked up his own courage and moved in among a group of men whose courage and resolve to do a soldier's duty had been found wanting—at least they thought it had. Only Bednarski did so much as look up at the sergeant stepping in to stand among them. "Listen to me," Weech said in a voice so quiet, it surprised them all. "You're American soldiers." He wasn't an orator. That kind of thing was best left to Captain Franklin or Colonel Chamberlain. But Weech knew that boys like his troopers didn't come easily to the idea of killing a man. Sure, some were hunters. Bednarski, he knew, made his living as a butcher, and he guessed that most of them had probably helped with slaughtering livestock on the family farm. Most likely every one of them had used a long-bladed butcher knife at home on the farm to slit an animal strung up on a hook and had watched the entrails spill on the ground. Sights and smells like those revolted some people. But that was far, far different than killing a man, maybe even a relative—a friend. "Stand up and look at me," he ordered with a confidence he didn't really feel. They shuffled to their feet.

Facing the twisting question forced them all to wrestle with the blunt choice of killing or being killed. But confronting didn't solve the matter. Eventually Wieczorek knew he'd have to take them beyond the uncertainty and self-doubt. "We gonna talk about this a lot before we face them Germans, 'n by the time it comes to killin' 'em, you gonna be more scared of me than 'a pullin' that trigger."

Wieczorek wasn't entirely satisfied with that little speech, but he knew he'd told the truth: that killing people would be something they would eventually face—again and again. His men couldn't be allowed to wallow in indecision. "OK. Let's get this place policed up," he said.

⌖

Officers' call began quietly—at Colonel Chamberlain's direction. His primary purpose was to give them the background first, so that they had the whole picture before he divulged the good news. If he didn't do it that way, they'd begin celebrating immediately and their attention would be lost for days, and his chance of their actually understanding what happened would be lost. Since Centaur had talked to the army chief of staff at about noon the day before, the people who were in the know about what was up had swelled to about ten. Of course, Sergeant Long knew—doubtless through the invisible efficiency of the sergeants' network. Of course, Lieutenant Colonel Newman, Major Perkins knew. And Sergeant Roper knew too, as well as Captain Michael and probably a few more.

Major Perkins spoke unemotionally, letting them in on more than what they could glean from the papers or the radio, but the atmosphere in the meeting crackled with energy. An observant captain, the Machine Gun Troop commander, elbowed Walter Franklin, steering his attention to the senior officers seated at the table in the front of the room. "Look. See their eyes?" Centaur and his exec stared into the distance through eyes widened to the size of tea-cups, concentrating on giving nothing away by showing emotion.

Captain Michael had worked through the night, stoked up on cup after cup of coffee to stay awake, to get this brief done the way Centaur wanted it. He held his pointer to keep his hands from shaking while he covered the basic stuff about the increase in the number of convoys carrying war materials to the beleaguered British and the noticeable increase in German U-boat activity in the Atlantic and the Gulf of Mexico. While he spoke, two sergeants displayed annotated maps depicting the intensification of activity the captain was talking about. "Take a good look at this," he said, pointing to the Mexican port city of Veracruz. "Draw a line from there to Galveston and it goes right through here." This time the pointer was on Matamoros and Brownsville. "Get the idea?" They got the idea all right, but Centaur wanted them to hear what the Border Patrol had been telling him—the same information that won over the generals in the War Department—and one other thing.

While his assistants took down the maps and rolled them tightly to be slipped into long metal cylinders, Michael put away his pointer and faced the officers seated on the chairs. Hands on hips, he said to them, "You think you know all this and you're bored with the brief. I can read it in your faces. You want something new, don't you?" He paced back and forth, waiting for the sergeants to remove the maps.

"OK. Those Germans across the river know a lot about us—too goddamn much for it to be a coincidence. We've gotten word from the Mexican police that some soldiers from Fort Brown were over there last night brawling with Germans in a bar called Die Lili Marlene or Die Lorelei, something like that." He scanned the faces of the men seated in rows of chairs, careful not to stop at any one face too long. "Now listen to me." In general terms Michael accused them all of talking too freely about the business of the 124th. People across the river, hostile people and probably not all Germans, knew a lot of detail about how the Fort Brown patrols were conducted and when they had been dropped in favor of infantry training. Doug and Danny, sitting together as usual, watched Michael like a pair of hawks, to see where his sweeping eyes would stop. They couldn't have been the only ones in that part of Matamoros. Could they?

The captain must have seen something in all those faces—not enough to accuse a single man, but he came close to doing it. "Let me be clear and direct. Some of you, or some of your men, may be unwittingly giving away information you should be keeping secret. God, I hope it isn't deliberate," said the S-2, letting them know he suspected a member of the regiment was guilty of doing it inadvertently. They had to be shocked into understanding what a breach of security might mean, because the colonel was about to divulge something important.

Centaur took the lectern the moment Captain Michael stepped away. The debilitating effects of months of uncertainty fell away in an instant. Overnight, his hollow-eyed, thousand-yard stare was gone, dropped like a bad habit. In three strides from his chair to the lectern, he was transformed—no longer a reluctant superintendent of ground-pounding infantry training, but once again Centaur, born to command horse cavalry. Elation emanated from his entire being. "Late yesterday, I went riding," he pronounced slowly into the microphone, enjoying the expectant looks from his officers. Only with great effort did he force himself not to give in to his emotions. Never did he consider allowing his officers to think that the respite General Marshall gave him was anything like a final decision to retain horse cavalry permanently—but it was a chance. "Calling for my horse was my first official act in response to an order directly from the army chief of staff himself to put away the infantry equipment. And now it affects you too. As of this instant, we're once again horse cavalry!"

They jumped to their feet, applauding, slapping each other on the back, cheering.

"Make the most of it," Chamberlain shouted into the noise. The celebration was still going when he left his operations officer in charge.

Major Perkins wasted no time laying out a new operating schedule. "I'll give you a moment to get your notebooks out. I have a lot to cover before we resume patrolling this afternoon." For nearly an hour, he detailed a schedule for an entire month. Before he excused them to pass the information to their troopers waiting in the barracks, Perkins described what Colonel Chamberlain called a gift from the gods: a war game proposed by the cavalry generals. General Marshall had already approved it. "It's a life or death opportunity to convince the army to keep any horse cavalry at all." He waited for the note taking to stop before stressing the gravity of the challenge, "But should we fail, it's the end of the horse cavalry, forever."

The two lieutenants climbed into Danny's car for the short ride to the barracks. Their hasty departure from Die Lorelei was still very much on Cameron's mind, but for all Danny mentioned about it, their little adventure might never have happened. Captain Michael all but named names right there in officers' call, or maybe it was the two uniformed troopers the S-2 knew about. Still, the act of going to that specific bar wasn't, in itself, against any law he knew about. He watched Danny driving, eyes unblinking, smiling, probably thinking about horses or women—maybe both. This Irish boy was an enigma. If Flynn ever got his mind focused, he'd be unbeatable. Nobody on the post could touch him as a rider. He had a sense with horses—his troopers too, for that matter. Look what he'd done to make a soldier of that sergeant of his. Drinking, he could hold as much tequila as anybody without showing the effects. It was with women, though, that Danny Flynn was unsurpassed. Never were his special powers so sharply focused as when his mind was on women—which was almost always. Take the look on his face right now. Was she one of those Michael had mentioned?

Two minutes after hearing it, Danny wasn't giving one damn about that warning. "Did you debrief with the S-2 people about wiping up that bar with those Germans?" asked Doug, attempting to break into Danny's reverie.

"Talk to the S-2? Why would I do that?"

"You randy SOB!"

Flynn was probably no more preoccupied with women than were most of the men in the 124th, but something about Danny made them want to jump into bed with him—that's what got under the skin of the lieutenants of the caucus. If he were truly honest about it, Doug would have admitted he was as jealous of that enviable gift of Flynn's as anybody. "They suspect it was us over there last night. But they're not sure," Cameron said.

"Who?" Suddenly Danny was interested.

"The S-2! You knew damn well the two troopers would come back to the post talking about the lieutenants in the bar. It's a good guess that they went to another bar and blabbed about what they had seen."

Captain Michael had collared Doug during a short break in the drawn-out officers' call to ask a few questions. The two troopers they had sent away from Die Lorelei hadn't gone far. One of Michael's men did overhear a sketchy account in the barracks, but it could have been secondhand information.

"According to Captain Michael, some redheaded lieutenant is becoming a legend in the barracks," Cameron said. "The S-2 thinks it's got to be you. You should go talk to him."

Flynn ignored the suggestion, asking, "When he talked to you—did you tell him it was us?"

"No." Doug squirmed uncomfortably. "He asked a lot of questions. For instance, he asked me how often I went to Matamoros and where I went." In their interview, the captain fished for some critical details, like the street name and the exact name of the bar, so Cameron had been able to avoid giving direct answers. "And then he asked me about rumors that you go there a lot. I told him that you didn't talk about where you go."

"Well now. And why wouldn't he be asking me about those things?"

"I think he'd be grilling you in his office right now, if it hadn't been for this reprieve for the horse cavalry. I'd bet the man is on to you."

Danny parked his car at the barracks. "Tell me about this."

"Flynn! I don't go around interrogating the S-2." Cameron warned Danny about suspicions that somebody might be having Danny followed. Almost immediately he felt he shouldn't have admitted his suspicions, but he still felt a lingering sense of responsibility for the new lieutenant. "It's not easy talking to a man who's either on a horse or in bed with the first woman who comes along," he said.

Flynn glared indignantly at Cameron, "She's a lady, bucko." He shook an accusatory finger. "She's an Irish lady, a nurse. How many times do I have to tell you? Besides, I hardly see her. She's away from Matamoros a lot—at a clinic in some village."

Cameron threw up his hands. "For months you and that Blankenship woman were shacked up in her apartment. Now, she hasn't seen you at all, so she calls me twice a day to ask where you are." He gave Danny a shove, and sniped away. "Your pal Doug doesn't know where you are. Your dog robber covers for you. You've got something secret going over on the Mexican side, and I'm left to tell lies to Molly and give evasive answers to the S-2. Come on, Flynn. Come clean." Danny ignored him and hurried away to his waiting platoon.

chapter

FIFTEEN

Washington: U.S. Navy Department awards contracts for 210 new ships, including 12 aircraft carriers and 7 battleships.

White-coated waiters pumped furiously at the handles speeding the shuttle back and forth, struggling to keep pace with the orders. Centaur had broken his long silence to celebrate the reprieve, but if horse cavalry were to be retained permanently in the army, the War Department would have to be made to see things in a new light. After joyously announcing the miraculous deliverance from a life of ground pounding, the Colonel holed up in his office again. Common wisdom held that he was working doggedly on the all-or-nothing exercise wrested from George Marshall.

Truscott and Herr, the principal cavalry generals, did their best for Sam Chamberlain at the War Department, arguing for rules supporting the role of horses in a mechanized army. Now it was up to Centaur and the men from Texas.

Captain Walter Franklin collected his three platoon commanders at a table to share his vews on the news from regimental headquarters. Most of the troop commanders were doing the same thing.

"Drink up, gentlemen," he said, "This has been a long, thirsty day." Major Perkins had kept the captains for most of the afternoon, going over the fat document that laid out the specifics of the war game designed as a crucible to test the necessity for horse cavalry. The troop commander brought out his notebook and described the burden on the 124th in a bare few words. "Centaur will not permit us to fail."

They pulled their chairs up, giving him their attention. "First of all, the exercise is going to be in a large desolate area described as being north of Fort Ringgold and south of Fort Clark," began the captain. "You may have suspected that." He thought aloud for the benefit of his lieutenants who hadn't yet been that far north. "Probably, it'll be east of Eagle Pass, where Fort Duncan is located." Once, when the Twelfth Cavalry was still at Fort Brown, he'd been out there for about a week—awful-looking country full of broken limestone hills covered with cactus and thick brush. "Used to be Comanche country—and not so long ago," he said.

Franklin tore a sheet of paper from his notebook to sketch a rough map depicting the Rio Grande and four border forts. Across the river he drew a line that meandered from somewhere in Mexico, east to Fort Clark and farther into Texas. He labeled it the Comanche war road, cautioning the lieutenants that the so-called road didn't appear on maps.

"A fellow at Fort Clark told me about the Comanche, before the cavalry finally got them corralled." Local history held that not even the Comanche could force a passage into Texas from Mexico through the pitiless thickets without a dependable war road leading from their safe haven in Mexico to the new settlements in Texas. In reality, it was more of a path widened into a road by heavy travel on horseback. When the army got the job of putting a stop to the Indian raids, they built Fort Clark right smack on the Indian road, atop the highest hill for miles.

Franklin waved his hand vaguely northward, in the general direction of the rugged lands of Texas once ruled by the Comanche. "So we'll be hearing about the terrain up there," he said. All he was sure of was that to assure plenty of room for maneuvering, the army's agents were out there now, negotiating with landowners for the temporary use of thousands of square miles of ranchland.

George Kincaid came to the table to chat with the lieutenants' caucus, as he did occasionally. He too had to been to Fort Clark before the 124th came. He rolled his glass in his fingers, watching the amber whiskey roll down the surface. "Yeah, Captain, that's the better part of three hundred miles by road. We don't have anywhere near enough portees to get all our horses up there." Referring to Danny, he said, "We gonna have our transportation expert take our horses up there on the train?" He guffawed, enjoying his joke, banging his hand on the table hard enough to make the glasses rattle. "Flynn might decide to whip some poor trooper on the way up there. This time we all could watch."

Kincaid could get under Danny's skin with almost no effort at all. Flynn jumped to his feet. "Maybe they'd like to see you and me have a go, George," he hissed, tensed and full of fight.

"Get back to your troop, George. This is E Troop business," ordered Franklin. He had no patience for squabbling lieutenants. "Now, pay attention."

The captain agreed with Kincaid about the distance. "It's a long way, but not as bad as some might think. Now I'll tell you what the major put out about the movement." Dutifully the lieutenants took out their notebooks and pencils.

"Well, gentlemen, here are some things you need to know before we begin," said Franklin in the folksy turn of speech he employed when he wanted to make something plain. "There's generals and then there's other generals. What happened, most likely, is that the head man in Washington said, 'Give the cavalry a fair shake.' Sounded good, but then another one in San Antonio read the orders and said, 'Screw, 'em. General Marshall may be the boss, but he's a long way off.'" They understood, in a vague sort of way, but Franklin knew that with lieutenants, complex points frequently require painstaking explanation. "There's more to these maneuvers of Centaur's than meets the eye," he said, warning them that this was his own opinion and nothing more. "Sure, the man at the very top of the army gave a clear, direct order, and every aspect of this exercise has been chewed over exhaustively, I assure you. But the haggling's just begun, and it won't be over until the day the final report is signed. And maybe not even then."

Franklin tasted his drink, considering how to get across to his eager lieutenants that this lingering controversy between horses and armor would tempt any general interested in the outcome into twisting the rules to suit himself. He put the matter into practical terms. "Nobody's going to bring tanks to South Texas for this—too expensive, and the issue of what you can do with tanks isn't in doubt any longer. So Colonel Chamberlain has been selected as the army's champion to demonstrate that horse cavalry is indispensable on the battlefield, but it will mean being creative. Even without tanks, that might mean competing with motorcycles and trucks, or airplanes." He leaned back in his chair and stretched his booted legs out under the table. "I don't know, but I think our key will be to look for every opportunity to prove our effectiveness."

Franklin ticked off the rules. "To begin with, no mechanical transportation for the horses—and we take all our healthy ones." The sheer size of the enterprise taken on by Centaur was beginning to dawn on the lieutenants. "Each troop takes an equal share of the extra animals." It came to a straight-line distance of well over two hundred miles, depending on exactly where the exercise was conducted, across some nasty country. Franklin shifted uncomfortably. "I have to presume it won't all be out in that devilish brush around

Fort Clark," he guessed, but this exhausting cross-country travel was to be completed a few days before the actual exercise began.

Frowning, Danny asked Franklin to verify a point, "Is it a race then, sir?"

Franklin nodded grimly, expelling his breath through gritted teeth. "Yep, that's how I see it."

Doug Cameron finally broke the thoughtful silence, whispering barely audibly, "Jeezus H. Christ! We'll be all broke down by the time we get there. Horses and men both."

"I wish I could say it won't be that way," said Franklin, admitting his pessimism. "But Centaur inserted this provision himself. He wants us to go for a record, even if the effort kills us before we get started maneuvering in that rough country."

"But Captain, this is more like a cattle drive than cavalry work," said Mike Pinelli, who'd been unusually silent until now.

Danny asked, "How're all the supply people and the clerks and the medics going to get there?"

"Trucks," said Franklin, weary of hearing this point argued for hours in the troop commanders' meeting. "He wants to use everything in this exercise—the general who's going to run the exercise put his foot down on that—but for us, the horses are the focus, so we start off with a long-distance race."

Danny waved to the waiter. "Gin and tonic and whatever these gentlemen are drinking." While their orders sped on their way to Mexico, he began to outline an idea. "This may not be as bad as it seems." By buying the round of drinks, Danny had purchased the privilege of leading the discussion and for the moment, at least, Franklin's intention to explain the rules that favored the use of horses was tabled.

"What the hell do you mean, 'It's not that bad,' Flynn? You got some kind of magic spell?" asked Cameron. "We know how god-awful that country is. Right, Captain?"

Franklin's sour expression expressed his doubts.

It wasn't magic at all. Danny did know something about transporting horses through that wicked terrain, and he waited, calm and unflappable, until they were done with their blathering. "It's been done before." He gave them a moment to digest the thought. "I've talked to somebody who knows how to do it. Sergeant Long, at the stables, told me about it one afternoon."

Pinelli made a hand motion as if to brush off Long as a doddering old geezer. Flynn, though, remained insistent. "He said they used to cover long distances like this all the time—before they got trucks—but the hard lessons were quickly forgotten. Everybody had a private theory: slow, fast—they had any number of ideas, but here's one that works." Long suggested to Danny, while they discussed the details, that it might have been written up once in the *Cavalry Journal*. "He was right. They had done it right here in the Rio Grande Valley. The secret is a floating picket line—that is, speed and a floating picket line."

Franklin suspected a joke. "What's a floating picket line?"

Flynn tore a sheet of paper from his notebook. "Look here." He diagrammed a length of rope that would be attached at its forward end to a singletree hitched normally to a lead horse. Its length would be determined by the number of horses to be led. "Now, down here, the tail end: we'd fix it to the pole of a spring wagon, drawn by two horses." According to the *Journal* article, the light wagon would have a driver who could steer the tail end of the line of horses. "And you could carry a light load in the wagon," said Danny, expecting some response.

Pinelli stood up from his chair and walked around the table to study the diagram over Danny's shoulder as he drew it. His head bobbed with quick nodding motions as Danny described the concept. "It's ingenious," Danny said. "See, then you can attach the spare horses to this line in pairs and assign mounted troopers as outriders. This is the way it was laid out in the *Cavalry Journal*. Sergeant Long and I went over it together."

"Let me see that," demanded Franklin.

While the troop commander studied the diagram, Danny went over more of the detail from the article, "The idea is to move along at a pretty good speed. The man who wrote this swore that you could take rest stops hourly and still average better than five and a half miles an hour. Start early and be in camp by noon."

The idea took hold in Franklin's mind. "Interesting. Who else knows this? Around here, I mean?" He looked at the groups like his seated at tables around them to see if they had been listening. Flynn's information was intriguing and he wasn't about to share it—at least until they had tried it where prying eyes wouldn't steal the idea.

Danny shrugged. "I dunno, sir. People have been marching horses over long distances for thousands of years."

"But," offered Cameron, "If this crusty sergeant knows about it, maybe a lot of people know about this one. When and where exactly was it tried?"

"According to the *Journal* article, they did it in nineteen twenty-two, from around Del Rio to Fort Brown. Hell, that's over four hundred miles and the author claimed they did it without so much as a sore back."

Franklin picked up the small diagram to study it more closely. "Tell you what. Let me keep this and give it a good chewing over." He tapped the eraser end of his pencil on the table. "Maybe I'll have a chat with Sergeant Long over a glass of whiskey."

Danny drove his car slowly across the bridge into Matamoros, cautiously threading his way through the chaotic traffic to the hospital to collect a package of urgently needed supplies Maureen requested. Her note said, "Pick up a box from the orderly in the maternity ward. You'll have no trouble understanding him because he's Irish, like you. He'll be expecting you."

Not so long ago, finding Maureen Gallamore in Matamoros would have been about as unlikely as finding fields of Rose of Sharon growing lush and green on the banks of the Rio Grande; and now, at her bidding, he was on his way to meet another Irishman at the hospital. It still seemed odd, this medical thing that placed an IRA agent, if that's what she really was, here in Mexico. And now that Captain Michael had warned them about the disquieting presence of a growing number of German agents, Danny found it troubling, in a way. Still, she did have that letter from the archbishop, and wasn't he talking to Francis X. Riley right here in the hospital with all these pregnant Mexican women around.

Riley handed him a package marked "Medical supplies—Navidad" on its brown paper wrapping, and made excuses for not taking time to talk. A woman just beginning her labor required his attention. "She's going to have a Cesarean. Otherwise she wouldn't have come here," he confided.

Danny hefted the package and turned it over in his hands, trying to guess what kind of medical supplies he would be carrying. The contents of the box sloshed a little: medications of some kind, he guessed. Following Riley's sketchy directions, he pointed his Ford north, through irrigated fields and citrus groves that gave way to open country. The farther he drove along the military road, the rougher and more desolate the road and the land along it became. The Mexicans hadn't built anything like the military road that stretched along the river on the American side. Eventually the pavement gave way to oiled sand and then to a narrow, rough stretch where the biggest holes were filled with rock coarsely crushed with a hammer or simply left unfilled altogether.

Several hot, dusty hours north of Matamoros, he rolled to a stop, satisfied by a sign that he'd reached Navidad. Danny got out of the car, wiping his face with his red bandanna, congratulating himself that he hadn't suffered any real calamities along the way. Changing a flat tire cost him about half an hour. He left the punctured tire to be repaired at a little crossroads workshop where he gave the man some pesos, telling him he would return the following afternoon. Before resuming his journey, Danny sat in the driver's seat worried if the tire, or the red rubber inner tube itself, might prove too much of a temptation in a time of world rubber shortages. He went back inside to leave a few more pesos as a bribe to assure the security of his tire until his return.

To say that Navidad was built around a plaza would be stretching a point. At best the central area was little more than a rubble-strewn field laid out in a generally rectangular form. Danny stopped his car on the eastern, downhill end, just off the dusty ruts he had been following for eleven miles since leaving the main road. Stretching his legs, he counted fewer than a dozen stores or offices, most fitted with solid wooden shutters that could be closed at night, occupying spaces on three sides. An adobe church with cracked white walls and a small iron bell stood on the upper side. The priest's house, a few yards distant from the church, was the largest residence in the town or for many miles around, quite probably. On the north side, the major building housed the Alcalde's cramped one-room office. An even smaller iron cage, serving as a jail, occupied nearly half the official structure. Across the plaza from the Alcalde's, a tiny school, built in 1935, according to the numbers pressed into the adobe over the door, sat surrounded by a dusty play yard, from which the stones had been thrown aside to make the ground smoother for the children. In front of the school, two roughly crafted swings dangled from a rough wooden frame.

In the center of the plaza, as their crowning civic glory, the citizens of Navidad had dug a communal well and built a watering trough for the farmers' animals and a wooden bench where the old people could sit and pass the time. No one in Navidad remembered when the well was dug, only that it was long after the twice-weekly market was first held here. Paths wide enough for most farmers' carts and wagons drawn by animals or small tractors cut an irregular pattern of radial roads and footpaths converging on the well through the gaps between the buildings.

Danny walked along one of those paths to the well, lowered the bucket and brought up a little water. A tin cup sat on the brick wall around the well, connected by a cotton cord to a nail to keep it from falling into the dust. The first cupful of water, he swirled in the cup to wash away any dust and threw it on the ground. He drank the second cupful thirstily, his eyes closed with enjoyment. The next he sipped while carefully surveying Navidad's buildings, watching for a face in a window or any sign of activity at all. Maureen's directions were to, "Stay in the plaza. I'll know you're there and I'll come to find you."

He sat on the bench, watching the children at play in the schoolyard. Two or three of the braver ones crept closer to peer at the gringo with the red hair. A little girl in a worn red dress that had probably been her sister's smiled at him when he waved. Then he heard Maureen coming. Not Maureen herself, actually—it was the chattering and laughing of the children who had gone to find her leading the way back. She came toward him, walking in the long stride of country people, with the little ones clinging to her skirt for courage. As she came nearer, she called to him, "Danny! What a dear you are to drive all the way up here!" Had she not called out in English, he might have taken her for one of the local women coming to purchase some domestic necessity. Maureen, the Dona Marina of Matamoros society, wore a long loosely fitting dress like the ones he'd seen worn by women working the fields near the road on his northbound journey. She spoke to the children in rapid Spanish, answering their curiosity about the man who'd come in the car to visit her. When it was time, Maureen shook her long apron, making a game of shooing them back to the school.

To reach her house, Danny drove about a quarter mile toward the river, to an area of irrigated orange orchards. "It's just here," said Maureen of a stone and adobe house with a red-tiled roof and peeling plaster walls—quite a large house, actually, framed by palms. Handsome but crumbling landscaping lent a palatial air to the house, which dwarfed the sunbaked huts Danny had seen on his drive from Matamoros. She explained the house to him; "The people here call it a hacienda, perhaps because it was once entirely surrounded by a low wall with a gate." But the gate had been taken from the gateposts and part of the wall knocked down to permit farm vehicles to pass through on their way to the orchard just beyond the house. Perhaps the landowner took the gates away to a larger home.

Danny parked the car on the hard, bare earth in front of the house and stood with Maureen, taking in all the signs of her charitable enterprise. A sign in Spanish printed by an unsteady hand on a single board proclaimed the presence of a women's clinic. "Some days as many as a dozen women come to see me," she said, studying Danny's face for his reaction.

"At the moment, Maureen, I'm here to see one woman." He kissed her before she could begin another word and she pulled him eagerly to her. He felt her pressing against him, and heard her hotly whispering in his ear, "Oh. I see. Would you like to come in, Lieutenant Flynn?"

It wasn't until the sun was well up the next morning that he walked the bare earth around Maureen's hacienda while she prepared a breakfast on a stove stoked with wood left from pruning the orchards. Danny wandered slowly among the orange trees, fascinated by the loads of fruit clustered on branches bending under their weight. In New York, shopkeepers piled oranges like these in neat pyramids, to be sold as festive treats.

Here, however, a riot of trees bore fruit he could admire and touch, especially the well-irrigated and neatly tended ones in the orchard that began outside the crumbling remnants of the stuccoed wall. The few trees inside the wall had been planted years ago to enhance the grounds, but as the house aged and passed into the hands of less fastidious owners, they were allowed to grow untended. Even in their uncultivated state, they lent a certain stately grace to the aging hacienda. He plucked an orange from a low branch, feeling the fresh, thick skin; savoring the fragrance of the fruit and leaves. A few moments later, Danny found himself between the first few rows of the meticulously kept orchard, admiring the precise, geometric spacing of the trees and the large, perfect fruit. How long he'd been away from Maureen's kitchen, he wasn't sure, but a wisp of white smoke rising from the kitchen stove reminded him that he should be returning.

Approaching the hacienda, he noticed tire tracks leading toward a nearby stand of native trees: Maureen's car, probably—she would need a car to make her rounds. Out of curiosity, he followed them: a hundred yards at most. There, among a scattering of oil cans in a little clearing, stood a dusty blue De Soto with Texas license plates.

His imagination flashed back to that terrible day of his first patrol when first platoon had nearly been suffocated in the dust tossed up by a car like this driven by a black-haired gringa. In every clearly remembered detail, this was that same car—in fact, the one that caught his eye in the Matamoros market. He made his way to the house with heavy steps, wanting urgently to confront her, yet not willing to do it for fear of what she might reveal. Surely she knew where he had been walking. Could she possibly think he hadn't seen the car? He had to know.

He found Maureen at the stove in the simply furnished kitchen, stirring a pot of beans. If she held any concerns about what he might have seen, she gave no sign of it. She wiped a bit of perspiration from her forehead with a corner of her apron, motioned toward the table with her hand and set a plate of tortillas and beans at one of the chairs. As he drew a chair up she said a few words regarding the homely fare. "Usually the women want to pay, and they share a bit of their food with me."

Without a word, he sipped coffee from a dented tin cup like the one at the well. To him, tortillas and beans made a surprisingly tasty breakfast—far more appealing than the monotonous field rations he and his troopers carried tied to their saddles.

Danny ate quietly, aware of her eyes following him. Maureen was leaving it to him to choose the time to discuss questions that had been waiting for months. Putting it off any longer would be pointless. He pointed in the direction of the littered clearing with his coffee cup. "Your car?" he said, more as an assumption than a question and she returned his gaze steadily.

"Yes, it is, Danny," she answered in a voice soft and quiet

He chewed thoughtfully on a tortilla to give himself time to think. To rush through this might be disastrous. "You use it in your work, I guess?" he ventured finally.

"I do."

The morning sun sent a glow of light through a corner of the window, highlighting the serenity of her face. Outside a flock of songbirds flitted through the Orange trees. A confused, helpless feeling settled over Danny. He was the uncertain one, not Maureen. With his elbows on the table, he held the cup in both hands, tipping it for a tiny sip. Did he love this woman, he asked himself? But he knew the answer. Carefully, as if picking a path through a menacing stand of prickly pear, he sorted through the questions swirling in his head, searching for ones that might have answers he could bear. But it was impossible. After one more tentative sip, he went right to the core of it. "That was you at the sale in Matamoros, wasn't it?"

"Of course," she whispered huskily, eyes downcast.

Yes, of course. How gullible he had been. Danny sat up, confronting her. "That wasn't Francis Riley, the Irish hospital orderly, with you that day on the road? I met him yesterday." He ran his fingers through his hair. This was so difficult. A question emerged from him like a groan. "It wasn't an Irishman at all, was it?"

She barely whispered, "No."

He raised an eyebrow, wanting to ask who.

"I cannot tell you," she said. "I'm bound not to."

So now it was a matter of scruples. "What exactly are you doing in Mexico then?"

"I'm a nurse," she said calmly, holding her head high, eyes flashing the same fire he'd seen in that tumultuous meeting in the Upper Room.

"A nurse, you say. All right, you're a nurse. I'm prepared to believe that. Haven't I seen the letter after all? And I've been to the hospital for the package of medicine." He interrupted himself with a sudden thought. "I forgot to give you the package Riley gave me." He frowned. "It was urgent, you said."

She smiled, glancing through the kitchen window at his car. "I knew it was there. Earlier this morning, while you slept, I brought it in and put the contents away." Surprisingly, she brought him back to his questions. "You were inquirin', I believe?"

"Maureen, I'm in love with you, and I want to believe whatever you say, but now I know you're far more than a nurse. Why are you here, lass?"

"You shouldn't ask to know too much," she warned him.

Unsure of his footing, he bolted his breakfast without raising his eyes. When he finally looked up to speak, she interrupted in a voice hoarse with emotion, barely a whisper, "I'm an agent of the IRA. You know that, you soft-headed Irishman. I could tell you were fallin' in love with me, so I let you believe whatever you wanted. To tell the truth, since that Sunday at the corrida, I've been feeling the same thing for you, but I can't—no, I won't—let that get in the way of the Cause." She waved away another of Danny's attempts to speak. "What is important for you to remember now is that you swore an oath." The hoarseness had left her voice. In its place he heard the same strength and firmness felt by the Faithful that night, "You freely and unconditionally swore that oath to help me wherever you happened to find me."

He breathed deeply, disturbed by the boldness of her declaration, and yet he was surprised to hear himself responding calmly, explaining his dilemma. He didn't deny his oath, but events beyond their control had complicated the situation. "I see that oath in the Upper Room as being in direct conflict with another I made just as freely: my oath as a second lieutenant in the United States Army, to defend the Constitution of the United States against all enemies..."

Wanting a little time to think, she stood and walked noiselessly to the stove to bring the coffee pot to the table.

The woman fascinated him, even in the simple act of pouring coffee into a battered cup. These ordinary movements were no less graceful than her elegant Spanish manner-isms as Dona Marina in a clinging dress and mantilla in Matamoros. Yet something about the coarse fabric and utilitarian lines of her apron and long-hemmed dress of the country-side inserted something fundamentally different into her manner—something that gave her words a power rising from roots set firmly in the earth. "Daniel Flynn," she said in a voice gone throaty again, "your blood is as Irish as mine, and as your father's. None of that can be altered by the mere geographical accident of where a person was born. You may have been born in America, but your soul was conceived in Ireland. It cannot be washed from you nor can it be cast aside like a sin forgiven by a priest in the confessional. At birth you inherited a duty to the Cause to free a people who have been downtrodden for centuries—your people—ground by the English into the very turf they stole from its rightful owners." Danny felt those green eyes boring deep into him, probing the bottom of his soul. He heard her words driving her point home, "You have an ancient, sacred duty, and I am a witness to your oath to support the cause of freeing the land of your forefathers."

No response offered itself. He sat numbly, unable to tear his eyes from Maureen's face, flushed and animated with emotion, her chest heaving with an undiluted fervor for her cru-sade. The need to know who was with her at the Matamoros car sale was gone—evaporated from his mind. Trembling slightly at his scrutiny, she breathed, "Ye'd better go now, Danny, so you can think about what I've been sayin'."

"The chaplain will see you in a few minutes, Lieutenant Flynn," said the secretary, indicating the closed door. "He is expecting you, but I think he's putting the finishing touches on his sermon." She smiled reassuringly at the uneasy visitor sitting stiffly in a chair.

Danny had spent most of a sleepless night preparing for this visit, yet even now he couldn't say precisely what he wanted from the chaplain. He fidgeted nervously in his chair, frowning at some imagined imperfection in the shine of his boots. "Coffee, Lieutenant Flynn?" asked the secretary, trying to put him at his ease.

"Thank you. No," said Danny.

The secretary, a pleasant woman in a flowered dress—about forty, he guessed, with her dark hair pulled back in a bun—tried another tack at making him more comfortable. She adjusted her glasses to read from the appointment card she had made out for Chaplain Murdock's information, but it wasn't helpful. "Personal," it read simply. Taking the cryptic information Danny had hesitantly left with her, she suspected this might have been something to do with Molly Blankenship, but a few discrete calls to a few ladies on the post let her know it most likely was not about a wedding. "Can I tell the chaplain what you'd like to talk about, sir?"

"No, ma'am," said the nervous lieutenant, more sharply than he intended. Danny's social and ethical problems had become complicated beyond his powers to solve them—and he needed help. It was that simple, and that complicated. Actually, beyond the two conflicting oaths, it might be that he also faced a professional problem, too. According to his way of thinking, he could go to jail for aiding and abetting the enemy. How would he have been able to tell her all that?

Danny felt terribly alone with his dilemma. Other than his father, who could possibly understand that his problem was rooted in swearing those two oaths? This called for... what? Circumspection was a word that came to him. Oh, it was more than that, but could he tell the chaplain about his fears that he had unthinkingly passed information to a foreign agent? That is, if she truly was an illegal foreign agent. Something in Danny's soul told him both those oaths were real and valid. Maureen had been correct about the first being rooted deep in his heritage. If he broke it, he would suffer the eternal torments reserved for those who break ancient trusts. On the other hand, if he were to break the more recent one to defend the Constitution of the United States, the consequences would hardly be internal or limited to turmoil. He could easily find himself in a cell at Fort Leavenworth. His soul or his freedom—what was a man to do? So far, the answer hadn't been forthcoming.

The decision to come to the chaplain's office for help had come only after an ordeal of mental torment. For the hundredth time, it seemed, the same questions surfaced. How long had he been in the army? A very short time: only a few months, really. How long had he been Irish? Maureen was indisputably right; his Irishness went back to some misty age. What might this visit to the chaplain cost him in the long run? Would he gain anything? Might he lose no matter which way he selected? It occurred to him that this was indeed possible.

So what was it he feared most? Was it the vague, yet real notion of breaking his inborn trust? Or was it the quite corporal punishment of being slammed into prison? Such was the power of being cursed by an idea as old as time. Now he was on the threshold of going to someone outside his family for help in working through these deep moral questions. Partly it was going to see a chaplain at all that concerned him. His experience with the black-cassocked Jesuits wasn't very instructive just now. At home in New York, he went regularly for ritual absolution from a faceless man behind a screen in the confessional. He went because the sisters had taught him it was the right way, but never had he truly found ease and comfort in it. They weren't really faceless, the priests behind the screen. They were the men he saw every day. He knew them and they knew him. So after confessing the details of following the powerful natural urges that drive young men, he found it nearly impossible to face his confessors on the campus without visible embarrassment, because he felt they were still judging him for things he didn't think sinful at all. After he stopped going to confession, he felt better.

But now he wrestled with a problem that no one else could possibly understand—unless they both supported the Cause and served in the army. These questions focused combined forces on his conscience: one weighed down with moral gravity, and the other with dire legal consequences. Here, far from his family and his old friends, his choices were few. Physical torture would have been far preferable to airing his questions to the lieutenants of the caucus during an afternoon of belting back nickel margaritas: not even to Doug Cameron. And certainly, going to Molly Blankenship was out of the question. Where should he go then, if not to a chaplain? Go talk to the chaplain was the standard advice dished up when troopers had problems they found impossible to discuss with their officers. At least a chaplain, even this one—the only chaplain on the post—could be trusted to keep his problems in confidence. Couldn't he? He had to have relief, but the question of what it might cost him bore down on him heavily.

"You can go in now, Lieutenant Flynn," said the woman in the flowered dress.

Negotiating the few steps to the door took an effort of will in moving his leaden and unresponsive legs and arms. Apprehensively, he turned the knob and pushed the door open. A roundish man in khakis with silver captain's bars on his collar, nearly bald except for a fringe of dark brown hair, sat at his desk, writing intently on a yellow legal pad. Danny recognized Captain Murdock as one of the more awkward riders he'd ever seen astride a horse.

The chaplain stabbed a final period onto the paper with his fountain pen and pushed the yellow pad away from him. Smiling, he stood to greet his visitor, extending his hand. "Lieutenant Flynn. How good to see you."

Without waiting for an invitation, Danny sat heavily on the sturdy, leather-covered chair and grasped the armrests with moist hands, breathing heavily to keep his head clear.

"Here, Lieutenant Flynn," he heard a voice saying. "Take this water. You nearly fainted." Chaplain Murdock's face came into focus. "Are you well, Lieutenant?" the chaplain was asking.

Danny took the glass and drank gratefully. "Sure, Father, I think I'm OK. I skipped breakfast today, that's all."

Murdock smiled at Danny's excusable gaffe and allowed him a few moments to regain his composure. He tried a bit of light conversation to put his visitor at ease. "At last I have an opportunity to meet the regiment's finest horseman face to face. It's truly a pleasure to watch you ride. Frankly, I think you're a more gifted rider than even Colonel Chamberlain. What is it I hear him called: Centaur?"

Feeling a bit steadier, Danny smiled, accepting the compliment gracefully, "Colonel Chamberlain is the best horseman there is, anywhere, without a doubt—but thank you all the same, sir."

"I like to ride a little myself," said the chaplain modestly. "I'm not very good at it, but I want to get better. It's important to me to be able to understand what the men of the 124th do in the course of their day. Maybe you could give me a little instruction occasionally."

Now it was Henry Murdock who found himself uncomfortable about coming to the business of Danny's visit. On his own, the chaplain had learned that this lieutenant's name came up frequently in conversations with the troopers and with the senior officers as well. "That kid who put the sergeant in his place," someone said. Another time, the exec was heard to say, "All kinds of things happen wherever Lieutenant Flynn happens to be." So why was he here? From his secretary he already knew that this wasn't to arrange a wedding, so...

"Of course, sir. Anytime, sir," said Danny about the riding lessons.

Murdock returned to his seat behind his desk and squared his shoulders. "What shall we talk about, Danny?"

Flynn began uneasily, "I have an ethical problem, sir—at least I think that's what it is."

"Would you like to tell me about it?"

"I'm going to try, sir, though it won't be easy," said Danny, forcing himself to relax his steely grip on the arms of the chair. He stretched his legs forward a bit to cross his ankles, forgetting about his spurs. He uncrossed them with care; no harm done. In his uneasiness, however, none of his rehearsed openings would come to him, and he simply couldn't work out for himself exactly how his relationship with the captain behind the desk should be conducted. He settled on an opening that occurred to him in the waiting room. "What should I call you, sir? Is it Father, or Captain, or what?"

"I can understand your uneasiness, Lieutenant Flynn. In your case particularly, things are muddled and that stands in the way of conversation." Murdock furrowed his brow, considering the question of protocol. "Call me Henry. Yes, let's be Henry and Danny. That would be best." Henry paused, his mouth in a thoughtful pucker. "I gather you're a Catholic, but I...am a Methodist." He added hastily, "Still, I should be able to help you with a question of ethics. Why don't you begin?"

Danny's mind searched through the opening statements he'd been rehearsing. If only I hadn't met Maureen Gallamore, I wouldn't be in this fix, he thought, clutching at straws. He decided on a slightly different way, "When I was still in college, I swore an oath." Now he was able to lay it out for the chaplain: his heritage, his father's own service in the Cause, the meeting in the Upper Room. "So, when I was asked, I swore an oath without a thought," he summarized.

Henry Murdock nodded, encouraging Danny to continue. "You haven't told me anything that would pose much of a problem."

I hope he knows his business, thought Danny, tapping his forefinger nervously on the arm of the chair. "Let me tell you about this oath, sir," he suggested to Murdock, whose keenest interest had been aroused. "It was to help a particular woman who is an agent of the IRA, wherever I might encounter her." He stopped short of describing Maureen's unexpected appearance in Mexico, at least until he could see Henry's reaction.

The chaplain sat unmoving and expressionless. "I see," he said.

Danny made an impulsive decision. He would make the chaplain see. "Even though I was born in New York, I've lived among immigrants fresh from Ireland. Maybe I think too much like a European. I tried to go to Europe, volunteering as a pilot to help keep Hitler from overrunning Europe, but the RAF wouldn't take me. Neither would the Air Corps, but a recruiter talked me into the cavalry."

"They're very opportunistic, those recruiters," said Murdock, nodding sympathetically. He poured himself a glass of water and offered another to Danny, who refused it with a shake of his head.

"So I found myself at Fort Reilly, learning to shoot and ride horses. I found I had natural talent for both of them. And then they gave me a commission as a second lieutenant."

"Yes, yes," said the captain, urging Danny on.

"Well, Henry. As you're aware, the commission has an oath attached to it." Danny looked at the chaplain carefully, hoping to catch any change, any nuance of his expression. "And I stood there and took the oath. You know, 'To protect the Constitution' and all that."

Henry nodded. Yes, he knew the oath well. "So where's your ethical problem? Or have I missed something?"

Danny proceeded warily. "Shortly after I arrived at Fort Brown, I was invited to a bullfight in Matamoros, by Maureen Gallamore." He didn't tell the chaplain about any of the other things—certainly not about Navidad.

Murdock's eyes opened slightly. "She's the Irish agent?"

Danny nodded.

"What's she doing in Mexico?" asked Henry, sipping at his glass of water.

"That's the whole point of coming to you, sir. She says she's a nurse, but I'm pretty sure she's helping German spies enter Texas."

Murdock expelled his sip of water in an explosive breath, coughing heavily. Danny stood to offer assistance, but Henry waved him away. "I'm quite all right. Thank you."

The chaplain held both his hands, palms up, signaling Danny to stop. "Don't say another word. Relax. Let me talk while you listen." He closed his eyes briefly to compose himself. "Yes, Lieutenant, you do have a problem, and if you say more, I'm certain I know what you'll tell me. Then I'm going to have a problem." He raised a warning finger. "She's holding you to the oath. I can tell. That may be OK, in itself, as long as you helped her in doing something innocent, but if that woman is actually helping the Germans insert spies into this country, you've got to turn her in. Is that clear?"

Danny sat in the chair feeling like a trapped rabbit. He seriously considered bolting out of the office.

Henry, out of his chair and excited, paced back and forth, speaking rapidly, "Look, Danny, I have to tell you that as of this moment, I'm acting as a military chaplain. I have to warn you that there is no longer any confessor-penitent privilege in our conversation."

Danny heaved a breath. What a mistake he'd made coming here!

Chaplain Murdock sank heavily into his swivel chair, muttering more to himself than to Danny. "Good thing you didn't pass any information—or heaven help us—give her any assistance—yet."

Danny reached for the water Henry offered him earlier and gulped it down.

The chaplain turned businesslike, sitting erect with his hands on the desktop blotter, speaking slowly, gravely. "Listen to me very carefully. I'm willing to remain silent on this because of what we'll call a technicality—I stopped you short and called this a matter of conscience. As of this moment, I do not want to know about any of her association with Germans. I most surely do not want to know if she's asked you to help her in what I will call her alleged activities."

Then he was up again. Twice he paced across the room, sliding a hand across the desktop as he passed. "Look. I promised I wouldn't divulge any of this, but what you've told me may explode into something much more serious than an ethical problem. It could happen at any time." The chaplain looked beseechingly at Danny. "My God, man! You know the regiment and the Border Patrol are combing the valley for Germans."

"Yes sir."

Henry Murdock, shoulders sagging under the weight of the share of Danny's burden he now shouldered, warned, "If you aren't very careful, you'll be looking for a lawyer, not a chaplain. He held his finger pointed steadily at Danny's chest, warning, "And if you don't go to Captain Franklin or Major Perkins about this, I'll have to call the colonel and advise him of what I've learned."

chapter

SIXTEEN

London: As threatened, German Luftwaffe warplanes commence night bombing raids on London.

Every man in the regiment knew which troop had reached the exercise area first, and the men of E Troop swaggered around among the tents scattered on the rugged terrain, bragging and collecting on bets. Just being able to watch their slower competitors straggle in with their horses spent in the unforgiving conditions of the long race, was the thing that really mattered, not the approbation of generals and colonels.

Walter Franklin, their jubilant commander galloped straight from the pre-exercise meeting to the First Platoon tents, carrying the division commander's congratulations. Right out in front of the general and his team of senior officers who came from Washington as observers, Colonel Chamberlain had proudly announced the winner. "Gentlemen, Captain Franklin here commands the best troop in the 124th," he said. He was especially proud of E Troop because of their splendid achievement of marching their horses—off road, in terrain where trucks can't go—more than two hundred and thirty-five miles at a rate of better than six miles per hour. He spoke slowly to be understood. "Please note that the speed I quoted was an average over the distance, including overnight stops for rest." In the event the point might have been lost on the armor and infantry colonels from Washington, Chamberlain made a most emphatic point, "That demonstrates why the army still needs horses."

The colonel's announcement fit the general's purposes perfectly. He wanted every single soul with the slightest influence on the exercise or any part in writing the final report to understand. "Gentlemen," said Burton, speaking loudly so that everyone at this pre-exercise meeting could hear him over the racket of trucks shuttling back and forth from the supply dump, "I'd like to see E Troop's accomplishment set the tone for what we do in the next few days. If we all can be as innovative in our thinking as Colonel Chamberlain's captain is, the entire army will benefit." His audience knew that the general's actual goal was that the War Department be persuaded to retain at least a token number of horse cavalry units in the army.

Burton briefly reiterated his final directions for the exercise and seated himself at the table to preside over the final discussion of rules. Most of the hard bargaining had already taken place in the Fort Clark Post Theater in a day and a half's worth of meetings. It was getting late and the two force commanders faced a long night of preparation before the exercise began officially.

The senior officers mingled for a few extra minutes after the meeting, congratulating Centaur on having the balls—and the contacts—to get this exercise approved. Privately, many of them harbored their own personal agenda, but before they boarded the sedans for the dusty thirty-mile ride to the comforts of Fort Clark for the night they took pains to shake Chamberlain's hand and wish him well. Afterward, Eddie Burton stayed behind for a companionable private chat with his friend Sam Chamberlain. Neither the colonels sent by the War Department to assess the contribution of the horses, nor the independent group of officers and sergeants assigned to umpire the tactical contest needed to hear what he wanted to discuss. "Let's talk, Sam—just you and me."

"My, tent's right over there, sir. The one under the tree," Chamberlain said, keeping up the public formality. "I think my dog robber may have packed a flask of medicinal spirits."

Burton accepted the invitation and fell in with Chamberlain for the short walk, sharing some thoughts. "I've got to hand it to you, Sam. You made the right decision a number of years ago. I'd swap my stars for eagles in a heartbeat for the opportunity to command the mounted regiment fighting to influence the army's decision to keep horse cavalry around." To the senior officers who served with Chamberlain through the bad old days when a penurious Congress wanted almost no army at all, it wasn't a secret: Chamberlain had passed up almost-certain promotion to general for a slim chance at being exactly where he was right now. That's the way it was in War Department politics. Sam gambled and it paid off. Now he was in the center of a struggle between armor and cavalry—tanks and horses. To horse cavalrymen all over the army, Sam was their champion in the contest. All he needed now was one more break to assure him of glory in cavalry annals. But the other side wasn't by any means sitting idle. That's why General Burton had come out two days early—to spend time with the participating commands to assure himself that all that could be done to enhance Chamberlain's chances of winning a reprieve for the horses was being done. As the exercise orders worked their way down the chain of command, one general at a time, the masters of artful bureaucracy had modified the look of the war game to suit their purposes, knowing full well that the junior commanders no longer had a hope of appealing success-fully to General Marshall.

Over glasses of Chamberlain's medicinal whiskey, the two men sat on folding camp chairs by the light of a gasoline lantern and talked. "Somebody far above my pay grade changed the rules and got them approved. Now they're set in stone," Burton was saying with disappointment sounding plain in his voice. Here in the scrubby rangelands of South Texas, Sam and his troopers would have to make the best of an exercise shriveled in scope from full divisions of infantry and armor to several battalions of infantry and no armor at all—just a few dozen trucks to simulate tanks. Cavalry had been cut short, too. All that remained were two regiments: Chamberlain's 124th and another already depleted in strength prior to shipping out to be trained in tanks. That poorly equipped, understrength regiment might be worse than no help at all in showcasing the utility of cavalry.

Somewhere in Washington, after a day of facing the bright lights in a Congressional committee room on Capitol Hill, asking for the funds to buy modern tanks and aircraft for a growing army, General Marshall was satisfied with what he'd done for the cavalry. In the limestone dust of South Texas, however, the flame of hope for rejuvenated mounted cavalry units sputtered feebly.

"You're the last chance for the war horse in the U.S. Army, Sam. Good luck," said Eddie Burton, shaking Centaur's hand.

Walter Franklin dismounted at the First Platoon tents hoping to relay Centaur's con-gratulatory statement to the lieutenant who inspired the winning effort—only to find the camp quiet. Picking his way through the maze of tents in the faint moonlight, he found a handful of troopers tightly circled around Sergeant Wieczorek, listening to him expound-ing his theory on where E Troop would most likely encounter the opposing force in the early afternoon of the opening day. Franklin stopped behind a scrub cedar tree, eavesdrop-ping on the enigmatic sergeant.

"Listen t'me," Weech was saying. "We bin heah two, three times since I bin in th' regi-ment. They say it's a new place we usin' this time...but, really it ain't." He shook his head slowly for emphasis. The sergeant's sixth sense told him that, even with all the importance the general was putting on this war game, some things were going to be shaped by practical matters—like getting the supply trucks up to where the troops were. "Sh'nuf," he said with his great forefinger raised, "somethin' gonna happen at San Agustin. I don' know why. I guess it's the way the land lays 'round heah."

Interesting, thought the captain, the sergeant may have something there, but intuition was no substitute for planning. "Sergeant Wieczorek!" he called, entering the clearing.

"Yes suh."

"Where's Lieutenant Flynn?" inquired the Troop commander, riding up to the First Platoon tents.

Betting on the race had put more than a month's pay in the platoon sergeant's pockets, and that put him in an expansive mood. Weech climbed nimbly through the limestone rubble to join the captain and saluted. He pointed over his shoulder with his thumb, in the general direction of the river. "He and his dog robber rode outa heah a' coupla hours ago, sir, headed for the rivuh to do a little reconnoiterin'." Wieczorek really didn't know what they were up to, but reconnoitering sounded like a constructive thing for the lieutenant and his trusty dog robber to be doing on the day before the action began.

"That's fine, Sergeant. What I have to say will keep."

⇥⇤

Now that they were in Mexico, Garza lowered his voice. "Not far now, *Teniente*. You forded the Bravo just like the locals do it." He didn't know why exactly, except that he and the lieutenant were armed and in uniform, making an incursion into another country which suddenly seemed foreign. Had they been in civilian clothes, nobody would have cared much.

Danny opened his map for a quick try at determining his position, but he refolded it and followed closely behind Garza, who had already begun climbing up and away from the river, leading both their horses. Common sense told him that on this side of the river, it was better to rely on Pancho Garza's local knowledge than to use a map that could be inaccurate. Together, the pair moved soundlessly through the labrynthine growth of thorny plants, following narrow animal paths and the occasional natural breaks between the heaviest patches.

Once mounted, the two khaki clad riders worked their way through the thorny brush without speaking for about half an hour, moving far enough away from the river to reach the boundary of land under cultivation. Garza stopped to listen. "We're getting close now. It might be better if we try to stay in these mesquite and huisache trees," he whispered. With a working familiarity with the general details of the river's course and its banks, and making regular double checks with his compass, Flynn satisfied himself that allowing for negotiating dry washes and patches of forbidding growth since leaving the river, they had maintained a generally westerly route. He heard nothing himself, but his resourceful orderly and guide must have.

Garza slowed the pace, finally stopping for a long time to listen.

Danny held his breath, listening intently until he made out a faint ringing of a tiny bell and the plaintive bleating of an animal—a goat, most likely. Garza gave a low whistle and waited. From off to the right and rather near, they heard the whistle repeated. The orderly turned for the teniente's approving nod before proceeding any farther. Even then he remained cautious and alert, venturing out of the cover to cross a field cleared for farming.

"Panchito?" a man's voice called out.

"Si, Tio. Panchito y Teniente Flynn."

Not much farther, a half mile maybe, a prosperous-looking collection of white-washed buildings, including a small adobe ranch house and a corral, came into view. The uncle, Rudolfo Garza, greeted them in Spanish and practically dragged his nephew from his saddle and handed him over to his wife to be hugged and covered with kisses. Turning to Danny, he said, "You are welcome, Senor Teniente." Rudolfo making unnecessary apologies, begged forgiveness for not speaking English well, "I know only what I learn when I go across the Bravo." Garza's aunt spoke only Spanish, but in the way of genuinely hospitable women who can always make themselves understood about essential things, she bustled the men into her small kitchen and began preparing food. "You will stay the night with us, no?" inquired the uncle.

Danny, who knew only the Spanish learned since arriving at Fort Brown, ventured a hesitant, "No, gracias." Then he lapsed into English to explain that they could stay only briefly to enjoy their hospitality. He looked to Garza to translate.

No need. Rudolfo understood, "Si, si."

At the open doorway, a procession of cousins collected for a look at the gringo teniente, fascinated by his tall boots and the gold bar on the collar of his shirt. The oldest might have been twelve. The little ones interpreted Pancho's introduction as permission, and one by one they crowded near, inspecting Danny and his bright hair with wide eyes. Tia Esmerelda smiled and bustled around the table, urging them in Spanish words and expressive gestures to eat.

For several minutes Rudolfo eyed Danny as if seeing something familiar. He beckoned to his nephew to come nearer, and they spoke rapidly in Spanish, gesturing with their hands, nodding and shrugging. Panchito appeared to be taking the negative side of the discussion, but Rudolfo knew what he'd seen, pointing to Danny's hair as proof that his memory hadn't failed him.

The orderly glanced at the lieutenant and looked again to his uncle. There must be some kind of mistake. "My uncle says he has seen you before—at the store in San Martin—

with a flat tire. He wants to know if you are the man who visits Dona Marina?" To hide his shock, the lieutenant gulped water from an enameled cup. The uncle saw his answer in Danny's discomfort. To avoid embarrassing a guest, he dropped the subject and spoke to his nephew a bit longer, pointing toward San Martin and the river.

Garza translated this latest information. "My uncle says he has seen well-dressed men: gringos, but not Texans. They speak English and ask about the Bravo. Sometimes they speak another language: German, he thinks. Maybe it's because Carlos Kreutzer's big farm is two or three miles that way." Pancho Garza pointed toward the afternoon sun. "Karl is a Mexican citizen who has been living there a long time, but the Kreutzers still talk German at home."

Uncle and nephew spoke together in brief sentences, repeating some words to get details straight. The orderly turned businesslike, "My uncle is nearly positive they're not Americans because they're trying too hard to look as if they belong here. In English, they ask about crossing the river here, and sometimes of going up to Piedras Negras or one of the other major crossings. These gringos try to look as if this is a natural thing, he says, but they're always nervous. And they never say anything about coming back this way."

For a while the visitors ate and chatted with the Garzas with their nephew translating. The aunt and uncle beamed while Panchito laughed and chatted with his young cousins, who were curious about his uniform and the frightening .45 strapped to his waist. Danny knew from the length of the shadows that it was time for them to get back across the border. He wanted to thank the uncle for his hospitality and the information, and to explain his impatience, saying that he had much to do in preparation for the next day's mock warfare. "Can you translate that, Pancho?" Calling his dog robber by the familiar nickname wasn't exactly what the army wants to hear from a lieutenant, but, under the circumstances, it seemed right.

Rudolfo Garza spoke directly to Danny, "He doesn't need to translate, Lieutenant Flynn," assuring his nephew with a brief nod that they could carry on in English. Sometime it was useful to pretend when talking to gringos. He smiled shyly, confessing, "I went to American schools for two years—when I picked cotton with my brother." People who lived and worked along the river knew about these cavalry maneuvers, and Rudolfo knew that the American army did things by the clock.

The family spilled out of the house to help Panchito and the Teniente saddle up, wishing them a safe journey with kisses and handshakes. Rudolfo shook Danny's hand warmly. "Adios, Senor Teniente," said the hospitable farmer. "Come again when you are on your way to Navidad. She is a beautiful woman, yes? Dona Marina. She speaks Spanish very well."

At his command post, an impatient Colonel Sam Chamberlain struggled to view the confusion with equanimity, but one niggling miscue after another had put him into a foul mood. He and Major Perkins, in their field gear, including helmets and sidearms, stood by their portable map tables, listening to the frowning, distraught radiomen straining to sort intelligible information out of the squealing noise in their headsets. Without smooth radio communications, the 124th would be forced to fall back on shuttling messengers to control unit movements in this rugged terrain.

Irritably, Perkins hitched up the white cloth band pinned to his left sleeve. An uncomfortable damned thing to have hanging there, but if one of the umpires caught him without it, they'd mark him in the White Force column as a casualty and send him to Fort Clark, to sit out the remainder of the exercise. He tried to put the commanding officer in a better frame of mind with a little small talk. "You know how it is in these games, sir. Every commander has been trying to get a head start before it officially begins." He was right, of course. Some of their own troopers had been out during night, taking advantage of the moonlight to string miles of telephone wire through thickets and across dry creek beds, and by sunup most of the 124th was deployed far from where they had last been seen by the umpires.

That's the way it would be in a war too. Both Chamberlain and Perkins knew it and factored it into their thinking. The more critical problem—the worst by far, in fact—was the damn radios. "Colonel, you think some of those Brown Force fellows've figured out some way to screw up our radio communications? Colonel Hall's something of a specialist at that kind of thing, isn't he?" mused Perkins.

Chamberlain winced at a sharp howl from one of the radios being tuned by a frantic radioman. At the moment, nobody in White Force knew for sure where any other unit was. He blamed it on a disastrous incompatibility of the new radios with some of the obsolete equipment still around. "Dammit, Wilmer. I'll bet Ghengis Khan and his horde could communicate better than we're doing this afternoon. Of course the old Mongol was smart enough to depend on horses."

The frustrated colonel pointed to the low-flying aircraft circling overhead. "Look at that pilot up there: useless as tits on a boar hog. We have a man with a pair of sharp eyes in a perfectly good aircraft. He's right there in plain sight, and we can't talk to him."

Some of these difficulties were to be expected, but complete radio failure could kill his chances before he got good and started. His best idea of how his troops were positioned came from the messengers shuttling back and forth on horses. The motorcycles helped, but Chamberlain had only four of those smelly, noisy things. The rest were shuttling the referees around the battlefield. Centaur moaned his frustration. "Talk about ridiculous!"

Right off the bat, neither of the forces hesitated to employ the dashing, swift-moving tactics learned from studying the war in Europe. In a fluid, rapidly changing situation like this one, stringing more wire, no matter how fast it was done, couldn't help much in keeping command posts in contact with units scattered across the dry washes and rockslides of the hostile landscape. In a matter of less than an hour, miles of the wire strung in anticipation of the opening moves of the exercise lay tangled and useless in the scrub cedar and cactus.

It was one of those inevitable moments when a military commander is powerless to redirect the forces he's set in motion. He can only wait to see what unfolds. Colonel Chamberlain sat with Major Perkins in a corner of the command post, isolated from the activitiy around them. Neither spoke. Staring at the wall of the tent with unfocused eyes, Centaur felt the anxious, pleading stares of every horse soldier in the army trusting in him—expecting him to act in their behalf. The crushing burden of their trust left him seriously questioning his ability to bring this off.

Perkins, reading the colonel's stare, guessed at his thoughts. He thought it would help if he asked a question. "I wonder what our troopers are thinking right now, sir. Don't you? Do they really give a damn about busting their butts, playacting at war?"

At the moment, the question did bring Centaur out of his temporary malaise. "Wilmer, it doesn't matter what they think. If I've done my job well, they'll go out and do theirs," he said, silently hoping for good luck. Chamberlain swirled his coffee cup and threw the cold dregs to the ground.

To Sergeant J.R. Roper, this frustrating loss of communications might be an opportunity for the colonel to take a bit of breakfast. The man probably hadn't slept all night, and Roper knew for certain he hadn't eaten. "How about some breakfast, Colonel?" he asked. "It won't quiet down for a long time."

Chamberlain nodded. Breakfast might help his disposition. He stood and stretched to ward off the stiffness and fatigue threatening to lull him to sleep. If the tent sides hadn't been rolled up for air to flow through, he wouldn't have seen the battered civilian truck bouncing up the road into the command post with a load of fence-mending tools rattling in metal boxes in back. "What the hell is that?" he shouted to no one in particular. "That damn truck, I mean."

Oscar Rankin stopped his vehicle amid the collection of tents, mad as a wet hen and not the least bit impressed by all the vehicles and people collected in the clearing his vaqueros used for handling cattle at various times during the year. He jerked the handle on the parking brake in his dusty little flatbed truck, blocking a line of heavy supply vehicles waiting to be waved through the camp. The wiry, bowlegged driver jumped out of the cab, slammed the door and headed for the command post, trailing smoke from his hand-rolled cigarette. "Colonel," raged Rankin without introducing himself, "Yew gotta teach yore loo-tenants some manners—or I'm gonna start shootin'."

The angry little man with sunburned wrinkles earned through years in the hard Texas climate knew exactly where the incident happened and the time. No chance of a mistake, so Chamberlain listened politely and quietly. Rankin slammed the map table with his hat—the same way he did with balky cattle to persuade them to move down a handling chute. "Dammit! I told th' army they c'd use my land, but then I seen this lootenant 'n his min stringin' wahr." He waved his hand to show he had no objection to telephone wire or whatever it was on the spool. "Now that's all right," he allowed, but he made it very clear it wasn't all right for the lieutenant to be "cuttin' my bob wahr." Chamberlain prayed for patience with this man whose ire showed no signs of abating. "This lieutenant looked at me like Ah wasn't no more'n a cow pile n' he said, 'Ah'm a lieutenant in the U.S. Army, 'n Ah go where Ah want.'" Rankin held his hand about a foot above his pale bald scalp to show how tall the lieutenant was. The rancher searched angrily around the tent as if expecting to find the trespasser among the men updating the maps with the scanty information coming in by messengers on horseback. Out of view behind Rankin, Perkins gritted his teeth. He knew who it was: D troop, Second Platoon, but he didn't dare say a word to Rankin. But the major did make a mental note to have a talk with the D Troop officers.

Rankin had yet to disclose what he considered an even greater outrage, "See, Colo-nel, Ah let 'em go and went about my business. Then, by god, Ah found them bullet holes. Somebody'd bin takin' tahgit practice on one a my winmills." In those arid acres, water from the windmills meant life for the livestock. "Now, you're a horseman, Colonel. You know what water means to a' animal." If the noise of the radios and engines hadn't been so loud, every trooper at the command post would have heard the irate Rankin threatening, livid with rage. "Yew k'n tell yore troopers they better treat them winmills with respect, else Ah'll take tahgit practice on *them*!" The wiry cattleman sent the maps flying with a swipe of his wide-brimmed felt hat and stamped out into the glare of the sun.

On the way to his truck, Rankin stopped abruptly to inspect a pair of powerful new Indian motorcycles parked near his dusty truck. The machines, each fitted with a side-car, had come in while he was venting his rage at Colonel Chamberlain. The tough little rancher shook his head to condemn them as something distasteful and decadent. Trucks might be all right, but..."Your's?" Rankin inquired of a pleasant, round-faced trooper bent over one of the bikes wiping dust off it with a rag.

"Yes sir."

"Who rides in these heah side cars?" Rankin wanted to know.

The soldier pointed across the clearing to a tent the umpires were using as their field office. "They do, out to where our guys are dug in."

"This what you do at Fort Ringgold? Drive people around?"

"No sir. I'm at Fort Brown, but I'm a trombonist in the band. When we're in the field, the musicians act as messengers."

Rankin cleared his throat and drew a sack of tobacco and a packet of cigarette papers from his shirt pocket, taking in the spectacle of all this stuff the army had crammed into his little clearing: horses by the dozen on picket lines, sacks of grain piled high; a field kitchen surrounded by trucks loaded with boxes, sacks of potatoes and crated field rations; a fuel truck; and all those trucks and motorcycles. He held one of the papers between his fingers to form a kind of trough, filled it with tobacco, moistened an edge of the paper with his tongue and rolled his cigarette into a tight cylinder with his fingertips. Unbelievable, he thought, all this equipment, right here where his hired hands worked cattle. He lit the cigarette with a match, squinting in the smoke and bright sunlight. "What's in them trucks?" He meant the heavily loaded convoy grinding up the grade in a low gear.

"That's a field hospital. They're gonna set up pretty soon," the messenger told him.

Rankin walked slowly to his truck alone, shaking his head in a way that could have meant anything.

Relieved to see the rancher's truck bouncing down the rocky road, stirring up a plume of white dust, Centaur turned to his cold oatmeal and coffee. He nibbled at a slice of bacon. All it would take to lose the fight to keep the horse cavalry alive would be Rankin showing up in the middle of a crucial maneuver to give somebody a piece of his mind about how the army was using his property.

Centaur lit a cigarette to help him concentrate on getting the 124th into the fight. Damn! Rankin was still on his mind when Major Perkins ran up from the communications tent, shouting excitedly, "We're in business, Colonel! Hot-to-mighty damn, we're in business!"

While Oscar Rankin was pinning their ears back with his complaints about the army's manners, a messenger had ridden in with a key bit of information. A simple but profound error of some kind had resulted in sending the wrong radio frequencies to the White Force units. "Somebody on the general's staff figured it out," said Perkins, his face creased with smiles.

They couldn't afford any more of these stupid mistakes. With a jerk of his head toward the group of umpires idly drinking coffee near the field kitchen, waiting for some action to begin, Chamberlain shouted to Perkins, "Remind those people that the command error was rectified by a messenger on horseback carrying the correct radio frequencies." Centaur was hot to get going. Fearful that one damn column of erroneous numbers might have sounded the death knell for the horse cavalry, he snatched the paper from Perkins's hand. "Let's see that, Wilmer."

The best radiomen in the regiment strained to catch every dot and dash, and now a steady stream of information flooded into the command post. Minutes later Perkins returned with more information, rapidly transcribed in pencil, offering a sampling of what was coming in. "You'll like these, Colonel," said Perkins.

⚹

The musician who answered Oscar Rankin's questions kicked his motorcycle engine to life and tore recklessly over a steep, rutted path, scattering limestone fragments and clouds of dust behind him, to deliver specific instructions to the E Troop commander. A scout from the 124th reported what looked like infantry, a battalion at least, pushing through the hills as fast as they could over the tortured, rockstrewn terrain. An airborne observer had gotten a good look at them. The White Force commander recognized a golden opportunity for Centaur's troopers. E Troop was in the best position to set up an ambush.

All those hours of outrage and foul cursing at having to load machine gun and mortars on packhorses were suddenly forgotten. Not one word of complaint about loading the hand-cranked radios that suddenly were the best means of communicating. Machine guns and mortars would be a deciding factor. Franklin's troopers got them loaded without a problem. In a last-minute decision, Captain Franklin ordered his platoons to abandon the heavy portable walkie-talkie radios: ancient, clumsy things designed to be seated in a socket on the stirrup and held vertical by the mounted trooper. Those tall antennas would have gotten hung up in the brush anyway. "Leave 'em behind. They'll only be useless burdens in these tight little canyons," he decided.

E Troop went out loaded for bear. This was classic stuff—the way it was supposed to work according to basic cavalry doctrine. By the time they heard the noisy progress of Brown Force infantry making their way up the dry washes chosen as an infiltration route, E Troop waited silently in a deadly ambush. They understood this country: how the meager soil responded to shovels and picks and what it took to camouflage a position among clumps of scrubby cedars. All they had to do was to wait. They were dug in with fields of fire checked by the lieutenants and platoon sergeants. Behind the ridge, where they could be brought up in a hurry, the horses waited in the care of a few troopers designated as horse holders. The Brown Force intruders were walking right into the trap, but they wouldn't know it for a while—not until after they moved far enough up the slope to be declared casualties or prisoners by the referees.

After the bleakness of the early hours, when White Force's twentieth century ambitions were thwarted by communications working at an eighteenth century pace, Centaur finally sensed things going his way. The burden of being the last hope of the horse cavalry suddenly become easier to bear. Now he wanted E Troop off their hillside position and working toward their new bivouac area, keeping scouts out, probing for a hint of the next Brown Force move.

Lieutenant Flynn, his platoon sergeant and six troopers waited in the meager shade of a few low scraggly trees hanging over the nearly dry streambed. The rest of his troopers toiled on the brush-covered hillside, sweating and cursing the heat and thorns. When one pair of scouts came in to report their observations, Danny would dispatch two more and give the sweating riders and their spent horses the opportunity to rest, get a little water and cool off. "Careful how much water you let your horses drink. Don't let them drink directly from the stream." He knew the troopers hated carrying the canvas water bags uphill to the horses. They also knew the consequences of a horse drinking too much water, but tired men with exhausted mounts are prone to take ill-advised short cuts.

A mounted messenger arrived in cloud of dust with a message from Captain Franklin. Without dismounting, the trooper brushed the brim of his steel helmet in a salute and delivered his message hurriedly. "Lieutenant Flynn. Captain wants you to bring your platoon in to the rendezvous point at San Agustin crossroads well before sunset. He wants to get us to the supply trucks before those thieving rascals in F Troop arrive."

Danny returned the salute. "Tell the Captain we'll be there."

The shadows were already lengthening before a First Platoon scout finally saw the windmill and heard the supply trucks in the distance somewhere, grinding their way up the snaky turns of the road. The weary, dusty trooper had gotten quite near San Agustin, the critical crossroads, without being seen before he galloped away to deliver his report. "Lieutenant Kincaid and Corporal Bennington from F Troop are already there, sir." The breathless trooper had seen something else. "Otherwise, the place is empty." The supply trucks were late for the rendezvous.

Well, wasn't that a revolting development. Danny's first thought was of Kincaid, that George had simply broken away from the exercise to be at the assembly point early. "Typical," he muttered to himself. But if the supply people weren't in place by now, the situation was becoming confused. If First Platoon were to be there in strength when the supplies finally arrived, he might be able to nose out old George and his single trooper, and E Troop could still get their supplies first. He waved Wieczorek to start inbound to the San Agustin rendezvous point. "Sergeant, get the troopers in there and make sure we get our share of the fodder for the horses. I'm right behind you." Hurriedly he sent a mounted messenger to describe the situation to Captain Franklin, collected the remainder of the platoon and fell in behind Wieczorek, urging his mount to catch up. But the poor exhausted animal didn't have a race in him.

A crossing of two faint roads marked the sketchy little settlement on the army maps, making it appear to be much more imposing than it really was. A crumbling shrine that gave the place its name stood almost unnoticed in a grove of cedars, but the most prominent building was a little adobe store that sometime carried a few necessities. Otherwise San Agustin consisted of a well with a windmill and cistern and a couple of drinking troughs for animals. The total population couldn't have been a dozen people living in four or five small houses roofed with cracked red tiles patched with sheets of rusting corrugated metal and a few scattered sheds where Oscar Rankin's ranch hands could store some equipment when working his cattle. Other than being easy to find on the map, San Agustin offered one major asset: a broad flat clearing, practically the only place for miles around suitable for assembling a troop for resupply.

Hidden in the brush, where their wary mothers sent them to be out of the way of the men in khaki, a couple of small children shyly watched the two soldiers on their massive, dark horses. Off and on during the day, the natural peace of the clearing had been shattered by groups of mounted men bursting out of the brush thickets, yelling and cursing, pausing for a few minutes to water their horses and refer to the maps, then dashing off again, leaving the handful of people who lived there temporarily in peace. Right now there were only these two, probably waiting for more like them. One dismounted and wandered into the trees to relieve himself. The larger trooper sat on his horse, watching the setting sun, impatiently checking his watch over and over again. Full of curiosity, a little mongrel dog emerged from among the cedars near the dilapidated dwellings, barking at the horse. Suddenly it darted out at the huge black animal, yapping furiously, making a stand for possession of its domain. When his horse shifted its feet anxiously and raised its head, Lieutenant George Kincaid returned his timepiece to its pocket to keep a watchful eye on this feisty little yapper. The dog continued it barking and made another bold move for the horse's ankles. Surprised and annoyed, the horse snorted and reared up on his rear legs. "Hey, get away, y'little mutt," yelled the lieutenant. But the little mongrel stood its ground, neck hair standing on end, teeth bared, barking aggressively. Kincaid would have no more of it. He drew his .45 and fired. The heavy slug threw up a geyser of dust and sand, sending the animal tumbling and squealing, but not killing the dog outright. Sighting more eliberately than he did with the first shot, he prepared to put the wounded dog out of its misery.

A small boy in tattered shorts bolted from his hiding place without thinking, running toward the dog writhing on the sand, howling in pain. Impulsively the boy's smaller sister followed a few steps behind him. The darting children were only a step or two from the animal by the time Kincaid fired again to quiet the dog for good. The little girl screamed in fear, wetting the dust in her fright. Kincaid howled with laughter. When he saw the children frozen in terror, he sent them scrambling back with another shot, this time into the ground near their feet.

Wieczorek barreled into the clearing at a full gallop to investigate the sounds of shooting. What he saw was a dead dog and Lieutenant Kincaid firing the shot at the feet of the children. "Stop, stop," he shouted. The children froze when they heard the new rider yelling, but raced for the concealing brush at seeing the muzzle of the lieutenant's .45 being pointed in their direction.

Whether he heard Wieczorek's plea or not, the lieutenant fired into the rocky soil twice more, yelling, "Get on back to the bushes, you little greasers." The sergeant reacted instinctively to stop the shooting, diving at Kincaid like a bulldogger in a rodeo. His momentum carried the lieutenant off his saddle and sent them both rolling into the dust. The terrified children vanished into the cedar thicket behind the shacks, shooed farther into the trees by their anxious mother following closely behind.

Kincaid scrambled to his feet, spitting dust and loosing a barely controlled stream of foul oaths at Wieczorek. "I was only having a little fun with that Meskin' kid," shouted the fuming lieutenant.

Wieczorek staggered through the dust toward Kincaid, not quite sure of all that happened as a result of his impetuous act. His only purpose had been to prevent an accidental killing. Now, confronted by a sputtering officer picking himself out of the dust, the realization struck him that what he did instinctively might be taken for an assault. "Lootenan' Kincaid. I'm sorry! The children!" said the sergeant by way of explaination, his face aghast, shocked at the result of his impulsive but innocent act. Wieczorek shook with fear, shouting apologies, barely aware of Kincaid's blustering threats.

The lieutenant yelled, "You stupid ape. I don't give a damn what you thought I was doing. You're incapable of thinking. If you could think, you wouldn't have made the idiotic mistake of assaulting me. That's striking an officer." Kincaid pointed at the shaken sergeant with a gloved hand. "You'll be on bread and water for this one, Wieczorek." He walked shakily around the crossroads area, collecting his pistol from the sand where it had fallen, and ran a few more steps to take the reins of his horse. "Get back on your horse, Sergeant," he screamed, pointing his weapon at Wieczorek. "You're under arrest and I'm taking you to the command post to prefer charges."

Only at that second did the two antagonists hear the hoofbeats of Flynn's sweating horse being reined to a stop. Flynn shouted, "No, George. I saw it. You don't have grounds to arrest Sergeant Wieczorek."

"Hell I can't. I just did," said Kincaid, swinging his arm to point the pistol at Danny. "If you want to keep this up, I'll take you in too, for interfering with me."

Danny, seeing Kincaid as a man acting irrationally, quite capable of being dangerous, said quietly, "Go with him, Sergeant. I'll be there as soon as I can."

※

"I'll give you credit for being an optimist, Sammy," said Colonel Orlen Washburn. "This exercise is one hell of a test for a guard regiment federalized only a few months ago."

"They're good soldiers, Orlen. All of them are very aware they'll be in a war soon," said Chamberlain, accepting a veiled compliment. "But be honest. What do you think now that we've gotten the first day's action under our belt?" He offered Washburn a seat on one of the canvas folding chairs in his tent. The visitor tossed his hat on the table, settled himself comfortably and produced his pipe with a packet of tobacco. From long years of friendship, Washburn knew Chamberlain to be a cigarette man, but as a neighborly gesture, he offered a pipeful of the fragrant mix before beginning the elaborate process of filling and tamping. Motioning with his unlighted pipe toward the busy team of officers and sergeants compiling the day's results and explaining them to a group of Washburn's team of observers, he said, "Those fellas over there are getting into a lot of detail that we'll want to go over later." Washburn allowed himself a smile. "But, I'm very pleased by what I see. Your troopers are pretty well advanced in handling their new weapons. I know you were a little embarrassed by the communications breakdowns, but a realistic exercise like this one will expose human weaknesses."

Chamberlain, rising irritably from his camp chair, excused himself to Washburn. "Forgive me for interrupting you, Orlen. My exec is signaling to me there in the tent entrance. I'll be right back."

Newman drew Chamberlain aside to allow the work of sorting out the results of the exercise to go on. "I got this from San Agustin, sir. It's from F Troop. Colonel, Lieutenant Kincaid has brought Sergeant Wieczorek in, under arrest. He's charging him with striking an officer." Newman saw the shock on Chamberlain's face. "You know this man, sir. He's Lieutenant Flynn's platoon sergeant."

Striking an officer! The news left Chamberlain momentarily thunderstruck. Yes, he remembered the sergeant. He swore, "For Christ sake, that's the same troublemaker who instigated the incident on the train to Fort Reno." He looked anxiously around at the frenetic activity among the tents, not sure what he expected to see.

"He's not here yet sir," said Newman. "Lieutenant Kincaid and the sergeant are being brought in on a supply truck."

Centaur nodded, agreeing with the action. "Best I don't get involved in this right now." He chewed at his lip nervously, thinking of the two men involved—Kincaid and Wieczorek. "I don't want to let this situation get drawn out. I have a feeling about what probably happened. Do you think you can get them together and send them back to work?"

Newman missed Chamberlain's insightful thought. He shook his head, "No, sir. This is too much of a coincidence with that man. Remember? At first we thought it was simply a case of Wieczorek and Lieutenant Flynn having a personal thing, but it could be that the sergeant hates officers; or he's a born troublemaker. Maybe both."

If this were to go to a court-martial, or even if he ended up handling this under his disciplinary authority as a commanding officer, Chamberlain knew he had to be careful about what he said. But there was that questionable reputation of Kincaid's. "George is no saint, Jerry," he reminded Newman.

"Very true, sir," said the circumspect Texan, "But are we going to get Lieutenant Kincaid to agree that there was a reason for Wieczorek to act as he did? Or that it was an accident? I doubt it."

Chamberlain went over in his mind the disastrous effect an affair like this could have on the troopers' morale. "Well, if we leave it to a full-blown legal proceeding, it's going to have to be at Fort Brown. Think of what this exercise means to us—the whole damn cavalry! I'm not going to let this incident interrupt the progress of the entire regiment. Damn!" He smacked his right fist into the palm of his left hand. "What they're doing out here today is the result of many months' work and training. We've got to do something," he said, still hot about the affair, but exactly what to do wasn't that clear. He had some options, but even if this were an isolated incident, it would still be a powder keg. Striking an officer could go to a court-martial, so he couldn't just throw the case out without an investigation. Or if Kincaid could be persuaded to back off and reduce the charges, maybe, then the air might clear without affecting the exercise. That wasn't likely, Chamberlain judged. But he was wasting time dithering. Something had to be done right now. Being in the field with a platoon sergeant under arrest for everybody to see was a recipe for confusion and disorder.

Newman waited quietly, appreciating the burden on the commanding officer as the single man with the power to dispose of this with a decision that might, in turn, destroy the morale of his command. He watched, bemused as Chamberlain opened his cigarette case, hesitated, and then closed the case without removing a cigarette.

Centaur beckoned to Newman, who had stepped away to leaf through a stack of incoming communications. "I'm reluctant to take action too quickly, but we can't keep the sergeant here. We'll have every sergeant in the regiment with nothing else on their mind but this guy. Put him in a truck right now, and hold him in the guardhouse at Fort Brown until we get back."

Newman wondered about George Kincaid. "What'll we do with him?"

Chamberlain was finding the whole matter distasteful. "My first impulse is to put him in the same truck with Sergeant, ah, what's his name?"

"Wieczorek."

"Right." But he decided against sending both men away in the same truck. "We can't do that. Get Kincaid out of F Troop for the meantime and find something for him to do here at the command post. Put him in charge of the horses, maybe," he suggested irritably. "Now, when the truck gets here with the two of them, take care of the details." This time, Centaur took the time to light his cigarette before returning to his conversation with Orlen Washburn, a man whose impressions on this mock battlefield could affect so much.

Danny's first thought was to take the matter to Captain Walter Franklin, but the captain had been summoned to the command post by radio before he could reach San Agustin. That changed matters for the worse. It might mean the colonel wanted to take some kind of action tonight. If his bosses were going to be discussing that unfortunate altercation between Weech and George Kincaid, Flynn knew his best chance of helping his platoon sergeant lay in going to the command post himself. Hurriedly he beckoned to Corporal Wilson. "Now listen to me carefully." This young man needed some reassuring. The lieutenant put his hand on Wilson's shoulder to buck him up for the challenge. "I'm putting you in charge of the platoon until I straighten this out with the colonel. Your first responsibility is for this platoon, but if Captain Franklin does, by some chance, visit the platoon on his way to see the colonel, he needs to know there's a serious misunderstanding."

It was almost dark by the time Danny dismounted near Centaur's command post. He'd been riding for most of an hour in hopes of tracking down Captain Franklin. Vexed, he left his mount with a trooper with scarcely a civil word. Nearby, where the glaring gasoline lanterns cast their pools of light, sweating supply clerks moved boxes of field rations brought up the steep grade by the heavy trucks and sorted them to be distributed to the troops setting up their evening bivouacs. A noisy, sputtering generator supplied electricity for essential lights through a tangle of black cables. The engineers had little choice but to snake them along the ground because the low, desert growth offered few trees strong enough to bear their weight. Mounted messengers continued to shuttle in and out because three motorcycles had broken down. Under naked light bulbs dangling from the wooden rails of an empty supply truck, a crew of mechanics, stripped to their waists, worked feverishly with bits and parts of disassembled motorcycles laid out on shelter halves.

In his command tent, with the sides rolled up in the hope of catching a little breeze, Centaur sensed that things were improving after that troublesome episode involving the sergeant striking an officer. A growing knot of captains, most of them troop commanders, gathered nearby to talk, waiting for the umpires' assessment of the day's maneuvering. Some of them turned curiously for a look at the dust-covered lieutenant dismounting a little way out from the tents, just outside the glare of the gas lanterns.

Lieutenant Flynn caught up with the E Troop commander standing alone. Only then did he see the anguished look on Franklin's face: he hadn't been apprised of the trouble between Lieutenant Kincaid and Sergeant Wieczorek until minutes before.

Franklin explained, "Wieczorek had been right there in the tent, under arrest, until just before I got here. I've been told Colonel Newman had been standing there, talking with the sergeant and Lieutenant Kincaid. By then, the two of them were already out of the exercise and Weech was climbing into the truck."

Those words sent a surge of alarm through Danny. Already, he was too late to help. "Where's Weech now, sir?"

"On his way to Fort Brown," said Franklin, looking down the rocky trail, watching the truck's barely visible lights. "Shake it off, Flynn. Don't worry about him. He's done it to himself."

Danny knew a mistake had been made: More than a mistake—a terrible error! "Everybody's got it wrong! He didn't do it!" he shouted, breaking into a sprint for the command tent.

Franklin called him back, "It's all over until we get back—after the exercise," speaking in his command voice to penetrate the lieutenant's anxiety. "Return to your platoon, Lieutenant Flynn."

It didn't take long before rumors and flurries of official inquiries circulated like a whirlwind.General Burton ordered a cease fire, halting the exercise for twenty-four hours—for the sake of safety, although he knew very well the confusion was small compared to that of the haze of actual combat.

Some things, at least, were still the way that made First Platoon the envy of the regiment. A barbecue augmented the plain fare of the field rations issued at the supply trucks, and almost certainly there was beer to slake their dusty throats as only a beer can; but if it was being drunk by the troopers, then it was privately in the darkness outside the fires' glare.

First Platoon could see their brooding lieutenant wasn't a man to be approached. Danny sat alone on the ground, his back to a tree trunk, scribbling furiously in his notebook. He ripped out a page from the book and handed it to Private First Class Garza whose guitar lay silent in its unopened case.

During the night Centaur altered his decision to leave the sergeant's accuser in the battle. Lieutenant Kincaid, too, was now on his way to Fort Brown. For two more sweltering days in the superheated air of south Texas, the 124th fought the make-believe battle with a grim determination driven by Centaur's hope that it mattered and fueled by the rumors surrounding the incident involving Sergeant Wieczorek.

If Max Gindler had been there, he would have seen a new maturity in the way the troopers went about their soldiering, an altered spirit that compelled them to work like devils despite the stifling effect of a flood of camp rumors. Gindler would have seen it because these men were the people he had written about daily, still Texans to the core. The dismal atmosphere clutched at the men returning from the field, dragging their spirits down. Even if they refused to talk about the unfortunate case, their families could read in their faces a weary resignation that meant something had gone wrong.

Two weeks earlier the 124th had marched away from Fort Brown in a competitive mood, fired up by lively martial music, ready for what amounted to a horse race up the Rio Grande Valley. Today it was different. If asked how the exercise went, most any trooper would have answered with a grin, "We whipped 'em." But for some undivulged reason, they didn't ride the horses back. Most of the regiment had boarded a long convoy of trucks. They'd been arriving at Fort Brown throughout the night after a long, uncomfortable ride. The musicians and medics labored together with the supply clerks unpacking the field hospital supplies, but most of the exhausted troopers took an opportunity to rest or read mail. The horses would be days shuttling back in the overtaxed portees. The troopers felt the 124th should've ridden back to Fort Brown and there was still the looming matter of the charges against the sergeant.

They weren't expecting a rousing speech from Colonel Chamberlain and they didn't get one, but there was some good news to brighten the ominous mood hanging over them. Word spread quietly through the lieutenants and sergeants that the regiment had four days off, effective immediately after morning muster. The four-day pass didn't apply to the Headquarters Troop or the senior officers. Sergeant Roper expected the commanding officer to be in his office early, ready for a busy day on the telephone to Washington trying to learn what the War Department had made of the exercise. But an unexpected visitor waited outside the colonel's office, refusing to leave without seeing him.

Throwing his briefcase on his desk, Chamberlain growled at Roper, who followed him into the office with a cup of coffee, "What's Lieutenant Flynn doing out there?"

"He was standing in the hall outside the office when I came in this morning to make coffee, sir. He says it's imperative that he see you immediately. I told Lieutenant Flynn it would be impossible to see you today under any circumstances." The sergeant made a motion of helplessness with his hands. "He said he'd wait here in the building until you do have time to see him."

"Is Colonel Newman in?" asked Chamberlain. He knew what the lieutenant's business was: the charges against Wieczorek.

"Yes, sir. Shall I ask him to come in?"

"No, not yet at least, but send in Lieutenant Flynn," said the colonel. "And call Major Perkins. Tell him I'll be five minutes late."

"Stand at ease, Lieutenant Flynn," said a haggard Centaur who appeared to have aged several years since taking his command into the field. "Is this about Wieczorek? It looks as if that sergeant of yours is up to his neck in trouble this time." He spoke to Danny like a consoling father. "Don't be disappointed in the man. That's one of the good things about being in the field—you find your weak links. It's a good thing we found out about him before we face a hostile enemy."

Danny interrupted, shaking his head, "I don't know what George Kincaid told you about what happened at the San Agustin, sir, but I'll bet it's wrong."

"Make your point quickly, Lieutenant," said Chamberlain, taking his seat. His own professional world was turning upside down and a pair of wet-behind-the-ears lieutenants seemed to be dragging their commanding officer into their personal spat. Morale had suffered enough over this Wieczorek thing. Still, maybe Flynn did have something to say.

Centaur reached for his coffee cup and sipped slowly, taking a bit of time to review a copy of Kincaid's accusatory account. Through a cloud of cigarette smoke, he recounted the salient points gathered by the investigating officer. "Lieutenant Kincaid said the Mexican family at San Agustin sent two young hoodlums and a pack of dogs to attack him and his horse. He felt forced to draw his pistol to save his mount from harm. Your sergeant, who for some reason has an abiding animosity for officers, saw his chance to attack him without witnesses, knocking him off his horse to put him at the mercy of those people and their dogs. Kincaid thinks Wieczorek was sly enough to think he could attack an officer and have the blame fall on those Mexicans." He looked at Danny for comment.

"That's not right, sir. George is wrong on a lot of counts."

Centaur looked up from the paper at Danny over his glasses. "Let me get this straight. Is it correct to say that you're here to speak on Wieczorek's behalf?"

"Yes, sir," said Flynn firmly.

"I'll be damned." Putting his tight schedule aside, he gestured impatiently for Danny to speak his piece.

"First of all, sir, there were at least two witnesses."

Chamberlain raised his eyebrows. "You aren't counting the sergeant and the lieutenant as witnesses, are you?"

Danny shook his head. "No, sir, but I'm a witness. I saw it." He didn't wait to be asked for his account. "I was following Wieczorek into the clearing when this happened, and George's corporal can tell you about it too."

Centaur was scribbling notes.

"I saw George, ah, Lieutenant Kincaid, shoot the mongrel—it was a feisty little mutt—twice. And when the little children came running for their dog, he proceeded to terrify them by firing at their feet. Three shots. I saw Wieczorek galloping toward George and what looked like a terrible situation. He yelled at Lieutenant Kincaid, but the warning hadn't stopped him from shooting, so the sergeant did the only thing he could have done in time to keep him from firing any more—and maybe killing one of those children. He knocked George off his horse. And Corporal Bennington was there through the whole thing: dismounted in the bushes. I saw him. Has he told you anything, sir?"

The colonel sipped his coffee thoughtfully, trying to picture the situation at the crossroads that evening. "Nothing yet, but now that I know he was there, I'll talk to him myself." The more he thought about it, the less Lieutenant Kincaid's account appeared to be the true picture. He pressed an intercom button for Sergeant Roper at his desk. "Ask Colonel Newman to come in, please."

The executive officer entered a few seconds later.

"Who has custody of Lieutenant Kincaid's weapon?"

"I do, sir," said Newman.

"Has it been unloaded and cleaned?"

"Unloaded. Yes, sir. I removed the magazine, but it's in my safe with the pistol. Frankly, I locked it up. It was so late, I forgot to have the Provost Marshal come pick it up."

If the omission had been an error, it was forgivable as far as Chamberlain was concerned. "It's a good thing you held on to the weapon. Can you unlock it and check the ammunition remaining? I want to know how many rounds have been fired." He pointed at Flynn. "How many times did he fire? Three, did you say?

"No, sir. Five, all told," said Danny.

Centaur turned expectantly to Newman returning with the pistol and its magazine.

"Assuming the magazine was full, five rounds have been fired, sir," said the Executive Officer.

Chamberlain relaxed visibly. "Very well, Lieutenant Flynn" he said, "from what I've been hearing from you, this is a very different matter than the one described to me earlier. We'll take your statement and double check what you've said—particularly the observations of Corporal Bennington. If everything adds up then, I won't let this go to a court-martial." Taking another sip from his coffee cup, he encouraged Danny. "I hope I can let Wieczorek go." He thumped his fist on his desk blotter. "Damn. It would be better for everybody," he said, excusing Flynn with a nod.

"Thank you, sir." Danny saluted and left the office. Before the door closed completely, he heard Chamberlain speaking to Newman. "Jerry, what the hell are we going to do with Kincaid?"

A relieved Lieutenant Flynn returned to his quarters, exhausted by lack of sleep and uncertain about...well, just uncertain. He pushed aside the boots and gear he'd left dumped on the floor in a hurry to make himself presentable before setting up a vigil in the headquarters building. He and his dog robber would handle that—later.

The first thing he wanted was a hot shower. The rushed run under the shower several hours earlier had helped remove the grime and filth accumulated in two weeks without once being able to take a bath, but did almost nothing to take away the aches and deep weariness, and his face felt raw from the hasty shave; so did his neck and head, where Garza had hurriedly plied his clippers and scissors.

Now he would sleep before setting himself to thinking about Molly's expectations of marriage, and Maureen, who may have led him into treason. Ah, no, he couldn't sleep just yet; a handful of letters lay on his bed, a two-week accumulation of mail.

The bright afternoon sun glaring through the window awakened him where he had fallen asleep with his mail lying on his chest. A single unopened envelope remained, put off until last. This would be in response to a letter he wrote to his father after his visit to the chaplain. He could feel his pulse racing, for, unopened, this letter carried enormous potential to bring him peace or to push him deeper into his dilemma.

Danny hefted the envelope in the palm of his hand, feeling its weight, considering its thickness. This firm packet, he felt certain, held his father's thoughts on the questions consuming him that night. No one who knew him could doubt Michael Flynn's love of words, or fail to be beguiled by his speech. Neighborhood stories recounting the elder Flynn's eloquence at the pub had brought a broad respect for his wisdom.

As a very young lad Danny would sometimes sit listening to the voices of the neighborhood men, watching his father enjoy his pipe, tamping the slowly burning tobacco and its cover of ash with the tip of his calloused finger. It was when the talk turned inevitably to matters of the Cause that he grew pensive, preferring to listen until he felt compelled to contribute. When he was ready to speak, the veteran of the Troubles emitted a signal puff of tobacco smoke and spoke eloquently; melodically some said, and people listened. And the son recalled one of the neighborhood women saying to another, "Ooch, when that Michael Flynn talks to you in the Irish, it makes you want to drop your knickers." They were enjoying one of their few luxuries, squandering a bit of time to gossip, thoughtless of the possibility that Michael's young son might be listening. To the bright lad, it meant only that the ancient Celtic gods had blessed his father with the gift of the blarney. To the son, a soldier in Texas, the recollection brought a roguish smile in appreciation of another man's powers of persuasion.

A tingle of anxiety prickled along his back as he felt for a small pocketknife with a horn-covered handle. Carefully he slit the top of the envelope, then the side, to remove the ruled pages more easily. Lying open and smoothed by Danny's hands, the humble, porous paper released the magical aroma of Michael Flynn's pipe. Though two thousand miles and a fortnight's travel removed from the Flynn kitchen table, Danny found himself under the older man's influence. The salutation read, "Dear Son," but Danny visualized his father exhaling a final breath of smoke and clearing his throat. "Ummghh, umh." He wasn't conscious of reading the penciled words. It was his father's voice delivering the message.

"Well, now, boy," the voice was saying, "you've presented me with a thorny problem. If I have the right of it, you have freely and fully sworn two oaths: one to aid and assist Maureen Gallamore, a fighter in the Cause, wherever you encounter her; the other to defend the Constitution of the United States against all enemies, foreign and domestic."

Michael must have paused to consider his thoughts and to sharpen his pencil, because now the words were formed with a finer point in tighter, firmer strokes. Danny held his pocketknife, identical to the one his father had used, firmly in his hand as a token of contact and read further. "Let us think now, Danny. What do these oaths mean?"

Merely allowing the question posed by his father to lodge in his mind stimulated his thinking. Time after time, hadn't the elder Flynn reminded his son that, to generations of Flynns, a spoken promise represented an obligation, one to be kept unless absolved? But an oath was another, even more profound thing. "To us," his father would declare, raising a forefinger, "a man must never swear an oath until he is certain he has the means to keep it."

Michael knew his son had long ago absorbed that lesson, but he wrote it again. "This is the difference between boys and men. Only when you have the freedom and strength to keep it can you take such a step, for an oath is a thing of utmost gravity, graven into a Flynn's soul. To break an oath is unthinkable." The pencil left a dark slash under the last word.

Michael Flynn began again on a new page. "Now, then. You have been unlucky, or unwise enough, to swear two oaths." His son visualized Michael shaking his white mane in disbelief. "To me it seems inconceivable that a Flynn could contrive, no matter the circumstances, to enter upon two oaths more in opposition. You want to know what to do, but the matter can never be made perfectly clear.

"Now, I've thought on this for a long time. I've gone to the friends who stood by me in the time of the Troubles. I've sought the advice of my confessor and besotted myself, futilely seeking wisdom in the essence of the fermented oat. But from all this, I've concluded nothing more than that you have created a moral cauldron for yourself, a bit of hell on earth, for you are obliged to live with them both." Over and over, Danny read the sentence. The words gave him no latitude whatsoever. The next few lines bore no consolation either: only the guidance he expected from a man whose life had asked as much of him as Michael Flynn's. "If I found myself in this predicament, the oath sworn on the blood of my ancestors would have to be honored first. Only then would I look after the one sworn to defend and uphold a scrap of paper."

Danny put the letter down, unable to read more, at least not at the moment. In his closet, he found a nearly full bottle and poured a generous amount of the amber Irish whiskey into the heavy tumbler the army provided for his use. Reputed as the inspiration of poets and philosophers, the elixir withheld any powers it possessed to clarify his thinking. In his agitated state, it tasted so sour that he poured it down the drain of his enameled sink before returning to his seat on the bed. After a time, he smoothed the pages and began to read once more. "Be in mind that this is America, not Ireland, and you are an American born and educated, serving in the Army, while I am still and forever an Irishman," wrote his father. "So, Danny, my dear son, you must consider your own argument that if Maureen Gallamore is aiding Germans, who if not at war with the country you serve, will soon be, she is your enemy. First make sure that is the case, then think again." The father surprised the son with a barbed insight. "Your words did not say it, but you are in love with this woman, aren't you? That makes this far, far more difficult." Again the renewed fineness of the pencil point told of a long, thoughtful pause.

At that moment Danny accepted Michael's enlightened sense of the difference between the Irish father and the American son. The son only now saw in Maureen's mission what the father felt viscerally, that she felt an unlimited freedom in seeking allies against a nation of people who for nearly a thousand years made it their privilege to grind the Irish into the soil stolen from them. Michael's words said, "The English have enslaved and impoverished the Irish, deported and forced them to emigrate to the ends of the earth." Once more Danny read the words without consciously seeing them. In them he hear the tears in the voices of the old ones recounting a history of ancient oppression and the awful lament carried by the mournful melodies of their songs.

He returned to the firm flow of words that read, "I brought your mother here to this country, not because I turned my back on Ireland—how could I do that to a country where I shed my own blood, as did my father himself, for the sake of its people? I was weary of the fighting and the killing, and I knew to my core that I had done all I could. We Irish had won a country, part of it at least, but the country couldn't provide for growing families. I came to America because your grandfather had almost nothing to leave his sons. Your uncle, my elder brother, would receive his few acres, but to me all he had to give was his blessing to go, because there was nothing else." Here the writing stopped again where the pencil had been put to the paper several times, while Michael Flynn collected his thoughts.

When the writing resumed, its tone had changed. "'Tis true, your mother and I have a house and a few belongings now, but it is ours, only by scratching for it and being battered and cursed almost as badly as we were by the English. Still, we owe America something." A softer, apologetic tone crept into the words. "You have been blessed to have your mother's aptitude for study, and with marvelous agility and dexterity. No other Flynn has gone to college, yet here in New York, the Jesuit fathers took you in and gave you an education. And for that too, I call this a blessed country." The hint of his father's tobacco smoke that still clung to the paper pulled Danny into imagining Michael puffing his pipe, concentrating on what he would write. He forced himself to follow the penciled words further. "So your soul is scribed with two indelible messages. To me, the first holds you to a cause, the cause of a people scratching in the soil with bleeding hands to force it to feed them—giving their lives for the freedom to live as they please on their own land. The second, you tell me, is to the Constitution, not necessarily to the soil of America or to the patriotic sacrifices of blood and life, but to the words that express the magic ideas that give us those freedoms—for no other reason but that we are here. In the coming days, your soul will be tormented, twisted between the two.

"By age and accomplishment you are a grown man, with the power to keep either, or both, of these oaths. So in the end, you must face them yourself." The words blurred again, and Danny heard his father's voice. "Y' must seek to honor them both—as best y' can, for y' cannot simply choose one and leave the other."

His father's advice left him grappling with a suffocating, formless burden. If he failed to honor his oath as an army officer, he would profane the sacrifices of those who won the life that the immigrant Flynns now enjoyed, and he would face the might of the U.S. government: penalties he was unable to bear. In the other, the first oath, his father was right: Failure to keep it was tantamount to forfeiting his soul. But maybe he could find a way to keep her requirements reasonable. Or maybe he could ask her to absolve him of the oath, or...Oh, God, what could he do?

chapter

SEVENTEEN

London: British Admiralty reports HMS Hood sunk by German battleship Bismarck.

The green-eyed beauty opened the door—a slight crack at first—peering out cautiously. Then she opened it wide, took him by the arm and pulled him inside. Maureen held him closely, trembling. "Danny, love. You've been away from me so long, I thought I'd lost you," she said, her voice brittle with worry. "Come, come. Let me have a look at you, my beautiful man." She held him by his shoulders, regarding him with a look of the most genuine concern. "Ah, you're not well, are you?" She caressed his cheek with her long, soft fingers. Two weeks of hard riding, irregular meals of those abominable field rations—cold, like as not—and intermittent sleep on the stony ground had left him thin and haggard. But her intuition must have seen the tortured soul, wracked by nights of feverish deliberation. She kissed his mouth, his deeply sunburned face, and then his eyes. Clinging tightly to him, she saw in those eyes a visceral urge to take her to bed at once. It could have been love—she wasn't sure about that, but feeling his body stirred her just as strongly. Somehow, both felt a sort of troubling tenseness preventing them from acting. Her mind went back inevitably to that strained morning conversation in Navidad. Caressing his cheeks with her hands, she implored, "What it is that torments you? Don't you be hating me for what I must do."

"You're a witch the way you can read my mind, woman. You know why I had to come today," he said, holding her by the waist with his hands. "And you must know it's the oath I've been thinking of since I left you in Navidad."

She nodded, eyes downcast.

"Almost from that moment I left you that day, I've been learning more and more about you and what you're doing." He hesitated, searching for words. "It's a picture puzzle. Could you be a patriot? A spy? Maybe you're my sworn enemy. The pieces don't tell me exactly who this woman I love really is."

"I'm so sorry, love," she murmured, raising her eyes, and lowering them again, unable to look into his.

He concentrated on resisting a natural inclination for his voice to become shrill. "When I talk to you now, am I speaking to Maureen Gallamore, the nurse...or is it the shadowy Dona Marina, the spymaster of Navidad?"

"Spymaster!" She smiled at the thought of being called such a thing by a man she loved, but she parried the question, "Which do you think, Danny?"

He hung his head with a miserable sigh, and he let his words escape slowly. "I'm afraid it's the latter." At his admission, she remained motionless, pale and silent.

After a few seconds of thought, he allowed a pent-up question to escape. "Who was that man with you at the car sale in Matamoros and why were you with him?"

Lowering her eyes, she asked, "Can you accept the truth?"

"Yes."

"Leutnant Helmut Fischer of the *Kriegsmarine*, captain of a U-boat being replenished at Veracruz." Her green eyes sought his and held them. "More?" she asked.

He nodded.

"The car he bought, the one you saw in the orange grove, carried us to Galveston and the ports near the oil refineries. Helmut reconnoitered the waterfronts, taking notes on ships being loaded with oil, estimating when they would be ready for sea. In the bars he would pose as an able seaman looking for work, asking questions about their destinations. Then I brought him back to Matamoros."

Depressed by this confirmation of his fears, he forced himself to raise his head. "Did you and he...?"

She was certain he wanted to know if she had shared her bed with Leutnant Fischer. Her lips formed the word, "No."

He felt relieved, wanting to believer her, but many disturbing thoughts still lodged in his mind. For a while Danny stared at the floor of the small room, reviewing the alternatives boiling in his restless mind since the night before. "Indelibly etched on your soul," the words from his father's letter flashed through him with energy so intense that the revelation stood out clear and simply: the solution to his disquieting question lay not in his oath, but in his soul! The new knowledge conferred a calm he hadn't felt for many days. "Listen to me," he said with a conviction that surprised her. "It's true. I was born with an Irish soul that burns for the Cause, as you've reminded me. Last night I heard the voices of my ancestors."

In his mind he was in the Upper Room, speaking against Maureen's firebrand speech. "Remember my warning that making common cause with the Germans would result in another enslavement of the Irish people," he said to her.

Something in her eyes told him her memory of it still stung freshly.

"So, Maureen, dearest, if one of us is betraying the ancient cause of Irish freedom, it is you." He put it to her directly. "I cannot help you."

If his bold revelations shocked her, she showed no evidence of it. "What gave you this insight, Danny?"

He sat on one of the simple straight-backed chairs at the table, straddling it, clasping the slats against his chest. "I've sought counsel," he explained. "My father his thoughts about my conflicting oaths, and he opened my eyes to the part a man's soul plays in his life."

"Has someone else counseled you?" she asked.

He hung his head, letting his gaze fall on his clasped hands. "Another man, an army chaplain. He tells me I must inform the army about you, lest I face going to jail."

She didn't understand. "A priest would do that? After you confessed to him?"

"I didn't exactly confess." Danny tried to explain to her that he had simply gone to Captain Murdock for advice, and not all chaplains are Catholic. "He tells me he's a Methodist. It wouldn't matter, though. As an army officer, he has to turn me in and tell them what he knows about you—and I could go to jail. Or..."

"Or?" she asked.

"He tells me I have to tell the Army what I know about your activities."

For a time she said nothing, leaving Danny to wonder how this woman he loved could listen to him exposing his soul and take it all so coolly.

After what seemed a very long time, Maureen asked, "What will you do?"

"Maureen, my hands are tied. Think of what the army chaplain said. If I remain quiet about what you do and don't tell them about how the Germans are crossing the border, he'll inform the commanding officer and I'll be tried by court-martial, for treason, quite probably."

She sat impassively, waiting for Danny to work his way through the tangle. "If I go to the Intelligence Officer before the chaplain does, it would mean that I did my duty by my country. Either way, the Army and the Border Patrol will know about it."

"I see," she said in a small voice, closing her eyes for a moment. When she opened them, her face was strong and firm and she spoke as she did that night in the Upper Room. "You tell me you've renounced a binding oath to help me, and your second oath forces you to alert the authorities to my work for the cause." She waited for an answer.

"Yes," said Danny simply.

"What do you think my response should be?" she asked.

Much of Danny's agonized thinking had fixed on Maureen's situation. "I think you have a choice. You could continue your nursing work in Matamoros and Navidad. That way you'd likely be safe here in Mexico." The second did not appeal to him. "You'd be free to return to Ireland," he said.

Maureen sat motionless, considering his words before she countered, "But what about you, Danny love? When you act as your officer counseled you to do, won't they be forced to arrest you after they find you have helped me?"

From his expression, Danny appeared genuinely puzzled at her question. "But I haven't helped you at all, except to bring supplies for your clinic. The clinic is real, isn't it?"

Maureen closed her eyes, drawing a deep breath. This was far more complicated than this lusty but principled man she loved could recognize. "You sweet, naïve thing. Yes, the clinic is real. The people of Navidad are grateful for what I try to do for them, and they honor me by calling me Dona Marina. I am truly a nurse, and you did bring boxes of medicine." She pressed her lips together tightly, searching for the gentlest way to put the truth. "But some of those boxes held something else, a small, crucial shipment you might call contraband." Danny felt a terrible sinking feeling deepening as she explained, "For a time the men I helped across the border were satisfied with the Irish passports we provided, but after some were caught, they insisted on American identities to be a little safer when they roamed the port cities. The documents took little room under a false bottom in each of the boxes." The truth was out now. Her eyes steadily on his confirmed the realization falling on his shoulders. "You were transporting blank American passports and driver's licenses to match the men who were coming to me to be inserted into Texas." She opened her hands to express the inevitability of it all. "So you see, you have already been helping me."

He sat helplessly, his face in his hands, thoughts racing between visions of the stockade at Fort Leavenworth and rage at his own gullibility, and he remained lost in those overheated thoughts for a considerable time. Maureen gently caressed his neck and head, whispering, "I'm needed in Navidad—at the women's clinic."

The stricken Flynn moved hastily away from the table, aching with the piercing awareness he'd never see her again. "Don't go, please, Maureen," he pleaded.

She kissed him on the forehead. "Dear Danny, remember that I love you, but you've given me little choice. The things I'm certain you will say to the authorities in the next few hours will make me a fugitive." Before the door closed, she whispered, "Stay as long as you like. Senora Gomez will lock the door."

He bolted for the door to call to her. "Wait, Maureen," he shouted. At the foot of the stairs, she paused for only a moment. "Tell me this, please. If you expected me to keep my army oath, why did you have me carry the passports to you in Navidad?"

"You'll never believe me, Danny, but it's the truth. You were such a safe way to deliver them, and I didn't want you to know. I thought..." Eyes misting, Maureen felt her composure crumbling. Danny took several steps down the stair. "No, no. Don't come," she pleaded. She motioned toward the street, where a car waited with the engine running. "The car is here," she explained lamely, tears streaming down her cheeks. "Will I see you again, Danny?"

Wretchedly, Danny stood stammering, at a loss for words, now keenly aware of the steps he'd have to follow in exposing Maureen's spy ring. He heard the beguiling vixen say, "Please."

She ran to a car now altogether too familiar, the blue De Soto, driven by a sandy-haired gringo.

⚜

In some basic ways, this Texas Guard unit was no different than any army unit that ever existed: With hard training and discipline, its troopers would do their jobs under the most appalling conditions. When morale was high, though, the regiment came alive with an energy every trooper could feel. History is replete with cases of highly motivated soldiers performing near miracles. Colonel Chamberlain sensed the fragility of that elusive spirit in the 124th. These days he found himself brooding constantly over his troopers and how they might be affected by the case of Sergeant Wieczorek and the army assessment of how well the horse cavalry had acquitted itself in the harsh limestone country south of Fort Clark.

Lieutenant Danny Flynn sat alone in his room in his underwear, with the artificial breeze from an oscillating electric fan playing over him, brooding over the mess he'd allowed his life to become. The visit to Maureen in Matamoros had brought his emotional foundations crumbling. Who knew when she might emerge again, or whether he'd ever see her at all, unless she was arrested and named him as a sworn accomplice. Rather suddenly, it occurred to him that, in his lustful pursuit of the scheming Maureen, he'd been behaving shabbily to Molly. His most recent pang of conscience came the night he and Doug ventured into the twisted alleys of Matamoros. Dear Molly, how must she feel about being ignored for another woman?

A glance at his watch told Danny it was now almost exactly twenty-four hours since his impetuous effort to exonerate Weech, yet nothing had been heard from Colonel Chamberlain. In fact, rumors sputtering around the post held that the sergeant remained locked up in the guardhouse. Could it be taking that long to verify his statement that Wieczorek had acted to protect the children in San Agustin from harm? He'd done his best for the man. His mind was clear on that at least, but these other worrisome things churned chaotically in his mind. He could be arrested as a traitor! But, he reasoned, nothing was likely to happen until the regiment came back to work after the four-day pass.

For a time he lay on his bed, sipping the whiskey neat from the heavy glass. Then he napped for a while. In midafternoon, with the fan not doing much to blow away the heat, he evacuated his room with no particular plan in mind. He drove slowly through the nearly deserted streets of Fort Brown, thinking, talking to himself, practicing what he'd say when he turned himself in. The idea of driving to Padre Island for a run in the surf came to mind, but he dropped that idea too. Ignoring his problems for a few hours wouldn't do any good. He had to work through them, and soon.

Without realizing where he'd driven or why, he parked his Ford at the stables with the vague thought of walking among the stalls to think, or maybe even to take a solitary ride. In the doorway, he paused to let his eyes adjust to the dim light. Three troopers in baggy blue denim killed time between their routine duties with the horses. Two privates from B Troop sat on sacks of grain at a checkerboard set up on an upturned bucket. A sergeant stood nearby watching the game, sipping coffee from an enameled cup. At first the checkers players remained absorbed in their board, unaware of the arrival of an unexpected visitor; but the sergeant, a man Danny recognized, saw Lieutenant Flynn, and saluted hastily, greeting him. "Hahdy, Lieutenant. Still here on the post, are you?" To the privates, he said, "This here is Lieutenant Flynn," as if the lieutenant with the flaming red hair could be anybody else.

Off and on during the day, Wieczorek's time in the guardhouse had popped up for discussion. In fact, not long before Danny interrupted their afternoon checkers game, the troopers on the stables detail had been in a heated conversation mixing an assortment of fact and speculation. Their thinking ran generally that Weech had been screwed by the system. In their opinion, the whole affair between Lieutenant Kincaid and the sergeant showed how the army's double standard—a benign, permissive one for officers, but one of cynicism and hard knocks for troopers—had worked as it always did. Lieutenant Flynn, though, was all right. He was the one person willing to stand up for Weech.

Danny returned the salute and tried to make some optimistic small talk about a hope that Wieczorek would be out soon, but the stiff, edgy atmosphere made conversation difficult. "I think maybe I'll go riding for a while," he said.

One of the privates volunteered to saddle a horse for him. "It'd be a help, Lieutenant. Horses need some exercisin'. How 'bout ol' Baldy?" Private Biggs was suggesting one of Colonel Chamberlain's favorites; his best jumper. The soldier talked as he led the way to the long, low building near the office—the one where the CO's horses were stabled. "Lieutenant, we know it ain't you." The private nodded to emphasize his point. "We know y'done right by Sargint Weech." While the lieutenant followed his unfailing routine of checking the horse's feet and letting Baldy hear his voice, the trooper talked. "Guess y' want yer nice saddle, right, sir? Up there in that rocky country 'round Fort Clark, y' didn't have a chance ta ride anything but them ol' troop horses." Private Biggs approved the match he was arranging. "Y' got a hour 'til water call, sir." Biggs understood the restorative powers of riding a horse like the colonel's jumper. A mount like Baldy could improve a man's outlook on life. The horse had a way of imparting confidence to his rider. Of course, not just any rider was capable of appreciating Baldy's talents.

Only a few minutes on Baldy's back set Danny feeling noticeably more in tune with himself. The familiar mixed experience of the smell of grass and the feel of a powerful horse galloping under him had a therapeutic, awakening effect and it helped him think more clearly. And Baldy? An agile, athletic, smart horse trained by Sam Chamberlain felt a superb rider on his back allowing him to run and stretch his powerful muscles in a way no mere exercise rider could. When Baldy told him he was ready, Danny took him through a series of jumps. He put that splendid mount in position, and Baldy did the rest, springing off his mighty hind legs, alighting as gracefully as a bird. And time flew.

Judging that he still had a bit of time to let Baldy cool down before water call, Danny circled the parade ground at a gentle trot, watching the children playing across the street. At one of the houses, a kneeling figure in a faded uniform shirt and fatigue trousers waved for attention. Danny recognized Major Perkins with his gardening tools scattered around him, struggling to coax a bed of begonias into surviving the heat. The sight of the operations officer clicked in Danny's mind. What luck. The major might be the one to whom he could bare his soul.

He walked Baldy across the street and dismounted on the tiny, lush green lawn of the Perkins bungalow. After only the briefest attempt to "make his manners," Danny blurted. "Would you happen to have some time today, sir? I've got a problem."

Perkins stabbed his trowel into the earth and stood up stiffly, rubbing garden soil from his hands. His bemused smile transmitted his opinion that lieutenants always have problems, but he spoke reassuringly to the agitated Flynn as if he were a nephew. "If it's about your sergeant, the papers to let him out were sent to the guardhouse earlier this afternoon. He may already be in Matamoros. Go out and enjoy the days off. It may be a long time before you get more."

"Yes, sir. Thank you, sir, but the sergeant's only part of it. There's a lot more." Danny wiped his face with his red bandanna.

Perkins squinted at the visitor loosely holding the reins of the colonel's jumper. "What do you mean, Lieutenant Flynn?"

"I'm afraid I could be arrested for treason, sir."

Had it been any other lieutenant, Perkins would have laughed and shooed him away to think the matter over until the regiment was back at work. But this lieutenant whose mount was grazing on his small, carefully tended lawn was Danny Flynn, one of those gifted men who seemed to go through life overdramatically steering between the extremes of glory and doom. Perkins decided to have the talk with him. "Finish your ride. When you're done, drop by the house—in civvies. We'll make sure this'll be a social call—so Captain Franklin won't think we've bypassed him." Perkins winked. "I'll have some cold beer ready so we can talk," he said, hoping he sounded reassuring.

Danny walked the short distance between his quarters and the major's house, rehearsing what he'd say. When the very nervous young officer knocked, a beaming Ruby Perkins met him at the door. "Ah, Danny. So nice to see you," she gushed with sincere pleasure. "Please come in where it's cool. We have the electric fans going." She took him by the elbow to lead him to the little room the Perkinses were using as the major's den and office. "We haven't seen you for ages. Wilmer is expecting you." She chattered cheerily about how long it had been since the last official social event, completely oblivious to the consternation showing plain on Danny's face.

Perkins, in his den, wearing civilian clothes, didn't look nearly as imposing as he did with gold oak leaves on his collar. The major forced a cheery smile to put his caller at ease, but he had an uncomfortable feeling about what he might hear from Danny. Making certain they wouldn't be overheard, he called to Ruby, "We may be talking for a while, dear. I think we'd best not be disturbed."

"I know, dear," Ruby called pleasantly on her way to the kitchen. "Tell the dear boy he'll be having dinner with us tonight. No excuses." Danny heard a pleased giggle in her voice as the door closed.

"Have a seat then, Lieutenant Flynn, and let's get to this problem," said Wilmer Perkins, offering his apprehensive visitor a glass of beer poured a few minutes earlier. "Treason," young Flynn had said. He'd see. Perkins sipped carefully, concentrating on keeping his face an impassive mask.

Danny, fully convinced he'd be pleading his case for freedom, bared his soul. God, how he hoped Major Perkins would believe him and understand how his contorted ethical views on swearing oaths could have caused such a snarl. Somehow he found himself describing Maureen more as a hardened veteran IRA agent than as the bewitching vamp who had lured him away from Molly. It was in the spirit of getting to the truth, he reasoned.

Right from the beginning, this disclosure to Major Perkins moved along more easily than the one with Henry Murdock. Stands to reason, Danny thought, a soldier would have a different view on these things than a chaplain. If Perkins understood, Flynn planned to beg to be spared from court-martial and a stretch in Leavenworth. "Major, let me try to explain how these two oaths trouble me," he pleaded. At an encouraging nod from Perkins, Danny called on his father's words to help his listener appreciate the ancestral pressures that made him see his actions, not as promises deliberately made in diametric opposition, the way others might see them, but as actions with meanings as different from one another as the inborn duty to help a needy parent is from a promise to pay rent to a distant landlord. He produced the letter from his father and read it to Perkins, feeling his eyes misting, hoping it didn't show. How could he be considered a traitor? Didn't it make a difference that he'd been duped and that, under the circumstances, he couldn't have known that he was carrying treasonous material in the unmarked boxes?

Perkins had long since dropped the sham of impassivity. One after another, he fired questions to satisfy himself of the details. Who in the regiment knew of this besides the chaplain, he wanted to know?

"That's all, sir. Just the chaplain."

"How about Miss Blankenship?"

"Oh, no, sir. No, sir," said Danny, shaking his head vehemently. He felt beads of sweat popping on his forehead.

"Danny, this is very ticklish stuff for Captain Murdock, but he did exactly as he should have. It was your duty to inform us of your suspicions of this agent's work, not his. Now what was this agent's name? Gallagher, wasn't it?"

"Gallamore, sir, but Major..."

Perkins stopped him lest another digression take them well into the evening. The two had been wrestling with the details for more than an hour—Ruby had knocked twice, and once the front doorbell had been rung.

To ease Danny's anxiety about baring his soul, Perkins had taken no notes, but he did have a plan in mind. "Listen to me, Lieutenant Flynn," he said. "You're not a traitor, I know that. But if someone who doesn't know you and your ethical dilemma heard only the basic points of the story you've been telling me, it could easily have taken that you acted treasonously. What if the FBI or some other lawmen caught the Irish woman and got her to name names?" Flynn would've been in hot water. "Look, Lieutenant," Perkins said to him, "the army doesn't have an understanding of opposing oaths. Neither does the law, as far as I know."

By talking so long, they had already imposed on Ruby's good humor. Perkins was no philosopher and neither was Danny. They were alike in seeing much of the world in terms of black and white. Lieutenant Flynn's views—young man's views—were almost certainly shaded by instinct or distorted by passion.

The major waved his hand as if to brush away the fuzziness of what he was trying to explain. What he meant to get across *was* imprecise, but in a way, that was the point. Perkins leaned from his armchair to speak earnestly. "With this thing that you've gotten yourself into, it's good that we're in the Army. As people and not automatons, it's particularly easy for you and me to understand each other and find ways to handle this without it becoming a matter of law or regulation." Something about the major's view of his predicament sounded reassuring to Danny.

Perkins's prescription for putting the matter to rest turned out to be simple and typically direct. "I'll notify the CO about this, and give him my thoughts and a recommendation. But I think it's best that you talk to Captain Michael, the S-2. Do it tomorrow, so it's a matter of record before the full regiment gets back to work. I'll call him to make sure he can set time aside for you. Expect the interview to be very thorough."

Perkins leaned back comfortably in his chair, satisfied that he'd done his duty to set the young lieutenant straight. Thirstily, he gulped the now-tepid beer remaining in the glass. Ah, but he'd forgotten one point—an additional bit of advice. Actually, it was more of an order. "Stay out of Mexico for a while, whatever you do," he said. Hearing Danny's, "Yes, sir," Perkins smiled, more relaxed now, pleased that he'd gotten to the bottom of Lieutenant Flynn's problems. Emotionally drained, Perkins finished his beer. "Let's go join the ladies," he said, standing.

"The ladies, sir?"

Perkins ignored the question, leading the way down a short hallway to a cramped dining room nearly filled to capacity by a table set for four. Already a steaming bowl of mashed potatoes occupied a place on the table awaiting the long-postponed entrée.

Have I ruined your plans for dinner, sir?"

"No, no," the major said casually, concentrating on his new role as the genial host. "Ah, here's Ruby."

Mrs. Perkins emerged from the kitchen with a roast on its platter, apparently unfazed that her dinner had been delayed so long. She offered a litany of excuses and urged the men to the table. "We're so pleased that you're here, Lieutenant Flynn," she said cheerfully with a wink at her husband. She called into the kitchen. "Is the gravy ready, dear?"

"Yes, it is, Ruby," said a voice from the kitchen. He recognized it. Molly Blankenship!

Obviously she'd been here for nearly an hour. He wasn't ready for this, and it panicked him. Why hadn't he called her? If Doug's hints were true, she'd been seen with George Kincaid. But here she was, carrying a gravy boat to the table.

She nodded to Danny with her slow smile. "Lieutenant Flynn. So nice to have you among us again," she said.

chapter

EIGHTEEN

Tokyo: Imperial Japanese Finance Ministry begins freezing American financial assets.

Sergeant Roper slipped quietly through the door to alert the colonel, "The division commander's on the phone for you, sir."

A call from the new general could mean only one thing. After days and days of sterile official silence, this was certainly the official news. The War Department had chosen his old West Point friend to give Sam Chamberlain the word that he needn't torment himself with false hope any longer. If the thinkers in Washington had been entertaining any thought at all of retaining even a token regiment of mounted cavalry in the army, the congratulatory calls would have been burning up the wires. Instead, the unofficial rumor network carried nothing at all to him about a decision from General Marshall. Most of the conversations were carefully businesslike—certainly nothing lighthearted—and no news. Too proud to make direct inquiries, Chamberlain stoically kept his own counsel.

In the days immediately after the exercise, Chamberlain had been rehashing that disturbing Wieczorek incident and analyzing all the tactical moves to a fare-thee-well. But the realist in him saw far more important factors shaping the future of the 124th and its commanding officer. Most disturbing was the news that General Herr was gone—the chief of cavalry, out of the army—let out to pasture, just like that. And why? Herr had given an "Over my dead body" ultimatum to the mighty George Marshall. A step like firing a three-star general usually signals a cascade of disruptive changes. This one sealed the fate of the horse cavalry and dashed the hopes of many men who'd given their professional lives to it.

Chamberlain reached for the telephone with the slumped shoulders and drained features of a man facing the gallows, saying, "Thank you, Sergeant Roper. I've been expecting this call." But he pulled himself up to sit erect and heaved a sigh. "Give me a few seconds before you tell his office I'm on," he said.

Sergeant Roper knew his telephone etiquette as well as anybody, but if Centaur was concerned with the fine points, it was already too late. "The general is waiting for you, sir. He said to tell you it's Eddie Burton."

Chamberlain's premonition of the hammer falling and quashing his hopes had been dead center on the target. Sergeant Roper didn't hear the general's words delivering the bad news, but Chamberlain's responses told the story. "Yes, sir. I understand. I know it has to be that way."

The two old friends must have put all that unhappy official business behind them in short order and moved on to other things, for the sergeant overheard the two chattering and gossiping about the flurry of changes going on. Then he heard them laughing. Roper left his desk to find Lieutenant Colonel Newman, who was expecting the news too. He'd be relieved to know that Centaur was taking this in good humor.

Roper sharpened a few pencils and turned his steno pad to a fresh sheet—there was always dictation after the regiment heard from a general by telephone. But Centaur burst from his office waving a sheet of notepaper, looking cheerful for the first time in days, relieved of the ordeal of waiting for the bitter medicine.

"The new division commander's coming to visit us," Chamberlain said. "My old friend is coming to help say farewell to the best horse cavalry regiment in the army."

Life at Fort Brown improved for everybody when the regimental commander smiled.

Chamberlain passed his notes to the sergeant. "I had some ideas, but Eddie has the stars, and here's a tentative schedule for two weeks from now—the first weekend in December. I want you to get this typed up with some copies. Then make the calls to set up a meeting in my office."

Collecting paper and new carbon sheets, Roper read the colonel's neat printing:

Fri:	MGen. Burton arrives	Parade Ground
	Reception	Officers' Club

Sat:	Regimental Parade	Parade Ground
	Field Day	Various at Ft. Brown
	Dining Out	Officers' Club
Sun:	Sunday Service	Chapel
	MGen. Burton departs	Parade Ground

Newman had met Burton only once, at an army function in San Antonio, and he asked about the new general who was coming visiting.

"Eddie and I were at West Point together," Chamberlain said, lapsing into a rambling recollection. "Burton acquired a reputation as an innovator, even when he was Master of the Sword at Fort Riley, not too long after George Patton held the job and took credit for designing a new saber. They even named the damn thing for him. The Patton saber! What a piece of junk that was, a straight-bladed weapon made for thrusting—a sleazy way to get a little notoriety. Eddie wouldn't do that," said Chamberlain, who didn't think much of Patton, because the man had sold himself out to the armor faction, but that was a view he kept to himself. Now Eddie Burton was a man Chamberlain genuinely respected. "These days he's pushing airplanes, insisting on incorporating aircraft reconnaissance as an integral part of his divisional training." Centaur laughed briefly, recalling smugly how pleased Eddie was at seeing the use of aircraft in that unfortunate war game at Fort Clark.

Newman, whose home was in San Antonio, had friends in the Air Corps, and he recalled the army's experiments with aircraft nearly two decades before. "Black Jack Pershing had aircraft available when we were chasing Pancho Villa in the twenties, but we didn't know how to use them," he reminded Chamberlain. He also avoided mentioning that the famous bandit eluded his army pursuers, aircraft reconnaissance or not, because at the time, communication between the pilot and the pursuers on the ground consisted of hastily scribbled notes dropped from the aircraft.

A comfortable hour before the general's plane was to land, Centaur and his regimental sergeant major walked together, making a final painstaking scrutiny of every detail of the arrival. The day couldn't have been more beautiful: a warm, clear, comfortable, early-December day in far South Texas. A scattering of troopers—the ones not working at the stables—and the families who lived in post quarters waited in the shade of the orange trees to watch the general's airplane land on the parade ground.

In an expansive mood, Chamberlain strolled over to chat with the ladies of the Officers' Wives' Club seated on folding chairs. He was making small talk with Ruby Perkins when a rising noise resembling the sound of a peevish wasp approached from the southeast, where the Rio Grande flowed into the Gulf. Centaur turned toward the sound, spotting an oncoming biplane barreling along barely above the palm trees—low and dropping lower until it skimmed with its wheels only a few feet above the parade ground.

Forgetting their composure, Lieutenant Colonel Newman and Major Perkins, with several other officers of the official welcoming party, craned their necks to keep the maneuvering aircraft in sight, whooping their appreciation. Newman pointed across the parade ground to the tops of trees and peaks of roofs visible above the heads of the two men in the open cockpits. "He wasn't more than three feet off the grass," shouted Perkins, grinning delightedly. The colonel hurried to rejoin his officers.

The pilot, a flight instructor from one of the Air Corps fields in the vicinity of San Antonio, selected for his skill and experience to fly his special passenger, pulled the agile trainer's nose up steeply into a graceful wingover, rolling the aircraft gracefully so that briefly, the spectators on the ground could see the airplane outlined against the sky. He continued the rolling turn toward Fort Brown, diving for another low pass. This time he showed them a loop, leveling off at the lowest point of the maneuver with a snappy aileron roll not more than a few hundred feet above their heads. Another smart turn positioned the aircraft for a landing on the grassy expanse where Colonel Chamberlain and much of Fort Brown waited. He placed the aircraft lightly on the smooth green grass in a three-point landing and let it roll out almost to the border of oleanders before taxiing back to stop before the reviewing stand precisely as the minute hand hit twelve. Damn, it made a beautiful sight, sitting silently on the grass: blue, yellow and silver. In the appreciative silence, Centaur led his officers out to greet their visitor as he climbed from the aircraft.

The general, an agile athlete, released the buckles of his safety harness and flung the straps back with a practiced ease. Conscious of the curiosity of hundreds of men in khaki, he climbed unassisted from the front cockpit and let himself down the lower wing. Beaming with unconcealed delight, Eddie Burton strutted toward his old friend Sam Chamberlain and a few members of his staff, waiting until he was almost in handshaking distance before pushing his goggles up on his forehead and removing his flying gloves to return their salutes. At the waiting sedan, Burton pointed to the aircraft ringed by appreciative viewers. "There's the future, Sam. We have to admit it...but let's have a hell of a time celebrating the past."

***

In marked contrast to the festive air created by officers in dress uniforms and their ladies in frocks and broad-brimmed sun hats in the clear, balmy afternoon, a haze of profanity hung over the stables, where preparations proceeded at an intense pace. So much was still to be done, even though the entire regiment had been practicing and preening for three solid days. Without let up, the troopers had been sweating through long daily drills.

Sometimes it was by individual troops. At other times, the entire regiment passed in review over and over in tight formation under the unrelenting gaze of Centaur himself: ranks were never the sharp lines they should have been, postures not as erect nor guidons perfectly aligned. Loudspeakers squealed a list of discrepancies to be corrected. A slight dissatisfied nod of the colonel's head was enough to start the entire process anew. And every day Chamberlain stood where the general would review the parade on Saturday, supervising until impatience got the best of him. Then he would ride past the rectangular blocks of mounted men in ranks with Major Perkins and say curtly, "Keep them at it until they get it right, Major."

The morning's practice was the last opportunity to get everything perfect, or at least moderately so. The parade ground was crawling with captains and sergeants taking notes and picking away at tiny little details. Afterward, platoon by platoon, lieutenants and their sergeants copied the lists of sins: troopers' hats, horses' manes and hooves. At noon, Major Perkins relented and sent the regiment to the stables with orders to "work out these little odds and ends."

Lieutenant Flynn drank water from a galvanized cup, going over the items in his notebook, listening to the voices of First Platoon getting back to work that had been interrupted by the aerial display marking the general's arrival. Word was already going around among the troopers that the general was having lunch with Colonel Chamberlain in some cool room at the officers club.

As they did naturally, the troopers collected to talk among themselves, only now it didn't sound so secretive to him. He heard one griping, "Sarge, I don't care a damn bit about playing a baseball game tomorrow afternoon. The season's over anyhow. If it's so damn important to the general, why couldn't we play the damn thing now, before my pitchin' arm goes dead from polishin' all this brass 'n leather"?

Since being exonerated in the fracas involving Lieutenant Kincaid, Weech enjoyed an elevated status throughout the 124th. His troopers held him in a kind of awe, as a man who had played with fire and escaped without being burnt. The other sergeants deferred to him and were quick to buy him a beer and ask his advice. Elwin Wieczorek was a changed man—not in outward appearance, of course—but his threats and intimidation were gone, replaced by the more comfortable air of a man who expects to be obeyed because his word is law. He walked among his discontented troopers laboring in the heat, many bare from the waist up, sensing their moods, keeping them at their work with a joke or a word of encouragement, but equally ready to urge them to activity with a bruising kick in the butt if required. With the lieutenant too, things had improved remarkably since the court-martial threat disappeared. Wieczorek had found a quiet moment to come to the office to say his thanks for getting the charges dropped. Running his fingers through his thin brown hair, the sergeant did the best he could, "Lootenan', I wanta thank you fuh savin' my neck." From Wieczorek, a statement like that meant a conversion—not quite complete, however—because indelible memories of that night on the train still lay hidden inside both men. An easy working relationship might never come, but these days there was at least open and forthcoming mutual respect, and that was the important thing.

Private Billy Chapman, a recruit from Iowa, one of the replacements sent to fill the regiment's vacancies, had been sweating with a brush and a bucket of thick black paint, a chore assigned by Corporal Tony Wilson. "Good job, f'r a rookie f'm Iowa," said the corporal as if merely mentioning the state's name left a sour taste in his mouth.

Soaked with sweat from working in the latrine and covered with filth, Chapman waved a paintbrush clotted black with paint and sand. "It ain't polishin' the tack that bothers me so much," he complained. "It's paintin' these goddamn horses' hoofs that sticks in my craw." Largely ignored by the Texans and chafing at getting all the worst details, he grumbled under his breath about having to pick up the horses' feet to paint the hooves and keep them clean until the black stuff dried into a hard shine. "Iowa horses work. These horses are just like you Texans: prissy and pampered."

Private Clement Sevcik, face spattered with paint when the horse whose hooves he was painting kicked the brush with a twitching hoof, yelled, "Hey, you Iowa Yankee." He could conceive no worse insult. "You think you the only one workin'?"

It took only that little spark to set him off. Chapman flicked his paintbrush, slinging a black swath across Sevcik's chest.

"You son of a bitch," screamed the outraged Sevcik, jumping up to kick sand on the hooves of Chapman's horse. The Iowan tossed the thick black paint remaining in the bucket at Sevcik and grabbed his suspenders to pull him down into the sand. The platoon gathered to watch the two rolling and kicking at each other. "Hey! Fight! Fight! Give 'em room," the cry went up.

Sergeant Wieczorek, saw no need to hurry for a fight like this one. That Yankee kid started it. Besides, deep inside, he shared their objections at having to paint horses' hooves, so he ambled unhurriedly over to the two outraged troopers wallowing in the sand.

"Enough," the sergeant bellowed, and went into action before either of them could react. Grabbing Chapman by the back of his baggy fatigues, Weech hoisted him off Sevcik's back, and dropped him into a watering trough. Sevcik scrambled to attention to avoid the water, but his posture simply made it easier for the sergeant to dunk him too. Weech lined the two dripping privates up before him to deliver his judgment. "You git back to work," he growled. "But tomorrow, after the parade, while everybody else is swimmin' in the river 'n playin' baseball, we gonna have a little boxin' match to settle this—out behind the stables. I'll be there with the gloves. Heah me?"

Lieutenant Flynn, who'd been observing Wieczorek's lessons in practical leadership called from the high steel fence, "A word with you, Sergeant, if you're done with your, ah, instruction."

Wieczorek walked across the deep, soft sand, shouting over his shoulder to the lieutenant's dog robber bent over a hoof, examining the paint. "Garza," he called, searching for the dog robber. "Got the lieutenant's horse saddled? He's here to practice."

Danny nodded toward the two troopers climbing soggily out of the water. "Who's doing the fighting, Sergeant? Tomorrow, I mean."

"Each other, I think, Lootenan'. If they won't fight each other, they gonna have to fight me," he said.

Even before the final horse in the final rehearsal for the pass in review left the parade ground, the post engineers had already begun a last-minute manicuring treatment for tomorrow's program, setting out the water sprinklers and connecting long hoses for a final irrigation pumped from the reliable Rio Grande.

A lush, verdant lawn is no natural sight in the arid desert climate of far-south Texas, but the parade ground is a showcase for a cavalry regiment and its skills. Its condition says much about the stewardship of the post and its buildings. In the distance, a detail of soldiers toiled with the steeplechase obstacles, giving them a final touching up for the field day following the tomorrow's parade.

Many of the competitors were exercising their horses, getting them accustomed to the bright paint of the freshly repainted jumps. Danny Flynn, like the others, wanted a few extra minutes to exercise his mount. There wouldn't be time tomorrow.

Behind sprinklers, sharply standing out against the backdrop of bald cypress trees, the brightly painted biplane from Ellington Field sat quietly, gleaming in the afternoon sun. The driver of a flatbed truck from the fuel farm carefully cranked the handle of a portable pump, transferring fuel into the wing tanks from steel drums. Another soldier held the brass nozzle at the filler neck. The anxious pilot paced anxiously. He didn't trust these horse soldiers near his airplane. "These crazy people would probably start a polo match or sure as hell, they'd try to build a platform or some kind of jump right in front of it," he said to someone who inquired about the fueling process.

"Hey! Watch it. You almost dropped the nozzle on the fabric," he yelled at the soldier with the fuel hose, genuinely concerned that one of these men would try straddling the aircraft fuselage wearing spurs.

As soon as they got the fueling done, he'd get the engineers to move the sprinklers, clearing a takeoff path for his return flight to San Antonio. For a few moments he watched the riders taking the jumps. Jesus, but that redheaded kid can ride like a dream, he thought to himself. Why's he wasting coordination like that on horses? He'd have made a great pilot!

Molly Blankenship sat in Danny's car, parked on the street that ran in front of the officers' houses. She adored her cavalryman, and now that she had him back from that Mexican woman people talked about, whoever she was, she meant to keep him. She knew how much he loved riding his jumper, and she had become accustomed to waiting patiently, as she was now, until Danny was ready to escort her to the reception at the officers' club.

What a sight they were! Danny-and-his-mount, panting and sweating, muscles tensed and pulsing from exercise. That's the way she would think of them, like a single word, when they took the jumps of the steeplechase course. No matter how hard she tried or how patiently Danny coached her, she hadn't been able to achieve anything like that marvelous balance and fluid grace of his. Molly found herself thinking about her lieutenant at odd times, like when her students were working on an essay, thinking of what a fluid art form riding could be when practiced by a gifted, instinctive horseman like Danny. Was the horse trained to respond to subtle messages from his rider, she asked herself, or was it the animal that in some mysterious way transmitted to his rider that he was ready for the jump? Once she'd asked Danny which way it was, but he said he didn't know for sure.

Danny dismounted and led his mount, drawn irresistibly to the plane. This probably was as close as he'd ever approached an aircraft. Had he been alone, he would have walked up to the brightly colored fuselage to drum his fingers on the tight, glossy fabric. Maybe he would have climbed into the cockpit, to belt himself into the seat and put his hands gingerly on the stick, imagining himself flying it. The pilot, she saw, recognized the rider's fascination.

She stepped down from the car, following at a distance, along the parade ground boundary maintaining a discrete distance. Under one of the bald cypresses, she hesitated, appreciating a special moment—the cavalryman and the aviator sizing each other up. A slight breeze carried a blend of earthy scents: orange trees, water, damp sod disturbed by hooves, crushed grass, horses, and the intrusive aroma of aviation gasoline.

The aviator felt a trifle uneasy at the approach of a saddled horse being led too close to his fragile airplane. Perhaps he felt diminished by the effortless control of the rider over his massive mount, and by sensing the slight vibrations of hooves on the earth as the animal walked and by an animal smell he'd never experienced. His instinctive reaction was to step back to grasp one of the struts between the wings, seeking the comfort of his own métier. He struck a haughty, defiant pose in his leather flying jacket and helmet with the goggles pushed back. In this moment, alone among these dinosaur soldiers, dashing and mysterious as they might be, he would never have surrendered his helmet and flying jacket, no matter how hot it might have been in this southern desert. This was the view Molly captured with her boxlike black Kodak camera.

Danny saw the pilot's double silver bars, tossed him a casual salute and swung down lightly. "Captain, I'm Danny Flynn. I'll trade you this horse for that airplane."

The aviator proffered his hand. "Well, Danny Flynn. Come here Sunday, early—before I fly the general on to El Paso—and I'll give you the ride of your life."

To Sam Chamberlain, this visit from his old friend Eddie Burton marked a high point in his army career. Not that Sam didn't cling to personal aspirations to a general's star of his own; but Eddie's visit was a heaven-sent opportunity to assure the 124th and its commanding officer a place in history. These few days of tradition and festivity were to be savored, chronicled and remembered. To Centaur, it meant that for the coverage to be complete, he wanted professionals on hand: a team from the Historian of the Army, another from the University of Texas Department of History, gladly provided by the governor with his best wishes, but he also wanted Max Gindler, the enterprising reporter from the *San Antonio Express,* to be here with his camera and portable typewriter, so that the citizens of Texas would be aware of the role their men were playing.

Army people are not accustomed to doing their job in the light of popping flashbulbs or answering questions from reporters, but the troopers accommodated the photographers and interviewers with a remarkable élan and grace. Newsreel crews perched on special towers, training their cameras on the pageantry of what they had been informed would probably be the final cavalry parade in the U.S. Army. Their cameras caught Sergeant Frank Tibbs opening the field day, riding at full gallop with a foot on the back of each of two horses, holding Old Glory aloft in his right hand. Gindler's men took hundreds of still photographs, neglecting nothing, not even the track and field events and dozens of troopers swimming in the Rio Grande. Younger reporters concentrated on interviewing the soldiers from the small towns of Texas, while Max Gindler spent most of the day with Colonel Sam and General Eddie Burton.

The three were making a brief visit to a baseball game between A and D troops when a duty officer arrived with an urgent message. He called Centaur aside to say, "A few minutes ago I took a call from the Border Patrol, Colonel. The patrols the people at Fort Ringgold are taking for us?" Chamberlain nodded. He was quite aware. "They caught some Germans less than a mile from the American side of the river up north of here. They got 'em by watching a suspicious car parked on a little ranch road."

Chamberlain listened to the details, nodding his head as the lieutenant reeled them off. "Did anybody get hurt?" he wanted to know.

"They didn't say. But according to the Border Patrol, there was some shooting. They captured two, but one got away into Mexico with the help of the agent who may be planning these things. So did some of her helpers."

"*Her* helpers?" Chamberlain wanted to be certain he had it straight. "You don't suppose that's the woman Lieutenant Flynn told the S-2 about?"

The duty officer had no way of knowing about female spies in this incident. "The report was very terse, sir. It didn't contain anymore information about the woman," he said.

The colonel stood quietly, staring at an imaginary spot in the outfield for several moments, thinking over the report. "Thanks. I'll tell the general. He'll want to know," he said to the Duty Officer.

⌘

The Fort Brown officers' wives had made their wishes known. Mrs. Chamberlain put her foot down, insisting on an evening party in a garden setting, and on this Friday evening, the officers' club accommodated them, a transformation as nearly miraculous as the artistry resident in a cavalry post could make it. Landscaping had been irrigated and manicured. Potted trees, Japanese lanterns and newly touched-up garden furniture completed the project. Indoors, a combo from the regimental band fussed with their instruments, preparing to play music during dinner and later, for dancing. While the guests arrived and chatted, Sergeant Marcus Cohen, the band director at New Braunfels high school, strolled from group to group, serenading with his violin.

Danny knew by now how lieutenants were expected to behave at these affairs. Conscious of the scrutiny he would get from Captain Franklin and others who knew about that woman in Mexico, he was doing a credible job of appearing civilized, gracefully guiding Molly through the decorations and out to enjoy the view of the Rio Grande roiling beneath the broad platform. But there was the obligatory reception line. Like all others, this one was stiff and contrived, and lately Danny and Molly had become one of the hot gossip topics. There'd be all those senior officers whose wives were certain to give him the once-over—this renegade who threw dear Molly over for some lusty senorita in a rundown adobe village. Running that genteel gauntlet would be more bearable if he could fortify himself beforehand. "Let's get a glass of punch, why don't we?" he suggested.

Danny steered Molly to the back bar where the club manager had thoughtfully stationed a bowl of the reddest, indisputably authentic cavalry punch—for enjoyment by purists. "No, thank you. But you have one if you like," Molly said. She too sensed pressures tonight, just as Danny did. One cup in the fresh air and a few minutes of quiet to compose himself would have been understandable, but when he tossed the potent drink back in several large gulps, she placed her hand demurely on his arm to distract him from downing a second. 'Danny, dear, shouldn't we go in to the reception line now? They're expecting us."

Refusing a second cup of the lethal stuff required self-denial in heroic proportions, but he conceded Molly was right. He turned away from the expectant waiter with an apologetic smile

Fortified by the alcohol, Danny smiled and made small talk with the officers' ladies. Several were quite direct about the plans making the rounds of the Wives' Club: wedding plans for Molly and her lieutenant. Ruby Perkins was even less guarded. "Oh, you lucky man, Lieutenant Flynn," she gushed. "We ladies are so excited."

Once they reached Lieutenant Colonel Newman, Danny felt the greatest dangers of the Wives' Club gauntlet safely behind him, but now he faced the challenge presented by the senior couples. He hated that, especially when introducing Molly formally to the Chamberlains and then General Burton. He rehearsed some polite remarks Walter Franklin suggested, but with the Newmans, the talk took a dangerous turn. Newman greeted Molly as if she was family—and Mrs. Newman hung Danny out to dry. "Molly, dear. We haven't seen you recently. Do tell me about your wedding plans!"

Molly lowered her eyes demurely. "You've been keeping Danny very busy, Colonel," she said in an evocative tone. Danny mumbled something about the hard work of training.

Helen Chamberlain's tone was a bit more circumspect, but not much. "Molly dear, will you join the ladies at tea this Wednesday?

Molly, the picture of poise and decorum, accepted as if her attendance was completely normal and customary. "Of course, Mrs. C."

By the time he was introduced to the guest of honor, Danny's mouth and throat felt strained and parched. In the midst of a haze, he heard the general saying with the broadest of smiles, "Well, I am pleased, Miss Blankenship. I've heard about your plans from the Chamberlains." Danny, perspiring, forced a smile.

During the quiet period while dessert was being served, Danny whispered to Molly and pushed his chair back, nodding to their dining companions, making apologies. "I'll be back in a few minutes." He seemed well enough, but Doug followed hastily, suspecting that the wicked cavalry punch might have proved too much for even Flynn's cast-iron disposition. But Danny waved Doug away and hurried across the spacious ballroom to the broad doors separating it from the hallway. Outside, near the manager's office, he stopped at a small desk to use the telephone, jiggling the hook impatiently for the post operator.

Holding his hand over the receiver to prevent his conversation from being overheard by the manager, who stood nearby at a small standing desk reviewing some papers, he spoke in a voice hardly more than a whisper. "Get me the stables sergeant." The operator reminded him that the stables office was closed, but he was insistent. "Yes, I know it's late, but he'll be there." To himself he thought, he'd better be right by the phone, or he's dead.

The manager, intrigued by a call to the stables at this time of night, stared at a display of framed photographs on the wall, pretending not to be eavesdropping, but the small, fearful man scuttled away at Danny's scowl. From inside his office, the inquisitive manager heard the lieutenant say, "Just as soon as you can, Sergeant. I'll be waiting." What were these celebrating soldiers going to do in his club? Inside, the band stopped playing. Mr. Torres breathed with visible relief when Colonel Chamberlain began his prepared speech. If the commanding officer was speaking, he reasoned, the revelers would be less likely to start some club-wrecking craziness. But the colonel's balky microphone began making pesky, squealing noises. Torres reluctantly tore himself away from his eavesdropping to look into getting the microphone working correctly.

Outside, at the foot of the broad entrance steps, Flynn anxiously searched the dimly lighted parking lot. A match flared in the shrubbery at the far end. Sergeant Amos Long, who possessed firsthand experience with practically every scheme or prank that could be committed from horseback, wouldn't do anything to spoil this one. Not until he was certain it was Lieutenant Flynn approaching did the usually taciturn Long emerge from the gloom, beaming his delight in this little conspiracy. "I got Peggy back there, tethered to a tree limb," he whispered, chuckling. For the occasion Long had actually abandoned his faded blue fatigues for a real uniform, complete with a tie. And, in the excitement, he'd forgotten his pipe. If he hadn't just stepped out of the shrubbery leading a saddled horse, he might have been taken for one of the musicians taking a break during the speech.

"Is she ready, Sergeant?" Peggy was a good, steady, calm horse, one of the colonel's favorites.

Long smiled broadly. "Oh, yessir. We did a little warm-up work and I wiped 'er down, jes like we talked about."

Peggy was one of two horses in the stables fitted with rubber shoes, a crucial point in her selection, but Danny checked anyway, to be certain nothing had changed. One by one, he picked up her feet to have a look. "Just right," he said to no one in particular.

Long approved of the lieutenant's thoroughness.

"Good girl, Peggy," Flynn spoke quietly to the black mare and patted her on the neck and shoulder. He drew his watch from its pocket. "OK, Sergeant, mount up. I'll lead the way and you ride."

Long didn't move. "You got to ride 'er, Lieutenant," he insisted. As usual, he had a good reason. "You ride a lot more like C'unnel Sam than I do. They won't be so much change in weight, y'see."

Flynn swung into the saddle with an order to Long. "Lead on, Amos. Don't keep Sam Chamberlain waiting."

With Long clearing the way, the lieutenant rode her up the steps, gently reassuring the horse, leaning forward to caress her shoulders and neck. "Good Peggy." She reacted calmly to the lights and noise as if attending noisy parties was something she did every day. At the high double doors, they allowed a few seconds to accustom her to bright lights and tobacco smoke—as well as the shouting and music. Peggy placed her feet delicately on the carpet runner stretched across the polished floor leading to the ballroom as if this were nothing new, but neither the carpet nor her rubber shoes could muffle the rhythmic thudding of hooves against the wooden floor.

The incredulous manager heard, or perhaps he felt, the mounting ruckus in the lobby. He raced for the ballroom doors, uncertain of what he would encounter out there. These cavalry people were crazy; Alfonso Torres knew that much for a fact, but the spectacle of a spirited half-ton mare with a mounted rider being led through his painstakingly decorated club was too much for him. Fearfully, he retreated to his office and slammed the door.

Through the ballroom entrance doors, the colonel could be heard concluding his speech. Danny dismounted and listened for his cue to lead Peggy in. Long turned, walking toward the club entrance, where he planned to wait discretely until Peggy was ready to leave the party.

"Don't you leave, Sergeant," Flynn said to Long. "You've got to see this. Walk in with me and stand on the bandstand when the colonel mounts."

"The final chapter of mounted cavalry in the U.S. Army is about to close," Colonel Chamberlain said to his officers and their ladies, speaking his closing lines from memory. Over the heads of his listeners, he saw the door crack open slightly, the signal that Peggy was in position. The colonel concluded his speech. "What we accomplish in the next few months will do much to change the course of America's history." He grasped the lectern firmly and his voice boomed with the charge, "Let those of us here in this room strive to end our days as military horsemen ensuring that history remembers us in the brilliant light of glory."

The officers of the 124th and their ladies applauded, not fully aware as yet of the doors swinging open and of Peggy being led through the ballroom by Lieutenant Flynn and Sergeant Long. Centaur stepped forward to take Peggy's reins, and the ballroom echoed with shrieks of surprise and approbation at the spectacle of a saddled horse looming above tables covered with white tablecloths.

Suddenly Centaur was in the saddle, riding the length of the floor, slowly at first, allowing Peggy to get her footing on the polished wooden floor, gauging distances, feeling the plucky little mare's confidence growing. Hoofbeats thundered up and down the open dance floor, almost drowning out the applause and shouts urging the colonel to jump the dinner tables.

Centaur and his faithful Peggy didn't disappoint. A few powerful steps and up they went, over the first, then the second and even a third table. Except for one major, a doctor who lost his nerve and ran to avoid the spectacle of a horse soaring overhead, the diners held their seats. Some shrank involuntarily, or held hands over their heads, but oh, how that horse could fly! So nimble and graceful getting under herself for jump after jump! And such confidence in the man in the saddle! The colonel guided Peggy through a tight turn and judged the approach for a second series of jumps. The officers and ladies hurriedly took their seats. They watched without moving while Peggy's rubber-shod hooves whistled by, barely a foot above their heads. Bravado? Yes, certainly, but one of those events in cavalry lore that would never be repeated, and for Centaur, a climactic moment in his life as a cavalryman. He gave Peggy a slow circuit of the floor to accept her ovation. Major Perkins, grinning broadly, shouted, "Curtsey, Peggy. Curtsey."

Centaur dismounted to the sweetest sound he would ever hear, his officers screaming their approval. He seized a glass, raised it and called out to them all, "Charge your glasses to drink to the moment, and toast the 124th, the greatest horse cavalry regiment in the history of the United States Army."

Without further speeches, Centaur entrusted Peggy's reins to Amos Long, who led her down the length of the ballroom floor to a rolling ovation.

chapter

NINETEEN

Honolulu: Waves of carrier-based Japanese Navy aircraft in surprise strike at U.S. Pacific Fleet at Pearl Harbor.

In his post chapel office, before the Sunday service, chaplain Henry Murdock offered a heartfelt, private prayer of thanks for the presence of General Burton, for if the two-star hadn't announced his plans to attend, the chapel pews would have been nearly vacant. Murdock himself could attest to the lethal qualities of the cavalry punch. With a soft "Amen," the chaplain went out to do his duty for God, country and the United States Cavalry. In his sermon he reminded his distressed listeners of the war clouds looming over Europe and the impending dangers to America. He spoke eloquently of the special trust the nation placed in the armed forces and of a soldier's duty to his country. Concluding, the chaplain asked God to bless the men and the families of the 124th through the dangers to come, and with a glance at Centaur and the general suffering silently in their pews, he asked that He give the leaders of the nation fortitude and wisdom. Finally, Murdock requested the congregation to bow their heads, asking for blessings on those who had already given the supreme sacrifice while serving their country. The chaplain led them all in three verses of "Battle Hymn of the Republic" and bade the general a safe journey.

In the open cockpit of the aircraft carrying him to his evening appointment at Fort Bliss, General Burton expected to be aloft for several hours. To him the time wouldn't be lost. In fact, he and his pilot had carefully plotted a course allowing for a personal aerial reconnaissance of the remote, isolated country along the Mexican border—his responsibility to defend.

Flying low over the Davis Mountains and the Big Bend country, Burton rode in undisturbed peace, unaware of an attack by Japanese aircraft on the United States Naval Base at Pearl Harbor, but reports had reached Washington and the army communications circuits were abuzz with the news.

The customary formalities for an arriving general had already been canceled by the time they landed at the remote border fort near El Paso. The grim-faced men who met his plane broke the news brusquely. "I'm afraid you've arrived to some bad news, General. The Japanese hit us a couple of hours ago—at Pearl Harbor, at first light. From all reports, it was bad. The army circuits are full of it. We're at war."

The news didn't particularly surprise him. "I've got to get caught up," General Burton said simply. The army sedan whisked him away to the briefing room, where shifts of men had been sorting through stacks of reports flooding in by telegraph.

⌖

At Fort Brown, the gates had been closed to unofficial traffic. In the 124th, the Headquarters Troop worked furiously, getting word to men off post on passes or away on leave, ordering them to return immediately to Fort Brown. Bednarski and Warnken had left for Matamoros, but they were turned back at the Fourteenth Street Bridge by the border guards. Two more, Bohuslav and Reimers, were sent back to the barracks by the gate sentries. Lieutenant Flynn reported to the headquarters building with all the other officers to learn of the events that had thrust the nation suddenly into war. Waiting for the colonel to arrive, the officers jostled noisily before a wall map, pointing out the vast and unfamiliar reaches of the Pacific Ocean to one another.

Sergeant Wieczorek called in his muster report to the E Troop office. "Onliest one missin' now is Private First Class Garza," he informed the sergeant keeping track of the remaining absentees. "We think he went to Mexico to visit his family ovah theah."

"Mexico?" asked the voice at headquarters. "That's not so good. The bridges are closed to traffic from Mexico."

Weech reassured him. "Oh, Garza kin git back all right. He don't need no bridge." But the dog robber's pass was for two days. Finding him in Mexico wouldn't be easy. Who knew if he'd get news of the war? The Mexicans hadn't been attacked.

The news came as a shock to the men in the barracks; not that the president declared war, that was expected, but that it was Japan who attacked rather than Germany. The Germans had been audaciously sinking American ships without any declaration of war. And why would it be the Japanese? Three troopers sat near a radio, listening to the news.

Hours had gone by since the news came, and still the mood remained somber, with none of bravado First Platoon felt upon learning of submarine attacks on American shipping. These young, unsophisticated men, confined to their barracks on a balmy South Texas Sunday afternoon, turned especially thoughtful. They talked wistfully among themselves, speculating about the war threatening to consume them in ways they couldn't yet understand. "Where do you think they'll send us, Sarge?" drawled the slow-talking Sevcik, looking up from laying out everything he owned, refolding undershirts, polishing and repolishing boots and shoes to perfection, repeating a question that had already been asked a half dozen times.

Wieczorek dutifully fielded the question again, as he would many times more before taps: a different man than the one who ruled by intimidation and fear in the misty days at the River Camp. His troopers looked to him for an answer he couldn't find. A sergeant with all those stripes, and he was helpless to explain how fighting the war would affect them in any understandable way. The best he could do was to repeat his answer as many times as one of them felt the need to ask. "It's just like ah bin sayin'. We gonna be fightin' Germans, in Europe," he said to Henry Moore. "What th' hell d'ya think they'd send cavalry soldiers to the Pacific for? It's all watuh. Th' Navy's gonna be fightin' th' war 'gainst th' Japs." Where they'd be sent was a question they were utterly powerless to control, and at the moment it had no definite answer anywhere—not even in Washington. The crucial question, the one they couldn't bring themselves to ask was: Will I be able to kill a man when the time comes? The topic had come up regularly, as it must when young soldiers train with weapons that kill. Today, chances were vastly increased that they'd be facing a live enemy very soon.

Idling away time in the barracks while the fires still raged through the crippled American fleet in Pearl Harbor affected each of them differently. Mattijetz, Reimers and Bohuslav sat on footlockers writing letters. They'd been at it since being sent back to the barracks. Bednarski, who hadn't written a word since the 124th arrived at Fort Brown, addressed his third envelope; brow furrowed, he scribbled with a stubby pencil he sharpened every now and then with his pocketknife. Thoughtful Henry Moore sat on his footlocker, brooding on the shocking notion of a license to kill. To kill a man: that's what all this business of soldering was about, wasn't it—when you stripped away parades and stripes and shiny boots, and laid the reality of having to take lives against years of churchgoing and learning the Ten Commandments by heart? How many times had they heard, "Thou shall not kill" and never thought for an instant how the message would someday apply to them personally. In all their training, the army message had been to work hard, learn to shoot straight, and take care of your horses—but not too much was ever said about taking a human life without remorse. One by one the troopers working their way through this self-questioning by doing menial little tasks or writing home, stopped to hear the sergeant's words.

Three of the young troopers from the Czech communities interrupted Weech's conversation with Henry Moore to ask his permission to go to the chapel to recite the rosary.

"Sure," said Weech grinning self-consciously. "I'd go with yuh, but I gotta stay here, yuh know." He leaned against one of the heavy wooden structural beams spaced regularly through the open barracks bays, returning to Moore, who wanted to know how it might be that shooting a man could ever seem natural, even if he were confronted by a Japanese or a German—or an Italian, for that matter. Weech tried his best to make it clear. "Henry, those people bin killin' Americans fuh a long time, now—sinkin' them ships and all. And we ain't done a thing about it. Now, we gonna git 'em!" He smacked his fist into his palm.

Knowing that the president had declared war laid the question bare, like raising the curtain on the school play. Moore wanted to get his arms around what it all meant. "Tell me something then, Sarge," asked Moore, thinking hard about those Germans across the river—the ones the lieutenants roughed up in *Die Lorelei*. "Could First Platoon go across the river to Matamoros and shoot all those people and be rid of a few enemies?" he asked. He made the question sound so reasonable.

By now most of his troopers were listening to the exchange between Wieczorek and Moore with an intense interest. Weech fumbled for something to say, "Well, they got these rules tellin' yuh when it's OK to kill our enemies, see." The sergeant wasn't prepared for this kind of discussion, but they were depending on him. He wasn't clear on the fine points of exactly where you could kill an enemy or precisely what kind of clothing he must be wearing before it was legal to shoot him, but he knew the army couldn't afford to have its soldiers thinking too much about such problems.

Wieczorek's awkward explanation prompted Private Reimers to ask for more clarification, "So we can't go to Matamoros to get them Germans, right, Sarge?"

Wieczorek nodded. "Yep. 'At's right." Really, he didn't know why. All he knew was that it was so.

Matthijetz, who'd simply been taking in the discussions, piped up, "But them U-boats bin sinkin' our ships and gettin' people drownded, ain't they?"

Moore asked another question, "Right, Sarge. Don't the Germans have rules too?"

"Yeah, Henry, but they the bad guys."

Bednarski finally barged into the conversation with his opinion. "If a U-boat can kill Americans, then dammit, when we git ovah theah, I'm gonna shoot any kinda German I see. That's how it's gonna be." He slammed his fist on the bench he was using as his writing table.

The legal issues being raised ranged far beyond the sergeant's power to explain, but the troopers couldn't leave the question alone. He felt pressed into issuing his final judgment. "You better be careful," Wieczorek admonished, shifting his gaze from face to face. "Shoot the wrong German and y' could git yuh ass court-martialed." Never in his life had Weech been faced with questions like these, and the mental wrestling to find answers made him uncomfortable. He walked to the window to see if the lines at the telephone booth had dwindled. "Where's Zientek?" he snapped irritably. "Didn't he go out to the phone an hour ago?"

Tony Wilson, the corporal, reminded him, "Yeah, Sarge. And he came back while you were drawing a cup of coffee. You want me to go stand in the line for you? Then you can call your mother." Two or three troopers, amused by the thought of Sergeant Wieczorek having a mother, laughed nervously.

"Nah. Sergeants don't need to call their mothers." No one laughed, not even a snicker.

Every man in the platoon stopped what he was doing to listen when Gerhard Reimers answered the ringing telephone. "Yes, sir," he said, nodding and pronouncing the words carefully, the way he did when he met his English teacher in town. This had to be either headquarters or the troop office. "Yes, sir, I'll tell the sergeant." Reimers knew he was relaying the first orders of the war to the rest of the platoon. "It's from Lieutenant Flynn. He's with Major Perkins. He says f'r us t'git our gear ready. We load horses for transportation at 0600 hours tomorrow."

"I volunteered us to do it," Danny told his troopers when he returned, omitting anything of his personal interest in the matter. "We'll go up to the north in trucks and portees tomorrow morning, set up a camp for three days—more if we find anything—patrolling to show our presence during the day and setting ambushes at night." They were being sent to the area where the 156th had gotten into a scrape and shot up some people suspected of being foreign agents. "We've been there before, but Centaur wants us to get some of those agents...and so do I," he said.

This wasn't Europe and certainly not the watery wastes of the Pacific Ocean, but it was real. No questions, no wisecracks; the entire platoon felt the excitement of facing an enemy they might have to kill. Danny and Weech stood together, critically observing the men loading the horses, discussing plans for the operation. They went over the platoon roster. Garza had come in during the night after fording the river in the dark and thumbing a ride to Brownsville. "Have those people from the Machine Gun Troop shown up?" asked the lieutenant, momentarily picturing Esteban keeping a lookout while Panchito waded across.

The sergeant called the troop office with an all-present report. He found Lieutenant Flynn to let him know his troopers were now loading the machine gunners' weapons and ammunition into a truck. "And we got their horses n' packsaddles." Weech handed Danny a list with six extra names penciled in: four men with their machine gun and bulky ammunition cans, and two more with a radio to keep them in touch with Fort Brown. While the lieutenant went over the list, Wieczorek made an observation. "Centaur's a little bloodthirsty, ain't he, sir? Sendin' us out theah with th' machine gun, I mean."

Danny grunted something about fighting a war against the Japs now, not caring too much that a change in enemy probably didn't make sense to Weech. He felt edgy about the operation, questioning his own motives in volunteering First Platoon. Was he trying to catch Maureen at her work to prove he was no longer bound by his oath to help her? Maybe it was only because the woman he loved had used him in espionage, discarding him when he was no longer useful. That the United States was in a declared war didn't figure into his thinking very much just yet. With so many practical details to worry about, he couldn't dwell on it.

Garza's return was a great relief: Well, sure, a lieutenant could get along without a dog robber, but Garza's skills made the First Platoon lieutenant's job much easier. And, if he were truthful about it, he'd admit how highly he valued Garza's judgment in a lot of things.

"Mark these positions," said Danny, spreading the map for the sergeant. "Here's where I want you to put people—across here." He drew an imaginary line with his finger. "Spread them out far enough so they have to use hand signals. I don't want any chattering back and forth. This way, by the time it gets dark, we'll be all set in our positions without giving ourselves away by making noise." He flipped through the pages of his notebook, checking a list of points he copied at the briefing. "While they're getting set up, I want you to have two mounted troopers scout these little roads—for cars—parked cars. It's key to this whole operation. If either of them finds a car, one should come back immediately, while the other keeps searching." Danny saw Weech's quizzical look. The sergeant thought Lieutenant Flynn was going crazy.

"Cars?"

"Sergeant, listen to me," said Flynn, annoyed; "Cars." He reminded Wieczorek that a car had been involved in many of the known insertions of German agents. "Sometimes one of them drops off a car with Texas plates, and these people jump into it to drive away."

"Cars it is, Lootenan'," mumbled Wieczorek, not sounding very convinced.

"Take my word for it," Danny said, without explaining why he was so confident. "If they find a car, have them look it over, but leave it there. We want to be sure we know where it is, so we can keep an eye on it at night."

To avoid having to explain his reasoning in the car business any further, Danny turned his attention once more to the map to refine the details of the ambush. "Our people have to be in position before dark." He put a mark on the sergeant's map with a marking pencil.

"Here. Put the machine gun here—so it can sweep the ford." Danny clenched his fist for emphasis. "There may well be some traffic from across the river, but we've got to be sure it's not some innocent Mexicans. Tell the gunners not to open up with that thing unless these guys start shooting first." Flynn felt his own pulse racing. He wanted his troopers to know that not everybody trying to cross the river would be a foreign agent. "So don't be too quick to shoot." He felt himself rattling along too rapidly to be understood, and he worked consciously to slow it down.

By the time Weech returned to the camp, the sunset was only a faint glow in the west, and a fat moon—about a week from becoming full—hung three fingers above the eastern horizon. Garza was speaking earnestly to Flynn when the sergeant came up.

"We made a lotta noise gettin' in position," said the sergeant. "It's gonna be a bright night. Nobody gonna try nothin', except maybe some Mexican tryin' t' get home t' his wife." They shared a low chuckle.

In the quiet, a sending key tapped coded messages to Fort Brown. Danny lowered his voice so only his orderly and the sergeant could hear. "Garza's been roaming the area in civilian clothes, talking to the local people to see what they know. He got a little word through his family and a friend named Esteban. Something's up on the other side."

Garza spoke up. "But this isn't any solid word, *Teniente*. Only something Esteban said. 'Be careful tonight, Panchito,' he told me."

Danny assured his dog robber that he knew about the information, but he respected Garza's faith in Esteban. "Listen to me, both of you. We want to go carefully on this—especially tonight—until we get a feel for what we're doing. But if we see somebody in the river bottom who isn't obviously a local, I want him."

That much was simple and direct, but the lieutenant had been working on another plan. "If one of these agents gets across—and then goes back to the Mexican side to save his ass from being shot, I'm going after him. See, that way it'll be a case of hot pursuit." Holding up a hand, he cut off questions, speaking directly to the sergeant. "If that happens, you are to stay put, Weech. On this side of the river, I mean. The less you know about this, the better."

He had a different assignment for the dog robber. "Garza, you stick to me like a dirty shirt, and I'll take four more with me, riding straight to where I think this is being masterminded. It's four or five miles from the ford." Seeing questioning looks from the sergeant, Danny repeated, "We'll go straight there, learn what we can and get right back."

Weech's eyes narrowed with curiosity about this business of a foray into Mexico. The lieutenant had been pretty damn clear he was on to something. As platoon sergeant, he thought he should know more about it, but he remained silent.

To placate the sergeant, Flynn reached for his map and marked it with a slight dot on the Mexican side. "Don't worry. We'll be back. Be careful who you pass this information to." Just to be sure his orders were clear, he repeated the final point to his platoon sergeant. "Don't you cross the river." Satisfied that they understood, he said, "I'm going to try to sleep a little now. Around midnight I'll come down to the gunners' position. Make sure these troopers are down there, ready to go with me." He handed the sergeant a folded scrap of paper. Wieczorek read the names to himself, nodding his understanding.

By First Platoon standards, tonight's camp was a spartan affair, without any of the comforts Garza would have normally arranged. Danny sat on an ammunition container, prying his supper out of a can of preserved beef with the blade of his pocketknife. He waved Garza over to him. "Don't bother trying to get something fancy stirred up. Get some rest if you can. I want to get over there tonight—before it's too late." He soaked a corner of the hard biscuit in a cup of coffee and looked expressionlessly ahead, mulling over his plans.

"Just copied this message, sir." The radio operator handed him a small sheet of paper. "Now it ain't only the Japs. The Germans've declared war on us. Italy, too. So have a few other countries."

Danny sighed wearily. "So we're taking on everybody at once. Well, it makes things clearer for me." He handed the message back to the private who brought it up from the tent. "Show it to Sergeant Wieczorek and let him spread the word."

Danny awakened Garza and went over his map in minute detail, sipping at a cup of coffee while the dog robber saddled the horses. Including himself and the indispensable Garza, his little force numbered six: Sevcik, Warnken, Matthijetz and Moore, all good marksmen. "Let's move quietly, leading the horses." He pointed to a clump of brush. "Try to get yourselves and your horses hidden in that mesquite." The lieutenant motioned with his hand toward the river bottom. "I'll be down there with the gunners. Take turns staying awake and sleeping. Come instantly with the horses if I click this three times." He held a little cricket clicker between his fingers.

"Si, Teniente, si,"said Garza excitedly, "and how 'bout if I hear shooting first?"

"Then get down the slope to me as fast as you can."

A few minutes later, Flynn slipped into the gunners' observation post concealed behind a fallen tree and draped with Spanish moss. "See anything?" he hissed.

Sergeant Belden and the other gunner had been watching the ford, catching naps. "Nothing, sir. Not a thing. And pretty soon, it's been hard to see anything, 'but we'll have a better moon a bit later," the sergeant whispered.

"All right. I'm going to try to sleep. Wake me if anything happens—anything," whispered Flynn.

An hour and a half or so passed with only the sounds of insects and nightbirds to break the utter silence. The gunner put a hand on the lieutenant's shoulder to awaken him. "Look, sir. I b'lieve I see a woman and a little boy, sir...tryin' to cross."

"A little boy, at this time of night? And a woman? Let me use your glasses."

"Right over thah, sir—dressed up like a peon, sure as hell, but that's a woman. She's leading the little boy," Belden whispered a little louder. "A mother and her son," he repeated.

Danny exhaled slowly. "All right. I see them." The woman in the broad straw hat stood scanning the bank where the faint footpath ran in the direction of First Platoon's well-hidden positions. The two figures standing in the shallow water showed no interest in going any farther. Apparently satisfied with what she was seeing, the woman turned away from the American side and led the boy back toward the shadows. "Don't shoot. But be ready. Something's going to happen."

The gunners looked up from the machine gun at Lieutenant Flynn. What the hell could he possibly know about what those people on the other side would do?

Another half hour passed before the first shape could be made out dimly moving down the bank. It wasn't the woman this time. Danny watched the man in his glasses, a full-grown adult, moving cautiously toward the river. Sergeant Belden sensed the lieutenant's rising excitement. He shook the other gunner awake and carefully sneaked his finger onto the trigger.

The man didn't walk like Garza's family and most of the Mexican workers. Danny whispered to Garza. "Not a Mexican, is he?"

The dog robber shook his head no, without ever taking his eye off the figure.

Danny remembered Garza's friend in his little house not far away. He whispered to Garza, "How about Esteban?"

"That's not Esteban, sir. He's safe. If they don't live around here, people wouldn't ever know where he lives."

The man waded into the water without hesitation until it came nearly to his waist. Then his manner became more tentative; he felt his way along the bottom for dangerous holes. If he was armed, the weapon wasn't evident. Once on the dry sand on the U.S. side, he turned momentarily to look back across the river, most likely toward a companion waiting up the bank, in the brush perhaps, or maybe to look for a signal.

Belden, itching to use the machine gun, looked to Lieutenant Flynn, who signaled him to hold his fire. Dripping with river water, the man studied the footpaths leading up the American bank toward First Platoon, but he didn't move away from the water as they expected him to. Danny got a look at his face through the glasses before he hid himself behind a clump of brush. Whoever he was, he wasn't Mexican.

Half a minute passed without anything happening. Then another figure, smaller than the first, slipped out of the tangled brush at the top of the far bank, keeping near cover as long as he could. A third followed a few yards behind. Both were smaller than the man waiting in concealment. Evidently these two expected trouble. One carried what looked to be a pump action shotgun, and the other appeared to be carrying a short-barreled revolver. Very probably then, all three were armed.

Something startled the first man, the one already across. Danny couldn't tell what he might have heard or seen. Maybe he felt the eyes of the First Platoon troopers. He crouched to stay hidden as much as possible and ran, not back across the river, but upriver, where most of Wiezcorek's troopers lay hidden and waiting. Either he had no inkling of the ambush or he was confused.

On the lieutenant's signal, the machine gun erupted in a short, frightening burst of tearing sound. On the Mexican side, about halfway up the bank, Belden's carefully planned shots passed above the heads of the two waiting in the water and tore into the sand, sending echoes cascading along the river bottom for miles, startling the birds and animals. The thinking was that shooting behind the men would drive them across toward First Platoon, but the intruders in the river bolted for the cover of small trees behind them and to one side. The lieutenant gave the order, "Take them."

Belden sprayed the trees with two long bursts. "All right. That's enough, for me," Flynn said. He was on his feet, moving, giving rapid-fire orders. "Moore, Sevcik. Follow the runner on our side. Give him a chance to surrender. Shoot him if he refuses. Warnken, Matthijec; come with me. We're crossing the river. Be ready with your weapons. Garza, you too, bring the horses."

Hardly more than a minute after the machine gun chewed up the sandy soil of the riverbank, Danny and his troopers were in Mexico, weapons ready, shining their lights into the heavy brushy cover where the armed pair vanished. The other four dismounted, leaving Garza with the horses. The lieutenant drew his pistol, motioning Matthijetz and Warnken to follow him up the bank. Every few steps they stopped to listen, for anything: a twig breaking, maybe, or footsteps. Danny heard something running through the underbrush—far too fast to be a man moving through thick, thorny stuff like that—probably a deer. Hard to believe that Belden's fire hadn't killed somebody outright. Danny scanned the ground with his flashlight, searching for footprints or some other sign that somebody had scrambled through the tangled grass and cactus. He knew he wasn't good at following tracks, and the chances of finding footprints in these difficult conditions were small. He was reluctant to send a trooper into the thicket to be shot by a desperate wounded man.

From the distance, he heard the sound of an engine starting. "Damn!" he said, shaking a fist in frustration. "I'll bet it was the woman! She left a car waiting up there." A disappointment, but at least it gave him an ironclad excuse for hot pursuit.

Danny called his men together before moving deeper into Mexico. "Garza, take the horses to the ford so they can drink some water while I talk to these two." He spoke quietly to the troopers, both shivering with excitement at going into Mexico chasing full-fledged enemies. "We're going to cross the farms between here and Navidad, staying off the roads. No need to let the world know the U.S. Army is roaming in Mexican territory. The house I want is on the edge of an orange grove a few miles from here. When we get there, we'll surround the house and capture whoever's there. Understand?"

"Yes, sir," they said, grinning, almost jumping with excitement. The lieutenant regretted sending Sefcik and Moore to run down the man who had come across, but what was done was done.

In the dark, Warnken opened his mouth to ask something about the car they heard earlier, but Garza was coming up with the horses. Danny raised his hand to stop any further conversation: "Too late for questions now."

An hour later, Danny and his small force knelt behind the hacienda wall covering both the front and rear exits. A brief search of the land around the house assured him no automobiles were hidden among the trees, but fresh tire tracks suggested strongly to him that at least one car had been hidden there recently. With Garza aiming his rifle at the door from behind the adobe wall, Danny walked cautiously toward the house, pistol drawn. "Maureen. It's Danny. I'm coming in," he called.

Hearing no response, he called again, "Hello, the house. We're coming in." He ran up the steps, prepared to kick the door down, but he found it ajar. A cautious look over his shoulder assured him that Garza had jumped the wall behind him on the lookout for people approaching the house. He heard his troopers at the rear of the house moving in. The door swung open with an easy push. Through the vacant house, he heard Matthijetz entering the kitchen from the other side. The place looked deserted. Flynn had them go through the few remaining items of Maureen's effects thoroughly, ransacking the place searching for some clue that could suggest how the house had been used recently. The signs in Spanish still told local women Dona Marina would be available to tend to their needs from Monday through Friday. Danny felt a pang of emotion seeing the bed he and Maureen shared—unmade, but it satisfied him that only one person had been using it. The other rooms had seen hard use—beer bottles piled in a corner; cigarette butts ground out on the floor; pieces of peon's clothing like the men at the ford had been wearing, lying in a heap. Danny pried open the locked cabinet where he knew she stored her medications, pulling out boxes, searching their contents. Heart pounding, he tore open one closely resembling some of those he carried with him from Matamoros and threw out the small vials. He used his pocketknife to dislodge the flimsy wood bottom, which came up easily. There, tied in neat stacks were six U.S. passports and several Texas drivers' licenses. He stuffed them into his pockets. She must have overlooked them in her hurry to leave.

"Matthijetz! You find anything?"

"No, sir. Nothin' more'n a lot of trash, sir. We gonna burn this place?"

Why not? He liked the idea. Sure. Why not burn the damn place, he thought? It would serve her right. But he sensed his thinking becoming erratic in the excitement of exacting revenge. No. If he wanted to tell every Mexican for a hundred miles about his little incursion, burning the house would do the job. He scratched his chin thoughtfully. "Leave the house be," he said, shaking his head.

Outside, Garza called, "Everything all right in there, Lieutenant?"

Danny walked over and opened a window. "Sure, we're fine," he said. Checking his watch, it alarmed him that so much time had passed. "We need to move out and get back across the river.

With Belden pointing out the brushy area where he pumped thirty eight rounds, Weech sent three troopers into the brush to search for results, but they found nothing, except split and shattered tree trunks, large holes torn by bullets smashed into the sand and a few tracks verifying some men had crawled through. The troopers couldn't be sure how many.

The machine gunner and the platoon sergeant stood together in the gathering light, getting a better look at the damage done to the terrain around the ford. Belden wet his lips, commenting to Weech, "Ain't so easy to do good shootin' when it's a man that's out there in th' bushes."

Moore and Sevcik bagged the one who'd made it across the border about two hundred yards up the river, trying to escape on foot through the heavy brush. They called for help in dragging the body out of the thick, thorny growth into an open space on the sandy riverbank and stretched him out on his back. Wieczorek went through the dead man's pockets. A circle of wide-eyed troopers jostled each other, chattering in amazement at the sight of four neatly placed bullet holes punched through his chest. "Looka heah," said the sergeant, holding a bloody passport. "He's gotta be a German." Who else would be wading across the river carrying an American passport with an address in New Braunfels? Otto Kleiber, it said his name was. They'd done their job in the river bottom. Nothing much to do now but take the body up to the camp and wait.

Weech sat motionless in his saddle, staring intently up the bank where the lieutenant and the other three had gone. He satisfied himself he was still following his orders if he rode only as far out into the water as he could without getting his boots wet, and no farther. If the lieutenant hadn't been so specific about not crossing into Mexico, he'd be over there by now, following his tracks looking for him and the troopers. Weech squirted tobacco juice into the dark water, sorting through the questions facing him: Where was the lieutenant? What we gonna do with that dead guy now? What about the car on the road? Damn! The radio operators were after him for something to send in the morning report. "They'll be houndin' us fer sure if we don't send 'em somethin'," urged one of the radiomen.

"Don't send nothin' till I tell yuh to send it," snapped Wieczorek irritably. He had a plan in mind. If the four over in Mexico didn't show up in another half hour—it would be light enough to do it by then—he'd send some people across to look for Lieutenant Flynn and the others. He'd stay at the camp, as directed.

But in the way things like this work, as soon as his plan was made, the problem resolved itself. He heard the horses a little while before he saw the lieutenant's head coming into view above the bank. In a few more seconds, all four were in sight, working their way down the steep sandy slope. From the looks of them, horses lathered, men sweating and covered with dust, they'd been pushing it. But they were back.

Weech had been anxiously keeping an eye on the time. "Three hours and twenty-six minutes, Lootenan. Yuh sh'nuff had me worried," he said.

They rode to the camp together, the sergeant pumping the lieutenant for an account of his hot-pursuit foray to Navidad, but the preoccupied Flynn remained noncommittal. Warnken and Mattijetz could tell the sergeant all he wanted to hear. At the camp, troopers dropped what they were doing to crowd around the lieutenant and his three-man force, as inquisitive as a yard full of children about what went on in Mexico. But all that had to be put off for the more pressing business of sending the long-delayed reports. They could always claim they had to repair some problem, and who would know? In fact, Flynn had been so intensely occupied in the quarter of an hour since his return that the fate of the man who had crossed the river hadn't crossed his mind: Then his eyes found the prostrate shape of a body laid out under a blanket a few yards from the crates of field rations.

He carefully raised a corner of the blanket, half expecting the corpse to come to life. He recognized the face as the man he saw through the glasses. "Well, for the love of...I thought he would have come out as soon as he knew his traveling buddies were running back to Mexico." Maybe it was the fearful sight of bullets tearing into the far bank that kept him from escaping to Mexico. Flynn replaced the blanket over the body, feeling the weight of a realization that a man lay dead on his orders. "First things first," Danny said to his sergeant, who paced anxiously nearby, not sure what he meant by it.

Garza brought the lieutenant his breakfast and a cup of coffee and left to get his own meal. Over a plate of hot beans and canned beef, Danny asked the sergeant for his observations. For several minutes he listened to Wieczorek excitedly retelling his version of chasing the one now lying under the blanket. "We yelled at him to stop—in English and German. Reimers did. Somebody tried a little Mexican. He knew we had him, but he nevuh would surrender. I saw him pull a little pistol out of his pocket, and he started poppin' away at us. That's when I ordered Sevcik and Moore to fire." Wieczorek speculated that the dead one's job was to lead the rest to a designated pickup spot, but when the machine gun tore the place up, he changed his mind, and the mistake cost him his life. "But he ain't all that happened," Weech admitted sheepishly. "We found a car 'bout a mile from here. Jus' like you said, Lootenan.'"

It still amazed the platoon sergeant that Lieutenant Flynn knew about the car. Once it was found, what to do with it became the problem—but only briefly. Without any of the illegals alive on this side of the river, Weech couldn't be certain the car had been left for them. What if it belonged to one of the ranchers? "I drained the gas tank." He grinned, pleased with his own ingenuity. Almost as an afterthought, he reminded Danny of the urgency of sending a radio report back to Fort Brown. He waved one of the radiomen in to take the lieutenant's report. "Heah's Corporal Berry, Lootenan'. He's been lissenin' to that machine all mornin'." Weech exhibited little embarrassment over his nearly complete ignorance of what the radio did. It mystified him that, even if it could transmit messages all over South Texas, the radio couldn't even bring in a little music from Brownsville or somewhere. "They can get these reports all the way up to Fort Bliss," he announced proudly. He strutted away shaking his head in amazement.

After all this activity, shooting a man to death and an unauthorized three-hour military foray into Mexico, Danny felt surprisingly calm. He told the radio operator, "Send this: 'Situation normal. One foreign agent dead.' And sign it, Flynn."

Danny stood squinting at the sun and the shadows cast by the scrubby little trees to find a suitable spot of shade. "Good job here in the camp while I was gone, Sergeant. Everything is going well, so I'm going to take a nap." He watched Berry clicking away with the sending key. "We'll be attracting a lot of interest with that message, I'm thinking. When he gets some messages to read, be wakin' me."

❧

About an hour later Wiecorek shook the lieutenant from his nap, waving a sheaf of messages from the radio operators. "You were right, Lieutenan'. All of a sudden, we got lotsa readin' matter."

Danny stretched and yawned. He took a seat on a sack of oats and pulled an empty ammunition can toward him to use as a table. Then he scanned the handprinted copies in front of him and scribbled in his notebook. The sergeant sat nearby, ready with his pencil. Shuffling the papers into some kind of order, Danny could infer from the messages that Fort Brown must be a bedlam. "You'll see what I mean, Sergeant. Here's the way I read them."

In the terse language of military communicators, the first messages informed them that First Platoon was to stay where they were, expecting representatives from the Border Patrol, the FBI and the county coroner's office. "Give these officials your complete cooperation and await further orders," it read. Another was from division headquarters to the regiment at Fort Brown. Still another relayed a War Department decision bringing the curtain down on the 124th as mounted cavalry. "Effective immediately, cease mounted cavalry operation except for any units still in the field. Orders specifying dismounted training will follow." The words plainly pronounced the War Department's final judgment on the fate of the 124th. Wieczorek's stricken face and slumped shoulders left nothing to hide about the news and how it affected him.

Danny reminded the dejected sergeant that the army thinkers had already changed their minds at least once before. Maybe Colonel Chamberlain could pull another rabbit out of a hat, but it didn't seem likely, he admitted. Flynn leafed through the communicators' handwritten translation of dots and dashes. There were still two more to read. The first was more of the same: When released by the Border Patrol, the platoon would return to Fort Brown. Unsaid was what they all knew: Getting back home would spell the end of their lives as military horsemen. This time no reprieve could be expected.

Reluctantly he began to read the final message, but it turned out to be good news. He motioned to the sergeant. "This is a list of troopers promoted from private to private first class," he said, handing over the list. "OK, Weech. Our privates have been promoted to PFC—every one of them. Get 'em together and put out the word."

Danny had a sudden thought. "Weech. The German. Who has his effects? Whatever he was carrying."

"We put evahthing back in his pockets, Lootenan'," said Weech. It seemed logical at the time that whoever came to get him would want the papers.

"Have Garza uncover him while I get something I found at the house on the other side. He can stay and be a witness while I look him over." Danny returned carrying the passports and drivers' licenses. "Why is he still covered?" he asked Garza, working busily examining Danny's saddle. Garza shrugged and looked away. The dog robber, for all the toughness acquired growing up as a migrant worker's son, refused even to look at the blanket-draped shape on the ground.

Danny drew a deep breath. He'd gone with his parents to plenty of funerals at the parish church, but there the deceased was usually somebody he knew well, laid out peacefully with flowers so the neighbors and relatives could file by to pay their last respects. Everybody knew everybody else, so the atmosphere was one of a family gathering—not at all like this. So this was his first time too, really, to touch a dead man. Hell, he'd already done this earlier with the same man. Swallowing hard, he pulled the blanket back All right. Not so bad. The corpse looked surprisingly calm and peaceful, for being shot and dragged up the sandy riverbank. The face looked clean, so somebody had probably washed him up. Could this be the first German killed by Americans in the newly declared war?

Danny counted four wounds, all in the chest. Sevcik and Moore did that, probably two shots each. The realization that two of his youngest troopers could act so steadily in their first test of fire gave him a stronger determination to complete this examination. He felt the man's shirt pockets, finding nothing, so Weech had put the papers in his back pockets.

He hated to do it, but there was nothing to do but turn him over. Flynn didn't bother to look for Garza and Wieczorek. He took an arm in one hand and a leg in the other and heaved the corpse over on its face, finding it stiff and surprisingly cold to the touch when he searched carefully for identification or any other information. He felt the passport in a rear pocket, stained from the man's bleeding wounds. Kleiber: The name matched the one on the scrap of paper Weech tucked inside. Carefully he copied the passport number into his notebook and compared it with the six still in the box taken from Maureen's hacienda. No surprise that the number was in sequence with those of the passports in the box. For an instant, he felt the burning sensation of acute embarrassment at allowing himself to be used by Maureen. He turned the dead man over onto his back. "Let's cover him up. Take the other side of the blanket," he said to his orderly, but the dog robber was gone. Looking around, he saw Garza bent over, heaving behind a half-buried river snag.

Danny walked through the little camp rehearsing the story he would tell the investigators when they arrived. Waiting in camp for the Border Patrol gave First Platoon a welcome rest from the strenuous schedule of patrolling and ford surveillance ordered by Major Perkins in his orders. Most of the troopers busied themselves doing the little things that would keep life "on the road" a little more comfortable. Some had gone out, optimistically collecting wood for a cooking fire, expecting Garza to bring in a steer, or at least a goat to be barbecued. Several others had begun stacking the field rations, setting the generally hard, dry, tasteless stuff aside, to be eaten only in case of emergency. Out on the picket line, Corporal Wilson supervised the men caring for the horses.

Flynn took off his hat and ran his fingers through his coppery hair, scanning the camp. "They're good soldiers," he said aloud. For a fact, they had come a long way since his first encounter with them when the train to Fort Brown lay trapped by the flood. Now that the promotion list had arrived, not one of his troopers was without at least a PFC's single stripe to sew on his sleeve. They were good men, quiet and unassuming, with a work-manlike approach to soldiering, but there was much more to it than being thorough and methodical. Ever since the exercise up north, where they set the pace for the entire regiment, First Platoon troopers swaggered, with no more justification than simply being First Platoon, and everybody knew who they were. At the slightest opportunity, Weech had them standing in their stirrups at a gallop. It was much the same out here in the dry brush. When they pissed, they made a contest of seeing who could piss higher, or farther. When they bitched, they complained loudly and creatively so everybody could hear it. Damn, he loved leading a cavalry platoon!

The Czechs, the Fayette County boys, were cooking sausages—as they always did when the platoon was away from the post. How they came to have those dark, peppery *klobase* after several days away from Fort Brown remained a logistical mystery. Like the Polish and the German speakers, they still felt most comfortable laughing and joking among themselves in their first languages, but today Private First Class Jerry Bohuslav, sitting with his back against a scrawny tree trunk sewing a button on his shirt, turned talkative. Perhaps it was the promotion. Only when showing the trooper his name on the promotion list did the lieutenant learn that his name was really Jaroslav. "Can your name really be Jaroslav V. Bohuslav? What's the V for?" asked the lieutenant.

He sounded it out for Flynn. "Vahtslaf, sir."

"How do you spell it?"

The young man whose curly mane was nearly as vivid as Danny's, smiled shyly and spelled the name slowly. *Vaclav.*

Flynn seemed puzzled. "But it spells, 'vaklav,' doesn't it? Isn't that right?"

The new PFC shrugged. "It's kinda like Sevcik. We pronounce his name 'Shevchik,' not 'Sevsik.' It's not easy to speak Czech, sir. But I think it's easier than trying to figger out what the Army is doing to us. Jesus Christ, Lieutenant. First we were cavalry, like we signed up to be, then we was'nt no more than a bunch of dogfaces leading mules, setting up mortars and machine guns. Now we cavalry again—but only 'til we get to Fort Brown." Bohuslav fixed his gaze on something in a scraggly willow tree. "An' we don't really know when we'll get there, do we, sir?"

This time Danny took more care with the trooper's name. "Bohuslav, ah, Private First Class Bohuslav, why are you pestering me with all these questions? Hasn't the sergeant been telling you why we're being moved north? Pointing to the form under the blanket, Flynn said. "There are more in Mexico like that one." The new PFC forced himself to stare at the shape under the blanket and held the needle still for a moment. Danny laid his hand on the PFC's shoulder briefly to steady him. "I don't like it either, but let's make the best of our last days of being horsemen." Hard to be eloquent at a time like this, he thought.

The two-vehicle official convoy didn't find First Platoon for a full four hours. The county coroner led the way in his black van because he knew the country better. The FBI agent and the Border Patrol agent rode together in a Dodge sedan, also black. From their surprised expressions, they must have been expecting the First Platoon camp to be something far grander than a pile of crates and sacks, plus a few tents scattered under scrubby trees and blankets spread out to air on tree limbs and the remains of a long-abandoned barbed wire fence.

Without wasting much time on amenities, the man in the Border Patrol uniform, Officer Puckett, came directly to the point. "We think the Germans and their helpers over there are moving north." He pointed across the river. "That your German?" he asked about the body shape lying in full view.

The coroner went to work without hesitation, kneeling to examine the man now dead for nearly twelve hours, carefully noting the location of his wounds on a printed form.

Puckett and FBI agent Kelvin questioned Danny and Weech for the better part of an hour. For one thing, they wanted to know why Danny ordered his troopers to shoot the man without knowing exactly who he was. And why did Danny go directly toward Navidad, and what was the result of his pursuit?

Before Danny answered, the dapper FBI agent in a business suit, a snap-brim straw hat, and dusty, but well-shined shoes, did a little speculating. "This couldn't all have been intuition, now could it?" Both the Border Patrol and FBI scribbled furiously while Danny gave them an abbreviated version of the report he made to the S-2 at Fort Brown, including a highly edited description of his visits to Maureen. "It's all a matter of record," he assured them.

They bought Weech's logic in identifying the man as a German. The FBI agent wrote out a receipt for the passport and the keys to the car and sent the coroner away with the body strapped on a stretcher in the rear of his black vehicle.

Officer Puckett, a longtime resident of South Texas who had taken a listener's role in the questioning, expertly rolled a cigarette and lighted it, keeping his gimlet stare on Danny. "It might interest you to know, young fella, that we bin onta that gal fuh a good while," he said.

Danny nodded, acknowledging that what the man said might be so.

"You didn't ride up to her house to tip her off, did you?" asked Kelvin, still sniffing for something.

Danny bristled at the insinuation. The Border Patrol, or the FBI for that matter, didn't know as much as they thought. These men were tipping their hand. "The woman I told you about—the one in the ford with the little boy—that was Miss Gallamore," he said firmly to Officer Puckett. "By recognizing her, I knew for certain what was happening, and

I knew I was the only one with a Chinaman's chance of capturing them, because I had a rock solid reason to cross the river." On an impulse, he omitted mentioning the passports he found in Maureen's house.

Agent Kelvin dropped his cigarette and ground it into the dirt with his toe. He nodded to the direct, guileless Puckett, who fumbled for an envelope he had left in the pocket of a jacket laid over a seat in the black sedan.

It was for Lieutenant Flynn. "This here's a paper that put's down what I'm about to tell you," he said as a preamble to a speech he'd been rehearsing since early in the morning. In his way of thinking, the Mexican woman's operation had been completely disabled, and she was most likely planning to hide somewhere south in Mexico. He dismissed her as a factor. "We prob'ly ain't gonna see her again."

Puckett agreed that the Border Patrol was anticipating a quick push by the Germans to get twenty or more agents into Texas, fording the river between Rio Grande City and Piedras Negras before the border was sealed by U.S. Government actions. "We asked the Ahmy to get theah best people into the Rio Grande bottoms for the next few days, and heah you are." A momentary smile crinkled the crows' feet at the corners of his eyes. "I b'lieve you the only people who acksh'ly got a real spy."

Danny anticipated what was coming next. "The papers in this envelope order you to temporary duty with the 156th—up at Fort Clark." Puckett knew what he was doing in dealing with army bureaucracy. He'd gone directly to General Burton to approve the assignment. "Listen to your radio for verification," he said to Danny.

The two lawmen shook hands with Danny and Sergeant Wieczorek. On the way to the car, Puckett remembered a crucial bit of information. "What them papers in the envelope don't say is that the ahmy trucks'll be heah at first light. I expect 'em t'have y'all back in the valley up no'th sometime this evenin'." With no further information to offer, he and Kelvin drove away.

chapter

TWENTY

San Francisco: *Sixteen U.S. B-25 bombers take off from USS Hornet to strike at Japan.*

Just to hear it, the plan made such good sense. What could go wrong with First Platoon getting a lift in portees and trucks dispatched from Fort Ringgold to a clearly designated drop-off farther to the north, in the area usually patrolled by troopers from Fort Clark? Fort Ringgold was the nearest army post to both the pickup and the drop-off. The trucks would drop them off with supplies for the troopers and their horses, and First Platoon could rest while awaiting further orders. So much time would be lost if it were done any other way.

"The drivers know where to drop you; the portee driver was up there a few days ago," Captain Burr assured them. The captain was a staff officer who had come out with the small convoy of vehicles dispatched from the brigade headquarters at Fort Ringgold. He was a Quartermaster Corps officer, far more interested in Danny's signature for the supplies and the trucks than he was in any questions the lieutenant might have about the orders being issued to First Platoon. "You'll have to trust the drivers and the maps in the packet I gave you," he said.

Before he dared order First Platoon to load the portees, Danny examined the maps in the packet handed over to him to be sure he understood the location of their new camp. It was with the maps that he found his first premonition of something being not quite right. His major concern was that the maps didn't cover the new area in the detail he needed for this kind of work. Without good maps that depicted the terrain in great detail, he couldn't be clear on exactly what his platoon was to do after they were dropped off. A telephone call to Fort Ringgold placed from the rectory of a country church didn't help either. Even if they had better maps, it would take half a day to get them to him. "Why don't you try Fort Clark?" he was told. Danny adamantly insisted that the maps given to him were inadequate, but the captain who answered the telephone didn't appreciate this unknown lieutenant's fears. All he could offer was, "Lieutenant Brooks, with a platoon of the 156th, will meet you there with what you need." He tried to sound reassuring, but the man made it clear that a single platoon from Fort Brown under orders specially issued by division headquarters far to the north in El Paso wasn't something he wanted to meddle with. It was their problem. His far-too-hearty, "Good luck," didn't help much either.

As far as the distracted quartermaster captain was concerned, he'd done all he could for this nervous Nellie lieutenant. He spoke to Danny as he would to a slow-learning school-boy. "Set up your camp as near the drop-off point as is convenient, Lieutenant Flynn, and wait for the rendezvous. I'm not going to waste any more time debating with you." Checking the time, the captain signaled the drivers to start their engines and climbed aboard the lead vehicle. Once the sound of the departing truck engines faded in the distance, only the shouts of the troopers sorting out the supplies left by the drivers broke the silence.

For a quarter of an hour, Danny walked the ground, inspecting the terrain, the trees, the angle of the afternoon sun, even the direction the birds were flying, but he couldn't make it fit with what he saw on the maps. He asked the sergeant to try his luck at verifying their position. The written orders didn't mean much to Wieczorek. He wasn't an avid reader, and only fair with maps, but the man had an uncanny nose for impending trouble. From the way the sergeant moved his feet nervously and shrugged, Danny could see he wasn't satisfied. "It's wrong, isn't it, Sergeant? Do you feel it?"

Wieczorek scratched his white forehead, looking over the place the drivers had dropped them off. Just before the vehicles departed for Fort Ringgold, one of the drivers, a young private, offered his opinion. He didn't think they had left the paved road at the right place—but the lead driver pulled rank on him. The sergeant squinted, giving the place a once-over before offering his opinion. "Yes, suh. Sure do. Onliest thing good about it is that broke-down wind-mill ovah theah. Least we c'n git some water, prob'ly. What do y'wanta do, sir?" At least they had water for the horses, and it looked as if somebody had been burning platoon-sized cook fires. But, no, it wasn't the right place. It was still early—a little after noon. No need to panic.

Flynn chose the obvious action. "Take care of ourselves first. Set up the camp and get the radio operating. Stay on those operators. Make sure they keep a record of all incoming traffic, but make damn sure they don't send anything until I say so."

Danny took some satisfaction watching his troopers quickly transforming a pile of gear and crated supplies into an efficient camp: not very comfortable, but workable. The main thing was that they were working, trusting their lieutenant to solve this unsettling uncertainty. Silently, he prayed for an inspiration to leap out at him, clear and bold, from the vague written orders the Border Patrol had given him. Wilson could be heard moving among the men, getting the camp organized.

Weech called four troopers to saddle up and wait for the lieutenant's instructions. Flynn gave them the simplest orders he could contrive for this essential task. The first received very simple instructions: "Go west until you reach the Rio Grande. I want to know exactly how far we are from it. Take note of whether it runs straight or if there's a bend, and how wide it is. I want details like that to compare with my map. Remember, keep going west."

Weech added a little practical advice. "Keep the sun in front of you. Like this," he said, facing the general direction and pointing out the track the sun would make through the afternoon.

Instructions to the remaining three were even simpler: to go out north, east, and south, on tracks as nearly straight as possible. "Go out until you find something like a creek, or a road, or a village." If they found anything prominent enough to appear on a map, they were to return immediately. In the unlikely event they found nothing significant after an hour, they were to return. "It shouldn't be so hard to find our exact position," Danny said to Wieczorek with more optimism than he felt. Sipping cautiously at fresh cups of hot coffee, the lieutenant stood with the sergeant near the radio operators, going over the possibilities for locating Lieutenant Brooks and his platoon.

The scout sent to the west returned first. Flynn fired questions while he wolfed down beans, hard bread and coffee. Wieczorek squatted on his haunches, chewing on the end of a Johnson grass stem, listening. Finding the river hadn't presented any difficulty, but it turned out to be more like two miles, rather than the half mile the driver had estimated it would be. And the river ran generally straight instead of making a sharp bend as it should have if the position were right. He did find what looked like a fordable place, where the river appeared a little narrower than it was down south. But the scout hadn't seen any tracks or any other sign of recent use. The report wasn't definitive, but at least it was a little something to go on.

As further observations came in, Danny learned that no ranch buildings of any kind were located in about a five-mile radius, although all the scouts had been spotting a few head of cattle and tracks. The cattle sightings probably meant many more somewhere in the thickets. By all rights there should have been some buildings.

Also, First Platoon's scouting showed the nearest paved road to be more than five miles away. Danny looked to Garza, sitting on a crate of rations, asking if some of his populous kin might not live nearby, but this time the dog robber wasn't sure he could help. "Sorry, *Teniente*. My people live a good piece south of here," said Garza, standing hurriedly, volunteering to do a little scouting. "I'll saddle up to look for some little settlements, if you want."

"Not yet," said Flynn

He regretted the decision within minutes. The day would be lost entirely if they didn't find some likely fords to observe during the night. Danny took out his notebook to draft a long overdue report. For a good half hour, he scribbled at a first attempt that turned out to be a rambling criticism of the events that got First Platoon stuck out in this situation. It wouldn't do. The platoon from Fort Clark would be arriving soon anyway. Then his troubles would be over.

The required report had to be something terse and to the point. "First Platoon, E Troop in position. Commencing operations. Awaiting arrival Lt. Brooks." Satisfied, he left the scrap of paper for Corporal Berry to transmit and went searching for Wieczorek. The sergeant had been inspecting the shoes of the horses on the picket line. The rocky soil around here could raise hell with horseshoes.

"Now then, Sergeant," the lieutenant said, "let's get some people moving upstream to look for any sign of the people from the 156th or anything at all interesting." He sought the sergeant's concurrence. "Wouldn't you say ten miles ought to do it?

"Yessuh," said Wieczorek, removing his hat to scratch his forehead. "I cain't figger a better plan."

If patrolling out to ten miles didn't produce some helpful information, all they could do was to keep trying to get some help from somewhere. At Fort Brown, the 124th was busy complying with the order to cease mounted operation. The staffers at Fort Ringgold washed their hands of the 124th as an operational command and showed no interest in one platoon. A plea for help from Fort Clark didn't help either. The 156th seemed to have lost them in the confusion of having to expand their coverage of the border. Disappointment approached frustration as the day wore on: A desultory string of messages described the confused situation:

"State position."

"Unknown. Required maps not delivered by Lt. Brooks."

"Lt. Brooks unkn at Ft. Brn."

From Fort Clark they received, "First Platoon not located. State position."

Danny, thoroughly disgusted with the blundering that left First Platoon wandering forgotten in the valley, ordered Garza to mount up to see what he could find. To kill the time it would take to get responses from another round of radio transmissiions, he left Weech in charge and rode to the river alone to survey the ford. After about a half hour of surveying the river bottom and testing the depth of the water, he concluded this was an unappealing place to cross at night. A little too deep for a man on foot, it seemed to him, but nothing would keep the damn spies from using horses.

Garza was back by late afternoon with a scrawny little goat trussed up and slung behind his saddle. He dismounted and pulled the bleating animal off the horse's back. Two troopers from Lee County, both of them Polish men, carried the goat away to have Bednarski butcher it.

On his reconnoitering ride, Private First Class Garza had slipped easily into the role of Panchito when he chanced upon two vaqueros tending a fire. The men had seen these oversized army horses before, but they'd never had an opportunity to examine one closely—or to sit on one of those useless army saddles. A man couldn't do much cattle work with equipment like the army saddle on his horse, they said. What good was a saddle without a horn if a man roped a good-sized steer? "You got to take a turn around the horn with your *riata* to keep the steer from pulling you off the horse," one of them said, demonstrating the lightning-fast move needed to get the rope around the saddle horn. From the vaqueros, Garza learned that the property for miles around was the Sholtz Ranch, but the hard-working hands were more familiar with the villages across the river than they were with the gringo towns to the north. They described landmarks and explained how to find the places where they crossed the river to visit their relatives in the tiny villages of Aquila and San Isidro: two spots, both a little deep, but the bottom was firm, they said, and nobody cared much who crossed. With his polite thanks for the goat, Garza warned them to be careful using the fords for the next day or so.

"*Teniente,* here's what I can tell you about the land up north a little way," Garza said on his return. But the map didn't show either Aquila or San Isidro on the river anyplace near Danny's best estimate of their position.

By evening water call, the mysterious platoon from Fort Clark had yet to make any contact with First Platoon. Danny checked with the troopers operating the radio. Nothing was heard of them on the net they were monitoring either. Flynn's best guess was that the platoon from the 156th was most likely monitoring a different frequency than the one First Platoon was using. Without being able to communicate directly, the two platoons were groping for each other like blind men. He scribbled on a page and gave it to the troopers at the radio for transmission, "Two possible fords found on Sholtz ranch, roughly opposite Mexican villages of Aquila and San Isidro. Will est. obs. post opposite San Isidro." He and

Wieczorek concurred that the S-2's people would have to be deliberately ignoring them if they couldn't find them with that much information.

Fort Clark still wasn't making the connection. "State position," was the unvarying response. "Saints preserve us," yelled Danny in exasperation, "if the S-2 people can't find Aquila and San Isidro on their maps, what am I to do with the useless scrap of paper they gave me?" He sat on the ground near the radio operators, watching them decode the incoming traffic.

An hour later, Wieczorek returned from setting up positions on the bank overlooking one of the new fords—the southern ford, almost the same way as when they caught the Germans earlier. As they'd discussed earlier, Wieczorek concealed the machine gun and two riflemen with commanding views of the fords. "Everything go well, Weech?" asked Danny.

"Yessuh," he said, but his face showed signs of doubt. "Yuh know, Lootenan'. It's a purty long way up to them fords f'm heah. We could cover both fords better if we was up North a little ways. Think we oughta move the camp?"

The lieutenant gave the suggestion some thought, but moving wouldn't simplify the problem finding the other platoon in the slightest. Besides, without a truck moving crates of food and ammunition would be a tedious effort. No point in going through all the labor of shifting the camp from one uncertain location to another. And how would the platoon from the 156th find them then? "Let me think this through a little more, Sergeant."

They could coax enough water from the well for the horses now that the decrepit windmill had been repaired. Without the rancher's hardware, they might have to camp right on the river to find water. Tomorrow maybe, if they could locate a wagon or something. Water was always a consideration.

For the sergeant's benefit, he made a show of being satisfied with their progress, putting his heels up on a sack of oats. "Smell the goat roasting?" he said to Wieczorek. "In another hour or two, we'll have a fine meal. We've done pretty damn well for a lost platoon, don't you think?"

Wieczorek made a meaningless grunting noise. It was a little better than five miles to the San Isidro ford—a long way to go changing the teams of men observing it. And what if they needed help? A nearly full moon up since midafternoon would set early. It meant a good dark night for anybody wanting to cross the river unseen. "We gonna have hell figgerin' out who's trying to cross," he muttered, ambling over to where his troopers sat grumbling, smoking and drinking coffee to kill time. Nothing he heard from them could be called optimistic. Morale is a fragile thing, even with seasoned troopers. If the lieutenant and the sergeant are fidgety about something, it affects everybody.

After a meal of hastily roasted goat and beans, Danny slept.

"Better wake up, Lootenan'." It was Weech shaking him. Danny sat up, dazed, staring into the dark, only half rested.

"Christ. What time is it?"

"'Bout two thutty, suh. Bohuslav jus' rode in from the ford we watchin'—'crost from San Isidro." Wieczorek pounded a fist into the palm of his open hand. "I thought I heard firin' a little bit ago. Damn. I shoulda mounted up and gone myself."

The diminutive Bohuslav, wide-eyed with excitement and sweating profusely, had ridden as fast as he could in the darkness. "Corporal Wilson sent me back here to report, but I don't know exactly what happened," he said, trying to catch his breath. His mouth was so dry, he could hardly talk. He gulped frantically at a canteen somebody handed him, until he could talk more easily. "There was some shootin' from 'cross th' river. We shot back, 'n then we seen somebody movin' down low, next to the water—on our side. I wuz about to shoot again, when them bufflo sojers popped up outa the brush." His eyes rolled up momemtarily; he'd been so close to opening fire at the source of the sounds. "I knew we was going to work with bufflo sojers, but I didn't know what they was, really. They're nothin' but plain old..." Weech bellowed, "Calm down! What happened?"

The sweating trooper unscrewed the top of another canteen somebody handed him and guzzled more water. "Oh, shit! Excuse me, sir. We was set up in the brush just like the other night. We seen somebody workin' his way down the bank on the Mexican side—it was hard as hell to see without any moonlight. Then all of a sudden, there was a shot." In his excitement, Bohuslav's sentences simply tangled around his tongue.

"Calm down, Jerry," urged Weech.

"Right, Sargint." Bohuslav closed his eyes and drew two or three deep breaths to get control. "Then, for a minute, there was shootin' all around."

This didn't sound right. Lieutenant Flynn asked, "All around? What exactly do you mean, Bohuslav?"

"There was shots from the other side'f the rivuh, 'n we fired back, sir. I dunno how many rounds. I fired at some of the flashes on the Mexican side. I think I mighta hit somebody. I seen a lot of muzzle flashes down below us, too. Close. Awful close. And then the bufflo sojers jumped up out of the brush down there, screamin' and yellin'. Some was shootin' in the air."

Danny smacked his hand on a wooden bench that was part of the rancher's handling pens. "Slow down, Trooper. Tell me where the buffalo soldiers were."

"Below us. Right down at the water. In the brush."

"You never knew they were there until then?"

"No sir."

"Oh, Jesus! Anybody hurt?"

"I don't know, sir. Lotsa people was yellin'. Our guys 'n the bufflo sojers, both. Could be some fightin' goin' on by now—between us 'n them—fist fightin', or knives, I mean. Corporal Wilson sent me back to get you."

Roused by the commotion, the entire camp came alive with men talking excitedly, repeating scraps of information, collecting gear and saddling horses. The lieutenant yelled for his dog robber. "Garza, I need my mount, on the double. Field gear too."

Danny shouted over his shoulder, "Sergeant Wieczorek, make damn sure the radio team copies every squawk that comes in while we're gone. I'll send Wilson back here to run the camp. You come down to the river as soon as he gets here."

At the ford, he found two small groups of troopers angrily facing off in threatening semi-circles, exchanging distrustful glares and screaming accusations of stupidity and incompetence. They hadn't moved much from where they had been when the first illegal showed himself. The buffalo soldiers of the 156th stood with their backs to the river—the white boys from the 124th collected a little farther up the bank. So far no further shots had been fired. Apparently, the two groups had at least convinced themselves they were all in the U.S. Army. Maybe they'd been talking through how it all happened. He couldn't tell. At the moment at least, the bare-knuckle brawling Bohuslav reported had stopped. Flynn used his flashlight to get a better look. A few might need some cleaning up—and a stitch or two. Danny assumed the buffalo soldiers of the 156th—that's who these men had to be—had sent a mounted messenger to find their officer. Wherever he might be, there was no white officer in sight.

"Who's in charge here?" he demanded of the black troopers.

A slight, bow-legged banty rooster of a man with sergeant's chevrons stepped forward, clenching his fists angrily, outrage and aggressiveness showing plain on his face. "I am, sir," he said, gritting his teeth with obvious revulsion at the turn of events. Lurching toward the newly-arrived lieutenant, he growled through his clenched teeth, "I'm Jeremiah Fox, platoon sargint."

Now that this white lieutenant showed up, the situation was different. Fox dropped all pretense of controlling his rage, pointing at the men of First Platoon, screaming, "These stupid bastahds up here on the bank damn near killed us." According to Sergeant Fox, these Texans had carelessly placed his people in peril, nearly killing him, in fact, by shooting in panic. "You in command of these sorry-assed excuses f' sojers?" What kind of soldiers would get themselves lost on a damn riverbank? The whole screwed-up affair appalled the sergeant and offended his professional sensibility. He kept up his screaming at the lieutenant from Fort Brown. "Sheeit, you the stupid, dumb-assed people I been looking foah' since Lieutenant Brooks broke his shoulder and had to go back to Fort Clark."

By the time Danny heard the last of Fox's agitated string of grievances, he realized that the key to the lethal confrontation lay in the feisty sergeant's screaming. The more he heard from Fox, the clearer it became. So close to a bloodbath, and if Bohuslav was right, there might be a man dead on the ground in Mexico, and if that were the case, it could be anybody. Might be a German spy, but the way things were going, it could be a Mexican civilian. As far as he knew, any thought of having him identified by the confused groups screaming at each other had been lost in the scuffling and screaming.

It terrified him to think it could have been Maureen and the little boy! To collect his thoughts, Danny sat on a large piece of driftwood deposited by the river in some long-forgotten flood, but this last possibility simply wouldn't go away.

What if all the shooting had been heard on the surrounding farms, or even in San Isidro? Would the Mexican police be on the way? Maybe, but the prospect of Mexican authorities arriving was practically nothing compared to the potential for another fight starting between First Platoon and the buffalo soldiers. If he didn't get this mess cleared up pretty damn quick, it could become a disaster.

Flynn breathed deeply to calm himself before turning to the pugnacious Fox. "These are my men, Sergeant, and they want to know what you're doing in territory assigned to us." Still tensed and full of fight, Fox puzzled over his options until he heard the lieutenant asking him, "Aren't you forgetting your manners, Sergeant Fox?"

Surprised to hear talk of manners, Fox stared blankly.

"If you're in the same army I am, I'm due a salute," Danny reminded the sergeant.

Slowly, grudgingly, Fox saluted, and his troopers relaxed visibly. Reverting to army custom had the desired calming effect. Flynn inquired if any of Fox's people were injured.

Fox shook his head. "No, suh," he said quietly. They weren't, at least not badly.

Danny called Corporal Wilson to join him and Sergeant Fox. "You two were in charge here during the shooting. We have two problems. First, it's possible our platoons shot at each other. Then again, maybe not. But nobody is wounded, so we'll work it out later. There may be a dead man on the bank across the river. What can you tell me about those people on the other bank?"

Wilson spoke first. "I think I saw one go down in the bushes on the other side when my guys started returning fire, sir. But'cha cain't see into that brush when ya don't even have the moon."

Fox thought so too. "I think all my troopers fired up there, sir," the sergeant said, pointing at the taller growth on the higher part of the riverbank." Danny thought carefully. To go across now would be a second foray into Mexico in three days, but if they didn't go, things could be worse. "Sergeant Fox, I want you to mount up with six men, three of yours and three of mine, and get across the river to see what's there. Bring back whoever you find:

live, dead or wounded. Sing out if you run into trouble, and we'll be right there. When you get back, you and I will make out a report."

While Fox and his six men searched the opposite bank, Danny sat with his notebook open, thinking about what to send in his report. Maybe it should say something like, "Contacted Sgt. J. Fox. 156th Cav., at a point opposite San Isidro, Mex. Combined platoons opposed illegal agents attempting to enter U.S." Satisfied, he penciled it into his notebook, tore out the sheet and gave it to the men at the radio.

"Lieutenant," Fox called out from across the river, "we got one dead and one wounded. The wounded man's nearly dead."

In Flynn's mind there was no time for hesitation. Daylight might bring heavy foot traffic from the Mexican towns to see what all the shooting was about. "Bring 'em over," he called out. "Hurry." In the flickering light of a newly built fire, he watched the troopers preparing to cross, picking their way down to the water single file. Sergeant Fox, swiveling his head toward every new sound, led his mount to the water's edge with two inert forms draped like sacks over the horse's back. Both could be dead by now, for all he knew. He waited for all six of his troopers to cross before he waded into the water. To Flynn standing on the riverbank, the men slung across the horses looked small and dark-haired. Mexicans, probably, he thought. Could be bad.

Fox gave orders to unload the two injured men and lay them out on the clean sand beneath the overhanging limbs of gnarled oak heavily festooned with Spanish moss. He beckoned to one of his troopers, explaining to the lieutenant, "Corporal Hicks here was a hospital orderly once. He's the best we got...unless you got a medic with real training."

"No. Let Hicks have a look at them."

Holding a flashlight, Flynn bent over the corporal's shoulder, watching his hands tearing away the shirt of the man whose sucking chest wound bled profusely with every breath. The man's eyes stared blankly—it could have been a look of terror, but Danny couldn't tell what it might mean. It didn't look good for the man. In the poor light, he could see both were Caucasians who must have used some kind of dye on their hair to look like Mexicans making convenient river crossings. It looked like a surge of agents trying to force their way into Texas.

Hicks, with an ear to the chest of the one clinging to life, said, "This one's still got a weak heartbeat, but the other one is already getting cold." Sergeant Fox produced a small medical kit. Hicks rummaged through its contents. Ripping open a sealed package, he applied bandages to the pulsing wound, shaking his head at the futility of it. "He's been bleedin' bad. Nothin' I can do for him."

Danny made a snap decision. "All right, then. We're getting away from this ford. Heave 'em both on horses and get them to First Platoon's camp. Sergeant Fox, your troopers can return to your camp, but you come with me."

The earlier peacemaking completely forgotten, the pugnacious little sergeant planted himself in front of the lieutenant, legs spread wide. "No! I ain't goin', Lootenant," he pronounced, pointing a long finger at Flynn's chest. "An' them are my prisoners—them Germans. This is my territory."

"In a pig's ass, Fox. Cut out all the play-actin' crap, and set an example for your troopers," bellowed Wieczorek, joining the confrontation. "You don't get your platoon loaded and mounted up, I'll drag your scrawny butt up to our camp and write you up for insubordination."

Fox made a long, low, hissing sound, but he and his troopers followed Weech's interpretation of Lieutenant Flynn's orders.

A few quiet words were enough to get the dead and wounded collected and set the two mounted columns in motion. Wieczorek waved for Reimers to come to him. "Stay with this wounded guy for a while, 'n lissen' to him in case he says somethin'."

Lieutenant Flynn nodded his approval. "Yes, and Sergeant Wieczorek, send a trooper ahead to tell Corporal Wilson we're on our way with company for breakfast." Danny, with Sergeant Fox following closely behind, rode directly to the radio tent waving a page from his notebook. "Send this now: 'Contacted 156th. Two men fired upon in illegal crossing; one dead, one critically wounded.'"

The lieutenant's stark message reporting more dead and wounded in the Rio Grande Valley stripped away the languor and confusion clogging communications for the past fifteen hours. A series of coded messages flew back and forth, requiring a flurry of laborious work with codebooks. A final, bureaucratic radio message put it all together. "Remain in position for arrival of Border Patrol. Sgt. Fox and Third Platoon, B Troop, 156th Cav. report to Lt. Flynn, First Platoon, E Troop, 124th Cav. When released by Border Patrol, report to Commanding Officer 156th Cavalry at Fort Clark earliest. Transportation not available."

Lieutenant Flynn spread the handwritten copies of radio messages on an empty field rations crate to lay out the situation to the two platoon sergeants. "Well, Sergeant Fox. Here's the message that tells us plain and simple what to do. Like it or not, you work for me, and they want us to stay here until the Border Patrol comes to collect these men. Then we go cross country to Fort Clark on horseback because they won't send the trucks to get us."

Four hours had passed since Bohuslav arrived in the camp with his report of gunshots along the river and the general confusion that followed, but to the lieutenant, it seemed like days. Suddenly remembering the two men lying on the sand, Flynn turned to Wieczorek. "What about those two? Any papers?"

"They both dead now, suh," said Weech, fumbling in his shirt pocket. "An' we got papers too. Same kind as the othuh one that said he wuz from New Braunfels: American passports, sure as hell. This'n said someplace in Louisiana, I think." He handed it to Flynn.

Shuffling through the passports to check the numbers against the list he carried, Danny called to Wieczorek, "What about the one who died on this side? Did he say anything to Reimers?"

The sergeant beckoned. "Did he say anything, Gerhard?"

"Oh, yeah, Sarge, but it was kinda crazy talk in German. I heard him say somethin' like, '*Ich sollte dich umbringen, du gruene augige Hexe,*'" said the young blond trooper unscrewing the cap of his canteen. "It's German, sir."

The lieutenant looked up from his notebook. "What's it mean, Reimers?" he asked. "I don't speak German."

Reimers replied, "Don't mean nothing, I don't think, sir. Just some wierd stuff about how he shoulda killed some green-eyed witch."

"Well, ain't no way to know now," said Weech. "What'sa mattah, Lootenan'? You OK?" he asked.

Danny remained seated, staring at the sand between his feet, thinking

⚜

Flynn halted his platoon on the stone bridge spanning the clear, spring-fed stream separating Fort Clark from the town of Brackettville, where a few lights shone in windows. From that point, the chalky, crushed limestone road began its climb to the gate. The men of First Platoon were filthy, sweaty and exhausted from many days of independent operating: unshaven and gaunt from hard riding and living on field rations and the occasional calf or goat Garza could acquire through guile and charm. Up there, perched atop a limestone hill, no more than a quarter mile away, lay the honey-colored stone buildings illuminated by the setting sun. Lieutenant Flynn collected his men for a quiet moment. Up ahead they could see Sergeant Fox's smartly formed platoon passing through the gate at a trot.

Nobody talked about it much, once they began their final cross-country journey from the border, but entering the gate up there meant many things. For one, it meant good food, hot water, rest and maybe a pass to Piedras Negras. For another, it might mean official recognition for what they had accomplished on their own for ten days. Most significant to them, the reality rising like a bitter lump in the throat, was that their lives as mounted troopers would end when they dismounted at Fort Clark. After that they'd become common dogface infantry like the rest of the 124th at Fort Brown.

Danny closed his eyes briefly, fighting back tears, reminding them of their accomplishments. "Troopers," he said, "They're going to be telling stories about First Platoon for a long time. You've drawn first blood in our homeland against a declared enemy nation—three men! As far as we know, the rest of the army and the Border Patrol put together don't have a single one!" He wiped his eyes on the sleeve of his filthy shirt. "One last time, Weech. Let's show Fort Clark who we are," he said.

Sergeant Wieczorek appealed to his men in his own unique style. "This ain't some common ordinary pissant platoon." Every single trooper and their lieutenant agreed with him. "There ain't gonna be any slouching when First Platoon rides through them gates. Understand?" Of course his troopers understood the sergeant's meaning. For the last quarter mile up the steep grade, they put aside the weariness and soreness of days in the saddle and sat erect as if passing in review, through the gate, and across the parade ground, coming to a halt facing the headquarters building.

"Take charge, Sergeant," said Lieutenant Flynn, "As soon as the horses are taken care of, get the troopers into the barracks. I'll see about getting you passes to go to Piedras Negras for a little fun. You deserve it." Returning Wiezcorek's salute, Flynn dismounted and ran up the steps to report as directed, not sure whether he was to be congratulated or to have his ass chewed, or what—especially when he stepped inside.

He hadn't been under a roof of any kind for about ten days—eight, if the raid on Maureen's hacienda counted as being under shelter. Here, in these highly polished hallways, everything seemed so clean. A starched and polished collection of self-absorbed officers and clerks scuttled about in the lighted offices, too engrossed in the papers on their desks to notice the arrival of the sunburned, unshaven lieutenant, stinking to high heaven of sweat, unwashed uniforms and horses.

A captain looked up impatiently once it became apparent this apparition didn't intend to go away. It could have been the odor. "Who the hell are you, Lieutenant?" he asked.

Danny saluted. "Second Lieutenant Daniel Flynn, reporting as ordered, sir." Apparently the name meant nothing to the captain, so he added, "124th Cavalry."

"Tell me again why you're here?" asked the captain, his nose wrinkling in disapproval. "We've got a crisis going on here, Lieutenant. Germans are trying to get across the border."

Danny stood erect and proud, wearing his crusty khaki uniform like a badge of honor. "I was ordered to report here with my platoon after we turned the Germans we shot over to the Border Patrol, sir."

The captain snapped a series of questions: "Orders? What orders? What Germans?"

Danny pulled a rumpled stack of tattered, limp sheet of paper from a leather case—the radio operator's transcription of the coded dots and dashes, printed hazily in pencil—and gave the captain the best answers he could. "The Border Patrol is examining the dead Germans at the hospital, sir. And I'm here to report to the commanding officer of the 156th Cavalry Regiment."

The captain looked at the ragged paper intently, trying to put this flood of scattered facts together. Danny waved a wad of rumpled, much-thumbed copies of radio messages written out in pencil. "The order you need to help you figure this problem out is the top one in this stack of subsequent directions we copied." He dropped the grimy bundle of transcribed, coded radio traffic onto the captain's clean desk blotter.

The captain snapped his head up from the piles of rumpled paper, finally realizing that this was the lieutenant with the German killers. "Flynn!" he said, standing up to shake the lieutenant's hand. "We didn't expect you until tomorrow morning. This is good news! Come with me," he said finally, rubbing his hands together. He led Danny up a flight of stairs and left him waiting in the hallway outside an office door lettered "Commanding Officer." "This shouldn't take more than a minute," he said apologetically.

Danny paced slowly on the polished tile floor, looking through the open doors, gawking at the black Headquarters Troop clerks toiling away on typewriters, passing the papers to two white officers, a colonel and a major.

Breaking away from a conversation with a major, the commanding officer looked up over the eyeglasses balanced on the bridge of his nose, taking in the sight before him. "So you're Flynn of First Platoon? The radio messages you generate make you out to be larger than life." Removing his glasses to get a better look at the field-weary Flynn, he said, "And now that you're here in the flesh, I'm not disappointed." The colonel extended a welcoming hand. "I'm Archie Dowling," he said. "Let's go into my office."

Danny drew the conclusion that he might be safe, for a while at least. A colonel introducing himself by name can be taken as a positive sign.

"Good job out there, Lieutenant: over a week in the field, dumped in the wrong place without maps." The colonel clucked and puttered like a proud mother hen with her chick. "This thing has gotten big!" Archie Dowling caught himself, remembering First Platoon knew firsthand exactly how important it really was. "But you certainly know the situation better than we do." Dowling was a man with a tight schedule, but he, more than most, was aware the situation along the river wasn't all glory.

The colonel turned deadly serious, donning his glasses again to glance at a paper filled with typewritten notes. "You were badly served by us here and other headquarters up and down the border. We've been looking into the terrible incident you reported—the one where your men inadvertently clashed with Sergeant Fox's men.

"Put your mind at ease, you did your best to get us to see the problem. And it's no fault of Fox's either. The problem is far above your pay grade. I'll ask to keep you here for a few days in case we need to ask you some questions." He shook Danny's hand again. "Here, go next door to talk with my intelligence officer Captain Dunagan," he said, turning to take a waiting telephone call.

Danny wouldn't let the man who ordered him to Fort Clark desert him so easily. "Colonel?"

Dowling held the telephone expectantly. "Yes, Lieutenant Flynn. Did I forget something?"

"Perhaps, sir. I've got a mounted platoon of troopers who've been on the road for a long time. They're hungry, dirty, and very thirsty, among other things. I'd like to give them passes to Piedras Negras for a little recreation."

"Of course, Flynn. Your troopers can go." Colonel Dowling wagged a finger. "But not you."

chapter

TWENTY-ONE

Honolulu: In the Philippines, General Wainright surrenders the fortified island of Corregidor and 12,000 U.S. troops to the Japanese forces.

Danny leafed through his notebook, checking for details the debriefer would surely want to go over, and assessing his chances of getting a bath and a shave before the grilling began.

"No, Lieutenant. You're not leaving here until we're done getting the best possible detail of your report," said Captain Dunagan. He wanted to get to the bottom of the breakdown in communications that created the nearly fatal encounter between the two platoons. Working with extremely detailed maps, the kind First Platoon needed in the first place, Flynn and Dunagan determined that the drop-off point had been roughly twelve miles too far to the south, and Lieutenant Brooks's disabling riding injury exacerbated the mixup, creating the nearly fatal confrontation. As to why the various headquarters staffs muddled the radio communications; that was for a separate, much more detailed investigation.

Dunagan got right down to the meat of the matter. "I'd say the two platoons were forgotten in a bureaucratic screwup." But that was history. Right now he wanted to know something about how the spies were being inserted.

The captain listened attentively, monitoring the turning spools of the wire recorder taking down every detail the lieutenant could remember of the mix-up. Satisfied that his record was as complete as he could get it, Dunagan had another requirement.

"I know you'd like to get cleaned up, Lieutenant, but we want to know something about the woman's operation. We'll need it immediately, so we can brief the division commander as soon as he arrives." He motioned to a desk in a corner behind those of the clerks. "Give it to my sergeant over there for typing when you're done."

Dunagan already had his recorded thoughts on the wire recorder, he knew, but taking his time to provide additional comments to support his actions might save him from being charged with assisting Maureen in her work.

It was already dark outside by the time Danny felt satisfied that his report was complete and all the details written out the way he wanted them. Even so, he was still afraid of what they might make of his association with Maureen if somebody saw the need for a scapegoat. A lieutenant wouldn't stand a chance if colonels and a general got into a finger-pointing match.

But now the weariness was setting in; he considered having a beer and turning in. Maybe he'd wait until tomorrow before going to Piedras Negras. He tried the door to the S-2's office. It was unlocked and the lights burned brightly, but the captain was no longer at his desk. Gone to his quarters, maybe? A major was still there, though, referring to a small area on a wall map of the Rio Grande Valley, frowning at what he was hearing on the telephone.

The major's face brightened when he saw First Platoon's lieutenant. "Flynn! You're still here in the building," the major called out, beckoning for Danny to come into the office. He shouted the news of his good luck into the telephone. "We thought we were out of lieutenants, but we forgot about Lieutenant Flynn." Holding the black telephone receiver aside, he said, "Don't go anywhere, Flynn. We need you."

Danny slouched into an oak swivel chair behind a vacant desk, eavesdropping on the conversation. With First Platoon's encounters, plus a few less successful brushes farther to the north, the Border Patrol people were convinced that what remained of a group of specially trained agents using American passports would attempt another push to get into Texas, and they were appealing to Washington for the army's strongest efforts in searching the Rio Grande Valley for them.

So here was the German infiltration problem, refusing to die. The immediate problem was that Fort Clark was nearly empty—most of the troopers were forty or so miles away in Piedras Negras for a normal Saturday night's fun in the Mexican border town. Earlier in the day, General Burton ordered the commanding officer of the 156th to mount a maximum effort to collect every off-duty trooper they could find. "Goddamn it, Dowling.

We're at war with those German bastards," he yelled into the telephone moments before he and his pilot took off for Fort Clark.

No way could Danny be persuaded that this crisis, as they were calling it when he first arrived in the headquarters building, was his personal problem. He wasn't in the habit of disputing orders, but First Platoon had done their share. It was that simple. "Major, my guys have been out there for a week and a half," he complained. "They've covered hundreds of miles on horseback. They're worn out and they want to go to town too."

The major waved away Flynn's objections. "We're wasting time. Now listen to me. Your platoon can rest...but they can do it here at Fort Clark—no passes for them, or for you either. I am not going to give your platoon, the men who know most about finding these agents, the opportunity to get lost over there on the other side." He watched Danny's face for a sign that the inevitability of his decision had sunk in. "Right now, it's you I want, Lieutenant. We need another officer to go over there and collect every trooper who can be found—black, white—it doesn't matter." He wasn't going to spend more time in useless discussion. "Your personal desires, and those of your platoon, are overcome by the needs of the army, Lieutenant Flynn."

Stopping only to use the latrine, Danny found himself seated in the cab of a portee hastily daubed a drab olive green. The driver, a buffalo soldier who introduced himself as Lukas, had the motor idling. He already knew the story about the redheaded lieutenant just in from the field. "Poor devil hasn't had any luck at all today," said the sergeant. "Wait for him."

While waiting to be dispatched, Flynn asked the driver about vehicles like this one, and he learned that they'd been slightly modified to be personnel transporters by installing some benches along the sides, and now were the standard transportation for Fort Clark troopers to the Mexican border towns.

Guiding the portee out of the back gate, Lukas pointed a long finger toward the lights of Brackettville lying in the dark valley off to the right. Like Brownsville, it was one of those towns that spring up around isolated army posts. Over the noise of grinding gears, the driver said, "See, Lieutenant, the army wanted a fort out here to keep the Commanches from crossin' the river into Texas to make raids on the towns farther on into Texas. They put it right smack on the Commanche war road. That much makes sense, don't it?"

Danny nodded. Almost anything can make sense to a man dead on his feet.

"Then the town got built." The lanky driver laughed at the thought that anybody could be so opportunistic to think there was money to be made in this desolate country by supplying the needs and desires of troopers who were paid so little in the first place. "You say you ain't seen the town yet?" asked Lukas.

Danny shook his head no, but he'd gotten an earful about it from Wieczorek. The closer they got to Fort Clark, the more lurid the stories had become. "Why does the army take troopers all the way to the border, if there's a town here?" he asked Lukas. "Isn't there drinking and dancing and other things in Brackettville?"

"Oh, yes, suh," Lukas laughed at the thought of such a naive question. "They's one street in that town that's set like this." He described a diagonal with his right hand. "They got every kinda dance hall, ho' house, saloon 'n gamblin' joint y' kin think of—but it's jus' one street."

Army lore was full of stories about towns with special streets like this one. "So why the portees?" inquired the lieutenant. "It's not like the army to provide transportation just for variety's sake."

"Well, there wa'ant any transportation 'til the buffalo soldiers came," explained the driver.

"So the flesh pots of Brackettville won't take the buffalo soldiers' money. Is that it?" Flynn asked.

"They used to, a few yeahs ago," Lukas drawled. "All them places wuz happy enough to take money from the buff'lo sojers." He pounded the steering wheel with the heel of his hand. "But then, when the town got a 'lil bigger, some folks said they didn't want no mo' buff'lo sojers in town." His shoulders sagged as they must have a hundred times before, reflecting on the inevitability of the whole thing. "Seems kinda strange, don't it?" he told the lieutenant. "Lotsa stories about how that came about, but that's the way it is right now."

Suddenly black troopers were no longer welcome in Brackettville, Texas, not even to walk through to buy a lunch on the way to Mexico like white troopers did. So the army used the portees to keep the black soldiers and the citizens of Brackettville separate by simply transporting them around Bracketville and on to Piedras Negras.

Lukas went on with his story. "Until a year or so ago, there was another regiment here—a white one. The way the army saw things, the white boys was allowed to walk into Brackettville, to go to the stores and churches, and down that street with the ho'houses and bars, so they didn't need no transportation. But after a few days watching these here oversized horse trailers going around Brackettville, taking the buffalo soldiers to the border towns, it dawned on nea'ly everybody that there wasn't that much to do in Brackettville anyway—the real fun was in Piedras Negras—'cross the border. Now the buffalo soldiers had this regular, free transportation and the white soldiers had to make they own way."

Lukas laughed, recalling how it was. "See, them white boys don't wan' be walkin' or paying fer no taxi when the buff'lo sojers gets rides." Lukas glanced at the white lieutenant to get an idea if the man could possibly understand. Maybe this Irishman did, he guessed. Anyway, he had a captive audience. "Right off, they was yellin' and the officers listened to 'em." Again,

Lukas signaled the inevitability of these things with that melancholy way he had of moving his head and shoulders. "So then we stahted carryin' them white boys over there in these here hoss trailers, too."

According to Lukas, who was still amused at the prospect of the white boys wanting what the buffalo soldiers had, the troops got along well in Piedras Negras. "Maybe there's somethin' about not bein' on they own ground. Oh, the white boys call us some pretty bad things. I can tell you f'm up north—but don't tell me you ain't heard them things. Now, in PN they do go to differn' bars n' differn' houses, 'cept f'r the Black Bull. Ev'body got to go there at least once." Lukas shrugged at the inevitability of it. "So it worked out prett' good."

Danny fell silent, mulling over Lukas's story, and neither spoke after that. The exhausted lieutenant slumped against the door and didn't awaken until the portee came to a halt in a cramped, dimly lighted plaza scattered with small groups of soldiers waiting for transportation to Fort Clark. Lukas shook him awake, "This is it, Lieutenant: Piedras Negras."

Drugged by the effects of a sound sleep far too short to be refreshing, Danny extended his hand. "Well, I guess it's good-bye then. Thank you." He became aware that Randolph Lukas, in a uniform identical to the ones he and the First Platoon wore, was not simply a buffalo soldier, another kind of soldier in the same uniform, but he was just another soldier who happened to be a Negro.

"Lieutenant," Lukas said slowly, "for some reason I think you understand how life is twisted by unexpected circumstances. Good luck to you in the war." He engaged the clutch and the portee rolled slowly around to where about half a dozen MPs struggled to keep order among the mob of disgruntled troopers whose night of revelry had been cut short.

Captain Leo Zamora, one of the few officers still assigned to Fort Duncan, the lightly staffed army post directly across the river in Eagle Pass, had been in the plaza since the recall started. For hours he'd sent teams of lieutenants and MPs fanning out through the streets of Piedras Negras, stopping every trooper they found and escorting them to the little plaza for transportation. But far too many were still unaccounted for. Zamora was pretty certain most of those were missed because they were holed up in the dark seamy areas the teams had been avoiding throughout the evening. Well, who could blame them for not wanting to go into those dismal places? To locate more would require sending more MPs and lieutenants untrained for this kind of work into the dark, smelly hellholes of Piedras Negras. "Hell, this is hard, nasty, dangerous work. None of these guys' mothers would believe their boys were hiding out in places like this," Zamora quipped to one of the lieutenants.

He sorted through the new arrivals spilling out of the portee from Fort Clark: Three musicians—a handful of black soldiers with bugles standing together in one group testing the sound of their instruments, and one smelly, ragged lieutenant with a disreputable growth of unshaven red whiskers. Things must be worse at Fort Clark than he thought. Otherwise he had a few MPs and two other lieutenants who had already made one sweep of the Mexican streets. One of Zamora's MPs moved around quietly, making sure that the musicians had loaded sidearms and that they remembered essential points, like how to reload the unfamiliar weapons. "If you're being threatened, Trooper, use that forty-five. I don't care who it is," he told a wide-eyed bugler.

Danny walked over to talk to the other lieutenants to see what he could learn about how it was out there on the dark, winding streets, but Captain Zamora wasn't wasting any more time. Only a few minutes earlier, a major from Fort Clark telephoned with word that General Burton's airplane had landed and the division commander was personally putting on the heat. "Don't coddle those men. Dig them out of whatever hole they're in," the man said, not mincing words.

"Listen up, gentlemen," said Zamora edgily to the lieutenants. "I'm going to match each of you with a bugler and an MP who can lead you to sections of Piedras Negras we haven't searched before. The buglers will sound "Boots and Saddles" as often as you think necessary. The idea is, no trooper can possibly be too drunk to recognize such a familiar bugle call, and they'll come out of these dives to see what's happening. Any soldier you see, order him to get moving down here to this plaza for transportation. The MP will help with handling the drunks, but the troopers are going to scream bloody murder, telling you they have passes to be over here in these places." He shook his head. "They can forget it. Those passes have been cancelled. None of them, not one, has a valid reason to stay behind in Piedras Negras, so don't waste time haggling."

In his days at Fort Duncan, Zamora had seen most of the worst places. Yes, some were full of people preying on soldiers, and others would protect their customers from being disturbed by military authorities, but an armed lieutenant should be able to bring the troopers out and into the street. "I want those people right here!" The captain emphasized the order, jabbing with his index finger. As a final comment before he sent his three-man teams out into the alleys of PN, Zamora looked at his wristwatch, holding the face toward the streetlight to be sure of the time. "The last portee leaves here in two hours. I repeat: the last portee leaves in two hours. Get my meaning?"

White or black, it made no difference; soldiers didn't go to Piedras Negras, or any of the border towns, for elegant entertainment. What they wanted could be found in a not-too-large maze of dimly lighted, narrow, winding streets and dingy alleys lined with low, mostly adobe buildings. Up and down the streets, garish, brightly painted signs offered cheap hooch in a flood of beer and tequila—drugs, too, very likely. And for a change from army mess hall fare, they could buy all the hotly spiced Mexican street food they wanted for a few nickels. Here they could get drunk and gamble and find plenty of willing Mexican women. The district in which the soldiers were likely to be enjoying themselves had grown haphazardly over the years into a warren of dark malodorous alleys lined with noisy, sinister places trafficking in a prodigious variety of immorality and vices. The Mexican police did no patrolling there. If they ever did venture into those depraved areas, it was in response to an emergency call from a madam or a drug dealer, with the expectation of a substantial bribe.

The disreputable looking lieutenant in the filthy uniform and his bugler followed the MP, heading for a section of Piedras Negras specified by Captain Zamora, and, heeding his opinion that the cleaner law-abiding places had already been searched, Danny avoided them. Every so often, he looked through all kinds of doorways into raucous, smoky places with names like "Hussar's Haven" or "The White Horse Bar," finding them emptied by the recall. Here the jukeboxes blared Bob Wills's Texas swing instead of the German music that blared from the establishments of U-Boot Alee in Matamoros. Out of curiosity, as much as any sense of duty, he poked around in dark, littered alleys stinking with the sour smells of stale beer and urine, just to see, but no men in uniform turned up.

The MP led the lieutenant and the bugler through successively narrower passages, stopping occasionally to allow the bugler to rip through the rousing notes of "Boots and Saddles." It never failed to attract a few staggering troopers in disheveled uniforms. When ordered to the collection point in the plaza, they usually shrugged passively and complied. But not all obeyed the orders. Some responded with obscenities and turned back into the dens of vice as soon as the lieutenant was out of sight. Letting them get away with it was a matter of practicality. One lieutenant with one MP had no way to restrain more than one or two belligerent troopers. If he were to succeed in rounding up troopers in significant numbers, he couldn't waste his time on ones and twos.

It was while standing in the darkened doorway of a bar closed for lack of customers, keeping an eye on a trickle of men in khaki lurching drunkenly toward the plaza that the MP sized up his lieutenant. "You up for a look at *El Toro Negro,* sir?" he asked. As far as he knew from the other MP's, none of the teams had made it that far.

The bugler's wide eyes told what he thought of the suggestion.

Ignoring the bugler's obvious opinion, Flynn pulled out his watch. "We don't have much time. Let's not waste it." Rely on an MP to know where to find the flesh pots, thought Danny, matching the corporal's hot pace through the largely deserted streets. On the way, he ordered plenty of troopers toward the portees and in a surprisingly short time, there it was: *El Toro Negro*, spelled in red neon letters across the painted brick front of the legendary pleasure palace of Piedras Negras. According to the old hands of the 124th, the brightly lighted red sign mounted on the roof stood out like a beacon to soldiers who might have been disoriented by overindulgence in the many enticements available in soldier bars. There was a catch, however, explained the MP. The dim streets and dark corners in the streets surrounding the Black Bull, were thick with pickpockets and thugs known to cut a drunken soldier's throat for a few dollars.

At three stories, El Toro Negro towered over the low adobe buildings of the surrounding district. "Wait here just a minute," said Danny to the two troopers. Anticipating they'd be very busy before long, he walked around the building. Occupying one brick wall, an immense painting of a black fighting bull with curving, needle-pointed horns done on a vivid red background, stretched across the entire side wall of the building. In front, the only side with windows, an ornate second floor balcony overlooked the street. Exactly as Lucas had related the scene; a very young, bosomy woman with a red rose in her glossy black hair, leaned out, blowing kisses and beckoning to men in the street.

Three soldiers, one white and two black, stood in the street negotiating for something with a Mexican man in a slurred mixture of English and Spanish. One pointed at the lieutenant and his assistants. Leaving the other two to carry on the discussion, he stalked stiff-legged up to the lieutenant, threatening: "This ain't army territory. We don't give a damn about no recall. We ain't going back." He shook a fist under Danny's nose. "Ya'll get outa heah."

The MP approached, speaking quietly and firmly, nodding toward Danny standing with his bugler. "Look at this guy." He meant Lieutenant Flynn. "He ain't a man who's gonna leave just 'cause you say so. Get'cher asses down the street to the plaza."

One of the unsteady troopers in the street got the MP's message that the recall was serious business. "I ain't stayin' in this place," slurred the trooper, weaving in the general direction of the plaza. The others moved toward the open door of El Toro Negro, never expecting to be followed.

From the volume of sound blaring into the night and a glance at the indistinct figures, dancing with Mexican women to brassy music from a jukebox, Danny judged the place to be packed with drunken men in khaki uniforms.

Forewarned by the confrontation in the street, Danny unsnapped the holster of his .45 and said the first thing that came to him, "Bugler, sound 'Boots and Saddles.'" The bugle's blast rang through the street for a few long seconds, temporarily stopping everything except the jukebox. "We're going in," he said to the troopers. "Draw your weapons."

This was a bit too much for the bugler. "I'll stay out here in the street, if that's all right, Lieutenant," he said, hanging behind.

"The hell you will," snapped the MP, swallowing apprehensively. "You stick close with your weapon and watch our backs."

Inside, the only light came from a neon sign and some small bulbs at the base of the jukebox. Otherwise, the thick, acrid atmosphere obscured the dark mass of writhing bodies. Flynn and the other two could barely see across the small room.

At the sight of three men with drawn pistols elbowing their way into the murky atmosphere redolent of smoke, spilled beer, sweating bodies and cheap perfume, the crammed room turned to pandemonium: the panicked screaming of prostitutes and the cursing of outraged men drowned out the jukebox. A mass of panicky soldiers strained against a crush of protesting bodies blocking their way to the door. Danny felt crushed glass grinding under the soles of his boots. Upset tables and chairs lay on the floor, and shadowy, threatening figures in khaki pressed in on him, intent on pushing the three armed men back into the street. Certain that he and the other two were about to be assaulted, the lieutenant fired a shot into the ceiling. Suddenly, there was quiet—except for the jukebox. The bugler followed the MP's order to work his way around the walls to snatch the electrical cord from the wall, killing the blaring music and its lights as well. In the near darkness voices rose again,—sounding uncertain now rather than belligerent.

Temporarily at least, Danny and his two troopers had escaped a mauling. The frightened women fled hurriedly, disappearing somehow—it seemed almost magic—through doors leading somewhere into dark maze of narrow hallways and tiny rooms.

"Into the street," the lieutenant shouted. "Get them into the street, and keep them out there," he ordered the MP and the bugler. Grudgingly the disturbed revelers gave way, emptying the room.

A stout Mexican woman, wide-eyed, trembling in agitation, emerged through a side door. She cried out in relief at the sight of armed soldiers herding the rioting mob outside. "Ah! Senor Teniente! How lucky you are here!" she said in a border town mélange of languages. This could only be the madam, a woman in a plain, loosely fitting smock, hair streaked with fine lines of silver: far more a businesswoman than a working prostitute. She tugged at Danny's sleeve, making it plain that there was more trouble upstairs.

"Is it trouble between the white ones and the black ones?" Danny asked.

She shook her head, looking upward with wide, frightened eyes, saying, "Oh, no, Teniente." Through gestures and a mixed tumble of words, she got across the idea that a single unrestrained trooper was causing mayhem in an upstairs room. She searched for a word and pantomimed a striking motion with her fist.

"Hitting?" Danny suggested, "Beating?"

"Si, si, si." She agreed, nodding her head vigorously. "He hits Isabella."

"Where are they now?"

The woman pointed toward the stairs. From a deep pocket, she produced a large room key, making a twisting motion. Upstairs, Isabella must have locked the door after the trouble, whatever it was, began. She made the most of her limited border English. "*Con* Isabella. I think he breaks, ah, ah…" The madam needed help with a word.

"Furniture?" She did not comprehend. He pointed at some of the broken furniture on the floor, "Chairs, beds?" he suggested.

She brightened. "Si, chairs."

"We'll get him out." Danny smiled to assure her.

From somewhere, she produced a coiled, braided leather bullwhip—new and supple. She spoke rapidly in her Mexican dialect: words he could not understand, but from her hand and body motions, she let him know that the owner of the bullwhip, the man now locked in the room, had been terrifying her employees and patrons, threatening to use it, until one brave girl, Isabella, lured him up to the room.

Danny felt himself sweating, realizing he had just agreed to face a man locked in a room with an unwilling woman, a rampaging trooper who carried a bullwhip for fun. Leaving the armed bugler downstairs with the MP, he followed the madam up the narrow dark stairs into a hallway reeking of cigarette smoke and heavy, cheap perfume. Heart pounding, he cursed himself for his stupidity in getting into this.

"Aqui," said the woman, stopping a foot or two outside the room.

He drew his .45 again and listened with his ear to the door. No sounds from inside. "This is Lieutenant Flynn, and I'm coming in on official business," he said, trying to sound calm and authoritative.

No response from either the trooper or the woman. He nodded to the madam, who unlocked the door. He pushed the door open with his foot, entering with his weapon levelled. In the light from the hallway, he found a well-muscled man standing naked over Isabella, who lay cowering on the floor covered partially by a khaki shirt with sergeant's stripes on the sleeves. The sergeant, thoroughly inebriated, menaced the intruders with the sharp, broken legs of a partially destroyed chair.

What now? Oh Lord, what now? Danny thought to himself. He needed help. Without taking his eyes off the naked trooper, he called loudly for the bugler to go out into the street for the corporal. They would need some way to restrain the sergeant.

"Wait, Teniente," said the madam, who had obviously seen this kind of situation before, reaching into her pocket to produce a pair of handcuffs.

At the sight of the cuffs, the sergeant unleashed a stream of profanity and protestations, cursing the treachery of the younger woman who'd tricked him into the room, as well as the madam who kept handcuffs in her pocket. He became considerably more cooperative when the unshaven lieutenant leveled his pistol directly at his chest. "Better cooperate, Sergeant," said Flynn quietly, "or I'll turn you over to the Mexican police."

The madam confidently stepped behind the naked soldier to lock the cuffs around his wrists.

"Get the key from the madam and let's get out of here," Danny said to the bugler, who had returned without the MP. "Any more soldiers?" he asked the madam while she gathered up the sergeant's clothes and handed them to the bugler.

"*No, Teniente,*" she said, shaking her head.

At the entrance she stopped him, "*Momento, por favor, Senor Teniente.*" She handed him the bullwhip, slammed the door and bolted it firmly. With the MP helping the bugler, they got the whip-wielding sergeant into his trousers and boots and out into the street. The bugler draped the sergeant's shirt over his shoulders while the lieutenant checked the time.

With this unexpected delay at the Black Bull, he was already too late to reach the plaza at the stated time. What difference would it make to take another minute or two? The street talk would get the word to Zamora and the last portee would have to wait.

Running footsteps told Danny of some soldiers who had decided to fade away into the dark alleys, but when things settled down, eight troopers spouting shrill profanity and the one half-subdued sergeant milled outside in the red glare of the lights of El Toro Negro, and the plaza was still far away. Danny sent the MP and the Bugler ahead to the plaza with the nine. "I'll be right behind you," he assured them.

Word that Captain Zamora's search would be over in two hours had spread like lightning among the troopers rollicking in the streets and alleys. All they had to do was to avoid the search teams for two hours. After that the officers sent to collect them would be gone and the good times could resume. What was wrong with just waiting it out? The army had given them passes, after all. If the renewed activity and rising volume of music in the alleys was an indication, the recall effort had missed scores who had simply hunkered down in a bar with an accommodating proprietor who turned off his lights, ignoring the buglers until the last portee was gone.

"Out into the street with ya," Flynn ordered six soldiers he surprised in one smoky den, and in another, three more. In the second, a massive master sergeant threw a beer bottle at him, cursing him for being a hard-ass, but he came along grudgingly nevertheless.

Along the street Danny encountered a few more, and now he had more than a dozen in the street. He was still carrying the bullwhip coiled over his shoulder, thinking it might help explain why he brought in a sergeant handcuffed by a whorehouse madam, but if this growing mob of shirkers gave him trouble, he might be able to use it to control them. The quality of the leather and the workmanship told him the whip was the real thing, not merely a tourist souvenir. From what he'd seen of men herding cattle, the things an expert could do with a whip like this were frightening. A strong, practiced vaquero could make it crack like a gunshot. Wielded with accuracy, its snapping sound alone could make a reluctant, balky steer move wherever a man wanted it to go. Or the lash could inflict a hideous cut on a man's skin.

Of course, Danny wasn't practiced at all with a whip like this one, but he knew it presented little threat if he carried it tightly coiled over his shoulder like a tourist, so he loosened the coils and carried it over one arm with the handle in his other hand, making it looked more businesslike. Not one of the riled and pickled soldiers was thoroughly convinced that the lieutenant was good enough with the whip to use it as a weapon, but they weren't brave enough to try him either: not yet, anyway. But when Danny rousted two more from one of the soldier bars that earlier gave the impression of being deserted, he found that one of his original group had run off while he was inside. If only he could get the damn whip to crack, the noise might keep this growing rabble under control, so he rolled it out on the street and tried swinging it around overhead. It felt good and looked threatening enough to keep the mob of troopers guessing about his abilities with it—for a time at least.

By the time the MP assured him the plaza was less than fifteen minutes away, his collection of unsteady, argumentative troopers had grown to an unwieldy nineteen. He tried one swing overhead and then a tossing motion with a hard snap of his wrist. To his surprise it worked! The crack surprised him—loud, if not awe-inspiring. But it was enough. He kept cracking the whip every now and then, improving as he went. The crazy lieutenant brought his nineteen forcibly recalled troopers grumbling and cursing into the plaza for transportation to Fort Clark...but the place was deserted. No portees; no transportation of any kind—Captain Zamora and his people were nowhere to be seen—gone back to Fort Duncan, presumably. Sure, Zamora had said two hours. But the son of a bitch wouldn't have gone and left him and the two troopers to fend for himself, would he?

"Look what I found ignoring the recall, Corporal," he called to the MP who had brought in his nine, including the half-dressed sergeant. Another eight had come into the plaza on their own accord, and more were trickling in.

The corporal wiped sweat from his face on the shoulder of his shirt. "What now, Lieutenant? The portees are gone. So're Captain Zamora and his sergeant."

"Not one? You mean to say they were all gone by the time you arrived?" Danny asked the corporal, who had arrived at the plaza a few minutes earlier.

"Yes, sir," said the MP, eyeing the unruly, filthy lot apprehensively. "Maybe we should just let 'em go, sir," he said.

Danny thought about his predicament. They'd risked too much and worked too hard to send the troopers back into the street. As the MP said, the mouthy troopers were threatening to bolt for the alleys, or to break the lieutenant and his helpers in half for forcing them here. To him it looked as if Zamora just left him and his two men to fend for themselves in a foreign country. Damn! This screwed up situation smelled to high heaven: even worse than the bungling that left First Platoon deserted in the valley. Abandoned, in a Mexican border town, dammit! Sent out there into those stink holes to bring these troopers back and then left to rot!

Flynn wanted to scream, to hit something; preferably the man who deserted them, but Zamora was gone, he realized, so he resorted to his habit of asking himself what his father would do. At first nothing came to him, except the realization that he'd begun thinking rather than raging uselessly. But the MP was nervous about holding these troopers. "They haven't done anything all that wrong, I don't think, sir," argued the anxious corporal.

Danny's response was pure Michael Flynn. "But the army wants them back at Fort Clark," he said, coolly scanning the plaza in the dull lighting from the neon lighting of the cantina.

The cantina! If it was open it might have a telephone. "Take charge of these men. Get some of these sergeants to help you, maybe one or two of those who walked in on their own," he ordered. Coiling his whip, he looked around at the buildings fronting the plaza. "I'm going over here to that little cantina to call for some help—more people, or at least another portee to take these guys to the post," he said, motioning to it with the leather coils. Over his shoulder he encouraged the troopers, "If they get nasty, fire a couple of shots in the air, and I'll come running."

The cantina did have a telephone. That much was positive. But simply being able to see the lights of the United States on the opposite side of the Rio Grande didn't mean that making a telephone connection to an operator in Eagle Pass was easy. He didn't have the slightest idea of a number and probably wouldn't be able to speak to the Mexican operator anyway.

Danny threw the bullwhip on the bar and tossed his hat on top of it. He offered the startled man at the bar most of the money he had to arrange the connection to the Fort Clark operator. From his assurance in handling the matter, Danny took the man to be the owner. "Have a seat, senor—over there, please," the owner said, pointing to a small, inconspicuous table in a dim corner. "It will take a few minutes for the telephone. Perhaps you would like a cerveza?" he asked, jiggling the hook to summon the operator.

With nothing to do but to wait to be connected to the Fort Clark operator, Danny thought about that cerveza. For many days now, the only liquid available to slake his burning thirst was tepid water drawn from shallow wells or straight from the river. What could it hurt if he had a small glass of beer?

Curious to see who might be watching, he glanced warily around the room. The only customers he saw occupied a single table: three Mexicans who looked to be businessmen who had lost their evening's customers because the recall emptied the streets and bars of soldiers, and all the shouting and cursing and grinding of truck engines had chased away the mostly timid tourists. The bullwhip cracking like a pistol had probably done its share to clear the plaza of the rest of its nightly tourist traffic. Danny stood to signal for the cerveza. Only then did he glimpse his reflection among the liquor displays behind the bar. He barely recognized the unkempt image staring back at him from the mirror.

Daniel Flynn, Second Lieutenant, United States Army, pistol on his hip, with the bright brass of .45-caliber ammunition in magazines winking from green webbing pockets on the belt, haggard and emaciated by a fortnight of gobbling scanty rations standing up, was a frightening sight. No wonder those troopers gave him room on the streets.

Through gaps between the letters painted on the windows, he watched the lone MP and his armed but scared bugler, gamely struggling with a noisy mob of belligerent drunks to keep them from straggling away. Troopers were continuing to trickle in. Occasionally one would succumb to the irresistible need to urinate, pissing in a prodigious arc, letting it splash on the pavement.

Even if his two troopers were doing a valiant job controlling the mob, the situation was obviously becoming critical. The only solution he saw was to get transportation out of Piedras Negras. Should he have been the one to stay out there? No. It had to be this way. It was the lieutenant who had to make the call, and Danny sat wearily at the table offered by the proprietor, leaving the whip and his hat hung on the back of a vacant chair.

A short, slightly plump woman in a flowered dress, cut low in front, arrived with the cerveza. Danny fumbled for money to pay for the beer, watching her lean over to place the bottle before him. With a slow smile, she touched his arm, nodding toward the bar where the owner stood, speaking rapidly into the telephone. "*Momento*," she said. The connection would be complete in a moment. Reflecting on the effects of too many days in the wicked, thorny thickets of the Rio Grande Valley, on thirst and a man's urges, he consumed the cold beer in three or four long gulps.

The owner waved the receiver at the end of its cord. Fort Clark was on the line. Sergeant Fields, the Fort Clark operator, waited.

"I'm Lieutenant Flynn, and I want to speak to Captain Dunagan or the colonel," he demanded. Another cerveza appeared at his elbow.

"That'll take a minute, sir."

Danny waited, composing in his mind a description of what he needed in the way of help. Across the plaza, the corporal was visibly losing confidence in his ability to control what appeared to be about thirty disgruntled soldiers whose self-appointed mission for the evening, to get roaring drunk—or laid—preferably both, had been abruptly interrupted. Being herded to this godforsaken little wide spot in the road by some crazy bullwhip-wielding white lieutenant made matters worse. The powerfully built black sergeant who had thrown the beer bottle was making things difficult for the white corporal. The little bugler was doing his best to help, but handling mobs wasn't his usual line of work. The few civilians who couldn't avoid the plaza scuttled through as fast as possible, giving the drunken soldiers a wide berth. The only positive aspect of the struggle for control was that some of the troopers were sleeping or passed out probably, lying wherever they happened to go down—either on the sidewalk or on the street.

"Come on, operator, get me somebody," Danny shouted.

"Lieutenant, I'm trying my best, sir. It's getting late, you know."

"Dammit, Sergeant, if what you're doing isn't working, start at the top of the list."

"That's General Burton, he's visiting from Fort Bliss," said Fields. That kind of suggestion usually stopped lieutenants who called this time of night.

"Get him," shouted Danny. Might as well get the general, now that he thought about it; He didn't remember the colonel's name anyway.

"This is General Burton," said a voice with studied gruffness—but a tone of concern came through. "What's all this about, Lieutenant? You have troubles in Piedras Negras? Why didn't you make the last portee?"

Danny sighed to himself, feeling the effects of profound weariness and two beers. Common sense told him to be tactful, but matters out there in the plaza were deteriorating rapidly. "Well, now, General, listen to me, please. I've been in the saddle for nearly two weeks—and most of today too. They sent me over here to herd soldiers back to the post, and I've got nearly three-dozen drunken troopers here in the Plaza—that's where the last horse truck left us. Those people knew damn well that some of us were still out in those stinking alleys. One massive sergeant is about to take my MP corporal apart because, in his state, he doesn't want to understand the reason for being dragged out of a whorehouse. This isn't the fault of any one of us on this side of the river. We're here because some half-baked orders created this mess. I've got all these otherwise good troopers who are mean and nasty and about to get into trouble. Some are passed out, they're that drunk. I'd march them back to Fort Clark if I thought they could make it. I need a portee. Any kind of goddamn truck will do, and I'll bring them back. If you can't send one, tell me so now, and I'll let these soldiers go. The corporal and I—and the bugler—will walk back and swear we never saw them...Are you hearing me, General...sir?"

For perhaps five seconds, the only sound Danny heard over the international connection was a hissing crackle. Then the general answered, "Sit tight, Lieutenant. I'll get you a goddamn truck if I have to drive it myself." A clicking sound must have meant that the general had hung up, but Sergeant Fields was still on the line. Do you need any more calls, sir?" he asked.

It took a great leap of faith to believe that a general was coming to help him, but that's what the voice said. Danny said to Fields, "No, and I'm thanking you, Sergeant."

The lieutenant handed the telephone back to the owner, shrugged and finished the remainder of his cerveza, hurriedly collecting his hat and the bullwhip before going out to face the mob.

In the mirror behind the bartender, Danny saw that, while he was speaking to Sergeant Fields, Maureen Gallamore had slipped from the shadows and sat down at his table! She looked smaller than he remembered, swallowed by a peon's shirt and trousers faded, hair stiff with dust and sweat, matted from wearing a sombrero, and weary—almost as tired as Danny, perhaps—but nothing could dull those expressive green eyes telling him of her fear. Her voice came to him; no more than a whimper, "God be praised, I found you. They're threatening to kill me if I don't get them all across the border in the next few days." Her chin dimpled slightly and trembled.

"Maureen, my girl. What did they do to you? Who was it?

"I was wrong," her voice quavered. She steadied herself with great effort. "The Germans are forgetting why I'm here. One called me an Irish cow and tried to rape me. The first time they threatened me, Danny love, for delaying in getting them across the river, I led some of them myself, straight to where I knew the Border Patrol and the army were waiting. Three of them are dead, but others may have crossed the river at places they found themselves. I don't know if they were successful. Some may have drowned." The distraught beauty's vivid green eyes filled with tears. She drew a bandanna from a pocket and used a corner to dry them. "Their plans are to drive to a place just outside Uvalde, north of here in Texas, to collect and wait. They have a house there, one they've used before when pursuit was hot. That's why you haven't been able to find them in Houston or Galveston. But you can find them at that house now."

In the plaza the corporal struggled to control the khaki mob shouting obscenities and threats. Two men had ripped the terrified bugler's instrument from his hands and were blowing through it, trying to produce sounds. The overtaxed MP was feeling more threatened by the minute, looking helplessly at the cantina for the lieutenant he felt certain was ignoring him.

The corporal would have to manage somehow. Danny took Maureen's hand and drew it toward him. "Come with me," he said with a slight move of his head toward the plaza.

She smiled sadly. "This is Mexico, love, not Texas. This is where I'm obliged to stay."

"I have the means to force you," he said, not sure he could force her to come with him at gunpoint.

A shake of her head told him she wouldn't cross the border, and she said with a sad, weary smile, "The man at the table just there across the room doesn't think you could force me." She lowered her head slowly, in a movement both exhausted and frightened. "I love you, Danny," she whispered, "but I want very much to live. He's ready to shoot you. I pay him very well to do a bodyguard's work."

How long ago the bodyguard had entered and taken a seat, Danny couldn't say, but there he sat with his right hand under the table, watching his client and the lieutenant with a businesslike stare.

"Don't let it end like this," she said, leaning across the small table, kissing him quickly on the lips.

He pulled her close to him. He wanted to take her with him—right now—but he knew she wouldn't come to Fort Clark. "Maureen, love. I want to be with you. I'll find you when this is over. Not here, but in New York or Ireland." He realized suddenly that he wouldn't have the slightest idea of where to begin a search for her.

Her bodyguard was making insistent signs. Her safety was in danger. "Yes. Maybe in Ireland." she whispered hoarsely, her eyes filled with anxiety. She brushed her lips hastily on his and followed the bodyguard into the dark alley behind the cantina.

He crossed the plaza on the run, shaking out the bullwhip, cracking it again and again. All that noise and the return of the bearded lieutenant restored a little order. It would take some time for the truck to get here, even if those people at Fort Clark found one immediately. Flynn shouted, "Sit down and we'll take you back to Fort Clark peacefully. Sit down or you're gonna be in trouble. We're gettin' a truck to take us back to the post."

In the distance a siren wailed. It sounded so faint, it probably was in Eagle Pass on the Texas side. "Hear that? They're on the way." He was guessing, of course, that the small convoy of olive drab vehicles had been cleared at the border crossing to enter Mexico.

The wailing siren crossing the bridge became increasing louder, giving Danny some assurance that help was at hand. A staff car, followed by two portees, careened over the bumpy streets and braked abruptly to a stop. A passenger in civilian clothes jumped out of the staff car, staring at the dirty, unshaven lieutenant with a bullwhip coiled around his shoulder. "Lieutenant Flynn? I'm General Burton," said the man in civvies.

Danny saluted the man he recognized, relieved to see four MPs piling out of a portee. "Yes, sir. I'm Lieutenant Flynn."

Burton looked Danny over carefully, certain he'd seen him before. "So you're the Flynn who seems to be able to smell out German agents." The general snapped his fingers in recognition. "I know you," he said. "You're Centaur's champion. Get in the car."

chapter

TWENTY-TWO

London: The Japanese begin their second Burma campaign, sending strong forces down the strategic Burma Road.

"I never heard'a this place wheah you said we goin', Lootenan'," admitted Weech, struggling to awaken a dim memory of a worn map in a two-room country schoolhouse. Geography wasn't a particular strength among the men of First Platoon. "Is it a country, or what?" asked the sergeant.

"Burma," said Danny, "is a country south of the Himalayas from China." Lest they think this was some sort of joke, Danny waved the notes he'd made at officers' call and read, "It's Burma." He spelled it for them letter by letter. It's been in all the papers and on the radio too. The Japs are moving south and west toward India along a highway the world is calling the Burma Road, and the army is sending us over there into the jungle to stop them."

The enormity of being plucked from their native Texas and flung into a hellish jungle to turn back the rampaging Japanese Imperial Army was lost on these men, who knew almost nothing of lands west of California. Sevcik, the steady marksman of the river-bottom encounters with the Germans, stood with his fellow sharpshooter Moore, squinting, struggling furiously with his own questions about far-off Burma. The two had been inseparable since two different regiments recommend them for medals for shooting those enemy agents. Danny singled out the little PFC, asking, "Out with it, man. What's bothering you?"

"Well, sir. You said there's Japs in this place. What did you call it?"

"It's Burma, you dumb Bohemian," growled Moore, elbowing Sevcik.

Sevcik accepted the gentle insult goodnaturedly. "But that ain't nowhere near Germany. We suppose' to be goin' to fight Germans, no?"

"Sit down, Anton. Don't be stupid," shouted somebody else. PFC Arnold Adamcik, the shy plumber who repaired the windmill at the camp near San Isidro, interrupted to divert the attention from Sevcik. He explained the situation as he saw it. "This is the army, see. We bin' out here in the desert, trainin' n' huntin' these German agents. I bin' thinkin' about this, see. Th' Lootenant said Burma's got jungles. Don't it make army sense that we gonna go fight in a jungle when all we know is desert?" A scattering of fretful laughter told Danny the plumber's ironic humor captured their feelings pretty accurately.

⋈

Pretty Molly, lovely Molly: She waited there for him the evening they came back from Fort Clark. Alerted by the uncannily efficient intelligence network of the Wives' Club that Danny and his men were scheduled to be home in the late afternoon, she watched from the shadows when First Platoon led their horses into the stables and unloaded their gear, working somberly and silently. She took her cue from the married women.

Pearl Wieczorek and some of the other soldiers' wives stood apart from their men, waiting patiently. Molly didn't understand the women's reluctance to rush to their menfolk. Pearl confided to Molly that ordinarily she would've run to Erwin to hug him and give him a kiss after an absence as emotional as this one had been, but today's reunion was profoundly different from anything she'd seen before. Pearl hoped Molly could understand how it was affecting them all.

First Platoon received word to turn in their horses and board trucks to take them back to Fort Brown to catch up with the rest of the 124th after missing a month of dismounted training. But General Burton relented after a personal request sent up the line from Lieutenant Flynn and Colonel Dowling. "Oh, hell, why not? Take your horses with you to Fort Brown, Lieutenant Flynn." It was a considerate gesture and the troopers appreciated it.

Weech had his troopers practicing behind the stables before loading up at Fort Clark for the long ride home. First Platoon felt a unique right to a little celebration as the last mounted unit at Fort Brown.

On Lieutenant Flynn's orders, the portees pulled off the road at a gas station just north of Brownsville to allow them to unload and saddle their horses. If this was to be the last time they returned to the fort as cavalrymen, it was going to be done right, so they took their time. While the troopers brushed the horses and changed into fresh uniforms, Weech used the station's telephone to call home, asking Pearl to spread the word to the families.

Led by a car driven by Brownsville Police Officer Lorenzo Cardenas, who had gone to high school with Pancho Garza, they rode along the Military Highway and through the streets of Brownsville, riding tall and proud. At the front entrance, the sentries, properly warned by Pearl Wieczorek, swung the gates wide. Following Weech's lead, they rode standing in their stirrups for the final time—as First Platoon—not dogface infantry. Danny led them past the headquarters building, saluting, in the likelihood that Centaur was watching from his office.

Even after hearing Danny dismissing his platoon for two days free of duty, Molly waited discretely, watching him stand alone at the stables, his spurred boot on the lowest bar of the wide steel gate. She guessed he was listening to the quiet sounds of the horses standing patiently in their stalls, unable to pull away from them. These were his horses: every one of them handpicked at the remount station. In his short time in the army, Danny and the men who rode these horses had been through much together.

Molly left her place in the shadows, approaching silently to put her arm around her man's waist. But felt somehow that Danny never truly noticed; not even as he moved his arm around her and held her closely. They stood silently and almost motionless, her head on his shoulder, until he could accept the finality of losing the life of a mounted soldier. Then they walked out of the pool of light into the balmy darkness of the evening.

Danny luxuriated in a tub of hot soapy water, allowing Molly to scrub his back, to fuss over him, her man. Her insight told her not to demand inclusion in his reveries tonight, but rather to allow him to sort out his feelings, even if it meant giving herself to a man whose thoughts might still be with another woman.

⊰※⊱

Late in the morning, she awakened with a start. Where was Danny? The sound of the kitchen radio and the aroma of coffee told her he was listening to the news of the war in the Pacific. A few minutes later, Molly followed him to the tiny kitchen, dressed...well, she was wearing his underwear—to stunning, arousing effect. Her nipples showed clearly through his knit undershirt, tied in a knot below her breasts, and a pair army-issue shorts clung temptingly low on her hips. She ran her fingers through his thick coppery hair, refilled his cup with fresh coffee and poured one for herself. She sat in the chair next to him, laying her claim to his undivided attention. He ogled her slowly with his eyes, not missing a detail, but to be sure, she allowed her hand to glide over the skin of his knee. "Like what you see, Danny?" she asked softly, her voice barely above a whisper.

"Oh! Yes, indeed!" he said, reaching out to take her by the wrist. "How enticing you are, Molly. Irresistible," he said, and allowed her to verify that he was indeed aroused.

"Ooh, now *that's* irresistible." She said it gently—invitingly. With her hand in his, Danny stood to lead her to the bedroom.

But Molly had other ideas. She didn't intend to budge from the chair. "Sit down, Danny. It's time for a conversation," she said with a firmness that took him by surprise. She was full of questions about how matters stood between them. The world was changing rapidly, even in the sleepy southern tip of Texas. Molly Blankenship did not intend to go on allowing Danny Flynn to share her bed, yet holding her love at arm's length. She reminded him about the time they met. "A little over a year ago, a redheaded Irish Adonis came into my life and changed it forever."

The fires of war threatening civilization spread around the globe, reaching Americans in every city and hamlet in the country, spreading fear, disrupting lives, even shaking the foundation of their beliefs. Millions of Americans, mostly men, left their homes answering the call to arms, while millions more, their women, remained behind, to live with their fears for the changes that a violent future might bring. At Fort Brown, the 124th prepared constantly for combat in Burma, leaving their families to work out the plans for riding out the war. But one thing hadn't changed for Molly Blankenship. She loved Danny Flynn, but she wasn't yet his family, and she wanted to know where she stood before he left.

She took the chair opposite him, waiting for him to look into her eyes, wanting him to see what she held in her soul. "The one thing that's been constant since you came to Fort Brown is that I love you," she said. Danny sat motionless, challenged by Molly to listen to her, rather than talk. In these tense days, no time remained for coyness and lighthearted courtship, and Molly came to the point. "I thought for a while I had lost you," she said. "I know you had a woman in Mexico, but you never told me about her. I learned of her through rumors, so I don't know who she is or what she meant to you." For a few seconds, Molly held his face in her hands. "From the look in your eyes," she said, "I think she's gone." He opened his mouth to speak, but she held her finger to his lips. She had more to say. "But you came back to me. You're here with me now, and that's what I want more than anything."

First Platoon's women had been including Molly in the news from their menfolk. From the ladies of the 124th, she knew many things about the war she hadn't heard from Danny, beginning with the grinding agony of cavalrymen forced to become foot soldiers; and she had learned the rumors of the dark specter of the men being shipped out for the steaming jungles of Asia to become fodder for the Japanese juggernaut. They'd even shared the rumors of a threatened campaign for control of the Burma Road.

She was determined to tell Danny of her ache at being at the very fringes of the wives' circles and of being his woman, yet not quite his wife. "I don't want to be without you again," she said, meeting his eyes again with hers. "When you leave, I don't want to feel that the only thing I have to remember you by is your underwear in my bedroom drawer." The chair creaked under his shifting weight and they could hear the kitchen clock ticking. She waited, but when he didn't speak, she broke through his silence. "Danny, before you go to Burma, I want to be married to you and I want to be pregnant with your child."

Danny took a long time swallowing his sip of coffee. "And I would like to be married to you," he said haltingly.

Molly took Danny's guarded statement as an engagement to be married, despite having to drag it from him. Even if it wasn't delivered on a bent knee the way they did it in the movies, she threw herself to him, hugging him to celebrate. "Wonderful. You've made me a happy woman, Danny," she whispered breathlessly between kisses.

Molly and her man Danny had become an urgent project for the Officers' Wives Club. In these last few weeks, the ladies became a font of wisdom and information, stirred into action by strong rumors of shipping out earlier than expected, with new rumors arriving almost daily. Some unfathomable source, call it women's intuition, did the rest. "These men get so caught up in themselves, they forget about the women who support and comfort them," said Helen Chamberlain at a morning tea scheduled to give encouraging advice to the wives of the Texans who had never faced the pangs of their men shipping out, as had the ladies of career officers, but they all understood her to mean Molly and her lieutenant.

"Yes," agreed Ruby Perkins, tossing her head primly, inserting a remark aimed directly at Molly. "If we don't get you married before he goes, you'll be without financial support." At the delicate, subtle pressure of an elbow, Ruby quickly moved her hand to her mouth and dropped the critical counseling. "Well, you know what I mean," she said. Of course the meaning had been abundantly clear.

At their urging, Molly made discreet inquiries into the availability of the chapel—for a wedding. She drew the line at calling on Chaplain Murdock, but it was these sessions that prepared her to act on Danny's declaration when it was fresh and simple. "I'm sure we can be married in the next week or so—just as soon as my parents can get here from Longview," she confided to the ladies.

The son of Michael Flynn would not long be found at a loss for words, and he was certainly not a man to take to his heels in the presence of a woman wearing his own underwear. "Of course we should be married as soon as possible," he declared emphatically, "but you may be forgetting centuries of Flynn tradition. I'm a Catholic, bound by Holy Mother the Church to be married in a consecrated church, by an ordained priest. Naturally I want my parents to know and to attend, but they live in New York. And then the priest will have to publish the banns of marriage. That itself will take several weeks."

Nothing since the news of Pearl Harbor had produced such a smashing psychological effect as the words of the drill sergeant standing on the platform before a larger-than-life image of a dark, menacing Japanese soldier in jungle battle gear—wrap-around leggings and a helmet camouflaged with leaves and vines. Yellow, buck-toothed, bespectacled and squinty-eyed, the barely human monster brandished a rifle fitted with a long-bladed bayonet. "It comes down to this," the sergeant's amplified voice screamed through tinny loudspeakers, as he waved a U.S. Army issue bayonet: simple and workmanlike, even inoffensive in its hard sheath, but deadly nevertheless. His strident voice assaulted their ears, driving home the urgency of developing the mental toughness essential to success in hand-to-hand combat. "This son of a bitch is going to kill you unless you want to kill him more than he wants to kill you." The instructor continued his shrill scream lest his audience think that his point was not absolutely the most important thing in the world. He waved the weapon high over his head in his hand, asking "Are you ready to use this?" His contemptuous sneer convinced each of them of his doubt that they were, but he gave them no time for self-examination.

"Now, let me see your bayonets, soldiers. Hold 'em up. Let me see the steel." Exactly as he expected, they were clumsy and unaccustomed to the task—even to thinking about it. "Now look at your bayonet closely," he demanded. "When was it sharpened last? In the factory—or did you do it?" All over the parade ground, every last man of the 124th, sweating in new, chafing green fatigues, carefully fingered the edge of his bayonet blade. An assistant turned down the volume, and the sergeant's voice took on an understanding tone. "You're Americans, taught by your mothers to play fair and be nice boys, so I understand that you wouldn't want to play with these nasty knives." The volume increased again and the speakers screamed, "So not one of you would have survived meeting this murderous bastard who's been killing men and raping women all over Asia," and he thrust his bayonet into the belly of the contemptible Jap soldier vividly depicted on the drawing in garish colors. Giving them a few seconds to meditate on their inadequacies, he paced back and forth between displays of rifles, machine guns and mortars, talking to them. "All of you are qualified with these—on the range. You can kill people from long distances. You know this because you've punched holes in targets hundreds of yards away and watched the dust fly behind them. You think you're good at it because you have a certificate that says so." Then up came the volume again. "But you can't see hundreds of yards in the green hell of a jungle. You might bump up against one of these Jap killers not more than a yard away." He knew what the sweating soldiers on the grass were thinking. He allowed them another few seconds to torture their minds with it.

For the love of Christ himself, Flynn thought furiously, can I do it? I know I've got to get myself ready mentally, but will I do it? He looked at the men of First Platoon standing on the grass at precisely measured distances from one another. At least two of these men had already killed foreign enemies—shooting them at a distance. Which of them were capable of wrestling that Jap down to the mud and sticking him with the knife?

The drill sergeant knew he had their attention—the idea of sticking an enemy with a knife had that kind of effect. In a strong, but slightly softer voice, he drew them into his confidence. "In a few precious days, you'll be boarding that train for Fort Riley. You'll be there for some training—I can't talk about it here. Then there'll be another train for Fort Mason in San Francisco, where you'll ship out into the Pacific. I can teach you how to fight with your bayonet, and even these," he held his hands like the weapons he wanted them to envision, "but the killer has to be here." This time he pointed to his chest. "I want you to learn to hate this Jap, and every damn one of them."

The speakers screamed again, "All right. Pair off with an opponent. Fix bayonets."

Why the hell did Chaplain Murdock have to pick First Platoon for his conditioning partners today? Even without weapons and a pack, pudgy Henry Murdock was sure to slow them down. And why today of all days, when Major Perkins was having times recorded?

Breaking away for a private word with Walter Franklin, Danny pleaded, "My boys want to go for a regimental record. Why don't you take him with you, Captain?"

"He specifically told me he wanted to go with First Platoon," the troop commander said. "He may go into the jungle with us in Burma, and you don't want him to be holding you up then." Franklin posed a challenge. "Give him a test, then, Lieutenant Flynn. You have a vested interest in it."

As Flynn walked away to find the chaplain, he heard the captain shout, "Don't you let him drown in the resaca." Since the trouble with German agents attempting clandestine crossings of the Rio Grande, the army no longer practiced river crossings into Mexico. Instead, they rerouted the conditioning courses to ford the oxbow-shaped lakes made by the meandering river. There were plenty of those, and since they had been part of the river at one time, the steep banks had the look and feel of the river.

Danny went away to find the chaplain, grumbling under his breath about his bad luck, imagining how Murdock would look in combat gear—most likely awkward and very uncomfortable in his pot-like steel helmet and brand-new boots. And if he were to show up in his field gear and a pack, he'd be nothing more than dead weight. But by the time he finally caught sight of Murdock, the chaplain had already found the platoon and introduced himself to the men. At the moment he was chatting amiably with Garza in Spanish, waiting for the lieutenant to arrive.

He'd give the man credit—Murdock looked ready. From all the signs, he was no stranger to these conditioning hikes; like every other soldier in the regiment, his face and hands were burned to a dark brown by the sun, and he stood comfortably in his boots. Regular marching had stripped so much weight off him that his green uniform hung loosely from his frame. Danny saluted. "Good morning, sir. Ready to march with us?"

Murdock smiled confidently as Danny approached. "Ready to go, Lieutenant."

Danny and Weech wanted that record. First Platoon's reputation was at stake. If they went out at a torrid pace, that would show Henry how hard real soldiers worked. Then, if Murdock didn't do the decent thing and drop out, they'd slow down to the chaplain's pace, letting the regiment know whose fault it was that First Platoon failed. "Step it out up there, Weech," shouted the lieutenant, consulting his nickel-plated watch. For the first quarter mile, the whole platoon worked eagerly but clumsily, somehow unable to settle into an efficient, mile-eating stride—inexperience, maybe.

Twice Danny sneaked a glance to see how Murdock was faring. Each time he was surprised to find something in the man's face that hadn't been evident in his prim little office. The chaplain's smile exuded a confident, hard strength Danny hadn't noticed before. "Don't worry about impressing me, Lieutenant Flynn. Your men are having trouble, though. Set the pace you need," he said. Danny decided to postpone interrogating Chaplain Henry Murdock about his reasons for selecting First Platoon.

The march today was far more rigorous than the morning hikes of the gentler, uncertain times of a few months ago. This one was ten miles out along the Rio Grande toward its mouth at Boca Chica, then to whichever resaca had been selected for the required river crossing, and back to Fort Brown. That would be twenty-five miles altogether, with a fording of the uncertain waters of the resaca thrown in. Flynn pretended to be absorbed in a sketch of the route in his notebook, and for a time Murdock left him alone. After a mile or so of strenuous marching, Danny could see the sweat stains spreading on his troopers' backs, even in the breeze from the Gulf. Weech was urging them to keep a creditable pace—an impressive rate, in fact, for the men of a recently dismounted platoon. The chaplain, however, strode blithely along, showing no sign whatsoever of fatigue.

Under the extra burden of his pack, plus weapons and ammunition, Danny felt himself laboring to keep his breathing even. Eventually he accepted the likelihood that Murdock wouldn't drop out. Grudgingly he complimented the captain, "Nice to have you with us today, sir. Why are you out here when you aren't really a combatant?" He regretted the question immediately. Now you've done it, Laddybuck, he thought to himself. You just gave the chaplain the opening to launch a lecture about making an honest woman of Molly Blankenship.

But Murdock surprised him. "This is part of my job now, Lieutenant," he said, speaking without difficulty. "I've done this at least twice a week. I never miss one of these tougher marches—not even on Sundays, if the men are out there. It's practically the only training I can take part in, except for shooting on the ranges or that kind of thing. So I march every day one of these is scheduled." The chaplain pulled back a sleeve to check his army issue wristwatch, with a dull finish and a green wristband. "I'd say you've got your platoon on a record pace." Danny adjusted the fit of his gear, keeping his eyes straight ahead and his mouth fixed in a straight line. "By the way, Danny, I saw you referring to your watch earlier. It's quite handsome. Keepsake?" inquired Murdock.

Danny bobbed his head slightly. "M' father, Michael Flynn," he said, making sure his speech sounded normal, without gasping.

The chaplain wondered aloud if Danny had ever thought about how the shiny case might glint in the sunlight—even in the jungle—and give away his position to a vigilant enemy. Danny felt his face flaming under his sunburn, chafing at being corrected on his battle gear by a chaplain.

To Henry Murdock, this was as good a time as any to get to the purpose of his selection of Danny's platoon today. "War has changed life for us all, hasn't it?" He paused a second to rephrase. "I mean to say, it's put a different complexion on everything we do."

Danny wiped the sweat from his face and glanced skeptically at Henry from under the rim of his heavy steel helmet. This wasn't at all the opening he expected.

The chaplain obviously thought it was not only normal, but something he felt obliged to say. "After the hand-to-hand combat training began, I met with a lot of soldiers who were very troubled at the idea of killing another man with a knife, or even their bare hands. Your man Moore was one of them," he said, aware that PFC Moore was one of the kraut killers. "It's upsetting, I know."

Danny concentrated on stretching his stride, allowing the chaplain to work toward whatever point he was making. Murdock seemed to feel a need to explain himself somehow. He adopted an apologetic tone, remarking that as a chaplain he was forced to adapt his pastoral methods to accommodate what the drill sergeants were driving into the soldiers daily—that their duty was to kill enemies of the United States, no matter what God's commandments said. He tossed at nights wrestling with responsibilities heaped on him by the tortuous combination of part soldier, part man of God. In conversations with his fellow soldiers in shallow holes dug into the dusty desert soil with small folding shovels, as well as in his clerical robes delivering Sunday sermons in the Post Chapel, he constantly felt it necessary to focus his comments on easing their consciences, telling them and their families that it wasn't a sin to kill in wartime. Murdock very much wanted to be a man who could be true to his long-held principles while supporting his uniformed flock with a heartfelt rationale for waging war, even by its most basic, primitive means, but he was torn between what he felt and what he must say. "Danny," he said in a rather plaintive tone, "these days I can finally truly understand the ethical torment you felt when you came to my office. Now

I know what it is to have duties conflicting with inborn scruples and how living with them can be a hell on earth."

Murdock's frank confession flatly surprised Danny. A chaplain, an older man senior in military rank, was sharing these personal torments with a young man who normally kept his private, contemplative side to himself, sharing only his most exuberant feelings. Though he understood the compliment implicit in this frankness, he found it impossible to reciprocate with anything more than a shy, "Thank you, sir."

Referring to his map, Flynn noted a first aid station they would reach in the next half mile, conveniently placed at a point where men being pushed hard were likely to require medical help. More than half of the grueling course had been completed in a very good time, and the exhausting toil of slogging through the murky waters of the resaca was coming up soon. Danny half-expected Murdock to drop away before putting himself through anymore marching. It would have been easy for him to drop out to catch a ride in one of the aid station vehicles with his dignity intact, but he didn't. Either he intended to march with them at this brutal pace, or he could still claim urgent business when they reached the resaca and conveniently accept a ride back to the main post. Danny hoped to heaven Murdock didn't intend to broach the subject of Molly at precisely the time he became preoccupied with getting his platoon into good order for getting through the water.

Murdock surprised Flynn again. With the resaca crossing in sight, the chaplain ran ahead, calling over his shoulder, "We're on a very good time here at the fording. I'll go ahead to test the mud on the bottom and look for snakes." Murdock waded into the brown water without hesitation and took a position in the middle, where the greenish-brown water darkened his fatigues up to his armpits, urging the platoon on. "Keep moving, men. The bottom isn't like the river. It's muddy, but it doesn't get any deeper," he shouted repeatedly, urging the troopers on.

Danny heard Weech up ahead, laughing at the spectacle of Murdock directing the crossing. "Looky, theah, Lootenan'. The chaplain's takin' my job!"

Clear of the simulated river, Danny halted the platoon for a few minutes—for a brief rest, to check feet for blisters and to gulp a few mouthfuls of food and a little water. Weech moved around from man to man, to gauge for himself if each man had it in him to make a final push to the finish. Satisfied, the lieutenant and his platoon sergeant exchanged nods, and the men of First Platoon were up and on the road again, before they were aware of their near exhaustion and the stiffness set in.

Only then did Murdock draw Danny aside again. All the familiar easiness of an hour earlier was gone. "I think you've probably guessed what my original purpose was in coming with you today," he said.

Hesitating, Danny asked, "Molly?"

"Yes, of course," said Henry Murdock, comforted to a degree that he wasn't springing a surprise. "Hardly a day goes by without one of the ladies calling or visiting my office." Danny feared that the chaplain was about to unveil some inescapable genteel ambush plotted to get him married to Molly Blankenship in a lavishly contrived swirl of showers, teas and receptions. Inwardly he groaned, Lord, help me. Spare me from the Wives' Club.

But the chaplain wanted Danny to know he was on his side. Murdock urged him to drive the men to the finish line. "Pick it up, man. You've got a record going here." Ignoring the colorful curses rising from every man in the platoon, Henry reluctantly unburdened himself of the pressures he was getting from the ladies. "They want me to impress upon you an appreciation of your duty to do right by Miss Blankenship."

Danny, finding easy speech difficult at this pace, gasped, "And Molly? What does she say?"

"Miss Blankenship apparently has no hand in this—although I'm sure the ladies' plans and telephone calls reflect her wishes." Seeing Danny's agreeing nod, Murdock said, "Let me get right to my point of view—I want it crystal clear. From our conversations on the matter of your dilemma with the conflicting oaths, I think I know your view in this matter—that you do not truly desire to be married—to anyone right now, correct?"

Danny grunted, "Uh huh."

Satisfied, Murdock said, "You might say I've taken up your defense as a lawyer might. We chaplains make it our business to know a bit about all faiths, so I've reminded them of your firm Catholicism and your family's heritage." Henry hesitated. He needed a breath too. "You probably know that a Catholic bishop will sometimes dispense with the requirement to announce the banns of marriage, especially for soldiers who are shipping out." Danny didn't know that, and he felt a pang of fear strike. Henry anticipated the reaction and reassured him, "I ignored what I've learned from the bishop's offices, and I also informed Mrs. Chamberlain of all the things that had to be done before you could possibly be married here." The chaplain cleared his throat and spat into the weeds on the side of the road. He appeared concerned with, perhaps embarrassed by, a matter of delicacy. "She isn't pregnant, is she?" he asked.

"No sir. I don't think so," croaked Danny, his eyes rolling upward.

If Henry Murdock had ever heard anything to the contrary, or if he had any reason to doubt Danny's assertion, he gave no indication. The chaplain sucked deeply for breath and said, "A marriage entered under pressure is worse than no marriage at all, in my opinion." For a few moments, the sounds of men marching, straining and gasping for air, made the only discernible sounds.

For a variety of reasons, only the chaplain appeared physically comfortable and mentally at peace with himself. He walked shoulder to shoulder with the lieutenant so that his words wouldn't be overheard. "So far, they've accepted my arguments," he said to comfort Danny. "But it's up to you to make your peace with Miss Blankenship. Understand?"

"Yes, sir," said Danny, hugely relieved.

"Then let's move out."

Walter Franklin relayed the commanding officer's specific orders to his reluctant lieutenant. "I told him that your first trip to Fort Reno in charge of the horses was enough experience for anybody, but Centaur didn't give a damn for that kind of talk. All he said to me was, 'This is part of our preparation for war, Captain. Wieczorek can handle First Platoon for you.'"

To be truthful about it, Colonel Chamberlain had been reluctant to snatch Danny from his platoon in these crucial days of training, but Flynn was his best man to move the horses, and he couldn't bring himself to trust transporting the animals to anyone else. This time the 124th's transportation would be high priority: faster, no delays on remote sidings, direct routing, and newer cars. But new cars meant that their designers had given no thought whatever to transporting a cavalry regiment's horses; the cars they needed simply weren't available. Even if those horses were destined for the bone yard, Colonel Chamberlain was determined not to mistreat them. He wanted Danny's ideas considered in reconfiguring the cars, and he wanted him in charge of the troops handling the horses. So, until the 124th arrived in Fort Riley, that's how it would be.

Building the train that would take the 124th Cavalry Regiment away from its native Texas took nearly a week. For one thing, it was a complicated matter because in reality it was two trains—the new and the old trains, the planners called them. Only on the final day, when everything else had been done, would they be coupled together in the Brownsville railroad yard.

The new train consisted mostly of passenger cars that would carry the men of the rearmed and reorganized 124th to war. Immediately behind these would be a string of cars carrying new weapons and equipment to their next training site. After that, whenever they went to the field, their supplies would go with them on trucks or on the backs of mules. The new train was short, compact and efficient. The 124th could fight with the loads in those cars. Thus it would not be broken up under any conditions.

The old train took far longer to load than the new one because it carried a far heavier burden, and not only in the way of sheer weight. A line of flatcars hauled outmoded weapons and ancient vehicles not changed appreciably since the Great War. Giving up those trucks was no particular loss. Once they had transported food, ammunition and field hospitals—even horses. Some were so old, they ran on wheels with wooden spokes. The cars carrying them would be shunted off early, consigning their cargo to scrap heaps as raw material for the rearming effort.

Of course there were the horses, unmistakable symbols of a way of warfare many thousands of years old. The battle to keep them in the army had been long and emotional. Yet even the most diehard cavalryman recognized the superiority of the technologically advanced Axis powers in aircraft and tanks. That struggle now lay behind them, and in concentrating on fighting the Japanese in Burma, the emotional baggage of having to part with their beloved animals was ebbing away. These, cars too, would be split off, to Fort Riley probably, for disposal of their cargo.

What took so long in preparing the old train was the internal strain of putting away everything familiar. All the gear unique to working with warhorses, personal equipment especially, received the same emotional care a child's outgrown baby clothes receive from an adoring mother. Some would be mailed to personal addresses, the rest marked for disposal.

⚜

The men of First Platoon, because of almost a month's absence, were forced to shift for themselves in preparing their saddles and tack for shipment to storage, along with their personal property. Not a single useable box remained after the rest of the 124th had crated their gear up for shipment several weeks earlier, and the post engineers' shops were nearly bare of materials. It took Flynn's resourceful troopers most of a day scrounging in warehouses to build their own storage boxes.

By now Danny shouldn't have been amazed that carpentry was another hidden skill of the remarkable Pancho Garza. They worked well together, collaborating as they had for many months, cutting the wood according to the pattern in the carpenters' shop and fitting it together. Doing without a dog robber would be an inconvenience, but losing Private First Class Francisco Garza's daily assistance as an advisor on the cultures of the Southwest, a translator of Spanish, and a confidant on matters of leading a platoon, would be a burden. Once, Danny turned away abruptly to drink deeply at the shop water fountain, hoping it would help him retain his composure. After the wooden boxes were painted, stenciled and packed, only memories remained to remind First Platoon of Fort Clark and their brief flirtation with fame.

Now everything was done. One telephone call would set it all in motion; loading the horses could be done in a matter of an hour or two. The entire regiment waited tensely on short alert. At Centaur's orders, the 124th was confined to the post, awaiting orders to board the train. Once again, the Bachelor Officers' Quarters and barracks were filled beyond capacity, forcing some to sleep in tents. This time it wasn't a drill to prepare for some future exigency, but to be ready to board the train on a moment's notice. Those with quarters on the post paid conjugal visits to their homes, and Molly slipped quietly into Danny's room.

But now a train of heavily burdened cars stood ready. Far ahead, the locomotive's shrill steam whistle signalled the beginning of an epic journey into an uncertain future. A cascading racket of brakes being released, and the heavy shuddering of couplings accepting weight, rattled more than a mile from the locomotive down the entire length of the massive train.

Far from the straining locomotive, Danny and Molly stood embracing on the crushed stone roadbed. With a long embrace and a final kiss at the door of the car he would ride in, Danny said tenderly, "I'll write. We'll be married just as soon as I can come back to you here." Behind him he heard the mechanical complaints of rolling stock straining to overcome inertia. Standing in the open door of the car, he said, "Bye, Molly dearest. I'll think of you every day." They waved good-bye until an army warehouse blocked her from his view and left him engrossed in the stark reality of going away to war, absorbed in an unknown future.

The train hadn't yet attained walking speed when Danny became aware of a sea of serious, anxious faces; some streaming tears, many beaming messages of pride, all struggling with fear and uncertainty: the families of men who'd become closer to him than his own family. They stood resolutely where they'd last seen their soldier, not willing to depart until the entire train receded from view. By now the new train was long past where these people stood, and still they shouted and waved their hands or handkerchiefs and small flags.

Nearing the end of the loading dock, a small isolated group of young, dark-haired women in dark skirts and colorful shawls clustered apart from the others. These women, most certainly unmarried—at least not to army men—knew their soldiers in a more commercial context than those who stood where the waving throng was thickest. Some, he was quite sure, were citizens of Mexico. But now that the entire world was feeling the touch of war, they had come in response to a basic sense of sharing the danger faced by the men being shipped away to fight an enigmatic enemy in a place with a strange name. Who knew how they managed to be here when the gates of the post had been sealed to unofficial visitors? Love, regardless of its social standing, has its ways. Maintaining a delicately discreet distance from the acceptable and legal friends and loved ones, these shy young women moved slowly away to avoid questioning stares. Danny smiled, recognizing a few faces.

One of them stood alone, apart from the rest, face partly hidden by a black kerchief that covered her head and draped loosely over her shoulders. Steadfastly ignoring the troop cars now long past, but intent on the approaching cars, she grew visibly expectant as the end of the train neared, alertly searching every window of each car. Standing on a step at the door where he boarded, Danny watched her tear off the kerchief, shaking free a cascade of raven curls, allowing them to fly in the wind. Who else could it be?

Maureen, ecstatic, green eyes flashing, dashed the few steps across the nearly deserted platform, approaching perilously close to the rolling cars, waving frantically at the man she'd risked her freedom to see for this one moment. Seeing her dispelled anything else from Danny's mind. He waved from the step, so she'd be certain to see him.

The train brought him closer—near enough to see every detail of her face and to hear her calling again and again. Was she shouting, "I love you?" Yes, he was certain of it! She inched still closer to the extreme edge of the loading dock, so tantalizingly near, stretching out with the kerchief in her hand. He leaned out as far as he dared, barely grasping the black fabric fluttering from her fingers. "Come back to me, Danny Flynn," he heard. Their worlds, brought together for this single instant, drew apart faster and faster.

Maureen lingered, watching the train carrying Danny away until it receded to a speck. He remained at the open door, leaning out, waving until her figure disappeared in the distance. The dark, glossy fabric felt soft in his hand, and the eddying wind brought the faint hint of jasmine to him. Urgently he gathered it tightly in his hand to stuff it into his pocket before her fragrance was lost—and he felt the crinkling of a tiny paper sewn into a corner. He tore open the stitches and unfolded the note.

Farewell for now, love. When this war is over, I'll come to you in New York. Ask for me at the Bantry Maid.

Maureen

www.ingramcontent.com/pod-product-compliance
Lightning Source LLC
Chambersburg PA
CBHW080821250626
47160CB00008B/2818